1632

Baen Books by Eric Flint

Mother of Demons

The Belisarius series, with David Drake:
An Oblique Approach
In the Heart of Darkness
Destiny's Shield

1632

Copyright © 2000 by Eric Flint

A Baen Books Original

Baen Publishing Enterprises
P.O. Box 1403
Riverdale, NY 10471

ISBN: 0-671-57849-9

Cover art by Larry Elmore
Interior maps by Randy Asplund

Distributed by Simon & Schuster
1230 Avenue of the Americas
New York, NY 10020

Typeset by Windhaven Press, Auburn, NH
Printed in the United States of America

1632

ERIC FLINT

To my mother,
Mary Jeanne McCormick Flint,
and to the West Virginia
from which she came.

THE HOLY ROMAN EMPIRE

The Central Regions

0   50   100

Scale In Miles

Brandenbvrg

Berlin

Magdebvrg

R. Elbe

R. Oder

Harz Movntains

Thvringia

Saxony

Halle   Leipzig

Dresden

R. Werra

Eisenach   Erfvrt Weimar

Anstadt   Jena   Gera

Grantville

Badenbvrg

Saalfeld

Svhl   Thvringian Forest

Pragve

R. Main

Ottoman Empire

Nvrnberg

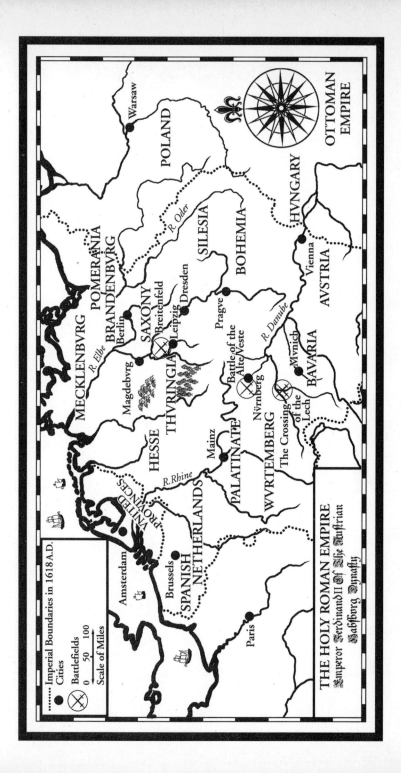

THE HOLY ROMAN EMPIRE
Emperor Ferdinand II Of The Austrian
Habsburg Dynasty

Imperial Boundaries in 1618 A.D.
Cities
Battlefields
0   50   100
Scale of Miles

POLAND
Warsaw

OTTOMAN
EMPIRE

HVNGARY

MECKLENBVRG
POMERANIA
BRANDENBVRG
SILESIA
BOHEMIA
AVSTRIA

Berlin
Magdebvrg
SAXONY
Breitenfeld
Leipzig
Dresden
R. Elbe
R. Oder

Pragve
Vienna
R. Danube

THVRINGIA
HESSE
Battle of the
AlteVeste
Nvrnberg
Mvnich
BAVARIA

R. Rhine
Mainz
PALATINATE
WVRTEMBERG
The Crossing
of the
Lech

UNITED
PROVINCES
Amsterdam
Brussels
SPANISH
NETHERLANDS
Paris

Prologue

The mystery would never be solved. It would simply join others, like the Tunguska event or the Square Crater on Callisto, in the catalogue of unexplained occurrences. The initial worldwide excitement waned within a few months, as it became clear that no quick answers would be found. For a few years grieving relatives would, with some success, press officialdom to maintain the studies and inquiries. But there were no lawyers to keep the fires stoked. The courts ruled soon enough that the Grantville Disaster was an Act of God, for which insurance companies were not liable. Within ten years, the Disaster had devolved into another domain of fanatics and enthusiasts, like the Kennedy Assassination. Thereafter, of course, it enjoyed a near-eternal half-life. But few if any reputable scientists in the world held out any hope for a final explanation.

Theories, of course, abounded. But the vague traces on instruments were impossible to decipher clearly. A small black hole, passing through the Earth. That was one theory. Another—popular for a time until the underlying mathematics were rejected in the light of later discoveries—was that a fragmented superstring had struck the planet a glancing blow.

The only man who ever came close to understanding that a new universe had been created was a biologist. A junior biologist by the name of Hank Tapper, attached almost as an afterthought to one of the geological teams sent to study the disaster. The team devoted several months to a study of the terrain which had replaced what had once been part of West Virginia. They came to no conclusions other than the obvious fact that the terrain was not indigenous to the area, but that—this eliminated the once-avid interest of the SETI crowd—it was clearly terrestrial.

The size of the foreign terrain was mapped, quite precisely. It formed *a perfectly circular hemisphere about six miles in diameter, approximately half that deep at its center. Once the team left, Tapper remained behind for a few more months. Eventually, he identified the fauna and flora as being almost identical to those of parts of Central Europe. He became excited. That matched the archaeological report, which—very, very diffidently—suggested that the ruined farmhouses on the new terrain had a vaguely late-medieval/early modern Germanic feel to them. So did the seven human corpses found in one of the farmhouses. Two men, two women, and three children. The remains were badly charred by the fire, but marks on the bones indicated that at least two of the people had been murdered by some kind of large cutting implements.*

The dental evidence suggested that the dead people were not modern. Or, at least, had somehow never been given any kind of dental treatment. But medical examination determined that the murders were very recent. And the farmhouses were still smoldering when they were found.

Tapper teetered on the edge of the truth. Then, after several more months of work failed to turn up any matching piece of disturbed terrain anywhere in central Europe, he abandoned the study altogether. He had suspicions, but—

The only possible explanation was a transposition in time as well as space. Tapper was a junior biologist. His budding career would be ruined if he advanced his suspicions without evidence. And there could be no evidence, if he was right. Whatever remained of the area of West Virginia which had vanished was lost somewhere back in time.

So, Tapper accepted the loss of a year's work, and went in search of greener pastures. He published his findings, to be sure; but only as dry factual accounts in obscure publications. He made no attempt to draw conclusions, or posit theories, or draw any kind of public attention.

It was just as well. His career would have been ruined—and for no good purpose. No one would have believed him. Even if someone had, the most extensive archaeological search of central Europe would never have discovered the matching hemisphere. It was there, of course, in that region of Germany called Thuringia. But it was there almost four centuries earlier, and only for an instant. The moment those hemispheres had been transposed, a new universe split off from the old.

And, besides, the truth was far stranger than even Tapper ever imagined. Even he assumed that the cause was some kind of natural cosmic disaster.

In reality, the Grantville Disaster was the result of what humans of the day would have called criminal negligence. Caused by a shard of cosmic garbage, a discarded fragment of what, for lack of a better term, could be called a work of art. A shaving, you might say, from a sculpture. The Assiti fancied their solipsist amusements with the fabric of spacetime. They were quite oblivious to the impact of their "art" on the rest of the universe.

The Assiti would be exterminated, eighty-five million years later, by the Fta Tei. Ironically, the Fta Tei were a collateral branch of one of the human race's multitude of descendant species. Their motive, however, was not revenge. The Fta Tei knew nothing of their origins on a distant planet once called Earth, much less a minor disaster which had occurred there. The Fta Tei exterminated the Assiti simply because, after many stern warnings, they persisted in practicing their dangerous and irresponsible art.

Part One

Tiger! Tiger! burning bright
In the forests of the night

Chapter 1

"I'm sorry about my parents, Mike." Tom gave the two people in question a look of resentment. "I'd hoped—" He broke off, sighing faintly. "I'm sorry, I really am. You spent a lot of money on all this."

Mike Stearns followed his gaze. Tom Simpson's mother and father were standing near the far wall of the cafeteria, some fifty feet away. Their postures were stiff; their faces, sour. Their very expensive clothing was worn like suits of armor. They were holding the cups of punch in their hands by thumb and forefinger, as if determined to make as little contact with the surrounding festivities as possible.

Mike repressed a smile. *Ah, yes. The dignitaries from civilization, maintaining their savoir faire among the cannibals. They'll hold a cup of blood, but damned if they'll drink it.*

"Don't worry about it, Tom," he said softly. Mike's eyes moved away from the haughty couple against the wall and surveyed the crowd. The gaze was filled with satisfaction.

The cafeteria was a very large room. The utilitarian gray and cream walls had been festooned with an abundance of decorations, which made up in cheerfulness and festive abandon whatever they lacked in subdued good taste. Many of the cafeteria's plastic chairs had been moved against the walls, providing a bright orange contrast—those few of them that were not holding someone. Long tables ranged near the kitchen were laden with food and drink.

There was no caviar, and no champagne. But the crowd which packed the room wouldn't have enjoyed the first—*fish eggs, yuk!*— and the second was prohibited by high-school regulations. Mike was not concerned. He knew his folk. They would enjoy the simple fare which was piled on the tables, thank you, even if it *was* beneath the contempt of wealthy urban sophisticates. That was true of the adults, even, much less the horde of children swarming all over the place.

Mike gave the younger man standing at his side a little pat on the shoulder. It was like patting a slab of beef. Tom was the first-string nose guard for West Virginia University's varsity squad, and looked the part. "My sister married *you*, not your parents."

Tom scowled. "Doesn't matter. They could at least— Why did they even bother to show up at my wedding, if they were going to act like this?"

Mike glanced at him. For all Tom's immense size, Mike didn't have to look up. Tom was barely over six feet tall, about Mike's own height, even if he outweighed him by a good hundred pounds.

Tom was back to glaring at his parents. His own face was as stiff as theirs. Unobserved, Mike studied his new brother-in-law.

Very new brother-in-law. The wedding had been held not two hours earlier, in a small church less than a mile away from the high school. Tom's parents had been just as haughtily rude at the church as they were being now at the reception. *Their* son should have been married in a properly discreet ceremony in a proper Episcopalian *cathedral*, not—not—

This yahoo preacher! In this yahoo—*shack!*

Mike and his sister had abandoned the stark faith of their ancestors in favor of quiet agnosticism. Years ago, in Mike's case. But neither of them had even once considered having Rita married anywhere else. The pastor was a friend of the family, as his father and grandfather had been before him. The Calvinist fundamentalism of the ceremony had bothered them not in the least. Mike choked down a laugh. If nothing else, it had been worth it just to see the way the pastor's fire and brimstone had caused obvious constipation in Tom's sophisticated parents.

His humor faded quickly. Mike could sense the pain lurking within Tom's eyes. An old pain, he thought. The dull, never-ending ache of a man whose father had disapproved of him since he was a small boy.

Tom had been born into one of the wealthiest families in Pittsburgh. His mother was old Eastern money. His father, John Chandler Simpson, was the chief executive officer of a large petrochemical corporation. John Simpson liked to brag about having worked his way up from the ranks. The boast was typical of the man. Yes, he *had* spent a total of six months on the shop floor, as a foreman, after he retired from the Navy's officer corps. The fact that his father owned the company, however, is what accounted for his later advancement. John Chandler Simpson had fully expected his own son to follow in those well-worn footsteps.

But Tom had never fit his family's mold and expectations. Not when he had been a boy, and not now when he was of age. Mike knew that John Chandler had been furious when his son chose WVU over Carnegie-Mellon—especially given the reason. *Football? You're not even a quarterback!* And both his parents had been well-nigh apoplectic at their son's choice for a wife.

Mike's eyes scanned the room, until they fell on a figure in a wedding dress, laughing at something being said by the young woman at her side. His sister, Rita, sharing quips with one of her bridesmaids.

The contrast between the two girls was striking. The bridesmaid, Sharon, was attractive in a slightly heavy and buxom sort of way. She was very dark complected, even for a black woman. Tom's sister was also pretty, but so slender that she bordered on being downright skinny. And her complexion—very pale skin, freckles, blue eyes, hair almost as black as her brother's—betrayed her own ethnic origins. Typical Appalachian mongrel. The daughter and sister of coal miners.

Poor white trash. Yup. That's what we are, all right.

There was no anger in Mike's thought. Only contempt for Tom's parents, and pity for Tom himself. Mike's father had a high school education. Jack Stearns had worked in a coal mine since he was eighteen, and had never been able to afford more than a modest house. He had hoped to help his children through college. But the mine roof-fall which crippled him and eventually caused his death had put paid to those plans.

The quintessential nobody. On the day he finally died, Mike had been like a stunned ox. Years later, he could still feel the aching place in his heart where a giant had once lived.

"Let it go, Tom," he said softly. "Just let it go. If it's worth anything, your brother-in-law approves of you."

Tom puffed out his cheeks, and slowly blew out the breath. "It is. Quite a bit."

Abruptly, he shook his head, as if to clear his mind for other concerns. He turned to face Mike squarely.

"Give it to me straight, Mike. I'm graduating in a few months. I've got to make a decision. Do you think I'm good enough to make it in the pros?"

Mike's reply came instant and firm. "Nope." He shook his head ruefully. "Take it from me, buddy. You'll be right where I was—the worst possible place. *Almost* good enough. Good enough to keep hoping, but . . ."

Tom frowned, still *hoping*. "You made it. In a way. Hell, you retired undefeated."

Mike chuckled. "Sure did. After all of eight professional fights as a light heavy." He reached up and stroked the little scar on his left eyebrow. "My last fight I even made it to the second card at the Olympic Auditorium. Pretty big time."

The chuckle came again—more of an outright laugh. "Too big! I won—*barely*—on points. The kid demanded a rematch. And that's when I finally had enough sense to quit. A man's got to know his limitations."

Tom was still frowning. Still *hoping*. Mike placed a hand on his thick arm. "Tom, face it. You'll get no farther than I did. Realizing that you only beat the kid in front of you because you were a little more experienced, a little savvier, a little luckier." He winced, remembering a young Mexican boxer whose speed and power had been well-nigh terrifying. "But that kid'll learn, soon enough. And the fact is that he's a lot better than you'll ever be. So I quit, before my brains got scrambled. You should do the same, while you've still got healthy knees."

Again, Tom puffed out his cheeks and, again, blew out a slow breath. He seemed on the verge of saying something, but a motion caught his eye. His brand-new wife was approaching, with people in tow.

Tom was suddenly beaming like a child. Watching that glowing smile, Mike felt his own heart warming.

Hell of a sweet kid, to come from such cruddy parents.

Rita arrived with her usual thermonuclear energy. She started by embracing her new husband in a manner that was wildly inappropriate in a high-school cafeteria—springing onto him and wrapping both legs around his thighs. Wedding dress be damned. A fierce and decidedly unvirginal kiss accompanied the semi-lascivious embrace. Then, bouncing off, she gave Mike a hug which, though it lacked the sexual overtones, was almost as vigorous.

The preliminaries done, Rita spun around and waved forward the two people lagging behind her. Outside of the accompanying grin, the gesture resembled an empress summoning her lackeys.

Sharon was grinning herself. The man next to her wore a more subdued smile. He was a black man somewhere in his fifties, dressed in a very expensive looking suit. The conservative, hand-tailored clothing fit the man perfectly, but seemed at odds with the smile on his face. There was something a bit rakish about that smile, Mike thought. And he suspected, from the man's poised stance, that the body beneath the suit was far more athletic than its sober cut would suggest.

"Mike, this is Sharon's father. I want to introduce you." She reached back, more or less hauled the parent in question to the fore, and moved her hand back and forth vigorously. "My brother, Mike Stearns. Doctor James Nichols. Be very polite, brother of mine. He's a surgeon. Probably got four or five scalpels tucked away somewhere."

An instant later she was charging off, hauling Tom and Sharon toward a cluster of people chattering away in a corner of the cafeteria. Mike and Dr. Nichols were left alone.

Mike eyed the stranger, unsure of how to open a conversation. He opted for low humor. "My new brother-in-law's in for a long night," he said dryly. "If I know my sister."

The doctor's smile widened. The hint of rakishness deepened. "I would say so," he drawled. "Is she always this energetic?"

Mike shook his head fondly. "Since she was a toddler."

Having broken the ice, Mike took the time to examine the man next to him more carefully. Within a few seconds, he decided his initial impression was correct. Sharon's father was a study in contradictions. His skin was very dark, almost pure black. His hair was gray, kinky, cut very short. His features were blunt and rough-looking— the kind of face associated more with a longshoreman than a doctor. Yet he wore his fine clothing with ease, and the two rings on his fingers were simple in design and very tasteful. One was a plain wedding band, the other a subdued pinky ring. His diction was cultured, but the accent came from city streets. Then—

James Nichols was not a big man. No more than five feet, eight inches tall and not particularly stocky. Yet he seemed to exude a certain physical presence. A quick glance at the doctor's hands confirmed Mike's guess. The faint scars on those outsized hands had not come from working in the medical profession.

Nichols was returning Mike's examination with one of his own. There seemed to be a little twinkle in his eyes. Mike guessed that he would like the man, and decided to probe the possibility.

"So, Doc. Did the judge give *you* a choice? Between the Army and the Marines, I mean."

Nichols snorted. There *was* a twinkle in his eyes. "Not hardly! 'Marines for you, Nichols.' "

Mike shook his head. "You poor bastard. He let me pick. Since I wasn't crazy, I took the Army. I wanted no part of Parris Island."

Nichols grinned. "Well . . . You were probably just up for assault and battery, I imagine. One brawl too many." He took Mike's smile for an answer. His own headshake was rueful. "They couldn't prove it, since I fumbled the thing like a Laurel and Hardy routine, but the authorities had their dark suspicions. So the judge was hard as stone. '*Marines*, Nichols. I'm sick and tired o' *you*. Either that or six years downstate.' "

The doctor shrugged. "I admit, that judge probably saved my life." His expression became filled with mock outrage. The accent thickened. "But I still say it ain't armed robbery when the dumb kid drops the gun on the way into the liquor store and gets caught running five blocks away. Hell, who knows? Maybe he was just looking for its rightful owner. Not realizing, the poor cherub, that it was a stolen piece."

Mike burst into laughter. When his eyes met those of Nichols again, the silent exchange between them was warm and approving. The way two men, meeting for the first time, occasionally take an instant liking to each other.

Mike glanced toward his new in-laws. He was not surprised to see that his riotous gaiety had drawn their disapproving eyes. He met their stern frowns with a smile whose politeness barely covered the underlying mockery.

Yeah, that's right, you rich farts. Two scapegraces, right before your eyes. As close to outright ex-cons as you can get. Heavens!

Nichols' voice broke into Mike's silent test of wills with the Simpsons.

"So you're the famous brother," the doctor murmured.

Startled, Mike's eyes left the Simpsons. "I wasn't aware that I was famous," he protested.

Nichols shrugged, smiling. "Depends on the circle, I imagine. From what I can tell, listening to them gabble over the last couple of days, every one of your sister's college friends has a crush on you. You're quite a romantic figure, you know."

Again, Mike was startled. And, again, it must have showed on his face.

"Oh, come on, Mike!" snorted Nichols. "You're still in your mid-thirties, and look younger than that. Tall, handsome—well, handsome enough. But, most of all, you've got that glamorous *history.*"

"Glamorous?" choked Mike. "Are you nuts?"

Nichols was grinning, now. "Give me a break. You can't fool *me.*" He made a little sweeping gesture with his hands, indicating himself. "What do you see here? A very prosperous-looking black man in his mid-fifties, right?" His dark eyes glinted with humor and knowledge. "*And what else?*"

Mike eyed him. "A—let's call it a *history.* You weren't always a proper doctor."

"Certainly wasn't! And don't think, when I was your age, that I didn't take full advantage of it." Nichols' wide grin changed to a gentle smile. "You're a classic, Mike. It's that old tale which always tugs at sentiment. The reckless and dashing black sheep of the family, leaving town before the law could nail him. An adventurous lad. Soldier, longshoreman, truck driver, professional boxer. Disreputable roustabout, even if he did manage to tuck away three years in college. Then—"

The smile faded away completely. "And then, when your father was crippled, you came back to take care of your family. And did as good a job of that as you'd done scaring them to death earlier. Quite respectable, now. Even managed to get yourself elected president of your local miners' union a couple of years back."

Mike snorted. "I can see Rita's been telling tales." He started looking for his sister, ready to glare at her, when his eyes fell on the Simpsons. They were *still* frowning at him, so he bestowed the glare on them.

"See?" he demanded. "My new in-laws don't seem to feel any 'romantic attraction.' Me—*respectable*? Ha!"

Nichols' own gaze followed Mike's. "Well . . . 'Respectable' in an Appalachian sort of way. Don't think Mr. Blueblood over there is mollified that his new daughter-in-law's brother is a stone-hard union man as well as a damned hillbilly. Not hardly."

The Simpsons were still maintaining the stare. Mike was matching it, and adding a grin to the bargain. The grin was purely feral. A sheer, brazen, unyielding challenge.

Nichols would remember that savage grin, in the years to come. Remember it, and be thankful.

The Ring of Fire came, and they entered a new and very savage world.

Chapter 2

The flash was almost blinding. For an instant, the room seemed filled by sunlight. The accompanying thunder rattled the windows.

Mike ducked, hunched. James Nichols' reaction was more dramatic. *"Incoming!"* he yelped, flinging himself to the floor and covering his head with his arms. He seemed utterly oblivious to any possible damage to his expensive suit.

Half-dazed, Mike stared through the plate-glass windows of the cafeteria. The afterimage was still glowing in his eyes, as if the greatest lightning bolt ever heard of had just struck right next to the school. But, blurrily, he couldn't see any actual damage. The windows hadn't even been cracked. None of the multitude of cars and trucks in the parking lot seemed damaged. And if the people in the parking lot seemed like a bunch of squawking chickens, none of them seemed to have been hurt.

The men in the parking lot were mostly coal miners from his local, who had come in from all over the area for his sister's wedding. Partly, that was because the United Mine Workers of America never missed a chance to flaunt their solidarity. *The UMWA sticks together.* Mike thought that almost every single member of his local had shown up for the wedding, with their families in tow.

The sight of the startled men in the parking lot almost caused Mike to laugh, despite the sudden shock of that incredible—*sheet lightning?* What the hell *did* happen? The men were clustered at the back of several pickups, making precious little attempt to hide the fact that they were sneaking a drink in clear and flagrant violation of the high school's firm policy against alcoholic beverages anywhere on the premises.

A motion in the corner of his eye caught Mike's attention.

Ed Piazza was scurrying toward him, frowning like Jupiter. For a half second, Mike thought the high-school principal was about to lecture him on the unseemly behavior of the coal miners in the parking lot. He choked down another laugh.

No, he's just wondering what happened too. Waiting for Ed to reach him, Mike felt a moment's warmth for the man. *Wish he'd been the principal when I was in school. Might not have gotten into so much trouble. Good-humored, Ed is.*

"I know they're gonna drink in the parking lot, Mike," Piazza had told him the day before. *Snort.* "Bunch of coal miners at a wedding reception? But *puh-leese* keep 'em from waving the bottles under my nose. I'd feel downright stupid, all five and a half feet of me, marching out there to whack 'em with a ruler."

Ed was at his side now. "*What happened?*" The principal glanced at the ceiling. "The lights are out too."

Mike hadn't noticed until Ed mentioned it. It was still broad daylight, and the plate-glass windows lining the entire side of the cafeteria made the room's fluorescent lighting almost redundant.

"I don't know, Ed." Mike set his cup of punch—unspiked; he hadn't felt he could break the rules himself—on the table nearby. Dr. Nichols was starting to rise. Mike lent him a hand.

"Lord, do I feel stupid," muttered the doctor, brushing his clothes. Fortunately for his finery, the cafeteria floor had been mopped and waxed to a shine. "For a moment there, I thought I was back at Khe Sanh." He, too, asked the inevitable question. "What the hell was *that?*"

The large and crowded room was now in a muted uproar, everyone asking the same thing. But there was no panic. Whatever *that* was, nothing immediately disastrous seemed to have occurred.

"Let's get outside," said Mike, heading toward the cafeteria's door. "Maybe we'll get a better idea." He glanced around the room, looking for his sister. He spotted Rita almost at once, clutching Tom's arm. She seemed a bit alarmed, but was obviously unhurt.

By the time Mike reached the door, Frank Jackson had pushed his way through the babbling crowd. Seeing the stocky, gray-haired form of the union's secretary-treasurer, followed by five other miners from the local, Mike felt a flash of pride. *UMWA. Solidarity forever.*

Meeting Frank's eyes, Mike shrugged and shook his head. "I don't know what happened either. Let's go outside and check around."

A few seconds later, the little group of men was passing through the entrance to the high school and making their way onto the parking lot. Seeing him come, dozens of Mike's local union members started moving in his direction. Most of them even had enough self-possession to leave their drinks behind in the vehicles.

Mike's first concern was for the high school itself. His eyes ranged up and down the long row of buildings, looking for any signs of damage. But none of the beige and white structures seemed to have been harmed at all.

"Everything looks okay," muttered Ed with heartfelt relief. The relatively new consolidated high school—built not much more than two decades ago, using a lot of voluntary labor—was the pride and joy of the rural area. For no one was that more true than its principal.

Mike looked to the west, toward Grantville. The town itself, two miles away, was hidden behind the hills which gave northern West Virginia its distinctive landscape. But Mike couldn't detect any obvious indications of trouble in that direction either.

His eyes moved to the south. The high school had been built on a gentle slope north of Buffalo Creek. At the bottom of that slope, just beyond the end of the parking lot, U.S. Route 250 ran parallel to the small river. The hills on the other side of the little valley were steep, covered with trees, and uninhabited except for a handful of trailers.

Nothing. His eyes began following the highway at the bottom of the slope, toward the large town of Fairmont some fifteen miles to the east.

Stop. There was a hint of smoke...

He pointed to the hills southeast of the school. "Something's burning. Over there."

Everyone followed his finger. "Sure enough," muttered Frank. "C'mon, Ed. Let's call the fire brigade." The union's secretary-treasurer and the high-school principal started moving toward the double doors leading into the school. Then, seeing the man coming through those doors, they stopped.

"Hey, Dan!" Frank pointed to the thin columns of smoke rising in the distance. "See if you can get hold of the Volunteers. We've got trouble here!"

Grantville's police chief didn't waste more than two seconds staring at the smoke. Then he was hurrying toward his vehicle and its radio.

The radio wasn't working, for some reason. Nothing but static. Cursing under his breath, Dan looked up and spotted Piazza.

"You'll have to use the phones, Ed!" he shouted. "The radio isn't working."

"The phones aren't working either!" responded Piazza. "I'll send someone down there in a car!"

The principal hurried back toward the school. "And get hold of Doc Adams while you're at it!" the police chief shouted to his retreating form. "We might need medical help!" Piazza waved his acknowledgment.

By then, Mike and Frank and several other coal miners had already started up their trucks. Dan Frost was not surprised at their instant assumption that they would be accompanying him to see what the problem was. In truth, he took it for granted.

Dan had once been offered a position in a large city's police force, at a considerably larger salary. He hadn't thought for more than three seconds before turning it down. Dan Frost had seen police work in big cities. He'd rather stay in his little town, thank you, where he could be a cop instead of an occupying army.

As he climbed into his Cherokee and started the engine, Dan checked the interior of the vehicle quickly. The shotgun was in its gun case in the back, and there was extra ammunition for his pistol in the glove compartment. Satisfied everything was in place, he leaned out of the window. Mike Stearns pulled his truck alongside. Dan was surprised to see a black man riding in the passenger seat.

"Dr. Nichols here is a surgeon," Mike explained, half-shouting. "He volunteered to come along." Mike hooked a thumb over his shoulder. "His daughter Sharon will ride with Frank. Turns out she's a trained paramedic."

Dan nodded. An instant later, he was driving the Cherokee down the asphalt road leading to Route 250. Three pickups and a van followed, carrying eight coal miners along with James and Sharon Nichols. Behind them, in his rearview mirror, Dan could see a mob of people pouring out of the high school. There was something slightly comical about the scene. Squawking chickens, wearing their Sunday best for the wedding.

Once he reached the road, Dan turned left. Route 250 was a well-built two-lane highway. Even winding through the hills and hollows, it was easily possible to drive fifty miles an hour at many stretches. But Dan took it more slowly than usual. He was still uncertain what was happening. That flash had been truly incredible. For a fleeting instant, Frost had been certain that a nuclear war had started.

Everything seemed normal, though, as far as he could see. He was driving alongside Buffalo Creek now. On the other side of the creek, at the foot of the hills, railroad tracks ran parallel to the road. He caught a glimpse of two house trailers nestled away in the woods. They were old, weather-beaten, ramshackle—but otherwise unharmed.

Coming around a bend, Dan threw on the brakes. The highway ended abruptly in a shiny wall, perhaps six feet tall. A small car had skidded sideways into the wall, caving part of it—*dirt*, Dan realized—over the hood. Dan could see a woman's face staring at him through the driver's side window. The woman was wide-eyed.

"That's Jenny Lynch," he muttered. He stared at the wall across the road. "What in the hell is going on?"

Dan got out of the Cherokee. Behind him, he could hear the miners' trucks coming to a halt and doors opening. When he reached the car, he tapped on the window. Slowly, Jenny rolled it down.

"Are you okay?" The youngish, plump-faced woman nodded hesitantly.

"I—I think so, Dan." She reached a shaky hand toward her face. "Did I kill anybody? I don't know what *happened*." The words started coming out in a rush. "There was a flash—some kind of explosion— I don't know . . . Then this wall, where did it come from? I hit the brakes, car started skidding—I . . . I don't know what happened. I don't know what happened."

Dan patted her on the shoulder. "Relax, Jenny. You didn't hurt anybody. I think you're just a little shaken up." He remembered Nichols. "We've got a doctor with us. Hold on just—"

He started to turn, but Nichols was already there. The doctor gently shouldered Dan aside and gave Jenny a quick examination.

"I don't think there's anything serious," he said. "Let's get her out of the car." He opened the door. A moment later, he and Dan were helping Jenny. Other than being shaky and pale, the woman didn't seemed harmed.

"Come here a second, will you Dan?" said Mike. The union president was squatting by the strange wall, digging into it with a pocket knife. The police chief walked over.

"This thing is just *dirt*," Mike stated. "Nothing but plain old dirt." He spilled another scoop out of the wall. As soon as the cohesion was broken, the shiny substance turned into nothing but a pile of soil. "The only reason it looks shiny is because—" Mike groped for words. "It's as if the dirt's been cut by a perfect razor." He poked at the wall again. "See? As soon as you break through the surface, it's nothing but dirt. What the hell could have done that? And where did it come from?"

Mike glanced right and left. The "wall" continued on both sides of the road. It was as if two completely different landscapes had suddenly been jammed together. He could see the side of a typical West Virginia hill to the south—except the side was now like a perpendicular cliff. Just as shiny as the wall across the road, except where pockets of soil were falling loose.

Dan shrugged. He started to say something when he heard a sudden shriek. Startled, he rose and stared at the wall. An instant later, a body hurtled over the top and crashed into him.

The impact sent Dan sprawling on the pavement. The body—a young girl, he realized dimly, a raggedly dressed teenager—landed on top of him, still shrieking. The girl bounced off him and scrambled down the bank, heading for the creek. Still screaming.

Half-dazed, Dan started to rise. Mike was at his side, extending a hand. Dan took it and got back on his feet.

Everything was happening too fast. He had just started to turn, looking for the girl, when he saw two new figures appear on top of the wall.

Men. Armed.

Mike's back was toward them, half-blocking Dan's view. Dan pushed him off and reached for his pistol. One of the men—then the other—began raising his rifle. *Rifle?* What *was* that strange-looking weapon?

Dan's pistol was clear of the holster. Coming up. *"Halt!"* he shouted. *"Drop your weapons!"*

The first rifle went off. The gun made a strange, booming sound. Dan heard the bullet ricochet off the pavement. He caught a glimpse of Mike throwing himself down. Dan had his pistol up—levered the slide—two-handed grip—

The round from the second rifle slammed into his left shoulder, knocking him sideways.

His mind felt suspended. Dan had never actually fired his weapon in a live situation. But he was an instructor in police combat tactics, and had spent uncounted hours on the firing range and in simulated drills. His training took over. Using his right hand, he brought the pistol back on target.

Detached, his mind recognized that the man was wearing some kind of armor. And a helmet. Dan was an expert shot. The range wasn't more than thirty feet. He fired. Fired again. The .40-caliber rounds practically severed the man's neck. He flopped backward, out of sight.

Dan swung his pistol to the left. The other man was still standing on the wall, doing something with his weapon. He, too, was wearing armor. But he had no helmet. Dan fired. Fired again. Fired again. Three shots, in less than two seconds. The head which absorbed those rounds was nothing but a ruptured ruin. The man collapsed to his knees, dropping his weapon. A second later, both the man and his firearm were sliding over the wall. The firearm landed on the pavement with a clatter. The body landed with a sodden thump.

Dan felt himself slumping. He sensed that his arm—his whole body—was soaked with blood. Mike caught him and lowered him to the ground.

He was fading out now. *Shock*, he realized. *I'm losing a lot of blood.* Dimly, he recognized the face of the black doctor, looming over him. His vision was getting blurred.

There was something he had to do. Urgent.

Oh, yeah. "Mike," he whispered. "I'm deputizing you. You and your guys. Find out what the hell—" He faded out, back in. "Just do whatever you've got to . . ."

Faded out.

"How is he?" Mike asked.

Nichols shook his head. The doctor had pulled out a handkerchief and was trying to staunch the wound. The cloth was already soaking through.

"I think it's just a flesh wound," he muttered. "But—*Jesus*—what did that bastard shoot him with, anyway? A shotgun slug? Damned near ripped his shoulder off. Sharon—*come here. Quick!*"

As his daughter hurried up, Nichols was relieved to see she was carrying a first-aid kit. Frank Jackson must have had one in his truck. The doctor spotted another miner hauling a first-aid kit out of his own vehicle. *Thank God for country boys,* came the whimsical thought.

While Nichols and his daughter started tending to Dan Frost, one of the other miners picked up his assailant's weapon. Ken Hobbs, that was. He was in his early sixties and, like many of the men in the area, was an enthusiast for antique black-powder guns.

"Will you look at this thing, Mike?" he demanded, holding up the firearm. "I swear to God—this is a fucking *matchlock!*"

Noticing Sharon working at her father's side, Hobbs flushed. "Sorry, ma'am. 'Bout the bad language."

Sharon ignored him. She was too preoccupied helping her father. Dan's eyes were closed. His face was as pale as a sheet.

Mike turned away. Hobbs came up to him, extending the captured weapon. His wizened face, scrunched up with puzzlement, was a mass of wrinkles. "I *swear*, Mike. It's a matchlock. There's pictures of them in one of my books at home."

Another miner, Hank Jones, came up. "You oughta be careful handling that," he muttered. "You know. Mess up the fingerprints."

Hobbs started to make some vulgar retort. Then, remembering Sharon, turned profanity into a simple hiss. "For what, Hank? So we can nab the culprit?" He gestured at the corpse lying at the foot of the peculiar embankment. "Case you didn't notice, Dan already blew the SOB's head off."

Another miner had scrambled onto the wall, and was studying the corpse of the other man. He barked a harsh laugh. "Same here! Two rounds, right through the neck."

Darryl McCarthy was in his early twenties. He had none of Hobbs' old-fashioned qualms about using bad language in front of a woman. Not under these circumstances, anyway. "Only thing holding this asshole's head to his body," he announced loudly, "is maybe three little strips of meat."

McCarthy rose. Standing on the lip of the wall, he stared down at Dan Frost's unconscious form. His look was full of approval. "Both rounds hit the bastard right in the throat. Blew his fucking neck all to hell."

All the coal miners were gathered at the scene, now. All of them were staring down at Frost. All of them with approval.

"Remind me not to lip off to him at the Happy Trails, next time he says I've had enough," murmured Frank Jackson. "Always heard he was a hell of a shot."

Mike straightened up, remembering the girl. His eyes ranged down the creek where she had fled.

"She's probably half a mile away, by now," said Hank. He pointed southwest, across the creek. "I saw her scramble over to the other side. Creek must be low. She went up somewhere into the trees."

Hank's face twisted into a ferocious scowl. "The whole back of her dress had been ripped off, Mike." He glared at the corpse lying on the pavement. "I think those guys were trying to *rape* her."

Mike's eyes went to the corpse. Then looked at the wall and the unseen territory beyond. Thin columns of smoke were still rising.

"Something bad is happening here, guys," he stated. "I don't know what it is. But it's bad." He pointed at the corpse. "I don't think this is all of it."

Frank stalked over to the corpse and stooped over it. "Look at this weird armor. What do you think, Mike? Some kind of crazy survivalists or something?"

Mike shrugged. "I've got no idea, Frank. But if there were two of them, there's no reason can't be more." He gestured at Dan. Dr. Nichols seemed to have the blood flow stanched. "You heard the chief, guys. He deputized us, and told us to do whatever's got to be done."

The miners nodded, and crowded a little closer.

"So get your guns, boys. I know damn well you've all got something stashed in your vehicles. We're going hunting."

As the men started moving toward their trucks, Mike reconsidered. "Except you, Ken. You've got to get Dan back to the high school. They've got a clinic."

Seeing the elderly Hobbs' look of suspicion, Mike elaborated curtly. "Don't argue with me! It's not your age, dammit. You've got the only van here." He pointed at Frost. "Better than tossing him into the bed of a pickup."

Mollified, Hobbs nodded. "I'll get my gun. Leave it with you guys."

Mike heard Nichols murmur something to his daughter. A moment later the doctor was rising.

"Sharon can do as much for him right now as I can," he said. "It's just a flesh wound. Big one, but nothing worse. She'll go back with him to the clinic."

Mike cocked an eyebrow. Nichols smiled thinly. "I'm coming with you." Nichols nodded toward the wall. "Like you said, something bad's going down here. I suspect you'll need me down the road a ways."

Mike hesitated. Then, studying the hard, rough face—a *very* thin smile that was—he nodded. "Okay with me, Doc." He looked down at Frost. "Can you get that holster off him? You better have a weapon yourself."

While Nichols occupied himself with that task, Mike went over to his own pickup. It was the work of a few seconds to haul his gun from its place of concealment behind the seat. And a box of ammunition. He hefted the big .357 magnum. The weapon was a Smith & Wesson Model 28 Highway Patrolman fixed-sight revolver, tucked into a clip holster. Fortunately, Mike had insisted on dress pants using a belt instead of suspenders. He attached the holster to the belt and shoved the ammunition in the rented tuxedo's deep pockets.

Then he went over to Dan's Cherokee and took out the shotgun. He also found two boxes of ammunition. One of them contained rounds for the .40 caliber. The other held double-ought buckshot. The same rounds would be in the shotgun's magazine. He pried out a half dozen shotgun shells and stuffed them in his pants pockets. The box of .40-caliber ammunition he kept in his hand. Between the revolver and all the ammunition, he felt like a waddling duck.

Screw it. I'd rather be a well-armed duck than a sitting one.

By now, Sharon and Hobbs had gotten Dan into the back of the van. Jenny Lynch had recovered enough to lend them a hand. Less than a minute later, the van was turning around and heading back to the high school.

Mike's union members were gathered around him. All of them were armed. Most of them with pistols, except Frank's beloved lever-action Winchester and Harry Lefferts'—

"For Christ's sake, Harry," Mike snapped, "don't ever let Dan catch you with that."

Harry grinned. He was the same age as Darryl—they were best friends, in fact—and shared Darryl's carefree youthful attitudes. "And what's wrong with a sawed-off shotgun?" he demanded. He jerked his head around, pointing to everyone else with his chin. "It's not as if every damn one of these guns isn't illegal, when you get right down to it. So what's another concealed weapon—among friends?"

A little chuckle swept the group. Mike made a face. "Yeah, well— you better be damn close, with that thing. Don't forget these guys were wearing armor."

He turned now to the doctor, and handed him the box of .40-caliber ammunition he'd found in the glove compartment. Nichols put down the first-aid kit he was carrying. Mike was not particularly surprised to see the quick and expert way in which Nichols reloaded the automatic pistol.

"Well-trained, you Marines," he murmured.

Nichols snorted. "Marines, my ass. I knew what to do with one of these before I was twelve." He hefted the automatic. "This is Blackstone Rangers' training. I grew up within spitting distance of Sixty-third and Cottage Grove."

Suddenly, the black doctor was beaming wickedly at the white men around him. "Gentlemen," he said, "the Marines are at your side. Not to mention Chicago's worst ghetto. Let's deal."

The miners grinned back. "Nice to have you along, Doc," announced Frank.

Mike turned, and strode toward the embankment. "Like you said. *Let's deal.*"

Chapter 3

Mike used Jenny's car, still dug into the embankment, as a stepping stone to climb onto the embankment. When he planted his foot on the peculiar wall, it immediately gave way, showering more dirt on the car. He sprawled awkwardly, cursing under his breath, and dragged himself over the edge.

Once he arose, he gazed down at his tuxedo. Between his recent mishap and the effects of throwing himself onto the pavement when the shooting started, the elegant outfit was looking more than a little scruffy.

The rental company's not going to be happy with me, he thought ruefully. *But—*

Mike gave Frank a hand climbing up. "Be careful," he urged. "That wall looks solid because it's so shiny, but it's nothing but loose earth."

Once Frank was atop the wall, he turned to help the others. Mike took the moment to examine his surroundings.

His *new* surroundings. What he saw confirmed his suspicions.

But I think a ticked-off tuxedo rental company is probably the least of my problems.

The "wall" wasn't a wall of any kind. It was simply the edge of a plain stretching into the distance. Everything about that landscape was wrong. There was no level stretch that size anywhere in northern West Virginia. And the sun—

Frank vocalized the thought. "Mike, what's happening? Even the damn *sun's* in the wrong place." He pointed to the south. "Should be over there."

Or is that the south? wondered Mike. *At a guess, I'd say we're facing north instead of east, like we should be.*

He thrust the problem aside. Later. There were more pressing problems to deal with. Much more pressing.

The plain was heavily wooded, but not so much so that Mike couldn't see one–two–three farmhouses scattered among open fields. One of the farmhouses was not more than a hundred yards away.

Close enough to make out some details . . .

"*Jesus*," hissed Frank.

The two farmhouses in the distance were burning fiercely. The one nearby was not. It was a large and rambling structure. Unlike the wood-frame farmhouses which Mike was familiar with, the construction of this one leaned heavily toward stone. Hand-fitted stone, from what Mike could see. If it weren't for the fact that the farmhouse had all the signs of current occupancy—that unmistakably ragged-respectable air of a place where people *worked*—Mike would have sworn he was looking at a something out of the Middle Ages.

But he didn't spend more than two seconds studying the farmhouse itself. The farmhouse was still being "worked," but not by farmers.

His teeth were clenched. He could sense that Frank, standing next to him, was filled with the same outrage. Mike looked around. All of his miners were on the plain now, standing in a line staring at the scene.

"All right, guys," he said softly. "I count six of the bastards. May be more inside. Three of them are assaulting that poor woman in the yard. The other three—"

He looked back at the horrendous sight. "Don't know exactly what they're doing. I think they've got that guy nailed to his door and they're torturing him."

Slowly, as softly as possible, Frank levered a round into the chamber of his rifle. Despite its incongruity with the suit he was wearing, the action was quietly murderous. "So what's the plan?" he demanded.

Mike spoke through tight jaws. "I'm not actually a cop, when you get right down to it. And we haven't got time anyway to rummage around in Dan's Cherokee looking for handcuffs." He glared at the scene of rape and torture. "So to hell with reading these guys their rights. *We're just going to kill them.*"

"Sounds good to me," snarled Darryl. "I got no problem with capital punishment. Never did."

"Me neither," growled one of the other miners. Tony Adducci, that was, a beefy man in his early forties. Like many of the miners in the area, Tony was of Italian ancestry, as his complexion and features indicated. "None whatsoever."

Tony, like Mike, was holding a pistol. He reached up with his left hand and quickly removed his tie. Angrily, he thrust it into a pocket.

The rest of the miners did likewise with their own. None of them took off their jackets, however. All of them were wearing white shirts and all of them were experienced hunters. Their suit jackets, gray and brown and Navy blue, would make better camouflage. After removing their ties—a bow tie, in Mike's case—the miners simply loosened the top collar buttons. For the first time in their lives, they would "hunt" in their Sunday best, wearing dress shoes instead of boots.

Mike led the way, working toward the farmhouse through a small grove of trees. *Birch trees*, a part of his mind noted idly. *That's odd too.* Most of his mind was simply wishing that the slender trees provided more concealment. Fortunately, the criminals at the farmhouse were too preoccupied with their crimes to be paying any attention to the area around them.

The miners got within thirty yards of the house without being spotted. They were now squatting down, hidden in the trees at the very edge of the farm yard. The woman being raped was not more than forty feet away. Mike's eyes shied away from the sight, but his ears still registered her moans.

And the coarse laughs of the men assaulting her. One of them, the man holding her arms to the ground, barked a jeering remark at the man on top of her. The rapist grunted some sort of reply.

Mike couldn't understand the words, but they sounded German. He'd been stationed in Germany for a year, while he'd been in the Army. But he remembered little of the language beyond the essential phrase, *ein bier, bitte.*

"Those guy are *foreigners*," muttered Darryl. The young man's face was tight with anger. "*Who do they think they are, coming here and—?*"

Mike made a short, curt gesture, commanding silence. He went back to studying the criminals.

All of them wore that same peculiar armor and those weird helmets, although the men assaulting the woman had removed theirs. The discarded gear was lying on the ground nearby. The men torturing the farmer still had their armor and helmets on, but they had stacked their firearms against the wall of the farmhouse. From a distance, the "rifles" looked like the same kind of weapons carried by the two men killed by the police chief.

The helmets and armor reminded Mike of pictures he had seen of old Spanish conquistadores. The helmets were metal pots, basically, with flanges tapering into points toward the front and back. The armor, if he remembered right, was called a *cuirass*. Steel breast and back plates, tied on with leather strips. Outside of the antique-looking firearms, the only weapons they had in their possession were—

Swords? *Swords?*

He looked back at the three men asaulting the woman. They were not wearing swords, but now that Mike knew what to look for he spotted the weapons immediately. The scabbarded blades had been unbuckled and tossed onto the ground near the firearms. Mike had never once in his life considered the practical mechanics of rape, but he could understand why a sword would be awkward. These men, he was suddenly quite certain, were not committing this crime for the first time. There was a relaxed and practiced casualness about their activity.

You are dead men. The thought was grim, final.

He turned his head and whispered in Frank's ear. "You've got the only rifle. Can you take out the bastards at the door? Don't forget, they're wearing armor. Can't go for a body shot."

Mike and Frank stared at the three men torturing the farmer. The heavy door of the house had been opened wide and pressed against the wall. The farmer's wrists were pinned to the door with knives. A man in front of him was digging another knife into the farmer's thigh, while his two companions shouted at him. The shouts, Mike thought, were some kind of interrogation. It seemed a pointless exercise. The farmer was screaming with pain, oblivious to any questions.

"Forty yards?" Frank snorted. "Don't worry about it. A .30-caliber slug in the ass will take anybody down."

Mike nodded. He turned the other way and motioned toward Harry Lefferts. Harry crept up to him.

Mike scowled at the sawed-off double-barreled shotgun in Harry's hands. "Forget that stupid thing. We've got innocent people mixed up with these thugs." He handed Harry the riot gun he'd taken from the Cherokee. "Use this. It's loaded with buckshot. The magazine's full—I already checked. When Frank shoots those guys at the door, you back him up. He's going to be aiming for their legs, on account of the armor. You finish them off after they're down."

Harry nodded. He tucked the sawed-off shotgun under a nearby shrub and took the riot gun. After passing over the additional shotgun shells in his pocket, Mike glanced around at the rest of his men. All of them, like himself, were armed with nothing more than pistols and revolvers.

He decided there was no point in developing any more of a battle plan. Besides—

I can't bear listening to this any longer.

"Just back me up, guys," he whispered. To Frank: "Don't start shooting till I do."

A second later, Mike rose to his feet and strode out of the trees toward the rapists. He held the revolver in his right hand. His steps

were quick, but he was not running. Mike hadn't boxed profession-
ally in years, but the old training and experience had taken over.
Steady, steady; don't lose your cool; it's just another fight. A stray,
whimsical part of his mind told him how foolish he looked, marching
toward mayhem in wingtips and a tuxedo, but he ignored it.

The first man who spotted him was the one squatting on his heels
about three feet from the woman. The man had been simply watching
the scene, leering. When Mike's movement caught his eye, the man
turned his head. His eyes widened. He was not more than thirty feet
away, turned sideways.

Mike stopped. He crouched slightly, in a firing-range stance, bringing up the revolver. Some part of his mind noted the instant reflexes
of the man he was going to kill, and was impressed. No tyro, he. The
man was already rising, shouting a warning.

*Both hands, firm grip, cock the hammer. Steady, steady. Center of
mass. Squeeze the—*

As always, the magnum went off with a roar and bucked in Mike's
hand. He watched just long enough to see that the slug had slammed
into the man's turning shoulder and knocked him flat. A split second, no more. The man might still be alive, but he was clearly out
of the action.

Mike could hear the flat crack of Frank's Winchester, and Harry
shouting. He ignored the sounds, blocking them out as easily as he
had blocked out the roar of the crowd while he was in the ring. He
was swiveling, now, ready to take out the man holding the woman's
arms. That one was facing him squarely. Mike could see the man's
mouth gaping wide open, but his face was a blur. The man was still
on his knees, but he had released the woman's arms and was rear-
ing back on his heels.

*Just another fight. Cock the hammer—single-shot's more accurate.
Center of mass . . .*

Again, the .357 roared. The shot took the man square in the chest,
slamming him back as if he'd been run over by a truck. Mike knew
he was dead before he hit the ground.

One left, and he's tangled up in his dropped trousers.

The rapist was shouting something. Again, Mike couldn't understand the words. Nothing registered except fear. The man was scrambling off the woman. He tried to rise, tripped on his trousers, sprawled
on his face.

But he was clear of the woman now. Mike raised the revolver, ready
to kill him, but stopped when he saw Dr. Nichols was already there.
There was something surgically precise about the way Nichols, from
close range, leaned over and shot the man in the back of the head.
Once, twice.

So much for that. Mike turned away, looking to the farmhouse. He could remember, now, hearing several shots from Frank's rifle.

All three men at the door were lying on the ground. One of them was not moving. He was on his knees, sprawled against the wall of the farmhouse. His buttocks were covered with blood. Mike was certain that he was the first one Frank had shot. For all that he teased Frank about that silly damned lever-action, Frank was both an excellent marksman and one of the most reliable men Mike had ever met. Got his deer every season, usually on the first day. Frank would have shot for the lower spine, just below the cuirass.

Paralyzed, for sure. Probably dead or dying.

The other two were writhing on the ground, screaming, clutching their legs. They didn't scream or writhe for long. Harry was already there, racing forward. The young miner stopped abruptly, a few feet away. He pumped a shell into the chamber, aimed the shotgun and fired. For all that Harry was obviously in a rage, he hadn't lost his composure. He aimed for the neck, unprotected by either helmet or armor. The man was almost decapitated. The buckshot sent his helmet bouncing off the farmhouse wall, the straps broken and flailing about.

Harry swiveled. Pump, level, fire. The other man was silent. Unmoving, dead. Blood and brains everywhere. Another helmet sent flying, straps flapping. For good measure—there would be no mercy here—Harry pumped another round, stepped forward, and shot the paralyzed man sprawled against the farmhouse wall. The range was not more than three feet. This time, the helmet stayed on—but only because the man's head was removed entirely. Blood gushed out of a severed neck, painting the rough stones with gore.

Mike caught a glimpse of motion, somewhere in the darkness within the farmhouse. He ducked.

"Harry—down! Fire in the hole!"

Mike's warning probably saved Harry's life. The young miner was lunging aside when the gun in the farmhouse went off. The bullet took him in the side and knocked him down, yelping. On the ground, Lefferts clutched his ribs, still yelping. But there was more surprise and outrage in the sound than anything else. Mike was pretty sure the wound was superficial.

"Cover me, Frank!" he yelled, racing to the side of the door. He could hear Frank's Winchester firing again. He couldn't see the shots themselves, but knew that Frank would be firing through the door, driving back whoever was inside. In the corner of his eye he saw James Nichols and Tony Adducci leveling their pistols and firing shots into the small windows alongside the farmhouse. He could hear the wooden shutters splintering.

Once he reached the door, Mike pressed himself against the farm-house wall. He was on the opposite side of the door from the farmer. The man was unconscious, now, soaked with blood and sagging. His weight—he was a middle-aged man, heavy in the gut—was tearing his wrists badly. Blood spurted everywhere.

Christ, he'll bleed to death. Mike's decision was instant. He sprang across the doorway to the farmer's side, momentarily exposing himself to fire from within the farmhouse. But there was no gunshot. Two quick powerful jerks withdrew the knives. As gently as he could, Mike lowered the man to the ground.

That was all he could do for him at the moment. Mike hesitated, then, for a second or two. The interior of the farmhouse was so poorly lit it was impossible to see anything inside. Caution and his Army training urged him to wait until his companions could come up in support. On the other hand—

All these guns are those weird antiques. Single-shot muzzle-loaders. I'll bet that son of a bitch hasn't had time to reload.

Again, decision was sharp, immediate. Mike dove through the door and landed rolling.

Good decision, bad luck. His enemy *hadn't* had time to reload. Unfortunately, Mike rolled right into him.

For a moment, everything was chaos. Mike felt a body landing on top of him. The surprise, as much as the collision, jarred the pistol out of his hand. Frantic now, he lunged to his feet, hurling the man off his back.

Tried to, at least. The man, whoever he was, clutched Mike like a wrestler. Mike snarled and slammed his elbow backward.

Damn! He'd forgotten the cuirass. His left elbow was aching from the impact. But at least he'd knocked the man loose.

Mike had never been in a gun battle before in his life. He had a boxer's training and instincts, not a gunfighter's. He didn't even think to look for his pistol. He just pivoted and drove a right cross into his enemy's chin.

Eight pro fights. The first seven had been won by knockouts, none of them later than the fourth round. Mike had quit the game because he'd realized he didn't quite have the reflexes. But nobody had ever said he didn't have the punch.

The thug, whoever he was, sailed across the room and slammed against a heavy table. His jaw hung loose, broken. His head lolled to the side.

That dazed helplessness brought no mercy. Neither that, nor the fact that the man was quite a bit smaller than Mike. This was not a fight governed by Marquis of Queensbury rules. Mike bounced for-ward on his toes and slammed another right hand, low into the man's abdomen below the cuirass. Another. If there'd been a referee, Mike would have been disqualified by either punch. His next blow was a left hook, which shattered the man's jaw and lifted him right off his feet. Mike was a very strong man, and—unlike most—he knew how to fight. The blows were like sledgehammers. Mike started to slam another right into the thug's face but managed to stop the punch.

Christ, Stearns—enough! He's done.

He forced himself to step back, as if being driven off by an invisible referee. The trained reaction brought some clarity to his thoughts. Mike was shocked to realize how much fear and rage had taken possession of him. He felt like a vial of pure adrenaline.

His opponent collapsed to the floor in a heap. Mike dropped his arms and let his fists open. His hands hurt. He'd forgotten how much punishment bare-knuckle fighting inflicted on the victor as well as the vanquished.

He was starting to tremble now, from delayed reaction to the entire fight. The gunplay was affecting him more than anything else. For all that he'd been something of a roughneck in his youth, Mike had never killed anyone before.

A hand fell on his shoulder, turning him around. He saw Dr. Nichols' concerned face. "Are you all right?"

Mike nodded. He even managed a wan little smile, and held up his hands. Three of the knuckles were split and bleeding. "Far as I know, Doc, this is all that's wrong with me."

Nichols took the hands and examined them, kneading the joints. "Don't think anything's broken," he muttered. The doctor cast a quick glance at the unconscious thug on the dirt floor of the farmhouse. "But as hard as you punch, young fellow, I'd really suggest you use gloves from now on. That bastard looks like somebody took an ax handle to him."

For a moment, Mike felt a little light-headed. He could sense other miners ranging through the farmhouse, looking for more enemies. But there weren't any. The blood rushing through his ears blurred the words they were speaking, but Mike could sense from the tone that all danger was past.

He took a deep, almost shuddering breath. Then, with a quick shake of the head, he cleared away the sensation of dizziness. Nichols released his hands.

"Thanks, Doc," he said softly.

Nichols' face broke into a sudden smile. "Please—call me James! I believe we've been properly introduced."

The doctor turned away. "And now I've got some badly injured people to deal with. I think I've tattered the Hippocratic Oath enough for one day." In a mutter: "Christ, Nichols. 'First, do no harm.'"

Guiltily, Mike remembered Harry Lefferts. And the farmer and the woman he assumed was his wife. He started after Nichols, ready to lend assistance. Then stopped and turned, looking for Frank.

Jackson was standing by a large fireplace, slowly examining the interior of the room. Most of the farmhouse seemed to consist of a single chamber, although Mike could see a slender staircase--more like a ladder—leading to the upper story. Very little light filtered into the farmhouse, since the few windows were tiny. But Mike could see that the place was a complete shambles. The thugs had obviously been looting, along with their other crimes. Now that he'd seen how thoroughly the farmhouse had been ransacked, Mike realized that the farmer had been tortured in order to reveal whatever hidden treasures he might possess.

Not much, from the looks of this place. For all its size and painstaking construction, the house was poorer-looking than any farm Mike had ever seen. There wasn't even any interior lighting. Nor plumbing, from what he could tell. No glass in the windows. Even the floor was simply packed earth.

Frank's eyes met him. "I'll see to this, Mike. Tony's already checking upstairs. You go help the doctor."

Outside, Mike found Nichols working on the farmer. The doctor, having apparently gone through all the bandages in the first-aid kit, had removed his suit jacket and was tearing his shirt into strips. He was now bare from the waist up. For all that Nichols was in late middle age, there was almost no fat on his wiry musculature. The hard black flesh, covered with a thin film of sweat, gleamed in the sunlight.

Mike looked around. Darryl was tending to Harry Lefferts. Lefferts also had his shirt off, and was goggling at the wound in his side. It was quite spectacular—his entire thigh and hip were soaked with blood, along with his ribs—but Mike didn't think it was really serious. The wound was already bound with a bandage roll. The bandage was bloodstained, but Mike thought the bleeding had stopped.

"It's just a flesh wound," he heard Nichols say. Mike turned. The doctor had cocked his head toward him. "I treated Harry first thing. He'll have a truly amazing scar to boast to his grandkids about, but the bullet just traveled along one rib before passing out. No internal bleeding, so far as I can tell."

Nichols' head jerked toward the woman. She had rolled over onto her side, her hands covering her face. Her knees were drawn up to her chest, in fetal position. She was sobbing quietly and steadily. Her shabby dress had been pulled back down over her legs and two jackets were covering her further. The miners who had contributed those jackets—Don Richards and Larry Masaniello—were squatting nearby.

Their expressions were confused and distressed. Beyond what they'd done, they obviously had no idea what other help they could give her.

"She'll be all right," murmured Nichols. His face tightened. "As much as any gang-rape victim, anyway." He looked back down at the farmer. "But this guy might not make it. There are no major arteries severed, but he's lost an enormous amount of blood."

Mike squatted by the doctor. "How can I help, James?" He saw that Nichols had bound up all of the farmer's wounds. But blood was already soaking through the cloth. The doctor was tearing more strips from his ruined shirt, ready to add new bandages.

"Give me your tuxedo jacket, for starters. See if there are any blankets inside. Anything to keep him warm. He's in shock."

Mike took off his jacket and handed it to the doctor, who spread it over the farmer. Then Nichols blew out his cheeks. "Get me an ambulance, so we can take this poor guy to a hospital. Short of that, I've done all I can here without medical supplies and facilities."

The doctor raised his head and slowly studied the surrounding area. "But somehow I've got a bad feeling that ambulances and hospitals are going to be hard to come by."

His eyes met Mike's. "Where the hell are we, anyway?" He managed a smile. "Please don't tell me this is what West Virginia's really like. My daughter's been pushing me to move my practice here." Again, his eyes ranged about. "Not even that movie *Deliverance* was this crazy. And that was somewhere in the backwoods, if I remember right. We're only an hour and a half from Pittsburgh."

Mike copied the doctor's examination of the surrounding area. Softly: "I don't think we're in West Virginia anymore, Toto." Nichols chuckled. "Nothing's right, James—not the landscape, not the trees, not the people, not—" He jerked a thumb over his shoulder, pointing to the farmhouse which loomed behind them. "There's nothing like this in West Virginia, I'll tell you that. For all the poverty of this place, the farmhouse itself is no rickety shack. Anything that big and well-built and old would have been declared a historical monument fifty years ago."

He leaned over and seized one of the thugs' guns, still leaning against the farmhouse. After a quick scrutiny, he held it out for Nichols.

"You ever seen anything like this?" The doctor shook his head. "Neither have I," mused Mike. "Ken Hobbs says it's a matchlock. He'd know, too. He's made a hobby of antique weapons his whole life. They haven't made guns like this in—oh, must be two hundred years. At least. Even by the time of the American Revolution, everybody was using flintlocks."

He eyed the weapon's bore respectfully. "Look at this thing, will you? Must be at least .75 caliber."

He started to add something else, but was interrupted by Frank, coming out of the door.

"All clear," he said. Jackson seemed as unflappable as ever. Some of that was simply his personality, but some of it was due to the fact that the union's secretary-treasurer was the only one of them besides Nichols who had real combat experience.

Mike examined the other men he could see. All of them except Jackson and Nichols, now that the fight was over, were starting to react. Lefferts was lying on his back, clutching the bandage to his side and staring at the sky. The young miner, who had been so murderously ruthless in the heat of the action, seemed like a stunned steer. His eyes were wide, empty of all thought. Kneeling next to him, Darryl's head was slumped between his shoulders. He was gripping his knees so tightly that his knuckles were white. Off to the side, near the rape victim, Don Richards and Larry Masaniello were no longer squatting alertly with their guns in their hands. Both men were now sitting flat, their legs sprawled out in front, supporting themselves with their hands. Their weapons were lying on the ground. Both men were breathing heavily. Richards was cursing softly. Masaniello, a devout Catholic, was muttering the Lord's Prayer.

Mike blew out his breath almost like a whistle. "I think most of us are in a bit of shock, James. Except you and Frank."

The doctor barked a little laugh. "Don't kid yourself. Sometime tonight I'll wake up in a panic. So will Frank, I imagine."

Jackson, leaning against the door post, shook his head. "Not tonight. Not tomorrow night, either. But the day after that'll be real bad. I'll get the shakes, sure as shooting." He surveyed the scene grimly. "Christ, this was a worse firefight than anything I saw in Nam."

He shrugged himself off the doorpost. "But at least we did almost all the firing." He stared down at Mike, who was still squatting next to the doctor. "And how are you?" he demanded. Before any reply could come: "And don't give me any shit, Mike. You're not that tough."

Mike chuckled humorlessly. "I wasn't about to claim it. Truth? I feel like a truck hit me. Still trying to figure out how come I'm still alive." He had a flashing image of himself marching forward into the farmyard like a killing machine, cold as ice. *Bang. Bang. Just like that. One dead, one—*

He looked over at the body of the first man he had shot. In the shoulder. He didn't need to be a doctor to know that the man was dead, dead, dead. The magnum round must have blown right through into the heart.

Well, that's why you bought that monster in the first place. Stopping power, they call it. Jesus!

He pursed his lips, trying to decide exactly how he felt. Frank cut through the fog.

"Don't," his friend said. "You won't make any sense of it today, Mike. Trust me. Let it go for a time."

"Truth," echoed Nichols. The doctor rose to his feet. The motion reminded Mike that he was supposed to look for blankets.

"Sorry," he muttered. Mike got up and started toward the farmhouse door. "Frank, did you notice any blankets while you were—"

Suddenly, a shout came from above. Tony Adducci's voice. Mike looked up. Tony was leaning out of a small upper-story window, pointing his finger.

"We got more trouble!" he exclaimed. Mike followed the pointing finger. There was a small dirt road leading away from the farmyard, bending around a grove. From the ground, Mike couldn't see anything past the trees.

Apparently, Adducci could see over them. "There's a—ah, hell, Mike, I swear it's true—there's a *stagecoach* coming this way, escorted by four horsemen. They aren't more than a quarter of a mile away. Be here any second."

His voice rose with excitement. "With about another twenty men pounding after them on foot! Some of those are carrying goddamit huge spears! I kid you not—*spears*, for Christ's sake."

Leaning over the window sill, Tony glared down at the dead thugs lying in the farmyard. "Look just like these bastards. So do the ones riding the horses, for that matter."

Mike stared in the direction Tony had pointed. The dirt road was more in the nature of a cart path. Two furrows worn into packed earth. The trees blocking his sight of the area beyond were twenty yards away. But Mike could now hear the sound of pounding hooves.

Seconds later, four horsemen came into view around the trees. These men were also wearing helmets and cuirasses, with swords scabbarded to their waists. Mike could see what looked like very large pistols slung from the saddles.

The lead horseman spotted him and shouted something. All four riders drew up the reins, bringing their mounts to a skittering halt. A moment later, they were followed around the bend by a vehicle drawn by a team of six horses. The driver frantically sawed on the reins, barely bringing the vehicle to a halt before it rammed into the stationary outriders. As it was, the vehicle slewed sideways across the road. One of the wheels caught a furrow, almost tipping the thing over.

Tony had called it a "stagecoach," but it was like no stagecoach Mike had ever seen—not even in a movie. The vehicle, for all its elegant woodwork and ornate trappings, reminded him more of a small covered wagon.

Again, the lead horseman shouted something. As before, the words were foreign, but Mike was now almost certain that the language was German. At least, if his memory wasn't playing tricks on him.

A moment's silence followed, as the horsemen stared at the Americans. The two miners by the woman had risen to their feet and were holding their guns half-raised. So was Darryl. So were Frank and Tony. Nichols rose to a half-squat, the police pistol held loosely but easily in his hands. Even Hank, still sprawled on the ground clutching the bandage to his ribs, was groping for the riot gun. The last miner, Chuck Rawls, was in the farmhouse. Mike heard him whisper through the door: "I've got 'em covered, Mike. Just say the word."

Mike held out his hands. "Hold everything! Let's not start shooting without cause!"

He could see the four horsemen reaching slowly for the pistols slung at their saddles. Mike remembered—uneasily and belatedly—that his own weapon was lying somewhere on the floor of the farmhouse.

That moment, the curtain on the side of the coach was drawn aside. A face popped through, staring at Mike. The face was that of a young woman, looking very distraught. A few strands of long black hair had escaped the cap over her head. Her eyes were brown and her complexion was dark, as if she were Spanish. She was also—

Mike suddenly smiled. Cheerful as could be. Strangely so, perhaps. But, then again—perhaps not. Instincts will work sometimes, after all, even when logic and reason have fled.

"Ease up, guys! I think we've got a damsel in distress here. The way I see it, that makes figuring out which side we're on a piece of cake."

Frank chuckled. "You always were a romantic. And a damn fool for a pretty face."

Mike shrugged. Still smiling, he started moving slowly toward the carriage. He kept his hands widespread, so that the outriders could see he was unarmed.

"You call that face 'pretty'?" he demanded over his shoulder. "You're nuts, Frank. Me, I think we just got promoted. We were on the set of that movie *Deliverance.*" With a snort: "Or maybe it was *Texas Chainsaw Massacre.* Now—"

The woman's face was closer. "Now we're in *Cleopatra,*" Mike said. The words came out much more softly than he'd intended. And he realized, with a little start of surprise, that he was no longer joking at all.

Chapter 4

The carriage's sudden lurch threw Rebecca against her father. Balthazar Abrabanel hissed with pain.

"Gently, daughter!" he admonished. He pressed his hand more firmly against his chest. Balthazar's gray-bearded face was drawn and haggard. His breath came short and quick.

Rebecca stared at him. Her own heart was racing with a fear so great it bordered on panic. *Something was wrong with her father. His heart . . .*

The sound of a shouting voice came from outside the carriage. Rebecca recognized the voice. It belonged to the leader of the small group of Landsknecht whom her father had hired in Amsterdam to escort them to Badenburg. But the man's German was so thickly accented that she didn't understand the words themselves. Clearly, though, the man was startled by something.

Another shout. This time she understood. "Identify yourselves!"

Balthazar moaned softly. Then, with an obvious effort: "See what is happening, Rebecca."

Rebecca hesitated. Her father's condition was frightening. But, from long habit, she obeyed within a moment.

She fumbled with the sash which held the curtain closed. The hasty action brought its own exasperation. The carriage was open-sided. Rebecca would have preferred to keep the curtain open at all times, to enjoy the breeze. But her father had insisted on making the entire trip closed off from exterior view.

"This journey will be dangerous enough, child," he'd told her, "without men getting a look at *you*." The statement had been accompanied by an odd smile. Fondness and pride, partly. But there had been something else. . . .

When she had realized what that "something else" was, Rebecca had been startled as much as shocked. The shock came from understanding the crime her father feared. *Do men actually do such things?* The startlement, from realizing that even her father thought she was beautiful. Others had told her so, but— The notion still seemed odd. She herself never saw anything in the mirror but a young Sephardic woman. Olive skin, long black hair, a nose, two dark eyes, a mouth, chin. Yes, the features were very regular and symmetrical. More so than most, perhaps. And she sometimes thought, in her rare moments of vanity, that her lips were attractive. Full, rich. But still—*beautiful? What does that mean?*

Finally—it took but seconds, though it seemed an eternity—she had the sash undone. She brushed the curtain aside and thrust her head through the window.

For a moment, she did not understand what her eyes were seeing. Her mind was still fixed on her father's plight. *His heart...!*

Then, she saw. She gasped and drew back. A new terror came, crashing onto the old. Some of that fear was caused by the sight of bodies scattered everywhere. Or so it seemed to her, in that first glimpse. Rebecca had never witnessed scenes of violence before. Nothing beyond scuffling ruffians, at least, and the authorities in Amsterdam tolerated little even of that. She had certainly never—

Blood everywhere! And that's—that's a head *lying over there. And that woman—what? Has she been—? Oh, God!*

But so much only caused fear. The terror—the hot spike sent down her spine—was caused by the sight of the man standing right before her. *Advancing* toward her. Not thirty feet away, now.

Rebecca watched the man come, paralyzed. Like a mouse watching a serpent.

An hidalgo! Here? God save us!

"What is it, child?" demanded her father. Hissing: "What is *happening?*" She sensed him lurching forward on his seat behind her.

She was torn between fear of the hidalgo and fear for her father. Then—*was there any end?*—came yet another terror. She heard the leader of her father's hired Landsknecht shout again.

"Let's go!" she heard him cry. "Come on! We're not getting paid enough for this!"

Rebecca heard pounding hooves set into motion. An instant later she felt the carriage rock and realized that the driver had leapt off also. She could hear him thrusting through the bushes alongside the road, racing off.

They're deserting us!

She turned back into the carriage, staring wide-eyed at her father. Her lips began to open. But the gentle and wise man upon whom she had relied all her life would be no help to her now. Balthazar Abrabanel was still alive. But his eyes were shut, his jaws tight with agony. Both hands were now pressed to his chest. He was slipping off the cushions onto the floor of the carriage. A faint groan came.

The child's terror overrode the others. Rebecca was on her knees in an instant, clutching her father. Desperately trying to bring comfort and aid, not knowing how she could do either. She stared at the heavy chests resting on the seat bench opposite her. Those contained her father's books. His translation of Galen's medical writings was in one of those chests. But it was hopeless. There were thirty-seven volumes of Galen. All of them written in Arabic, which Rebecca could only read poorly.

She heard a voice. Startled, she turned her head.

The hidalgo was standing at the window of the carriage, pushing his head through the window. The man was so tall that he had to stoop a bit to do so.

Again, the voice. The words registered, barely. She thought she understood them, almost. But it was not possible. He couldn't be speaking—

The hidalgo spoke the same words. This time, they registered fully. Most of them, anyway. His accent was very strange, unlike any she had ever heard in that language.

English? He speaks English? *No hidalgo speaks English. It is beneath their contempt. A tongue for pirates and traders.*

She stared at him, now as confused as she was frightened. The man was every inch the hidalgo. Tall, strong, erect, handsome. He exuded the certainty and self-confidence which only a Spanish nobleman possessed. Even his clothing, a ruffled white shirt—silk, she was sure of it—over dark trousers, was not dissimilar. True, she thought there had been something odd about his boots, but—

He smiled very widely. *Who else has such perfect teeth?*

And then, he spoke again. The same words, repeated for the fourth time. "Please, ma'am, do you need help?"

Rebecca Abrabanel would always wonder, in the years to come, why she spoke the truth then. Spoke it—babbled it. She would spend hours remembering that moment, sitting quietly by herself. Wondering.

Some of it, she would decide, was ancient heartbreak. For all the savagery of the Holy Inquisition and the pitilessness with which the hidalgos enforced the expulsion, Spain and Portugal's Sephardim would never be able to forget Iberia, the sun-drenched land they had come to love, spending centuries helping to build, convinced that Jews had finally found a place of welcome and refuge. Until Christian royalty and nobility decreed otherwise, and they were driven out to wander again. Yet they retained the language, and recited the poetry, and cherished the culture for their own. Ashkenazim could huddle in their ghettos in central and eastern Europe, shutting the outside world from their souls. But not the Sephardim. Almost a century and a half had gone by since their expulsion from the land they called Sepharad, but it was still the highest praise, amongst them, to call a man *hidalgo*.

So she would conclude, as the years went by, that some of her response had been a child's, discovering—hoping to discover—that legends were not lies, after all. That there did exist, somewhere in the world, a nobility that was not simply cruelty and treason, veiled beneath courtesy and custom.

But there was more. That, too, she would conclude. There had also been the reaction of a woman.

For there had been the man himself. Handsome, yes, but not quite in the hidalgo way. Even in that moment of terror and confusion, she had retained enough of her wits to sense the difference. The man had possessed none of a hidalgo's raptor beauty. Simply a good-looking man—almost a peasant, come to it, with that blunt nose and open smile. And if his eyes had been such a pure blue as to give despair to hidalgos, there had been nothing in them but friendship and concern.

So Rebecca Abrabanel would conclude, over the years. But she would still find herself wondering about that moment. Hour after hour, at times. It was self-indulgence, perhaps. No other moment in her life, when she looked back, would ever bring quite such a glow to her heart.

"Yes—*please!* My father . . ." She lowered her head for a moment, shutting her eyes. Tears began leaking through the lids. Softly: "He is very ill. His heart, I think."

She opened her eyes and raised her head. The man's face was blurred by the tears.

"We are alone," she whispered. "No one—" A shuddered breath. "We are *marranos*." She sensed his puzzlement at the term. *Of course. He is English.* "Secret Jews," she explained. To her surprise, she managed a chuckle. "Not even that now, I suppose. My father"—she pressed her fingers down, as if to safeguard the gray head in her hands—"is a philosopher. A physician, by trade, but he studies many things. Maimonodes, of course, but also the arguments of the Karaites on the Talmud. And Averroes the Moslem."

She realized she was babbling. *What did this man care?* Her lips tightened. "So he was expelled by Amsterdam's Jews for heresy. We were on our way to Badenburg, where my uncle lives. He said he could provide us shelter." She jarred to a halt, remembering the silver hidden in the chests of books. Fear came again.

The man spoke. Not to her, however. He turned his head and shouted: "James, get over here! I think we've got a very sick man here."

He turned back. His smile was thinner, now, not the gleaming thing it had been earlier. But even through the tears Rebecca could sense the reassurance in it.

"What else do you need, ma'am?" he asked. His face tightened. "There are some people coming this way. Men carrying weapons. Who are they?"

Rebecca gasped. She had utterly forgotten about the band of mercenaries they had encountered earlier.

"Tilly's men!" she exclaimed. "We didn't think they had come so far from Magdeburg. We encountered them two miles up the road. We were hoping to escape down this path, but—"

"Who is—*Tilly*?" the man demanded. The smile was gone completely. His face was tight, tense, angry. But the anger did not seem directed at her.

Rebecca wiped the tears away. *Who is Tilly? How can anyone not know? After—Magdeburg?*

The man seemed to sense her confusion. "Never mind," he snapped. There came a shout from a distance. Rebecca couldn't make out the words, but she knew they were in English. A warning of some kind, she thought.

The man's next words were quick and urgent: "I only need to know one thing. Do those men mean to do you harm?"

Rebecca stared at him. *Was he joking?* The honesty in the face reassured her.

"Yes," she replied. "They will rob us. Kill my father. Me—" She fell silent. Her eyes flitted toward the place where the woman had been lying on the ground. But the woman was not there now. She was on her feet, walking slowly toward the farmhouse. Two of the hidalgo's men were helping her along.

She heard the hidalgo's voice, snarling. "That's good enough. *More than good enough.*" She was startled by the sheer fury in his tone.

An instant later, the door was being opened. A black man, naked from the waist up, was climbing into the carriage. In one hand, he held a small red box emblazoned with a white cross. Despite her astonishment, Rebecca made no protest when the black man gently moved her away from her father and began examining him.

The examination was quick and expert. The man opened the box and began withdrawing a vial. Rebecca, a physician's daughter, recognized another. She felt a vast sense of relief. *Thank God—a Moor!*

Her father thought well of Islamic medicine. His opinion of Christian physicians bordered on profanity.

The Moor turned to the hidalgo. The hidalgo, after shouting a few commands—Rebecca, preoccupied with her father, had not caught their meaning—had his head back in the carriage.

The Moor spoke in quick and curt phrases. His accent was different from the hidalgo's, and he used strange words. Rebecca could only understand some of his English.

"He's having a (meaningless word—*coronation?*—that made no sense). Pretty bad one, I think. We need to get him to a (hostel?) as soon as possible. If we don't get some (meaningless phrase—the first part, she thought, sounded like 'clot-busting,' but what could dirt have to do with anything?) into him, there won't be any point. The damage will have been done."

Rebecca gasped. "Is he dying?" The black physician glanced at her. His dark eyes were caring, but grim. "He might, ma'am," he said softly. "But he might make it, too." ('Make it?' *Survive*, she assumed. The idiom was strange.) "It's too early to tell."

Another shout came from one of the hidalgo's men. Rebecca thought it came from the farmhouse. This time she understood the words. "They're coming! Take cover (meaningless—the hidalgo's name, she thought)!" *Maikh?*

The hidalgo was staring down the road. Rebecca could now hear the sounds of racing footsteps and other shouting men. Germans. *Tilly's men.* Baying like wolves. They had spotted the carriage.

The hidalgo shook his head and shouted back. "No! You all stay in the farmhouse! As soon as they come up, start shooting. I'll draw their fire away from the carriage!"

Quickly, he thrust his head into the carriage, extending his hand toward the physician. "James, give me your gun. I haven't got time to find my own."

The Moor reached back and drew something out of the back of his trousers. Rebecca eyed it uncertainly. *Is that a pistol? It's so tiny! Nothing like those great things the Landsknechte were carrying.*

But she did not doubt her guess, from the eager way the hidalgo seized the thing. Rebecca knew very little about firearms, after all, though she was struck by the intricate craftsmanship of the weapon.

Now the hidalgo was striding away. Not more than five seconds later, he had taken his stance many yards from the carriage. He stopped, turned. Briefly, he inspected the pistol, doing something with it that Rebecca could not make out clearly. Then, squaring his shoulders and spreading his feet, he waited.

Rebecca was at the carriage window now, watching. Her eyes flitted back and forth from the farmhouse to the hidalgo. Even as inexperienced as she was, Rebecca understood immediately what the hidalgo was doing. He would draw the attention of Tilly's men to himself, away from the carriage. His men in the farmhouse would have a clear angle of fire.

The mercenaries charging toward the farmhouse were on the other side of the carriage. Rebecca could hear them but not see them. All she could see was the hidalgo, facing at an angle away from her.

In the battle which followed, she watched nothing else. Her eyes were fixed to a tall man in a farmyard, standing still, in a ruffled white blouse and black trousers. A humble setting, and there *was* something odd about his boots. But Rebecca did not care. Samuel ibn Nagrela, reciting Hebrew poetry to the Muslim army he led to victory at the Battle of Alfuente, would have been proud of that footwear. So, at least, thought a young woman raised in the legends of Sepharad.

So confident he seemed—so certain. Rebecca remembered lines from Nagrela's poem celebrating Alfuente.

> *My enemy rose—and the Rock rose against him.*
> *How can any creature rise up against his Creator?*
> *Now my troops and the enemy's drew up their ranks*
> *Opposite each other. On such a day of anger, jealousy,*
> *And rage, men deem the Prince of Death*
> *A princely prize: And each man seeks to win renown,*
> *Though he must lose his life for it.*

The hidalgo fired first. He gave no warning, issued no commands, made no threats. He simply crouched slightly, and brought the pistol up in both hands. An instant later, to Rebecca's shock, the gun went off and the battle erupted.

It was short, savage and incredibly brutal. Even Rebecca, an utter naif in the ways of violence, knew that guns could not possibly be fired as rapidly as the hail of bullets which erupted from the hidalgo's pistol and the weapons of his men. She could not see the carnage which those bullets created, in the small mob of mercenaries, but she had no difficulty interpreting their cries of pain and astonishment.

Literature kept her soul from gibbering terror. She took courage from the hidalgo's own, that day, and the poetry of another at Alfuente.

> *These young lions welcomed each raw wound upon*
> *Their heads as though it were a garland. To die—*
> *They believed—was to keep the faith. To live—*
> *They thought—was forbidden.*

She held her breath. Not all the weapons fired belonged to the hidalgo and his men. She could recognize the deeper roar of the mercenaries' arquebuses. She fully expected to see the hidalgo's white shirt erupting with blood.

The hurled spears
Were like bolts of lightning, filling the air with
Light . . . The blood of men flowed upon
The ground like the blood of the rams on the corners
Of the altar.

But there was nothing—nothing beyond an unseen wind which tugged the hidalgo's left sleeve and left it torn and ragged. She hissed. But there was no blood. No blood.

No blood.

Suddenly—as shocking, in its way, as the beginning—the battle was over. Silence, except for the sound of footsteps running away and the shouts of fearful retreat. Rebecca heaved a deep breath, then another and another. The motion drew the physician's eye. After no more than a glance, the Moor turned back to her father. A slight smile came to his face. Rebecca, recognizing the meaning of that smile, flushed from embarrassment. But not much. Just an older man, whimsically admiring a young woman's figure. There was no threat to her in that smile.

Rebecca collapsed, falling back from her own crouch onto the cushioned seat of the carriage. She burst into tears, covering her face with her hands.

Some time later—not more than seconds—she heard the door of the carriage opening again. She sensed the hidalgo entering the carriage. Gently, he eased himself onto the seat next to her and put his arm around her shoulder. Without wondering at the impropriety of her action, she leaned into the shoulder and turned her face into his chest.

Soft silk, over hard muscle. *No blood.*

"Thank you," she whispered.

He said nothing. There was no need. For the first time since the terror began that day, Rebecca felt all tension and fear fade away. For the first time in years, perhaps.

Has a flood come and laid the world waste?
For dry land is nowhere to be seen.

It was odd, then, what came to her mind. Recovering from terror in the shelter of a strange man's arm, all she could think of was a sun-drenched land of poetry and splendor, which she had never seen once in her life. Drying her tears on a silk shirt, she remembered Abraham ibn Ezra's ode to his cloak:

I spread it out like a
Tent in the dark of night, and the stars
Shine through it: through it I see the moon and the
Pleiades, and Orion,
Flashing his light.

Chapter 5

The hidalgo did not stay in the carriage for long. Two minutes, perhaps. Rebecca was not certain. Several of his men came up the carriage. There was a rapid exchange of words. Rebecca could not understand much of it, partly because of the accent and partly because they were using terms unfamiliar to her. Odd, that. Rebecca had been born and raised in London. She had thought herself familiar with every flavor of the English language.

But she understood the gist of their discussion. And that, too, she found peculiar. The hidalgo and his men seemed puzzled, as if they were disoriented by their location. They were also confused, apparently, as to what course of action to pursue.

Strange, strange. Again, fear began to creep into Rebecca's heart. The hidalgo's men, for all that they clearly respected him and sought leadership, were not addressing him as a nobleman. That meant, despite his courtesy of manner, that he must be a leader of mercenaries. A bastard son of some petty baron, perhaps, from one of England's provinces. That would explain the accent.

Rebecca shrank back in her seat. Mercenaries were vicious, everyone knew it. Criminals in all but name. Especially here, in the Holy Roman Empire, which had been given over to the flames of war.

Her eyes flitted to her father. But there was no comfort to be found there. Her father was fighting for his life. The Moorish physician was holding him up and giving him some small tablets from the vial he had taken out of his box. Rebecca did not even think of protesting the treatment. The black doctor exuded an aura of competence and certainty.

The hidalgo came back to the carriage. Timidly, Rebecca turned her head toward him.

Relief. There was still nothing in his eyes but friendliness. That, and—

She found herself swallowing. She recognized that look. She had seen it before, in Amsterdam, from some of the more confident young men in the Jewish quarter. Admiration; appraisal. Desire, even, veiled under courtesy.

But, after a moment, she decided there was no trace of lust. At least, she *thought* not. Lust was not something Rebecca was really familiar with, except the flowery version of it which she had found in some of her father's books. The romances which she tucked into great tomes of theology, reading in the library of their house in Amsterdam, so that her father might not notice her unseemly interest.

She felt a flash of pain, remembering that library. She had loved that room. Loved its quiet, its repose. Loved the books lining every wall. Her father's mind lived in the past, and tended to be disdainful of the present. But for one modern device her father had nothing but praise—the printing press. "For that alone," he was wont to say, "God will forgive the Germans their many crimes."

And now here they were, in the land of the Germans. Adrift in time of war, seeking shelter in the eye of the storm. Or so, at least, they had hoped. She would never see that library again, and for a moment Rebecca Abrabanel grieved the loss. Her childhood was gone with it, and her girlhood too. She was twenty-three years old. Whether she wanted them or not, the duties of a grown woman had fallen upon her shoulders.

She straightened those shoulders, then, summoning determination and courage. The motion drew the hidalgo's eyes. The admiration lurking within those blue orbs brightened. Rebecca didn't know whether to cringe or smile.

As it happened, she smiled. And did not, somehow, find that unthinking reaction strange.

The hidalgo spoke. His words came clipped, full of peculiar contractions and idioms. Automatically, Rebecca translated into her own formal English.

"With your permission, ma'am, we need to use your carriage. We have injured people we must get to proper medical treatment."

"And *quickly*," muttered the Moor, still crouched on the floor next to her father. "I've given him some—" *aspiring?* Rebecca did not understand the word.

The hidalgo's eyes moved to the chests and crates piled on the other side of the carriage's interior. "We'll have to remove those, to make room."

Rebecca started. *Her father's books! And the silver hidden within!*

She stared at the hidalgo. As he recognized her fear, she thought to see a flash of anger. But if so, it was gone in an instant.

The hidalgo's large hand tightened on the carriage door. His right hand, she noted idly. One of the knuckles was split, scabbed over with blood. An injury from the battle?

But it was his face that she was concerned with. The hidalgo looked away for a moment, scanning the distance. His jaws seemed to tighten. Then, with a faint sigh, he turned back to her.

"Listen to me, lady." Pause. "What is your name?"

"Rebecca—" She hesitated. "Abrabanel." She held her breath. Of all the great family names of Sepharad, Abrabanel was the most famous. Notorious.

But the name, apparently, meant nothing to the hidalgo. He simply nodded, and said: "Pleased to meet you. My name is Mike Stearns."

Mike? Then: *Oh. It's those bizarre contractions again. Michael.*

The hidalgo flashed a smile. Then, as quickly as it came, the smile vanished. His face became stern and solemn.

"Listen to me, Rebecca Abrabanel. I do not know what this place is, or where we are. But I do not care." Fiercely: "*Not one damn bit. As far as I am concerned, we are still in West Virginia.*"

Rebecca's mind groped at the name. West—*what?*

The hidalgo did not notice her confusion. His eyes had left her for a moment. Again, he was scanning the countryside around them. His look was fierce. *Fierce.*

Growling, now, almost snarling: "You—and your father—are under the protection of the people of West Virginia." His eyes moved to his men, clustered nearby. They were watching him, listening to him. The hidalgo's jaw tightened. "*Specifically,*" he stated, "you are under the protection of the United Mine Workers of America."

Rebecca saw the hidalgo's men lift their shoulders, swelling their own determination and courage. Their sleek, delicate-looking weapons gleamed in the sunlight.

"*Damn straight!*" barked one of the younger men. He cast his own hawk glare at the countryside.

Rebecca was heartened by that reaction, but her confusion deepened. *America?* Her jaw grew slack. *There are almost no English in America. True, that little wretched colony of theirs is called Virginia, if I remember correctly. But America is—*

Hope flared. *Spanish, of course. But Sephardim are there too. Since the Dutch took Brazil, eight years ago, America has been a refuge. My father told me there is even a synagogue in Recife.*

Rebecca stared at the hidalgo. *Was he a hidalgo?* She was completely adrift, now. Her mind groped for reason and logic.

Her confusion must have been apparent. The hidalgo—*Michael, think of him as Michael*—chuckled. "Rebecca, I am just as puzzled as you seem to be."

The brief moment of humor passed. Severity returned to his face. Michael leaned forward, placing both hands on the open window of the carriage. "Where *are* we, Rebecca? What place is this?"

Her eyes went past his shoulders. She could not see much, they were so wide. "I am not certain," she replied. "Thuringia, I think. Father said we had almost reached our destination."

Michael's brows furrowed. "Thuringia? Where is that?"

Rebecca understood. "Oh, of course. It's not well known. One of the smaller provinces of the Holy Roman Empire." His brows were deep, deep. "Germany," she added.

His eyes grew wide, almost bulged. "Germany?" Then, half-choked: *"Germany?"*

Michael turned his head, staring at the landscape. "Rebecca, I've lived in Germany. It's nothing like this." He hesitated. "Oh, I suppose the countryside's a bit the same. Except for being so—so raggedy-looking." He frowned, pointing a finger at the corpses still lying in the farmyard. "But there are no men like this in Germany."

Michael barked a sudden laugh. "God, the *Polizei* would round them up in a minute! Germans love their rules and regulations." Another barked laugh. *"Alles in ordnung!"*

Rebecca's own brows were furrowed. *"Alles in ordnung?" What is he talking about? Germans are the most unruly and undisciplined people in Europe. Everybody knows it. That was true even before the war. Now—*

She shuddered, remembering Magdeburg. That horror had taken place less than a week ago. Thirty thousand people, massacred. Some said it was forty thousand. The entire population of the city, except the young women taken by Tilly's army.

Michael's blue eyes were suddenly dark with suspicion. No, not suspicion. Surmise.

"Guess not, huh?" He shook his head, muttering. "Later," she thought he said. "Deal with it later, Mike. For now—"

There was a shout. Several. Michael pushed himself away from the carriage, looking toward the woods. Rebecca leaned forward, craning her neck.

Many more men were coming out of the woods. For an instant, Rebecca was paralyzed with fear. But seeing the odd costumes and weapons, she relaxed. More of Michael's men. More of these—*Americans?*

Then Rebecca saw the first women coming through the trees, their faces filled with worry and concern. Like a child, she burst into tears.

Michael. And women.
Safe. We are safe.

For Rebecca, the rest of that day—and the next, and the next, and the next—passed in a daze. She was lost in legends not even Sepharad had ever dreamed. All she ever remembered were glimpses and flashes.

Bizarre vehicles, not drawn by anything other than a roar from within. But those roars, soon enough, she understood to be machinery. She was more fascinated by the speed of the vehicles—and still more by the smoothness of their progress. A carriage traveling at that speed would have been shaken to pieces. The secret was only partly contained in the incredible perfection of the road itself. There had also been—

When she climbed out of the vehicle, in front of a huge white-and-beige building, curiosity overcame concern for her father. She stooped to examine the vehicle's wheels. Odd-looking, they were. Small, squat, bellied—almost soft-looking. She poked the black substance with a finger. Not as soft as she thought!

"What is that?" she asked the hidalgo. He was leaning over her, smiling.

"Rubber. We call those 'tires.'"

She poked it again, harder. "It is filled with something. Air?"

The smile remained as it was. But the hidalgo's eyes seemed to brighten. "Yes," he replied. "That's exactly right. The air is—ah, *pumped*—into them at high pressure."

She nodded, and looked back at the tire. "That's very shrewd. The air acts as a cushion." She looked back up at him. "No?"

There was no reply. Just a pair of bright blue eyes, staring at her intensely. Very wide, too, as if he were surprised by something.

What? she wondered.

Into a room now, buried somewhere within the labyrinth of that huge building. The building was a school, she realized. She had never heard of a school so big.

The equipment was odd, dazzling. Rebecca realized that she was in the presence of a people who were master mechanics and craftsmen—far more so, even, than the burghers of Amsterdam.

But she had no time to wonder. The room was filled with people, urgently moving furniture and equipment aside in order to create a makeshift hospital. The badly injured farmer and his wife were being attended by several women. The doctor was easing her father onto a table covered with linen and removing his clothing. There was a rapid exchange of words between him and the women. Rebecca couldn't follow the conversation. Too many of the words were unknown to her. But she understood the meaning of the womens' head-shaking. Whatever the doctor wanted was not available. She saw his black face tighten grimly.

Despair washed over her. She felt the hidalgo's arm go around her shoulder. Unthinkingly, again, she leaned into that comfort. Tears began filling her eyes.

The doctor saw her face and came over to her, shaking his head. "I think he will survive, Miss—ah—"

"Abrabanel," said the hidalgo. Rebecca felt a moment's surprise that he had remembered the name.

The doctor nodded. "Yes. I think your father will live. But—" He hesitated, making vague gestures with his hands. As if groping for something. "We do not have the medication that I wanted most. The"—again, that strange term: *clot-busting?*—"drugs."

The Moor sighed. "He will lose some of his heart capacity. But I have sent people into town to get"—she recognized the Greek term *beta*; not the rest; and there was a substance he called *niter*-something. "That will help."

Hope flared. "He will *live?*"

"I think so. But he will be incapacitated for some time. Days, possibly weeks. And will have to be very careful thereafter."

"What can I do?" whispered Rebecca.

"For the moment, nothing." The Moor turned away and went to the farmer. A moment later he was back at work, surrounded by assistants. She saw that he was going to suture the man's wounds, and was deeply impressed by his obvious skill and confidence. She felt her anxiety begin to lift. Whatever could be done for her father would be done.

The room was now packed with people. Rebecca realized that she was in their way and edged to the door. A moment later, unprotesting, she allowed the hidalgo to lead her out of the room. Out of the room, down a long corridor, down another, into a library.

She was stunned by the number of books. There were many young people gathered in the library, talking excitedly. Most of them were young women—girls really. Rebecca was amazed to see so many prostitutes in a library, wearing clothing more immodest than any permitted even in Amsterdam's notorious brothel district.

She glanced up at the hidalgo. *Odd.* He seemed to take no notice of the girls.

They are not prostitutes, Rebecca realized immediately. *That scandalous show of bare leg is simply their custom.*

She pondered the matter, as the hidalgo gently steered her onto a couch. "I will be back in a moment," he said. "First I have to make a"—*garble*—"call, in order to arrange for you and your father. They've got the"—*garble*—"system working again."

He was gone for a few minutes. Rebecca pondered the strange term he had used. She recognized the Greek prefix "tele." *A long call?* she wondered. *No. Distant.*

Mainly, however, Rebecca spent the time trying to settle her nerves. It was not easy, with all those youngsters staring at her. They were not impolite, simply curious, but Rebecca was relieved when the hidalgo returned. He sat next to her.

"This all seems very strange to you," he said.

Rebecca nodded. "Who are you?"

Fumbling, obviously confused himself, the hidalgo began to explain. They talked for at least two hours. Rebecca became so engrossed in the conversation that she was even able to ignore her fears for her father.

By the end, Rebecca was answering far more questions than she asked. She seemed to accept the reality, in some ways, much better than the hidalgo. She was surprised, at first, because of the man's obvious intelligence. But eventually she understood. He had none of her training in logic and philosophy.

"So you see," she explained, "it is not really so impossible. Not at all. The nature of time has always been a mystery. I think Averroes was right—" She flushed, slightly. "Well, my *father* thinks—but I agree—"

She stopped abruptly. The hidalgo was no longer listening to her. Well, not exactly that. He was listening to *her*, but not to her words. Smiling with his eyes even more than his lips.

Blue eyes held her silent.

"Keep talking," he murmured. "Please."

Flushing deeply, now. Silent. Flushing.

The Moorish doctor rescued her. He strode into the library and came up to them.

"Your father is stable, Miss Abrabanel," he said. "The best thing to do is get him into a bed and make him comfortable." The doctor smiled ruefully. "Away from this madhouse." He cast a questioning eye at the hidalgo.

Michael nodded. "I already sent word into town." He gave Rebecca a glance which combined care with—puzzlement? "Under the circumstances, I thought—"

There came another interruption. An elderly couple was entering the library. They spotted the hidalgo and approached. Their faces were creased with concern.

Michael rose and introduced them. "Miss Abrabanel, this is Morris and Judith Roth. They have agreed to provide lodgings for you and your father."

The rest of the day was a blur. Her father was carried into a large vehicle shaped like a box. The words "Marion County Rescue" were emblazoned on the sides. She followed with the hidalgo, in his own vehicle. The hidalgo's men had already loaded all of the Abrabanels' possessions in the back of the vehicle. In a very short time—so fast! so smooth!—they drew up before a large two-story house. Her father was carried up the stairs on a stretcher, into the house, up the stairs into a bedroom, and made comfortable. Rebecca and he whispered for a few minutes. Nothing more than words of affection. Then he fell asleep.

The hidalgo left, at some point. He murmured something about danger needing to be watched for. He gave her shoulder a quick reassuring squeeze before he went. His departure left her feeling hollow.

Everything was rolling over her now. Her mind felt adrift. Mrs. Roth led her downstairs into the salon and eased her into another couch. "I'll get you some tea," she said.

"I'll get it, Judith," said her husband. "You stay here with Miss Abrabanel."

Rebecca's eyes roamed the room. They lingered on the bookcase for a moment. For a longer moment, on the strange lamps glowing with such a steady light.

Everything seemed vague to her. Her eyes moved on to the fireplace. Up to the mantel.

Froze there.

Atop the mantel, perched in plain sight, was a menorah.

She jerked her head sideways, staring at Judith Roth. Back to the menorah. "You are *Jewish*?" she cried.

A day's terror—a lifetime's fear—erupted in an instant. Tears flooded her eyes. Her chest and shoulder heaved. A moment later, Judith Roth was sitting next to her, cradling her like a child.

Rebecca sobbed and sobbed. Desperately trying to control herself, so she could ask the only question which seemed to matter in the entire universe. Choking on the words, trying to force them through terror and hope.

Finally, she managed. "Does he *know*?" she gasped.

Mrs. Roth frowned. The question, obviously, meant nothing to her.

Rebecca clutched her throat and practically squeezed down the sobs. "*Him*. The hidalgo."

Still frowning, still uncomprehending. Hope burned terror like the sun destroys a fog.

"Michael. Does he *know*?" Her eyes were fixed on the menorah. Mrs. Roth's gaze followed. Her own eyes widened.

"You mean *Mike*?" The elderly woman stared at Rebecca for a moment, her jaw slack with surprise. "Well, *of course* he knows. He's known us all his life. That's why he asked us to put you up, when he called. He said he thought—he didn't understand why, he just said he had a bad feeling—but he thought it would be best if Jewish people—"

The rest of the words were lost. Rebecca was sobbing again, more fiercely than ever. Purging terror, first. Then, touching hope. Then, caressing it. Embracing it, like a child embraces legends. *Hidalgo true and pure.*

With the morning, blue eyes came again. As blue as the cloudless sky, on a sun-drenched day. In the years after, Rebecca remembered nothing else of the two days which followed. Simply blue, and sunlight.

Always sunlight. Drenching a land without shadows.

Chapter 6

Gustav II Adolf, King of Sweden, had a form given to him by his ancestry. His skin was pale, perhaps a bit ruddy. His short-cut hair, eyebrows, upswept mustache and goatee were blond. His eyes were blue, slightly protruding, and were alive with intelligence. His features, dominated by a long, bony and powerful nose, were handsome in a fleshy sort of way. He was a very big man. He stood over six feet tall. His frame was thick and muscular, and tended toward corpulence. He looked every inch the image of a Nordic king.

So much came from nature and upbringing. The rest—the spirit which filled that form at the moment, striding back and forth in his headquarters tent pitched on the east bank of the Havel River—came from the hour itself. The chalk-white complexion came from horror. The closely shut eyes, from grief. The trembling heavy lips, from shame. And the manner in which the king of Sweden's powerful hands broke a chair in half, and hurled the remnants to the floor, came from outrage and fury.

"God damn John George of Saxony to eternal hellfire!"

The king's lieutenants, all except Axel Oxenstierna, edged away from their monarch. Gustav Adolf's temper was notorious. But it was not the rage they feared. Gustav's anger was always short-lived, and the king had long ago learned to keep that rampaging temper more or less under control. An excoriating tongue-lashing was usually the worst he permitted himself. And, on occasion, venting his spleen on innocent furniture. This occasion—this monumental occasion—was shaping up to be a veritable Sicilian Vespers for the seating equipment.

Gustav seized another chair and smashed it over his knee. The sturdy wooden framework dangled in his huge hands like twigs.

No, it was not the rage which caused those veteran soldiers to quake in their boots. And they were certainly not concerned with the chairs. Axel Oxenstierna, the king's closest friend and adviser, never stocked Gustav's tent with any but cheap and utilitarian furniture. This was not the first time, since they arrived in Germany, that the Swedish officers had seen their monarch turn a chair into toothpicks.

"And may the Good Lord damn George William of Brandenburg along with him!"

It was the blasphemy which frightened them. Their king's piety was as famous as his temper. More so, in truth. Much more. Only Gustav's immediate subordinates ever felt the lash of his tongue. Only those of his soldiers convicted of murder, rape or theft ever felt the edge of his executioner's ax. Whereas many of the hymns sung by Sweden's commoners, gathered in their churches of a Sunday, had been composed by their own king. And were considered, by those humble folk, to be among the best of hymns.

The chair pieces went flying through the open flap of the tent. The two soldiers standing guard on either side of the entrance exchanged glances and sidled a few feet further apart. On another occasion, they might have smiled at the familiar sight of broken furniture sailing out of the king's headquarters. But they, too, were petrified by the blasphemy.

The king of Sweden seized another chair, lifted it above his head, and sent it crashing to the floor. A heavy boot, driven by a powerful leg, turned breakage into kindling.

"God damn all princes and noblemen of Germany! Sired by Sodom out of Gomorrah!"

The blasphemy was shocking. Terrifying, in truth. None of the officers could ever recall their monarch speaking in such a manner. Not even in his worst tirades. It was an indication of just how utterly enraged Gustav was, hearing the news of Magdeburg.

The king of Sweden stood in the middle of the tent, his great fists clenched, glaring like a maddened bull. His hot eyes, glittering like sapphires, fell on the figures of three young men standing a few feet away. The men were all short and slim, and dressed in expensive clothing. Their hands were clutching the pommels of their swords. Their own faces were pale.

For a moment, Gustav Adolf glared at them. The bull challenging the yearlings. But the moment was brief. The king of Sweden inhaled deeply and slowly. Then, expelling the breath in a gust, his heavy shoulders slumped.

"Please accept my apologies, Wilhelm and Bernard," he muttered. "And you, William. I do not, of course, include *you* in that foul tribe."

The king had blasphemed in Swedish, but he spoke now in German. Gustav was as fluent in that language as he was in many others but, as always, his accent betrayed his Baltic origins.

The dukes of Saxe-Weimar and the landgrave of Hesse-Kassel nodded stiffly. The tension in their own shoulders eased. Very quickly, in truth. For all their aristocratic lineage, they were more than ready to accept Gustav's apology in an instant. The three noblemen were the only German rulers who had rallied to the Protestant cause, in deed as well as in word. In large part, their attachment to Gustav was due to youthful hero worship, plain and simple. Italians were beginning to refer to Gustav II Adolf as *"il re d'oro"*—the golden king. Wilhelm and Bernard of Saxe-Weimar and William of Hesse-Kassel would put the matter more strongly. As far as those young men were concerned, Gustavus Adolphus—as he was known to non-Swedes— was the *only* European king worthy of the name.

So, it was more with relief than anything else that they accepted his apology. Their own easing tension was echoed by everyone in the room. Gustav's temper, even today, was proving to be as short-lived as ever.

The king of Sweden managed a smile. He glanced around the interior of the large tent. There were only two chairs left intact. "Best send for some more chairs, Axel," he murmured. "I seem to have outdone myself today. And we need a council of war."

Axel Oxenstierna returned the smile with one of his own. He turned his head, nodding to an officer pressed against the wall of the tent. The young Swede sped out of the tent like a gazelle.

Gustav blew out his cheeks. His eyes flitted around the room, as if he were assessing the quality of the twelve men within it. Which, indeed, he was.

It was a quick assessment. More in the nature of a reassurance, actually. None of those men would have been in that tent in the first place, if they had not already matched the king's high expectations of his subordinates.

"Very well, gentlemen, let's get to work." Gustav's gaze went immediately to Wilhelm and Bernard. "The imperialists will march on Saxe-Weimar next. That is a certainty. The two of you, along with William, have been my only German allies worthy of the name. Emperor Ferdinand will demand your punishment."

Wilhelm, the older of the two dukes of Saxe-Weimar, winced. "I'm afraid you're right, Your Majesty." A trace of hope came to his face. "Of course, Tilly is on Maximillian of Bavaria's payroll, not the emperor's, so perhaps—"

William of Hesse-Kassel snorted. Gustav waved his hand. "Abandon that hope, Wilhelm. And you, Bernard. Maximillian is even greedier than the emperor himself. He has already demanded the Palatinate for his services to the Habsburg dynasty and Catholicism. He will certainly want to add Thuringia and Hessen. Parts of them, anyway. The emperor can hardly refuse him. Since Ferdinand dismissed Wallenstein, Tilly's army is the only major force left at his disposal."

Wilhelm sighed. "I can't possibly stop Tilly," he said, wincing. "He will ravage the Thuringian countryside and take every one of its cities. Weimar, Eisenach and Gotha, for sure. Erfurt may be able to buy him off." The nobleman's face was drawn and haggard, giving him an appearance far beyond his tender years. "The people will suffer greatly."

Gustav clasped his hands behind his back and squared his shoulders. His face was heavy. "I can do nothing for you. I am sorry, bitterly sorry, but that is the plain truth." The next words came leaden with anger. And, yes, shame. "I will not make any promises I cannot keep. Not again. *Not after Magdeburg.* I simply don't have the forces to save Thuringia from Tilly. And the geography favors him entirely. He is closer and can use the Harz Mountains to shield his flank."

Bernard nodded. "We know that, Your Majesty." He straightened, clutching his sword pommel. "My brother is the heir, and he must remain here with you. But I will return to Weimar, and do what I can. I will reestablish contact with you by courier as soon as I can, but—"

"*No.*"

Startled, Bernard's eyes went to Axel Oxenstierna. The Swedish chancellor spread his hands apologetically.

"Excuse my abruptness, lord. But that is really a very bad idea." Axel raised his hand, forestalling the duke's impetuous protest. "Please, Bernard! I admire your courage. All the more so, since courage seems a rarer substance than gold among the German aristocracy."

Again, the Swedish officers in the room barked angry, sarcastic laughter. Axel plowed on:

"It would be a very romantic gesture, Bernard. But it would also be sheer *stupidity.* You can accomplish nothing in Thuringia beyond dying or being captured. You have few forces of your own, and—"

Axel fixed the young nobleman with keen, intent eyes. "You are inexperienced in war, lad." He almost added "*a virgin, in truth,*" but bit off the words.

Bernard of Saxe-Weimar's face was pinched, tight. His eyes flitted to Gustav Adolf, pleading.

Gustav breathed heavily. Then, stepping forward, he placed a huge hand on Saxe-Weimar's slender shoulder. "He's right, Bernard." The king's face broke into a sudden, cheerful smile. "Stay here instead. *With me.* I would be delighted to add you to my staff, along with Wilhelm. I am certain you would be an asset"—Gustav blandly ignored the barely veiled skepticism on the faces of his Swedish officers—"and, in exchange, I believe I could teach you something of the art of war."

The last part of the sentence did the trick, as Gustav had expected. Saxe-Weimar's adolescent admiration for the king's military prowess had become a minor embarrassment.

Bernard's eyes moved to the other men clustered about. Veterans, all. Men of proven valor. Plain to see, the young man was concerned for his reputation. His gaze settled on the youngest Swedish officer in the tent. That was Lennart Torstensson, the brilliant commander of the Swedish artillery.

Torstensson chuckled. "Have no fear, Bernard. Let the imperialists taunt you as they will. Soon enough—within a year—they will taunt no longer."

The laugh which swept the tent, this time, was neither angry nor sarcastic. Simply savage and feral. So might northern wolves bark, hearing that reindeer questioned their courage.

Torstensson's response, and the accompanying laughter, was enough. Saxe-Weimar's nod turned into a deep bow, directed at the king. "It would be my honor and privilege, Your Majesty."

Gustav clapped his hands together. "Excellent! In the meantime—" He turned to one of his cavalry commanders, Johann Banér. "That small garrison is still at Badenburg, I trust?"

Banér cocked his head. "The Scots, you mean? The cavalry troop under Mackay's command?"

"Yes, them. *Alexander* Mackay, as I recall. A promising young officer."

Oxenstierna, judicious as ever, refrained from commenting on that last remark. *You spent less than an hour in his company, Gustav. Based on* that *you call him "a promising young officer"?* But he left the words unspoken. The king, he was quite sure, was under no illusions. He simply wanted—almost desperately—to bring confidence and good cheer into a day of gloom and horror. Besides, unlike Banér, Axel knew of Mackay's real mission.

Gustav continued: "Send a courier to Mackay, ordering him to remain in Thuringia. I don't expect him to hold Badenburg against any serious assault, of course. If he's pressed, he can retreat into the Thuringen Forest. I simply want him there to report on Tilly's movements." He gave Oxenstierna a quick glance. "But have that courier report to me, before you send him off. I'll have more detailed instructions."

Banér nodded. The king turned to Hesse-Kassel.

"William, I can provide you with nothing in the way of direct assistance either. But your situation is less desperate. Tilly will move on Thuringia first, not Hessen. And—"

Hesse-Kassel snorted. "And Tilly moves like a slug under any circumstances. The great and mighty General Slow."

Gustav smiled, but the smile faded very quickly. "Don't underestimate the man, William," he said, softly and seriously. "He may be slow, but remember this: Jan Tzerklas, Count Tilly, has been a professional soldier all his life. Most of that time as a commander of armies. He is over seventy years old, now—*and has yet to lose a major battle.*"

The king's face grew solemn. "He is the last, and perhaps the greatest, of a breed of generals going back to the great Gonzalo de Cordoba."

"The butcher of Magdeburg," snarled Torstensson.

Gustav glanced at his artillery officer. When he spoke, his tone was sad. "Yes, Lennart, so Tilly will be known to posterity. And everything else forgotten." The king squared his shoulders. "I do not say it is unjust, mind you. A general is responsible for the conduct of his troops, when all is said and done. But all reports of Magdeburg are agreed that Tilly attempted to restrain his soldiers. He certainly had no reason to put the city to the torch."

Torstensson, accustomed to the ways of Swedish monarchy— Gustav's Sweden, at least—did not retreat. "So?" he demanded. "Tilly *chose* to lead that army. No one forced him out of retirement. An army of sheer wickedness. He cannot complain if his devils got loose." The young artilleryman's anger became mixed with admiration. "*Your* army, Highness, has no Magdeburg to stain its banner. Nothing even close."

Gustav's temper began to rise, but the king forced it down. He did not disagree, after all. "I am not of that old breed, Lennart," he replied mildly. "But I can still admire it for its virtues. So should you."

Then, smiling wryly: "I believe I have started a new line of generals. I hope so, at least."

Several of the officers chuckled. The Swedish chancellor did not.

"You, yes," murmured Oxenstierna. "A new breed. But Wallenstein is doing the same, my friend Gustav. Don't forget that. Some day you will break Tilly and his legacy. Only then to face Wallenstein. Like you, he scorns the old ways. And—like you—he has yet to find his master in the art of war."

Mention of Wallenstein brought silence. The great Bohemian general had retired to his estates, since the emperor dismissed him at the demand of Austria's nobility. The Catholic lords of the Holy Roman Empire despised the man, as much for his low birth as his great wealth and power. But Wallenstein was still there, lurking, ready to be called forth again.

Gustav's face grew ruddy, but his response was very calm. "You are quite wrong, my friend Axel. I have always had a master, in war as in peace. His name is Jesus Christ." The piety in that statement was deep, simple—and doubted by no one who heard. "Wallenstein? Only he knows his master."

Torstensson looked down between his feet. "I can guess," he muttered softly. The officers standing on either side chuckled.

Gustav turned back to Hesse-Kassel. "William, your forces are much stronger than Saxe-Weimar's, and you should have months to prepare your defenses. So I think you will be able to hold Tilly at bay."

There was a small commotion at the tent's entrance. A squad of soldiers was bringing in new chairs.

The king glanced at them, smiling. "Actually, I think those may be unneeded. I don't believe there's much more to discuss. Not today, at least."

Gustav looked past the incoming soldiers, to the plains of central Germany. His jaws tightened. "For the moment, William of Hesse-Kassel, the best assistance I can give you is to put some steel into the spines of certain Protestant rulers. We will start with the Prince of Brandenburg."

"Steel in his spine?" demanded Torstensson. "*George William?*" He sneered. "Impossible!"

Gustav's smile was a thin spreading of lips across still-clenched teeth. "Nonsense," he growled. "He *is* my brother-in-law, after all. He will see reason. Especially after I give him a simple choice. 'Steel in your spine—*or steel up your ass.*'"

The tent rocked with laughter. Gustav's thin smile became a shark's grin. He turned his head to Torstensson. "Prepare for the march, Lennart. I want your cannons staring at Berlin as soon as possible."

The officers in the tent took that as the signal to leave. Hesse-Kassel and the brothers Saxe-Weimar lingered behind, for a moment. The first, simply to shake the king's hand. The others, to present themselves for their new duty. Gustav sent them scurrying after Torstensson.

Soon enough, only Oxenstierna was left in the tent. Gustav waited until everyone was gone before speaking.

"There has been no word from Mackay?"

Oxenstierna shook his head. The King scowled.

"I *need* that Dutch money, Axel. As of now, our finances depend almost entirely on the French. *Cardinal Richelieu.*" His heavy face grew sour. "I trust that three-faced papist as much as I'd trust Satan himself."

Axel shrugged. He tried to make his smile reassuring. Not with any great success, despite his skill as a diplomat.

"The French—Richelieu—have their own pressing reasons to support us, Gustav. They may be Catholics, but they're a lot more worried about Habsburg dynastic ambitions than they are about reestablishing the pope's authority in northern Germany."

The king was not mollified. "I know that!" he snapped. "And so? What Richelieu wants is a long, protracted, destructive war in the Holy Roman Empire. Let half of the Germans die in the business—let them all die! Richelieu does not want us to *win*, Axel—far from it! He simply wants us to bleed the Austrian Habsburgs. And the Spanish Habsburgs, for that matter." He scowled ferociously. "Swedish cannon fodder, working for a French paymaster who doles out the funds like a miser."

He slammed a heavy fist into a heavy palm. "I *must* have more money! I can't get it from Richelieu, and we've already drained the Swedish treasury. That leaves only Holland. They're rich, the Dutch, and they have their own reasons for wanting the Habsburgs broken."

It was Oxenstierna's lean and aristocratic face which grew heavy now. "The Dutch *Republic*," he muttered sourly.

The king glanced at his friend, and chuckled. "Oh, Axel! Ever the nobleman!"

Oxenstierna stiffened, a bit, under the gibe. The Oxenstiernas were one of the greatest families of the Swedish nobility, and Axel, for all his suppleness of mind, was firmly wedded to aristocratic principles. Ironically, the only man in Sweden who stood above him, according to that same principle, was considerably more skeptical as to its virtues. Gustav II Adolf, King of Sweden, had spent years fighting the Polish aristocracy before he matched swords with their German counterparts. The experience had left him with a certain savage contempt for "nobility." The Poles were valiant in battle, but utterly bestial toward their serfs. The Germans, with some exceptions, lacked even that Polish virtue. Most of them, throughout the long war, had enjoyed the comforts of their palaces and castles while mercenaries did the actual fighting. Paid for, naturally, by taxes extorted from an impoverished, disease-ridden, and half-starved peasantry.

But there was no point in resuming an old dispute with Axel. Gustav had enough problems to deal with, for the moment.

"If Mackay hasn't reported, that means the Dutch courier hasn't reached him yet," he mused. "What could have happened?"

Axel snorted. "Happened? To a courier trying to make it across Germany after thirteen years of war?"

Gustav shook his head impatiently. "The Dutch will have sent a Jew," he pointed out. "They'll have provided him with letters of safe-conduct. And Ferdinand has made his own decrees concerning the treatment of Jews in the Holy Roman Empire. He doesn't want them frightened off, while he needs their money."

Oxenstierna shrugged. "Even so, a thousand things could have happened. Tilly's men are rampaging through the area already. They don't work for the emperor. Not directly, at least. What do those mercenaries care about Ferdinand's decrees, if a band of them catch a courier and his treasure? Much less Dutch letters of safe-conduct."

The king scowled, but he did not argue the point. He knew Axel was most likely right. Germany was a witches' sabbath today. Any crime was not only possible, or probable—it had already happened, times beyond counting.

Gustav sighed. He laced thick fingers together, inverted his hands, and cracked the knuckles. "I worry sometimes, Axel. I worry." He turned his head, fixing blue eyes on brown. "I worship a merciful God. Why would He permit such a catastrophe as this war? I fear we have committed terrible sins, to bring such punishment. And when I look about me, at the state of the kingdoms and the principalities, I think I can even name the sin. Pride, Axel. Overweening, unrestrained arrogance. Nobility purely of the flesh, not the spirit."

Oxenstierna did not try to respond. In truth, he did not want to. Axel Oxenstierna, chancellor of Sweden, was eleven years older than his king. Older—and often, he thought, wiser. But that same wisdom had long ago led the man to certain firm conclusions.

The first of those conclusions was that Gustav II Adolf was, quite probably, the greatest monarch ever produced by the people of Scandinavia.

The other, was that he was almost certainly their greatest soul.

So, where the chancellor might have argued with the king, the man would not argue with that soul. Oxenstierna simply bowed his head. "As you say, my lord," was his only reply.

Gustav acknowledged the fealty with his own nod. "And now, my friend," he said softly, "I need to be alone for a time." Regal power was fading from his face. Anguish was returning to take its place.

"*It was not your fault, Gustav,*" hissed Oxenstierna. "*There was nothing you could do.*"

But the king was not listening. He was deaf to all reason and argument, now.

Still, Axel tried: "*Nothing!* Your promise to the people of Magdeburg was made in good faith, Gustav. It was our so-called 'allies' who were at fault. George William of Brandenburg wouldn't support you, and John George of Saxony barred the way. How could you—?"

He fell silent. Hopeless. The human reality which the warrior king had put aside, for a time, was flooding into the man himself.

The huge, powerful figure standing in the center of the tent seemed to break in half. An instant later, Gustav Adolf was on his knees, head bent, hands clasped in prayer. His knuckles were white, the hands themselves atremble.

The chancellor sighed, and turned away. The king of Sweden was gone, for a time. For many hours, Axel knew. Many hours, spent praying for the souls of Magdeburg. Oxenstierna did not doubt that if his friend Gustav knew the names of the tens of thousands who had been slaughtered in that demon place, that he would have commended each and every one of them to the keeping of his Lord. Remembering, all the while, the letters they had sent to him, begging for deliverance. Deliverance he had not been able to bring in time.

Many hours.

At the entrance to the tent, Oxenstierna stared out across the plains of central Europe. Millions had already died on those plains, since the most horrible war in centuries had begun, thirteen years before. Millions more, in all likelihood, would die on those plains before it was over. The horsemen of the Apocalypse were loose, and drunk with glee.

There was some sorrow in his own eyes, but not much. The chancellor did not pretend to have his king's greatness of soul. He simply recognized it, and gave his unswerving loyalty.

So the eyes were hard, not soft. Cold and dry with future certainty, not warm and wet with past knowledge. Better than any man alive, Axel Oxenstierna understood the soul kneeling in prayer behind him. That understanding brought him all the solace he needed, staring across the plains.

I would damn you myself. But there is no need. A greater one than I—much greater—is bringing you something far worse than a mere curse.

A new breed has come into the world, lords of Germany.

Tremble. Tremble!

Chapter 7

The high school's gymnasium was designed to hold 1,500 people. Looking around, Mike estimated that twice that number were packed into the place. Almost the entire population of the Grantville area was present, with the exception of a handful of men at the power plant and perhaps two dozen members of Mike's mine workers.

The disaster—what everyone had taken to calling the Ring of Fire—had occurred three days ago. Since then the UMWA had become, willy-nilly, the area's impromptu defense force. There was no other body of armed and well-organized men available to patrol the area. Grantville's police force consisted of only five officers, including its chief. Even if Dan Frost had not been wounded, he couldn't possibly have handled the problem of overall defense. Grantville's police force was more than busy enough as it was, maintaining order in the town itself.

There had been no major problems with the townsfolk themselves, beyond an initial run of panic buying which the town's mayor brought to a halt by a quick and decisive order to close all the stores. The police department was patrolling the town, to make sure the order was obeyed, but there had been no significant opposition. Privately, everyone admitted that the mayor's decision had been sensible.

The real problem—which was developing very rapidly—was the influx of refugees who were beginning to creep into Grantville's outskirts. It appeared that the entire countryside was being ravaged by undisciplined mercenary soldiers. So far, none of the soldiers themselves had come near the town, but Mike's men were alertly watching for any sign of trouble.

Mike was standing on the floor of the gym, next to one of the tiers of seats near the entrance. Frank Jackson, along with a small group of other miners, were clustered about him. To his immediate right, perched on the edge of the lowest tier of seats, sat Rebecca Abrabanel. The Jewish refugee was still in a bit of a daze, confused by the strange people—and stranger technology—around her.

Perhaps fortunately, Rebecca had been too preoccupied with her father's medical condition to panic at the bizarre experiences she was undergoing. Most of the other refugees were still cowering in the woods surrounding the town, fleeing from any attempt to coax them out of hiding. But Mike suspected that the woman's steadiness was innate. While Rebecca had all the earmarks of a sheltered intellectual, that did not automatically translate into cringing helplessness. He chuckled ruefully, remembering their conversation in the library. He had barely understood a word, once she plunged into philosophy. But he had not sneered—not then, not now. Mike decided he could use some of that philosophical serenity himself.

Still, Rebecca was hardly blasé about her situation. Mike watched as, for the tenth time in as many minutes, Rebecca self-consciously smoothed her long, pleated skirt, tugged at her bodice, touched the full cap which covered her hair. He found it mildly amusing that she had adjusted well enough to her circumstances to be concerned about her appearance.

The person sitting next to Rebecca, a small gray-haired woman in her sixties, reached out and gave the refugee's hand a little squeeze of reassurance. Rebecca responded with a quick, nervous smile.

Mike's amusement vanished. Understanding Rebecca's fears concerning her Judaism—if not the reasons for it—he had asked Morris and Judith Roth to take Rebecca and her father into their house. The town's only Jewish couple had readily agreed. Balthazar Abrabanel had been there ever since. He had survived his heart attack, but both James Nichols and Jeff Adams, Grantville's resident doctor, had agreed that he needed plenty of bed rest. Balthazar had barely survived the experience as it was.

The next day, when Mike dropped by for a quick visit, Rebecca seemed calm and almost relaxed. But Judith had told him, privately, that the Abrabanel woman had burst into a flood of tears when she spotted the menorah perched on the Roths' mantel. She had spent the next half hour collapsed on a couch, clutching Judith like a drowning kitten.

Mike glanced again at Rebecca. The woman was listening intently to what the town's mayor was saying. He was relieved to see that her expression was simply calm. Intent, curious. Wondering, at what she was hearing. But without a trace of panic.

Mike scanned the sea of faces in the gymnasium. *Truth is, she's doing way better than half the people here.*

The thought was whimsical, in its origin. But the accompanying flush of fierce, half-possessive pride alerted Mike to a truth he had been avoiding. His feelings for the Abrabanel woman had obviously taken on a life of their own. The image of runaway horses came to his mind, bolting out of a broken corral.

Good move, Stearns. As if you didn't have enough trouble! The runaway horses paid as much attention to his admonition as they would have to a field mouse. Since the first moment he saw her, the exotic beauty of the woman drew him like a magnet. Some men might have been put off by the obvious intelligence in Rebecca's dark eyes, and the hint of sly humor in her full lips.

Mike sighed. *Not me.* With difficulty, he forced himself to look away and concentrate on the mayor's concluding remarks.

"So that's about it, folks," Henry Dreeson was saying. The mayor nodded toward a small group of people sitting on chairs near the podium. "You heard what Ed Piazza and his teachers told us. Somehow—nobody knows how—we've been planted somewhere in Germany almost four hundred years ago. With no way to get back."

A man stood up on one of the lower tiers. "Are we sure about that, Henry? The 'getting back' part, I mean? Maybe whatever happened could—you know, happen again. The other way."

The mayor gave a glance of appeal to one of the teachers sitting next to the principal. Greg Ferrara rose and stepped up to the microphone. The high school's science teacher was a tall, slender man in his mid-thirties. His speech patterns, like his stride and mannerisms, were quick and abrupt—and self-confident.

Greg was shaking his head before he even reached the podium's microphone. "I don't think there's the proverbial snowball's chance in hell." He gripped the sides of the podium and leaned forward, giving emphasis to his next words. "Whatever happened was almost certainly some kind of natural catastrophe. If you ask me, we're incredibly lucky we survived the experience. Nobody suffered any serious injuries, and the property damage was minimal."

Greg glanced at the fluorescent lighting on the ceiling of the gym. A fleeting smile crossed his face. "The power plant's even back on-line, so we've got all the conveniences of home. For a while, at least." The smile vanished. "But we're still in the position of a trailer park hit by a tornado. What do you think the chances are of another tornado coming by—*and setting everything back the way it was?*" Greg took a deep breath. "Personally, I'd have to say the chance is astronomically minute. Let's hope so. Another Ring of Fire would probably destroy us completely."

The crowd jammed into the gymnasium was silent. Greg took

another deep breath, and concluded with simple, forceful words. "Face it, folks. We're here to stay."

A moment later, he had resumed his seat. The mayor took his place back at the microphone. "Well, that's about it, people. As far as that goes. What we've got to do now is plan for the future. The town council has been meeting pretty much nonstop for the past three days, and we've come up with a proposal we want to put before everybody." He paused for emphasis, just as the teacher had done. "We'll have to *vote* on it. This is way beyond the council's authority. So every registered voter here—"

The mayor stumbled to a halt. "Well, I suppose *everybody* here, registered or not." The sour look on his face caused laughter to ripple through the gym. For as many years as anyone in Grantville could remember, Henry Dreeson had been admonishing people to register to vote.

The mayor plowed on. "We need to figure out a proper structure to govern ourselves by. We can't just stick with a mayor and a town council. So what we want to propose is that we elect an emergency committee to draw up a plan—kind of a constitutional convention. The same committee should oversee things in the interim. And we need to elect somebody as the committee's chairman. He—or she—can make whatever immediate decisions are needed."

Someone in the crowd shouted out the mayor's own name. Dreeson shook his head vehemently. "Not me! The town council raised that idea already, and I turned 'em down. I'm sixty-six years old, folks. I'm a small-town mayor, that's it." The elderly man at the podium stood a little straighter. "Been pretty good at it, if I say so myself, and I'll be glad to stay on in that capacity. But there's no way I'm the right man to—" He waved his hand. The gesture was neither feeble, nor hopeless. But it conveyed the sense of impending catastrophe nonetheless.

A motion at the edge of the crowd drew Mike's attention. John Simpson, his sister's new father-in-law, was stepping forward to the microphone. The well-dressed man moved with the same self-confidence with which he had addressed numerous stockholders' meetings. He did not push the mayor aside so much as he forced him to yield the microphone by sheer authoritativeness.

"I agree with Mayor Dreeson," he said forcefully. "We are in an emergency. That calls for emergency management."

Another, less self-confident, man would have cleared his throat before proceeding. Not John Chandler Simpson. "I propose myself as the chairman of the emergency committee. I realize that I'm not well-known to most of you. But since I'm certain that I am better qualified than anyone here, I have no choice but to put myself forward for the position. I've been the chief executive officer of a major corporation for many years now. And before that I was an officer in the United States Navy. Served in the Pentagon."

Next to him, Mike heard Frank Jackson mutter: "Gee, what a self-sacrificing gesture."

Mike repressed his own snort of derision. *Yeah, like Napoleon volunteering to take the throne. For the good of the nation, of course.*

Quickly, he scanned the faces in the crowd. Mike could detect some signs of resentment at a stranger's instant readiness to take command. But not much. In truth, Simpson's decisiveness was obviously hitting a responsive chord. People floating in the water after a shipwreck are not inclined to question the origin of a lifeboat. Or the quality of its captain, as long as the man seems to know what he's doing and has a loud voice.

He brought his attention back to Simpson. "—first thing is to seal off the town," Simpson was saying. "Our resources are going to be stretched tight as it is. *Very tight.* We're going to have to cut back on everything, people. Down to the bone. We certainly aren't going to have anything to spare for the refugees who seem to be flooding the area."

Mike saw Simpson cast a quick glance toward him and his little cluster of coal miners. Simpson's face was tight with disapproval. Over the past three days, Mike and his coal miners had made no effort to drive away the small army of refugees who were beginning to fill the surrounding woods. Once he was satisfied that a new group was unarmed, Mike had tried to coax them out of hiding. With no success, so far, except for one family which had taken shelter in the town's outlying Methodist church.

"I say it again," Simpson drove on. "*We must seal the border.* There's a tremendous danger of disease, if nothing else." Simpson pointed an accusing finger at the south wall of the gymnasium. The banners hanging there, proudly announcing North Central High School's statewide football championships—1980, 1981, and again in 1997— seemed to be surrogates for his damnation. "Those *people*—" He paused. The pause, as much as the tone, indicated Simpson's questioning of the term "people." "Those creatures are *plague-carriers*. They'll strip us of everything we own, like locusts. It will be a toss-up, whether we all die of starvation or disease. So—"

Mike found himself marching toward the podium. He felt a little light-headed, as he always had climbing into the ring. Old habit forced him to ignore the sensation, drive it out, bring his mind into focus.

The light-headed sensation was not nervousness so much as sheer nervous energy. *And anger*, he realized. That too he drove aside. This was no time to lose his temper. The effort of doing so brought home to him just how deeply furious he was. Simpson's last few sentences had scraped his soul raw.

First thing we do, we put the lawyers and the suits in charge. Then we hang all the poor white trash. As he approached the podium, he caught sight of James Nichols standing next to his daughter. *Oh, yeah. String up the niggers too, while we're at it.* The image of a beautiful face came to him. *And fry the kikes, of course.*

He was at the podium. He forced Simpson away from the microphone with his own equivalent of assertive self-confidence. And if Mike's aura carried less of authority, and more of sheer dominance, so much the better.

"I agree with the town council's proposal," he said forcefully. Then, even more forcefully: "And I completely *disagree* with the spirit of the last speaker's remarks."

Mike gave Simpson a glance, lingering on it long enough to make the gesture public. "We haven't even got started, and already this guy is talking about *downsizing.*"

The gymnasium was rocked with a sudden, explosive burst of laughter. Humor at Mike's jest was underlain by anger. The crowd was made up, in its big majority, of working class people who had their own opinion of "downsizing." An opinion which, unlike the term itself, was rarely spoken in euphemisms.

Mike seized the moment and drove on. "The worst thing we could do is try to circle the wagons. It's impossible, anyway. By now, there are probably as many people hiding in the woods around us as there are in the town. Women and children, well over half of them."

He gritted his teeth, speaking the next words through clenched jaws. "If you expect mine workers to start massacring unarmed civilians—*you'd damn well better think again.*"

He heard Darryl's voice, somewhere in the crowd. "Tell 'em, Mike!" Then, next to him, Harry Lefferts: "Shoot the CEO!"

Another laugh rippled through the gym. Harsher, less humorous. The title *Chief Executive Officer*, for most of that blue-collar crowd, vied in popularity and esteem with *Prince of Darkness.* The Four Horseman of the Apocalypse, rolled into one, wearing a Brooks Brothers suit and holding a pink slip in his hand.

Sorry. No room in the Ark for you. Nothing personal. You're just useless in today's wonderful global economy.

Mike built on that anger and drove on. "His whole approach is upside down and ass-backwards. 'Seal off the town?' *And then what?*" He swept his hand in a circle. "You all heard what Greg said earlier. He estimates the disaster—the Ring of Fire—yanked an area about six, maybe seven miles in diameter with us. You know this countryside, people. We're talking hills, mostly. How much food do you think we can grow here? *Enough for three thousand people?*"

He let that question settle for a moment. Simpson started to say something, angrily pushing toward the microphone. Mike simply planted a large hand on the man's chest and pushed him back. Simpson stumbled, as much from the shock of being "manhandled" as the actual shove itself.

"Don't even think about taking this microphone from *me*, big shot," growled Mike. He hadn't intended the statement to be public, but the microphone amplified his words through the gymnasium. Another laugh came from the crowd. Almost a cheer, actually—as if they were applauding a dramatic slam dunk by the high school's favorite player.

Mike's next words were spoken softly, but firmly. "Folks, we've got to face the truth. We're here, and we're here to stay. *Forever*." He paused. "Forever," he repeated. "We can't think in terms of tomorrow, or the day after. Or even next year. We've got to think in terms of decades. Centuries."

Simpson was gobbling something. Mike ignored him. *Drive on. Drive it home.*

"We can't pretend those people out there don't exist. We can't drive them away—and, even if we could, we can't drive away the ones who'll come next." He pointed a finger at Melissa Mailey, the high school's history teacher. "You heard what Ms. Mailey told us earlier. We're smack in the middle of one of the worst wars in history. The Thirty Years War, it's called. Not halfway into it, from what she said. By the time this war is over, Germany will be half-destroyed. A fourth of its population—*that includes us, now, 'cause we're here in the middle of it*—dead and buried. There are gigantic armies out there, roaming the countryside. Plundering everything, killing everybody. We've seen it with our own eyes. Our police chief's lying in his bed with half his shoulder blown off." He glanced at Lefferts, up in the stands. The young miner was easy to spot, because of his bandages. "If Harry had any sense, he'd be lying in bed, too."

Another laugh rang through the gym. Lefferts was a popular young man, as much for his boundless energy as anything else. Mike turned and pointed to Rebecca. "She and her father were almost massacred. Robbery, rape and murder—that's standard operating procedure for the armies roaming this countryside.

"You don't believe me?" he demanded. He gestured angrily at the door leading out of the gym. "Ask the farmer and his wife we barely kept alive. They're not thirty yards from here, in the makeshift hospital we set up in the school. Go ahead, ask them!"

Simpson was still gobbling. Mike turned to him, snarling. "I guess this clown thinks we can keep those armies off by blowing hot air on them."

Another roar of laughter. Most of the crowd was with him now, Mike could sense it. Rooting for the home team, if nothing else.

"Sure, we can fight them off for a while. We've got modern weapons, and with all the gun nuts living around here"—another mass laugh—"we've got the equipment and supplies to reload for months. *So what?* There's still only a few hundred men who can fight. Less than that, once you figure out how much work's got to be done."

Now he pointed to Bill Porter, the power plant's manager. "You heard what Bill had to say. We've got enough coal stockpiled to keep the power plant running for six months. Then—" He shrugged. "Without power, we lose most of our technological edge. That means we've got to get the abandoned coal mine up and running. With damn few men to do it, and half the equipment missing. That means we have to make spare parts and jury-rigged gear."

He scanned the crowd. When he spotted the figure he was looking for, he pointed to him.

"Hey, Nat! How much of a stockpile do you keep in your shop? Of steel, I mean."

Hesitantly, the owner of the town's largest machine shop rose to his feet. He was standing about half a dozen tiers up in the crowd.

"Not much, Mike," he called out. "We're a job shop, you know. The customer usually supplies the material." Nat Davis glanced around, looking for the other two machine shop proprietors. "You could ask Ollie and Dave. Don't see 'em. But I doubt they're in any better position than I am. I've got the machine tools, and the men who can use them, but if we aren't supplied with metal—" He shrugged.

A voice came from across the gym, shouting. That was Ollie Reardon, one of the men Davis had been looking for. "He's right, Mike! I'm in no better shape than Nat. There's a lot of scrap metal lying around, of course."

Mike shook his head. "Not enough." He chuckled. "And most of it's in the form of abandoned cars in the junkyard or somebody's back yard. Have to melt them down." He emphasized his next words by speaking slowly. "And *that* means we have to build a smelter. *With what? And who's going to do the work?*"

He paused, allowing the words to sink in. Simpson threw up his hands and stalked angrily back to his seat. Mike waited until Simpson was seated before he resumed speaking.

He suppressed a grin. *Kick 'em when they're down, by God!* Mike gestured toward Simpson with his head. "Like I said, I disagree with everything about his approach. I say we've got to go at this the exact other way around. The hell with *downsizing*. Let's build up, dammit!"

Again, he swept his hand in a circle. "We've got to expand outward. The biggest asset we've got, as far as I'm concerned, is all those thousands of starving and frightened people out there. The countryside is flooded with them. *Bring them in.* Feed them, shelter them—and then give them work. Most of them are farmers. They know how to grow crops, if they don't have armies plundering them."

His next words came out growling. "The UMWA will take care of *that*." A chorus of cheers came up, mostly—but by no means entirely—from the throats of the several hundred coal miners in the gym.

Drive it through. "We'll protect them. They can feed us. And those of them with any skills—or the willingness to learn them—can help us with all the other work that needs to be done."

He leaned back from the microphone, straightening his back. "That's what I think, in a nutshell. Let's go at this the way we built America in the first place. 'Send me your tired, your poor.' "

Angrily, Simpson shouted at him from the sidelines. *"This isn't America, you stupid idiot!"*

Mike felt fury flooding into him. He clamped down on the rage, controlling it. But the effort, perhaps, drove him farther than he'd ever consciously intended. He turned to face Simpson squarely. When he spoke, he did not shout. He simply let the microphone amplify the words into every corner of the gymnasium.

"It will be, you gutless jackass. It will be." Then, to the crowd: "According to Melissa Mailey, we now live in a world where kings and noblemen rule the roost. And they've turned all of central Europe—*our home, now, ours and our childrens' to come*—into a raging inferno. We are surrounded by a Ring of Fire. Well, I've fought forest fires before. So have lots of other men in this room. The best way to fight a fire is to start a counterfire. So my position is simple. I say we start the American Revolution—*a hundred and fifty years ahead of schedule!*"

Before Mike had taken more than three steps away from the podium, a large part of the crowd—a big majority, in fact—was on its feet applauding. Not just shouting and clapping, but stamping their feet. He almost laughed, seeing the look of consternation on Ed Piazza's face. The principal was clearly worried that the stands might give way—but not so worried that he wasn't clapping and shouting himself all the while.

So much Mike had hoped for. Even expected, down deep. He knew his people—a lot damn better than some arrogant big shot like John Simpson.

But what he hadn't expected—certainly not hoped for!—was the immediate aftermath. He heard Melissa Mailey's voice behind him, speaking into the microphone. Melissa was in her mid-fifties, and spoke with all the self-assuredness of a woman who had been teaching her whole adult life.

"Mayor Dreeson, I'd like to nominate Michael Stearns as chairman of the emergency committee."

Mike stopped in his tracks and spun around, his jaw dropping. The crowd's applause deepened, grew positively fierce. Through the din, he heard Ed Piazza quickly second the motion.

Then, behind him—*et tu, Brute?*—he heard the stentorian voice of Frank Jackson: "Move the nominations for chairman be closed!"

Frank's motion drew more applause. Mike's brain was whirling around like a top. He hadn't expected—hadn't so much as—

"The nominations are closed!" announced the mayor firmly. "Call for a vote."

Mike gaped at him. Dreeson was grinning like an imp. "Under the circumstances—running unopposed and all—I think we can handle this with a voice vote." He pulled out a gavel from the shelf underneath and smacked the podium once. Firmly. *"All in favor?"*

The shouts ringing through the gymnasium were like a deafening roar. In a daze, Mike found himself staring at John Simpson and his wife. He was relieved to see that they were scowling as fiercely as mastiffs.

Well, thank God. At least it's not unanimous.

Moments later, Mike found himself shepherded up to the podium by Melissa Mailey, greeted cheerfully by Ed Piazza, and having the gavel thrust into his hand by Henry Dreeson. Before he knew it, he was chairing the town meeting.

That task, in itself, posed no particular difficulty. Mike had chaired plenty of UMWA meetings. Coal miners were as famous for their knowledge of the arcane forms of Robert's Rules of Order as they were for the often-raucous content with which they filled those forms.

No, the problem was simply that he hadn't caught up with the reality of his new position. So, after a time, he stopped worrying about what he was going to *do*, and simply concentrated on who he was going to do it *with*.

"This isn't going to work, folks," he said forcefully at one point. "You've already nominated a hundred people for the committee, and I don't doubt half of them will get elected. I've got no problem with that—but I'm still going to need a *working* committee to actually help me out. Fifty people can't get anything done. I need a—a—"

He groped for the right term. Melissa Mailey provided it: "You need a *cabinet.*"

He gave her a sour glance, but she responded with nothing but a cheerful smile. "Yeah, Melissa. Uh, right. A cabinet." He decided not to argue the point at the moment. *Remember, Mike—it's just a temporary committee.*

Mike scanned the crowd. "I'm willing to pick the—uh, cabinet—out of the people elected to the committee." Half-desperately: "But there are some people I've just *got* to have."

A loud male voice came from the stands: "Who, Mike? Hell, just name them now! We can vote in your cabinet right here!"

Mike decided to accept that proposal as a motion. And the crowd's roar of approval as a second. *All in favor? The ayes have it.*

The gymnasium, for the first time, became silent. Mike's eyes scanned the crowd.

His first selections came automatically, almost without thought.

"Frank Jackson." Several dozen coal miners whistled.

"Ed Piazza." Hundreds of voices applauded—many of them teenagers from the high school. Mike felt a moment's whimsical humor. *Not too many principals in this world would get that kind of applause. Most would have gotten nothing but raspberries.*

His eyes fell on the teachers sitting next to Piazza. Mike's face broke into a grin. "Melissa Mailey." The history teacher's prim, middle-aged face broke into a moue of surprise. *Ah, sweet revenge.* "And Greg Ferrara." The younger science teacher simply nodded in acknowledgment.

"Henry Dreeson." The mayor started to protest. "Shut up, Henry! You're not weaseling out of this!" A laugh rippled through the gym. "And Dan Frost, of course, when he's up and about."

Mike's mind was settling into the groove. *Okay. We need production people, too. Start with the power plant. That's the key to everything.*

"Bill Porter." The power-plant manager's face creased into a worried frown, but he made no other protest. *Machine shops. Critical. I'd rather work with Ollie, but his shop's the smallest.* "Nat Davis."

Need a farmer. The best one around is— Mike spotted the short, elderly figure he was looking for. "Willie Ray Hudson."

His eyes moved on, scanning the sea of faces. Mike was relaxed, now. He was accustomed to thinking on his feet, under public scrutiny.

Need some diversity, too. Nip that in-group crap right in the bud. Out-of-town and— He spotted the face he was looking for. Which was not hard, since the face stood out in the crowd. "Dr. James Nichols."

Okay. Who else? Like all union officials, Mike was no stranger to politicking. It would be a mistake if his cabinet appeared too cozy and cliquish. *I need an enemy. In appearance, at least.*

His gaze fell on John Simpson, still glaring at him. The gaze slid by without a halt. *No appearance there. I* don't *need an endless brawl.*

When Mike's eyes came to a burly, middle-aged man sitting not too far from Simpson, he had to force himself not to break into a grin. *Perfect!*

"And Quentin Underwood," he announced loudly. The name brought instant silence to the gym. Utter, complete silence. Followed, a second later, by Darryl's loud "Boo!"

And, a second later, by Harry Lefferts' even louder bellow: *"Treason! I say 'treason!' Mr. Chairman, what's the procedure for impeaching your sorry ass?"*

That produced a gale of laughter, which went on for at least a minute. Throughout, the newly elected chairman of the emergency committee exchanged a challenging stare—fading into a mutual nod of recognition—with the manager of the coal mine in which he had formerly worked as a miner.

Mike was satisfied. *He's a stubborn, pig-headed son of a bitch, pure and simple. But nobody ever said he was stupid, or didn't know how to get things done.*

Henry Dreeson's voice came from behind him. "Anybody else, Mike?"

Mike was about to shake his head, when a new thought came. *And there are the people outside. Thousands and thousands of them.*

He turned his head and stared into a corner of the gym. Then, pointing his finger, he named the last member of his cabinet. "And Rebecca Abrabanel."

To his dying day, Mike would claim he was driven by nothing more than logic and reason. But the counterclaim began immediately. No sooner had the town meeting broken up into a half-festive swirling mob, than Frank Jackson sidled up to him.

"I knew it," grumbled his older friend. "I knew all that stuff about the American Revolution was a smoke screen. Admit it, Mike. You just engineered the whole thing to impress the girl."

With great dignity, Mike ignored the gibe. With considerably less dignity—almost with apprehension—he stared at the girl in question. She was staring back at him, her hand still gripping Judith Roth's hand. Rebecca's mouth was open, in stunned surprise. But there was something other than surprise in her eyes, he thought. Or, perhaps, he simply hoped.

"Oh, come on!" he snapped. Even to him, the reproof sounded hollow.

Chapter 8

Mike and his "cabinet" held their first meeting an hour later, in Melissa Mailey's classroom. Mike began the meeting with a fumble. Of the hemming and hawing variety.

"For God's sake, young man!" snapped Melissa. "Why don't you just come out and say it? You want *me*—the only woman in the room, except Rebecca—to be the committee's secretary. Take the notes."

Mike eyed her warily. Melissa Mailey was a tall, slender woman. Her hair was cut very short, and its color matched the conservative gray jacket and long dress she was wearing. Her hazel eyes were just as piercing as he remembered them, from days gone by when he stammered out an unstudied reply to a stiff question. She looked every inch the stern and demanding schoolmistress. The appearance was not a pose. Melissa Mailey was famous—or notorious, depending on who was telling the tale—for her acid tongue and acerbic discipline.

She was also famous for being Grantville's most unabashed and unrelenting liberal. *Flaming irresponsible radical*, according to many. As a college student, she'd been a participant in the civil rights movement. Arrested twice. Once in Mississippi, once in Alabama. As a young schoolteacher, she had marched against the Vietnam war. Arrested twice. Once in San Francisco, once in Washington, D.C. The first arrest had cost her first teaching job. The second arrest had done for the next. Boston Brahmin born and bred, she'd wound up teaching in a small town in West Virginia because nobody else would hire her. Her first year at the newly founded high school, she'd organized several of the schoolgirls to join her in a march on Washington demanding the Equal Rights Amendment. A clamor had gone up, demanding her dismissal. She held onto her job, but she'd been treading on very thin ice.

As ever, Melissa didn't give a damn. The next year, she got arrested
again. But that was for denouncing an overbearing state trooper at one
of the UMWA picket lines during the big 1977–78 national strike.
When she got out of jail, the miners held a coming-home party for
her in the high-school cafeteria. Half the student body showed up,
along with their parents. Melissa even snuck out, halfway through the
proceedings, and joined some of the miners for a drink in the parking lot.

Melissa Mailey had finally found a home. But she was still as
unyielding and acerbic as ever.

"Look, Melissa," Mike muttered, "I know it looks bad. But we've
got to have accurate records, and—"

Melissa broke into a smile. That expression was not seen often on
her face. Not in Mike's recollection, at any rate. But it was quite
dazzling, in its own cool way.

"Oh, relax," she said. "*Of course* we have to keep meticulous
records." Again, the smile. "We're the Founding Fathers, you know.
And Mothers. Wouldn't do at all not to have accurate notes. I know—
I'm a history teacher. Historians would damn us for eternity."

The smile vanished. Melissa's eyes flicked around the faces gathered
in the center of the room. Her expression made plain just how slop-
pily and carelessly she thought *men* would keep important records.

When her eyes came to Rebecca, Melissa's frown deepened. The
young Jewish refugee, hands clasped nervously in her lap, was sitting on the edge of her seat. Her chair was pushed back several feet
from the circle.

Melissa stood up and pointed her finger imperiously to a spot next
to her own chair. "Young woman," she stated, "you move that chair
here. *Right now.*"

If Rebecca had any difficulty with Melissa's Boston accent—still
as pronounced as ever, after all these years—she gave no sign of it.
Hastily, like a thousand schoolgirls before her, she obeyed the voice
of command.

Melissa bestowed the smile upon her. "Attagirl. Remember: *United
we stand, divided we fall.*"

Melissa sniffed at the men. "Do something useful, why don't you?"
She pointed to a row of long tables lining the back wall. "Move those
together into the center of the room. Make a big conference table out
of them. Then push these silly desks away and go get us some real
chairs. Ed'll show you where they are. We'll be meeting here from
now on, I imagine. May as well set things up properly."

She turned away, briskly striding toward a cabinet. "I, meanwhile,
will demonstrate the marvels of modern technology." Over her
shoulder, with a snort: "Stenography. Ha!"

The next few minutes were taken up with a flurry of activity. When the meeting resumed, a large and expensive-looking tape recorder occupied a prominent place in the center of the jury-rigged "conference table."

Melissa turned it on, recorded the time and date, and turned to Mike.

"You're on, Mister Chairman."

Mike cleared his throat. "All right. The first thing I want to take care of is this 'constitutional convention' business. It's important, of course—more important, in the long run, than probably anything else. But we've got way too much emergency business to take care of for this entire committee to spend any time on it."

He could see Melissa's gathering frown out of the corner of his eye. Hurriedly: "So what I want to propose is that we set up a small subcommittee to work on it. When they come up with a proposal, we can discuss it. Until then, the rest of us will concentrate on immediate matters."

"Sounds okay to me," said Nat Davis. "I wouldn't know where to start, anyway. Not with that problem. Who do you want on the subcommittee?"

Mike's first two names came instantly. "Melissa and Ed. She's the history teacher and Ed used to teach civic affairs." Pause. "One or two more people."

Everyone's eyes glanced at everyone else's. Melissa cut through the hesitation. "Willie Ray. He served a few terms as a state representative, way back in the Stone Age. Give us some practical experience, even if he was a chiseling politician like all the rest of them." Everyone chuckled except Hudson, who laughed aloud. "And Dr. Nichols should be on it too."

Nichols' eyes widened. "Why?" he demanded. "I don't know anything about constitutional law." He cocked his head. The gesture was both quizzical and half-suspicious. "If it's because I'm the only—"

"Of course it's because you're the only black man in the room!" snapped Melissa. Her eyes challenged Nichols, and then the other men. "*Grow up*—all of you. I didn't propose him out of tokenism. There's a good and simple reason to include someone whose people had a different history than most of ours. Whether he knows any law or not, I suspect Dr. Nichols won't be quite as complacent as everyone else about the received wisdom of the ages."

Mike wasn't sure he agreed with Melissa's reasoning. In general, that is. But he realized that he would feel a bit more confident himself, knowing that Nichols had a hand in shaping their new constitution.

"I've got no problems with that. James? Do you accept?"

Nichols shrugged. "Sure, why not?" Grinning: "Man does not live by chitlins alone, after all."

When the laughter died down, Mike moved on to immediate business. He started with the power-plant manager.

"Bill, the way I see it, power is the key to everything. As long as we have electricity, we'll have a gigantic edge over everybody else in this new world of ours. All the way from modern machine tools to computers. So—*how long*? And what can we do to keep the power coming?"

Porter ran fingers through his thinning hair. "I don't know how much anybody here knows about power plants. The truth is, the design of steam–water cycle power plants hasn't changed much in a long time. They're simple machines, when you get down it. As long as we're provided with water and coal, we can keep running until we use up our small stock of critical spare parts. That'll probably happen somewhere between a year and a half and two years from now. After that, we're shut down for good."

He shook his head. The gesture was both rueful and half-amused. "We've got enough coal stockpiled to last for six months. Water's not a problem at all. We used to get it from the Monongahela. The Ring of Fire cut the pipes, of course, but it turns out—talk about blind luck!—that there's another river pretty much right in the same place. Not as big, but it'll do."

"I don't understand about the spare parts," said Frank. "Can't we make them? We've got three machine shops in town."

Porter shook his head. "That's not the problem, Frank. I wish it was! We've got four machine shops in town, actually. We have a maintenance shop in the plant itself." He glanced at Piazza. "And now that I think about, I just remembered the high school's technical training center has a pretty good shop, too."

Piazza nodded. Porter turned to Davis, the machine-shop owner. "Tell 'em, Nat."

Nat Davis was a pudgy man in late middle age. When he puffed out his cheeks, he bore such an uncanny resemblance to a frog that Mike almost laughed.

"Not a chance, folks. Bill's right." He shrugged. "Oh, sure, I could make lots of parts. Shafts, you name it. But some things—like gears, and bearings, and mechanical seals—are specialty work. I don't think there's a job shop in the country that could handle that stuff. Not without spending years at it. We just don't have the tooling."

Silence. "A year and a half," Ed muttered. "Two at the most." His frown conveyed both worry and exasperation.

Mike leaned forward, tapping the table with a stiff finger. "I don't think the situation's that bad. Remember, we don't need to keep *that* power plant running. That monster's overkill, anyway. Just *any* power plant."

Porter stopped running his fingers through his hair. His head popped up. "You're right, Mike!" he exclaimed. Then, chuckling ruefully: "We've got the thing running on minimal load condition as it is. Our plant could have provided power to the whole of Marion County. Over fifty thousand people, *including* all the industry in Fairmont. We can keep Grantville supplied with anything it needs with what amounts to a trickle."

He was getting excited, now. "Hell, yes—Mike's right! We can use that year or two grace period to *gear down*." Seeing the blank expressions on several faces, Porter elaborated. "Remember what I said. The basic principle of a coal-operated power plant is damn near ancient. *We can build us a new one.*" Another chuckle, full of cheer rather than chagrin. "An *old* one, I should say. Forget about high-speed turbines and bearings. All we need, for our relatively modest purposes, is a good old-fashioned steam engine."

He looked at Nat. "We can build something like that, I imagine?"

Before Davis could respond, Willie Ray Hudson was laughing gleefully. "You *imagine*? Bill, I know of at least four men in this town who build steam engines *for a hobby.*" The old farmer was grinning from ear to ear. "The Oil and Gas Festival contest, you know." He shrugged. "They don't build anything as big as we'd want, of course. But they understand all the principles."

Hudson slapped the table with his hand. "And that's another thing! Let's not forget that this whole area started with natural gas and oil, before the coal mines started working." The farmer pointed to the floor beneath his feet. "We're still sitting on it. Natural gas mostly. I run my farm direct off the gas from my own land. All my vehicles are converted to operate on natural gas instead of gasoline. Don't pay the gas company a nickel for it. So we've got another energy source, right there!"

Frank joined in the excitement. "You're right. Now that I think about, the whole town's heat comes from that gas supply. Even the high school. Right, Ed?"

The principal nodded, but his face was creased with worry. "Yeah, but—" He looked down at the floor. *"Is it still there?"*

For the first time, Greg Ferrara spoke. "I'm pretty sure it is, Ed." The science teacher made an apologetic face. "I can't be sure, of course. But I examined what I could of the evidence left by the Ring of Fire. As near as I can tell, the—whatever it was—cut out a perfect circle. Right through everything. Dirt, trees—even rail lines and power cables—cut like a razor."

Everybody was staring at the floor, now. "I can't imagine anything that would have just skinned the planet's surface. It's far more likely that the Ring of Fire moved an entire hemisphere. Well, a *sphere*, actually—but the top half would have just been atmosphere."

Ferrara paused, studying the tiles as if the answer were to be found there. "I'm not positive, but I'll be surprised if we don't discover that we've got the same radius beneath our feet. Three miles down, at the center—maybe more. Way deeper than any gas and oil beds we'll be tapping into. Or coal seams."

"We'll know soon enough," said Mike forcefully. "Quentin, we need to get that abandoned coal mine up and running. Six months from now, the power plant's stockpile will be gone. We've got to get the coal moving by then."

Startled, the former mine manager looked up. "But that belongs to—" He broke off, chuckling. "Ah, screw 'em. I never liked that outfit anyway. And now I guess they're in no position to yap about property rights."

Quentin's harsh chuckle was echoed by others. The abandoned coal mine was located less than two miles out of town. It was practically brand new. The largest coal operator in the United States had built the thing, run it for a few months, and then closed it down. The company claimed it was due to "unfavorable market conditions." Everyone in the town—including Quentin, who managed a competitor's mine—was certain that the mine had been built as a tax dodge.

Frank was grinning. "Tell you what, Quentin. I'll get the bolt cutters, you bring the hacksaw. We'll have that sucker up and running in no time."

"No—*not you*, Frank." Mike's words were spoken softly, but decisively. "Put Ken Hobbs in charge of it. That old-timer almost goes back to the days of pick-and-shovel mining, anyway. Which is what we're probably going to be reduced to. I doubt very much if the company left any continuous-mining machines down there. Or any long-wall equipment."

He drove over Frank's gathering protest. "I need you *here*, Frank— not buried hundreds of yards down in the ground. We've got to build us a real little army now. I'm counting on you to show me the ropes. You're a real veteran of a real war, which I'm not."

Frank stared at him. Then at Quentin Underwood, then at James Nichols, and then at Ed Piazza. Those were the Vietnam War veterans in the room.

"I will be good God damned," he mused. "Whaddaya know? The Vietnam 'era' is finally classified as a for-real war."

The other vets chuckled. Quentin eyed Mike. "How 'bout me?" he demanded. "You going to insist on putting me in a uniform too?"

Mike shook his head. "No offense, Quentin, but you were stationed on an aircraft carrier. I need men with combat experience on dry land. James was in the Marines, but he's one of our only two doctors. Ed—"

The short, stocky principal laughed. "Not me! Spent my whole tour of duty as a rear-echelon motherfu—" He broke off the vulgar term, glancing warily at Melissa. She responded with a grin and a wagging finger. "The closest I ever got to action was being caught in a shoot-out in downtown Saigon between the police and some black market-eers. You want a real combat vet like Frank."

Jackson made a sour face. "I was in the Eleventh Armored Cav, Mike. I haven't noticed any tanks parked around town."

Nichols' eyes widened a bit. "You were with the Blackhorse?" he asked. "Good outfit."

Frank returned the doctor's compliment with a brief nod. "So were the Marines. By the way, which unit were you in?" He shook his head. "Ah, never mind. Later."

To Mike: "Sure, I had some experience with infantry tactics. But nothing like what we're going to be facing here." He snorted. "Can't hardly call in an air strike."

"That's still more experience than I've got, Frank," retorted Mike. "The only combat I saw in the service was barroom brawls." He scanned the other faces in the room. When he spoke again, his tone was deadly serious.

"Building our army has to take first priority, people. Without it, we're just another town ripe for plunder. I'm going to need every combat veteran I can get my hands on. That's true of most of the middle-aged miners, fortunately. But—sorry, Frank—they're getting a little long in the tooth for this sort of thing. I want to use them as a training cadre for the younger miners, and any of the younger men in town who aren't absolutely needed for something else. And—"

He took a deep breath. "We're going to have to call for volunteers." Another deep breath. "I'm going to pretty much want every boy in next month's high-school graduating class."

The room exploded with protests from Ed Piazza and Melissa Mailey. Ed gobbled semicoherent and indignant phrases about *his kids.* Melissa neither gobbled nor was incoherent. She simply denounced Mike. She avoided the term *warmonger*, but precious little else.

Throughout, Mike weathered the storm in suffering silence. When the protests began to die down, he opened his mouth to speak.

Greg Ferrara cut him off. "*Don't be stupid, Melissa.* You too, Ed. I agree with Mike completely. Most of the miners are getting on in years, you know that as well as anyone. The mines have done only a trickle of new hiring for the last decade." Bitterly: "*Downsizing.* Hell, at least half the working miners in this area are Frank's age. Late forties and up. You can't expect men that old to do all the fighting. Not for long, anyway."

Ed and Melissa were staring at their fellow school teacher, jaws open. Their thoughts were obvious: *Benedict Arnold.*

Seeing their expressions, the science teacher smiled ruefully. "Sorry. But facts are facts. Every country in history, when the fighting starts, depends on its youngsters. I can't see where we're any different."

He turned to Mike. "I know those boys, Mike. Every one of them will volunteer. Even the kids in the special education program."

He waved down Melissa's gathering storm of renewed protest. "Relax! We're obviously not going to put someone like Joe Kinney into the army." Mike nodded his firm agreement. Joe Kinney was a sweet-tempered eighteen-year-old boy. But he had the mental age of a five-year-old, and was never going to get any better.

Greg nodded at Nichols. "Dr. Nichols and Dr. Adams can screen out the boys who are just plain unfit. But most of them can serve, and all of them will. *For the duration*—just like in World War II."

He squared his slender shoulders. "And some of the male teachers should volunteer to lead them in. *Just like in the Civil War.* Let's start with me. I'm sure Jerry Calafano will volunteer also. And Cliff Priest and Josh Benton."

Half-unconsciously, the school principal nodded his agreement. Priest and Benton were the two younger coaches for the high school. Calafano was a math teacher in his late twenties. He and Ferrara were close friends, as well as mutual chess fanatics.

Melissa started to say something—a protest, from the sound of the initial stuttered syllables. Then, her shoulders slumping, she heaved a great sigh. "Oh, Lord," she whispered. "Oh, dear God." Her eyes filled with sudden moisture. There was nothing of politics in either the words or the wetness. Just the grief of a woman who had helped to raise another generation of children, and must now see them march toward the dogs of war. *Cry havoc!* Like so many generations before them.

Mike gave that grief a moment's respectful silence. Then, squaring his own shoulders, he pushed on to new business.

"All right. Greg, I appreciate the offer and I accept it. It'll help if several of the teachers volunteer along with the kids. Help a lot." For a moment, his mind sped off at a tangent. Ferrara, he knew, had organized a rocketry club with some of the science-oriented students in the high school. He could see possibilities—

Later. He looked at Willie Ray. "Willie, I want you to get all the farmers together and draw up a plan for food production. Inventory our resources, figure out what you're going to need—" He broke off.

Hudson had started nodding before Mike had finished the first sentence. The old man was a natural-born organizer. Mike could let him handle it from there.

To Quentin: "Frank will talk to Ken Hobbs and some of the older miners. We'll also see if we can get some retirees back to work. Break into that abandoned mine and see where we stand. Transporting the coal will be a problem, too. We got rail tracks leading most of the way from the mine to the power plant, but as far as I know there isn't a locomotive anywhere around. We may have to haul it by truck."

To Dreeson: "That brings up the problem of the gasoline supply. We need to inventory how much fuel we've got sitting in the underground storage tanks of the town's gas stations. Diesel and kerosene also. And anywhere else it can be found. Which will mostly be in the gas tanks of everybody's cars and trucks."

He paused, pursing his lips. "I can't see any way around it. Starting immediately, we've got to put a complete stop to people using their vehicles for personal transportation. As of *right now*, all motor vehicle fuel is a vital military resource."

Quentin nodded. "Absolutely!" He looked at Willie Ray. "How hard is it to convert to natural gas?"

Before Hudson could respond, Ed piped up. "Yeah! We could convert a couple of the school buses. Provide the town with a bus service." Apologetically: "Some of the old folks can hardly be expected to walk all the way to the grocery stores." His quick mind seemed to have a life of its own, tripping from subject to subject. "And that brings up the question of groceries. We can't keep the freeze on buying much longer. But how are we going to ration the food? And what do we use for money? I'm not sure U.S. currency's worth much anymore. And—"

Dreeson pitched in immediately, with a proposal to use the town's only bank—*85% community owned, remember?*—as their new financial clearing house. Quentin agreed. Melissa snapped something about protecting the town's poorer residents. Quentin snapped back. Before that argument could get started, Nat Davis chimed in with a concern for the town's resident businessmen. *Not the absentee owners, of course. Hell with them. Nationalize all that stuff. But I worked all my life—* Ed and Dreeson immediately assured him arrangements could be made. Property rights would be respected, but the demands of the common good—

On and on. Mike leaned back in his chair, almost sighing with relief. He had picked this team on the spur of the moment, driven more by instinct than conscious thought. He was pleased to see that his fighting instincts seemed to be as good in this arena as they had been in the much simpler environment of a boxing ring.

❖   ❖   ❖

The meeting broke up three hours later. There was still a lot to be done—all of the actual work, and most of the planning—but at least they'd agreed on an initial division of labor.

Overall command of the political and military situation: *Mike Stearns.*

Army Chief of Staff: *Frank Jackson.*

Coordinator of all planning and general factotum: *Ed Piazza.* The school vice-principal, Len Trout, would assume Ed's old duties in the interim.

In charge of drafting a proposed permanent constitution for the new—nation? Whatever it was. *Melissa Mailey.*

In charge of the town itself, rationing, finance, etc.: The mayor, who else? *Henry Dreeson.*

Medical and sanitation: *James Nichols*, with some help from Greg Ferrara when Greg wasn't too busy being the unofficial "Minister of the Arms Complex." (Which wasn't, of course, all that complex at the moment.)

Power and energy: *Bill Porter* and *Quentin Underwood.*

Agriculture: *Willie Ray Hudson.*

That left only—

Rebecca had been silent throughout the entire meeting. The refugee had simply listened intently. It was obvious that much of the discussion passed by her completely. But the one time that Mike began to explain an unfamiliar term, she simply shook her head and, with a firm little gesture of her hand, urged him to continue. Clearly enough, Rebecca had an excellent grasp on priorities. *Explain later. Right now, let's stay alive.*

Mike was pleased and gratified by that hand gesture. Quite powerfully, in truth. Charm and exotic beauty are all fine and good in a woman. So, of course, is intelligence. But, like many men born and bred in poverty's hills, Mike treasured hard-headed practicality even more. He could feel his attraction toward her deepening by the moment. Whether the sentiment was reciprocated, he had no idea. But he made the decision, then and there, that he was going to find out.

Rebecca Abrabanel did not speak until the very end. Then, softly clearing her throat, she asked: "I am uncertain. What is it, exactly, that you desire *me* to do?" Her English had a distinctive accent, a strange blend of Germanic harshness and something of Spain, but her command of the language was fluent and grammatically precise.

Mike hesitated, trying to explain. He blurted out the whimsical thought which first came to him:

"Basically, Miss Abrabanel, I need you to be my National Security Adviser."

Rebecca frowned. "I understand the words. Taken separately, I mean to say. But I am not certain—" She cocked her head slightly. "Can you explain what I am supposed to *do*?"

Melissa Mailey snorted. "That's easy, Miss Abrabanel. Just do the same thing every National Security Adviser I can remember always does." She pointed a finger at Mike. "Whenever he asks you what to do about any problem, just tell him: *Bomb it.*"

The answer confused Rebecca. But not half as much as the uproarious laughter which filled the room. When the laughter died down, Mike stood up and extended his hand.

"May I walk you home, Miss Abrabanel? I can explain on the way."

Smiling, Rebecca nodded and rose. By the time they had passed through the door and taken three steps down the wide corridor of the school, Rebecca's hand was tucked under Mike's arm.

Frank sidled over to the door and peeked after them. Then, chuckling, he turned back and spoke to Melissa. "In that new constitution of yours, I'd suggest you run a little lightly on the matter of separation of powers. We don't need another scandal in high places, right out of the gate."

Melissa arched her eyebrows. "Whatever are you talking about, Frank Jackson? *I* certainly don't see a problem with the chief of state walking his national security adviser home." She scowled. "In fact— might be a good idea to put in right there in black and white. The National Security Adviser *must* be female."

Greg Ferrara curled his lip. "Yeah, the gentle sex. Like Catherine the Great, or the Medici women. Or—what was her name? You know. The English queen who had everybody burned at—"

Melissa waved her hand airily. "Details, young man. Details! You can't get everything perfect. But at least we'd have a modicum of good sense." She scowled. "Not that I don't imagine Miss Abrabanel won't be advocating a certain amount of bombing."

The scowl deepened. "So would I, come down to it. We could start with half the palaces in Europe." *Scowl, scowl.* "I take that back. Let's start with *ninety percent*—and work our way up from there."

Chapter 9

When Rebecca and her companion reached his exotic vehicle perched on the flat expanse before the school—the *parking lot*, they called it—she watched him reach into his pocket for the keys. As if suddenly remembering something, he stiffened.

Rebecca heard him mutter. A suppressed curse, perhaps. She had noticed that American men seemed to avoid the use of obscene terms in the company of women. Quite reticent, they were, compared to the Londoners of her childhood and the men who swarmed in Amsterdam's streets. But she had also noticed how casually they allowed themselves to blaspheme. She found that combination odd.

Odd, and— *And what?* she asked herself. A bit frightening, of course. But, for the most part, Rebecca had decided that the casual blasphemy was reassuring. Men who did not seem to fear either the wrath of God or—more to the point—the wrath of their God-fearing neighbors, were men who would be less likely to persecute others for their own beliefs. So, at least, Rebecca hoped. And was even beginning to believe.

Michael was speaking to her. An apology, it seemed. "I'm sorry, but we'll have to walk. We just approved a decision to restrict gasoline to military use, if you remember."

She smiled. "Yes, we did. So? It is not far. The walk will be pleasant."

Rebecca almost laughed, seeing his little start of surprise at her answer. So strange, these Americans. They seemed to view the simple exercise of walking as the labors of Hercules. Yet they were quite healthy—much more so, in fact, than any other people of her acquaintance. They appeared to be physically fit, too, other than being even more corpulent than Dutch burghers.

On average, that is. Michael—

The man standing next to her was not fat at all. No more than any hidalgo of legend. Over the past three days, talking with the Roths, Rebecca had come to understand that Michael was not an hidalgo. Not of any kind, it seemed. Among their many other peculiarities, the Americans had a ferocious commitment to what they called "democracy." They reminded her of the old Anabaptists of Munster, without the bizarre excesses.

Not an hidalgo. But Rebecca, standing there, knew that she would always think of him as such. The knowledge brought a sharp sensation to her heart. Sharp, and confusing. The sensation was partly fear, of course, and partly uncertainty. But she would no longer hide from the rest.

She saw that Michael had, once again, crooked his elbow in a subtle invitation for her hand. Just as he had done, to her surprise, in the school's hallway. Her response then had been timid. Now—

An instant later, her hand was tucked on his arm and they were walking away from the school.

No longer hide from the rest. There is a reason, Rebecca, you are feeling that sensation in your heart and not in your head.

Understanding the risks and dangers involved—*he is a gentile, stupid girl!*—but not wanting to dwell on them, Rebecca hastily brought up a new subject.

"The 'gasoline' you seemed so concerned about. I spoke to Mister Ferrara on the subject. For a few minutes only, during one of the recesses in the meeting. If I understand him correctly, I think it is just purified naphtha. Distilled, perhaps. Am I correct?"

She was expecting him to be startled again. That was the normal reaction Rebecca got from older men—any men—when she asked one of her many questions about the natural world. Instead, to her surprise, the expression which came to his face was—

Pride?

"That's just about exactly right," Michael replied. "The distilling process is pretty complicated, you understand." He frowned. "Probably more than we can manage here, I'm afraid. In any large quantities, at least. But—yes, that's what gasoline is. Simple, really."

"And you then burn it inside the—*motors?* Is that the right word?" At his nod, she added: "And that is the source of the power which drives your horseless carriages."

Again, he nodded. And, again, that odd expression came to his face. Smiling very broadly he was, too.

Yes. It is pride. *Why, I wonder?*

The distance was almost three miles, from the school to the house owned by the Roths where Rebecca was now living. It took them well over an hour to make the journey, as slowly as they were walking. Most of the time—almost all of it—was spent with Rebecca asking questions. Michael answered them, of course. But his answers were usually brief. He was a good listener, and Rebecca more often than not managed to answer her own questions with new ones.

By the time they reached the Roths' home, that peculiar expression of pride seemed to have become permanently fixed on Michael's face. So had his smile.

But Rebecca no longer wondered at the reason. She knew. And found the knowledge as exhilarating as it was unsettling.

At the door, standing on the porch, she began to knock. Then, pausing, she turned to face Michael. He was very close to her.

This is insane! Insane, Rebecca—do you hear?

She lowered her eyes, staring at his chest. He was wearing a linen shirt today, well-made and dyed in blues and grays. But she knew that she would always see that chest in white silk, drenched by sunlight. For one of the few times in her life, Rebecca Abrabanel was utterly at a loss for words.

Michael spoke softly. "Rebecca."

She raised her eyes to meet his. He was still smiling. Not broadly, however. The smile seemed—*understanding*, she thought.

"This is difficult," he said. "For both of us, I think." He chuckled. "Sure as hell for me!" Chuckled again. "Dinner and a movie just doesn't seem appropriate, somehow."

She did not comprehend the precise meaning of that sentence, but she understood the logic. Quite well. She felt her cheeks flush, but fought off the urge to lower her eyes. She even smiled herself.

Michael spread his hands in a gesture which combined amusement, momentary exasperation, and—most of all—patience. Rebecca was dazzled by the charm of it. Relaxed, humorous—*confident*.

"Time," he said. "I think—yes. We need some time."

Rebecca found herself nodding, and fiercely tried to restrain the impulse. Hopeless. *Idiot girl!* The image of a rabbit came to her mind, sniffing the world's juiciest cabbage. The image, combined with her nervousness, caused her to burst into sudden laughter.

Then, seeing the quizzical expression on Michael's face, she placed her hand on his chest. "Please," she whispered. "It is not— I am laughing at myself, not you."

The humor faded. Staring into his eyes, now, Rebecca fought for the words. So hard, to speak those words, in a world of confusion and chaos. Too hard.

Time, yes. I am not ready for this.

"Do not be angry with me," she said. Softly, pleading: *"Please."*

Michael smiled and placed a hand on her cheek. She responded by pressing her cheek into the hand, as if she were an automaton. She did not even try to stop herself.

"Why should I be angry?" he asked. And that, too—that simple question—seemed as dazzling to her as the sunlight. His hand was very warm.

He was turning away. "Time," he said, still smiling. Very broadly, now. Very cheerfully—almost gaily. "Time, yes."

Rebecca stared at his departing figure. When Michael reached the bottom of the small flight of stairs, Rebecca blurted out his name.

He turned and looked back at her.

The words came, finally. Some of them, at least.

"I think you are the most splendid man in the world, Michael. Truly I do."

A moment later she was knocking on the door. Almost frantically. She did not look behind her, afraid of what she would see. Or, perhaps, she was simply afraid of her reaction to what she knew she would see. A smiling face can be the most frightening thing in the world. Her world, as she knew it.

The door opened, and she vanished into the safety beyond. Out of the sunlight.

For a time.

Time, yes.

Time—yes!

Chapter 10

Alexander Mackay was a Scotsman and, as such, a Calvinist born and bred. Even if he had lapsed a bit—more than a bit, in truth—from the faith of his fathers, he had not lost the ingrained habits of his upbringing. Thus, staring down at the newest batch of corpses, he did not blaspheme. But he had no qualms about using other terms, so long as the Lord's name was not taken in vain. Perched on the saddle of his great warhorse, the young nobleman cast a wide net of incredibly vulgar terms across the Thuringian landscape in general, and a certain unit of Protestant mercenaries in particular. "Whoreson craven jackals" was perhaps the least obscene.

His second-in-command, a half-bald, mustachioed veteran in his forties, waited patiently until the cavalry commander was finished. Then, spitting casually onto the ground, Andrew Lennox simply shrugged and said: "What d'ye expect, lad? Most o' t'men guarding Badenburg"—the word *guarding* was accompanied by a magnificent sneer—"ae deserters from Mansfeld's old army. T'most wort'less soldiers in t'world e'en 'fore Mansfeld died."

"Then why did the town fathers hire the bastards?" Mackay demanded hotly. His eyes, still studying the scene of carnage, fell on the corpse of a small boy, perhaps six years of age. The child's body had been charred by the collapsing roof of the burned farmhouse in which he had spent his short life, but not so badly that Mackay couldn't see his entrails stretching across the dirt of the farmyard. The end of his intestines had been pinned to the ground by a kitchen knife, several feet from the body itself. The grotesque display of torture was entirely typical of the way some of Tilly's mercenaries amused themselves.

For all that Mackay had become inured to such scenes in the year since his arrival in Germany, he was glad that the bodies of the farm's womenfolk had been in the house itself. The corpses had been burnt to skeletons in that inferno, so there was no way to determine the exact manner of their deaths. Mackay didn't want to know. At the age of twenty-two, he had learned enough of cruelty and bestiality to last him a lifetime. Even the lifetime of a Scotsman, a breed not noted for their squeamishness.

Lennox did not bother to answer Mackay's question. The question had been purely rhetorical. Young, Mackay might be, but he was not foolish. The cavalry commander knew as well as anyone why Badenburg's notables had "agreed" to hire Ernst Hoffman's small army of mercenaries. They had been given precious little choice. *Let them plunder the town all at once, or let them plunder it a bit at a time.* Like many other towns in war-ravaged Germany, Badenburg had taken the second option. By now, several years later, most of its citizens had come to regret the choice. Hoffman's men claimed to be "Protestant," but that had proven to be no boon for Protestant Badenburg. With individual exceptions here and there, Hoffman and his thugs could no longer even be considered "soldiers," in any meaningful sense of the term. They were simply a gang of extortionists. Criminals, in all but name.

Mackay's anger faded away, replaced by a weariness of soul which, by right and reason, belonged to a much older man. When it had become clear that Hoffman had no intention of sallying from the shelter of Badenburg's walls to stop the depredations of Tilly's mercenaries, Mackay had led his own soldiers forth to do what he could to protect the farmers in the area.

It was a pointless gesture, in all truth. Mackay and his Scots cavalrymen, employed by the king of Sweden, had arrived in Badenburg less than three months ago. Gustav Adolf had stationed them there as part of his far-flung effort to stabilize his control of Germany's Baltic provinces. But the king was strapped for men—badly strapped. The Protestant princes who had promised him such abundant aid upon his arrival in Germany had, with a few exceptions, proven to be misers with both men and gold. So Mackay had been given not more than a few hundred men to carry out his task. His *main* task, which was not to attempt the absurdity of guarding an entire province with a small cavalry force.

Memory of that task jarred him out of his bitter mood. He turned to Lennox. "Still no sign of the courier?"

Lennox shook his head. "Nae a trace. Tha' might be good news." The veteran swept his florid mustachios about, as if using the waxed tips as pointers. "Y'can see how little Tilly's swine care 'bout coverin' they crimes. They'll nae ha' buried a ransacked carriage. 'Tis possible t'courier is simply hiding out some'eres." Lennox pointed to the heavily forested hills a few miles to the south. "B'now, tha' must be thousands o' people hidin' in yon hills."

Mackay scanned the Thuringenwald, as that forest was called. He frowned suddenly. "That's odd," he mused. He pointed to a portion of the hills. "I don't remember seeing that before. That stretch there. Looks different."

Lennox squinted, then shrugged. "Sorry, lad. My eyes are nae what they were. I canna make out what ye're pointin' to."

Mackay pursed his lips, trying to think of how to describe that peculiar part of the landscape. Then, spotting movement, he thrust the problem aside. One of his soldiers was coming—at a gallop.

"Something's up!" he exclaimed. As ever, the prospect of *action* brought immediate cheer. Alexander Mackay was the illegitimate son of a minor Scots nobleman. Destined—doomed, most would say— to a life of penury and peril. But even if he'd been pampered roy- alty, Mackay would have been a high-spirited adventurer.

"Come on!" he commanded, spurring his horse to meet the oncom- ing rider. A moment later, Lennox followed. The veteran's mustachios twitched, covering his smile. Lennox approved of Mackay, which was unusual in itself. As a rule, the former peasant viewed nobility with as much enthusiasm as he did manure. Less, really. At least dung didn't give orders. But Mackay possessed little of a nobleman's haughtiness, and almost none of the stupidity. The rambunctious eagerness which remained was relatively harmless—and, in its own way, quite charming. Even for a skeptic like Andrew Lennox.

By the time Lennox came abreast of Mackay, the captain had already encountered the scout. The man was turned halfway around in his saddle, pointing back in the direction from which he had come.

"—bess sey fer youself, sar. Tis varra strange. Ever't'in' 'bout th'place."

Mackay was frowning. He stared at the distant farmhouse to which the scout was pointing. The fact that the farmhouse was still unburnt was odd enough. Tilly's men were ingrained arsonists, even when burning buildings was not in their own interests.

"But no bodies, you say?"

The scout rocked his head back and forth. The gesture was not a negative headshake; more in the way of an expression of uncertainty. "They's nae bodies ey cou'd see, sar. Boot they's ae fresh doog mound—biggun—'minds mey o' ae grafe."

Mackay reared his head back, frowning. "A *grave?*"

Lennox snorted. "Since when do Tilly's men boory they victims?" he demanded.

The scout shrugged. "Ey dinna say it made sense. Boot shar 'n' sairtain looks leyk ae grafe to mey. Wit' moor th'n one body buried in't. Somebey e'en planted ae headstone." The scout's face scrunched with puzzlement. "Leas', ey *think* 'tis ae headstone. Boot they's nae crucifix. An' somebey wrote somet'in' all o'er it."

Mackay did not bother asking the scout what the writing said. Many of the soldiers in Mackay's cavalry unit could read—and read well—from their habit of studying the Bible. But the scout's thick Erse accent was the telltale sign of an illiterate Highlander. He would certainly be illiterate in German. To the best of his knowledge, Mackay was the only Scotsman in the area who could read German as well as speak it.

"Let's take a look, then." Again, Mackay spurred his horse into motion. The scout led the way. Lennox followed, after checking to make sure that the cavalrymen behind him were maintaining skirmishers on the flanks. Lennox wasn't really expecting to encounter any of Tilly's men. The butchery they had seen since they left Badenburg this morning was several days old and had all the signs of undisciplined marauders, being too lovingly thorough for men operating under command. Still, things were often not as they seemed in war, and the stakes were very high.

By the time he finally caught up with Mackay, they were entering the farmyard. The house was still standing, but Lennox had only to glance at the door and the outer walls to recognize that murder had been done here. Done and done well, from the look of the bloodstains. Big splotches, now brown and black. Even the flies were sparse. He had also spotted old bloodstains on the dirt road near the house.

"Four days ago," he stated. Mackay nodded. But the gesture was only half-conscious. Mackay was far too preoccupied staring at the fresh mound of earth piled up in the center of the farmyard. And the large "tombstone" planted on its center.

A mass grave, sure enough. But the "tombstone" was no tombstone at all. It was a placard.

Mackay's eyes were practically bulging. He pointed a finger at the placard and turned to Lennox. "What in the world . . . ?"

Lennox shrugged. Then, slowly and warily, he gave the woods nearby a very close scrutiny. Whoever had written the warning on that placard was no one he was eager to encounter. Especially since he had no doubt whatever what was buried beneath the soil. He would have known even if it hadn't been for the placard.

Seeing no signs of life or motion, he brought his eyes back to the placard and read the words again.

Simple words. Puzzling words. Deadly words.

We don't know who these murdering raping bastards are that we put here. Don't much care either. If there are any more of you out there, be warned. This area is now under the protection of the UMWA. If you try to harm

OR ROB ANYBODY WE WILL KILL YOU. THERE WILL BE NO FURTHER
WARNING. WE WILL NOT NEGOTIATE. WE WILL NOT ARREST YOU.
YOU WILL SIMPLY BE DEAD.
WE GUARANTEE IT.
GO AHEAD. TRY US.

Mackay ran fingers through his short beard. "And just exactly *who*
is this—*the Umwa?*" His face was a study in confusion. "Sounds Polish.
Is there a Polish baron somewhere in this area?"

"Nae tha' I ken," responded Lennox. "And I canna say I e'er heard
tha' title before." He mouthed the words. "The Umwa." Grunted. "He's
nae bashful, whoe'er t'man be."

The rest of the cavalry unit was gathered around by now. Mackay
pointed to the mound of earth. "See if there are any shovels around.
I want that—whatever it is—dug up." Some of the men winced, but
none of them uttered a protest. Mackay was an easy-going officer,
as a rule, but when he gave a direct order he expected it to be obeyed.

The soldiers found digging tools quickly enough. And it didn't take
them all that long to excavate the mound. Whoever he was, the Umwa
had apparently not felt under any obligation to bury the bodies deeply.

They found over a dozen corpses before Mackay told them to stop.
The bodies were decomposing, of course, but the causes of death were
obvious enough.

Lennox straightened, as much to get away from the smell as anything else. "Well, so much for tha'. This Umwa fellow is nae one to
make empty boasts."

Mackay was still peering intently at the corpses. "Those are the
oddest gunshot wounds I ever saw," he mused. He pointed an accusing
finger to the wound on the chest of one of the corpses. "That hole's
no bigger than my finger!" Then, in a tone which brooked no opposition: "Turn him over!"

The soldier next to the corpse grimaced as he obeyed. When the
body was rolled over, exposing the back, a little gasp went up from
the soldiers standing around the shallow grave.

One of them even lapsed into blasphemy. "God in His Heaven,"
the man whispered, "fro' this side 't luiks like a three-pounder blew
'm apart."

Mackay straightened, shaking his head. "Never seen anything like
it. Have you, Andrew?"

But Lennox gave no reply. He was too busy cursing himself silently.
He had become so preoccupied with the excavation that he had
forgotten to keep an eye on the woods.

When he did speak, his voice was not loud. But the manner in
which he projected that half-whisper had all the experience of a

battlefield veteran behind it. Every man in the unit heard him very clearly.

"Do nae move. Do nae touch ae weapon. There are men in those woods."

Slowly, Mackay turned his head. He couldn't see anything until—

Motion. A man—no, two, three men—stepping out of the trees. They were wearing utterly bizarre costumes. For all his puzzlement, a part of Mackay's mind realized how perfectly those garments were dyed to keep the men almost invisible in the trees. Grotesque rippling patterns of grays and greens and browns, blending with the foliage.

All three men were carrying strange-looking weapons in their hands. Arquebuses of some kind, but like none Mackay had ever seen.

Lennox answered the unspoken question. "I've nae seen guns like tha' ayther, lad. Nor such costumes." Half-admiringly: "Clever devils."

He even managed a bit of humor. "An' how is y'r Polish, Alexander Mackay? I do believe we are about to meet th'Umwa, an' I hope there'll be nae misunderstandings." He saw the men, almost simultaneously, do something peculiar to the rear stocks of their weapons. Their quick hand motions produced faint, metallic clicks. Lennox had no idea, precisely, what they had done. But he had not a doubt in the world that those bizarre weapons were now loaded, primed, and ready to fire. Arquebuses which made finger holes going in, and cannon holes going out. "I *really* hope there'll be nae miscommunication."

Mackay's face was sour. "I don't speak a word of Polish, Lennox."

The veteran sighed. "Tha's what I was afraid of."

As it happened, Polish was unneeded. The strange men in their strange costumes, carrying their strange weapons, proved to speak the most familiar language of all. *English!*

Well. Sort of.

"Worst accent I e'er heard," complained Lennox. But the complaint was not heartfelt. Rather the opposite, actually, especially after a dozen more of the strangers came out of the woods and joined in the conversation. All of them were armed, and all of them were clearly ready to kill. And most of them—*God bless my soul!*—claimed Scots ancestry. Within a few minutes, Andrew Lennox knew he would live to see another day. The encounter between Scots cavalryman and—*Americans*, they called themselves—was turning into something much like a family reunion.

Within a few hours, he was beginning to wonder. Not whether he would live, but what that day would bring. *Anything*, he thought.

A young woman from Sepharad had found her legends here. So, now, did a man from Scotland. And if his Highland legends lacked the sheer poetry of Sepharad, they had their own attractions. Faeries, indeed, had come to life in the world. Some grim, obscure, pagan part of Andrew Lennox's Calvinist soul took pleasure in the fact. Took pleasure, not so much that faeries existed, but that they were every bit as dangerous as the ancient tales had sworn.

Chapter 11

"—engines are the big problem," Piazza was saying. "Can't really convert diesel to natural gas, and we've got damned little diesel to begin with. You can run diesel engines on vegetable oil, of course." He chuckled ruefully. "But there isn't that much vegetable oil left in the supermarkets, and it'll take us till next year to start making any in quantity. So in the meantime—"

Mike tuned out the rest. He'd already had a preliminary discussion with Ed and knew what the gist of the proposal was going to be concerning the proper use of the town's diesel equipment.

Same as everything else. Gear down, gear down. Use our modern technology, while it lasts, to build a nineteenth-century industrial base. Still put us way ahead of the game, here in the seventeenth century. Steam engines, steam engines. The railroads are about to make a big comeback in the world.

Mike smiled slightly. *Or is "comeback" the right word? Maybe I should say "come back around."*

He saw Rebecca was looking at him, and his smile widened. She responded with a shy smile of her own, but looked away almost at once. Her attention was back on Piazza. Riveted to his words, by all appearances. Rebecca's hands were clasped in front of her and resting on the big "conference table" in the center of the room. As usual, she was perched on the edge of her chair.

Mike still counted that smile as progress. It was the first time Rebecca had given him so much as a glance since their conversation on the porch the night before. It was plain as day that she was floundering in a strange sea of new emotions and customs, with a weight of her own traditions that Mike could only guess at. In the world he had come from, romantic liaisons between Jews and gentiles were so common as to hardly cause notice. But the seventeenth century, in many ways, seemed as different as another planet.

Remembering a discussion he had had with Morris Roth, two days earlier, Mike felt his jaws tightening. Morris and Judith had spent hours in conversations with Rebecca, since she and her father had moved into their home. Many of those hours had been spent in Balthazar's room, gathered about his bed. Balthazar himself had been too ill to do much more than listen, but he had participated enough to make clear that Rebecca's view of things was fully shared by her widely traveled father. She was not—definitely not—some ignorant country girl filled with mindless fears and superstitions.

"They're worried about the Inquisition, Mike, more than anything else," Morris had told him. "The Inquisition has agents—Jesuits and Dominicans, mostly—attached to all of the Catholic armies. It seems that two years ago Emperor Ferdinand decreed something called the Edict of Restitution. According to that Edict, all property taken from the Catholic church by Protestants since the Reformation has to be turned back over. And the emperor insists on the forcible conversion of Protestants back to Catholicism. The Inquisition is there to carry out the order."

Mike had been puzzled. "All right. But I still don't understand what they're worried about. I always thought the Inquisition was aimed at heresy. Rebecca and Balthazar aren't *heretics*, Morris. They're not Christians to begin with."

Morris stared at him for a moment, before wiping his face with a hand. "I forget," he murmured. "We Jews live with our history so closely, we sometimes assume that everyone else knows it as well as we do."

He took away the hand and gave Mike a weary look. "The Office of the Holy Inquisition was set up in 1478 specifically for the purpose of ferreting out *Jews*, Mike. The Spanish forced all Jews to convert, starting in 1391. Dominican monks led mobs in pogroms on the Jewish quarters. *Die or be baptized*: those were the choices. A lot of Jews chose baptism. *Conversos,* they were called. Then the Spanish monarchy, with the Pope's blessing, set up the Inquisition to hunt down the ones who were still privately practicing Judaism. Those people were called marranos. 'Secret Jews.' "

Mike remembered the term. Rebecca had used it in the carriage to refer to herself, the first time he met her. "And then . . . ?"

Morris looked away. "Trial by torture. *Auto-da-fé*. That's where they gathered the Christians in a town in order to watch the festivities, complete with sermons and parades. All the heretics were brought out from the prisons. Secret Jews, mostly, along with secret Moslems—those were called *Moriscoes*—and whoever else had come under suspicion."

Roth shook his head. "The whole thing was insane, Mike. One of the reasons Christians in that era—*this* era, God help us—were so filthy was because it was dangerous to pay too much attention to cleanliness and personal hygiene. Who knows? You might be a secret Jew or a Moslem. Better to remain in an ostentatious state of Christian grime. And when disease comes, blame it on witches or the Jews."

Again, he wiped his face. "The ceremony—the auto-da-fé—would be climaxed by having the heretics burned alive at the stake." Sarcastically: "If you can call someone who's been in the hands of the Inquisition 'alive,' that is. Plenty of them died in the Church's torture chambers. Those—the corpses, I mean—would be burned at the stake so the Inquisition could legally inherit their property."

Seeing Mike's little start of surprise, Morris had chuckled harshly. "Oh yeah, did I forget to mention that? They have some peculiar notions about legal impartiality, in this day and age. The Inquisition is mostly financed by the seized property of the condemned. So you can just imagine how many verdicts of 'innocent' they ever handed down. Didn't take those holy men very long to become rich."

Remembering that conversation, and the anger it had produced in him, Mike forced his mind back to the business at hand. *We'll see who burns who, in the new dispensation.* Piazza was moving on to a discussion of the refugee problem, but Mike interrupted.

"Excuse me, Ed, but there's something I want to bring up before we get into that." He turned to Ferrara. "Who's the best chemist in town, Greg? You?"

The science teacher shrugged. "Depends what you want, Mike. For some things, me. For others—"

"I want someone who knows how to make napalm."

Ferrara's mouth snapped shut. Opened. Closed.

"Nothing to it," said Melissa. "There's at least three homemade recipes that I know of."

Everyone, Mike included, stared at Melissa. The prim-looking, gray-haired schoolteacher shrugged. "I never made it myself, you understand." Sniff. "Didn't really approve of such tactics, even back then. But one of my college boyfriends was an anarchist. He used to meddle with the stuff all the time. Claimed we'd need it come the revolution."

Stares. James Nichols burst into laughter. "It's nice to know I'm not the only one here with a misspent youth!" He eyed Melissa approvingly. "But—*damn*—you white kids were ambitious. I never thought past a simple Molotov cocktail."

Melissa frowned. "What's the point of that?" she demanded. "Surely you didn't think—"

"Okay!" exclaimed Mike. "Enough, already!" He chuckled. "Christ, I didn't expect I'd be kicking off a sixties radicals' reunion."

Rebecca's brow was creased with frustration. Plainly enough, the conversation had once again taken a turn she was unable to follow. "Excuse me," she said softly. "What is—*napalm*?"

Mike's eyes fixed on her. "It's something we'll make to greet the Inquisition when they show up. Them and their goons." He smiled grimly. "Think of it as portable hellfire."

"Oh." Her dark eyes were very round. And then very bright. "Oh."

There came a knock on the door. Without waiting for a response, Darryl McCarthy came barging in. The young miner was carrying his rifle and was practically bouncing like a rubber ball.

"We got visitors, Mike! *Scotsmen!* Soldiers!" He caught sight of Rebecca and steadied down. "They say they're looking for you, Miss Abrabanel. Well, your father, actually."

Mike rose to his feet so abruptly that his chair tipped over. His right hand clenched reflexively. *"Why?"* he demanded.

Darryl stared at him, puzzled by the obvious anger in that curt question. But Rebecca immediately interrupted.

"Michael—*please.*" She smiled at him warmly, but shook her head. "It is not what you think. I imagine they—" She turned to Darryl. "Are these men in the employ of the king of Sweden?"

Darryl's head bobbed. "That's what they say, ma'am. Somebody named Gustav."

Melissa's jaw dropped. "Gustav?" The history teacher rose to her feet almost as abruptly as Mike had. "Are you talking about *Gustavus Adolphus?*"

Darryl was now utterly confused. "Who's that?" He threw up his hands with exasperation. The rifle, still in his right hand, was waving around like a stick. Frank was about to snarl something when Darryl realized what he was doing and apologetically lowered the firearm. He double-checked to make sure the safety was still on. Then, in a much-aggrieved tone, said: "I don't know what this is all about. All I know is that a whole bunch of horsemen—couple dozen, at least—showed up at that farmhouse where we had the shoot-out with those thugs."

He started to elaborate but broke off. "Oh, hell, why ask me? They're in the parking lot."

Now it was Frank's turn to lunge to his feet. "You let them through the perimeter?" he demanded angrily.

Darryl's face, at that moment, almost caused Mike to burst into laughter. The miner looked like a ten-year-old boy, aggrieved beyond measure by the quirks and whimsies of grown-ups. "They're *Scots,* for Christ's sake! Practically family. Of course we let them in."

Mike started for the door. "Come on, Frank. Let's just go see for ourselves."

The entire emergency committee trooped after him. Frank brought up the rear. As he passed Darryl, he commented sourly: "Your uncle Jake was family, too. Died in prison, didn't he, serving a murder sentence?"

A much aggrieved boy. "Only second-degree," he protested. "He would've been up for parole in a year, if he hadn't gotten knifed."

"Family," muttered Frank. "Wonderful."

They were there, all right. The Scotsmen had apparently arrived in marching order, three abreast, and were maintaining their positions. Twenty-six cavalrymen—there were only two men at the head of the column—still astride their mounts. The horses were skittish, stamping their hooves on the pavement nervously. But they were no more apprehensive than their riders, staring at the hill rising up behind the high school.

Staring at the backhoe and the bulldozer, more precisely. The big pieces of construction equipment were working away, engines roaring, clearing the area for the planned refugee camp. One of the camps, rather. The main refugee center would be built two miles away, next to the power plant, where the shelters could be provided with steam heat exhausted as a byproduct of the plant's operation. The camp on the hill above the high school would be heated from the school's own natural gas supply, with the added advantage that the inhabitants would be able to use the school's cafeteria.

As soon as he saw them, Mike had no doubt the Scotsmen were soldiers. True, their clothing was individually varied. But Rebecca had already explained that soldiers in this day and age rarely wore uniforms. Identification was usually provided on a battlefield by strips of colored cloth used as bandannas or tied around one arm—or even by the simple device of sticking leafy twigs in a hatband.

Everything else about them practically shrieked: *soldiers*. None of the men were wearing armor, as such. But their buff coats and leather boots were thick enough to protect against sword cuts and even, beyond close range, the heavy but low-velocity bullets of seventeenth century firearms. The boots were well made, and reached up to mid-thigh. The buff coats—armless vests, more often—had skirts which flared out over the hips and reached down just below the tops of the boots. A few of the men were wearing actual helmets, but most of them seemed satisfied with wide-brimmed leather hats. All of the men were armed with swords slung in baldrics, and all of them had at least two huge wheel-lock pistols jammed into saddle holsters. One man that Mike could see had as many as four.

Beyond their gear, the men had a certain grim and *dangerous* air about them. That was especially true of one of the two men at the

Eric Flint

head of the column. The man was middle-aged, heavily built, and sported a truly magnificent pair of mustachios. His face, despite its naturally florid color, was utterly expressionless. He, too, was staring at the construction equipment, but without a trace of the awe and trepidation which was so obvious on the other men.

Seeing Mike and his companions emerging from the school, the Scot tore his eyes away from the construction work and muttered something. His companion at the head of the column, a young man wearing somewhat more expensive-looking apparel, jerked his head around. Seeing him full-face, Mike realized that the man was very young. In his early twenties, he estimated. On the short side—even by the standards of the time, which Mike had learned were several inches shorter than the average American. His eyes were green, his hair was red, his mustache and goatee were on the sparse side, his face was pug-nosed, his complexion was pale and—just to make things perfect—he was flamboyantly freckled. He looked like the spitting image of Tom Sawyer. Or, at least, what Mike thought Tom Sawyer *ought* to look like, after he grew up.

For some peculiar reason, that appearance caused Mike to relax. There was no logic to his reaction, of course. But try as he might, Mike couldn't help but feel a certain warmth toward the young Scotsman.

Melissa verbalized his thoughts. "Good Lord," she chuckled, "I feel like I ought to set him to whitewashing my fence."

The quip caused Mike to smile, and it was with that friendly and cheerful expression on his face that he advanced toward the mounted men. Apparently, he was projecting the right attitude. He could sense the immediate relaxation in the two Scotsmen at the fore and then, moments later, the same easing of tension working its way down the line of horsemen.

As he neared them, the young Scotsman—the officer, Mike assumed; the man next to him had all the earmarks of a veteran noncom—pointed to the construction equipment and demanded: "What is *that*?"

The young man's head turned, bringing his green eyes onto Darryl's pickup truck. Mike had no doubt that Darryl had led them here behind it, and knew that the truck would have produced the same reaction in these Scotsmen that modern vehicles had on the Abrabanels. Days after arriving in Grantville, Rebecca still tended to stare at every passing motor vehicle.

Mike was impressed by the young Scotsman's ability to connect the construction equipment with the pickup truck. "Yes," he explained loudly, "they're basically the same thing. Motor-driven equipment, we call them. The motors themselves—they're just machines, that's all—are powered by burning naphtha."

The officer's eyes snapped back. "No sorcery then." It was a state-ment, not a question. Mike saw his shoulders ease a bit. "I had hoped as much," the young redhead added. "Expected it, actually. Your guns are extremely well made, I noticed. A craftsmanly folk. More so than any I've ever encountered in the world." His face flushed a little, highlighting the freckles. Plainly enough, the officer realized how absurd that statement must sound. *And just how much of the great wide world have you seen, at your age?*

The man at his side, apparently driven by an urge to support his young superior, immediately stated: "Well said, lad. Ne'er seen t'like meself."

Listening to the interchange between the two Scotsmen, Mike found himself grinning. That was probably an undiplomatic thing to do, but he couldn't help it. The Scotsmen's English was perfectly understandable, despite the heavy accents, distinctive inflexions, and frequent use of archaic terms. And why shouldn't they be? There was none of what modern Americans thought of as a typical "Scottish brogue." Instead, the cavalrymen's speech reminded Mike of nothing so much as that of real back-country Appalachian hillbillies.

Just like Darryl said—"family," by God!

"Why don't you all dismount," Mike said. The sentence was phrased like a question but spoken like a command. He pointed to the slen-der steel columns which held up the concrete awning sheltering the entrance to the school. "You can tie the horses up over there."

The Scotsmen hesitated. Mike waved his hand. "Come on, come on. I imagine you're hungry. We can feed you in the—" *Cafeteria*, he decided, was probably a meaningless word in this time and place. "In the dining hall," he concluded.

The mention of food did the trick. Within a minute, all of the Scots cavalrymen had dismounted, tied up their horses, and were being led into the school. By the time they got into the large hallway which served the school as its vestibule, a crowd had gathered. High-school students and their teachers, mostly—the Americans had decided to resume classroom instruction—but there were plenty of townsfolk there also. The high school had, willy-nilly, become Grantville's community center in the crisis. It was, by far, the largest and best-equipped facility in the area.

The corridor leading to the classrooms was jammed full of stu-dents. Others—boys in basketball trunks and girls from the cheer-leading squad—were pouring in from the gymnasium on the other side of the entry hall. The head cheerleader, Julie Sims, was leading that little crowd. She was clutching pom-poms, smiling broadly, and bouncing with excitement. With her pretty face, athletic carriage, full figure—legs bare from mid-thigh to ankles—she was a textbook illustration of the term *nubility*.

Most of the Scots soldiers ogled Julie and the other cheerleaders, but some had their eye on a few of the older girls in the corridor. Modern American women's clothing, by their standards, bordered on lasciviousness. Rebecca had told Mike that not even prostitutes, in this day and age, would display so much bare flesh in public.

One of the soldiers whispered something to a companion. Mike didn't quite catch the words, but he didn't miss the lewd tone. He was trying to decide how to handle this unexpected little problem, when the mustachioed veteran solved it for him. The man, as still-faced as ever, turned his head and hissed a few choice words of his own. Mike caught the last phrase: "—y'r own cocks f'r sausage. *D'ye understand?*"

His soldiers stiffened and turned their eyes away from the girls.

Mike smiled. *I do believe I'm going to get along with this very tough-looking fellow.*

The young officer had been one of those ogling Julie. He must have caught the same words, for he suddenly started and eyed Mike a bit apprehensively. He seemed on the verge of uttering some sort of apology.

Mike kept the smile on his face. "I realize that some of our—ah, *customs*—must seem a little strange to you." He nodded toward the cheerleading squad. "We're not much given to worrying about appearances. Just the *content* of morality."

The last words were spoken a bit grimly. Mike's smile faded away. Days ago, Mike had made his basic decision. He would not budge from it.

If the superstitious, flea-bitten, lord-and-priest-ridden bastards don't like it, let 'em choke to death. No surrender, no retreat. This is American soil!

A stray thought made him chuckle. During his three years in college, Mike had been a history student himself. Unlike Melissa, however, with her wide-ranging interests, Mike's attention had been rather narrowly focused on the American Revolution and the first few decades of the republic. The Founding Fathers, especially George Washington, ranked very high on his personal list of heroes.

He took the young Scots officer by the arm and began leading him toward the cafeteria. Up close, he towered over the man. Mike's next words were spoken loudly enough for everyone in the area to hear. "I might mention, as well, that we have certain fundamental political principles. One of those was neatly summed up by one of our early historical leaders, when our young republic was threatened by bandits."

The cafeteria was only a few steps away. Mike paused at the entrance, released the young officer's arm, and turned to address the entire crowd of Scots soldiers and American onlookers.

"Millions for defense, but not one cent for tribute!"

The Americans in the hallway burst into cheering applause. Julie Sims immediately began an impromptu routine with her pom-poms. "Give me a *D!*" Her squad mates and the basketball players grinned and responded with a roaring: *"Defense! Defense!"* A moment later, the entire crowd had joined the chant.

The Scottish soldiers flinched a little from the ruckus. All except the officer and his veteran subordinate.

The noncom, after glancing around, brought his eyes back to Mike. He didn't seem in the least intimidated by the American's six-inch advantage in height.

"Tha's ae proud boast, man. But can ye sustain it?"

Mike's own grin never wavered. "Care to try us?"

Slowly, the noncom matched the grin with one of his own. Crooked teeth gleamed under mustachioes. "No particularly, now tha' ye ask. Much prefer ae more—ah, friendly—arrangement."

Mike nodded. To the officer: "And you?"

But the officer had missed the exchange entirely. For a few seconds, his attention had been completely riveted on Julie Sims. Some of his fixation, of course, was due to the prettiness of the girl and the shapeliness of her very exposed figure. But most of it was caused by her sheer energy and athleticism. He had never seen a girl so—so *exuberant.*

By some odd causeway, that cheerleader's glorious vigor brought his mind to focus on the heart of the matter. So much so, in fact, that a born-and-bred Calvinist even lapsed into blasphemy.

"Who in the name of God *are* you people?"

Over lunch, Mike explained. Here, too, he had already made his decision days ago. *The truth, the whole truth, and nothing but the truth.* He would not stoop to superstition, or try to calculate the angles. Just tell it as best he could, based on what little the Americans knew themselves.

The conversation lasted for hours. Long before it was over, at Ed Piazza's initiative, miners had brought every one of Grantville's religious leaders to the cafeteria. By motor vehicle, not by foot—this matter qualified as a military affair.

As the town's preachers and priests began arriving, and joined in the discussion, Mike could see the slow easing of tension in the Scotsmen. It all seemed very strange, but—

Christians, then. Protestants, even, the most of them. Odd how they manage to live alongside Catholics and Jews and Moors and free-thinkers without quarrel. Still—

Many of the Scots soldiers, having seen the dogs of war and the carnage of religious strife, made their own mental nods of agreement. A sensible arrangement, when you come down to it. (And, oh, those lovely spirited girls!)

Not sorcery, then. No sign of witchcraft.

Master mechanics and artisans, true. And so what? Scotsmen already had their respect for such. Witchcraft was a thing of hailstorms out of season, and mysterious disease, and milk come sour right out of the cow. This milk was so pure it was like drinking nectar. Do these folk look sickly? Not a crone in the lot. Even the older woman—the schoolteacher—looked marvelous in her health. (And, oh, those lovely spirited girls!)

God's will, then. His doing, not Satan's. The Lord Almighty saw fit to bring these people here. Is that not a sign in itself? Plain as day, even to simple soldiers?

(And, oh, those lovely spirited girls!)

Chapter 12

When Rebecca ushered the Scots officer into the Roths' house, she was surprised to see her father sitting in one of the armchairs in the main salon. That was called the "living room." The odd name was typical of Americans, Rebecca thought. For all their near-magical powers, they were in many ways the most practical folk she had ever met. More so, even, than the hardheaded merchants of Amsterdam.

She was relieved to see him sitting up, for the first time since his heart attack. Indeed, Balthazar Abrabanel was having an animated conversation with both of the American doctors, James Nichols and Jeffrey Adams. Morris and Judith Roth were present also.

"Rebecca!" he exclaimed cheerfully, turning his head to his daughter. "I have the most marvelous news." Balthazar pointed to the doctors. "They have just—"

He broke off, seeing the officer standing behind Rebecca. His face, formerly so animated, froze into a mask. There was nothing hostile in the expression. It was simply the face of an experienced diplomat.

Rebecca's lips twitched. *Diplomat? Say better—an experienced spy.*

She knew her father's history. His branch of the Abrabanels had lived in London for well over a hundred years, since the expulsion of the Sephardim from Spain. Their existence was technically illegal—Jews had been officially banned from the island centuries earlier—but the English authorities made no attempt to enforce the ban so long as the Jews kept their community small and discreet. If for no other reason, English monarchs and high nobility preferred Jewish doctors to gentile ones.

With Elizabeth's ascent to the throne, in what Christians called the year 1558 *anno Domini*, the position of the Jews became quite secure. Elizabeth's own physician, Dr. Rodrigo Lopez, was Sephardic. The queen came to rely upon him to some degree for political as well as medical advice—particularly with regard to the dangers posed by Philip II of Spain. Dr. Lopez, acting as her intermediary, organized several members of the Abrabanel family to serve the English crown as spies. The Abrabanels, one of the great families of the far-flung Sephardim, were well placed to keep an eye on the doings of the Spaniards.

Rebecca's grandfather Aaron had so served, until his death, and had passed the mantle to his two sons, Balthazar and Uriel. Rebecca still had memories, from her early childhood, of being taken by her father down to London's great harbor to meet with Portuguese seamen and merchants, many of whom were marranos.

With Elizabeth's death and the coronation of James I, unfortunately, the political climate had changed. James was partial to the Spanish, and was inclined to grant their many demands. He even executed Sir Walter Raleigh to placate the Spaniards, though the official charge was treason. Jews were no longer welcome at the English court—not even privately—and the pressure on the Sephardic community intensified. In 1609, James again ordered their expulsion.

A few Jewish families remained, Rebecca's among them. They were sheltered by elements in the British government and, most of all, by the Puritans. The Puritans, a growing force in English society, were much more favorably inclined toward the Jews than the established church. Many of their scholars were keenly interested in the study of Hebrew texts, as part of their efforts to "purify" Christianity.

The Scottish officer stepped into the room and spoke his first words. As soon as Balthazar heard that unmistakable accent, his rigid face softened. Within seconds, Rebecca saw her father's normal warmth and wit returning.

She, too, had felt the charm of that northerly version of the English tongue. It was not the accent itself, but what lay beneath it. On two occasions, once when she was twelve and again when she was fourteen, Rebecca had accompanied her father and uncle to Cambridge, which was a hotbed of Puritanism. The presence of the two learned Jewish doctors—fluent alike in Hebrew and Greek—had been requested to clarify certain obscure passages in the Biblical texts.

"I bring you greetings from Gustavus Adolphus, Balthazar Abrananel."

Hearing that accent, Rebecca remembered those earnest Puritan scholars with fondness. Their branch of the Abrabanels had finally been forced to leave England, not long thereafter. Uriel, always the more adventurous of the brothers, had opted to seek his fortune in Germany. Her father, burdened with a sickly wife and a daughter, had chosen Amsterdam. There, among the Dutch cousins of the Puritans, they had found a haven.

Balthazar Abrananel nodded. "Please convey my deepest respects to His Majesty, uh—?"

"Mackay, sir. Alexander Mackay, captain in the king of Sweden's Green Regiment, at your service."

Stern and stiff they were, those Calvinists—as humorless and cold as the Sephardim were not—but they had a respect for the Bible not shared by the Catholics, or even the Lutherans. God had given the people of Abraham a place in the world. Who were they to question His will?

Behind her, Rebecca sensed Michael coming into the room. He came to stand behind her. Very near, he was. A bit more so, perhaps, than propriety allowed.

Rebecca found her lips curving into a smile, and forced the expression from her face.

Propriety. But whose, exactly? Not the Americans! They seem oblivious to the concept. The most shameless folk I have ever met. Remembering the treatment she and her father had been given: *And have perhaps less reason to be shameful, in all truth.*

Michael was *very* close. She felt an almost overpowering urge to lean back against him. Then, seeing her father's eyes upon her, she straightened.

The eyes were knowing. Rebecca had tried to keep her daily reports to her father free of any emotion. She had been especially careful—or so she thought—to keep any trace of warmth from her accounts of Michael and his doings.

Inwardly, she sighed. No doubt she had tried too hard. Balthazar Abrabanel was as shrewd a man as ever existed. She had never been able to hide anything from her father. In truth, she had never really tried before.

There will be a stern fatherly lecture coming, she thought glumly. *Very stern.*

Balthazar's eyes moved away from her and focused again on the Scots officer. Mackay had been bustled into a heavily upholstered armchair by Judith Roth, and was now resuming his conversation.

The Scotsman glanced quickly around the room. Clearly enough, the presence of the Americans was making him a bit reticent.

"You may speak freely, Captain Mackay," said Balthazar. "Our hosts are quite aware already of the treasure I was bringing with me." He bestowed a lingering look upon Michael. Rebecca was relieved to see that there was no anger in her father's eyes. Simply gratitude, and respect.

"Indeed, had it not been for them—Michael especially—the silver would now be in the possession of Tilly's monsters." He leaned forward and extended his hands. The spread fingers were heavily laden with bejeweled rings. "Along with these, cut from my body." Harshly: "And my daughter, of course."

Balthazar nodded toward the ceiling. "The chest containing the money for your king is upstairs in my bedroom. It is all there, every guilder. I have a receipt, of course."

Mackay waved his hand. The gesture was one of certainty and assurance. *No need, Balthazar Abrabanel. Your honesty is unquestioned.*

Perhaps oddly, Rebecca's reaction to that little movement was more one of anger than of pride. *Of course you trust the Jews with your money. And then, when the mood changes, you accuse us of foul crimes because we can turn a profit without cheating. Unlike your own bankers. Christians!*

But her anger was only momentary. In truth, it was misdirected. The various branches of the Calvinist creed were by no means free of intolerance toward Jews. But they had their own firm belief in the value of hard work and thrift, they encouraged literacy, and they tended to view people who acquired wealth more with admiration than envy.

It was not the Calvinists, after all, who forced us to leave Amsterdam's Jewish quarter. My father was expelled by orthodox rabbis, not Christian preachers.

She forced her mind to focus on the moment. Her father would want her advice and opinion. Especially now, in such deep and unknown waters.

Mackay, she saw, was staring at Michael also. There was respect in that look—and more than a trace of puzzlement.

"Why?" the Scotsman suddenly blurted out.

"Why *what*?" responded Michael. But the question was rhetorical. The American placed his hands on Rebecca's shoulders and gently moved himself around her to come to the center of the room. There, standing straight with his hands on his hips, he gazed down on Mackay. The gaze was almost a glare.

"Why aren't we rapists and thieves?"

Mackay lowered his head and shook it. "That's not what I meant." The Scotsman ran fingers through his thick red hair, his face crunched into a frown. Plainly enough, he was groping for words.

Rebecca's father found the words for him. "It is simply their way, Captain Mackay." Balthazar glanced at the Americans in the room. His eyes lingered on the black doctor for a moment.

"It's not that these Americans are lambs." He smiled. "Some of them, I imagine, have even been known to commit armed robbery. Attempt it, at least." James Nichols grinned.

Again, Balthazar's eyes studied the various Americans. They came to rest, this time, on Michael. "And other depredations, I have no doubt. Brawling, for instance. Drunk and disorderly conduct. Disrespect for the public authorities."

Michael was grinning, now. Rebecca did not understand why, but she was relieved to feel the tension easing from the room.

Balthazar's smile was quite warm when he turned it to Mackay. "But they are also a people who cherish their laws. Which they enact themselves, you know, with scant respect for lineage and rank. From what my daughter has told me, they are the most inveterate republicans since the ancient Greeks."

Balthazar spread his hands, as if demonstrating the obvious. "This is why, I think, that their instinctive response was to protect us, along with our goods. The law was being broken, you see. *Their* law, not the crown's."

The Jewish physician gave Michael another glance, lifting a finger at him. "Ask him, Mackay. Ask him again. But do not ask: *why*? Simply ask: did you even think twice? Or even *once*, for that matter?"

Mackay looked at Michael. The American, after a moment, let his hands fall from his hips. It was a weary gesture. But there was nothing weary in the way the large hands curled into fists.

"I don't know what kind of a world you people have created here, Captain Mackay," Michael growled. "But we will be no part of it. *None*, do you understand me? Wherever our power runs, the law will be obeyed. *Our* law."

"And how far does that power run?" asked Mackay.

Michael's response was instant. "As far as we can stretch it."

Mackay leaned back in his chair. "Some questions, then. My first." He pointed to the revolver at Michael's hip. "Are your weapons as good as I—as Lennox—thinks?"

Michael glanced down at the sidearm. "With a rifle, I can hit a one-inch bull's-eye at two hundred yards. Three hundred yards, with a scope. And I'm not the best marksman among us, not by a long shot." He stared out the window, as if examining the town. "There are other things, also, which we can make."

Michael brought his eyes back to Mackay. Blue and cold. "Your next question," he commanded.

Mackay jerked his head, pointing to the ceiling and the rooms above. "There is a small fortune up there, Michael of the Americans. It belongs to the king of Sweden, but he has authorized me to dispense it as I see fit. Will you take his colors?"

"No." Very blue and very cold. "*We are not mercenaries*. We will fight under our own banners, and no other."

Mackay stroked his beard, thinking. "Would you accept an alliance, then?" Hurriedly: "It needn't be anything very formal, you understand. Just an agreement between gentlemen. And with the funds I now have, I could cover the expenses."

The young Scotsman's gaze moved to the window. He tightened his own hands into fists, for a moment. And, for that moment, his green eyes held the same glitter as Michael's. "Think of us what you will, American. I take no more pleasure than you in seeing farmers and their children massacred, or their women subjected to vile abuse."

His right hand opened, and a finger of accusation pointed through the window to the north. "Tilly's beasts are pouring into Thuringia. They will be taking the larger cities soon, and then plundering the countryside like locusts. I cannot possibly stop them, not with my few hundred cavalrymen. But—"

His eyes fixed on Michael's revolver. Suddenly, startlingly, Michael clapped his hands together.

"Oh—*that* kind of alliance!" he exclaimed. Michael was grinning from ear to ear. The sheer good humor of the expression, for all the ferocity lurking in it, was like pure sunshine.

"Sure, Alexander Mackay. *We accept.*"

Less than a minute later, Michael was out on the street, where dozens of his coal miners were chatting amiably with the Scots cavalrymen. Mackay was at his side. A large crowd was gathered about, most of them students from the high school who had followed them into town.

Rebecca, watching through the window, saw Michael's lips moving. She could not hear the words, but knew he was addressing the coal miners. An instant later, the crowd on the street dissolved into an orgy of celebration and back slapping. Julie Sims and her cheerleading squad again started that bizarre little dance. And, again, the students responded with a roaring chant.

> *Two—four—six—eight!*
> *Who do we appreciate?*
> *Scotsmen! Scotsmen!*

The chant was loud enough to be heard through the window. More than loud enough. Rebecca thought the chant was bizarre, although she could not deny its raucous charm.

Then the cheerleaders began leading the crowd in a different chant and she was completely mystified.

Frowning, she turned to James Nichols. The doctor was on his feet, staring out the window, clapping his hands in time to the chant and muttering the same peculiar, meaningless words under his breath.

"Please," she asked, "explain this to me. What does that mean, exactly?" Her lips formed around unfamiliar words. *"On Wisconsin! On Wisconsin!"*

The doctor grinned. "What it means, young lady, is that a bunch of swaggering thugs are about to get a history lesson. In advance, so to speak."

He turned to her, still grinning. "Let me introduce you to another unfamiliar American expression." The white teeth, shining in a black face, reminded Rebecca of nothing so much as a shield of heraldry.

"We call it—*D-Day.*"

Chapter 13

In the hours that followed, the Roths' home became a whirlwind of activity. Michael and Alexander Mackay, along with Andrew Lennox and Frank Jackson, spent the entire afternoon at the large table in the kitchen, planning out their coming campaign. American coal miners and Scots soldiers trooped in and out as the hours went by. Bearing commands on their way out, and bringing questions on their way in. The Scots soldiers would come and go quickly, but many of the American miners would stay for awhile, chiming in with their own suggestions and opinions.

Julie Sims even showed up, bouncing into the kitchen to greet her uncle Frank and take advantage of that family connection to sate her eager curiosity. Mackay immediately lost his concentration on military affairs. Entirely. Julie had replaced her cheerleader's outfit with a blouse and blue jeans, true. But with her figure, and the energy which filled it, the change of clothing was irrelevant.

Then, seeing the smirk lurking in Lennox's eyes, Mackay flushed and tried to keep his eyes off the girl. But he still did not manage to bring his mind back into focus until several minutes after Frank shooed Julie away.

Mackay thought the extreme looseness of the American command structure—if such it could even be called—was extremely odd. But—

Everything about these Americans was extremely odd, when you came down to it. Yet there was no question that Michael and Frank had the final authority on any decisions. So, after a time, the two Scottish professional soldiers simply relaxed and—to use one of those peculiar American expressions—"went with the flow."

Others came also, to gather in the living room around Balthazar and Rebecca. The two doctors had remained, along with Morris Roth.

Judith, now and again, would sit in on their discussion, but she was generally too busy providing food and drink for the soldiers. Rebecca offered to help in that chore, but Judith wouldn't permit it.

"Melissa will be coming over, any moment," she explained. Smiling: "I'll catch enough hell from her as it is, catering to the men the way I am. If she sees you doing it too—you're the National Security Adviser, remember?—I'll *never* hear the end of it. Knowing Melissa, she'd probably start picketing my house."

Rebecca's look of incomprehension caused Judith to laugh. "You never heard of women's lib, I take it?"

Julie Sims was standing nearby, listening to the exchange. Judith smiled at her and said: "Explain it, why don't you?"

"Sure! Piece of cake!"

Judith went off to the kitchen. Grinning, Julie gave Rebecca a précis on the subject of women's liberation. And if the eighteen-year-old girl's version of it would have caused the more doctrinaire advocates of women's lib to blanch, they certainly couldn't have complained about the enthusiasm of the presentation. By the time Julie finished, the look of incomprehension was gone from Rebecca's face. Her expression was now one of pure and simple shock.

"You must be joking."

" 'Course not!" was Julie's reply. A moment later, her eye drawn by someone on the street outside the window, Julie charged out of the house. Haltingly, Rebecca took a seat on the couch and began to listen to the conversation among the doctors.

At first, her mind was elsewhere. *Women's liberation? Absurd!* But then, as she caught the drift of the discussion, all other thoughts were driven aside immediately.

And, again, Rebecca's face must have shown her shock and disbelief.

Her father smiled at her. "Yes, daughter. This is what I was about to tell you when you first arrived. So—what do you think of the proposal?"

She was at a loss for words. *Are they serious?* But a glance at the two American doctors made clear that they were.

It is unheard of! A medical partnership—between gentiles and Jews?

The older doctor, the one Rebecca had first thought to be a Moor, cleared his throat. "You understand, Dr. Balthazar, that while you will be entitled to your full share of the proceeds—one third of what the doctors take in, after the salaries of the nurses and other employees are paid—that you will still, in practice, be—uh—" Nichols hesitated. He was obviously trying to be diplomatic. "For a time, that is, not forever—uh—"

Balthazar held up his hand. "Please, Dr. Nichols!" Rebecca's father leaned over and picked up a book lying on the table beside the couch. "Dr. Adams was so good as to lend this to me yesterday. One of his many volumes on medicine—a textbook, he tells me, from his days as a student."

Balthazar cradled the heavy tome on his lap, almost caressing it with his fingers. "I have not been able to read much of it yet, I'm afraid. There are so many new words—not to mention new concepts—that each page must be studied carefully."

Rebecca stared at the cover of the book. The title was not what drew her attention, however. Something to do with introductory principles of medicine. Instead, her eyes were drawn to the names of the authors.

George White, M.D. Harold O'Brien, M.D. Abraham Cohen, M.D.

Cohen? Her eyes went to Morris Roth. The American Jew seemed to understand the question in her stare. So, at least, she interpreted his little smile and the nod which went with it. *Yes.*

Her father was still speaking. "—so I understand fully that I will have to learn everything anew."

Dr. Adams shook his head. "That's not true, Balthazar. Not even with regard to theory. Your notions about miasmas being the cause of disease are not that far removed from the truth. And your practical knowledge, in many ways, exceeds our own." He shrugged. "The truth is, I think you'll have much to teach us about the medications available in this time and place."

Nichols chuckled. "I certainly hope so! Just to give one example, our supply of antibiotics will be gone soon, and we can hardly call up the pharmaceutical companies for more." He made a sour face. "Then what? Eye of newt? Bat's wings ground up with coriander?"

Balthazar laughed. "Please! I have always found that Avicenna's great *Canon of Medicine* has remedies for almost every malady. Many of them even seem to work."

Nichols and Adams were peering at him skeptically. Dr. Abrabanel spread his hands. "Of course, you should examine the text yourself, before we prescribe anything." Hesitantly: "You *do* read Arabic?" Seeing the expressions on the faces of the two American doctors, Balthazar shrugged. "Well, no matter. I believe I have most of the *Canon* available in a Greek translation."

Nichols and Adams looked at each other. Adams coughed. Nichols looked like he was choking.

"Dr. Abrabanel," asked Adams, "just exactly how many languages *can* you read?"

"Fluently?" Rebecca's father wiggled his fingers. "Not more than eight, I'm afraid. Nine, possibly, depending on how you reckon 'fluency.' Hebrew, Arabic and Greek, of course, those being the principal languages of medicine. Spanish and Portuguese are native to my family. And English now, naturally. I spent most of my life on the island. German, French." Again, he wiggled his fingers. "My Dutch is becoming quite good, I think. But it would be boasting to say it was fluent as yet."

He paused, thinking, running fingers through his well-groomed gray beard. "Beyond that? I can manage Russian and Polish, with nontechnical matters. Italian and Latin, the same. I was concentrating on the Latin, actually, but I was forced to interrupt my studies due to the political state of affairs so that I could learn Swedish." He frowned. "It's a charming language, in its own way, but I almost hate to spend the time on it. There is nothing written in Swedish which is not already available in other tongues. Still—" He sighed. "I felt it would be wise, given the role I was asked to play—"

He cut off abruptly and leaned forward, his face filled with concern. "Dr. Nichols? Are you ill?"

"No, no," gasped Nichols, waving his hand weakly. "I am just—" Cough, cough.

"Jesus Christ," whispered Adams. "Almighty."

Rebecca leaned back in the couch. She managed—successfully, she thought—to keep the pride and satisfaction from showing on her face. Much as she had come to like and admire these Americans, she could not deny the pleasure it gave her to see them—*for once!*—absent their usual smug complacence.

Perhaps she was not as successful as she thought. Melissa Mailey marched in at that point, took one look at her, and demanded: "What are you looking so pleased about?"

Rebecca smiled. Demurely, she thought. Intended, at least. "Oh, it just seems that my father is a more accomplished linguist than these other doctors. Whatever else he may lack."

"Well, of course!" Melissa snorted. "Americans are ignorant louts when it comes to language." The schoolteacher planted her arms akimbo and gave Nichols and Adams the same glare which had cowed thousands of students over the years. "*What?*" she demanded. "Did you think you were actually *smarter* than these people?"

Then, spotting Judith scurrying from the kitchen with a plate of food in her hands, Melissa transferred the glare. "And what's *this*? Two hundred years of progress gone down the drain?"

The glare settled on Rebecca. "You and I are going to have a talk, young lady. *Soon.*"

The response was inevitable, inescapable. "Yes, ma'am."

Chapter 14

Much later that night, the Roth household was quiet and peaceful. Everyone had gone, except Balthazar, Melissa, and the Roths themselves. Even Rebecca was absent. Michael had insisted that she join the campaign planning effort, which had grown so large that it was being transferred to the high school.

Her father, in the event, was glad of her absence. It allowed him to raise a delicate subject freely, in the company of other Jews. And Melissa, of course. But Balthazar had already made his assessment of her.

"My daughter seems much taken by this Michael Stearns," he said. His tone was friendly and mild; the words themselves, an open invitation.

Morris and Judith glanced at each other. "He's a fine young man," said Judith hesitantly.

"Bullshit," snapped her husband. He gave the Sephardic doctor a look which combined apology with belligerence. "Pardon my language, Dr. Abrabanel. But I'm not going to dance around about this. Mike Stearns is the closest thing you'll ever find in this world to a genuine goddam *prince*, and that's all there is to it. Gentile or not."

Morris leaned forward, planting his elbows on his knees. "You read the book I gave you? The one on the Holocaust?"

Balthazar winced, and spread his hand as if to ward off demons. "As much of it as I could bear. Which was not much."

Morris took a deep breath. "The world we came from was no paradise, Dr. Abrabanel. Not for Jews, not for anyone. But if there were devils aplenty, there were also those who dealt with them."

He rose and stalked over to the mantelpiece. Perched next to the menorah was a small photograph, black-and-white, set in a simple frame. Morris took down the photograph and brought it over to Rebecca's father.

He pointed to one of the men in the picture. He was a small man, emaciated to the point of skeletonism, wearing a striped uniform.

"That's my father. The place where the photo was taken is called Buchenwald. It's not far from here, as it happens." He pointed to another man in the photograph. Taller, healthy looking despite the obvious weariness and grime—and wearing a uniform.

"That's Tom Stearns. Michael's grandfather. He was a sergeant in the American unit that liberated Buchenwald from the Nazis."

He put the photograph back on the mantelpiece. "Most people don't know it, but West Virginians—in terms of percentage, of course, not absolute numbers—have provided more soldiers for America's combat units than any other state in the nation, in every major war we fought in the twentieth century." He turned back to face Abrabanel. "That's why my father moved here, when he emigrated to the United States after the war. Even though he was the only Jew in Grantville when he first arrived. Tom Stearns had invited him to come, you see. Many others went to Israel, but my father wanted to live near the man who took him out of Buchenwald. It was the safest place he could imagine."

Morris stared down at Rebecca's father. "Do you understand what I'm trying to say, Balthazar Abrabanel?"

"Oh, yes," whispered the doctor. "We had that dream, once, in Sepharad." He closed his eyes, reciting from memory:

"Friend, lead me through the vineyards, give me wine
And to the very brim shall joy be mine . . .
And should I pre-decease you, friend, select
Some spot where vineyards twist, my grave to sink."

Morris nodded. The nod turned sideways, pointing. "My father is buried in the town's cemetery. Not far from Tom Stearns, and not far from Michael's father, Jack." His eyes came back. "And that's all I've got to say, Dr. Abrabanel."

Balthazar's shrewd eyes turned to Melissa. "And you?"

Melissa chuckled. "I'd *hardly* call Michael Stearns a 'prince'!" Then, cocking her head sideways, she pursed her lips. "Well . . . maybe. As long as we're talking about Prince Hal, the rapscallion."

Balthazar was startled. "The prince from *Henry IV*?" he asked. "You're familiar with the play?"

It was Melissa's turn to be startled. "Of course! But how did you—" Her jaw dropped.

"I saw it, how else?" replied Balthazar. "At the Globe theater in London. I never missed any of the man's plays. Always attended the first performance."

He rose and began pacing about slowly. "I was just thinking of it, in fact. Not *Henry IV*, but *The Merchant of Venice.*"

He stopped, smiling down at his audience. The expression on the faces of Morris and Judith Roth now mirrored Melissa's. Mouths agape, eyes bulging.

"The most wonderful playwright in the world, in my opinion." He shook his head. "I'm afraid you all seem to be misconstruing my question about Michael. I was not concerned over the matter of his faith."

Balthazar snorted, with half-amused exasperation. "Bah! I'm a philosopher and a physician, not a moneylender. What did you think? Did you really expect me to start wringing my hands over the prospect that my daughter might be smitten by a gentile?"

Suddenly, he clasped his hands and began wringing them, in histrionic despair. With the same theatrical flair, he twisted his head back and forth. *"O my daughter! O my ducats!"*

Melissa burst into laughter. Balthazar grinned at her. Morris and Judith just stared.

Balthazar dropped his hands and resumed his seat. "No, no, my friends. I assure you that my concern was quite mundane." For a moment, his kindly face grew stern, almost bitter. "I have no love for orthodox Jewry, nor they for me. I was cast out because I argued there was as much to be learned from Averroes the Moslem as from Maimonides the Hebrew."

He sighed and lowered his head. "So be it. I have found a home here, it seems. My daughter also. I only wish for her happiness. That was the sole purpose of my question."

"He's a prince," said Melissa softly. "In all that matters, Balthazar. In the way that such men truly come, in this true world."

"Such was my hope," murmured Dr. Abrabanel. He chuckled again. "It will be difficult for Rebecca, of course. I fear I may have sheltered her too much. Her head is full of poetry."

"We'll fix that," growled Melissa. "First thing."

Judith Roth finally managed to speak. "I can't believe it. You actually—" She almost gasped the next words. "You actually saw *Shakespeare*? In *person*?"

Balthazar raised his head, frowning. "Shakespeare? Will Shakespeare? Well, of course. Can't miss the man, at the Globe. He's all over the place. Never misses a chance to count the gate. Twice, usually."

Half-stunned, Morris walked over to a bookcase against the wall. He pulled down a thick tome and brought it over to Balthazar.

"We *are* talking about the same Shakespeare, aren't we? The greatest figure in English literature?"

Still frowning, Balthazar took the book and opened its cover. When he saw the frontispiece, and then the table of contents, he almost choked.

"Shakespeare didn't write these plays!" he exclaimed. Shaking his head: "Well, some of them, I suppose. In some small part. The ones that read as if written by committee. The little farces like *Love's Labour's Lost*. But the great plays? *Hamlet*? *Othello*? *King Lear*?"

Seeing the look on his companions' faces, he burst into laughter. "My good people! *Everyone* knows that the plays were really written by—" He took a deep breath, preparing for recitation: "My Lord Edward, Earl of Oxford, Seventh of that Name, and Seventh in degree from the English Crown."

Balthazar snorted. "Some people, mind you, will insist that Sir Francis Bacon is the real author, but that was a mere ruse to throw off the hounds. The theater is much too disreputable for the earl of Oxford to be associated with it. Hence the use of Shakespeare's name."

He looked down at the book. "Apparently, the fiction has become historical fact. So much for vanity and worldly fame!"

There was now a gleam of satisfaction in his eyes. "But perhaps it's simply justice. Edward was in some ways not the best of men. I know—I was his physician."

The stares were back. "Justice, I say. The earl owed me money, and refused to pay his bill."

Dr. Abrabanel stroked *The Collected Works of William Shakespeare*, like a man might fondle treasure. "This is so much more satisfying a revenge, don't you think, than a paltry pound of flesh?"

Part Two

What the hammer? what the chain?
In what furnace was thy brain?

Chapter 15

Hans Richter was awakened by a boot planted on his rump. The boot was abrupt, curt, and just barely short of brutal.

"Get up, boy," he heard Ludwig commanding. "*Now*. There's work to be done." The laugh that followed was more in the nature of a jeer. "You'll get your first taste of real fighting today, chicklet."

Dimly, Hans heard Ludwig clumping away. As always, the big man's footsteps were heavy and leaden. He sounded like a troll, moving about a cave.

Groaning, Hans rolled over on the dirt floor. His head was splitting with pain. For a minute or so, his eyes tightly closed, he fought down the urge to vomit. The struggle was fierce, not because he cared about the contents in his stomach, but simply because he didn't want to endure Ludwig's ridicule. Had Hans been alone, he would have gladly heaved up the remnants of his meal, even though it had been the first food he'd eaten in two days.

Most of that meal had been wine, in any event. Cheap, bad wine—the kind to be found in a peasant's farmhouse. The other mercenaries, led by Ludwig, had insisted that he drink his share.

More than my share, came the thought. *I drank more than my share, on purpose. It made them laugh, how quickly I got drunk. But that's what I wanted. It gave me an excuse.*

Memory of the night before came crashing in. Hans opened his eyes. He found himself staring at a corpse, not three feet away. The farmer, that was. The man was staring up at the ceiling of the farmhouse with sightless eyes. The rough clothing was caked with blood all through his midsection. Flies swarmed on the corpse.

Again, Hans felt the urge to vomit. And, again, fought it down desperately. His enrollment in the mercenary company was still very recent, and hung by a thread. If the soldiers decided he was unfit for their trade, they would cast him back into the pool of camp followers. Unarmed. Again.

Better anything than *that*. He still had what was left of his family to shelter. Ludwig protected his older sister Gretchen from the other soldiers, since he had taken her as his concubine. But Annalise, just turned fourteen, was already drawing their eyes. As a mercenary's sister, she would have some status. So would his grandmother. If Hans lost his place in the company, Annalise would be a tent whore before she saw another birthday. His grandmother would die in a field somewhere, abandoned and alone.

Hans decided he had mastered his stomach. He rose, and staggered toward the doorway. His eyes avoided the two corpses piled in a corner of the house. Those had been the old folk. The farmer's mother and his aunt, probably. Crones, of no interest to the soldiers. Hans remembered how casually Ludwig and another mercenary had murdered them, as if they were a pair of chickens.

He also kept his eyes away from the only bed in the house. That bed had been put to use by his companions, the night before. Hans had guzzled the wine as fast as he could force it down his stomach, in order to avoid the activity taking place there. Ludwig and his cohorts would have insisted that he participate. Drunkenness was the only acceptable excuse.

The bed was empty, now. The farmer's daughter had probably been dragged out this morning to join the camp followers, along with the boy. Her lot would be hard, and her brother's worse. Unlike Hans' sister Gretchen, the girl was not attractive enough to become a soldier's concubine. She would be a laundress and a prostitute. Her brother would be one of many camp urchins, available to run errands and do chores for the soldiers. Beaten for any reason, or, often enough, simply on a drunken whim. If he survived, the boy might eventually become a mercenary himself.

That was unlikely, however. Hans estimated the farm boy's age at ten years, no more. He would get less food than anyone, which was little enough. Hunger and disease would probably carry him off, long before he could reach the relatively secure status of being a soldier.

Hans stumbled out of the doorway into the farmyard. The bright sunlight, for all the pain it brought to his head, was a blessed relief. He could handle pain of the body. He had been a printer's son himself, once, not so far removed from the peasantry. Pain and hunger and hard work were no strangers. But he wondered, sometimes, how long his soul could endure this new world. The sunshine seemed to lighten that burden, a bit.

Ludwig and his men were gathering the camp followers, driving them into a semblance of marching order with shouts and blows. There were about fifty of them, mostly women and children, to service Ludwig's twenty mercenaries. Ludwig held no official rank in that band of soldiers. With his size and domineering personality, the point was moot. The informal arrangement was typical of Tilly's army. The officers didn't care, as long as the soldiers did their duty on the rare occasions when an actual battle had to be fought or a siege undertaken.

The camp followers were heavily laden with the mercenaries' gear and plunder. The "plunder" was pathetic, in truth. There was no gold or silver or jewelry to be found in peasant homes, and precious little in the houses of small German towns. Some of the "loot" would have caused Hans to laugh, if he didn't know of the carnage which had obtained it. One of the women—Diego the Spaniard's "wife"—was staggering under a wrought-iron bedframe. Diego had forced the poor creature to carry that thing for seven weeks now, even though he had no possible use for it. The Spaniard had been furious that the house had held nothing else of any value. He had spent two hours torturing the owner in an attempt to find hidden treasure. But there had been none. There almost never was. Only a bed. After Diego was finished, the pallet had been too badly soaked with blood to be salvageable. But he had insisted on taking the frame.

The small woman staggering under the bedframe stumbled and fell to one knee. Diego, seeing her mishap, snarled with anger. He strode up and delivered a vicious kick to her backside, sprawling her flat on the ground. She did not make a sound. Her face held no expression. She simply drew her legs under her and lurched back onto her feet.

Wincing, Hans looked away. In seconds, he spotted his own family. Gretchen, as always, was at the center of the crowd of camp followers, with his sister and grandmother nearby. His grandmother and Annalise were carrying bundles, but Gretchen always carried the largest, even though she was burdened with her baby. She was a big woman, and young, and strong, and had never allowed her good looks to go to her head.

Hans was not surprised to see the newest camp followers sheltered under Gretchen's care. The farmer's daughter seemed in a total daze. Her little brother was sobbing. There were no tears, however. The tear ducts would have been emptied hours earlier.

Hans took a breath and marched over. Ludwig would be demanding his presence within seconds. But he wanted to speak to Gretchen first.

As he drew near, threading through the little mob, Gretchen turned her head toward him. She was saying something to Annalise, but as soon as she caught sight of Hans her mouth closed. Her face, in an instant, stiffened like a statue. Her eyes, for all the natural warmth of their light brown color, seemed as cold as winter.

When Hans came up to Gretchen, he glanced at the farmer's children. Orphans, now. His words came in a rush.

"I didn't— I *swear*, Gretchen. I got drunk right away." Almost desperately, he nodded to the daughter. "Ask her. She'll tell you."

Gretchen's stiff face softened into quiet anger. "You think the poor girl remembers *faces*?" she demanded. Her eyes moved to the band of soldiers now forming into a loose column. The gaze was pure bitterness. "I didn't. Thank God."

The child nestled in Gretchen's left arm turned his head and stared up at Hans, with the unfocused eyes of babies. His mouth curved into a smile, seeing Hans' familiar face. The baby gurgled happily.

The sight, and the sound, melted away Gretchen's anger. Hans felt a surge of warmth toward the child, for bringing that break in the tension.

As he had often before, Hans wondered at that warmth. He had grown very fond of Wilhelm, in the months since his birth. Gretchen positively doted on him.

Odd, really. Wilhelm was Ludwig's son. Probably. After the first day, when their town was sacked by Tilly's army and Ludwig led his men into their father's print shop, Gretchen had been reserved for Ludwig's exclusive use. The baby certainly resembled his presumed father. Like Ludwig, his hair was very blond, his eyes blue. And already he was giving evidence that he might grow to Ludwig's size.

Gretchen's eyes came back to Hans. He was relieved to see that his sister's hostility was completely gone.

"It's all right, Hans. We do as best we can." A shout came. Ludwig's bellow, summoning him. "Now go," she said. "I will see to the family."

Hearing that word, the sobbing ten-year-old boy at her side was suddenly clutching Gretchen's hip. A moment later, his sister joined him, clutching Gretchen's arm. The dazed look in her eyes seemed to lift, a bit.

Hans' "family," plain enough, had just grown. He was not surprised. A third of the camp followers belonged to Gretchen. Adopted, as it were.

Ludwig's bellow came again. Angry, now. There would be a cuffing, sure enough.

"*Go*," hissed Gretchen.

The cuffing was not severe. Ludwig was in a good mood, insofar as that innocent expression can be applied to a troll in human guise. His gaiety, of course, was at Hans' expense.

"A real battle for you, chicklet!" roared Ludwig. "Some of our boys got bloodied down south a ways, so we're going to sack Badenburg to teach these Protestant fucks a lesson." The grin in the big man's bearded face was jeering. "No more lazing about in the lap of luxury. You'll be blooded before tomorrow's over. Or *bloody ruin* yourself!"

The veteran mercenaries standing nearby echoed Ludwig's guffaws. The laughter was good-natured, for the most part. But Diego the Spaniard's humor, as always, was sadistic.

"A gutted mess you'll be," he predicted. The sneer on his face became a leer. Diego grabbed his crotch. "Annalise's looking better by the day!" he chortled.

Hans felt a spike of rage run down his spine. He detested the Spaniard as he did no other man in Ludwig's band. More, even, than Ludwig himself. Ludwig was a brute, a beast, an ogre. Diego was something far worse. It was no accident that the Spaniard was always the man chosen by Ludwig whenever torture was to be done.

Yet Hans said nothing. He averted his eyes. He was terrified of Diego. The sallow-faced Spaniard was not a big man. Nothing compared to Ludwig. But he was as savage as a weasel, and just as deadly.

Hans braced himself for further ridicule. Fortunately, a small knot of horsemen came cantering up, diverting everyone's attention. The captain "in command" of Ludwig's band had arrived to give the orders.

Hans didn't even know the captain's name. It was meaningless. Hans took his orders from Ludwig. He only gave the captain and his three companions a glance.

But then, seeing the priest in the group, Hans' glance became a stare. Apparently, there was to be a sermon along with commands. The priest would almost certainly be a Jesuit, attached to the Papal Inquisition. He would exhort the troops to fight in the name of holiness.

Hans' guess was confirmed by Diego's muttered words of scorn. The Spaniard was contemptuous of the Jesuits and the pope's Inquisition. *Weak-livered punks,* he called them. Diego liked to boast about the Spanish Dominicans and their Holy Office of the Inquisition. The Spanish Inquisition answered to the crown of Spain, not the Vatican. They did as they pleased, and damn the pope's Italian lawyering. *Just burn the filthy heretics. They're all Jews and Jew-lovers anyway, the ones who aren't outright Moors.*

"Limpieza," the Spanish called it. Pure blood, to be protected from taint. That mattered as much to them—more, in truth—than the pope's concerns over religious dogma.

The captain finished his brief exchange of words with Ludwig. The priest urged his horse to the fore.

A sermon, sure enough.

❀ ❀ ❀

Hans tried to block the sermon from his mind. He did not even look at the Jesuit, lest his eyes betray him. He simply stared at the ground, hands clasped as if in prayer.

The priest was speaking of the need to safeguard the Catholic faith from heresy.

Hans could not help hearing the words. His thoughts seethed with fury.

Liar. We were Catholics ourselves. Our whole town was Catholic.

The priest was advocating the true faith.

We were kneeling in prayer when your "Catholic" mercenaries came into my father's shop.

Denouncing the Protestants.

The Protestants murdered my grandfather, and took away my mother. But it was your good Catholic Ludwig who drove a sword into my father's belly when he held up the rosary.

Denouncing sin, now.

And what was it, priest, when your soldiers sired a bastard on my sister? Was it hers, tied hand and foot to my father's bed?

The rest, he managed not to hear. Hans' thoughts moved far away. Bleak and hopeless. Utterly despairing thoughts, as only those of an eighteen-year-old young man can be.

Hans knew the truth. Satan's rebellion, stymied for so long, had finally triumphed. It was no longer God who sat on the heavenly throne. The Beast had replaced Him. It was the serpent's minions, not the Lord's, who wore the vestments of the clergy. All clergy, of all creeds. The creeds themselves were meaningless. Satan's joke, nothing more. The Lord of Flies was amusing himself, tormenting the land and its folk.

The sermon was done. Hans, had he still retained Gretchen's vestige of faith, would have thanked God. But there was no God to be thanked, any longer. There was nothing.

He managed, barely, to pull himself back from that brink. Suicide was at the bottom of that plunge. Hans had been tempted, often enough. But—

He flared his nostrils, and took in a deep breath. Still staring at the ground, still with his hands clasped before him.

The hands were not clasped in prayer, for all the strength with which he squeezed the fingers. Hans Richter was simply reminding himself that all was not lost. He still had something. Something to call his own, and something to give what he could.

Family. That I have. That I will protect, as best I can. Whatever else.

Chapter 16

"How many, d'you think?" asked Mackay.

Andrew Lennox squinted nearsightedly. Then, remembering his new gift from the Americans, he took out the spectacles and put them on. It took him not more than five seconds, scanning the field, to pronounce judgment.

"Two thousand. Divided two an' one. Maybe e'en less. Tilly is more conservative than Gustav Adolf, an' this'll be one o' 'is poorer an' weaker units. They've got nae artillery 't all."

Mackay nodded. "About my estimate."

Next to him, Mike cocked his head. "By two and one—?"

"Pikemen to arquebusiers," replied Mackay. The Scots officer pointed to the tightly packed mass of men slowly approaching their own forces. "See the formation? That's your typical Spanish-style *tercio*. All the Habsburg armies use it in battle, although the imperials prefer a higher proportion of arquebus than the Spaniards. Impressive, isn't it?"

Mike studied the advancing army. He had no difficulty agreeing with the word. *Impressive*, it most certainly was. The imperial army reminded him of a gigantic mastodon, bearing down with gleaming tusks.

And they're just about to become as extinct.

Tilly's mercenaries were packed into a rectangle approximately fifty files wide and forty ranks deep, covering not more than fifty yards of front. The men in the ranks were spaced every three feet, and the files were drawn up even closer. The formation was so tight that, even across the clear and level ground of what had once been plowed farmland, they could only move deliberately. Mike knew, from what Mackay and Lennox had told him, that if Tilly himself and his entire army had been here, the oncoming tercio would have been one of sixteen or seventeen such units. They would have been arrayed side by side, like a human glacier. Slow as a glacier, and just as unstoppable.

The pikemen formed the heart of the formation. Their great fifteen-foot spears, held erect, glistened even in the light of an overcast day. The five hundred arquebusiers were arrayed on either flank. The arquebusiers' principal duty was to fend off pistol-wielding cavalry and match volleys with enemy gunmen. But, as had been true for a century and more, it would be the press and charge of pike which would decide the day.

Such, at least, was the accepted theory and practice of the time. Frank Jackson, standing on Mike's left, echoed his own mental opinion. "Talk about candidates for extinction. One cluster bomb would take out the whole bunch."

"We don't have a cluster bomb," pointed out Mike mildly.

Frank snorted. "Neither did the NVA. But I'll tell you right now those tough little bastards in their black pajamas would have loved these guys. Mincemeat, coming up. Complete with *nuoc mam.*"

Mike grimaced at the image. Frank had brought home a Vietnamese wife from the war. In the decades since, Diane Jackson—she had Americanized her name—had blended in extremely well. But she still insisted on cooking at least one meal a month with that godawful Vietnamese fish sauce.

"Nuoc mam," Frank repeated. Under other circumstances, the obvious relish in his voice would have been odd. Much as he doted on his wife, Frank was no fonder of the fish sauce than any other native-born American.

Mackay, listening, understood the essence if not the precise meaning of Frank's words. "You are *that* confident?" The Scotsman pointed to the oncoming enemy. "They outnumber us two to one." He glanced to the left, where Ernst Hoffman's ragtag Protestant mercenaries were drawn up. About five hundred of them, more or less. Their formation was so irregular and undisciplined that an exact count was impossible. "That's counting that sorry lot, who'll break in a minute."

Mike shrugged. "I'm not relying on Hoffman's goons at all. I just insisted they be here in order to get them out of the town."

He cocked his head around. The little American/Scots/Protestant army was drawn up less than half a mile north of Badenburg. Unusually, for a town its size—the population was less than six thousand—Badenburg was walled. Those walls, as much as anything else, had determined Mike's political tactics over the past two weeks. Hoffman had been reluctant, to put it mildly, to risk bringing his mercenaries into the open field. But Mike had insisted, and Mackay had sweetened the pot with a portion of the king of Sweden's money.

When he turned his head back, he found that the young Scots

officer was giving him a very peculiar look. Well . . . Not so peculiar, perhaps. Mackay still hadn't quite gotten over his shock, once he realized the full extent of Mike's intentions. Defeating Tilly's mercenaries was only the first part of those plans. *Liberating* Badenburg, Mike had explained, required dealing with the Protestant mercenaries as well. Decisively and, if necessary, ruthlessly. Even Lennox, for all his grisly experience, had been impressed by Mike's cold-bloodedness.

"Yes, Mackay, I *am* that confident." Mike's eyes ranged up and down his own battle line. The UMWA members, reinforced by high-school seniors, were lying prone behind a log parapet. There were, by exact count, 289 Americans in that line. All of them were wearing hunting camouflage, and all of them were armed with high-power rifles.

Mackay had been skeptical, but he had agreed to let the Americans form up at the center. His cavalry, evenly divided, was marshaled on the flanks. Every one of those Scotsmen had been at least as skeptical as Mackay, once they understood what Mike had planned for them.

Pursuit? Cough, cough. *Doesn't that, ahem, presuppose that you've already defeated the enemy?*

Mike smiled thinly. A half hour from now, he didn't think the Scots would be skeptical any longer. His eyes moved to the enemy, now less than two hundred yards away. The tercio was marching across the open field almost as slowly as a turtle.

"If I wanted to, Mackay," Mike said softly, "I could end this battle right now. Your arquebuses can't hit anything much beyond fifty yards, even in a volley, and they take a minute to reload. I know you think our tactics are only suitable for skirmishers, but you've never seen breech-loading rifles in action. With our accuracy and rate of fire, we could have half that army dead before they could get in range."

Mike pointed to a small group of coal miners crouched in a rifle pit. The rifle pit was positioned on the left flank of the American line. "I want to do more than just win this battle. I want to terrify them completely—and Hoffman's goons with them. So we'll wait, for a bit, until the hammer falls."

Mackay stared at the men in the rifle pit. They were making last-minute adjustments to the weapon in the center. The adjustments were quite unnecessary, in all truth. But those middle-aged men were nervous. Their Vietnam days were many years behind them. It had been a long time since any of them fired an M-60.

Out of the corner of his mouth, Mike whispered to Frank: "I *still* can't believe you stole the damn thing."

Jackson was unabashed. "What the hell? I figured the Army owed me." He shrugged. "Hey, I was a piker. I knew one guy who smuggled a howitzer back from Nam."

Mike chuckled. Frank had shown him the machine gun less than three weeks ago. He had been a bit shame-faced, at the time, leading Mike and Dan Frost into the woods behind his house where he had buried it, years before, along with three boxes of ammunition.

"For Christ's sake, Jackson," Dan growled, after Frank hauled the carefully wrapped device out of its hiding place. "That thing is so goddam illegal I ought to put up MOST WANTED posters all over town." The police chief rubbed his left arm, still in a sling. "Good thing for you I'm officially on the sick list."

Yes, *then*, Frank had been embarrassed. "It's not like I was some goofy survivalist or anything," he'd tried to explain. "Just— Oh, hell. I was a kid. It seemed more like a prank at the time than anything else."

But that was then, and today was now, and Mike was glad to have the M-60. Delighted, if the truth be told.

Tilly's mercenaries were a hundred and fifty yards away, now. They were dividing their forces. The bulk of the formation continued to advance straight toward the Americans in front of Badenburg. But five hundred of them, approximately, were moving toward Hoffman's men. The Protestant mercenaries, skittish as kittens, had insisted on forming up some distance to the left. Right alongside the road leading back into Badenburg and the safety of its walls.

Mike took a last glance up and down the line. He turned his head, looking over his left shoulder to a small knoll some thirty yards behind. Standing on the top of the knoll, Greg Ferrara made a quick gesture. Thumbs up.

Mike looked away. He hoped the confidence of the science-teacher-become-artillery-officer was justified. Ferrara and his precocious students had designed and built the rockets themselves. Whether they would work, in an actual battle, remained to be seen.

Frank, apparently, shared Mike's doubts. "I just hope the damn things don't hit *us*," he muttered.

"They won't," came a voice from behind them. For all its youthful timbre, the words were spoken with great assurance.

Mike smiled, but didn't turn around.

Ah, yes. D'Artagnan, and the Three Musketeers.

The voice belonged to Jeff Higgins. Jeff was one of Ferrara's "whiz kids." Although he and his three best friends had played a big role in designing the rockets, they had a different assignment in this battle. Larry Wild, Jimmy Andersen and Eddie Cantrell probably had as much talent for science as Jeff himself. They *certainly* shared the same enthusiasm for off-road motorcycling. Mike had decided to use them for couriers today. Their dirt bikes would be perfect for the task.

Mike didn't really think he would need four couriers, but the boys were well-nigh inseparable. That had been true even before the Ring of Fire. Since the disaster, they had clung together ferociously.

Mike sighed, thinking about their situation. By and large, Grantville's families had come through the Ring of Fire relatively unscathed. Fortunately, the disaster had happened on a Sunday, when almost all the families were at home. Even the coal miners who had come into town for Rita's wedding had, with few exceptions, brought their wives and children.

Still—there were some heart-breaking exceptions. Bill Porter, the power-plant manager, had lost his whole family. He had been at the power plant, but his wife and children didn't live in Grantville. They had stayed behind, wherever "behind" was. A few others faced the same situation. Like Bill, most of them tried to bury their grief in hard work, consoling themselves as best they could with the knowledge—the hope, at least—that their families were still alive and well. Wherever—*whenever*—they were.

But there was no situation as bad as that of these boys. Jeff and Larry Wild were the only ones who lived in Grantville. They lived right next to each other, in two of the double-trailers in the trailer park next to the fairgrounds. Jimmy Anderson and Eddie Cantrell, who lived in Barrackville, had been visiting them. Jeff and Larry's families had all been gone for the day. The four teenagers had been taking advantage of the situation to enjoy an uninterrupted and adult-free game of *Dungeons and Dragons.*

None of them except Jeff had reached the age of eighteen. And now, orphans in all that mattered, they were adrift in a world more vicious than any fantasy adventure.

"About time," said Jackson.

Mike pushed all other thoughts aside. The enemy, he saw, was a hundred yards away.

"You're the expert, Frank," he said. "It's your call."

Frank cupped his hands around his mouth. *"Light 'em up!"* he bellowed.

The M-60 erupted, sweeping the front ranks of the tercio. The man firing the weapon was using the three- to six-round bursts of a veteran. The stuttering machine gun started ripping holes in the tightly packed front line of the enemy. At that range, the .308-caliber rounds could punch right through an armored man and kill the man behind him.

The M-60 had been placed on the left flank in order to maximize its effectiveness. The gunner had a semienfilade angle of fire and was taking full advantage of it. In less than two seconds, all of the men behind the parapet added their rifle fire.

The seemingly unstoppable tercio staggered. The front rank fell, like a glacier calving flesh instead of ice. The M-60 traversed back. Another rank spilled and shattered. Back again. Another. It was like mowing wheat.

Mike was amazed at the reaction of the soldiers taking that incredible punishment. He had expected them to break immediately. Instead, the tercio was stubbornly pushing forward. If anything, the pikemen reacted to the horrendous losses by stiffening their determination. The men in the rear ranks were stumbling over the bodies in front of them, but they were still coming on. Some of them even tried to dress their formation.

God, those men are tough! That's just pure balls keeping them up.

Something of his thoughts must have shown in his little shake of the head. Behind him, Jeff Higgins whispered: "That's what this kind of early gunpowder warfare was all about, Mike. Guts, sheer guts. There wasn't—isn't—much skill involved in being a pikeman or a musket-shooter. Slam it out until somebody quits. That's how they're trained."

Mike didn't doubt the words. He knew that military history was one of the enthusiasms shared by Jeff and his friends. But he had none of Jeff's "knowledgeable" nonchalance about it. Mike was *not* a teenager. He had a much better sense than the boys behind him of what it really took for those men to keep standing under that punishment.

Say what you will about those bastards. Murderers and thieves and rapists, some of them. But don't ever say they lack courage.

As he watched, the enemy arquebusiers on both flanks managed to get off a volley. Few if any of the rounds, at that range, came even close to the Americans. Before the mercenaries could reload, the M-60 hammered their neat front line into shreds.

Yet, for all the wreckage which the machine gun inflicted on the tercio, most of the casualties suffered by Tilly's mercenaries were actually caused by the rifle fire. Almost all the men shooting those weapons were experienced deer hunters. Many of the older ones were combat veterans. They were using modern rifles, firing into a pack of massed men at less than a hundred yards—point-blank range, essentially, for those weapons. Few of their shots missed a target, and the armor worn by the mercenaries was never designed to protect against high-velocity rounds.

By later examination, it would be determined that well over two hundred of Tilly's mercenaries were killed by rifle fire. The same number, wounded. All in less than a minute. The machine-gun rounds, in contrast, caused fewer than two hundred casualties—a majority of whom were simply wounded. If for no other reason, Frank had given orders to be sparing with the ammunition. Those three boxes were all they had.

But—

It was the M-60 that broke them. One in five of those rounds was a tracer. On that gray and cloudy day, the tracers blazed like streaks of magic fire. To Tilly's men, and the Scots who watched, it seemed as if a sorcerer's wand was smiting them down. Along with, seconds later, the spitfire of a dragon. Ferrara and Jeff's confidence proved to be warranted. The warheads on the rockets were not particularly powerful, but the missiles themselves sped swift and true.

The center of the tercio finally caved in under the M-60's blazing hammer blows. Holes were torn throughout the formation by the rockets. And, everywhere in the first five ranks—and then the next, and then the next, and then the next—men withered under the deadly rifle fire. In less than two minutes after the battle erupted, the proud and confident little army which had marched on Badenburg was an utter ruin.

Alexander Mackay was not the only Scotsmen, then—not by far—who committed the sin of blasphemy.

"Jesus Christ son of God," he whispered. *"Jesus Christ son of God."*

Andrew Lennox did not join in that violation of the commandment. Not because he was more saintly, but simply because he was more hard-bitten. His ruddy face might have paled, a bit. But his cold eyes never ceased ranging the battlefield.

"Hoffman's men are beaten," he announced. "They dinna fire more than one volley, th' wretchet cowards." His voice carried utter condemnation. Calvin and John Knox, speaking through a veteran, pronouncing the ultimate sin of a seventeenth-century soldier. *They did not stand and take it like men.*

Mike looked to the left. Sure enough, the Protestant mercenaries were retreating before their Catholic counterparts. Years of garrison duty had turned Hoffman's soldiers into a gang of simple toughs. Extortionists, now facing real soldiers on a battlefield. They were already scrambling toward the road, with Tilly's men lumbering in pursuit.

Mike bellowed an order; then, repeated it twice. Raggedly—his coal miners and school boys were hardly a trained army yet—the American riflemen shifted their aim and began firing at the separate Catholic detachment on the left. The distance was greater, but it was still within easy range for good riflemen. Those mercenaries began dropping too. The men in the rifle pit began shifting the machine gun, but Frank shouted at them to hold their fire. Plain enough, there would be no need for the M-60, and they had to husband the ammunition for the machine gun.

Mike turned to Mackay. "I think . . . ?"

Mackay was still too shocked to think. Lennox shook his arm.

"Yes, lad—he's right. Let's to it." The next word was spoken with sheer relish. *"Pursuit."*

Both wings of Tilly's mercenary army had collapsed by now, and the survivors were retreating in disorder. Mike called out the order to cease fire. A bit raggedly, again, the American riflemen obeyed the order. Mackay and his two hundred and fifty Scots cavalrymen poured onto the battlefield. Within seconds, they had overtaken the enemy and were calling on them to surrender. Those who resisted or continued to flee were ruthlessly sabered or shot down with wheel-lock pistols.

The battle was over. It had been Mike's first, and he was finding it hard to control his gorge.

"Is it always like this?" he whispered.

Frank shook his head. "This wasn't a battle, Mike. This was just a slaughter." The Vietnam veteran stared out at the bodies littering the field. Mounds of them, in places. "I almost feel sorry for the poor bastards, now. Almost."

Jeff Higgins interrupted. His voice was urgent. "Mike—it's starting." Jeff's finger was pointing to the left.

Mike followed the finger. Hoffman's Protestant mercenaries, seeing the complete and unexpected destruction of their seemingly triumphant opponent, were rallying. Mike could see Ernst Hoffman himself, astride his horse, waving his saber. The mercenary captain pointed the sword to the north. *Onward.*

Mike did not bother to squint into that distance. He knew what Hoffman was pointing to. The Catholic camp, now unprotected and ripe for the picking. Hoffman's mercenaries hadn't been worth a damn in a fight, but Mike didn't doubt for a moment that they would prove to be experts at plunder, pillage and rapine.

Mackay and Lennox had predicted this scenario, in the event the Americans won. Mike had shaped his plans accordingly.

The battle was won, but the fight wasn't over. He intended to *liberate* Badenburg. From *all* its enemies.

"Okay, Jeff," he said. "You and your buddies get over there. *Right now.* If you can, warn off Hoffman's men. But they probably won't listen to you, and I don't want you taking any chances. Don't do anything else until the reinforcements arrive."

As he straddled his bike, Jeff nodded. His three friends were already peeling off, their engines racketing.

Mike shouted after the rapidly receding boys: "Remember, dammit—*wait!*"

"Fat chance," muttered Frank. "You're looking at four knights in shining armor. Fucking *D&D* paladins, no less."

Mike turned to him, grinning. "Well, then, let's back 'em up. *Call out the armor.*"

Chapter 17

Gretchen knew the battle was lost as soon as she heard the machine gun start to fire. She had no idea what could be making that bizarre staccato sound, but it was nothing produced by Tilly's thugs. At the age of twenty, Gretchen had already learned life's basic lesson. *Expect the worst.*

She felt a moment's fear and anguish for her brother. Hans, poor little Hans, was somewhere up there. Near the very front he would be, too, since Ludwig's men were considered part of the "elite," as mercenaries gauged such things.

But Gretchen thrust that concern aside. There was nothing she could do for Hans, and she had other members of her family to protect. Quickly, she scanned the area, looking for a place to hide. The enemy would be here soon, rampaging in their victory.

Her first thought was for the woods, perhaps a mile distant.

Too far. Gretchen herself would be able to make it, before the beasts arrived. Annalise, too, perhaps. But they would have to abandon most of the family. Gramma, the children, the baby, the older girl with her bad leg, the new girl with her vacant mind...

No. What else?

They had pitched camp near a half-burned farmhouse. Gretchen had inspected it the evening before, as a possible sleeping quarters. She had chosen the open ground, instead. The farmhouse had been long abandoned, and she did not trust the condition of the half-collapsed ceiling.

No. The monsters will look there first. What else?

Her eyes fell on a small structure, dismissed it without thought, moved on. Stopped. Came back.

Her mind shrank in her skull, like a mouse huddling in a hole. A spike of horror ran down her spine.

Still . . .

Long abandoned. Maybe . . .

She strode over to the outhouse. The thin walls were rickety. Several planks had fallen away. The door hung loose on leather hinges. She pried the door aside and peered in.

She checked the smell, first. *Not so bad. Not used in some time.*

Then, the seat. It was just as described by one of the other girls in the family, the evening before when Gretchen had sent her to investigate. The wood, with the carved hole in the center, was half-rotted away. That was why they had not used the structure. Someone might fall in.

Gretchen almost tittered a laugh. *Might fall in!*

Horror and nausea steeled her will. She seized the plank and heaved it up. Looked down. Sighed with relief.

Almost empty. Drained away, the most of it. The stench is horrible, but there would be enough air now.

The hole was dark, but not so dark that Gretchen couldn't see the spiders perched here and there on the walls. She recognized one of them as dangerously venomous.

There are worse things than spiders. Much worse.

Her decision made, Gretchen turned away and stuck her head out the door. A moment later she was shouting orders. The family was confused, but they obeyed instantly. Within seconds, they were clustering around the outhouse, hauling the family's possessions.

As they were handed to her, Gretchen shoved the family's tattered bedding into the hole. It would provide some protection for bare feet. For a while, anyway.

That done, she made her triage. She thought there would be room for the girls old enough to be in danger. She started with her sister Annalise, taking Wilhelm from Gramma's arms and thrusting him into her younger sister's arms.

"Take him and hide in the latrine. *Now!*"

Annalise turned pale. But Gretchen's scowl was not to be argued with, and she obeyed from long habit. In less than ten seconds, she was being lowered into the pit by her strong older sister. Then, reaching up her hands, she took the baby handed down to her.

She flinched from a spider, whimpering.

"*Be still!*" hissed Gretchen. "They won't bother you if you don't move. And don't breathe deeply."

Annalise was very pale now, obviously fighting to control her stomach. The stench was truly horrendous. But Gretchen did no more than hold her breath. She was too concerned with gauging the size of the pit to worry about anything else.

Big enough for three more, she decided. Turning away, she called out for Elisabet and Mathilde, the two girls in the group of the same age as Annalise. They squealed and shrieked but, again, Gretchen's will was not to be thwarted.

Who else?

Her eyes fell on the young farm girl who had recently been forced into the camp. The girl was not pretty, not in the least. Her face was so plain it was almost ugly, and her figure was like a sack of potatoes. But she was young—not more than sixteen—and that would be enough.

Gretchen gauged the girl, for a moment. The dazed, half-vacant look on her face convinced her. *She will not survive another one. Not her mind, at least. Not this soon.*

"Get in," she ordered, pointing into the latrine. The girl stared at her, uncomprehending. "Get in," Gretchen repeated. She extended her hand.

The girl finally understood. Her mouth dropped open.

"Get in." Gretchen's voice was iron with command. "It's just filth, woman. Nasty, but it won't kill you."

The girl was still gaping. "Idiot!" hissed Gretchen. "It's the only place they won't look for women."

Comprehension came, and with it terror. Trembling, the girl came into the outhouse. Her legs were barely holding her up. Gretchen was a big woman, and very strong. She took the girl under the armpits, picked her up, and lowered her into the mess. Soon enough, the task was done.

Gretchen nodded with satisfaction. "If anyone starts to raise the lid," she commanded the four girls, "lower your heads and press against the sides, as far out of sight as possible. Never mind the spiders."

To Annalise: "And make sure you cover the baby's mouth if he starts to cry or scream."

Annalise's eyes were wide. "What if . . . ?" She took a little breath through pinched nostrils. "I can't cover his face for very long. He'll suffocate."

Gretchen shook her head. "If they open the lid, it won't be for more than a second or two. Not as stinky as *that* is. As for the other—"

Gretchen's face was blank. "There will be so much noise up here that no one will hear a baby."

It was time. Only half of Gretchen's mind had been on the sounds of the battle, but that half now surged to the fore. *The other side is winning. They will be here soon.*

Quickly, almost violently, she seized the lid and wrestled it back over the latrine. The only opening in the wooden cover was a squat-hole, too small to allow any light to enter the cavity below. The four girls and the baby hidden within were quite invisible.

Satisfied that she had done what she could for them, Gretchen left the outhouse and wrestled the door back into place. Then she gave the rest of the area a quick scrutiny. The entire camp, by now, was in an uproar. Hundreds of people were shouting and screaming. Many of them were starting to flee to the north.

For a moment, Gretchen was tempted to follow them. She was young enough and in good enough health that she could reach the cover of the distant woods before the enemy soldiers arrived. But she would have to abandon her grandmother, and the others.

No.

What else?

It didn't take her more than five seconds to come up with the answer. *Nothing. Survive, that's all.*

The small crowd was still clustered around her. Gretchen walked off a considerable distance from the outhouse. Then she ordered the older women to take the children and gather in a circle away from the camp's tents and possessions. There, they might be relatively safe. They would be of no personal use to the soldiers, and they obviously possessed nothing beyond the rags they were wearing.

For the rest—

One of the three younger women fell to her knees and began praying. Within seconds, the others had all joined her.

Gretchen remained standing. What was the point of prayer? She did not fear for her soul. The abuse of her body would end, eventually. She needed only to shield her mind. Prayer provided no help for that purpose.

Blank, blank. She began emptying herself of all thoughts. Nothing. A last glimpse of Hans, marching fearfully into battle, a last flash of grief. Empty.

All that remained was sensation. Eyes open, staring at the small figures of men charging forward from the distance. Her ears heard their whooping and hollering, but her brain made nothing of the words.

Mostly, she focused on the tactile sense. Feeling with her fingers the small knife which Hans had stolen for her many months ago. The knife was hidden away in her bodice, in a sheath under her armpit which she had sewn herself. The soldiers would not look there. They would not even bother to remove the dress.

The feel of the knife brought final emptiness. As she waited, Gretchen never thought once of suicide. She would survive, if at all possible. But the knife was there, should it be needed. If the soldiers— they were nearer now, much nearer—threatened her very life. Gretchen had long ago decided she would not leave this earth without taking a devil with her into the afterlife.

❖   ❖   ❖

It was the comfort of that knife, perhaps, which kept her mind blank for so many seconds after wonder appeared. Or, perhaps, it was simply the peculiarity of the wonder itself.

Gretchen had heard, once, a tale of knights in shining armor. Her grandfather had read her a story from a borrowed book. She had been ten years old. The war had just begun, and was only a rumor out of mad Bohemia. Yet even at that age, Gretchen had thought the tale was ludicrous.

She did not believe in knights. Armed and armored beasts, yes. Knights, no.

So it was hardly surprising that she found nothing strange in the four bizarrely costumed boys who raced toward her on the most bizarre—and *noisy*—contraptions she had ever seen. Nothing.

Devils, perhaps. She was not afraid of devils.

She fingered the knife.

Chapter 18

The first thing Jeff Higgins saw clearly, in the chaos of the camp ahead of him, was the figure of a woman. Alone, among the hundreds of people shouting and scurrying about, she was standing still. Still, silent, and very straight. Her hands were tucked under her armpits, and she was staring at him.

Jeff's motorcycle hit an unseen obstacle in the field, and he almost lost control of the bike. For a few frantic moments, he could concentrate on nothing else. Fortunately, his skill with a dirt bike was not much less than his boasts, and he kept himself from a very nasty spill.

When his eyes came up, he immediately looked for the woman.

She was still there. Still standing, still silent, and still staring at him.

There seemed to be no expression at all on her face, from what Jeff could tell at a distance. But something about her drew him like a magnet, and he steered his motorcycle toward her. Behind, his three friends followed faithfully.

Afterward, his friends would tease him about that instant reaction. But their jests were quite unfair. What drew Jeff toward her was simply that she seemed to be the one island of sanity in a world gone mad. A serene statue, towering over a horde of squealing people, scuttling through a rabbits' warren of makeshift tents and shelters.

It wasn't until he actually brought the bike to a skidding halt, not more than fifteen feet away, that he finally got a good look at the woman herself.

Goddam. She's— Goddam.

He was suddenly overwhelmed by shyness, as he always was in the presence of very pretty young women. Especially tall young women with an air of self-confidence and poise. The fact that the woman in question was wearing a dress that was not much more than a collection of sewn-together rags, was barefoot, and had a streak of dirt on her forehead, didn't matter in the least. All that registered on Jeff, and closed his throat, was the face itself. Long, blondish hair; light brown eyes; straight nose; full mouth; strong chin; and—

Oh God she's so lovely.

Choke.

Larry Wild's voice, coming from behind, didn't help a bit.

"Leave it to Higgins to spot her," his friend snickered. "Now watch him blow his opening line."

"Hey, lady," whispered Jimmy Anderson, loud enough to be heard in China, "you wanna see my computer? I got a really great Pentium—"

Jeff flushed. "Shut up!" he snapped, turning his head. The movement brought his eyes to bear on the Protestant soldiers they had swept past on their way to the camp. The mercenaries were much closer, now. Not more than fifty yards away and charging forward like—

He didn't want to think about that *like*. Jeff Higgins, for all his precocity, was still a small-town boy at heart. But he wasn't *that* innocent.

Neither were any of his friends. All three of them were turned around in their bike saddles, staring at the mercenaries pounding toward them.

"What do we do?" asked Eddie Cantrell.

"Mike said warn 'em off," muttered Larry. "But I don't think those guys are gonna listen to any warning."

Jeff brought his eyes back to the woman. She was still staring at him. Her face was totally expressionless. For all that he could tell, she hadn't moved a muscle since he first spotted her. Her mind seemed to be a complete blank. Was she mentally retarded or something?

Then—finally—Jeff noticed the women kneeling in a circle around her. Young women. All of them were babbling something. Prayers, he thought. And all of them were weeping.

His eyes rose back up and met the gaze of the standing woman. Light brown eyes. Empty eyes. Blank.

Understanding came, and with it a rage he had never felt in his life.

Over my fucking dead body!

Deliberately, slowly, he lowered the bike's kickstand and climbed off. Then he removed the shotgun slung over his shoulder. A twelve-gauge pump-action, it was, loaded with buckshot. It had belonged to his father, just like the 9mm pistol holstered to his waist.

Jeff began stalking toward the oncoming mercenaries. They were thirty yards away. He pumped a round into the chamber.

He heard Jimmy shout something about Mike, but he didn't catch the words. His ears were too full of the sound of his own rushing blood. He did hear Larry's response, and felt a moment's rush of comradeship.

"Mike can kiss my ass! Hold on, Jeff—I'm coming!"

Jeff didn't hold on. He didn't even think. When the first merce-nary was fifteen yards away, he brought the shotgun to his shoul-der. The mercenary stumbled to a halt. The ten or so men with him did likewise.

Jeff moved the shotgun, waving it slowly back and forth to cover the entire little crowd. Dimly, he sensed a tide of other mercenaries breaking around the knot he had stopped. They were spilling around the edges, moving toward other parts of the camp. But they were slowing, he thought. He caught a glimpse of several of them, off to the side, staring at him. One of them was reloading his arquebus. The other two were fingering their pikes.

The men in front of him were all pikemen, fortunately. They could run him down, but not before he killed several.

Then, Larry was standing at his left, his own shotgun leveled. And then, not a second later, Jimmy and Eddie were bracing him on the right. Both of them had their own shotguns up also.

Jeff heaved a sigh of relief. He had acted without thinking, on impulse. Now that some time had elapsed, he realized how insane his situation was.

Their situation, actually. Even with his three friends—even armed with pump-action shotguns—Jeff could no more have held off that mob of several hundred mercenaries than he could have stopped a stampede.

Yet—

He raised his head a little, taking his eye off the barrel of the shotgun, and swept his head around.

The mob *was* stopped.

Well...in a manner of speaking. The Protestant mercenaries had poured around the group which Jeff had halted in its tracks. The four American boys were now, for all practical purposes, sur-rounded. Dozens of mercenaries in the inner ring were staring at them. Others were pushing forward to look over their shoulders. Jeff had a sense that other mercenaries were starting to tear at the edges of the Catholic camp, but he wasn't certain. Everything was very chaotic.

"So what's the plan, *kemo sabe*?" hissed Larry.

Jeff hesitated. He had no idea what to do. He was amazed that the mercenaries hadn't already attacked them. He decided that they were simply too confused by the situation to know what to do.

So am I, for that matter.

Then, Jimmy's squeal of glee came. And then, the bellowing hoot of the first truck's air horn. And Jeff Higgins found himself fighting not to tremble.

The Seventh Cavalry had arrived, so to speak. In the proverbial nick of time.

The coal-hauling trucks which Mike and his men had converted into armored personnel carriers were not really off-road vehicles. But they would do well enough, on flat ground, as long as rain hadn't turned the soil into mud. The drivers were pushing their vehicles at a reckless pace, under the circumstances. It didn't help that the steel sheeting which had been welded over the cabs left them with only narrow slits to steer by.

In the cab of the lead truck, Mike was holding on for dear life. The driver had an air-cushioned seat, but all Mike had was a thinly upholstered one which provided almost no protection from the jolting ride.

The driver yanked on the cord over the door, blowing another blast through the air horn. "You want me to slow down?" he asked.

"No!" shouted Mike. He squinted through the slit in the steel plate over the window. "Damn those kids," he muttered. "Warn 'em off, I said. Instead—" An unseen furrow sent him lurching half off the seat. "They're making like Davey Crockett at the Alamo."

But for all the grousing in the words, his tone was not hostile. Not in the least.

Mike caught another glimpse of the four boys, staring down a huge mob of thugs with leveled shotguns, and felt a surge of pride.

My kids, goddamit!

"Hit that horn again," he commanded. "Just lean on it, lean on it. And step on the gas."

The ride got worse. "Where do you want me to park the truck when we get there?" asked the driver.

Mike laughed. "Don't park it at all. Just drive right into that crowd of goons and start circling the boys." Seeing the driver's frown, he laughed. "What? Are you worried about getting a ticket?"

Harshly: "I don't give a damn if you crush fifty of those bastards. Just do what I say."

He caught a glimpse of a man on horseback, floridly dressed. Ernst Hoffman. The mercenary leader was in the middle of the crowd, giving some kind of speech.

"You see him?" Mike demanded. The driver nodded. "Aim right for him. Try to run him down."

The driver looked startled. Then, seeing the grim and implacable look on Mike's face, he forbore any protest. A moment later, he even grinned.

"Yessir. One road kill coming up."

By the time the truck arrived, none of the mercenaries were staring at Jeff and his friends any longer. They had turned around and were gaping at the—*monsters?*—charging toward them.

In truth, few of those soldiers really thought the oncoming trucks were monsters. Men of their time were already accustomed to machinery and manufacture. Wagons, wheels, gears, crankshafts, glass—everything except rubber and the internal combustion engine. The Bohemian Hussites, more than a century earlier, had even developed their own version of armored personnel carriers. The machines of the time were primitive, of course, and the mercenaries wondered where the horses pulling the things were hidden. But they were still able to recognize the trucks for what they were. Vehicles, not magic beasts.

Still, the oncoming *things* were larger than elephants and they were charging forward faster than any vehicles those mercenaries had ever seen. As they neared, the armored cabs of the trucks loomed up like battlements.

Then the mercenaries spotted the slits in the front of the *things*—and the bigger slits along the steel sides—and they knew. *War machines.* Those slits would be spouting gunfire any moment—the same gunfire which had shattered Tilly's tercio.

They broke even faster than they had when Tilly's pikemen charged. In an instant, all thought of plunder and rapine vanished. The mercenaries were simply scrambling to get out of the way.

Jeff didn't start laughing until he realized what the driver of the lead truck was doing. Then, for the next several minutes, he and his friends were howling with glee. Their shotguns—on safety; they had all been well trained by their fathers and uncles—were lowered, held in loose hands.

The lead truck—and then another, and then another—were playing "tag" with Ernst Hoffman. The scene was utterly comical, for all its deadly potential. *None* of those truck drivers was trying to miss.

The portly mercenary leader's horse pitched him after the first truck roared past. Thereafter, Ernst Hoffman was waddling on his own. He lasted for five minutes, scampering through the torn-up fields of what had once been fertile farmland, before he collapsed from fear and exhaustion.

One truck roared up and stopped just a few feet short of crushing him. A figure clambered down from the passenger's side of the cab and stalked over to Hoffman. The mercenary leader looked like a pig, lying on his side, flanks heaving.

Even from the distance, Jeff could recognize Mike Stearns. He couldn't make out the face, but Mike's athletic stride was unmistakable. He saw Mike lean over, something glinting in his hand. It was the work of seconds to haul Hoffman's arms around to his back and put on the handcuffs.

"*Yes!*" shouted Jeff, his fist pumping. "*My man!*"

He looked around. All of the mercenaries within sight were surrendering. There had been twelve trucks in that charge. Three of them were near the Catholic camp, protecting it. The rest, except for Mike's truck, had formed a wide circle around the milling mob of Protestant soldiers. Some of the mercenaries, Jeff suspected, had managed to escape the encirclement. But most of them were lowering their weapons and raising their hands.

"A nice day's work!" exclaimed Larry. The boy—the young man, rather—was filled with elation. "Just like Mike planned. The Catholic mercenaries are whipped, and these so-called Protestant bastards—" He jeered at the huddling knots of soldiers, and jerked his thumb over his shoulder, pointing to Badenburg. Some of the surrendering soldiers were staring at the town also, obviously longing for the safety of its walls.

Too far, too far. They had been well and surely trapped.

Jeff stated the obvious. "Ernst Hoffman's reign of terror is *over.*"

Then, she was there. Jeff had quite forgotten her, in the excitement of the standoff.

She didn't say anything. Her face still seemed as blank as ever. She just stared at him. Light brown eyes.

She extended her hand. Her hand was large, for a woman, and not at all delicate. The fingernails were blunt, worn short by labor. When she took Jeff's shoulder and squeezed it, he was astonished by her strength.

She spoke. Her words were a pidgin mishmash. German and heavily accented English mixed together.

"*Bitte.* Pliss. I muss—need he'p."

She pointed to an outhouse nearby. To Jeff, the structure looked like something out of—

Middle ages. Probably when it was built, too. Yuck! Thank God for plumbing.

Insistently, the woman gave his shoulder a little shake. "Pliss. Need he'p. Pliss!"

Puzzled, Jeff slung his shotgun over his shoulder and nodded.

The woman led him toward the outhouse, striding quickly. Behind him, Jeff's friends followed. The cluster of older women and children huddled to one side rose and began running toward the outhouse.

What the hell is going on?

The woman ahead of him reached the outhouse first. She seized the door and practically wrenched it loose, almost snapping the leather hinges. For a moment, Jeff was dazzled by the strong, shapely figure outlined under the tattered and shapeless dress. Even the woman's dirty bare feet seemed lovely to him.

A moment later, the woman—frantically, now, no *almost* about it— had entered the outhouse and was lifting the wooden seat up. Wrestling with it, pitching it out the door. Jeff scuttled aside hastily, barely avoiding the horrid missile.

What the hell is she doing? Is she crazy or something?

Then, when he heard the first wail, he knew. He was so stunned, he couldn't move. Dimly, to one side, he saw Larry turn away and double up, vomiting. Behind him, he heard Eddie hiss with shock and horror. Jimmy came up alongside him, muttering. "I can't believe this, I can't believe this."

The woman bent over, extending her arms. A moment later, her back arched with effort. Effort. Effort.

Jeff saw her face turning toward him. Saw the look of silent pleading. *Pliss. Need he'p.*

Jimmy was still muttering. "I can't believe this. I can't believe this." Jeff was paralyzed.

The face. *Pliss. Need he'p.*

The breath blew out of Jeff's chest. He hadn't realized he'd been holding it. Jerkily, he scrabbled the shotgun off his shoulder and thrust it at Jimmy. "Hold this!"

An instant later, he was stepping forward. Then, seeing the straining frenzy in the face ahead of him, began running. He was at her side in seconds.

Looking over her arm, he saw the face of a young girl staring up at him from a black pit. The girl's expression combined terror and—

Christ, they must be suffocating in there.

Almost violently, Jeff thrust his arm into the hole. The woman crowded alongside him was holding the girl's hands. He seized the girl's wrist. Between them, heaving, they hauled the girl out in seconds. Jeff, flinching from the smell, almost threw her out the door. But he managed to transform the motion into a simple toss. The girl landed on her knees, gasping for breath. Then, almost immediately, she began vomiting alongside Larry. Her tattered dress was crawling with spiders.

Eddie and Jimmy were staring at him. Jimmy was still muttering. "I can't believe this, I can't believe this."

Angrily, Jeff pointed at the girl. "Help her, *goddamit!* At least get the spiders off of her!"

He didn't wait to see if they obeyed. He turned back into the outhouse and took his place alongside the woman. Another girl, another heave—*out.* This one didn't vomit, judging from the sounds coming from behind him. Just gasped and gasped, before breaking into sobs.

Another—*out.* He and the woman had the procedure down, now. Each take a wrist. Heave. *Get them out of here!*

Another—

Jeff almost lost it, then. *A baby?* Fortunately, the woman could handle the baby on her own. Jeff was locked into paralysis, fighting down his nausea.

Seeing another white face in the darkness—*the last, thank God!*— he managed to control himself. He didn't wait for the woman to return. Just bent over, seized, heaved. He drove off hideousness with humor. *Coach'd be proud of me.*

He did not toss the last girl out of the outhouse. Something in him rebelled, demanding that a measure of dignity be returned to a world swirling down into utter foulness. Holding the girl under the armpits, ignoring the spiders on her shoulders and the one crawling down his arm, he carried her out and set her gently on her feet.

The gesture was pointless, perhaps. The girl collapsed immediately and began retching. But Jeff still felt the better for it. He held out his arms, examining. One spider, no more. A quick flick of the fingers did for that.

Jimmy and Eddie were crowding around him. Then, backed away.

"Thanks a lot," grumbled Jeff. "Can you see any more spiders?"

After circling him for a few seconds, his friends shook their heads. Jeff was almost amused by the paleness of their faces. But not much. He didn't doubt his own face was just as pale.

He was feeling a bit giddy, now. He realized that he had been holding his breath. Trying to restore his calm, he turned his head back and forth, examining the scene around him.

The area was now packed with Americans. Two of the coal-hauling trucks had pulled up near the outhouse and disgorged the miners who had been inside manning the rifle slits. Other Americans had begun to arrive in pickups. All of them were being drawn by the commotion at the outhouse.

A young man pushed forward from the crowd. Harry Lefferts. His camouflage was bulked up in his midsection by the bandages he was still wearing from the first day's gunfight. He held his rifle in one hand, muzzle pointing to the ground.

"I can't believe this shit," muttered Harry. He shook his head, turned it, fixed his eyes on a German prisoner standing a few feet away. The man had his hands raised, clasped on top of his head.

"Little girls'd rather hide in a shithouse than deal with these fuckheads." Harry gave the German prisoner a very savage grin. "Go ahead, asshole!" he shouted, hefting his rifle. "Look at me cross-eyed, why don't you? Spit on the ground. Anything. Just give me an excuse so's I can blow your fucking brains out!"

The German obviously didn't understand the words. But, just as obviously, he understood the essence of them. He kept his hands firmly clasped on top of his head, and kept his eyes carefully away from Harry.

Smart move, thought Jeff. He looked around. All the German soldiers were now behaving as meekly as lambs. Harry's reaction to seeing the girls being hauled out of the outhouse was fairly typical. Many of the coal miners were taking the opportunity to express their opinion of Hoffman's mercenaries—usually right in their faces, obviously quite prepared to shoot if anyone gave them any trouble.

Trouble, needless to say, was conspicuously absent. The prisoners were thoroughly intimidated.

Mike Stearns arrived then. After hearing a quick muttered explanation from Harry, Mike walked over to the group of girls and stared at them. The girls were still on their knees, but they were not vomiting anymore. Jeff didn't think there was anything left to vomit. Just four girls, gasping for breath. Old women surrounded them, still brushing off spiders.

Jeff was standing close enough to hear Mike's whisper. "They can't be more than thirteen years old." His face was as pale as a sheet. Mike's faint freckles were normally almost invisible. Now, they shone like stars in the sky. Red stars. Antares—and Mars. Jeff could sense the big man's effort to control his temper.

Hearing the whisper, the young woman whom Jeff had helped stared up at Mike's face. She seemed to flinch, for an instant. Then, rising, she stood straight before him. Hands at her side, back stiff, shoulders square.

She was shielding her family again, Jeff realized. From the blows she expected to come from Mike. He saw her turn her face aside. Still level, but presenting the cheek.

Mike understood also. "Jesus Christ," he whispered. "What a nightmare world." He started to raise his hand, as if to comfort the young woman, but dropped it. The gesture seemed feeble, helpless. *What can you do? Say?*

❀   ❀   ❀

The leader of the strangers came up just as Gretchen and her family were cleaning the last spiders off of the girls. Gretchen was so relieved to see that all of them were unharmed—filthy, yes, but unharmed—that she never noticed his arrival. Not until he was standing right next to her and whispered something did she realize that he was there.

Startled, she looked up. Then, when she saw his face, she stood erect.

She recognized the leader. He was the one who had captured the Protestant chieftain. He was even bigger, up close, than she had realized. Not as big as Ludwig, but—

This man could have broken Ludwig in half.

Gretchen didn't doubt that for a moment. The American leader was the scariest man she had ever seen in her life. Much scarier—*much* scarier—than even Diego the Spaniard.

It was not so much the sheer size of the man—not even when that size contained nothing but bone and muscle—as he himself. He loomed above her like something out of old legends. She barely noticed the mottled clothing and the odd helmet. *(Why put a lamp on a helmet?)*

She saw only the face, and the anger in it, and knew the ancient warriors of Teuton myths.

Gretchen assumed that the leader was angry at her and her family. The Protestant soldiers also, of course. But mostly she. Because of her, some of his newly captured women were so foul no man would touch them. Not even soldiers.

She felt herself cringing, and fought it down. Cringing before men only fed the flames. She turned her head, bracing herself for the beating. She knew from experience that a blow on the cheek was the easiest to handle.

But the man simply turned away. He muttered something to the young man who had helped her. The young man nodded and turned toward Gretchen. She realized that the leader had instructed him to watch over her.

She glanced around. The victors' camp followers were arriving. She was astonished to see a Moorish physician in their midst. Only powerful people could afford Moorish or Jewish doctors. Then she saw two or three women moving through the camp, and was astonished again. Each of them was wearing a white armband with a red cross emblazoned on it. A religious order, apparently. Gretchen almost laughed. The piety of the insignia went very poorly, she thought, with those brazen bare calves. One of the women had a dress so short it showed her knees!

Then, another thought drove out all humor. She turned, looking for help from the same man who had provided it twice already. The man who had helped save her, and her sister, might help her save her brother. If Hans could be saved at all.

"*Mein bruder. Hans.*" The woman pointed toward the battlefield. Jeff, looking, saw that the distant field was now covered with people, moving slowly through—

He swallowed. There were so many bodies there. So *many.*

"Pliss," she repeated. "*Mein*—my—brutter. Hans."

Eddie Cantrell spoke hesitantly. "I think she's looking for her brother, Jeff."

Jeff looked back at the woman. She was not much shorter than he was, he thought. At least, her eyes seemed very level. Light brown eyes.

"Pliss."

"Sure, ma'am," he replied. "I'll be glad to help you look for your brother."

He ignored the chuckles, as he and the woman walked away. With great dignity, he thought. He even managed to ignore Larry's parting remark.

"See? *That's* an opening line, stupe. Flowers'll work, too." Then, half-shouting: "Beats the last stand at the Alamo, you crazy jerk!"

Chapter 19

As soon as Mike left Jeff and the young German women, he headed for Nichols. The doctor was moving through the crowd of frightened camp followers, quickly inspecting the women and children to see which might need immediate medical attention.

"James!" called out Mike. The doctor turned. Mike reached him in a few quick strides.

"I think you should look at those people first," he said, indicating the cluster of people by the outhouse. He gave Nichols a quick explanation.

The doctor winced. "In *there*? Jesus Christ almighty. What kind of a world—"

Nichols broke off. "They should be all right, if they haven't been bitten by the wrong kind of spiders. Lucky they didn't suffocate, though. And you're right, Mike—we need to get them to the sanitation center right away. I'll see that they get first priority."

"I already told Jeff and his friends to look after them," Mike explained. "So you can have them escort the girls—the whole family— to the school." Mike glanced back over his shoulder. Seeing the way Jeff was staring at the tall young blonde, Mike's spirits lifted. The sight of a young man so obviously dazzled by a young woman was quite refreshing. Innocence and sanity blooming in a field of lust and murder.

Nichols was observing the same tableau. He grinned. "From the looks of things, I'd have to pry him loose with a crowbar."

He began walking toward them. "I'll take care of it, Mike." James pointed into the distance, back toward the original American lines. His grin widened. "Rebecca's here, by the way. Speaking of prying people loose with a crowbar."

"Rebecca!" Mike spun around, staring in that direction. "What in the hell is she doing *here*?" For a moment, he began to charge off. Then, guiltily remembering his responsibilities, he forced himself to turn back.

For the next ten minutes, while he organized the disposition of the surrendered Protestant soldiers, Mike's mind was only half on his task. Half, at best. He was fretting over Rebecca.

What is that crazy woman doing on a battlefield?!

Fortunately for him, Harry Lefferts and Tom Simpson cheerfully took on themselves the nitty-gritty work. Between Harry's savage grin (*go ahead, Kraut—make my day*) and Tom's sheer size and extravagant musculature (*yeah, go ahead—I need an arm bone to pick my teeth*), Hoffman's mercenaries were quickly rounded up and organized into a column. Hands carefully placed atop their heads, eyes front, meek as could be.

Then Frank showed up, along with Lennox—Frank in his pickup and Lennox on his horse.

Lennox spoke first. "We've got t'Catholics neatly tied oop," he announced complacently. "Mackay's seeing to t'last o' t'strays. 'E'll be coomin' in a minute." Mustachioes bristled. "T'en we'll march this lot into Badenburg an' put'm under guard. Don' expect no trooble."

Frank had his arm perched on the open window of the truck. He was studying Mike with half-quizzical/half-amused eyes.

"Oh, why don't you cut the act?" he chortled. He hooked his thumb toward Grantville. "Just go see the lady, Mike. Lennox and I can handle the rest of this business."

Mike glowered. "What's she doing here?" he demanded. "She could have gotten hurt! She's got no business—"

"Are you *that* stupid?" snapped Frank. "She's worried sick about you, what do you think? *You're* the one went marching into battle, not her." Frank snorted. "She isn't alone, either. Half the women in town showed up, looking for their fathers and sons and husbands and boyfriends. Did you think they were going to stay home, waiting for a telegram—with a battle being fought practically on their doorstep?"

"Oh." Mike stared into the distance, looking for the log parapet. The parapet itself was not visible, but the small knoll where Ferrara had positioned his rockets made the location obvious. To his surprise, he saw that the knoll was now covered with people. American women and children, he realized, anxiously trying to spot their menfolk in the field below.

He winced, remembering the carnage on that field. None of the bodies were American, but the sight was nothing he wanted to inflict on children. He'd had a hard enough time with it himself.

"I guess I'd better get over there," he muttered. "Reassure everybody."

Frank grinned. "Yeah, guess so." He got out of the vehicle. "Here—take my truck. I can't bear to think of you tripping and falling all the way back. Fast as you'll be running and paying no attention to where you're going."

Mike was already at the wheel. "*Do* try not to wreck the thing, willya? It's only two years old—" Off with a roar, fishtailing in the dirt. Frank sighed. "So much for the paint job. Not to mention the shock absorbers."

Mike spotted Rebecca easily. She was standing on top of the parapet, balanced precariously, shielding her eyes from the sun with her hand. When she spotted the oncoming truck, her scrutiny focused on it. As soon as she was sure that Mike was the driver, she hopped off the parapet and began running toward him.

Mike brought the truck to a halt and climbed out. Not far away, to his left, was a scene of sheer ghastliness. Americans with medical experience, led by Doctor Adams, were picking their way through the battlefield looking for survivors. Mackay and his Scots, meanwhile, had organized the Catholic prisoners to start burying the corpses. But there were so *many* torn and ruptured bodies. The soil was literally soaked with blood. Flies swarmed everywhere.

But he had no eyes for that. Just for the figure of a woman, running. He had never seen her run before. For all the cumbersome nature of the long skirt, Mike was struck by the grace of her movements. He always thought of Rebecca as *stately*, because of the quiet poise with which she stood, walked, sat. Some part of him, finally erupting, realized that he was seeing her for the first time. His heart felt like it might burst.

Rebecca came to a halt a few feet away. She was breathing heavily. Her bonnet had fallen off, somewhere along the way. The long, black, very curly hair hung loose. A mass of glossy splendor. Her face glistened with a slight sheen of sweat, shining like gold in the sunlight that was beginning to break through the clouds.

"I was so afraid," she whispered. "Michael—"

He stepped toward her, extending a hand. The gesture was tentative, almost timid. Her own fingers slid into his palm. There they stood, for a few seconds, saying nothing. Then, so fiercely Mike almost lost his breath, Rebecca was clasping him in an embrace. Her face was buried in his chest. He could feel her heaving against him, and hear the quick sobs, and sense the tears starting to moisten his shirt.

He placed his hands on her shoulders. Gently, stroking. He felt the firm flesh under his hands, separated by nothing more than a thin layer of cloth. He could feel most of her body, she was pressed so closely. Breasts, belly, arms, shoulders, hips, thighs.

They had never touched before, except her hand on his arm during their daily walks. The passion that poured over him drove every other emotion away. Anger and horror and fear—the residue of battle— were like footprints obliterated by a wave. Paw prints. His arms enfolded her, drawing her more closely still.

Her hair was beautiful. Long, black, glossy, curly. He was kissing it fiercely. Then, gently but insistently, he nuzzled the side of her head. When her face came up—so quickly—he transferred the kiss to her lips. Full, rich, soft—eager. As eager as his own.

How long that kiss lasted—that first kiss—neither of them ever knew. As long as it took, before the cheers of the crowd startled them back to awareness.

"Oh," said Rebecca. She craned her neck, looking at the sea of grinning faces standing on the knoll nearby. Watching them. Cheering them. For a moment, Mike thought she was about to bury her face back into his shoulder. Trying to avoid that public exposure. But she didn't. She flushed, yes. But nothing more.

"Oh," she repeated. Then, smiling, she raised her lips again. "It is done," she whispered. "And I am so happy for it."

"Me too," Mike said. Mumbled, rather. Rebecca wasn't letting him get a word out. Not for some time. And he was so happy for it.

Chapter 20

The first one she found was Diego. Gretchen had known the Spaniard was incredibly tough, but even she was impressed. Despite his terrible wounds, Diego had managed to crawl forty yards from the front line where he was struck down.

He was even still conscious. "Give me water," he whispered, when she knelt by his side. He was lying on his back, his arms holding in his intestines.

Diego's eyes opened. They were not much more than narrow slits. "And get me my woman. Where is that stupid bitch?"

Gretchen raised her head and studied the scene around her. The battlefield was littered with bodies, especially where the tercio's front lines had been. Half of them, it seemed, were still alive. Men were moaning, groaning; a few were screaming.

Men, and now a few women, were moving through the field, inspecting the bodies. The men were all garbed in that peculiar mottled clothing which the boy near her was wearing. The women wore white.

Gretchen watched them long enough to make sure she understood their purpose. They were not killing the survivors, she saw. They were apparently trying to save the ones who might still survive. Even now, she could see several small teams of people carrying wounded men away on litters.

That might be good news. If Hans—

She pushed aside, for a moment, her fears and concerns for her brother. There was Diego to deal with, for the moment. And for *that*, the people around her might pose a problem.

Diego's spoke again, in a hoarse whisper. "Water, you fucking cunt. Are you deaf?"

Gretchen examined the Spaniard's wounds. She did not think that even Diego could survive them. But she was not certain.

Again, she studied the people around her. None of them were very close, except—

She turned her head and looked up at the boy she had asked to accompany her to the field. Almost like a cherub, he seemed, for all his size. The boy was tall, his body was on the heavy side—lots of fat there—and his round face was very earnest. An innocent face, with its plump cheeks and blunt nose. Almost a silly-looking face, with those peculiar spectacles. Gretchen had seen spectacles before, but only on rich old men. Never on a young man—and certainly never on a field of battle.

The boy's eyes, magnified through those lenses, were a very bright green. Healthy eyes. They were the one thing about the boy which did not seem childish in the least. Gretchen remembered the light which had flamed in those eyes, earlier, and the anger with which he had marched to confront the mercenaries.

A courageous boy, then. Perhaps now, also. And if not— Perhaps he was simply an innocent. Stupid, in the way such people are. She could remember, barely, being that stupid herself. Two years ago. A lifetime ago.

"Pliss," she said, mustering what little English she had picked up from some of the mercenaries. "Look—" She hesitated, trying to think of the word. Then, remembered. "Away."

He stared at her. "Look away," she repeated. Pleading: *"Pliss."*

She sighed. He obviously did not understand. His plump face was simply confused. Innocent, unknowing. Gretchen studied his eyes, and decided she had no choice but to trust them.

"Water!" hissed Diego. "And get me my bitch!"

Gretchen nodded to the wounded Spaniard next to whom she was kneeling. "He hurt—" She groped, trying to think of the future tense. Yes. "He *will* hurt *mein Schwester.*"

The boy frowned. Clearly, the words meant nothing to him. Again, Gretchen groped for the English term. Not finding it, she tried circumlocution: *"Mein*—my female *Bruder."*

His eyes widened. "Your sister?"

That was the word! Gretchen nodded. She drew the knife from her bodice. "Pliss. Look away."

The eyes widened still further. Very green they were. She realized they would be, even without the spectacles. The boy's heavy-lipped mouth opened, as if to speak a protest. Or a command.

But, after a moment, the lips closed. The boy stared at her.

"Water, you fucking cunt," said Diego. He added some words in Spanish, but Gretchen did not understand any of them except *puta.*

Apparently, the boy did. His face flushed with anger. Or, perhaps, it was simply that he was not so innocent after all.

Suddenly, he came down on one knee, looming over them. He leaned forward. In an instant, Gretchen realized that he was shielding her from the eyes of the other people on the field.

He said something in English, but she didn't understand the words. There was no need. His eyes were enough.

Gretchen had slaughtered animals since she was five years old. Diego took no more time than a chicken. The little knife slit the carotid artery as neatly as a razor. Blood started pumping onto the ground on the opposite side from where she was kneeling. Not a drop spilled on her. She was an experienced animal-slaughterer.

Diego was very tough. So, to be sure, Gretchen also drove the knife all the way into his ear. Then, for three or four seconds, she twisted the three-inch blade back and forth in his brains. Diego was not *that* tough. Not even the Satan who sired him was that tough.

When she was finished, she took the time to clean the blade on the Spaniard's sleeve before slipping it back into her bodice.

Killing Diego had pleased her immensely. Yet, oddly, she was even more pleased with the boy. He had said nothing, throughout. But his eyes had never looked away. Not once.

Healthy eyes. Very bright, very green. Gretchen decided the spectacles were actually rather charming.

She rose. One necessity accomplished, another remained. Perhaps two.

Only one, as it happened. Ludwig was already dead. Even his huge torso had been torn into shreds by the powerful guns of the strange men in their mottled clothing.

Gretchen stared down at him. She had been half hoping Ludwig would still be alive, so that she could have the pleasure of killing the man who had murdered her father and subjected her to two years of rape. For a moment, she was consumed by pure hatred.

Then she spotted the little arm—a third arm?—protruding from beneath the great gross body of Ludwig, and hatred was driven away by hope. Maybe, for the first and last time in his life, Ludwig had been good for something.

The boy helped her lever Ludwig's body aside. Beneath, like a kitten under a lion, lay her brother Hans. And he was still alive.

Barely alive. But alive.

As she rolled Ludwig off, Gretchen had seen the great wounds in his back. The strangers' gun—whatever that weapon had been with its horrifying dragon's stutter—had been powerful enough to shoot right through Ludwig and his armor and strike her brother standing behind. But apparently the bullets had been deflected enough, and lost enough of their force, that her brother's wounds were not instantly fatal.

Gretchen knelt by Hans and cut the straps holding his cheap cuirass. Then, as gently as she could, she probed his wounds with her fingers. The momentary surge of hope faded as quickly as it had come. At least one of the bullets had penetrated his chest wall. Even if it could be removed—she would try her best, with her little knife— the wound would almost certainly become infected with disease. She knew that disease. Men rarely survived it, even men much stronger than her spindly little brother.

Her eyes filled with tears, remembering Hans and his spindly little life. Remembering how hard he had always tried, cast into a world for which he was not suited in the least. He had been a studious boy, in love with books, and eager to follow his father into the printer's trade. He had often joked with Gretchen, telling her that if there were any rhyme or reason in the world *she* should have been the one in the family carrying a pike. Big, strong, tough Gretchen.

Through the tears, and the sorrow, and the hopelessness, Gretchen heard the strange boy's voice shouting something. He was not shouting at her, but at someone farther away. Her English was really very poor. The only word she understood was the last one, repeated and repeated. Over and again.

Now! Now! Now! Now!

Moments later, she heard the sound of clumping feet, rushing toward them. She raised her head and wiped away the tears. Two men were coming, followed very closely by a woman in white.

Then her eyes spotted what the men were carrying, and all other thoughts were driven aside. A stretcher. A thing used only, in her experience on many battlefields, to carry away the men who might be saved.

Startled, she looked up at the boy standing beside her. He was staring down at her. His face did not seem so young, anymore. Or perhaps it was simply his eyes. Green, clear, healthy eyes. There was promise in those eyes.

Chapter 21

After Hans was taken away, Gretchen was torn by indecision. A part of her wanted nothing so much as to accompany her brother, wherever the strangers were taking him. But she still had the rest of her family to look after. They would be relying on her, as always.

The boy made the decision for her. His eyes, rather. She decided she would trust those eyes again.

The boy was not showing any sign that he wanted to leave her. Quite the opposite. Everything in his posture indicated a kind of shy, uncertain, hesitant possessiveness.

Gretchen spent a minute or so thinking about that possessiveness, before she made her decision. The decision came easily enough. She did not really have a choice, anyway, except a choice between different evils. And—

She liked his eyes. That was something. The rest could be endured, easily enough. Anything could be endured, easily enough, after Ludwig.

The boy—

Stop. She forced her mind onto a different path.

"*Was ist*—" Damned English! "What iss *ihre*—you name?" She pronounced it in the German way: *nam-uh.*

He understood the question at once. "Jeff Higgins."

So. He is as intelligent as his eyes.

That, too, was a good sign. With intelligence there might also be humor. Good humor. Ludwig's intelligence had been that of a pig. His humor had reminded her of pig shit.

She pronounced the name a few times, until she was certain she had it right. *Jeff Higgins. Jeff Higgins.* Men—young men, especially—became sullen if you mispronounced their names. Gretchen could not afford any such obstacles. Not now, not here.

Not ever. For two years, Gretchen's life and that of her family had hung by the slenderest thread. But Gretchen had always been self-confident, even as a little girl. So long as there was a thread, she would hold it in a sure and capable grip.

She tucked her hand under his arm and began leading him back to the camp where her family waited. She tried not to make it too obvious. Men resented being led by women.

But the boy—*stop; Jeff*—didn't seem to mind at all. Soon, to her surprise, he even became very chatty. Fumbling with words, trying to find some mishmash language they could both speak. She was interested to note than he seemed more concerned with learning some German words than with teaching her English.

By the time they reached the camp, Gretchen was almost at ease. *This will not be so bad*, she decided. *He will be heavy, of course, as big and plump as he is. So what? Ludwig was like an ox.*

Then, shouting and threading their way through the chaos of the camp—the people were no longer shrieking with fear, but they were still very confused—three boys came running up.

Young men. Stupid woman. Not boys.

Gretchen recognized them. They were the three young men who had been with Jeff, and had stood by his side when he confronted the Protestant mercenaries. As soon as they arrived, Jeff and his friends began bantering. Gretchen could not follow the conversation, except for a few words here and there. But she quickly understood the heart of it. They were teasing him about his new woman, and he was responding.

She relaxed still further. The teasing was gay, not coarse. Almost innocent, in a way. And Jeff's response was—

Shy, uncertain. Fumbling and awkward and embarrassed. But most of all, proud. Very, very proud.

Gretchen studied that pride, what she could sense of it under the unknown words. She was accustomed to foreign languages—a mercenary army was a veritable Tower of Babel—and was quite proficient at separating meaning from its verbal sheath.

She relaxed. Ludwig had been proud of her. Like a pig farmer might boast of his sow. There was something else here. Something—fresh. Clean, perhaps.

A sudden image came to her, from a world she had long forgotten. A world she had banished from her mind. She remembered an evening, in her father's house, when he had been standing by the fireplace. Warming his hands, while her mother placed the food on the table. Her father had turned his head, and watched. Gretchen had been sixteen years old. Only four years ago, she realized. A lifetime ago.

Pride, in her father's eyes. Clear, shining, healthy eyes, full of possessiveness. A possessiveness so gentle, and so warm, that it had seemed to light the house more than the flames themselves.

To her shock, Gretchen found herself bursting into tears. Trembling like a leaf. She fought desperately for control.

Stop! He will be annoyed! Men do not like—

Arms came around her, drawing her close. A hand pressed her face into a shoulder. Like a child, unthinking, she wrapped her arms around the body and squeezed it tight. She sobbed and sobbed, feeling, all the while, the muscle under the fat and the bone under the muscle. Feeling—so strange—the sharp edge of the spectacles against her skull. Hearing the whispers and not understanding a word.

There was no need for words. Meaning, from its sheath, was all that mattered.

When she was done, finally, she drew her head away. Her eyes met his. Light brown; light green.

Not so bad at all.

Chapter 22

The first thing Gretchen's grandmother said, upon being informed that they were standing before a school, was:

"*Nonsense!*"

The stooped old woman peered up suspiciously at the young man standing next to Gretchen. He was holding a sheet of paper in his hands. "He's lying to you," Gramma pronounced. She spoke with the utter certainty of her age and wisdom.

Gramma twisted her head, studying what she could see of the huge structure. "There are not enough noble children in all of Germany for a school this big. *He is lying to you.*"

Gretchen was uncertain herself. She didn't think Jeff was lying to her. She barely knew the man, true, but a glance at his open face reassured her. Whatever vices and wickedness that face shielded, Gretchen did not believe for a moment that a capacity for cold-blooded dissemblance was among them.

Still—

There *wasn't* any logical reason for a school this big. At least, she hoped not. A *thousand* noble children at a time? That was the number Jeff had stated, proudly, in his stumbling German/English pidgin. Could there be that many, even in the entire Holy Roman Empire?

Gretchen almost shuddered. Her one faint hope, over the past years, had been that if enough noblemen killed themselves off the war might someday end. But if there were a thousand more ready to take their fathers' places—

She took a closer look at the sheet of paper in Jeff's hand. All of his friends held one just like it. So did the old woman who had emerged to greet them when they neared the school and handed the papers to the young men.

Gretchen studied the old woman. *A baroness, at the very least. Possibly even a duchess.*

To some degree, Gretchen's assessment was based on the woman's clothing. The apparel was simple in its odd and almost scandalous design, but it was very well made and of some unfamiliar fabric that practically shrieked: *king's ransom.* Mostly, however, Gretchen's conclusion was dictated by the woman herself.

No other women she knew could reach that advanced age without having long since been turned into crones by endless labor, deprivation and abuse. When she first saw the woman, Gretchen had thought her to be not much older than thirty, despite the gray hair. But the wrinkles around her eyes and mouth were those of a much older woman. Forty-five years old, perhaps even fifty. Almost the age of stooped and withered Gramma.

A duchess. The woman was as tall as Gretchen herself. She stood straight, without a trace of stooping. Everything about her blazed health and vigor. Behind her spectacles, the duchess' hazel eyes were as clear and bright as a young woman's.

Then—there was the self-confidence in her stance. Her posture, her bearing, even the way she held her head—all of them announced to the world in no uncertain terms: *I am somebody important. Valuable. Precious. Good blood.*

Gretchen looked away. Again, her eyes fell on the sheet of paper. It was covered with printed words.

She extended her hand hesitantly. "Pleez? Can I?"

Jeff was startled. But he made no protest when Gretchen took the paper out of his hand.

It took her no more than ten seconds to understand what she was looking at. Almost all of that lost time was simply due to the unfamiliar style of print.

How clever!

It was a miniature dictionary. Gretchen's father had published dictionaries, now and again. Great huge monstrous things. But this was simply one sheet, containing simple phrases in English and their German equivalent. The spelling of the words, of course, was not always what Gretchen was accustomed to, but that meant nothing. In her day, no languages had standardized spelling. Her father had often complained about the problem.

She spotted the one phrase immediately. *Oh yes!*

So there would be no misunderstanding, Gretchen moved next to Jeff and pointed to the phrase with her finger while she spoke the words.

"Would . . . you . . . like . . . some . . . food?" Her head began nodding up and down. *"Ja! Ja!"*

Immediately, Jeff's face was distressed. She saw him glance at the enormous stretch of windows covering the near wall of the building. Gretchen followed his gaze. She was impressed, again, by the sheer size of those windows. Inside the room beyond, she suddenly noticed that a few people were carrying trays to a table. *Food!*

She had not eaten in two days. And then, only some bread which Ludwig had plundered from a farmhouse. He had not left much, to be divided among the women and children. Hans had offered to share his small portion of food, but Gretchen had refused. Her brother needed to be strong enough to survive battles.

Jeff was looking very distressed. When he saw that the old duchess was marching toward them, his face sagged a little from relief.

There was a quick exchange of words between Jeff and the duchess. Gretchen's English was improving rapidly—she had picked up much more than she realized from some of the English-speaking mercenaries in Tilly's army—but she was still not able to follow an entire conversation. Only bits and pieces:

Jeff: "—starving, Miz Mailey." *Odd name for a duchess.*

The duchess: "Oh God," *how easily they blasphemed!* "—of me—didn't think." The duchess slapped her head with a hand, the way a person admits a stupid deed. Gretchen was astonished by the gesture. A duchess? In public? Before *commoners*? "I'm an idiot!" Gretchen's jaw sagged.

Jeff: "—we do?"

The duchess sighed, shook her head. Her own face was looking very distressed. "—have no—" Gretchen didn't quite catch the last word. *Choice?*

Again, the duchess shook her head. The distress was still evident, but it was overlain by determination. The royal assurance in her face was unshakable. Absolute. Despite her hatred for nobility, Gretchen was impressed. This was a woman for whom decisions—*authority*—came as naturally as breathing.

The duchess stared at Gretchen for a few seconds. There was no haughtiness in that expression, simply—

What?

When Gretchen finally realized, she was as stunned as she had ever been in her life. Not even the friendly (no—*comradely*) way in which the duchess took her arm and began leading her toward another building was as overpowering as that first moment of shock.

To her grave, Gretchen would carry the memory. Those royal—*imperial*—hazel eyes. The eyes of an elderly and powerful woman, shining bright with health and self-confidence—and, now, full of recognition. Friendliness also, yes; that, and kindness. But Gretchen had occasionally—not often—encountered a certain Christian charity, even among the powerful. And so? Peasants, too, could be kindly toward their livestock.

Never recognition. Never once. For the first time in her life, one of the world's mighty had gazed upon Gretchen Richter, and seen nothing but another human being.

Gretchen did not understand clearly any of the phrases which the duchess spoke as she led her toward the other building. She was only able to grasp the essence of the matter. The duchess seemed much concerned with disease.

Gretchen's entire extended family followed them, as did Jeff and his three friends. They were walking on a peculiar black substance which seemed to cover most of the area outside the buildings themselves. The substance served the same purpose as cobblestones, but it was wondrously flat. Gretchen thought the warm and gritty feel of it under her bare feet was marvelous.

She was puzzled, at first, by the big yellow lines which were painted all over the main expanse of the black stuff. What could be the purpose of that checkerboard pattern? Then, seeing the position of the few vehicles in the area, she realized that the yellow lines were to guide them to rest. Most of the yellow-outlined rectangles were empty. They stretched and stretched for yards and yards.

They own so many vehicles? To need that much space? These people are so rich!

She turned her head and glanced back at Jeff. He had been watching her, she realized. He met her eyes for an instant only, before looking away. Awkwardly, he hitched the sling holding his arquebus a little higher on his shoulder.

So shy. He's nothing but a young soldier, I'm sure of it. But he seems to take all this for granted. So he must be rich, too.

She turned her head back, facing front. Squared her shoulders and marched forward alongside the strange duchess. Heading toward a mysterious future she could not see, but with a fierce determination to bring her family through that storm intact. As intact as possible, at least. Whatever was necessary.

The duchess led them around the building. There, appended to the back, was a long edifice whose roof and walls were made of some unknown substance. Very shiny, almost like metal. But there was something soft-looking about the stuff. It was colored a light green, and Gretchen thought it was almost translucent. She was reminded, a bit, of the tinted glass in cathedrals.

For all the peculiarity of the design and the material, Gretchen knew at once that the edifice had been very recently constructed. The flimsy-looking metal pipes which protruded out of the building and ran off into the distance were still shiny, untarnished by time and weather.

The duchess led them to a small door in the side of the edifice. She opened the door and waved Gretchen forward into the room beyond. The duchess herself remained standing by the door. She seemed to be examining the other members of Gretchen's family as they obediently trooped through the entrance. Three of them she stopped with a gesture of her hand and motioned aside. Uncertainly, but obeying, the three boys stepped back. They were the three oldest boys in the group. All of them were past puberty—not by much—and all were laden with bundles carrying what little the family possessed beyond clothing.

When the rest of the family had entered, the duchess gestured toward the three boys and said something to Jeff and his friends. They, too, had remained outside. Jeff nodded and beckoned the three boys to follow him. He pointed somewhere down the edifice. Toward the other side, possibly.

Immediately, realizing what was happening, the women in the room began shrieking. All except Gretchen. Their words were not a protest—women of their station did not *protest* anything—so much as a simple wail of anguish.

Gretchen almost joined that squawling bedlam. Almost. But something in the duchess' expression closed her throat. The duchess' mouth was wide open. Her face registered nothing beyond incomprehension and shock.

In an instant, Gretchen realized the truth.

She has no idea what we are afraid of. None! She simply ... doesn't understand. How can anyone in this world be so innocent?

But it was true. She had no doubt of it. The image came to her mind, of a young man's green eyes, magnified by spectacles. She remembered those eyes. She had seen fury flaming in them, once, before he stepped forward to face a pack of beasts. Alone. With a strange and powerful weapon, yes, but still alone. Until his friends joined him, not hesitating for longer than a moment.

Gretchen stared through the open door. That same young man was still there. Staring back at her. His mouth, like that of the duchess, was gaping wide listening to the howls of women and children. Gretchen studied his lips. A boy's lips still, plump and soft.

Gretchen knew, then. *Knew!* Held-in breath erupted.

She had left behind the world of murder, and entered a new land. There were killers in this land, yes, fierce and terrible ones—*Oh yes! God still sits in Heaven!*—but no murderers.

Before she turned away, to take charge of her family, Gretchen's own light brown eyes shone a message at green ones. He would not understand, of course. Not yet. Perhaps not ever. But she wanted to make that promise anyway.

Gretchen had already decided to become his concubine. Now, she would be his woman also. A man barely past boyhood would get something no man ever had. Certainly not Ludwig.

She turned away and took command.

"*Silence!*"

Gretchen's bellow almost shook the walls. Instantly, all the children in the room closed their mouths. Snapped them shut. The women also, except the new farm girl. Gretchen sent her sprawling with a buffet. "*Silence!*" The new girl, landing on her rump, gaped up at her. The mark of Gretchen's hand flamed large and red across her cheek. But she was silent.

Gretchen turned back to the duchess. The woman's mouth was still wide. But the shock, Gretchen realized, had now been caused by her own action.

What? Has she never disciplined a child?

The duchess closed her mouth. Shook her head. The motion was quick, abrupt—a gesture, not of someone denouncing an action but simply trying to clear her mind of confusion.

Understanding that confusion, now, Gretchen haltingly tried to explain. The duchess was very intelligent. It did not take her more than a minute, even with the difficulty of the language barrier, to finally comprehend.

The duchess' eyes widened. Her pale face grew paler still. But she nodded, and turned her head. A few feet away, Jeff and his friends stood waiting. Huddled next to the door, almost at the duchess' feet, the three oldest boys of Gretchen's family were squatting down, staring up at her. Their faces were blank with terror. Numb, knowing death had finally come.

The duchess rattled off a string of sentences in English. She spoke too fast for Gretchen to follow. By the time the duchess finished speaking, the faces of Jeff and his friends were as pale as her own. They stared down at the three huddled boys. One of Jeff's friends touched the weapon slung over his shoulder, like a man might reassure himself that a house pet had not been transformed into a serpent.

The duchess barked another phrase, ringing with authority. Gretchen caught only the last two words.

"—do it!"

Gretchen found it hard not to grin, seeing the haste with which Jeff and his friends obeyed the duchess. *Well, no wonder. I bet she never has to slap a child. Not her!*

Almost frantically, Jeff and his friends unslung the weapons on their shoulders and leaned them against the wall of the nearby building.

A moment later, they had unbuckled the pistols and laid them down on the ground.

Gretchen stepped up to the door and addressed the three boys. "Follow them," she commanded, pointing to Jeff and his friends. "Do whatever they say. Understand?"

The boys stared up at her. Gretchen scowled and raised her hand. *"Now!"*

The boys scrambled to their feet. As confused and terrified as they were, that familiar voice cut through everything like a knife. They were not afraid of Gretchen, exactly. But *nobody*—no child or woman in the family, at least—would ever dream of disobeying her. They knew that large hand well, and everything behind it. The hand was hard. The muscles which wielded it were not much softer. But, most of all, the will which commanded the muscles was like iron itself. A steel angel, forged in the Devil's inferno.

Satisfied, Gretchen turned away. "It will be done," she told the duchess. "Lead us where you will."

There were still problems, of course, in the time which followed. The women squawled again, when the duchess ordered them to remove their clothing.

It's all we have! We own nothing else!

Gretchen silenced them with a bellow.

The duchess ordered them to place the clothing into large, metal baskets. Then, to push the baskets through a low door. Beyond, as best as Gretchen could understand, the clothes would be boiled and cleaned before they were returned.

The women squawled again.

They will be stolen!

Gretchen bellowed again. It was not enough. She raised her hand. But the duchess stopped her with her own, shaking her head. A moment later, the duchess began to remove her own clothing.

That wondrous act brought silence. The family stared, as nobility disrobed. The duchess did not linger over the task. Gretchen was surprised to see how quickly and easily the garments were removed. She would have thought a duchess needed maidservants.

She was even more surprised by the body which was revealed, once the duchess was naked. An old woman, yes. But if the breasts sagged, they were not withered dugs. If the buttocks were no longer firm and plump, they were still buttocks. And everywhere—arms and shoulders and legs and midsection and hips—the muscles were lean, almost taut. The duchess' body, for all its signs of age, seemed to vibrate with health. If she were a man, Gretchen knew, she would find that body desirable still.

The duchess carried her clothing to one of the baskets. For a moment, she seemed to hesitate. Then, with a wry little smile and a shrug of the shoulders, she pitched the royal garments onto the rags of destitution. She turned away and marched toward a further door, waving her hand in a gesture of command. Pushing the door open, she entered a room whose floor was tiled.

Thereafter, there was no further squawling.

Squeals, yes, when the duchess turned a knob and hot water began showering down upon the family.

Moans of fear, yes. When the duchess passed out bars of—soap?— and began demonstrating their use. *The Inquisition will think we are Jews! We will be burned!*

Blubbers of confusion, yes. When the duchess insisted that they scrub their hair with some harsh and caustic substance. It would kill fleas, apparently. Such, at least, was how Gretchen interpreted her words.

But no squawls. Gretchen was forced to bellow only once. That was to stop three of the children from their gleeful play, squeezing bars of soap at each other like missiles.

When the strange ritual was over, and they were all drying themselves with marvelous soft fabrics ("towels," they were called), the duchess came up to Gretchen. She studied her for a moment, her hazel eyes ranging up and down Gretchen's body. Gretchen wondered why. She wondered even more when the duchess started shaking her head. It seemed a wry gesture, almost rueful.

The duchess spoke softly. She seemed to be talking to herself rather than Gretchen. The tone of her voice held an unusual mixture of humor and worry.

Gretchen understood some of it.

"—this problem—what to do—dirt gone, she's a damned—" Here the headshake grew very rueful. "—built like a brick—" The duchess tilted back her head and laughed. It was a gay sound. "Jeff"—something—"drop dead"—something—"sees her!"

The humor faded. Worry remained. The duchess' eyes seemed to bore into Gretchen's, as if trying to probe her soul. Or, perhaps, simply to find it.

Gretchen straightened. The existence of her soul she did not doubt. And *damn* this duchess if she thought it was not there!

Apparently, the duchess was satisfied. The frown of worry remained, but the rueful twist of the lips returned. Gretchen understood, without quite knowing why. The duchess' concern, whatever it was, did not involve a condemnation of Gretchen. Simply a condemnation of the world which had brought her forth.

The duchess shook her head again. Not ruefully, but almost angrily. Quick, fierce phrases were muttered. "—that young man! —him straight! —be no taking"—something; *advance? adage?*—"of this poor girl!"

She turned and started to stalk away. Then, catching sight of Annalise, she stopped. Gretchen's sister, coming under that royal scrutiny, shied away a step or two. Hesitantly, she lowered the towel. Her body was fully exposed. Naked, the strips of cloth gone with which Gretchen had bound her chest and hips for the past year, the truth was obvious.

But there was no Diego the Spaniard any longer, from whom that truth had to be hidden. Gretchen had sent the Spaniard back to his homeland. His true homeland, a much hotter place than Spain. Diego was squatting at Satan's feet, now, leaking blood and brains over his master's iron flagstones. Gretchen took that moment to wish eternal agony upon his shade.

There was only a duchess to see, now. Whence that duchess had come, from what homeland, Gretchen had no idea at all. But not Diego's, of that she was utterly certain.

The duchess stared at Annalise. Turned her head. Stared at Gretchen. Ranged her eyes up and down. More muttering. "—her sister soon. Already!" She stared around the room, subjecting all the younger women to a quick scrutiny. "—half of them—that matter."

Her eyes fell on the new farm girl. Now that the dirt and dried blood were gone, and the bruises were fading, the girl's body did not seem quite so shapeless. But Gretchen, unlike the duchess, did not spend any time examining the body. She was much more interested in the farm girl's face. *Yes.* There was light coming back into those eyes. Not much, but some. For the first time since Gretchen met her, the girl even managed a shy little smile. *Yes!*

If anything, however, the smile seemed to increase the duchess' obvious agitation. She threw up her hands. The gesture combined despair, exasperation, fretfulness, and—yes, still, some humor.

The duchess marched over to a metal cabinet against a far wall and opened it. Within, hanging tightly side by side, were a row of garments. Very soft-looking and luxurious. She began pulling them forth. Robes.

To the amazement of the women and children, the duchess began handing them out. Hesitantly, at first, then with cries of sheer pleasure as they felt the fabric—*so soft! so soft!*—they donned their new finery. They stood quietly as the duchess stumbled through an explanation. Gretchen interpreted as best she could. The new clothing would be theirs only for a time. Until their old clothing was returned, and perhaps—Gretchen was not certain, here—new clothing might be forthcoming. But they would wear the wonderful robes for a while. Until others came, others like them, who needed that same comfort.

For all the acquisitiveness of desperately poor people, Gretchen and her family accepted the news willingly enough. They were not Diego the Spaniard, after all, to take pleasure in the pain of others. Certainly not such others as those, who were not other at all.

When they emerged from the building, Jeff and his friends and the three older boys were already standing outside, waiting. The three boys were attired in nearly identical robes. And, like the women and children, their hair was damp with moisture.

Jeff's friends were still dressed as they had been. But Jeff was not. He, too, stood there in a robe, his hair wet. He seemed awkward and ill at ease, especially when he saw Gretchen emerging. His eyes looked away instantly, as soon as he got his first glimpse of her.

Gretchen studied him, at first. But, soon, the study began to transform itself into something quite different. Something much softer and less calculating. Jeff, she realized, had done the same as the duchess. Quelled the fears of others by leading himself.

Something flared, for a moment, inside Gretchen. She was so *pleased* that it had been *him*, not one of the others.

She fought down a smile. He would have been awkward, she knew. Shy, fumbling, uncertain. Boylike. Embarrassed by his nakedness, of course. But much more embarrassed by his presumption of leadership.

She could see more of his body now. The robe covered much less than the mottled battlefield gear. A boy's body. A large boy, true, with more muscle than she had realized, lurking under the plumpness. But everything about it was still soft, rounded, childish.

She cared not at all. Quite the opposite. There had been nothing childlike about Ludwig's body. The rock-hard body of an ogre. An ogre, boasting of his manly form, and proving it by the bruises he left on his woman's body.

The flare returned. A little brighter, lasting a little longer. She was puzzled by the sensation.

Finally, Jeff brought his eyes back and looked at her. Then, stared. He was seeing Gretchen for the first time, in a way. Clean of filth, clear of ruin; a woman in a robe, not a murderess on a battlefield. His eyes widened and widened.

Gretchen glanced at the duchess. She was not looking. She glanced at Jeff's three companions. Neither were they.

Quickly, surely, she began to undo the sash and allow the robe to open. The center of her body would be exposed to Jeff's gaze, from her throat down to her ankles. Everything. Breasts, belly, abdomen, pubis, thighs. Everything. Those things meant nothing to her, beyond their health and vigor. But she had seen—more often than she wanted to remember—how instantly Ludwig could be aroused by the mere sight of her flesh. Instantly and ferociously.

Midway through, something stopped her. She tried to force her fingers to complete the task. They refused. It was as if her soul was bypassing her brain, commanding her body against her will.

Why? she demanded. *The family must be protected!*

No answer came, because no answer was needed.

After a moment, she let her fingers fall away. Gretchen had made a promise. A silent one, true, but a promise nonetheless. She had promised to be his woman, not simply his concubine. The boy—the man—was not Ludwig. She would snare him if she could, but she would not trick him with mere flesh.

The duchess was leading them all away, now, back toward the school building. There would be food, food! For all the hunger gnawing in her stomach, Gretchen did not follow immediately. She lowered her head, closed her eyes, took a deep breath. Luxuriated, for a moment, in cleanliness and softness. Softness of the robe, softness of the body, cleanliness of the heart. Even the black substance beneath her bare feet felt clean and soft.

She raised her head and opened her eyes. She would give Jeff a smile before she went. That much her promise permitted. A simple sweet smile, with just a hint of promise.

But when she saw him, she almost grinned. No pawing bull, here, snorting with lust. Just a young man, standing like a stunned ox.

Gretchen had triumphed, she knew. She had him now, she was certain of it. Snared beyond escape. No trick had been needed after all.

The knowledge brought satisfaction. Some part of it was warm, some cold. Warm, because she had not violated her promise. Cold, because the promise itself was calculation.

Such was life in a maelstrom. Once again, Gretchen had done what was necessary to shelter her family. Shelter it well, she thought. Very well. She hardly knew Jeff at all, yet. But one thing she knew already. The childlike half-boy would provide far more shelter than anything provided by Ludwig the troll. Far, far more.

But—there was something else. The flare came back, again. That sensation was strange. But the sensation which came to take its place was not. Gretchen recognized it at once, of course, and drove it down.

Mercilessly. She had lived with sorrow for years. Why should today be any different?

Chapter 23

Melissa Mailey ate with the refugees, still wearing her own robe. She felt foolish and awkward in that garb, eating in the same cafeteria where, over the years, she had shared thousands of meals with thousands of students. Dressed properly! Ed Piazza had obtained fresh clothes for her, but Melissa had refused to put them on. Not, she insisted, until the refugees were settled for the night and it was time for the committee meeting. The same stubbornness which had once sent a young Boston Brahmin to share a lunch counter with black people in the Jim Crow south, caused her older self to eat a meal in a robe with German refugees. Barefoot, just as they were, even if her own toenails were painted.

She had intended, also, to be there in order to guard against the inevitable danger of the half-starved refugees overeating. But there was no need. Not with Gretchen there, watching like a hawk.

Gretchen imposed food discipline with an iron hand. Melissa winced, several times, at Gretchen's methods of imposing that discipline. She had been opposed to corporal punishment all her life. But she did not protest.

Melissa Mailey was undergoing a conversion, as it were. Her mind was roiling, as she stolidly ate her meal.

She *still* did not approve of corporal punishment. But Melissa Mailey was not a fool, and could recognize reality when she saw it. Her eyes flinched, but she would not close them.

Gretchen, *not she*, had seen people eat grass to stay alive. Gretchen, *not she*, had seen those same people gorge themselves when unexpected plenty arrived. And then seen them die of surfeit, writhing in agony. She watched Gretchen buffet another child, stuffing food into his mouth with both hands, forcing him to sit with his hands in his lap for three minutes before he took another bite. She winced—the child's little face would be bruised tomorrow, and he was weeping bitterly—but she did not protest. Gretchen had kept that boy alive, again, in a world which would have slaughtered Melissa Mailey like a chicken. The boy was not even hers. Gretchen's baby was perched on her lap, feeding happily at her breast. Her own child was a rapist's bastard. The other—who knows? *Nothing. Nobody.* A piece of dust, sent swirling across a raging landscape by the hooves of noble chargers, until by good fortune it rolled against the dirty feet of a camp follower.

Melissa winced, too, seeing the glances which Gretchen continually sent to Jeff, sitting at the other end of the table. The glances were demure, in a way. Which only made them all the more effective. Jeff was a well-bred country boy. A leering, garish, raucous street prostitute would have scared him off. A young woman in a robe, poised, self-confident—her breast exposed only to feed a child—guiding her family through a meal—

Sending glance after glance—soft, shining, *promising*—to a boy only two years younger than she in age, but eons in experience—

Melissa almost laughed. *Leave aside that incredible figure!*

The conclusion was foregone. Given. By now, Jeff would be nothing but a raging mass of hormones. Burning with desire. Would he take advantage of the offer? *Ha!*

Melissa had a sudden image of herself, standing on a beach, ankle-deep in seawater. Queen Melissa—imperious, righteous—ordering the tide to retreat.

Melissa was opposed to sexual harassment. She was opposed to men taking advantage of the weaker position of women in society to satisfy their lust. She *was.*

She *still* was. But—

Despair washed over her. The world she had been plunged into was so far removed from the one she had known that no answers seemed possible. How could she condemn? How could she could reprove? And, most important of all, how could she point a way forward?

The boy Gretchen had buffeted was no longer crying. To the contrary, he was smiling. Looking at Gretchen, eager to catch her eye. Utterly oblivious, now, to the bruise forming on his cheek. Melissa realized that his Gretchen-imposed time limit was over. Gretchen, as if guided by some internal clock, met his gaze, smiled gently, and nodded. The boy stuffed a handful of food in his mouth. Started to reach for another, paused, glanced warily at Gretchen. Sure enough, she was watching him. Frowning.

Angels never sleep. The boy sighed and put his hands back in his lap. The angel smiled. The eyes moved on to another child, another woman—weaker than she—to a crone, feebler than she—and then, to a large American boy at the other end of the table. The promise in those eyes was not angelic in the least.

The eyes moved on. Watching, watching. Sheltering, protecting. Steel eyes, forged in a furnace Melissa could hardly imagine. The eyes of the only kind of angel that could possibly exist in such a place.

Melissa was paralyzed. In the showers, she had been firmly determined to speak to Jeff. Warn him—in no uncertain terms!—that he was *absolutely forbidden*—

Forbidden? Why? On what grounds?

The answer was a serpent, a snake, a scorpion. A cure far worse than the disease. Good intentions be damned, reality would be something different. Forbid American boys to copulate with German girls—girls who would be throwing themselves at them in order to survive—and you take the first step on the road to a caste society. The copulation would happen anyway, in the dark. On back stairs, in closets. Between *noble* Americans, and German *commoners. Whores again.*

Everything Mike—and she—were determined to prevent.

So what to do? Is there any light in this darkness?

Abruptly, Melissa stopped eating. Thoughts of corporal punishment and sexual harassment were driven aside by a wave of nausea. She closed her eyes, trying to control her stomach.

The nausea was not caused by the food. It was simply high-school cafeteria food, the same food she had eaten times without number. Nutritious, bland.

The nausea was caused by sheer horror. The horror, by a memory.

She had been able to block it out, for a time. The difficulty of coaxing the women and their children through the sanitation process had kept her busy. The fretting worry over how to handle the situation developing between Gretchen and Jeff—them, today; all the other girls, she knew, within a week, with other American boys carrying the guns which could protect them—had kept her mind preoccupied. A schoolteacher's habit, forged over decades, of maintaining decorum and discipline had kept her tightly focused.

But enough time had elapsed, now. The memory could no longer be held at bay. The memory of three boys, none of them more than fourteen years old, squatting at her feet like animals, their eyes blank, their faces numb, while their mothers and sisters and aunts wailed and shrieked like banshees. All of them, except Gretchen, utterly certain—

Utterly certain!

—that Melissa Mailey had come to murder them.

❧   ❧   ❧

She was going to vomit.

Not here! They'll think they've been poisoned.

Abruptly, she rose and strode away from the table. She waved away Jeff's look of concern. *Just thought of something I need to do, that's all.* Jeff, she knew, would reassure the others. He was a reliable boy. A *good* boy.

Once she was out of the cafeteria she turned left and pushed through the big doors leading to the outside. Melissa was almost running now. She couldn't hold it down much longer and she was determined to be completely out of sight of the refugees. Night had almost fallen, but there was still a bit of purple sky to illuminate the area.

She turned right, away from the cafeteria windows. Now, in the semidarkness, she began to run. Her bare feet slapped the walkway running alongside the school.

She couldn't make it to the bushes near the technical center. Not a chance.

This is far enough.

She stepped off the walkway and fell to her knees. Guiltless cafeteria food surged up, spewed, splattered innocent grass. Murder came out, rape came out, torture came out; cruelty beyond imagining covered the land. Horror spilled, anguish spread. The acrid smell of her own digestive juices was perfume, covering a stench so vile it could not be given a name.

By the time Melissa Mailey finished, her conversion was complete.

She leaned back and took a deep breath. Clean air filled her lungs. She probed her mind, pushing beneath the rage, searching for herself.

Still there, she realized, sighing with relief.

Barely. But still there.

Mike and Rebecca found her a few minutes later. They had arrived for the committee meeting early, as usual. What was *not* usual was that they were walking hand in hand. The sight of that affectionate handclasp helped to drive despair out of Melissa's mind.

Mike knelt by her side. "Are you all right?" He glanced at the vomit, glistening in the light of the rising moon.

Melissa nodded. "I'm fine." Then, realizing the absurdity of the statement, she chuckled harshly. "Physically, at least."

Her eyes welled with tears. "Oh God, Mike, they thought I was going to have them *killed*." A moment later, her head tucked into his sheltering arm, she began babbling the tale. As she spoke, Rebecca knelt alongside her also, listening closely.

When Melissa was done, she took another deep breath. "You know, I'm finding myself in a strange place. Mentally, I mean. Never thought I'd be here."

She tightened her jaws. The next sentence came between clenched teeth. "The way I feel right now, I'd have every single man in that army—*both* armies—lined up against a wall and shot. *Tonight*."

Mike smiled, and stroked her hair. "Take it easy, lady. You're the worst person in the world to have to make a decision like that."

Melissa tried to stop herself from laughing. Couldn't—and then realized she didn't want to stop. The humor was cleansing. "God, isn't that the truth?" she demanded. "Nothing worse than a convert when it comes to self-righteousness."

Mike was grinning, now. "Lord save us!" The grin faded. He shook his head. "Melissa, I just talked to James. He spent the last two hours checking over those men. The Scots took the Protestant prisoners into Badenburg. We've got the Catholics under guard out in the fair-grounds."

He blew out his cheeks. "You want to know what he told me? He said those men reminded him of all the tough kids and wild young men he grew up with, that's all. He comes from the ghetto, Melissa. You don't. A man like James understands a lot better than you do how men like that get produced. Put anyone in the right circumstances—*wrong* circumstances—and you'll get the same result. Some of them are genuine monsters, and probably would have been anywhere. The rest? Most of them?" He shrugged. "Just men, that's all. Fucking up in a fucked-up world."

She giggled. People were always so careful not to use profanity around her—schoolteacher! from Boston!—that it was refreshing to hear it. The truth was, for all her prim-and-proper appearance, Melissa Mailey was very far from a prude.

Mention of James caused her thoughts to veer aside, for a moment. She stared into the darkness, bringing his face to her mind. And now, for the first time since she'd met the man, realized how much she liked that face.

Immensely. Those rough, hard, blunt features would have been ugly, perhaps, on a different man. But with James' intelligence and humor shining through, they simply seemed very masculine.

Her thoughts must have been closer to the surface than she real-ized. "James," she murmured. The sound had a certain—*considering* air.

She didn't notice the quick, half-amused glance which Mike and Rebecca exchanged. Rebecca cleared her throat.

"A very attractive man," she said softly.

"A widower," added Mike.

Melissa snorted. "Michael Stearns, there is something absolutely preposterous about you being a matchmaker for your former school-teacher."

Mike grinned. "True," he admitted. "So what? You could do worse than James Nichols, Ms. Mailey."

"I *have* done worse," said Melissa. "God, my husbands—"

She shook her head ruefully. Since Melissa's second marriage had failed—as quickly and disastrously as the first—she had restricted her romantic liaisons to occasional, and very brief, encounters. Always out of town. Usually with other schoolteachers she met at union conventions. Very distant, very casual, very—safe. She was fifty-seven years old, and the last such occasion had been—

Again, she was startled. *That long ago? Five years?*

Old, familiar, half-forgotten sensations began welling up. Very powerfully. Melissa did not even try to stop the smile from spreading across her face. Not at all.

Well, by God. Whaddaya know? Guess I'm not such a dried-up prune after all.

Her spirits were lifting rapidly, now, as these new thoughts drove horror into the shadows. "I'll have to look into that," she murmured. Then, chuckling: "I notice that you two seem to have stopped dancing around."

Rebecca might have flushed a little. It was hard to tell, between the darkness and her own dusky complexion. But when she spoke, her voice was level and even.

"Yes, we have." She hesitated. "I hope my father—"

"I wouldn't worry about that," interrupted Melissa. Using Mike's shoulder as a support, she levered herself back onto her feet. "I'm glad to see it, myself. And I don't think Balthazar will feel any differently."

Mike and Rebecca rose with her. Slowly, all three of them began walking toward the school's entrance. Before they got there, moved by an impulse, Melissa walked out onto the parking lot. She wanted to see something bright and clean. She felt like looking at the moon. Mike and Rebecca followed.

"It's still so weird," she said, "seeing it come up from that direction. The Ring of Fire twisted us around, on top of everything else."

Her eyes came down, and fell on the cafeteria's windows. Beyond, she could see Gretchen and her family. They had finished eating, and were now staring at the fluorescent lights on the ceiling. Ogling them, to be more precise. All of them were standing, to get a closer look at these new marvels.

All except Gretchen. She was standing also—she stood taller than any of them—but she was not looking at the lights. She was looking at Jeff, smiling.

"Twisted us around," Melissa murmured. She probed, again, looking for herself. The rage was almost gone, and she found what she was looking for immediately.

Relief came again, and with it a sudden and clear understanding. She knew what to do, now. Melissa Mailey was teacher, not an executioner. A builder, a guide. A person who showed the way out, not a censor who barred the door.

She extended her hands. They were very slender, long-fingered. Elegant hands, for all that the nails were trimmed short.

"What do you think, Mike? Do these look like the right hands to hold the sword of retribution? Lay down the law? Ban this, ban that?"

Mike snorted. "Not hardly." He took a deep breath. "Why don't you leave that to me, Melissa? If there's one advantage to being a former professional boxer, it's that I'll know when I can pull a punch." He glanced at her aristocratic hands. "You won't."

She dropped her hands. "I have come to the same conclusion." The words were final, definite. She took Mike and Rebecca by their arms and began leading them to the door. "Wisdom begins with knowing your limitations. I know mine. I know what I can do, and what I can't."

Mike suddenly slowed. Melissa glanced at him, then followed his eyes.

Gretchen was clearly visible through the window. She was scolding one of the children, shaking her finger. Apparently, the boy had started to climb onto one of the cafeteria's tables in order to get a closer look at the lighting. The celerity with which he climbed down was utterly comical. The imp obeying the goddess.

She looked like a Teutonic goddess, thought Melissa. Bathrobe be damned. Clean, her hair was blond. Dark blond, but definitely blond. The long tresses framed a face that fell just outside of beauty simply because the features were so strong. The finger was shaken by the large hand of a shapely but powerful arm, attached to a shapely and powerful shoulder. Everything about her was cut from that cloth. Her breasts, as large as they so obviously were under the thin bathrobe, looked as if they were held up by armor. Melissa, remembering Gretchen's naked body, knew that the rest of her matched what was visible.

"Who is *that*?" asked Rebecca. Her eyes widened. "Is that the woman—?"

Happily, Melissa nodded. "Yeah, that's her. You heard the story, I take it?"

Rebecca nodded. "Michael told me. The woman who hid her sisters in a cesspool—and then stood there, straight up, waiting for—" She shuddered. "I can hardly imagine such courage."

Mike stared at Gretchen through the window for a moment longer, before adding: "Jesus, what a *Valkyrie*."

Melissa shook her head. "No, Mike. You're very wrong." She scowled. "Valkyries!" The word was almost a curse. "Leave it to the sick and twisted mind of Richard Wagner to glorify a Valkyrie."

Again, she took her companions by the arm and began walking toward the door. "A Valkyrie is just a *vulture*. A death-worshipper. 'Choosers of the slain,' they were called, as if that were something to be proud of."

She stopped abruptly, almost yanking them up short. Her finger, extended, pointed to Gretchen.

"*That* young woman, on the other hand, is something truly grand and glorious. That woman is a *chooser of the living*."

She sighed. "I know what I can do, and what I can't. I know what we need, and what I can give. I can help. I can teach. I can guide, hopefully. But I can't *do* it." A little shrug lifted her slender shoulders. "Even if I wasn't too old, I couldn't do it. I don't come from that world, and even if I did—"

She twisted her head, looking to the north. Beyond the hills was a battlefield. Her next words came in a whisper. "I never would have been tough enough, or had the courage. I'm not a coward, but—not a chance. I would have died myself, much less been able to save anyone else."

Melissa smiled. The expression was one of unalloyed satisfaction—the smile of a person at peace with themselves. "What this new world of ours needs is not a superannuated sixties radical. Except, maybe, as an adviser. We're back at the beginning, where it all started. The days of the abolitionists and the Underground Railroad. Seneca Falls and the pioneer women."

Her smile became a grin. "Melissa Mailey will sure as hell lend a hand, but she's not what we really need. What we *really* need is a new Harriet Tubman."

She beamed at the woman in the window. "And I do believe I may have found her."

Gretchen was glancing at Jeff again. He was no longer shying away from those glances. Oh no. He was staring back at her like a lamb. Begging to be slaughtered. "Of course, *first* I've got to stop her from selling herself to another soldier in order to keep her kids alive. That'll hurt her image, starting off her new life as a camp whore. Again."

Now Melissa was *marching* them to the door. Her bare feet struck the pavement like boots.

Mike chuckled. "I can't wait to find out how you're planning to do that."

"What is Seneca Falls?" asked Rebecca. "And who was Harriet Tubman?"

By the time they reached the door, Melissa had begun her explanation. She only had time to broach the topic, before the meeting started. But her words were enough to get Mike chewing on the problem, and Rebecca. And that was enough. The two finest political minds of the day—which they were, though they did not realize it yet—would take that germ and transform it into something mighty and powerful.

So, in the time to come, Melissa Mailey would take great comfort in the memory of a pool of vomit. Out of that nausea would come something precious to her soul—and just as precious to the souls of thousands of others.

The Inquisition, of course, would feel otherwise. So would a multitude of barons and bishops, and every witch-hunter in Europe.

Chapter 24

Melissa's concerns for Gretchen's image proved to be moot. In the end, the solution to that quandary was provided by another.

It was only a partial solution, of course, as solutions usually are, and addressed only one specific problem, as solutions usually do. But, as was often also true, it opened the door—if only a crack—for the multitude of solutions to follow.

Melissa, in a way, played a role in that solution. Not directly, not immediately. But a genuine role nonetheless. The same role that teachers—good ones, anyway, and she was truly excellent—have always played. The same role, in a different way, that parents play. Parents, uncles, aunts, grandparents—even, when you get down to it, the guy at the corner grocery who, in an idle moment, tosses off his opinion of how the world oughta be to a youngster come in to buy a soda.

Good boys, like bad ones, are shaped. The process is not perfect, and goes astray often enough. The mold is crooked, often warped, cracked—but it's still a mold.

Grantville, West Virginia was the mold that produced Jeff Higgins. All things said and done, it was as good a mold as any and a better one than most.

Add to that the boy himself. Sitting alone, now, at the cafeteria table, staring at a window. There was nothing to see in the window. Night had fallen on the countryside beyond the glass.

The others were all gone. Melissa had ushered Gretchen and her family into the classroom which was being used, temporarily, as a refugee quarter. The floor was covered with mattresses and blankets donated by the town's inhabitants. She had shown Gretchen how to operate the toilets nearby, and then hurried to the council meeting.

Jeff's friends were gone too. They were not far away—not more than a few yards. They were in the school's library. The library, like much of the school, was open twenty-fours a day now. Such a valuable resource could not be kept out of circulation for a moment. They were in there, heads hunched together, studying one of the school's few copies of a German language textbook. They also had the school's only copy of a German-English dictionary.

Under any other circumstances, Jeff would have been there also. But tonight he had a much more pressing problem to deal with. A German herself, not the language. A decision was before him, and he knew that it had to be made quickly. Gretchen would wait, for a bit, to hear his decision. She would not wait long. She had people to care for, and nothing to care for them with. She did not have the luxury of waiting. So, at least, it would seem to her. In truth, she had entered a world in which old courses of action were not necessary— but Jeff knew that she would not believe it. Not yet. Not soon enough.

Jeff Higgins was very far from stupid. He was innocent, more or less, but not really naive. Certainly not *that* naive.

Like all teenage boys, he had his fantasies. Some of those he exorcised playing D&D, others with war games, others on computer screens, others living a vicarious life in books, others on his dirt bike. Still others—especially those involving the female sex—mostly in his mind. And a rich and sometimes feverish mind it was, too. Wildly imaginative, and ready at an instant to take flight from reality.

But he could still, quite easily, separate truth from fiction. For all the fantasies about Gretchen which had raged through his hormone-saturated brain in the few short hours since he first met her—*today*— he understood the reality.

Jeff was not a virgin. But his two brief encounters had not given him delusions of being irresistible. He knew perfectly well that no beautiful young woman was going to fall head over heels in love with him in an instant. If ever. True—here his fantasies tried to rise in rebellion—he had met her in quite a dramatic manner. Rescuing her, almost single-handedly, from the proverbial "fate worse than death." A classic from fairy tales!

But—

He knew Gretchen. Well enough, at least. For her, that fate was not worse than death. She had already suffered it, and survived. And kept her family alive. He thought she appreciated—sincerely—what he had done. But he understand also that the woman he had watched murder a wounded man in cold blood in order to protect her sister—*her*, not her "virtue," which would soon be gone anyway—was not going to be bowled over by another brave soldier.

He paused over that, in his thinking. He *had* been brave, he realized. If he looked at it from the right angle, he could even say he had been heroic. He paused, there, and took deep satisfaction in the knowing.

For himself, however, not for Gretchen—or what she thought of him. It was good to know that courage lay within him. Very good. Courage, in this new world even more than in the old, was something he was going to need.

But he knew, without knowing any of the details, that the man who had formerly "possessed" her was brave as well, whatever his other characteristics had been. Jeff was not one of those foolish sentimentalists who thinks that courage is a monopoly of the virtuous. Like many boys his age, he was an aficionado of military history. The Waffen SS had compiled a criminal record almost unparalleled in modern history. Yet no one in their right mind had ever called them cowards. Certainly not more than once.

Gretchen did not care about his courage on the battlefield. He knew that for a certainty. She was no fairy-tale maiden, to swoon over her rescuer. She was what many people would call a camp whore, who had done whatever she found necessary to keep herself and her family alive. And, he knew, was doing it still. His fantasies could rage and bellow at every glimpse of her flashing eyes, gleaming promise at him. His hormones could rush like Niagara, knowing that her luscious body was his for the taking. But it was all a lie.

Jeff knew the truth. As much as the sight of her exposed breast had fired his imagination, his reason had seen what was real. The breast was real enough, of course. Far more real had been the baby suckling at it. A camp whore's bastard, that the whore would trade her body to keep alive, just as she had butchered a man to do the same for her sister.

He faced the truth, squarely, and came to his decision. Peace poured through his soul.

He was surprised, at first, to see that the decision had already been made. Surprised, and then, obscurely pleased.

He had been pondering nothing, he realized. Simply rationalizing an argument that could not be argued at all. It was not rational in the first place. He was quite certain that everyone he knew would be explaining that to him within the next few hours.

He did not care. It was the only decision, under the circumstances, that *he* could make. Others could think what they wanted, say what they would. He was who he was. Accidentally, in that moment, without knowing he had even done so, Jeff adopted for his own an ancient motto. *Here I stand. I can do no other.*

Anymore than he could have stepped aside, on the first battlefield of his young life, and let the choosers of the slain pass by, flapping their carrion-eater wings.

Jeff Higgins, too, would be a chooser of the living.

The decision made, it remained to carry it out. That would be difficult, but not impossible. Not by any means. He would have help. He knew that just as certainly as he knew the rest. Gretchen would help him.

He rose and marched into the library. Well, padded in. His big feet, flapping nakedly, were no more romantic than the rest of his heavy, awkward, intellectual's body. No one would ever confuse Jeff Higgins for a figure of martial glamour.

When he reached the cluster of his friends, he asked for the dictionary. They handed it over. Their eyes were full of question, but he gave no explanation. They did not press him, for which he was thankful. They would be pressing him soon enough, crushing him under ridicule.

With the dictionary in hand, he walked down the long corridor to the room where Gretchen and her family were preparing to sleep. At the door, he raised his hand. Hesitated, but only for a second, before knocking. Gently, so as not to wake whomever might be asleep, but firmly.

He was relieved when Gretchen herself answered the door. He was even more relieved to see that the room beyond her shoulder was quiet and dark. Everyone in the crowded room must already be asleep. That was not surprising, of course, given all that those people had been through that day. But he was still vastly relieved. He had been afraid he would have to wait while Gretchen went about the task of caring for her folk. The wait would have been very hard.

From the look of her face, he thought he had probably awakened Gretchen herself. But, if so, she recovered at once. Again, her eyes and lips were shining with promise.

At his gesture, she stepped out of the room and closed the door behind her. Jeff looked up and down the corridor, before deciding that this was as good a place as any.

He sat down on the floor, legs sprawled out before him. Gretchen immediately took the same position, by his side, and nestled against him sinuously. Feeling her body so close, nothing between them but two bathrobes, and seeing the long stretch of bare legs exposed under the robe—*long* stretch; she had seen to that deliberately, he knew— Jeff felt giddy for a moment. The passion raging in him was almost overwhelming.

But not quite. He took a deep breath, smiled awkwardly at her, and opened the dictionary. Moving from one page to the next, he began spelling out his purpose.

When she realized what he was doing, Gretchen gave a little gasp. Her eyes, startled from the word in the dictionary, came to his. Her mouth opened, shaping a denial. Her head began to shake.

Jeff, seeing that reaction, beamed from ear to ear. He was smiling like a cherub. "Yes," he said. "I do."

She stared back at the dictionary. She seemed paralyzed. Jeff twisted, rising to his knees, and took her face between his hands. Brought her eyes up to meet his own. Light brown; light green. "Yes, I do," he repeated. *"Ja, ich muss."*

Then, of course, Gretchen began nodding. Nodding. Nodding and nodding. Nodding and nodding and nodding and now she was beginning to tremble and then the tears began to flow and then she was clutching Jeff so tightly he thought for a moment his ribs might crack. It didn't matter. He couldn't have breathed anyway, he was so relieved.

The nodding meant nothing to him. It would later, but not now. That first little headshake gave him the world. He had been prepared to live without it, but his heart was singing knowing that he had it.

Her first reaction, when she understood, was the key. That instant denial, that unthinking shake of the head. *You don't have to do this!*

"Yes, I do," he whispered into her hair, cradling her. "Ja, ich muss." He could *feel*, now, the years of terror which caused the strong body in his arms to tremble like a leaf. Terror held under such tight control for so long that now, when it was finally breaking loose, the one who held it had no idea how to let it go. For all the tenderness of the moment, some part of Jeff wanted to shake her more violently still, just to hasten its departure. *It's over. It's over. I promise.*

An uncalculating denial, a little shake of the head. That was all he would need to keep him steady, in the hard years to come. It would not be easy for them. He was old enough to understand that much. But at least he could face those years without suspicion. A woman who had lived with no choices at all had still had the courage, at the end, to hold out one for him.

He had been trapped, snared, caught. But not tricked. The lamb was fair and truly slaughtered. But he could never claim, thereafter, that his executioner had not shown him the blade before he came, willingly, to the altar.

Chapter 25

Ed Piazza underlined the last word on the blackboard, with all the flourish of a former teacher, and marched back to the table. "That's it," he said. "That's the bottom line. Ten thousand people. Able-bodied and able to work. *Over and above*, you understand, the folks we've already got."

He clasped his hands on the table. "Some of them can include healthy old people and big enough kids. There's a few thousand jobs that don't require any kind of heavy labor. But most of it does. Especially the farming and construction work."

Mike leaned back in his chair and clasped his own hands behind his head. He studied the figures on the blackboard for a few seconds before speaking. "And if we don't get them?"

Quentin Underwood shrugged. The mine manager had been part of the team which, led by Piazza, had developed the production plan. "Then we have to change the equation the other way, Mike. *Subtraction.*"

"Driving people off, in other words," said Mike. "Push the extra mouths back into the furnace." There was no heat in the words, just clarification.

Quentin and Ed both looked uncomfortable. So did Willie Ray Hudson and Nat Davis, the other two members of the planning team.

Nat cleared his throat. "Well, I don't know as I'd put it that way."

"Cut it out, Nat," growled Quentin. "Mike's putting it bluntly, but that's exactly what we're talking about."

He sat up straight, half glaring. "I don't like it any better than you do, Mike. But that's the way it is. It's just an estimate, of course, but I think it's pretty damn close. We need ten thousand workers in order to build the infrastructure that'll keep everybody in this area alive through the winter. Food production and shelter are the big jobs. Even if we meet this schedule, winter is going to be a pure bitch. Pardon my language."

Mike lifted his hands off his head and made a little waving motion. "I'm not criticizing anybody," he said mildly. "I just want to make sure we're all on the same wavelength." He pursed his lips. "Does this include the labor force in Badenburg?"

Piazza shook his head. "Badenburg's not included on either side of the equation, Mike. We're just figuring the people already in town and our best estimate of all the refugees camped out in the area. A fair number of them are drifting in, now. All the churches are already packed to the gills. So's the community center next to the fairgrounds."

Dreeson, the town's mayor, looked alarmed. "That fast? What's that doing to our sanitation program?"

"Straining the hell of it," replied Ferrara bluntly. The science teacher leaned forward. "And that was true even *before* we got all these new-comers. The prisoners and the people from the soldiers' camp."

Dreeson was looking very alarmed, now. Bill Porter interrupted before the explosion came. "Relax, Henry! The refugee center by the power plant will be operational in eighteen hours. We've got a sanitation system up there that has way more capacity than anything in the town itself. We can cycle hundreds of people an hour through it, easily."

Melissa snorted. "And how are you going to get them through it, Bill? With cattle prods? You *did* notice that I was wearing a bathrobe earlier, didn't you? Is that the way you think I normally prance around in public?"

Porter shrank a little from the same piercing stare that had abashed teenagers over the years. Melissa relented, after a few seconds. "Folks, I just learned from bitter experience that these people coming in are so—so *traumatized*—that the only way I got them through the showers was to lead the way personally. Even then—"

She broke off, shuddering a little.

Mike took his hands from his head and set them on the table, palms down. The gesture had an air of authority about it.

"Okay, then. I've been trying to make a decision anyway, and it just got made. We're going to lean on the soldiers. The prisoners, I mean. We don't have any choice."

Ed cocked his head. "Lean on them?"

"*Rely* on them. There are well over a thousand able-bodied men in that crowd. When the wounded recover—those of them who do—that'll add maybe a couple of hundred more. That's the start of our labor force. We'll run them through the sanitation process at the power plant as soon as it's open for business."

The squawks started immediately.

"That's forced labor!" protested Melissa. "How are you going to get them through the showers?" demanded Underwood. "What about resistance?" queried Ferrara.

Mike scowled. "Melissa, give me a break! I've been a union man all my life, so I'd appreciate not getting any lectures about forced labor. Those guys aren't downtrodden workers. They're prisoners of war captured after launching an unprovoked attack on us. I'm not proposing to work them to death, for Christ's sake. But they *will* work."

He turned to Underwood, still scowling. "How? Simple. 'Take a shower or a bullet. Delouse your hair or we'll delouse your guts.' How's that for motivation?"

Melissa started to screech, but Mike slammed his hand on the table. The flat palm sounded like a rocket. "Melissa—*cut it out!*" His scowl was purely ferocious. "These aren't traumatized *women and children*, goddamit. These are the guys who did the traumatizing! Frankly, I don't care if they drop dead from fear. They *will* be sanitized, and they *will* work."

The scowl moved on to Ferrara. "What was that? Something about resistance?"

Ferrara smiled. "Ah—never mind. I think it's a moot point."

Melissa's mouth was still open, ready to speak. Her eyes were slits, her shoulders tense. She'd faced down bullies before, by God! Southern sheriffs and D.C. police and company goons. *If Mike Stearns thinks he can intimidate me . . . !*

Suddenly, she puffed out her cheeks. For a moment, she looked like a slender, elegant, sophisticated blowfish. Then, with a rush, blew out the air.

"Okay," she said.

Mike eyed her with suspicion. "What is this? Since when do you give up so quick? I was expecting you to throw up a picket line next."

Melissa grinned. "Well . . . Don't think I'm not tempted." The grin faded. Her face grew a little weary. "I don't like it, Mike. Not one bit. But I imagine you don't either. And—well, you're right, much as I hate to admit it. The alternative is just to drive them and their camp followers out."

Underwood cleared his throat. "Excuse me, folks, but I've got to say here that I think we *should* consider that alternative." Hastily: "Well, the soldiers anyway."

Frank Jackson started to speak but there came a knock at the door. Ed got up and went to open it. When he saw who was standing there, his eyebrows lifted in surprise.

Jeff Higgins. Flanked by his three friends, Larry Wild, Jimmy Anderson and Eddie Cantrell. All of their faces bore the same expressions. An equal mix of stubborn determination and deep apprehension.

"What's up, boys?" Ed asked. "We're in a meeting, you know."

Jeff took a deep breath and spoke.

"Yeah, Mr. Piazza, we know and I'm sorry to barge in like this but I thought—well, me and my buddies talked it over after I talked it over with them and"—a look of surprise and relief washed quickly across his face—"since they backed me up even though I thought they were gonna give me a hard time about it we talked it over and after we did we all agreed that I should come here first—they said they'd back me up—and tell you about it first on account of there's probably going to be all hell to pay—pardon my language, Ms. Mailey—so we might as well get it over with right away. So there it is."

He braced himself, obviously expecting some sort of onslaught.

Ed frowned, and turned his head to face the adults in the room. They responded with frowns of their own. In the doorway and the corridor beyond, four teenage boys braced themselves.

Ed shook his head. "Jeff, uh—what's this about, exactly?"

Jeff's eyes widened. "Oh. Yeah. Sorry." He took another deep breath and launched. "Well, it's like this and we've already agreed—both of us—and it's over and settled and done with and nobody can do anything about it because I'm legal age and my parents aren't around anyway and neither are hers either. So there it is."

The boys braced themselves.

Silence. Frowns.

Suddenly, Melissa started laughing.

"Oh, Lord!" She bestowed a look of sheer approval upon Jeff. "Young man, I want you to know that I've never inflated a grade in my life, but you are *guaranteed* an A in any class of mine you ever take."

Jeff frowned. "I'm about to graduate, Ms. Mailey."

"Silly! *Adult* education. Instruction in German, if nothing else. I've already started learning the language so I can help teach it."

She beamed at Jeff. "Had to use a dictionary, didn't you?"

He looked sheepish. "Well. Yeah."

Ed exploded. "What's this all about?" he demanded, throwing up his hands.

"Isn't it obvious?" Melissa pointed a finger at Jeff, wiggling it a bit. "He just proposed to Gretchen and she accepted." Grinning: "So. When's the wedding?"

All hell broke loose.

Chapter 26

"Yeah, Mr. Dreeson, I know she's only marrying me on account of she needs it to take care of her folks. So what? I've seen people get married for lots worse reasons."

"Yeah, Mr. Piazza, I know I only just met her and we hardly know each other. So what? The way I figure it, we'll have years together anyway with nothing else to do."

"Yeah, Mr. Ferrara, I know we'll probably just wind up getting divorced anyway. So what? Some of you folks have been divorced, haven't you?"

A moment's pause in the ruckus. Not much. Just a little stutter before the voices of adult wisdom plowed on.

"Yeah, Mr. Underwood, I know she's dirt poor and she's just marrying me for my money but that's a laugh because I don't have any worth talking about anyway. So what if I lose it? She's welcome to it."

"Yeah, Mr. Hudson, I know she's a knockout and that's probably at least half the reason I'm dumb enough to marry her. So what? I don't see where that's much different from lots of the other marriages I've seen in this town." Unkindly: "At least my girl *is* a knockout."

Driven off by the armor of youthful folly, adult wisdom turned on the eccentricities of maturity.

"*Melissa!*" roared Dreeson. "*Will* you please stop encouraging this child with your—what *are* you doing, anyway?"

Melissa paused in her awkward gesturing. "Give me a break. I know I'm not good at it. I was *much* too refined to be a cheerleader in high school. Got to ask Julie Sims to give me some pointers." She rose from her seat and took a dramatic pose, as if holding pom-poms. "*Two! Four! Six! Eight! What do we appreciate? Matrimony! Matrimony!*"

By now, James Nichols was laughing gaily. Mike, standing by the window staring out into the darkness, was grinning. So was Rebecca, sitting on her chair.

Frank Jackson, on the other hand, was glaring. Not at Jeff, however.

"All of you just *shut up*," he snarled. The genuine anger in his voice brought silence to the room. Startled, everyone except Mike stared at him. James stopped laughing and Melissa stopped gesturing.

When Frank continued, his voice was a low growl. " 'She's not good enough for you,' " he mimicked. " 'She only wants American citizenship.' 'She's too different.' 'It won't work.' " Snarling: "Jesus!"

He fixed Underwood with a cold gaze. Underwood had been the most vociferous—and crude—in his opposition to Jeff's announcement. "Let me ask you something, Quentin. Just where in the hell do you think I met Diane, anyway?"

Sarcastically: "You do know who I'm talking about, right?" He held up his hand, palm down, less than five feet from the floor. "Little-bitty woman, 'bout so tall. You may have seen her around town now and then. Woman I been married to for, what is it now, thirty years? Mother of my three kids." His anger faded, for just an instant, replaced by sorrow. Frank and Diane's three sons were all adults, and had moved out of town. The Ring of Fire had left them behind.

The anger returned, along with a half-sneer. "Yeah, Quentin, I'm curious. Did you think I met her at a gala reception at the embassy? Me in my swank uniform and her wearing a slinky evening gown imported from Paris? Did you think she was some kind of Vietnamese princess?"

Underwood looked away. "It's none of my business, Frank," he said, uncomfortably. "I never asked. Nobody knows, I don't think."

Frank snorted. He glanced at Mike. "He knows. A few others." Frank was in one of his very rare tempers. He leaned forward, clenching his fists on the table. "Well, I'll tell you what. I'm going to *make* it your business. I met Diane at—"

"*Frank!*" Mike's voice was not loud, just insistent. He turned away from the window and walked back to the table. He put a hand on his friend's shoulder. "Leave it alone. There's no need for this."

He looked at Jeff, still standing in the doorway. "If it's worth anything to you, Jeff, I think you're probably the smartest person in town at this particular moment. You already figured out something the rest of us are trying to catch up with. Except maybe Melissa."

His eyes fell on another figure. Softly: "Or Rebecca."

Startled, Rebecca's eyes widened. Mike smiled. "*Especially* Rebecca, I think. Why don't you explain it to them?"

Rebecca hesitated. She asked questions at these meetings, but, so far, had rarely offered an opinion. Mike's warm eyes—loving eyes—emboldened her.

"I am not sure, Michael. But I shall try."

She turned her gaze to the other people sitting at the table. "You have a choice here." She took a little breath, and closed a final gap. "*We* have a choice here. We can take one of two roads. Jeff's road—as 'foolish' and 'impetuous' as it may be—or a different road. Jeff's road leads to a country very much like the one I believe you once had." Sadly: "Like the dream my people once called Sepharad. The other—"

Her voice grew harsh and cold. That tone, coming from soft Rebecca, was quite shocking. "The other leads to a military aristocracy. A land of hidalgos and inquisitors. So-called 'pure-blood' Americans—*limpieza*—ruling over a horde of German peons."

She gestured with her head toward the window. "What are those people out there going to be for us? Those dirty, diseased, desperate people out there in the camps and the woods. Fellow citizens, neighbors, friends—*wives and husbands*? Or are they going to be serfs, servants, lackeys—*concubines*? That is the choice."

Underwood was ogling her. "What? You aren't—" His eyes were very wide.

Melissa's laugh was sarcastic. "Oh, for the sake of Christ, Quentin! *Of course* she's not proposing that we *require* anybody to get married. Grow up!" An impish gleam came to her eyes. "Although, now that I think about it—Alexander the Great did, you know? Made his Macedonian officers all marry Persian girls. Hmmm."

Mike chuckled. "Stop feeding the tourists, Melissa."

Quentin's eyes were still wide. Mike shook his head. "The *point*, Quentin, is not what this or that individual decides to do, but what stance we take toward whatever decision somebody does make. People can think or say or do whatever they want. That's not the same thing as what a society *sanctions*." He pointed at Jeff. "For the first time, an American young man is going to be marrying a German young woman. So what's it gonna be, 'Fathers of the Nation'? Is it going to be sanctioned, or not? Are you going to handle it publicly the way you'd handle any other wedding, regardless of your personal reservations? Or are you going to tell the world what an idiot he is and how the German girl's a worthless gold digger? *Scum*—not good enough for American blood?"

All the humor faded from his eyes. *"What's it going to be?"*

Willie Ray Hudson expelled the breath from his chest. "Aw hell, Mike. Since you put it that way." The old farmer leaned back in his chair and cocked his head at Jeff. "This girl of yours? Has she got a father to walk her down the aisle?"

Jeff's face fell. "I'm not sure, Mr. Hudson. But I don't—I don't think so. If I understood something she said, I think her dad was murdered a couple of years ago."

Hudson winced. "Jesus," he muttered, "I don't even want to think what that poor girl's been through."

"No, you don't," said Melissa forcefully. "Trust me on this one, Willie Ray. *You don't.*"

Hudson rose and walked over to Jeff. "Well, then. Jeff, you tell this girl of yours that—if she wants—I'd be more than happy to take her father's place at the wedding."

Jeff's face was suddenly eager. "Would you, Mr. Hudson? Everybody in town's known you their whole lives. Oh, that'd be great! I'll have to ask Gretchen, of course." He looked back at Larry. "You still got the dictionary?" Larry held it up.

The laughter in the room drew Jeff's eyes. "What's so funny?" The laughter got louder.

"This has *got* to be a record," chuckled Ferrara. "Meet a girl and propose in one day, maybe. But using a *dictionary*?"

Jeff flushed. Willie Ray patted him on the shoulder. "Ignore that lout, boy. I'm sure it's not a *record*. Just a contender."

That didn't seem to help, judging from the color of Jeff's cheeks.

"Ignore that lout, too," pronounced Melissa. She held up her wrist and examined the clock. "All right, that's enough. It's almost ten thirty. Let's not get crazy. We *did* fight a battle today, remember?" She gave James a serene glance. "And poor Dr. Nichols here has to be back at the hospital early in the morning."

"Real early," agreed Nichols. "Adams agreed to handle the cases tonight, but I've got to spell him first thing. We've got dozens of badly wounded men on top of everything else."

Mike nodded. "Yeah, I agree. Besides—" He looked over at Jeff. "Are you staying here tonight?"

Hesitantly, Jeff eyed Ed Piazza. "Well, if the principal doesn't mind." Jeff waved at his friends. "We decided we'd all like to camp out here. On the library floor, I guess. Gretchen and the others are asleep now, but they'll be waking up early and—and—" He stood a little straighter. "We're going to be their new family, now— all of us, since Larry and Ed and Jimmy live with me and they'll be I guess kinda like uncles or something—so we thought we should be here when they wake up. Just because—" He groped for words.

"Absolutely," agreed Piazza. He dug into his pocket and came up with a set of keys. Quickly, he began removing one from the key ring. "But don't use the library. There'll be people in there all night. Besides, my office has a carpet. You might actually get some sleep. Just try to be out of there before Len Trout comes in so he doesn't trip over you. He'll be groggy like he always is in the morning. Low blood sugar, you know. Makes him a little grumpy until he's had his coffee and you'll be right in front of the coffee machine."

Looking a bit alarmed, Jeff took the key. It was universally known by the high school's students that you did *not* want to arouse the vice-principal's ire before he'd had his dose of three cups of coffee, laden with sugar and cream. *Not.*

He and his friends sped on their way. Early to bed, early to rise.

When they were gone, Quentin Underwood heaved a great sigh. "Oh, hell. I still think the kid's crazy, but you know what? After this nightmare we've been plunged into, I swear I can't think of a single thing that'd be better for my soul than to watch a young woman walk down the aisle in a wedding dress."

Dreeson nodded. "Goes for me too. The whole damn town, for that matter."

His eyes widened.

Mike laughed. "I'm way ahead of you, Henry. If we can talk Jeff out of getting married as fast as possible—which won't be all that easy, let me tell you, 'cause I've actually *seen* the girl—then I'd like to hold the wedding four days from now."

Melissa looked startled. "Four days from now?" Her eyes fled to the wall. "What calendar are we using, anyway? Here in the seventeenth—"

"Don't care!" proclaimed Dreeson. "As far as I'm concerned"—he clapped his hands—"four days from now is *the Fourth of July!*"

Mike grinned. "Yeah, sure is. Just what we need. A celebration, parade, fireworks—and we'll cap it off with the biggest wedding this town ever saw."

Quietly: "It'll remind us what we're all about." He gave Rebecca a very warm smile. "And *not* about."

The meeting broke up then. As Melissa was walking down the corridor to the school entrance, she heard quick footsteps behind her. Turning, she saw that James Nichols was hurrying to catch up with her.

When he arrived, the doctor broke into a smile. "May I walk you home?" he asked.

Melissa grinned. "Shameless!" she exclaimed.

Nichols was startled. "Me? I was just—"

Melissa shook her head and took James by the arm. "Not you, doctor. I would be most delighted to have you walk me home." As they made their way down the corridor, she chuckled. "I was referring to a certain former student of mine. Prizefighter turned matchmaker. Shameless."

Nichols looked a bit embarrassed. "Oh." They walked on a little further. He cleared his throat. "Actually, it was Rebecca who gave me the elbow. Not"—a big smile, here—"that I hadn't been thinking about it."

Melissa turned her head and studied him. His smile, rather. She liked that smile. Immensely. It was a cheerful, happy, relaxed smile. The smile of a very grown-up man, well into middle age. He was fifty-five years old, she knew, only two years younger than she. Secure in himself, knowing himself well, and glad to be in that place. But also delighted to discover that he wasn't, apparently, all that old after all. As delighted as she was.

They were both smiling now. Both enjoying the relaxation of their age. Knowledge, certainty. Fumbling in the back seat was ancient history. Aches and pains of the body had come, but at least *guessing* was behind them.

Once they left the school and started walking down the parking lot toward the road below, James' arm slid around Melissa's waist. Gently, easily, he pressed her to his side. She leaned into him, covering his hand with her own. Her palm felt the wedding band on his finger.

Melissa knew that James was a widower, his wife dead in an auto crash, but she knew none of the details.

"How long ago—"

Apparently, he could read her mind. "Long enough," was his answer. "I grieved, Melissa. Long and hard. I loved her dearly. But it's been long enough."

As they approached the Roths' house—the Roth and Abrabanel house, now, since the arrangement had by mutual agreement become permanent—Rebecca turned and leaned into Mike. He folded her into his arms and they began kissing.

Five minutes later, more or less, they separated. Not far. Maybe half an inch.

"I must speak to your father," Mike said softly.

Rebecca nodded, her head against his chest. "How do you want to do this, Michael?" she whispered.

"Your father?"

She shook her head. "No, no, not that." She smiled, still against his chest. "I do not think, now, that will be the problem I once assumed. I am not certain, but after what Melissa said—"

She nuzzled his shoulder. "He has been reading this philosopher named Spinoza, lately. He smiles a lot. At me, especially. And now and then I see him smiling at you. As if he knows something we do not."

Mike chuckled. "He probably does, at that."

Rebecca leaned back and looked Mike in the eyes. "I will do whatever you wish," she said softly.

Mike studied her in the moonlight. Her eyes were like dark pools, soft, limpid, loving.

"You would prefer it slowly," he said. The statement was a simple declaration.

Rebecca hesitated. Then, ruefully: "Not entirely!" Her hands were suddenly pressing into his ribs, kneading, almost probing. Mike felt the passion flashing from her fingers down to his heels, back to his skull, down his spine. He swayed giddily, and pressed her close.

"Not entirely!" She laughed, turning her face eagerly to meet his. Five minutes more elapsed.

When they broke away—maybe an inch—she was smiling warmly. "But—*yes*. If you don't mind. I am still—" She hesitated, fumbling for the words.

Mike provided them for her. "You are in a new world, and pushing yourself as hard as possible to grow into it. You would like time, to fill every room properly, before you move into the house."

"Yes!" she said. "Oh, yes. That is exactly it, Michael." She stared up at him. "I love you so," she whispered. "Believe me that I do."

Mike kissed her forehead. "All right, then. That's how we'll do it." For a moment, feeling her shoulders under his hands, he almost hissed. *Desire*.

Then, laughing softly. "What the hell? My grandpa always used to say we youngsters didn't know what we were missing. *Anticipation*, he'd say. 'By the time you little twerps get married, you're already bored with sex.'"

Rebecca giggled. *How easily they talk and joke about this!*

Mike stepped back. Two inches, maybe three. "All right, then," he repeated. "We'll get engaged. A long engagement, just like in the old days. As long as you want, Rebecca Abrabanel."

He stepped back another few inches, slowly and reluctantly, but firmly for all that. "I will speak to your father tomorrow." Then, he was walking away.

Standing on the porch, Rebecca watched him recede until, with a last turn of the head and wave of the hand, he rounded the corner. Her head was straight, her hands clasped together, fingers pressed to her lips. Simply savoring the passion which flowed up and down through her body, like a surging tide.

Not so long as all that, Michael! Oh, I love you so. Oh, I want you so.

Chapter 27

Gretchen awoke in a panic. Disoriented in time, confused in space—but, mostly, petrified by a memory.

Her eyes sped to the door. Closed. For a moment, she was relieved. There was nothing in the door to say that her memory was false. She remembered closing that door, on a smiling face.

Still—

She sat up. Her eyes scanned the room. That act of long-practiced vigilance brought back a measure of calm. Her family was piled all over the floor, clustered in little heaps, arms and legs entwined in sleep. The automatic snuggling of people for whom winter was a familiar assassin. Even in midsummer, the feel of another body—*warm, warm*—brought a primordial sense of safety.

Smiling, Gretchen looked down. Her own baby was cradled in her arm. Wilhelm was still fast asleep. To her left, Annalise pressed herself against Gretchen's hip, reacting to the sudden absence of a shoulder. To her right, Gramma did the same. Muttering, now half-awake with the light hold on sleep of the elderly.

Gretchen's eyes went back to the door. The memory poured back in, demanding, insistent.

I must know!

As gently as possible, she disentangled herself from the others. Gramma awoke fully, then. The old woman was obviously confused and disoriented by their surroundings. Gretchen handed Wilhelm to her. Automatically, Gramma took the baby. The familiar act brought reassurance.

Gretchen arose and stepped to the door. She could hear the faint sound of voices coming from the corridor beyond. No words, just voices. She hesitated.

I must know. Firmly, decisively—almost frantically—she opened the door.

There were four young men there. Sitting easily, their backs leaning against the opposite wall of the corridor, legs stretched out before them. They had obviously been engaged in cheerful but quiet conversation.

The suddenness with which Gretchen opened the door startled them. Four faces jerked toward her.

She saw only the face in the middle. Smiling, now; beaming, now; rising to his feet; coming toward her—so eagerly—smiling, smiling. Green eyes like spring itself. Life, enlarged by spectacles.

Gretchen almost collapsed from relief. Shakily, she leaned against the doorframe, clutching it with a hand. A moment later, she was enfolded in his arms.

Safe.

She had noticed, without wondering at the reason, that one of Jeff's friends had hurried down the corridor as soon as she appeared from her room. A minute or two later, he returned. With him came several older people.

Two of them, Gretchen recognized—the duchess and the war leader. To her relief, they were both smiling broadly. Gretchen had been half certain that the powerful figures in Jeff's world would ban his marriage to such a one as she. Then, seeing the face of the young woman who accompanied them, her jaw almost dropped.

She had never seen one before—they had all been banned from her town long ago—but she had no doubt at all.

A court Jew—here?

That the woman was Jewish, Gretchen was certain. Her features, her skin tone, her long black hair—so curly!—fit the descriptions she had heard. And men always said Jewesses were beautiful, which she most certainly was.

That she was a court Jew, Gretchen was not so certain. She knew very little about noblemen, and princes and kings, and the life of their courts. But who else would have such poise?

Gretchen brought her surprised reaction under control immediately. She had no personal animus against Jews, and she had no desire to offend the woman. Leaving aside whatever influence the Jewess might have in the American court in her own right, Gretchen was quite certain from little subtleties in body language that the Jewess was the war leader's concubine.

The duchess arrived first, arms spread wide in greeting, and Gretchen lost her self-composure again. The duchess was *hugging* her!

Gretchen couldn't understand most of what the duchess was saying. She recognized many of the words, but the sense of them was simply gibberish.

"—get you some—*garble*—first thing! Can't have you—*garble*—laugh—in a robe! Then—*garble*—help us. *Garble*—need good men but—*garble*—wheat from the—*garble* (chaff?)."

The Jewess began to speak, translating the duchess' words. Her German was excellent. The accent was a bit odd—Dutch? Spanish?—and the intonation far more cultured than anything Gretchen was accustomed to, but she understood perfectly.

The words themselves, at least. The content of the words was insane.

Everything that happened that day was insane. And the next day, and the next. Gretchen obeyed, of course. She had no choice in any event, and the constant presence of Jeff kept her reassured. True, her husband to be was every bit as crazed as the other Americans, but Gretchen was learning to trust those green eyes. Very much.

By the fourth day, the day of her wedding, Gretchen would be reconciled to her new reality. And why not? There were worse things in the world than losing your mind and going to heaven. Much worse.

Chapter 28

Gretchen surveyed the scene in the large new building which the Americans had constructed next to what they called the "power plant." Part of her found it hard not to laugh. The crowd of mercenary soldiers packing the room looked absolutely miserable. Some of that misery was due to their wet condition. The Americans had obviously put them through the same cleansing process which Gretchen and her family had experienced. But she suspected they had been much more abrupt about it than the duchess.

And that, of course, was the major cause of their misery. Men— soldiers especially—wearing nothing but towels wrapped around their waists do not enjoy the sight of other soldiers holding weapons. Especially not those ferocious American guns with their bizarre mechanism for rapid fire. Pump-action shotguns, they were called. A few of the mercenaries had seen the weapons in action on the battlefield, and had quickly spread the word.

So they stood there, silent and unmoving. Shivering more from fear than the wetness.

Gretchen spotted a familiar face almost at once. Her amusement vanished, replaced by pleasure.

So he survived again! "Heinrich!" she called out, and plunged into the mob. "Heinrich—look! It's me—Gretchen!"

Watching her come toward him, Heinrich's jaw dropped. Gretchen grinned. She was not surprised by the reaction. Heinrich had seen her many times. But never so clean, and never wearing such clothing. Gretchen had just obtained them that morning, when the duchess took her entire family into something called the *Value Market*. The blouse was a bit odd, but not completely outlandish. But the rest!

It had taken Gretchen not more than two hours to make a

transition which, completely unknown to her, another world had already made in another universe. She *loved* her new clothing, especially the "blue jeans" and—marvel of marvels!—the *sneakers.*

And so, bouncing gleefully on magic feet, Gretchen approached the man who might have once become her own. Kind Heinrich, gentle Heinrich, canny and cunning Heinrich. Tough Heinrich, too. But not, alas, tough enough to dare challenge Ludwig.

Melissa gasped. "Is she crazy? We've got no way to protect her in that mob of thugs!"

Next to her, James shook his head. "Protect her? From what?" He pointed to the men beginning to cluster around Gretchen. Smiling men. *Relieved* men. "Look at them, Melissa. Do those look like thugs? Or—" He snorted. "Like kids running to their momma."

Melissa stared. The crowd around Gretchen was swelling rapidly. The young German woman was becoming the focal point of the entire room. Gretchen and the men around her were now engaging in a rapid verbal exchange. Melissa couldn't understand any of the words, but within seconds she grasped the essence. Much of it was questioning, of course. Frightened and confused men seeking explanations, reasons, bearings. *What is happening to us?* But then, more and more often, she caught the underlying banter.

"It's like you said," murmured Mike. "A natural born 'chooser of the living.'"

The first one she chose was Heinrich. Heinrich, and the twenty or so men who followed him. All of them had survived the battle. Completely uninjured, amazingly enough. Heinrich's group, like Ludwig's, had been in the front line. But they were arquebusiers, not pikemen. By good luck, they had been among the Catholic mercenaries ordered to attack Hoffman's men. They had not faced the M-60. And the ensuing enfilade rifle fire had struck the men on the opposite flank of their separate contingent.

Gretchen would have chosen Heinrich and his men first, under any circumstances. The fact that he spoke excellent English was simply an added bonus.

She introduced them to Frank Jackson personally. Then, allowed Heinrich to speak for himself. Ten minutes later, Jackson nodded and extended his hand.

The American army had just gained its first German recruits.

And so the day went. And the next, and the next. On the first day, the Americans were tense. On the second, watching the relief and joy with which the German camp followers who were now packing the area greeted the men who emerged from Gretchen's "choosing," they were beginning to relax. By the third day—

"Jesus," said Mike, wiping his face. "I don't know how much more of this I can take." He tried to block the sounds from his mind.

Grimly, the doctor surveyed the scene. Knots of women, children, old folks. Squatting on the ground outside the power plant, trying to cope with the news. These were the people who had come looking for men who were not to be found elsewhere. Hoping against hope that they might still be prisoners instead of battlefield casualties, and finding out otherwise.

"Yeah," agreed Nichols. "It's easy enough to kill a man. Something else again to listen to their families afterward."

Mike's eyes fell on a young boy, perhaps eight years old. The face was tear-streaked. Numb. *Daddy has gone away forever.*

Mike looked away. "How many are left?" he asked, nodding toward the new building attached to the power plant. The "processing center," as everyone was now calling it.

The third man in their party, Dan Frost, gave the answer. "Not that many. A lot fewer than I'd imagined, to tell you the truth."

"I'm not surprised, Dan," said Mike. "Not any longer. From what Rebecca and Jeff have told me, Gretchen and her people had the bad luck to fall into the hands of the worst types among the mercenaries. Most of them—"

James interrupted, pointing to a clot of people moving down the road, following a newly appointed American guide. At the center, still wearing nothing but a towel, was a man in his early thirties. "Most of them are like those." He smiled, cocking his head at Mike. "What did Melissa say you called it? 'Just men, that's all. Fucking up in a fucked-up world.'"

Mike nodded. "I'd say there won't be more than a hundred rejects left, in the end. Gretchen's being one hell of lot more charitable than I probably would have been."

"Are any of *their* women and children likely to complain?" asked Dan.

Mike and James sneered simultaneously. "Not hardly!" snorted Mike. He nodded toward the small crowd of miserable people squatting outside the processing center. "Those people are weeping for the dead, Dan. The ones who"—angrily—" 'belonged' to the *scum* still inside have already left. Practically dancing, once they got the news."

Nichols ran his fingers through his hair. "I saw one woman come up to Gretchen and ask her something. The whereabouts of her so-called 'man,' I'm pretty sure. The name Diego was mentioned. When she heard what Gretchen had to say, she just collapsed. Crying like a baby. She kept repeating two words, over and over."

His face was grim. "I don't know much German, but I know that much. *Thank God, thank God.*"

There was silence for a moment. Then the police chief cleared his throat.

"All right, guys. We've got to come to a decision here. I saw the body myself, before we buried it. Doc Adams was right. The man probably would have died anyway, but the fatal wounds weren't caused by gunfire. He was knifed. As neat a butchering job as you could ask for, too."

Mike glanced at him. "You know what my opinion is, Dan. Are you comfortable with it?"

Frost scowled. "Hell no! *Comfortable?* I'm a law-enforcement officer, for Christ's sake. I've got evidence suggesting first-degree murder and several witnesses placing two known people at the scene of the crime. And you wanna know if I'm *comfortable?*"

Mike said nothing. James, after looking away for a moment, asked: "Have you spoken with Jeff about it?"

The police chief was still scowling. "No," he said forcefully. "And I've got no intention of speaking to him, either. Not unless we decide to press charges."

Mike said nothing. James looked away again. Then, turning back: "Melissa told me that Gretchen had her younger sister all wrapped up in cloths. Keeping her figure hidden."

Dan spit on the ground. "Dammit, James, that's not the point! I don't have any doubt at all about what happened. Or why." He rubbed the back of his neck. "It's just the principle of the thing, that's all."

A little humor crept into his voice. "Truth is, any jury in this town would return a 'justifiable homicide' verdict in a heartbeat. Especially after I described the so-called victim. I swear, the guy looked so much like a devil I almost shot him two or three times myself, just to be sure he was dead."

Dan sighed. "But who needs a trial, when you get right down to it? Be great, wouldn't it? Do I arrest them right after the wedding tomorrow, or do I wait a day so the kids can get laid?"

Mike said nothing. James looked away. Silence.

The police chief's decision was inevitable. "The hell with it. If the principle bothers me too much, I can always remind myself that it happened out of my jurisdiction."

Mike nodded.

"Okay," said James. "There'll be rumors, of course. Adams is a very good doctor, but he's on the talkative side. By now, must be at least a half dozen people besides us who know the story."

Mike and Dan grinned simultaneously.

"Hell, yes, there'll be stories!" chortled the police chief. His eyes surveyed the surrounding hills admiringly. "We're mountain people, Doc. Always had stories. The more grisly the better. Ain't a man or woman around here who can't trot out their brag about some desperado in the family tree."

"My great-grandfather was a bank robber," bragged Mike. "They say he killed two guards in one holdup."

Dan sneered. "Oh, bullshit! The way I heard it he was just a petty horsethief." He drove over Mike's splutter of protest. "Now, if you want a *genu-ine* criminal, you gotta go to my great-great-aunt Bonnie's first husband, Leroy. Cut four men, they say, in a knife fight on a riverboat. That was just the gambling side of it. He's also supposed—"

"Pikers," sneered Nichols. "Hillbilly sissies. You want some *real* stories?" He rubbed his hands. "Welcome to the ghetto! Let's start with my second cousin, Anthony. A beast in human flesh, everybody says so. Started off at the age of thirteen—" He drove relentlessly over Appalachian outrage. "*Then,* no sooner did he get out of prison—"

By the evening of the third day, Gretchen's task was done. The town of Grantville found itself, almost overnight, doubled in population. Some of the soldiers, like Heinrich and his men, enrolled in the American army. But most of them seized the opportunity to take up new trades—or, often enough, return to long-familiar ones: farmer, miner, carpenter, craftsman.

Over the next few weeks, the crowds packed into the refugee centers would start thinning. One by one, hesitantly, tentatively, American families would start taking in German boarders. The process was initiated by men at work, usually. Discovering that the man next to them, for all that he spoke an unfamiliar tongue and was possessed of odd notions and whims, swung a pretty good hammer or dug more than his share of coal. Or, simply, was polite and had a nice smile.

The rest? The ones to whom Gretchen would not give the nod?

They expected to be executed, of course. Their actual fate was far more bizarre—and, truth be told, much more unsettling.

None of those men had ever seen a photograph before. Seeing one—seeing their own faces on it—was bad enough. The writing on the posters was worse. Many of those men could read. Most of them, actually, since Gretchen had a low opinion of officers. The ones who couldn't got a translation from their literate fellows.

The posters were identical, except for the photograph and the name.

WANTED—DEAD
THIS MAN IS DECLARED OUTLAW
IF HE IS FOUND ANYWHERE IN AMERICAN TERRITORY
AFTER JULY 5, 1631
KILL HIM
NO QUESTIONS WILL BE ASKED

Heinrich acted as interpreter.

"You've got two days," he growled. "Better move fast. You're on foot with nothing but the clothes on your backs."

The former commander of the tercio cleared his throat. "This is unclear," he whined. "Just how far does this—this 'American territory' extend?"

Heinrich turned to Mike for the answer. Mike said nothing. He just gave the commanding officer a stare.

A few months later, the officer found himself another employer. The Tsar. Russia, he thought, would be far enough.

Chapter 29

It may or may not have been July Fourth, depending on whom you asked. The division ran essentially along religious lines, but not entirely. The modern Gregorian calendar had been decreed by a papal bull in 1582, and was immediately adopted by Spain, Portugal, France and Italy. Within two years, most of the Catholic states of the Holy Roman Empire had followed suit, along with those portions of the Low Countries still under Spanish control. The Swiss started the process in 1583, but stalled immediately—the new calendar would not be accepted in the entire country until 1812. And the Hungarians took it for their own in 1587.

Then . . . Nothing, for a century. The Protestant and Orthodox nations dug in their heels and stayed with the Julian calendar.

So, what day was it? Well, according to the Scots cavalrymen and the Protestants from Badenburg who had come for the celebration, it most certainly was *not* the Fourth of July. Preposterous! It was—

No matter. Grantville was an American town, and the Americans said it was the Fourth of July. And besides—

Everybody loves a parade!

As official parades go, it was utterly disorganized. Henry Dreeson had tried desperately to bring rhyme and reason to the marching order, but the mayor had been overwhelmed by events and enthusiasm. Events, in that everyone was too preoccupied with integrating the former Catholic prisoners into their new world. Enthusiasm, in that the high-school students had their own opinion on the proper order of things. Especially Julie Sims, who led the rebellion with verve and élan.

The town's mayor was one man, in his sixties. He lost.

Cheerleaders first.

When they heard the news, the Scotsmen were delighted. They were less delighted—downright disgruntled—when they discovered their own assigned place in the parade.

Tha' far back? We'll nae see nothin' o' those high-steppin' knees! Ridic'lous!

So, the first little fray in the marching order began. Calvinists all, the Scots cavalrymen knew that man was born in sin and they were bound and determined to prove it. A full third of them had left their place in the parade before it even started. The parade route being jammed full of people, the Scots rebels cheerfully trotted their mounts down the side streets and alleys until they found the proper vantage points from which to *observe* the parade. And why not? It wasn't as if their horses needed the exercise.

Despite his own avid desire to admire Julie's knees, Mackay tried to stop them. But Lennox bade him still.

"Be a' ease, laddie," he said serenely. "Parades are a silly business anyway, an' t'Americans dinna seem to care. Besides—" He gave Mackay a sarcastic flourish of the mustachioes. "Ye look downright silly, wavin' tha' thing around as if t'were a saber on ae battlefield. 'Tis drippin' on y'buff coat, by th'by."

Flushing, Mackay rescued his ice-cream cone in the only manner known to the sidereal universe. He went back to eating it. Perched on his warhorse, a ferocious brace of wheel-lock pistols at his side, the Scot commander made as unmartial a figure as possible.

"Marvelous stuff," he mumbled. "How do they—*mumble*—it?"

Lennox took that as a rhetorical question, so he didn't bother with a reply. He knew the answer, as it happened, because Willie Ray Hudson had shown him. Simple, really, as long as you could make the ice.

Lennox studied the marching order ahead of them, trying to gauge when the parade would lurch into motion. He couldn't see much of it, however. The huge coal-hauling vehicle ahead of him—the Americans called it an APC, with their peculiar obsession with acronyms—blocked most of his vision.

Armored personnel carrier! Wha' ae laugh! Lennox didn't bother to restrain his grin. The rear of the vehicle was open, and American soldiers were hauling German children aboard for the ride. A few of the bolder German adults followed, curiosity and parental concern overriding their apprehension.

Lennox's grin faded. A glance at his commander, still happily chewing on his ice cream, brought back worry. Lennox had spent many hours in Willie Ray's company, over the past few weeks. The dour middle-aged Scotsman and the cheerful old American farmer had taken a liking for each other.

Ice cream, yes. Willie Ray had shown him the large stock of fla- vorings still available in the markets. *And we can tap the maple trees for sugar. The refined sugar's almost gone.*

So was the grain, and the vegetables, and the meat, and the eggs. Even with rigorous rationing, the food stocked in the town's super- markets had not lasted more than two months, just as their owners and managers had predicted. The small number of American farms which had come through the Ring of Fire could not possibly make up the difference. That had been true even before Grantville's popu- lation doubled, after the battle.

Lennox's mind veered aside, for a moment, snagged on another American eccentricity. They *insisted* on naming their battles.

That much Lennox could understand, even if the practice had fallen out of custom in his day. Most battles in the seventeenth century were sodden affairs. Bruising clashes between armies which collided almost accidentally as they marched across a ravaged landscape looking for food and shelter. No more worth naming than a dogfight in an alley.

But why call it the Battle o' the Crapper? He understood the ref- erence, but not the reasoning. They were a quirky folk, the Ameri- cans. Lennox could think of no other nationality which would have found logic in naming a battle in honor of four girls in a shit- house.

He didn't understand the logic, quite. The edges of it, perhaps, and the grim humor which lurked somewhere inside. But not the heart of the thing. It was too contradictory, too—

American. Only a nation of commoners, he decided, each of whom thought like a nobleman, could find logic there. An ice-cream nation, confident that the grain and meat would be found.

Lennox didn't understand it, no. But he had already made his decision, so the incomprehension was moot. He had never encoun- tered such confident people in his life, and confidence is the most contagious of all diseases.

The APC ahead of him lurched into gear.

"T'parade's startin', lad," he announced. Sourly: "It'd be ae fine thing if t'Scots commander c'd finish his ice cream 'fore he makes fools o' us all."

Mackay mumbled hasty agreement. But he did not relinquish the ice-cream cone until it had vanished, in the only suitable method known to the sidereal universe.

Ahead, somewhere in the middle of the parade, Mike and Rebecca walked hand in hand. They were more or less at the head of the UMWA contingent.

A flash of light drew his eye.

Rebecca smiled, and raised their clasped hands. "It's so beautiful, Michael. Where did you get it?"

Michael returned her smile with one of his own. "It's a secret," he replied. *And it'll stay one, too, if Morris keeps his mouth shut.*

Mike had intended to give Rebecca his mother's engagement ring. But it had been a paltry thing, in all truth, sentiment aside. When he brought it to Morris' shop for sizing, the town's jeweler had been aghast.

"*For Rebecca?* No way!"

Morris immediately made a beeline for the jewelry case which contained the finest rings in his collection. That case, as it happened, was the only one which still contained any jewelry. The Roths had turned over most of their stock to the town treasury weeks earlier. Roth Jewelry's gold and silver had provided the Americans with their first hard currency.

Morris opened the case and reached in. "I've got just the thing over here. Don't even think I need to size it."

Mike followed, scowling. "If it was good enough for my mother, I don't see why—"

Morris frowned. "Your mother was a fine woman, Mike Stearns. But—but—"

"Nothing but a coal miner's wife? Well, so what? *I'm* a coal miner."

"Yeah, but—" Still frowning, Morris shook his head. "Yeah, but."

Mike's irritation had vanished, then. He understood full well the meaning of that *yeah, but.* Understood it, and took pride in the knowing.

Yeah, but—she's also the closest thing this town's ever had to a princess.

There was something amusing in the thought. Rebecca's growing status in the town had precious little to do with heritage and "bloodline." True, the Abrabanels were ranked by Sephardim among their finest families. Finest of all, perhaps. But that meant little or nothing to Grantville's West Virginians. What they knew of the history of the Spanish Jews could have been inscribed on a pin.

Didn't matter. There was the *romance* of the thing!

And Dr. Abrabanel was becoming a familiar sight, taking his twice-daily walks through the town. Stopping, in his serene and courtly manner, to exchange a few words with every passerby. Everybody knew that he was a philosopher, and looked the part. Only philosopher in the history of the town, so far as anyone could remember. A *princely* gentleman, if you ever met one. A prince in exile is still a prince, especially when he has a beautiful daughter to prove it. So—

The high school's one-hundred-piece band was blaring away

gleefully not far ahead of them. But the sound didn't disguise the cheers that went up as Mike and Rebecca ambled their way down the route.

Hey, look—it's Becky!

So, in its informal way, did a town of West Virginians complete their adoption of an informal princess. And if the Germans standing alongside them thought the matter strange—a *Jewish* princess?— they kept their mouths shut. They were beginning, just beginning, to settle into an unexpected new world. One thing they had already learned. Their American hosts were not given to formalities and stiff propriety. But they took their principles seriously. Seriously enough, at least, to shatter a tercio. And seriously enough, before accepting new members into their world, to require them to listen to a recitation. The Bill of Rights, the schoolteacher had called it, before she stumbled through the words in newly learned German.

The name, and the concept beneath it, was still a bit bizarre to those commoners. But only a bit. They were quite familiar, actually, with many of the basic principles of democracy. The Dutch and Venetian republics had been in existence for decades, and the Puritan revolution in England was on the horizon. They had simply never seen all those principles put together in one place, and then—this was the key—*taken dead seriously.*

Odd, that. New. But the Germans had found nothing new or odd or bizarre in the confidence of the elderly woman who recited the phrases. A duchess, sure enough, with the authority to match the appearance. And the armed retainers standing at her side, with those terrible rifles, ready to enforce the appearance.

Here and there, scattered through the crowd, German accents came to join the cheers.

Ey luk—ist Becky!

"They should be cheering you," whispered Rebecca, frowning. "And the UMWA."

Michael's smile widened. "Hell, no. I like it this way just fine."

By early afternoon, the "parade" had dissolved completely. The official contingents of the parade fell aside and became onlookers. Onlookers marched. Soon enough, the fearsome APCs were pressed into service as tourist buses, hauling packs of German and American children all over town. By noon, Grantville's two downtown taverns were packed to the gills, especially after Willie Ray brought in his newly made stock of moonshine. He'd even provided labels for the jars: "Revenoo-ers Rue." Business spilled out onto the streets.

At that point, six American entrepreneurs formed an on-the-spot partnership with four German ex-soldiers. A Scots cavalryman acted as interpreter and, by the end of the negotiations, had parlayed himself into the partnership as well.

Three of the Americans were farmers who, like Willie Ray, had their own stocks of miscellaneous home brew. The fourth American, Ernie Dobbs, was a beer-truck driver. By bad luck, he had been in Grantville making deliveries when the Ring of Fire occurred. Since there was no one to say otherwise, he had retained possession of the truck's stock of beer—which he now contributed as his capital investment. The remaining two Americans agreed to provide the necessary equipment—which consisted, in the main, of card tables and folding chairs.

The Germans, former tavern-keepers, provided the experienced personnel. By noontime, having expropriated the small park next to the town's community swimming pool by mysterious means, the "Thuringen Gardens" were open for business.

"Ey am t'bouncer," pronounced the Scotsman proudly, as he ushered the mob onto the grounds. But he spent most of his time pressed into service as a lifeguard, after the children demanded the pool be opened also.

Henry Dreeson alone, stubbornly faithful to his civic duty, completed the assigned route. But the mayor spent no more than five minutes, glowering at the gas station on the edge of town, before retracing his steps to join the festivities. He didn't even raise a ruckus over the gross violations of several city ordinances represented by the "Gardens." Not even after he saw the German barkeeps, true to their own traditions, start handing drinks to youngsters. Soft drinks only, of course. But as far as the Germans were concerned, beer was a soft drink.

The only people who did not participate in the parade, in any capacity, were the members of the wedding party. Which, by then, numbered well over a hundred people.

Most of them belonged to the bride's party. In addition to Gretchen's own "family" of a couple of dozen or so, there were Heinrich and his men, and their camp followers—say, fifty people all told.

Then, there were the "advisers." Melissa occupied pride of place in that coterie, along with the owner of the town's bridal store. Her name was Karen Reading. The rest of the "advisers," truth be told, were gofers. Melissa's high-school students, mostly, along with Karen's two daughters and four nieces.

Karen took care of all the bridal preparations. Melissa took care of bridal discipline.

A difficult task, that last. Gretchen was generally very cooperative, and she was positively ecstatic over her wedding dress. Even after Karen explained that it was "only on loan." The difficulty—the battle royal—revolved around one question only.

Melissa, for the hundredth time: "You are *not* getting married in sneakers."

Gretchen, sullen: "You people iss *wahnsinnig*." Surly: "Zat means—"

Melissa, snarling: "I know what the word means! I looked it up, after the tenth time you used it. Insane or not, you are *still* going to wear them."

Gretchen, glaring at her feet: "Zese sings iss *torture*."

Melissa, sighing: "I know. I don't approve of them personally, mind you. But—"

Gretchen, gloomy, muttering, trying a few steps: "I vill fall *und* break *mein* neck."

Melissa, gloomy, muttering, watching: "I'm a traitor. A quisling." Then, snarling to her "aides": "And where *is* Willie Ray Hudson, anyway?"

The chorus replied: "In town, getting drunk."

"Get him! Now!" The high-school girls sped from the scene, a flying squad in search of a rascal. Gretchen stumbled. Melissa scowled.

Muttered: "Great. Just great. A bride in high heels and a drunk to give her away. We'll never make it down the aisle."

The groom's party was far smaller. Larry Wild was the best man, and Eddie and Jimmy the ushers. Beyond that, there were a handful of other high school boys, acting as gofers for the Grand Old Man of the group—Dr. Nichols.

James admired Jeff's tuxedo. "Good fit."

Jeff flushed. "Come on, Dr. Nichols. It isn't, and you know it." He stared down at the outfit. The tuxedo rental company being now in a different universe, the expensive suits had become the town's collective property, available "on loan" for whoever needed them. "This one was Mike's, 'cause he was the biggest. Ms. Reading *still* had to let it out. I look like a fat penguin."

James grinned. "What is *this*? You're getting married today to the prettiest girl in town and you're worried about your *weight*?"

Jeff's flush deepened. So did the doctor's good humor.

"Relax, Jeff. In a few months, it'll be a moot point anyway. None of us are going to get through this winter with any extra body fat."

Jeff's personal worries were overridden by a general concern. "What do you think? Are we going to make it?"

James peered through one of the windows of Jeff's trailer, looking to the north. "I imagine so," he replied softly. "There's a lot of food out there if we can just manage to bring it in. The area's farmers had finished their sowing before the mercenaries arrived and scared everybody off the land. So—"

He shrugged. "The truth is, it's not actually that easy to starve to death. The biggest problem with a low-calorie diet is that it weakens people, and it's usually deficient in vitamins and minerals. Leaves you wide open for disease."

His good humor returned. "Fortunately, while we're getting very low on food and medicine and antibiotics, the town's pharmacies and supermarkets still have a big stock of vitamins and minerals. We're going to establish a rigorous program of dietary supplements. That should get us through this first winter." He made a face. "Not that we won't be getting sick of gruel and porridge."

James decided to change the subject. He inspected the interior of the trailer. "Looks like you've done a good job here."

Jeff was just as eager as the doctor to leave worrying behind. "We worked our asses off, these past four days. Had lots of help from a bunch of the other kids from school, too. You like it?"

James hesitated, before opting for honesty. "*Like* it? That's not exactly the word I'd use. You're going to be as crowded as a basket full of kittens. But I approve, even if it does look like the strangest architectural design in the world."

"It'll work," said Jeff defensively. He pointed to the door. "All three of them have been hooked together, with good insulation for the passages."

In times past, that door had opened to the outside world. Now, it connected to a new trailer which had been laboriously inserted between this one and Larry's, next door. The "new" trailer was actually an abandoned one, donated by its former owner. Most of the last few days had been taken up by turning the three trailers into an interconnected complex, cleaning the new trailer, and re-designing the living space. As soon as the wedding was over, Gretchen's entire family would be moving from their temporary quarters in the high school into the complex. Between them and Jeff's three friends, the place would truly be crowded. But everyone would have a place, and—

"You're happy about it," stated James. "All four of you."

Jeff smiled. The expression combined pleasure with sadness. "Yeah, I guess. We've—" He sighed. "It's been real hard, not having our families. And now we're going to have the biggest family in town."

Worry returned, in full force. "I just hope it works out okay. I know it's going to be hard for all of us, getting used to each other."

James studied him for a moment. "You worried about Gretchen? Think she'll be unhappy?"

Jeff shook his head. "Not really," he admitted. "I showed her the place yesterday, you know."

His thoughts fell aside. James grinned. "Gorgeous, ain't she?"

Jeff nodded happily. But his fretfulness returned within seconds. "You know what she said, the minute she stepped in? 'You are so *rich.*'

" 'Rich'!" he snorted. "Look at this place, Dr. Nichols. It's nothing but a *trailer.*"

James reached up and placed his hand on the shoulder of the large boy—young man—standing before him. "Are you really worried about that 'gold digger' business?" he asked. "Myself, I think it's a lot of—"

"No, no. It's not that." Jeff hesitated. "I can understand why she'd think the way she does, coming from"—he waved his hand—"all that. It's just that—"

He lowered his head. The next words were sad, spoken in a whisper. "She doesn't love me, you know. I don't think she even knows what the word means. Not in the same way I do, anyway."

That very moment, as it happened, Melissa was discussing the same subject with Gretchen. When she finished her awkward, half-English/ half-German explanation, Gretchen frowned.

"Zat iss *für* nobles," she protested.

Melissa sighed. Gretchen studied her intently. "But you sink ziss iss important? Fü—for Jeff?"

Melissa nodded. "It will matter to him more than anything, Gretchen. Trust me. As long as he thinks you love him, he'll be able to handle anything."

Not certain if her words had made any sense, Melissa tried to stumble through a German semitranslation. But Gretchen waved her down.

"I understand." The frown on her face cleared away. "Iss not a problem, zen. I vill vork at it. Very hard. I am a good vorker. Very—" She groped for the word, for a moment, before finding it. "*Ja.* Determined. Not lazy."

Melissa couldn't help laughing. And if some of her humor was rueful, most of it was not. "That you most certainly are, girl!"

She examined the young woman standing before her. "That you most certainly are," she repeated. Smiling, shaking her head: "You know what, Gretchen Richter-soon-to-be-Higgins? I do believe this is one marriage that's going to fly."

Melissa laughed again. " 'Work at it!' I like that!"

Chapter 30

In the end, the wedding went off without a hitch.

Willie Ray showed up on time. And if he wasn't exactly sober, he had a lifetime's experience to lean on. So, stubby and half-inebriated as he was, he managed to get Gretchen down the aisle without mishap. True, it took her quite a while. But she didn't stumble once and the organist didn't mind having the time to show off.

Neither did the audience. The church was packed. Standing room only, and likewise the street outside. At least half the town showed up for the wedding, spilling off the sidewalks.

The huge crowd was in a very festive mood. More so, in truth—much more—than at most weddings. For all of those people, American and German alike, the wedding came like a burst of sunlight. Quentin Underwood had spoken for thousands. *After this nightmare we've been plunged into, I swear I can't think of a single thing that'd be better for my soul than to watch a young woman walk down the aisle in a wedding dress.*

That sentiment, everyone had in common. From there, the viewpoints diverged.

For the German participants and onlookers, the wedding came as something of a promise. Or, perhaps, a reassurance. Although they now numbered well over half of this new society coming into existence, the Germans—former refugees, mercenaries, camp followers—were well aware of their subordinate position within it. They were still groping to understand, much less accept—much less feel they *were* accepted.

The habit of centuries had shaped them. The acid of hereditary privilege had corroded their souls. Without even being aware they were doing it, the German newcomers automatically reacted to Americans as commoners to nobility. It didn't matter what the Americans *said*. Words are cheap, especially the promises of aristocracy to their underlings.

What mattered—what had always mattered, more than anything— was what people *are*. And the Americans, it was plain to see, were nobility. It was obvious in everything they said and did, and didn't say and didn't do. It shone through in their simple carriage.

Had they been told, the Americans would have been mystified. Their own centuries had also shaped them, and healed an ancient wound. Every American, on some level, took a fundamental truth for granted. *I am important. Precious. Human. My life is valuable.*

That attitude infused them, whether they knew it or not. And it was that unspoken, unconscious attitude which the German newcomers immediately sensed. They reacted automatically, just as Gretchen had instantly assumed that an American schoolteacher was really a duchess. Just as Rebecca had instantly assumed that a coal miner was an hidalgo.

Ingrained habits, beaten into people by centuries of oppression and uncaring cruelty, cannot be removed by words alone. Deeds are also necessary, especially deeds which cut to the heart of the thing.

Some people are really human. Most are not.

Good blood. Bad blood. That simple, vicious dichotomy had ruled Europe for centuries. For more than a decade, now, it had turned central Europe into a charnel house. The nobility, as always when they bickered over the price of their meat, presented the butcher's bill to the common folk. And why not? *Those people don't value life much anyway. They don't feel pain the way we do.*

Good blood, bad blood. Today, in the clearest way possible, the Americans were making a pledge to their new brethren. *We do not care. It means nothing to us.*

For the Americans who watched and participated, the thing was seen from a different angle. "Blood" was irrelevant. A goodly number of them, after all, had more than a little German ancestry in them. What *did* matter was a subtler definition of class.

Regardless of Jeff's plebeian Appalachian "stock," he was one of the town's *good* boys. Everybody knew it, for all that some of them— yahoos—might have ridiculed him in private as a "nerd" or a "geek."

Gretchen, on the other hand—

The word "trash" had been bandied about in private, often enough, in the days since the public announcement was made. To that coarse term, some had added others even worse. Slut, tramp—*whore.*

But, as Mike had rightly said, public sanction carries a powerful weight. So, the foul words were spoken only in private. And, even then, not so very often as all that. The days passed, and the terms faded away. By the afternoon of the wedding, they were forgotten by all but a handful. Grantville's Americans had been swept up in a tidal wave of romance.

Yes, yes, yes—it was all very peculiar. *So what?* There were a thousand fairy tales to fall back upon. Jeff Higgins was one of their own, after all. Everyone knew the story of how he and his friends had stood off a mob of thugs with their shotguns. If you looked at it the right way, he was a knight in shining armor. Appalachian style, of course— *and what's wrong with that?*

Gretchen? Rapunzel, by God, with the figure and the face and the long blond hair to prove it. Forget about the dirty feet. And if the story of how she had hidden her sisters in a shithouse was gruesome, it was also heroic in its own way. For hill people, at least.

Soon enough, too, the new story was worming its way through the populace, adding its own gory glamour. Oooh . . . so grisly! Mountain grisly!

The story was garbled, of course. Ludwig and Diego conflated, confused. A desperate young woman and her new paramour, in murtherous conspiracy, doing away with the obstacle to their love. Terrible, terrible, just terrible. On the other hand, the man was a fiend. A monster, whose villainy grew by the telling. The very picture of a devil. Hadn't Dr. Adams said as much himself? (Which he had, in his blabbermouth way. But the rumor that he drove a stake through the heart of the corpse was quite false.)

So, by the afternoon of the wedding, the American half of this growing society had come to accept it also. Embrace it, in truth. In one of history's little ironies, a commoner folk adopted the romantic mythology of nobility and used it to drive home their own purpose. Something new was being forged here, in a place called Thuringia. Something valuable and precious. Their own blood would go into the tempering. As it should, as it must. Good blood joining other. So are true nations made.

The wedding took place in the town's Catholic church, since it was the biggest. But the service was Methodist, and was done by Jeff's pastor. The arrangement was unusual, but had been agreed to by everyone. Neither Jeff nor Gretchen cared very much, so long as the wedding was "done right."

As for the pastor and the priest? They were good friends, as it happened. Their friendship had grown over the years, shaped by a mutual interest in theological discussion, foreign films, and—most of all—a shared hobby. Both of them were enthusiastic auto mechanics, in their spare time. They had worked together, often enough, rebuilding good cars out of junk. Let others worry about the fine points and the detail work.

True, Father Mazzare had fretted at one point.

"It's not the wedding that bothers me, it's—" He waved the wrench about. "Everything."

Rev. Jones grunted. His head was half-buried in the engine. "Are you *still* worrying about the pope?" He extended his hand. Father Mazzare passed him the wrench. His voice continued, half-muffled: "I looked it up, by the way. Papal infallibility wasn't proclaimed until 1869. So the way I see it, you've got almost a quarter of a millennium to argue with him." He grunted again. "Okay, that's done."

His face emerged, grinning, to meet the scowling visage of his friend.

"That's lawyering and you know it," growled Father Mazzare.

Still grinning, Rev. Jones shrugged. "Yeah, of course it is. So what? Lawyering'll work in a pinch."

Father Mazzare was *still* scowling. Rev. Jones sighed. "Larry, what else are you going to do? If you accept the current situation, you'd be pretty much bound to call in the Inquisition and demand the enforcement of the Edict of Restitution." He cleared his throat. "I'm afraid I'd have to take exception, if you tried to seize my church. Very least, I'd insist you return my copy of *Rashomon.*"

Mazzare chuckled. "Oh, well," he muttered. "We'll do the best we can. I *would* appreciate it, however, if you'd refrain from denouncing the Whore of Rome at the wedding service tomorrow."

Jones grimaced. "Give me a break!" Then, chuckling himself: "Not that the current pope doesn't deserve it, mind you, from all I've heard. But that girl's Catholic herself, and she's gone through enough already."

He peered into another crevice of the engine. "Hand me the quarter-inch drive, will you, with a three-eighth socket?"

As Mazzare rummaged in the rollaway, Jones continued. "Do you think they really did it?"

"That's between them and God," came the reply, along with the socket wrench. "I can't say I'm losing any sleep over it. The way I heard it, the man looked like a vampire."

"Wouldn't surprise me if he was," muttered Jones, diving back into his work. "How's the town stocked for garlic, by the way?"

Time, now.

Standing at the altar, his friends by his side, Jeff tried not to fidget. James Nichols, about to take his seat, paused and came back.

He spoke very softly, so only Jeff could hear. "You can still change your mind."

Immediately, Jeff shook his head. "No, I can't. You know that as well as I do."

Nichols studied the young face in front of him. "Just checking, that's all."

Jeff smiled. A bit ruefully, perhaps, but only a bit. "And I don't want to, anyway. I'm not worrying about the wedding, Dr. Nichols. Just—" His hand made a little motion. Groping.

"All the years after."

Jeff nodded. Nichols put a hand on his shoulder and leaned close. "Listen to me, boy. It'll work out or it won't. Doesn't matter, really, as long as you do your job. Forget all you ever heard about manhood. Your job is to give your people—your wife, your kids—a space where they can build their lives. A roof over their heads and food on the table is part of it. So's their own bed, for your old folks to die in. How much more you can do is up to you. Just try your best. If you do that, you can call yourself a man. The rest is all bullshit." He squeezed the shoulder. "You understand?"

The shoulder relaxed, and the man with it. "Yeah, Doc. I do."

"Good enough." Nichols left. A moment later, the organ began to play. In the back of the church, steadying herself on Willie Ray's arm, Gretchen made her appearance.

Jeff watched her come, the whole time. He never noticed her mincing, hesitant steps on treacherous heels. He was simply swept up in the ancient ceremony. And discovering, as untold millions of young men had discovered before him, that there is nothing in the world as beautiful as his bride approaching.

Doubts, worries, fears, anxieties—all vanished. *I do. Oh yeah, I do.*

Chapter 31

They were alone now. For the first time ever, Gretchen realized. After ushering them to the door of the trailer, the family had let Gretchen and her husband enter unaccompanied. For the rest of the day, and the night, the family would crowd into the other two trailers in the complex.

Silently, Gretchen took her husband by the hand and led the way into the bedroom. The bedroom had once belonged to her husband's parents. Now it would be theirs.

Once in the room, she closed the door and began to disrobe. The look on her husband's face stopped her. Very shy, very nervous. Gretchen had intended to get the matter over with as quickly as possible. Now, seeing his face, she realized that would upset her husband. The thought was unbearable. Whatever else, she owed kindness to this man.

So, smiling, she dropped her hands and held out her arms. A moment later, her husband had enfolded her in his own.

The practiced response with which Gretchen accepted that embrace changed almost instantly into something else. This was no Ludwig, to whose embrace she had both to submit and shield herself. Willingly, she lifted her lips to meet Jeff's. Her lips were soft, probing, open; not the shield wall of the past. She felt his tongue and sent her own to meet it. Fumbling the task, even more than he, because Gretchen had no experience at all in *kissing*.

She relaxed completely, now, and returned both the kisses and the caresses with her own. The hands roaming her body were becoming more and more enflamed. She could sense it. But she did not fear Jeff's passion. Not in the least. Soon, very soon, she would be satisfying it.

And so what? Satisfying a man's lust was a chore, true enough. But there were chores and chores. There was the chore of cleaning blood from a plundered pile of booty. The chore of shaving a rapist, controlling her hand with an iron will, lest her shrieking soul spill his life on the ground, and her family's with it.

And then, there was the chore of swaddling a baby. The chore of wiping spittle from a child. The chore of warming a grandmother in winter. Easy things, caring things. *Family* things.

There would be no bruises on her body from her husband's lust, she knew. Never. She was safe. But she also knew that she would be called upon to satisfy that lust far more often—*far more!*—than ever she had been called by Ludwig. The knowledge brought no fear, only a quiet satisfaction. Here, too, family things would prove themselves again. *Strong.*

What her husband would want, Gretchen would give. Gladly, if not eagerly. If nothing else, while she carried out the family chore, she could entertain herself mocking the shade of an ogre. Sneering at his ghost.

Then, Jeff was breaking away. Very reluctantly, she thought. To her surprise, Gretchen found that reluctance mirrored in herself. The reaction puzzled her. Even family chores, after all, are still chores. She was usually glad enough to be done with them.

She ascribed the reaction to lingering fear. Nothing more. That strange flaring sensation, likewise. Though that, too, was odd. Why should she feel this regret, now that it was fading? Fear was nothing to treasure.

Jeff was smiling. She could sense his growing relaxation and confidence, and was glad to see it come. Gretchen had promised the duchess—as she would always think of that woman, whatever her title—that she would work very hard at this odd thing which the Americans called "love." This, she realized now, was part of it. A husband was not a rapist. A husband should feel relaxed in the company of his wife. Confident, not in his power, but in his position.

Jeff sat on the bed and patted his hand next to him, inviting her to sit. Gretchen obeyed. Then, haltingly, he began to speak. She translated the broken words easily enough. She had much greater difficulty understanding his offer. It was the last thing she had expected.

Wait? Because of what I have been through? Until I am comfortable, and at ease? Myself willing?

Gretchen was utterly astonished. Her husband's offer, she knew at once, did not stem from lack of ardor. No, not in the least. She understood the difficulty with which he was restraining himself. Male desire was a thing she knew perfectly, and she did not think any man had ever desired her as much as the man sitting next to her on that bed did at that moment.

Her mind groped for meaning. Meaning came, immediately, but it was so obvious and simple that she ignored it without thought. Then, thinking, came back and examined it.

Yes. It is true. He simply cares.

Tears filled her eyes. A wave of affection more powerful than any she had ever felt in her life poured through her heart. Instinctively, without calculation, she embraced Jeff and drew him down upon her. Her lips pressed against his, soft and open, her tongue entering his mouth.

Suddenly, she felt very hot and flushed. She pushed Jeff away— softly, but insistently—sat up, and tried to remove her clothing. Her fingers fumbled at the cantankerous thing which the Americans called a "zipper."

No need. Her husband would do it for her. She returned his smile with one of her own. *Why not? It seems to please him. And I need not fear that he will tear my garments. Not this man.*

So, rolling and stretching, she helped Jeff in the disrobing. First herself, then him. When they were both nude, she writhed a little on the huge bed—"king-size," they called it, as if they were kings!— bringing herself to its center. She almost laughed, seeing the way that sinuous motion aroused him. Gretchen knew that her body could affect men so, but she had never seen Ludwig become as instantly inflamed as her husband.

For a moment, the sight of his erect manhood brought an old chill. She could feel the shield closing around her mind, and the blankness coming.

No! I will not be false to my husband. I promised the duchess. I promised him.

The struggle was brief, easy. So easy. Far easier than she would have imagined. She did laugh, now. Not with mockery or ridicule, but simple affection. Gretchen had always enjoyed keeping her family happy. This was simply part of it. No more to be dreaded than combing her sister's hair or feeding her child.

Jeff lay down beside her and began flooding her body with kisses and caresses. Another wave of affection poured through her. Then, an unexpected surge of pleasure. She was quite amazed by the latter. Gretchen was accustomed to caressing others, not being the recipient of that pleasure.

For a moment, she wallowed in the sensation. There had been precious little of sheer pleasure in her life.

It was too much. She shied away from it, recalled by stern duty.

It was time to satisfy her husband. Men demanded it. So, half-unwillingly—but not for the reasons of old—she began lifting her husband upon her.

Jeff resisted. Not fiercely, no, but firmly for all that. He moved his open mouth across her breast, and down her belly. Slowly, slowly, while his hand stroked her inner thighs. The hand—hot, soft—moved up. The mouth—wet, and softer still—moved down.

When his fingers reached their destination, Gretchen gasped. Partly from pleasure, but mostly from surprise. *So gentle. So—*

She realized, then, that he was not very experienced. He was fumbling, she thought. Only half-certain of his end, and less so of his means.

It mattered not at all. He was the only man who had ever tried. Half-accidentally, Jeff's fingers found their mark. Gretchen hissed. She sensed her husband's glowing satisfaction. Back again, trying, trying.

Hiss. *Oh!*

For the first time in her life, Gretchen felt her own eagerness arrive. She wondered, but only for an instant. Her body seemed to have a mind of its own. She gave it the rein and reached down herself. Guiding—or trying to. She was no more experienced in her own pleasure than her husband.

When the sharp sensation came again, she bit her lip. Then, realizing what she was doing, let the soft moan emerge. After the horror of the first day, she had never let a man hear her moan. Or make any sound. But this moan was the rightful property of her husband. It belonged to him, not her—and was freely given.

Now Jeff's mouth reached its goal, and Gretchen gasped again. With shock, this time. *What is he doing? Is he insane?*

She seized his head, ready to push him away. But her hands froze in the act. Jeff reacted to the pressure of her fingers in exactly the opposite manner to what she had intended. His mouth pressed down, and open. His tongue followed the path found by learning fingers. Sheer pleasure held her paralyzed.

Gretchen's mind was awhirl. Pleasure, confusion, joy, fear—all of them were contained in her sighing, moaning, wordless voice.

What to do?

Fear and confusion triumphed. Her mind fled down a different path. A well-worn, familiar, hated rut.

Just satisfy him and be done.

With her strength, Gretchen seized Jeff's shoulders and hauled him away. Up now! Across! Here, where you belong! She wrapped her legs around his own, pinning him to the rut.

That, too, he fumbled. But not for long, and even his awkwardness brought another wave of affection. For all his passion, Gretchen understood that Jeff was still trying to be gentle. The flare burst in her heart so brightly she thought it might consume her whole.

In, now. Oh yes! She laughed giddily, gaily, happily. Even in *this* her husband cast memory into the shade. *Oh yes!*

Duty fell away, replaced by ancient instinct. She felt her body reacting in ways she had never known. Her muscles stripped away the shield, her nerves broke it into pieces, her mind cast the pieces aside. Blankness filled with swirling color. There was nothing, now, between her and her husband. Nothing but skin and moisture. Nothing but his desire and her—

What?

Another wave of pleasure drove a hiss from her throat. She started kissing Jeff fiercely. The breath poured over her lips, down her tongue, into his mouth. She felt her husband respond, eagerly, avidly—

Proudly.

Gretchen finally understood Jeff's purpose, then. For an instant, she froze. Utter shock.

She moved her face away, pressing the back of her head into the pillow. Jeff lifted his own. They stared at each other. Light green; light brown.

Green glowed; brown questioned.

Is it possible? I never thought—

Green assured; brown—accepted.

I will try. Husband, I will try.

She was too confused, at first, to follow him down that path. She simply joined her body to the rhythm. But her mind, soon enough, found the way to join an old rut to a new destination. There was safety and security, for her family as much as herself, in keeping her man satisfied. This was what he wanted, as strange as it seemed. So—

She began by simply reacting, allowing Jeff's desire for her own pleasure to guide her. Waves of delight, she signaled with her mouth, her hands, her voice. Her husband responded. Learning, learning. The waves came closer, higher.

She was almost frightened, then, but drove away the fear with duty. *My husband wants this.* New desire found security in old habit. *Give him what he wants. Safety lies that way.*

Safety fell aside, duty fell aside, reaction fell aside. There was nothing left but Gretchen. The waves became a roaring surf and the surf became the tide. Unstoppable, now. When the end came, Gretchen even managed to accept it. Embrace it. Take it for her own, as something valuable and precious.

Glory in it, as if she were a duchess herself.

A refugee from Sepharad had found her sun-drenched legends in this place, and a Scots cavalryman his deadly faeries. Now, a young woman from broken Germany found her old wives' tales. They were true, after all. All that they had said. All that Gretchen had disbelieved, just as she had disbelieved the tales of knights and chivalry.

A new wife had found herself in her own pleasure. She repaid her husband with feverish kisses, tear-filled eyes, and a voice sobbing years of promise.

Satan, she repaid with laughter. Triumphant, exultant mockery, bouncing off the walls of a trailer bedroom and echoing down into the Pit.

Jeff, exhausted for the moment, lay by her side and watched her. Puzzled by the laughter, perhaps, but not caring. He was awash in his own satisfied pleasure and, still more, in the pride of his accomplishment. Whether he understood the savage humor filling his wife—and he didn't, not at all—he was reassured by the joy in her face and the warmth of her hands, stroking his body.

Finally, Gretchen understood the full extent of her victory. *Total, complete.* She had beaten the Devil. Whipped him like a cur.

She had saved *everything* from his dark realm. Even the one thing she had thought lost forever. The only thing she possessed of value to the Beast, which she had traded away to save her family. Now, at the threshold of her new life, she reached through the iron gates and snatched back her virginity. Gleefully, she robbed the Robber, and gave the treasure as a gift, to the man who had earned it.

Tears came, too—tears of joy and gratitude—but the laughter remained. Far below, deep, she could hear Satan's howl of rage.

I have been cheated! Swindled!

Laugh and laugh and laugh. Kissing and fondling her husband all the while. He was young, and clean, and glorious, and so fine, and so wonderful. Gretchen was not surprised to see how quickly he returned to her. Nor with what eagerness she joined him.

She had beaten the Devil. Now, she would torture the monster.

Satan's torment lasted through the night. Again and again, Gretchen lashed him with her pleasure. Hers and, even more, the delight she gave her husband. For hours, the Devil rampaged through his stone-glowing chambers. Shattering the walls with his horns, lashing the rubble with his tail, stamping his rapists under cloven hooves.

As her husband's ecstasy mounted—more from his wife's love in the doing, than from the doing itself—the Devil fled in despair. Out of his chambers he sped, down and down into the bowels of the Inferno.

Gretchen followed him, like a dachshund after a badger.

Go away! shrieked the Beast. *Leave me alone!*

But she was remorseless, merciless. *Watch, monster.* She cornered him in a grotto, dark and dank with refuse.

Satan cowered. *Stop it,* he whimpered. *You're hurting me.*

Watch. Her body—warm, wet, soft, loving—crushed vileness against the stones. *Watch.*

She was done with Satan, then. Done forever. Even Gretchen was satisfied with her triumph. Her husband's love filled her, purging every trace of the past. Gone now, all gone. Gone forever.

Gretchen believed in that love, now. It was like a pledge. Never again would she have to measure her life by how bad it might be. Only by how good.

There would be surprises in their life, she knew. Many of them, as they came to know each other. Some of those surprises would be unpleasant, of course. He would be petty at times; nasty; spiteful. Whatever. And so would she, at times.

No matter. There would be no surprises at the heart of their marriage. Of that, Gretchen was quite certain.

She stroked Jeff's face, gazing into his eyes. The green orbs glowed, like the buds of spring in a springtime face. Soft, young, full of promise. Wet, warm, full of life.

Gretchen was very pleased with herself, then. She had kept her promise to the duchess.

She laughed. *It had been so easy!* She had expected years of toil and struggle.

So easy. It was just family, she now understood. That's all. Nothing but the adoration which binds a family. Different in some ways, true. But every member of a family is different, and precious, and valuable. So to each one is given something special. To a baby, a breast. To a child, care and caresses. To a grandmother, comfort and an ear to complaints.

To a husband . . .

So easy! Just family adoration. Add orgasms.

Nothing to it. In fact . . .

Gretchen's practical mind worked on the problem, as her hand moved down, working on her husband's adoration. It did not take her long to reach the obvious conclusion. No longer than her hand.

Both felt the confirmation. Growing, firm, strong.

"I love you," she murmured. And set out happily to work on it some more.

Whatever doubts Jeff might have had were long gone by morning.

He awoke before she did, and gazed upon her. And discovered, as untold millions of men before him, that a wife is even more beautiful than a bride.

They made love again, first thing. After that, Jeff made them breakfast. It was just oatmeal, since that was the only breakfast food still available in the town. Even then, it took him quite some time. Gretchen was being very playful.

When the porridge was done, they wolfed it down and returned immediately to the bedroom. The rest of the morning was spent there. It was a happy morning, full of discovery. Trial and error, some uncharitable souls might have called it. But Gretchen and Jeff cared not the least. They welcomed the trials and laughed at the errors, and, most of all, simply savored the work. Love, like all growing things, also needs to be watered. Who cares if the bucket spills, now and then?

Come noon, the family's children could no longer be restrained, especially the youngest. They had fretted for almost a full day. Worried, fearful, anxious. The walls of the trailers were well insulated, but thin. Sound carried right through them.

None of the children had ever heard Gretchen make noises like that. *Never.* Not Gretchen!

They would have been utterly terrified, except for Gramma. The old woman had reassured them, soothed them, calmed them. *Nothing to worry about, children.* She had stayed up the entire night, just listening. Smiling, as she had not smiled in years.

Still—

Noon was enough! Enough!

The children poured into the trailer. Timidly, they approached the door. Timidly, knocked.

Moment! came the command. They heard people moving behind the door. Gretchen's voice, it sounded like, even though it was laughing. Something about robes.

The same cheerful voice—Gretchen's?—now bade them enter. When the children came into the bedroom, they stared at her. Eyes as wide as saucers.

Gretchen? Is that you?

True, the woman in the bed *looked* like Gretchen. Sort of. But there was not a trace of steel in that angel's face. No armored soul, in that soft body wearing a robe.

Uncertainly, their eyes moved away from Gretchen and settled on the strange creature lying next to her. Also in a robe. *And what was this?*

❖   ❖   ❖

It was the youngest of them who first understood. Little Johann, not five years old, his instincts still unencumbered by the memory of ogres. That large, round, friendly face—nestled cheek to cheek against the woman who had raised and sheltered them all—could be one thing only.

"Papa!" he squealed. *"Papa! Papa!"*

A moment later, he was scrambling onto the bed. A small tide of children followed.

Papa was back, sure enough. Right where he was supposed to be. Within seconds, Jeff and Gretchen were half-buried under happy children.

Little Johann, being the first, rightfully claimed pride of place. Like an eel, he wriggled himself between them. It took him not more than a minute to find the newest family treasure. Jeff's big, soft, warm feet.

"Papa," he murmured. Johann's eyes closed contentedly. Winter was no longer something to fear. Not with Papa's feet to keep him warm.

Chapter 32

Hans watched the angels of death for several minutes before he spoke. He was puzzled by the difference between them. It was not the fact that one was male and one female. It was simply that Hans had always thought of angels as being . . . ageless. So why should one of them resemble a young woman, and the other a gray-haired man?

Their hair seemed strange, too.

But he was not frightened. He knew they were angels of death because of their black color, but he could detect no evil in their faces. Only a sort of calm concern. They seemed to be watching over several souls.

Not Hell, then.

Hans' eyes ranged through the room. That, too, was odd. He would have thought a divine antechamber would have been better constructed. Or not constructed at all. Simply—*spoken* into existence. But he could see the nail heads holding the wooden framework together. Very sloppy workmanship, actually.

His eyes studied the filmy substance separating him from the dimly sensed soul of another. The other soul, like his own, seemed to be lying on some sort of cot. Hans admired the filmy substance. Very ethereal, he thought. But he was a bit nonplussed by the cot. It did not seem at all heavenly.

He was not dead yet, then. His soul was simply suspended somewhere, waiting to be reaped.

The filmy substance was suddenly brushed aside. One of the angels of death entered into his space. The young female one.

Hans studied her face. Her features were not what he would have expected on an angel. Very large, broad. But he decided she was quite beautiful. He liked the way her tightly coiled black hair framed her forehead. And her dark eyes seemed very warm.

He cleared his throat. "I am ready," he whispered.

The angel leaned closer, turning her head slightly to present an ear. "What did you say?" she asked.

Hans was puzzled. *Why would an angel speak English?* But he accepted the divine will, and repeated himself in English.

"Take me, angel," he repeated. "I am ready."

The words seemed to register. The angel's eyes widened. Her lips curved into a smile, the smile became a laugh. Hans got his next surprise.

" 'Take me!' " she mimicked. Another laugh. "I've heard of one-track minds before, but this—(strange idiom; something about a cake being taken)."

But English it surely was. Hans was quite familiar with the tongue. The only member of Ludwig's band that he had genuinely liked was a young Irishman. The Irishman was also dead, now. Hans had seen his brains explode.

The angel was still laughing. "You may be ready, honey," she exclaimed, "but I'm not!" Another laugh, quite gay. "Aren't you the randy one!"

She patted his cheek. "Welcome back, Hans Richter. I'll get your sisters."

They arrived within an hour, and Hans discovered that he was still alive. Alive—and healing well. But he had spent many weeks on the edge of death. It was now the month of August.

Other changes had taken place, he discovered, and still others were in the offing. By the end of the day, he met Gretchen's new husband. And his new employer.

"You don't have to be a soldier anymore, Hans," explained Gretchen. She gestured to a man standing behind her. He was a large man, rather young, with a friendly smile.

"This is Mr. Kindred. He is—*was*—the publisher of Grantville's newspaper."

"What is a newspaper?" asked Hans.

Gretchen frowned. "It's like a broadsheet, except it comes out once a week and tells people what's happening in the world."

Hans started to ask another question but Gretchen overrode him. "Later, brother. For now, Mr. Kindred could use your help. He is trying to build a print shop, so that he can resume his publication. But—" She hesitated. "His old methods won't work, so he needs to build one the way father did. He would like your help. Three other former printers have already joined him. If it goes well, you can become a partner if you want to."

Hans stared at the publisher. "I could be a printer again?" he asked, very softly. "Not a mercenary?"

Gretchen nodded. "They will ask you to join what they call the militia, and do some training every week. But unless you want to be a professional soldier"—she laughed, then, seeing the expression on her younger brother's face—"you don't have to."

"Be a printer again," Hans whispered.

The next day, the doctor he had thought was an angel of death released him from the hospital. Helped by his sisters and his new brother-in-law, Hans entered a new world.

It was all very strange, but Hans did not care. Not even when he was conscripted into the labor battalions the day after he moved into his new home. The battalions were being mobilized every day to bring in food from the surrounding countryside. Winter was coming, and the teeming town of Grantville was working feverishly to prepare for it. Hans understood the urgency. He understood winter all too well.

And then, acceptance turned into sheer joy. Because he was still weak, the Americans decided he was unfit for hard labor. They were on the verge of sending him home when one of them, hearing that Hans had been a printer, asked if he was comfortable around machinery. The next thing Hans knew he was being trained to operate the most wonderful machine he had ever seen. A "pickup," it was called. Hans fell in love with it immediately. Over the next few weeks, he learned to drive most of the American motor vehicles. And fell in love with all of them. He was almost sorry when he had to start his new job in the print shop.

But the print shop was urgent, now. The American leaders were determined, it seemed, to begin publishing newspapers and broadsides. And books, soon enough.

They called it "propaganda." After Hans read the first pamphlet which came off the press, he fell in love with propaganda also. He liked the Bill of Rights, even if he thought it was probably insane.

A mad, crazed new world. Hans loved all of it, especially after his wonderful new brother-in-law showed him how to operate the machine called a "computer."

The best of all, however, came on September 10. That evening, the strange machine in the trailer which his brother-in-law called a "television" came to life. For the first time, apparently, since the divine event which the Americans called the Ring of Fire.

Hans was gathered around the odd glass with the entire family. The room was packed with bodies. His brother-in-law, smiling, reached down and pushed a button. The glass—the "screen," it was called—suddenly came alive.

"Oh, look!" exclaimed Annalise. "It's Becky."

Gretchen pursed her lips, studying the image of the young woman on the screen. True, it looked like Becky. She was standing behind a table, whispering something to her betrothed. Yes, that was Mike, sure enough. But—

Gretchen was not certain. "She seems awfully nervous," she mused.

"That's nonsense," retorted her sister firmly. "Becky is *never* nervous."

Chapter 33

"I'm so nervous," whispered Rebecca.

She leaned her head on Mike's shoulder. He put his arm around her waist and gave her a quick reassuring squeeze. Then, nuzzling her ear, whispered in return: "Relax. You'll do just fine." His hand slid down, patting her upper fanny. Rebecca smiled and returned the pat with one of her own.

Janice Ambler, the school's television instructor, started hopping up and down with agitation, fluttering her hands frantically.

At the back of the high school's TV studio, Ed Piazza frowned. "Great," he grumbled. "We finally get this TV station back on the air and what's the first thing the audience sees? 'Grab-ass at North Central High.'"

Next to him, Melissa grinned. "You might remember, in the future, to warn her when she's going on the air."

"Why?" demanded Greg Ferrara. "If you ask me, it beats the old days. There's something nice about a National Security Adviser who lets her hair down in public now and then. In a manner of speaking."

"Good point," murmured Melissa.

Piazza was not mollified. "You people are sick, sick." He cleared his throat loudly. *"Uh, Becky, you're live."*

Startled, Rebecca raised her head and stared at the camera. The small audience in the room had to fight down a wave of laughter. She looked like a squirrel startled in the act of stealing food.

A moment later, Rebecca was scuttling into her chair. Mike ambled lazily out of camera range, smiling all the while. And a very smug-looking smile it was, too.

"Great," repeated Piazza. "You watch. Every kid and his girlfriend is going to be sneaking in from now on, trying to cop a feel on the air."

Ferrara started to make some jocular response, but fell silent. Rebecca was speaking.

"Good evening. *Guten Abend.* Welcome to our new television station. Thanks to the hard work of the school's teachers and students, we have been able to come back on the air for the first time since the Ring of Fire. Tonight, we will only broadcast for a few hours. But we hope, within a week, to be on the air for at least twelve hours every day."

She began translating into German. By the time she was halfway into the translation, all traces of nervousness had disappeared and Rebecca was her usual self.

"Smile," muttered Piazza. "C'mon, Becky, smile now and then."

"Naw," countered Ferrara. "I like it just fine the way she is. It's such a relief to see a news announcer who doesn't crack jokes every other line, like they were a stand-up comic or something. Just tell it like it is, Becky."

"Amen," agreed Melissa.

Rebecca resumed in English:

"Most of tonight's program will be entertainment. We felt everyone deserved an enjoyable evening, after all the hard work we have been doing. There is good news in that regard, by the way. I spoke to Willie Ray Hudson just an hour ago, and he told me that he is now quite certain we will have enough food for the winter. Rationing will be tight, but no one will go hungry. But he warned me—I felt I should pass this along—that our diet is going to be awfully boring."

Again, she translated into German. By the time, she was done, Rebecca was frowning. She added a few more sentences in German. Melissa, the only one of the Americans in the studio whose knowledge of the language was becoming passable, began laughing softly.

Piazza eyed her quizzically. Melissa leaned over and whispered: "What Becky said was that since Americans don't seem to be able to cook anything without a lot of meat, she just realized it might be a good idea for some German women to organize a cooking class and do it on TV. So she asked for volunteers. Congratulations, Ed. You've got your first new program for the season."

Piazza's face was a study in contradiction. Humor mixed with outrage. "She doesn't have the authority—"

But Melissa was laughing again. Rebecca, after pausing for a moment—still frowning—had just spoken another few sentences in German. "Now she said that while she's thinking about it we ought to have some German brewers come on TV and explain how to make real beer instead of that colored water Americans confuse with it."

Piazza started sputtering. "Amen!" exclaimed Ferrara.

Janice Ambler was scowling at them and making little waving motions with her hands. *Shut up! We're on the air!*

No use. Rebecca was now translating her latest impromptu remarks into English and the rest of the small crowd which formed the audience in the television classroom burst into laughter—all of which was faithfully picked up by the microphones and broadcast into hundreds of homes, trailers, and the still-packed refugee centers.

Grantville rollicked. The Germans' humor was heartfelt; that of the Americans, a bit chagrined.

By now, Mike had joined Piazza and the two teachers. He was grinning ear to ear. "I knew she'd be great."

Piazza shook his head ruefully. "So much for following the script."

But Rebecca was now returning to the planned program. She was still frowning, but the expression was now severe instead of thoughtful.

"We are starting to develop a problem with sanitation." *Frown, frown.* "Some of the newer members of our community are growing lax about it. We cannot have that! You all know that plague comes with the springtime, which is not so many months away. Later tonight, Dr. Abrabanel is going to come on the air and explain—*again*—why personal and public sanitation is so essential for warding off disease."

Ferrara was frowning, now. "I don't understand this," he muttered. "Why is Balthazar doing that segment? I'd think James or Doc Adams would—"

Mike interrupted, shaking his head. "No. You've got to remember, Greg, that the Germans are still skeptical about all of this weird stuff about germs. But the one thing they know for sure is that Jewish doctors are the best. That's why all the kings and high nobility have them. If Balthazar says it's true, they'll believe it."

Mike smiled at the expression on Ferrara's face. "Nobody ever said prejudice made any sense, Greg. Even when it's standing on its head."

Again, the television instructor was waving everyone silent. This time, the crowd obeyed. Rebecca, after translating the medical announcement into German, broke into her first smile since starting the program.

"But it is time we should enjoy ourselves. I will be returning with news announcements later, but for now let us watch a motion picture. I have seen it, and it is truly wonderful."

She fell silent, smiling into the camera. The television teacher's frown of displeasure didn't seem to faze her at all.

"She's supposed to explain what it's about," hissed Piazza.

Mike grinned. "She told me that was purely stupid. Buster Keaton explains himself."

Janice Ambler gave up her useless frowning, sighed, and started the movie. *The General* came on the air and Buster Keaton spoke silently for himself. Within minutes, Grantville was rollicking again—and no one harder than the Germans. True, they were not very familiar with trains. Many of them had helped to lay the tracks just coming out of the new foundry, but the first steam locomotive was still being built. It mattered not at all. Film critics had often argued that Buster Keaton's genius was universal. That speculation was now proven, beyond a doubt, in another universe.

While Keaton struggled with a refractory cannon, Mike and Rebecca conferred with Ed, Melissa and Greg on a different problem.

"I still think it might be smarter to let Simpson have what he wants," argued Ferrara. "He's been squawking for months about Mike's so-called 'rule of martial tyranny.' So let him have his hour of 'free speech.' "

Mike rubbed his chin uncertainly. But Rebecca was adamant. "That is absolute nonsense! Michael was elected unanimously. If we allow Simpson to proclaim himself the official opposition—and who elected him, anyway?—then we would have to do the same for everyone with a grievance. That is not democracy, that is simply anarchy."

Piazza immediately sided with her. "She's right. Besides, we've already announced that the founding convention is going to be held over the winter. There'll be new elections then. If Simpson and that gaggle of his want to run for office, let them do it at the proper time. Until then, he's just another grouser."

"He's got a pretty big crowd following him," countered Ferrara.

Melissa snorted. "Oh, come on, Greg! It's not that big. Three or four hundred maybe, out of three thousand. And that's only counting the Americans. How many Germans do you think would vote for him? Five, tops?"

"The Germans won't be voting in the next election," pointed out Ferrara. "We've already agreed we can't extend the franchise until the convention says it's okay."

Mike came to a decision and shook his head. "Doesn't matter. Even if he had more support than he does, he's still just another private citizen. When the elections are opened, he can get nominated if he wants. Then he'll have the same access to airtime as any other candidate. But Becky's right. If we give in to his demands now, we'd just be accepting political blackmail. Rules are rules. The loser can't demand they be changed after the fact."

Grudgingly, Ferrara nodded. "All right. I won't push it any further. But—" He gave Melissa a skeptical glance. "Three or four hundred?

Now, maybe. But you just watch what happens after Mike announces the first plank of his election platform. *Universal suffrage for everyone eighteen years or older, after three months residency.*"

Mike grinned. "Yup. And no lawyering, either. No poll taxes, no literacy tests, no language requirements—*nada*. If you've lived here for three months, you're eighteen years old, and you're willing to take the loyalty oath—you're a voter."

"The shit is going to hit the fan," predicted Ferrara. His expression was gloomy. "Right now Simpson's only got some of the older folks and the faint-hearts. But as soon as Mike makes that announcement, every bigot in town is going to be jumping on the Simpson bandwagon. And don't think there aren't plenty of them. You can start with those rednecks who hang out at the Club 250."

"*Those bastards,*" hissed Melissa. "I oughta picket the sons of bitches."

Piazza frowned. "What's this about?"

Mike was scowling now. "The owner, Ken Beasley, put up a sign last week behind the bar. 'No dogs and Germans allowed.' "

Ed's mouth dropped. Mike chuckled harshly—*very* harshly. "Yeah. When I first heard about it, I grabbed some work gloves and started on down there. Looking for sparring partners. But Becky stopped me."

Rebecca sniffed. "Stupid. So was Dan Frost's idea to close them down for violating the building codes. It took me an hour to talk him out of it." She gave her fiancé a glare and poked him in the ribs with a finger. "Especially since this one kept encouraging him."

"Why'd you stop him?" demanded Ferrara. "That rathole must have a thousand violations."

Mike shook his head. "No, Becky was right. It would have been a gross abuse of official power. It's not as if we haven't been cheerfully violating the fine points in the building code ourselves, with the all new construction we've been putting up. Besides, she came up with a better idea."

Melissa cocked her head, inviting an explanation. Rebecca smiled seraphically. "I spoke with Willie Ray—he owns that piece of land across the highway from the Club 250—and the partners who set up the Thuringen Gardens. I pointed out that with winter coming, they really needed to get themselves a permanent building. So—"

Mike grinned. "So Willie Ray's now a new partner and they're starting construction next week. A great big enormous German-style tavern they'll be putting up, right across the street. Frank and I are planning to raise the matter at the next local meeting. We want the miners to adopt the new and improved Thuringen Gardens as our unofficial watering hole. The partners have already agreed we can hang a big sign on the side of the tavern, quoting the relevant passage from the UMWA Constitution. The one we adopted back in the nineteenth century, banning racial discrimination."

Melissa burst into laughter. "Oh, that'll be perfect! Let those rednecks huddle in their rathole, with the town's biggest tavern doing a booming business right across the way."

Ferrara and Piazza were grinning themselves. "Won't be any rough stuff, that's for sure," said Ferrara. "Not even the bikers are crazy enough to piss off the UMWA."

"When do they expect to open?" asked Ed. "I'll make it a point to bring the whole family down for opening night. Even if it's standing room only, which it will be."

The television teacher scurried over and interrupted. "Becky!" she hissed. "You've got to start getting ready for the news broadcast."

Startled, Rebecca glanced at the clock on the wall. "It will not start for another—"

But Janet was not to be thwarted. She took Rebecca by the arm and began hauling her away. "We're going to *rehearse*," she hissed. "You *must* learn to follow the script."

"Why?" asked Rebecca. Her studious face was intent. She added something else, but she was too far away for the rest of her words to be heard.

Ed smiled ruefully. "Poor Janet. I think she's in for a rough few months."

"That's my girl," murmured Mike happily.

When Rebecca came back on, she followed the script for not more than three minutes. Then, frowning, she laid the sheets of paper to one side and clasped her hands in front of her. Staring intently into the camera, she said:

"I will return to all this news on the production projects later. The essence is that things are going well except for the new ice-cream factory, but I think we can all agree that that is really a little frivolous."

A hiss went up from the audience, a groan from Janet.

"Well, maybe not so frivolous," admitted Rebecca. "But it is still not so important as the news on the military front."

The audience fell silent. Rebecca paused for a moment to scan her notes. Then:

"You all know that Tilly's troops have been leaving Thuringia for the past several weeks. Mackay's scouts report that the last units of the Weimar garrison have also departed, as of two days ago. Now Mackay has received more news, from a courier sent by King Gustav."

She stared into the camera. "A great battle is looming, somewhere near Leipzig. Tilly is marshaling all his troops to meet Gustavus Adolphus on the open field."

She looked away, gathering her thoughts. When she turned back to the camera, her face was solemn and pensive.

"I am Jewish, as you know. Most of our citizens are Christians, and most of them are now Catholics. But I do not believe that anyone here can take sides in this coming battle based on creed. What is really at stake is not whether Protestant Sweden will defeat Catholic Austria and Bavaria, or the opposite. What is at stake is our own freedom and liberties."

There came another long pause. "I am supposed to present the news without commentary. That seems a bit foolish to me, since I do not know anyone who does not have an opinion on almost everything, including myself. But I will of course abide by the wishes of the television people. Nevertheless—"

Another groan from Janet. The audience—throughout Grantville—was utterly silent.

"My prayers tonight will be for the king of Sweden. In this coming battle, Gustav II Adolf fights for our future. Ours, and that of our children, and of theirs, and of theirs, and of theirs, and of theirs."

"Amen," whispered Mike.

Part Three

What the anvil? what dread grasp
Dare its deadly terrors clasp?

Chapter 34

In the centuries to come, they would call Gustavus Adolphus the Father of Modern War. Then they would take to quarreling over it.

For he wasn't, really. That title, if it can be given to anyone, more properly belongs to Maurice of Nassau. Gustavus Adolphus learned the modern system from the Dutch, he did not invent it. True, he refined Maurice's emphasis on the line rather than the square, and extended it to his arquebusiers. True, also, he gave particular emphasis to artillery. Here, too, myths would abound. People would talk of the famous "leather guns," never realizing they failed the test of battle and were soon discarded. The guns had a tendency to overheat and burst. Gustav brought none with him to Germany.

His greatest accomplishment, others would argue, was Gustav's creation of the first national army in the modern world. His Swedish army was an army of citizen conscripts, rather than mercenaries. But, again, the claim was threadbare. The Swedish system was actually pioneered by his uncle, Erik XIV. And, in truth, Gustav soon came to rely on mercenary soldiers—*värvade*, the Swedes called them, "enlisted" men—almost as much as his opponents. Sweden was a sparsely populated country, whose citizenry could not possibly provide the number of soldiers Gustav required.

So it went . . .

He introduced the light musket, which eliminated the clumsy musket fork. But many other European armies used light muskets, and as late as 1645 musket forks were still being issued to Swedish soldiers.

He abolished the bandolier and introduced cartridge pouches for his musketeers. Another exaggeration. The Stockholm Arsenal would continue issuing bandoliers at least until 1670.

He invented uniforms. Not true. Uniforms were already coming into existence throughout Europe. If anything, the ragged Swedish troops were more haphazardly garbed than any.

He shortened the pike to eleven feet, making it more maneuverable in battle. False—even silly. What use is a short pike to an infantry-man? That legend was begun by a parson, who mistook an officer's partisan for a pike.

Legend after legend. Gustavus Adolphus seemed to attract them like a magnet. For each legend refuted, two more would come to take its place.

He reintroduced shock tactics into cavalry warfare. He replaced the ineffective caracole, where cavalrymen would wheel around and fire pistols from a distance, with the thundering saber charge. There is an element of truth to this claim, but only an element. Many German armies were abandoning the caracole already, and Gustav learned the value of shock tactics from the ferocious Polish lancers that his army faced in the 1620s. In truth, the Swedish cavalry took many years to become an effective force. Sweden had never been a cavalry nation. Swedish kings—Gustav no less than his predecessors—leaned heavily on their half-civilized Finnish auxiliary cavalry. Even the Swedish horses were small and stout. As late as Breitenfeld, Tilly could still sneer that Gustav's cavalry was no better mounted than his own baggage-boys.

As late as Breitenfeld . . .

After Breitenfeld, of course, Tilly could no longer make the boast. All of central Germany was now open to Gustav, along with its magnificent horses. Soon enough, his Swedish cavalry was as well-mounted as any in the world.

Breitenfeld.

All the legends revolve around that place. They pivot on that day. Wheeling like birds above the flat plains north of Leipzig on September 17, 1631, they try to find sharp truth in murky reality. Never seeing it, but knowing it is there.

The legends would be advanced, and refuted, and advanced again, and refuted again—and it mattered not in the least. Breitenfeld remained. Always Breitenfeld.

After Breitenfeld, how could the legends *not* be true?

Breitenfeld was a rarity in those days. Pitched battles on the open field between huge armies were a thing of the past. For well over a century, warfare had been dominated by the *trace italienne,* the new system of fortifications developed in Italy and perfected by the Dutch in their struggles against Spain. War was a thing of long campaigns and sieges, not battles. The strength of nations was measured by the depth of their coffers, not the names of victories emblazoned on their standards. Attrition, not maneuver—and even there, attrition was measured in coins rather than lives. Lives were cheap, bullion was hard to find.

On the rare occasions when armies did collide in the open, the queen of battle was the tercio. Swiss pike tactics—with Swiss élan long gone—married to blocks of arquebusiers. Generals "maneuvered" armies only in the sense that the pharaohs maneuvered great stones to make pyramids.

The battle only happened because Tilly made a profound strategic error. Brought on, perhaps, by the overconfidence of seven decades of life without a defeat.

Tilly's greatest asset, since Gustavus Adolphus landed in Germany—on July 4, as it happens, in the year 1630—had always been the vacillation of Sweden's Protestant allies. The Saxons, in particular. Saxony was the most powerful of the German Protestant principalities, and it had always been Tilly's anchor.

One Saxon, rather: the elector of Saxony, John George. For whatever reason—stupidity, cowardice, or simply the cumulative effect of his constant drunken carousing—John George could never make up his mind. The Prince of Yes and No. The Knight of Doubt and Hesitation. Hamlet without the tragic grandeur; certainly without the brains.

John George had been one of the princes who invited Gustav's intervention; and then, when it came, foremost among those who quibbled and lawyered. Elector Hem and Haw. History would blame Tilly for the slaughter at Magdeburg, but the charge is more properly laid at the feet of the prince who was not there himself and would not allow another to come to Magdeburg's aid. When Tilly's soldiers ran amok, Tilly himself rode into the city to stop them. He failed, but at least he tried. And when nothing else could be done, the old soldier plucked a baby from the arms of its dead mother and carried it to the safety of his own tent. John George, secure in the safety of his palace in Dresden, saved not even the dregs of his tankard. As was the prince of Saxony's custom, he poured the dregs over the head of a servant, signaling his desire for another draught.

Tilly should have left him alone. So long as Saxony barred the way, Gustavus Adolphus was safely penned in Pomerania and Mecklenburg. Let the Lion of the North roar in the Baltic, far from the fertile plains of central Germany.

But Tilly grew too bold. Or, perhaps, he was offended by the constant complaints and the whispering sneers of the imperial courtiers. Tilly was past the age of seventy, now, and had never been defeated in battle. Who was this Swedish upstart—a man barely half his age—to sully that reputation?

So, when the Habsburg Emperor Ferdinand insisted that the Edict of Restitution be enforced—at long last!—on Saxony, Tilly was obliging. He marshaled his forces, pulling them out of Thuringia and Hesse-Cassel, and marched on Saxony. Along the way, as always, his soldiery ravaged and plundered. By the time his army reached Halle, on September 4, two hundred villages lay burning behind them.

Tilly moved on. Near Merseburg, his army went into camp and began devastating the region. Tilly sent his demands to John George. The Saxon elector was required to quarter and feed the imperial army; disband his new levies; place his troops under Tilly's command; formally recognize the emperor as his sovereign; and sever all ties to the Swedes.

Even now, John George vacillated. Tilly moved again, capturing the rich Saxon city of Leipzig after threatening it with the fate of Magdeburg.

The loss of Leipzig finally convinced John George he had no choice. He offered to join his army to Sweden's, and Gustavus Adolphus immediately accepted. The Swedish army joined with the Saxon forces on September 15 near the town of Düben. The next day, the combined Swedish-Saxon army marched from Düben to the hamlet of Wolkau. There was nothing between them and Leipzig but a level plain; vast, open, and unwooded. Ideal terrain for a battle.

On the morning of September 17, Tilly led his army into position before his opponents arrived. His left flank was anchored by the town of Breitenfeld; his right, by Seehausen. The old veteran's position was excellent. His army commanded what little high ground there was in the area, and he had the sun and the wind at his back.

His army's numbers are uncertain—somewhere between thirty-two and forty thousand, a quarter of them cavalry. The infantry was drawn up in the center into seventeen tercios—or "battles," as Tilly's men called them—massed side by side. Each tercio numbered between fifteen hundred and two thousand men. The cavalry was drawn up on the flanks. Pappenheim's famous Black Cuirassiers were on the left—the same men who had breached the defenses of Magdeburg, and initiated the city's massacre. On the right, under the command of Fürstenburg, was the newly arrived cavalry from Italy.

Later in the morning, the Swedish and Saxon armies arrived and took their own positions. The Swedes held the right and the center; the Saxons, the left. The Saxons were on the east of the road to Düben; the Swedes, to the west.

Like Tilly, Gustav Adolf concentrated his infantry in the center. His

right wing, mostly cavalry, was under the command of Field Marshal Banér. His left, also made up of cavalry, under Field Marshal
Horn. The core of his artillery was massed on Gustav's left center,
young Torstensson in command. But, unlike Tilly, Gustav Adolf inter-
spersed cavalry units among his infantry. The phrase "combined arms"
had not yet entered the military lexicon, but its logic had already been
grasped by the young Swedish king.

Of the Saxon formations, there is no record. They were simply "on
the left"—and not for very long.

The Protestant allies enjoyed a slight advantage in numbers, it
seems. And they held a definite superiority in artillery. But their
Catholic opponents were not fazed. No, not in the least. And why
should they be? Tilly's men had only to look across the field to see
that victory was certain.

The Saxon troops—well over a third of their opponents—were a
semirabble, untested in battle and obviously disorganized. The Elector
John George himself, surrounded by young Saxon noblemen wearing flamboyant scarves and cloaks, commanded the Saxon cavalry
on the far left. Resplendent figures, those newly equipped cavalrymen, with their polished arms and shiny uniforms. Tilly's veterans
were not impressed. A sheep looks resplendent, too, before it is shorn.

The Swedes presented a different picture, but Tilly's soldiers were
unequally unimpressed. True, the Swedes were arrayed in excellent
order, but—

What a ragged lot of vagabonds!

On this, every eyewitness account of the battle is agreed. The
Swedish troops, said one Scottish officer later, "were so dusty they
looked like kitchen servants, with their unclean rags." A Swedish
observer would say much the same, contrasting the appearance of
Gustav's men to Tilly's:

*Ragged, tattered and dirty were our men (from the continual labors
of this last year) besides the glittering, gilded and plume-decked
imperialists. Our Swedish and Finnish nags looked but puny, next
to their great German chargers. Our peasant lads made no brave
show upon the field when set against the hawk-nosed and mustachioed veterans of Tilly.*

Tilly's army had followed him for years, and had known nothing
but victory. In truth, those "hawk-nosed and mustachioed veterans"
included many neophytes. The desertion rate in armies of the time
was astronomical. But, because of the chaos which engulfed central
Europe, men who deserted would usually join other armies—or, often
enough, simply "recycle" through the army they had abandoned. And
there were always new men available for recruitment, due to that same

chaos. The formalities and rigidities which would characterize armies of a later day were almost entirely absent.

Yet even the rawest recruit, once they joined up, absorbed the mystique and prestige of the past. Whether veteran or not, hawknosed or not, mustachioed or not—they *acted* that way. And so, to those who faced them, there was nothing quite as intimidating as facing "Tilly's men" across a field of battle. The image may have been skewed, but it was an image carved out of history's true granite.

The Catholic soldiers began binding white scarves in their hats. As the old general—he was seventy-two, then, not a day less—trotted down the line on his familiar white battle-charger, shouts of "Father Tilly!" passed from tercio to tercio. And, along with it, the triumphant battle cry of the empire: *Jesu-Maria!*

Gustav Adolf likewise addressed his troops. The king was a famous orator—the best in Sweden, by all accounts—and his men greeted him with enthusiasm. Gustav Adolf was the boldest figure of his time. Not since Alexander the Great had a ruling monarch shown such personal daring—to the point of recklessness—on the field of battle. By the day of Breitenfeld, he bore the scars of many wounds on his huge body. He wore no armor, because he could not. A Polish bullet which had struck him four years earlier at the battle of Dirschau was still lodged in his neck. Armor chafed that wound, so the king went into battle protected only by his buff coat and the Will of his God.

As they listened, the Swedish troops tied green branches into their own helmets and headgear. When he finished, they roared their own battle cry: *Gott mit uns! Gott mit uns!*

At noon, the battle of Breitenfeld began. But for the first two and a half hours, it was simply an exchange of cannon fire. Tilly and Gustavus were still measuring each other.

As time went on, it became obvious that the Swedish artillery overmatched their opponents. The king had more guns, better guns, and better trained gunners. Most of all, he had Torstensson in command. Once they were into their rhythm, the Swedish artillerymen were exchanging three shots for one with their imperial counterparts.

Pappenheim, rash and impetuous as always, broke the impasse and led his Black Cuirassiers in the first charge of the day. Not waiting for Tilly's command, the commander of the imperial left launched a thundering cavalry charge on the Swedish right.

It was a foolish gesture, and Tilly cursed him for it before Pappenheim had ridden a hundred yards. "They have robbed me of my honor and my glory!" he cried, throwing up his arms in despair.

Pappenheim thought to outflank the Swedes and roll them up from

the side. But his Swedish counterpart, Field Marshal Banér, was prepared. His king's combined arms approach proved itself on the
defense as well as the offense. Pappenheim's cuirassiers were held off
by the salvos of the infantrymen, while Banér's Swedish and Finnish cavalry launched their own sharp sallies.

Seven times Pappenheim drove his men against the Swedish lines,
ignoring all of Tilly's commands to retire. Seven times he was driven
back. Then Banér launched a massive counterattack and drove the
Black Cuirassiers from the field. In complete disorder, Pappenheim's
heavy cavalry fled toward Halle. Banér made to pursue, but Gustav
Adolf recalled him to the line.

The king was cautious. Things were not going well on his left.
Seeing Pappenheim tangled up, Tilly sent the imperial cavalry on the
opposite flank into battle. Here, Tilly's forces met with far better
results. The Saxons, for all their glitter, did not have the years of Polish
and Baltic wars behind them that Gustav and his Swedish veterans
enjoyed. The very first charge of the imperial cavalry shattered them.

True to his nature, the elector himself led the rout. Seized with
terror, John George and his splendiferous noble bodyguard galloped
off the field, leaving their army behind. The army followed soon
enough. Within half an hour, the powerful imperial cavalry had driven
the entire Saxon army into headlong retreat.

The Swedish left flank was now open, bare, naked. The imperial
cavalry began curving in upon it. Disaster loomed, as certain as the
tide. The Swedish camp followers, panicked by the Saxons, began their
own scrambling dash for the safety of Eilenburg. Tilly, whose veteran's
eye immediately saw the coming glorious victory, gave the order for
his entire army to advance on his enemy's shattered front. The tercios
lurched forward, angling to the right in order to bring their full weight
to bear on the broken Swedish left. As cumbersome as a glacier, that
mass of tercios—and just as unstoppable.

There. Then. That moment.
That is where the legends pivot and wheel. Decade after decade,
century after century; never reaching agreement, but always circling.

The Father of Modern War, Gustavus Adolphus almost certainly
was not. But he may very well have been the Father of the Modern
World. Because *then*, at *that* place, at the moment when the Saxons
broke and the Inquisition bade fair to triumph over all of Europe,
the king of Sweden stood his ground.

And proved, once again, that the truth of history is always concrete. Abstractions are the stuff of argument, but the concrete is given.
Whatever might have been, was not. Not because of tactics, and

formations, and artillery, and methods of recruitment—though all of those things played a part, and a big one—but because of a simple truth. At that instant, history pivoted on the soul of one man. His name was Gustavus Adolphus, and there were those among his followers who thought him the only monarch in Europe worthy of the name. They were right, and the man was about to prove it. For one of the few times in human history, royalty was not a lie.

Two centuries later, long after the concrete set and the truth was obvious to all, a monument would be erected on that field. The passing years, through the bickering and the debates, had settled the meaning of Breitenfeld. The phrase on the monument simply read: FREEDOM OF BELIEF FOR ALL THE WORLD.

Whatever else he was or was not, Gustavus Adolphus will always be Breitenfeld. He stands on that field for eternity, just as he did on that day. September 17, 1631.

Breitenfeld. Always Breitenfeld.

Chapter 35

"Those bastards!" snarled Bernard. The younger duke of Saxe-Weimar glared at the Saxons racing toward the safety of Eilenburg. "Wretched cowards!"

Bernard shifted his gaze to the oncoming tercios, lurching at an oblique angle toward the ruptured left flank of the Swedes. He turned a pale face to Gustav Adolf. "We can hold them off, Your Majesty— long enough, I think, for you to organize a retreat."

Gustav's light blue eyes were alive and dancing. *"Retreat?"* he demanded. "Are you mad?"

The king pointed a thick finger at his left flank. "Race over there, Bernard—*fast as you can*—and tell Horn to pivot his forces to the left. Tell him to keep his right anchored to the center, but to form a new battle line at right angles to our own. Do you understand?"

Bernard nodded. An instant later, he had spurred his charger into a gallop. His older brother made to follow, but Gustav restrained him. "You stay with me, Wilhelm."

The king smiled. "Your impetuous and hot-headed brother is enough to pester Horn—who won't need the pestering anyway."

Wilhelm nodded obediently. Gustav twisted in his saddle. As usual, his small band of couriers were sitting their horses not many yards behind him. Most of these were young Swedish noblemen, but there were two Scots in the group. The king snatched the broad-brimmed hat from his head and used it to summon them forward. The flamboyant gesture was quite unnecessary, being due simply to Gustav's high spirits. For all the world, the king seemed like a man facing a ball rather than a disaster.

He spoke to the Scots first. "Tell Colonel Hepburn to move his brigade over in support of Field Marshal Horn. Understand?"

The Scots nodded. Hepburn's brigade, along with that of Vitzthum, formed the second line of the Swedish center. They constituted the bulk of the Swedish reserves. The king, logically enough, was now using them to shore up his threatened left.

The Scots had barely left when Gustav was issuing the same orders to two other couriers. *Vitzthum the same!*

The king eyed the center of the battle. Tilly's tercios were rippling slowly down the gentle slope where the veteran Catholic general had positioned them. Even with the advantage of downhill movement, across unimpeded ground, the imperial soldiers were making slow progress.

Gustav gave them no more than a quick scrutiny. He was quite confident that his infantry in the center, anchored by Torstensson's guns, could repel any direct charge. The Habsburg tercios would probably not even drive directly forward. The danger was on the left, and he had done what he could to support Horn against the coming hammer blow. The opportunity—

On the right!

Eagerly, Gustav examined his right flank. For a moment, he silently congratulated himself for having kept Banér from pursuing Pappenheim's broken cavalry. The temptation had been almost as great for the king as for his Field Marshal. But Gustav had distrusted the steadiness of the Saxons. Better to have Banér available if the battle went sour.

Which it most certainly had! But now—*now!*—Gustav could turn disaster into triumph. Banér and his men were back in line, organized and ready. Most of all, Gustav knew, those cavalrymen would be infused with self-confidence. They had already broken Pappenheim's famous Black Cuirassiers. Why should they not do the same to the rest?

"Why not?" demanded the king aloud. He grinned at the four couriers still around him. *"Why not?"* He waved his hat about cheerfully.

The young noblemen grinned back. One of them lifted his own hat in salute, shouting: *"Gott mit uns!"*

A few feet behind them, Anders Jönsson slid his saber an inch or so out of its scabbard, before easing it back. He did the same with his four saddle-holstered pistols. Those weapons would be needed soon, and he wanted to be certain they were easy to hand. The huge Jönsson was the king's personal bodyguard.

The dozen Scotsmen under his command followed suit. They knew Gustav Adolf. The king of Sweden was utterly indifferent to personal danger. There had been few enough battles in which the king was present where he did not lead a charge himself.

Clearly, this was not going to be one of them. His Scots bodyguards were about to earn their pay.

One of the Scotsmen tried to be philosophical about the matter. "Ah weel, he's a braw lad, no' like yon God-rotton Stuart king o' England." He spit on the ground. "Ae fuckin' papist, tha' one be."

"Aye. Near's ca' be," agreed one of his mates.

Gustav Adolf spurred his horse into a canter, and then a gallop. Duke Wilhelm of Saxe-Weimar rode at his side, with the couriers and bodyguards thundering just behind.

As they neared the Swedish right flank, Gustav could see Banér trotting out to meet him. But the king gave the Field Marshal nothing but a moment's glance. His gaze was riveted on a large body of cavalrymen waiting behind Banér, under green standards. Those were Erik Soop's *Västgöta*. Over a thousand horsemen from West Gothland, organized into eight companies. Gustav thought highly of them. *Just the thing!*

When he reached Banér, Gustav reined in his horse and shouted gaily: "And *now*, Johann? You see?"

The Field Marshal nodded his bullet head. "You were right, Majesty. As always."

"Ha!" cried Gustav. "So modest! Not like you at all!"

The king was grinning fiercely. His own combative spirit seemed to transfer itself to his horse. The great charger pranced about nervously, as if impatient for battle.

"I want you to take the Västgöta, Johann." The king pointed to the left flank of Tilly's battle line. With Pappenheim's cuirassiers routed, that flank was unguarded. Unguarded, and getting more ragged by the moment. Tilly's oblique advance, marching from left rear to right front across the field in order to fall on the Swedish left, was straining the rigidity of his tercios. The Spanish-style squares were not well suited for anything but a forward advance.

"I intend to do the same to Tilly that he plans for me," the king explained. "Ha!" he barked happily. "Except I will succeed, and he will fail!"

For a moment, Banér hesitated. The king was proposing a bold gamble. It would be safer—

As if reading his thoughts, Gustav shook his head. "Horn will hold, Johann. He will hold. Horn will be the anvil—*we the hammer*."

Banér did not argue. He trusted his king's battle instincts. Gustav II Adolf was young, by the standards of generalship in his day. He was thirty-six years old. But he had more battle experience than most men twice his age. At the age of sixteen, he had organized and led the surprise attack which took the Danish fortress of

Borgholm. By the age of twenty-seven, he had taken Livonia and Riga and was already a veteran of the Polish and Russian wars.

Banér had been with him there. Banér, Horn, Torstensson, Wrangel—the nucleus of that great Swedish officer corps. Along with Axel Oxenstierna and the more recently arrived Scots professionals—Alexander Leslie, Robert Monro, John Hepburn, James Spens—they constituted the finest command staff in the world. Such, at least, was Banér's opinion.

The king's also. "We can do it, Johann!" he cried. "Now be off!"

Banér turned his horse and shouted orders at his own couriers and dispatch riders. Within seconds, the neatly arrayed Swedish right wing erupted into that peculiar disorder which precedes coordinated action. Company commanders and their subofficers dashed about, shouting their own commands—unneeded commands, for the most part. The Swedish and Finnish cavalry were veteran units themselves, as such things were counted in those days. Within a minute, the scene was one of individual frenzy. Men jumped to the ground to cinch a girth, or checked the ease of a saber's draw, or changed pyrites in the jaws of a wheel lock, swearing all the while. Cursing their refractory horses and equipment, perhaps; or clumsy mates who impeded them; or their own clumsiness—or, often enough, simply the state of the world. Many—most—took the time as well for a quick prayer.

The Brownian motion of a real battlefield, nothing more. Logic and order emerged from chaos soon enough. Within five minutes, Banér and his West Gothlanders began their charge.

The king, in the meantime, had been organizing the heavier forces which would drive home the assault. Four regiments, numbering perhaps three thousand men.

The Smalanders and East Gothlanders were Swedish. Heavy cuirassiers, in their arms and armor, although the term was mocked by the puny size of their horses. The two Finnish regiments were more lightly armed and armored, but their Russian horses were much superior.

The Finns, like their mounts, favored the wild Eastern European style of cavalry warfare. What they lacked in discipline they made up for in fervor. They were already screeching their savage battle cry: *Haakkaa päälle!*

Hack them down!

Gustav would lead the charge, at the head of his Swedish regiments. He hesitated only long enough to gauge the battle on his left. He could see nothing now. The farmland dust thrown up by thousands of chargers, mixed with billowing gunsmoke, had turned the battlefield into a visual patchwork.

But he could hear the battle, and it did not take him more than a few seconds to draw the conclusion. Horn—good Horn! reliable Horn!—was holding Tilly at bay.

He drew his saber and pointed it forward. *"Gott mit uns!"* he bellowed. "Victory!"

The first imperial cavalry charge shattered against Horn's defense. The Catholic horsemen had been astonished at the speed with which the Swedes took new positions. They had been expecting the sluggish maneuvers of Continental armies.

Others could have warned them. The Danes and Poles and Russians had been bloodied enough, over the past twenty years, by Gustav's small army. The Danes could have told them of Borgholm, Christianopel, Kalmar and Waxholm—all places where a teenage Swedish king had bested them. The Russians could have told them of Angdov and Pleskov, and the Poles could have recited a very litany of woe: Riga, Kockenhusen, Mittau, Bauske, Walhof, Braunsberg, Frauenburg, Tolkemit, Elbing, Marienburg, Dirschau, Mewe, Putzig, Wörmditt, Danzig, Gurzno and the Nogat.

The haughty cuirassiers in Tilly's army never thought to ask. They were south Germans, in the main, taking the coin of Maximillian of Bavaria. The peculiar-sounding names of Baltic and Slavic battlefields and sieges meant nothing to them.

In all those years Gustav II Adolf had suffered defeats as well. The Danes had beaten him at Helsingborg, and the Poles at Honigfeld. But the Danes and the Poles could have warned the forces under the Habsburg banner of the incredible elasticity of the Swedish king. He rebounded from reverses with renewed energy, using defeat as his school.

Tilly's men would study in that school themselves—study long and hard, before this day was over. They were not, alas, apt pupils. Arrogant Pappenheim, now trying—and failing—to rally his cavalrymen somewhere on the Halle road, had learned one lesson. Pathetic the Swedish nags might be, but there was nothing pitiful about the men astride them. Neither they, nor the infantrymen who formed their shield. Seven times his Black Cuirassiers had charged the Swedish line. Seven times they had been beaten back—and then routed by a countercharge.

Not apt pupils, no. Now, on the opposite flank, the imperial cavalry failed the lesson for the eighth time. The first charge, headlong, exuberant, certain of victory—no caracole here!—broke like a wave against a rock. They had been expecting a confused and shaken enemy, disorganized by the sudden rout of the Saxons. Instead, the Catholic cuirassiers found themselves piling into a solid and well-positioned defense. Horn had even managed to seize and prepare the ditches alongside the Düben road.

The Swedish arquebus roared; the Swedish pike held firm. The imperial cavalry fell back.

Back, but not dismayed. Tilly and his men had won the first great Catholic victory in the Thirty Years War, the Battle of the White Mountain. Eleven years had since passed, and with them came many more triumphs. That army had been accused—and rightly—of many crimes over those years. Of cowardice, not once.

Again, they charged; again, with sabering fury. And, again, were driven back.

The infantry tercios lumbered nearer. The cavalrymen, seeing them come, were driven into yet another headlong charge. For them the victory! Not those wretched footmen!

No use. The tercios crept forward.

Finally, the imperial cuirassiers abandoned the saber and fell back on the wheel-lock pistol. They began wheeling in the caracole, firing their pistols at a distance and circling to reload. Those men were mercenaries, when all was said and done. They could not afford to lose their precious horses. And they had already learned, as Pappenheim's men before them, that the Swedish tactic against heavy cavalry was to aim arquebus and pike at the horses. They had been trained and instructed in that method by their king. Gustav Adolf had long understood that his Swedish ponies were no match for German chargers. So kill the chargers first.

The tercios advanced across the battlefield, at the oblique. Grinding toward the Swedish left, now bent at a right angle away from the original battle line. Like a glacier, those seventeen tercios seemed. Slow—and unstoppable.

But that too was illusion. The glacier was about to calve, under gunfire it had never before encountered. The finest artillery in the world was on the field, that day, under the leadership of the world's finest artillery commander. Torstensson had needed no orders. His king had not even bothered to send a courier. The young artillery general, as soon as he saw Gustav sending Hepburn and Vitzthum's men to reinforce Horn, had known what was coming. For all the Swedish king's strategic caution, he was invariably bold on the battlefield. Torstensson knew that a counterattack was looming, and it was his job to batter the tercios in advance. Batter them, stun them, bleed them. Like a picador in a bullring, he would weaken the beast for the matador.

"Swivel the guns!" he roared. Torstensson, afoot as always in a battle, raced to stand at the front. It was a day for hat-snatching, it seemed. He tore his own from his head and began waving it.

"Swivel the guns!" That second roar caused him to choke. There had been a drought in the area that summer, and the plains were dry. The dust thrown up by thousands of horses caught in his throat. Using his hat as a pointer, Torstenson silently emphasized his command.

His gunners were all veterans. Immediately, grunting with exertion at the levering spikes, they began swiveling the field guns to bring enfilade fire on the tercios crossing in front of them.

There were two types of guns in the batteries. The majority, forty-two of them, were the so-called "regimental guns." Three-pounders: the world's first genuine field artillery. These cannons were made of cast bronze, with a light, short barrel to make them easily maneuverable in the field. The Swedes, after experimenting, had discovered that by using a reduced powder charge the guns could be fired safely time after time. They were of no use in a siege, but were superbly effective on the battlefield.

The heavier field guns were twelve-pounders. Gustav Adolf had simplified his ordnance drastically over the past years, based on his experience in the Polish wars. He brought only three sizes of cannon with him to Germany—the light and heavier field guns, and twenty-four-pounders for siege work. He had dispensed altogether with the forty-eight-pounder traditionally used in reducing fortifications.

The three-pounders were firing within a few minutes. The twelve-pounders quickly followed suit. By the time Tilly's infantry neared the angle in their opponent's line, they were coming under heavy fire from the Swedish artillery.

Understanding that the battle had reached a critical moment, Torstensson was ordering a rate of fire which was just barely short of reckless.

"I want a shot every six minutes!" he bellowed, trotting up and down behind the line of his guns. "Nothing less!" He practically danced with energy, waving his hat. "I'll hang the crew who gives me less!"

His men grinned. Torstensson always issued blood-curdling threats on the battlefield. And never carried them out. Nor was there any need. His men were well into the rhythm again, and had already reached the round-every-six-minutes rate which was considered the maximum of the day.

They could not keep that up forever, of course. The problem was not with them, but the guns. The cannons had been firing for three hours, now. Each of them had discharged close to thirty rounds. After another ten rounds, at that rate of fire, the guns would be so hot that they would have to sit idle. For at least an hour, probably, to allow the barrels to cool enough to be used safely.

"Let the blasted things melt!" roared Torstensson. He flung his hat toward Tilly's tercios. *"I want those battles broken! Broken in pieces, do you hear?"*

The grins faded from his gunners' faces. Torstensson was dead serious now, they knew. If need be, he *would* keep the guns firing long past the point of safety. The artillerymen sweated through the rhythm. So be it. If a crew died because of a burst cannon, so be it. Torstensson himself would pick up the rammer.

Cannonballs began tearing great holes in the tightly packed Catholic formations. Torstensson's gunners were the finest in the world, and they knew what their commander wanted.

"Grazing shots!" Torstensson slammed the flat of one hand into the other, as if skipping a stone off a lake. "Nothing but grazing shots! I see two balls in a row plunge into the ground I'll hang the crew! Hang 'em, do you hear?"

His men laughed. Another idle threat. Almost every round they fired was the good artilleryman's sought-after "grazing shot."

The "grazing shot" was useless against fortifications, but against men in the field it was devastating. The balls landed dozens of yards in front of their target and bounced forward at a shallow angle, instead of burying themselves in the ground. From that first bounce, their trajectory was at knee-to-shoulder height. The cast-iron missiles caromed into the packed ranks of the enemy like bowling balls—except these balls destroyed men instead of knocking down pins. Even a three-pound ball, in a grazing shot, could easily kill or maim a dozen men in such close ranks. The twelve-pounders wreaked pure havoc.

Torstensson's artillery was ripping the tercios like an orca ripping flesh from a great whale. Blood began settling the dust. The men in the rear tercios slogged through mud left by their comrades' gore—and added their own to the mix. *Graze, graze, graze, graze.* Death wielded his sickle that day, and mercilessly.

Not even Tilly's men could shrug off that kind of fire. Courageous as always, the recruits following the lead of the veterans; they obeyed their orders and plowed stubbornly toward the angle in the Swedish line. But their formations became more and more ragged and broken. Pikemen were being injured by the weapons of their mates, now, as men stumbled over corpses and lost control of the great blades.

Tilly saw, and grew pale. Near the front of his advancing tercios, he reined in his horse and stared back at the carnage.

"God in Heaven," he muttered. Wallenstein had tried to warn him of the Swedish artillery. *Wallenstein—that black-hearted Bohemian!*

Aye, he—and a dozen Polish officers in Tilly's service. But Tilly had not believed.

"God in Heaven," he muttered again. For a moment, he thought of changing his attack. Wheeling, and driving down on those cursed guns.

Wheeling . . .

Tilly dismissed the notion instantly. His battles did not "wheel." *Could* not wheel. They were instruments of crushing victory, not clever maneuver.

"Victory," he growled. Seventy-two years old he was, not a day less. Seventy-two years, not one of whose days had ever seen defeat.

"Onward!" he bellowed. The old general drew his sword and trotted toward the front. He waved the sword at the Swedish left.

"Onward!" he bellowed. *"Victory is there!"*

The tercios obeyed, and obeyed, and obeyed—seventeen battles, down the line, slogged tenaciously forward. Not one of them faltered in their duty. Not one tercio, not one rank, not one file, not one man.

Torstensson splattered their entrails across the land. *No matter. Those men had marched through entrails before.* Torstensson painted the soil with their blood. *No matter. Those men had bled before.* Torstensson savaged them like no artillery in their grim experience. *No matter. Tilly had never failed them before.*

Murderers many of them were. Thieves and rapists too. Cowards, never.

The broken Swedish angle was in front of them now. Like a bear trailing gore, the tercios were about to mangle their prey.

At last!

"Father Tilly!" they bellowed. *"Jesu-Maria!"*

But the angle was not broken. Not any longer. Horn—*trusted Horn, trustworthy Horn*—had reformed the line even before his king's orders arrived. The Swedish left now formed a solid corner for the battlefield. The imperial heavy cavalry had already broken against that Baltic rock. The tercios lumbered up and did no better.

Pike against pike, the Catholics were easily the equal of their foe. But the Swedish king was a believer in firepower more than cold steel. He had studied the methods of the Dutch, and tested them in Poland and Russia.

At Breitenfeld, the Swedes had a higher arquebus-to-pike ratio than their enemies. More important, Gustav Adolf had trained them to fight in shallow formations, following the Dutch example. Tilly's arquebusiers were arrayed thirty ranks deep. Most of those arquebuses could not be brought to bear. Gustav's, not more than six—just enough to allow time to reload while the front ranks fired.

The Swedish pikes held the tercios at bay long enough for the Swedish preponderance in firepower to bring down them down. Tilly's men never buckled. But they made no headway against the Swedish line. They simply died. And meanwhile, the king of Sweden prepared the death stroke.

Tilly and his tercios could not *wheel*, but Gustav Adolf could. Could, and did.

Chapter 36

The king himself led the charge up the slope, heading toward the imperial guns. *"Gott mit uns!"* he bellowed, waving his cavalrymen forward with his saber.

Behind him, Anders Jönsson rolled his eyes with exasperation. Gustav Adolf carried two wheel-lock pistols at his side, holstered to his saddle. But he never used them in battle. He claimed it was because the weapons were too inaccurate, but his bodyguard was skeptical. The king of Sweden was sensitive about his myopia. Jonsson thought his unwillingness to use pistols was simply because Gustav couldn't hit the proverbial broad side of a barn.

Anders spurred his horse alongside the king's. "I'm supposed to be guarding *you*, Highness," he snarled, "not the other way around."

Gustav grinned. "Get a faster horse!" he bellowed. Again, he waved the saber. *"Gott mit uns!"*

Behind them, the Smalanders and East Gothlanders echoed the words. From either side—the Finns were already curling around the slower Swedes—came the blood-curdling Finnish battle cry.

"Haakaa päälle!"

Ahead of the cavalry charge, positioned almost at the crest of the shallow slope, were the imperial batteries. As slow as the tercios were, the big guns were slower still. Tilly's order for an oblique advance had caught the artillerymen by surprise. They were still hitching up the horses and oxen when Gustav started his charge.

The Catholic gunners stared at the thousands of Swedish and Finnish horsemen galloping toward them. They had no protection left beyond a small force of pikemen.

One of the gunners began hurriedly unhitching the lead horse from the trail of his six-pounder. "What are you doing?" demanded his comrade.

"I'm getting out of here," the gunner hissed. "You'd better do the same, if you're smart. Those Finns are as savage as Croats."

His partner blanched. The rammer had no experience with Finns, but he knew Croats. They formed a large part of the Habsburg dynasty's light cavalry, and were as famous for their cruelty as their horsemanship. Croats had no use for prisoners.

The gunner had unhitched the horse and was awkwardly climbing onto it. The horse had neither a saddle nor stirrups, and was guided by a simple halter. From a distance, his partner heard the faint sound of the Finnish battle cry. *Haakaa päälle*? He didn't know the words.

"That means 'hack them down,'" grunted the gunner. "In case you were wondering." He pounded his mount's flanks with spurless heels. The confused artillery horse broke into an awkward trot. Seconds later, inspired more by the fear and fury in his rider's voice than the naked boot heels, the horse lurched into a sudden gallop.

The gunner, riding bareback and without stirrups, was flung to the ground. He died soon thereafter. His broken neck was trampled by his partner's horse, as it made its own uncontrolled exit from the scene. Unlike the gunner, his comrade managed to stay on the horse's back by clutching the beast's mane. But it did him little good. The horse, unaccustomed to being ridden, was so terrified and confused that it galloped in a circle and brought the rammer into a knot of Finnish cavalrymen. *Haakaa päälle!*

Most of the imperial artillerymen lacked the option of fleeing—or trying to—on horseback. There were few horse-drawn six-pounders in Tilly's army. Catholic armies favored twelve-pounders and huge twenty-four-pounders, drawn by oxen. The gunners simply escaped on foot—successfully, in all but a few instances. For all their savage reputation, the Finns were under Gustav's command and were accustomed to his discipline. The king had a short way with cavalrymen who went off on wild charges when there was royal work to be done.

"Take the cannons!" Gustav roared. Ignoring the imperial gunners and rammers scattering to the rear, the Finns stooped onto the guns like hawks. The few knots of artillerymen still trying to stand their ground were butchered within a minute or two. By the time Gustav Adolf and the slower Swedes galloped onto the scene, Tilly's entire artillery had been seized.

Gustav trotted back and forth on his charger. He had scabbarded his saber and was back to waving his hat. "Turn them around!" he bellowed. His powerful voice, as always, carried well in a battle. "I want those guns turned on Tilly! Now, d'you hear? Now! *Move, move, move!*"

The Finns ignored the command, knowing it was not intended for them. While they maintained a guard against enemy cavalry, hundreds of Smalanders and East Gothlanders dismounted. Hurriedly, they picked up the spikes discarded by the routed Catholic gunners and began levering the great weapons around. Even before the guns were repositioned, other cavalrymen were already beginning to load the pieces.

They were slower and less adept than Torstensson's men would have been, of course. But, unlike the cavalry of other armies, Gustav's men were cross-trained to serve as artillery or even, if need be, as infantry. Swedish cavalry, like the cavalry of other nations, was dominated by noblemen. But the Swedish aristocracy had little in the way of continental hauteur—and what little they began with was soon drummed out of them by their king's training and discipline.

Soon enough, the huge cannons were brought to bear on their target. Gustav did not wait to fire a coordinated volley, as Torstensson's artillery was trained to do. Each gun fired as soon as possible.

The fire was ragged, slow, and indifferently aimed. It mattered not at all. Tilly's army was now a crumpled and half-broken thing, distorted almost beyond recognition by the pressure of the battle. The rigid formations of the tercios had collapsed, compressed between Horn's unyielding line and the battering of Torstensson's artillery. Now, adding to their destruction, came the heavy fire of their own cannons. The huge mass of Catholic soldiers—not much more than a mob—was a target impossible to miss, even for the cavalrymen manning the captured guns. And the size of the cannonballs made up for their lack of accuracy. Unlike Torstensson's well-trained and experienced gunners, the cavalrymen failed more often than not in making the grazing shot. But against thousands of men packed so tightly they could barely move, the twelve- and twenty-four-pound balls which landed caused pure havoc.

For one of the rare times in his life, even Gustav was not tempted to launch another charge.

Well . . . Not much.

"Perhaps . . ." Jonsson heard him mutter. "Perhaps . . ." The king was squinting at the distant enemy, raising himself up in his stirrups. His huge frame seemed like that of a brown bear, eyeing a crippled moose.

His bodyguard spoke hastily. "It's a done thing, Your Majesty." Jonsson pointed at the imperial forces with his saber. "They're finished. It's over."

The king took two or three deep breaths, and then eased himself back into the saddle. "Yes."

He heaved a sigh. "They should surrender now. Their cavalry has all fled. No chance of making a sally. They're trapped."

Jönsson said nothing. There was no chance at all of their enemy surrendering. Not with Tilly in command.

"Poor Tilly," mused Gustav. "Pappenheim has ruined him twice. The butcher of Magdeburg. And now—forever—"

The king's near-sighted blue eyes scanned a landscape that could have been nothing but a blur. But the sight still seemed pleasing to him.

"And now, forever. *Breitenfeld.*"

"God damn Pappenheim," hissed Tilly. The old general's face grew pinched as his aide tightened a bandage, but he made no sound of protest. Just another hissing curse:

"*God damn Pappenheim.*"

Tilly was lying on the ground near the center of his army. He had been wounded twice already. The first wound was minor, not much more than a bad bruise caused by a musketball glancing off his cuirass. The hip wound which his aide was now bandaging was more serious. A pike head sent flying by those infernal Swedish guns had torn him badly. His entire leg was soaked with blood.

Tilly's verbal curse was for Pappenheim. His silent one, for himself.

I should have listened to Wallenstein. So fast! So fast! I never saw an army move that fast. How did that Swedish bastard do it?

The old man was tempted to close his eyes, from sheer anguish and humiliation. But he resisted the impulse, even when—not forty yards distant—he saw another dozen of his men turned into a bloody, bone-splintered mess by a bouncing cannonball. No man would ever say that Tilly—*Jan Tzerklas, Count Tilly!*—could not face ruin with the same fearlessness with which he had always faced triumph.

Two of his officers approached and knelt at his side. The faces of both men were haggard.

"We must surrender, General," said one of them.

"There is no possibility of retreat," added the other, "not without cavalry to cover us. The Swedish cavalry and their Finns will butcher us."

Still lying on his back, weak from loss of blood, Tilly shook his head. For all the general's exhaustion and age, the gesture was firm as a bull's.

"*No.*" Hissing: "Damn Pappenheim and his precious Black Cuirassiers!" For a moment, he closed his eyes. Again: "No. I will not surrender."

The aides began to protest. Tilly silenced them with a clenched fist held high. His eyes reopened, staring at the sky.

"How soon is nightfall?" he asked.

One of the aides glanced up. "An hour. Perhaps two."

"Hold till then," growled Tilly. "Till nightfall. After that the men can retreat. It will be a rout, but in the darkness the damned Swedes will not be able to pursue. We can save most of the army."

"What's left of it," muttered an aide.

Tilly glared at him. Then at the other. Then at three more officers who had come to their side.

"Useless," he snarled. "As bad as Pappenheim. All glory and no stomach."

He turned to his aide. "Get me up," he commanded. "Onto my charger."

The aide didn't even think to protest. It was the work of a few minutes to lever the old general onto his horse.

From the saddle, Tilly sneered down at his officers.

"Surrender, you say? Damn you all! My men will stand with me."

And so it proved. Till nightfall, Tilly took his place near the front of the imperial line, holding his men by force of will and example. *Jesu-Maria!* they cried, dying. *Father Tilly!*

At dusk, Tilly was struck down again. No one saw the missile which caused the wound. A musketball, perhaps. But by the look of the terrible wound in his shoulder, it was probably another broken piece of the battle, sent flying by those horrible Swedish guns.

His aide and several soldiers rescued him. Improvising a stretcher, they hurried to the rear. Until he lost consciousness a few minutes later, Tilly cursed them for cowards. As the stretcher passed through the broken tercios, clusters of Tilly's soldiers formed a defense guard, escorting their commander to safety.

For the rest, Tilly's fall signaled the rout. The Catholic veterans could stand the butchery no longer. In less than five minutes, the lines which had stood unyielding for hours broke into a stampede. Discarding their weapons and gear, thousands of imperial infantrymen began racing for the shelter of darkness and distant woods.

Most of them made their escape. Gustav ordered no pursuit. Tilly's sheer courage, by holding the Swedes at bay until nightfall, had made the complete destruction of his army impossible.

As he knelt in prayer after the battle, the king of Sweden was not aggrieved and never thought to curse his foe. He understood what Tilly's purpose had been, in that seemingly insane stand, and found nothing in it except admiration.

And, truth be told, a certain satisfaction. The last of a great line had fallen. But he had toppled like a great tree, not rotted like a stump.

Something in the pious Lutheran king saw the hand of God at work, in the broken but glorious ruin of his Catholic enemy. God's will worked in mysterious ways, not understood by men. But Gustav thought he could detect something of that divine purpose, in the manner of Tilly's downfall.

No matter, in any event. Gustav Adolf had not completely destroyed his enemy, true. But he had won the greatest battlefield victory in decades, perhaps centuries. And if Tilly had prevented total ruin, the wreckage was still incredible to behold. The proud imperial army which had defeated every opponent they faced since the White Mountain was nothing but rubble.

At Breitenfeld, the Swedish forces suffered barely two thousand casualties. Their opponents?

Seven thousand dead.

Six thousand wounded and captured.

All the artillery, captured.

The entire imperial baggage train, captured.

Ninety battle flags, captured.

The road into central Europe was open. Vienna, Prague, Munich, Mainz—anywhere the king of Sweden might choose to go. Breitenfeld opened the way.

The Lion of the North was no longer penned in the Baltic. Emperor Ferdinand was penned, now. He and his cohorts in the Inquisition.

"Send for Wallenstein," Ferdinand sighed, when he heard the news. His courtiers began to protest, but the emperor scowled them down. "I distrust and despise the man as much as you," he snarled. "But what choice do I have?"

Silence. *No choice at all.*

Cardinal Richelieu did not sigh, when he was told of Breitenfeld. Sighing was not his way. He said nothing; his lean, intellectual's face remained expressionless; he gave no hint of his sentiments or thoughts.

He dismissed his assistants immediately. Then, sitting at his study, began to pen a letter.

> *My dear Wallenstein,*
> *Greetings, and may God's blessing be upon you. By now, you will have heard the news of Breitenfeld. You will recall, I am certain, a conversation which we had once. I regret that I did not listen more carefully to your advice and warnings. It seems to me that there might now be a mutual advantage in working toward*

*the end which you suggested at the time. I will say no more of
that here. Surely you understand my purpose without further
elaboration. If you are still of the same mind, send word to me
by courier.*

                                                    Richelieu.

While his enemies—open and hidden—plotted against him, the
king of Sweden solidified his hold on central Germany. He left Leipzig
to be recaptured by the chastened Saxons, while he himself followed
Tilly's retreating army. He captured three thousand more of those men
in a small battle outside Merseburg two days later. On September 21,
four days after Breitenfeld, he occupied Halle and allowed his army
to rest and refit.

The future was unclear, his ensuing course uncertain. Already the
king was being urged in many different directions by his various allies
and advisers.

No matter. Whichever course he decided upon, Gustav Adolf was
certain of one thing. At Breitenfeld, the world had changed forever.

Breitenfeld. Always Breitenfeld.

Part Four

On what wings dare he aspire?
What the hand dare seize the fire?

Chapter 37

Word of Breitenfeld reached Grantville toward the end of September. The town erupted in celebration, which went on for two full days.

The fact that the Catholics—who now constituted well over half the population—participated fully in the festivities was a sign of just how little religious affiliation lay at the center of the war. Germany's commoners, by and large, tended to be indifferent to their neighbors' Christian denomination. It was the aristocracy and the princes—above all, the Habsburg dynasty—who had forced the issue upon the Holy Roman Empire. And while each one of those noblemen claimed to be acting out of nothing more than piety, it was really their own power and privileges which were at stake. The great mercenary armies which ravaged central Europe were willing enough to enlist Protestants or Catholics into their ranks, regardless of their official allegiance. Any number of the "Catholic" mercenaries defeated by the Americans and then incorporated into their new society proved, once the dust settled, to be Lutherans or Calvinists.

So, everyone celebrated. Even Simpson and his coterie, for once, refrained from their usual recriminations and protests. Not even an ox was dumb enough not to understand that the king of Sweden's great victory at Breitenfeld removed most of the immediate military pressure from Thuringia.

Most, but not all. There were no official imperial armies squeezing the province any longer. But Tilly's army, in shattering, had produced a number of splinters. One of them, under the "command" of a self-appointed "captain," had decided to seek refuge for the winter south of the Harz mountains.

That ragged army numbered perhaps a thousand men, accompanied by twice that many camp followers. They marched—in a manner of speaking—into southern Thuringia, desperately seeking food and shelter from the coming winter. They had heard that the region was still largely unravaged by the war. They believed those rumors.

They had also heard that a band of sorcerers lurked thereabouts. But that rumor they dismissed. Witchcraft was a thing of old women, casting malicious spells on their neighbors—not powerful sorcerers shattering entire armies.

They learned otherwise before they got within thirty miles of Grantville, at a small crossroads not far from Jena.

Jena was a university town, famed throughout Germany as a center of learning. Its Collegium Jenense had been founded in 1558 with the help of the Protestant reformer Melanchthon. Jena had a population numbering in the thousands but, unlike Badenburg, the town was unwalled and essentially unprotected. When word arrived of an approaching army of mercenaries, the townsfolk were thrown into panic.

The notables conferred, debated, squabbled, bickered. *What to do?* The traditional remedy for the coming ill was to pay what amounted to extortion money. But there was no guarantee the measure would shield the town from such an undisciplined and half-leaderless force. It was a moot point, anyway. Jena's coffers had already been drained dry by Tilly.

Resistance? *With what?*

To be sure, the university's students mobilized in the streets, brandishing their cudgels fearlessly and demanding to be led into battle. The notables refrained from public sarcasm, since university students had a tendency to become riotous when mocked. But they did not take the offer seriously. A few hundred students armed with clubs—against a thousand real soldiers, armed with pike and arquebus?

Absurd.

Then, there came an unexpected offer of assistance. From the mysterious new town to the southwest called Grantville. A sorcerers' town, some said. A den of witchcraft and deviltry.

The notables consulted privately with the university's leading professors. Theologians, to a man. Experts on the Devil and his works.

The theologians, of course, also debated and bickered and squabbled. But not for long. Divine intention has a way of becoming very clear, when the alternative is a city sacked.

God's will. Accept the offer.

Three days later, the military contingent from Grantville passed by the town, on their way to confront the oncoming mercenaries. The townsfolk were relieved when the leaders of that force stated they had no intention of entering Jena. They were even more relieved when the leaders—"Americans," they called themselves; odd name—reiterated that they sought neither payment nor tribute. Only, as they had said in their offer, a desire for trade and commerce. Oh, yes—and a desire to exchange knowledge with the university's faculty and students, and take advantage of their famous printing facilities.

What could be the harm in that?

Half the town, and all the students, turned out to watch the Americans march by. They lined the road leading to Leipzig, cheering wildly. The applause was not diminished by the relatively small size of the American army. There were only four hundred men in that force, but they marched in good order and seemed full of confidence. So did the two hundred or so Scots cavalrymen who accompanied them.

The onlooking burghers and their wives were disturbed by the passing army. Well disciplined and unthreatening, yes. But the gear and equipment! Especially—

The university students, on the other hand, were not upset in the least by the huge vehicle which led the procession. To the contrary, they were quite charmed by the grotesque-looking thing. And once a few of their bolder number ascertained the name of the contraption, its further progress was greeted by a new cheer:

APC! APC! APC!

The older residents were less enthusiastic. Mutters were heard in which the name of the Devil was bandied about. But even the town's notables were ready enough to accept the explanation of the students. They had heard of Leonardo da Vinci, even if they had never seen his sketches.

The rifles, oddly enough, caused more distress. The coal-truck-turned-armored-personnel-carrier was too outlandish for the townspeople to gauge. But many of them were quite familiar with firearms, and the American-style arquebuses brought a chill to their spines. Not much to look at, true. But there was something reptilian and deadly about the serpentine slenderness of the things.

The camouflage hunting apparel also caused comment, as did the motorcycles. Couriers and scouts, apparently, although the onlookers were puzzled by the nature of the small black boxes into which the motorcyclists were seen to speak. The more perspicacious of the students spotted the similar device in the hand of the American leader riding in another vehicle. Inquiries were made, in stumbling English, to the passing American soldiers. Once it was ascertained that some of those soldiers were actually Germans themselves, additional charming acronyms were added to the students' cheers:

Four by four! Four by four!
CB! CB!

❧   ❧   ❧

Squatting in the back of the armored pickup, Mike grinned. Frank, the operational commander of the little army, was riding up front. As soon as Frank stopped talking on the radio, Mike leaned forward and hissed at him through the small window in the back of the cab.

"See?" he demanded. "What did I tell you?"

"All right, all right," grumbled Frank. "You don't have to rub it in."

Satisfied, Mike leaned back. But his grin never faded. He transferred it to the six other occupants in the back of the truck.

" 'Familiarity breeds contempt,' " he stated. "Give something a label and it stops being mysterious and devilish. It just *is*, that's all. That's why I told Heinrich and his guys to spread the word, if anybody asked."

The interior of the truck bed, enclosed by welded quarter-inch steel plate, was dark and gloomy. But there was enough light coming through the firing slits to allow Mike to see the faces of his companions. They responded to his cheerful grin with their own smiles, which were nervous in every case but one.

The nerveless—say better, insouciant—smile was actually quite wicked. The eyes above it gleamed with amusement and glee.

"You hear that, Frank?" the smile's owner demanded. " 'Familiarity breeds contempt!' "

Frank turned his head and glowered through the back window. At the nerveless smile, first; then, at the others.

"I still say girls have got no business here!" he snapped.

" 'Girls'?" snorted Gayle Mason. "I'm thirty-two, you old geezer. I remember you saying the same thing the first day I showed up at the mine. What was that—ten years ago?"

Frank glared; Gayle glared back. Gayle was an attractive enough woman, in a stocky and muscular manner. Her face was too plain to be considered pretty, but no one had ever suggested she was ugly. Still—excepting the absence of jowls—when she glared, Gayle bore a fair resemblance to a pugnacious bulldog.

"What *I* say," she continued, "is that broken-down old farts have got no business on a battlefield."

"Now, Gayle," murmured Mike. "Be nice."

Frank's eyes moved away from Gayle, and focused on the other women in the truck. "Gayle's hopeless," he growled. "She's doing this just to spite me. But you other—you *girls*—should have more sense."

The young women in the truck abandoned their nervous smiles, in favor of stubborn jaws. Except for Gayle, they were in their late teens or early twenties. The youngest of them, Julie Sims, managed a fair imitation of Gayle's glare.

"This is a hell of a time to bring up *that* argument, Uncle Frank!" she snapped. "We've already been through it, and it's settled."

Unkindly: "You're just pissed because I'm a better shot than you are, and you know it!"

Grumbling: "I'm tired of being a cheerleader."

"Beats being dead," came Frank's immediate reply.

"You were quick enough to put my boyfriend in the front line!"

Frank was just as stubborn as his niece. "That's different. He's a guy. And I'll tell you something else, young lady. If that stupid damned boyfriend of yours breaks ranks 'cause he's worried about you, there'll be hell to pay! That's one of the reasons I don't want—"

"Chip?" demanded Julie. "Ha! I already told him what'd happen if he did. He's hunted with me too, you know. I'll nail him before he takes a step."

Watching the interplay, Mike's grin faded. In truth, despite his genuine amusement at his older friend's knee-jerk outrage, Mike was uneasy himself with the arrangement. Mike thought he possessed little of any traditional "male chauvinism"—and what little there was had long ago been beaten out of him by his spunky sister—but he could still recognize a certain crude reality to Frank's opposition. It was a simple fact that, by and large, women were not as physically suited for infantry combat as men.

By and large . . .

Mike remembered a phrase from a play he had just seen two weeks ago. Shakespeare's *Hamlet*, staged by the high school's drama class in front of a packed audience in the school's auditorium, and then rebroadcast on TV. (They had kept the author's name. Balthazar had not objected; he had even had kind words to say about the performance, which, as was his custom, he had seen on the opening night.)

By and large . . .

Ay, there's the rub. What happens to the individual, when they get locked within that dangerous "by and large"? Generality is a slippery slope.

Mike studied the women in the pickup's bed, steadying himself with a hand against the truck's jolting progress down the dirt road.

Julie Sims, for all her cheerleader prettiness, had the physique of someone who was as well trained athletically as any of the boys she cheered on. Mike didn't doubt for a minute that she was in better physical shape than ninety-five percent of the men in the American/German army. Not as strong, no doubt, as many of them. But—

He eyed the rifle held casually in her hands. By universal acknowledgement, Julie Sims was the best rifle shot in Grantville. In all of Marion county, for that matter. Maybe even in the whole state. There had been talk of sponsoring her for the Winter Olympics biathlon. The talk had been serious enough that Julie had taken up cross-country skiing, and applied herself to it with her usual energy. Her skill on skis would be her downfall, she was convinced. Certainly not the shooting!

Mike's eyes met those of Gayle. The glance they exchanged was warm and friendly. When Gayle had started working in the mine years ago, she had encountered a certain amount of harassment from some of the male miners. Not much—and nothing in the way of physical abuse—but enough to make her defensive. "Defensive," for someone with Gayle Mason's temperament, was indistinguishable from *belligerent*. Then Mike had returned to West Virginia, gotten hired at his father's old job, and the harassment had ended within a week. They had wound up becoming good friends.

His eyes moved to the woman sitting next to Gayle, and the concern in them deepened.

"Relax, brother of mine," said Rita. "We'll stay out of trouble. I promise."

Mike smiled ruefully. *Promises be damned!* He knew his sister too well.

In the front, Frank was still muttering. "Damn Melissa Mailey, anyway," he was heard to grumble. "Stupid pinheaded liberal feminist peabrained—" On and on.

Bouncing around in the semidarkness of the truck bed, Mike and his sister exchanged grins. Melissa, of course, was taking the public blame for this latest outrage. Simpson, especially, seemed to spend half his time cursing her name from the rooftops. He had long since, in his relentless political campaign, elevated Melissa Mailey to the status of Ba'alzebub to Mike's Satan.

But Melissa was quite innocent, in truth. The middle-aged schoolteacher had been as surprised as anyone, when Rita and Gayle and Julie Sims advanced their demand to be incorporated into Grantville's armed forces. In the raucous debate which erupted in the emergency committee, Melissa had waffled and wavered—quite unlike her usual self. On the one hand, her feminism inclined her to support the proposal. On the other . . .

At bottom, Melissa Mailey had the soul of a pacifist. A semipacifist, at least. A Boston Brahmin, born and bred in a certain other-worldly atmosphere. The thought of carrying a gun *herself* had never seriously crossed her mind. Not even in her days as a radical college student, when she had been much more attracted by the tactics of civil disobedience.

No, Simpson could denounce Melissa all he wanted. Here, as in so many things, the rich man from the big city simply failed to understand the mentality of the "poor white trash" he had found himself placed amidst. Unsophisticated they might be, in some respects. But generations of poverty and hard times had also bred a certain hard-headed practicality, and a willingness to accept reality for what it was. Nor did the proposal seem all that strange, come down to it. Many of Grantville's women had already served in the U.S. military, after all, drawn by the same blue-collar motives which impelled their brothers and cousins to volunteer.

Our army's too small? Well, then—enlist women.

Squawk, squawk, squawk. By and large . . .

Fine. They've got to pass the same physical tests.

By and large, the women who volunteered failed to pass Frank's rigorous regimen. And Mike refused all pleas to ease the training. That far, he was not prepared to go.

By and large . . .

Ay, there's the rub. Because a fair number of women *did* pass even Frank's disgruntled scrutiny—and some of them with flying colors. Six of them, to be precise. All six were now riding in the pickup with the army's official commander. Mike had decided he should accompany them, in their first test in actual battle.

"Just stay out of trouble," Mike said, loud enough to be heard by all the occupants in the back of the truck. "Do us all a favor, will you? Stay out of trouble."

Gayle and Julie grinned. The other three girls smiled. Rita seemed to ignore the remark completely. She was peering through one of the firing slits.

" 'Stay out of trouble,' " she mimicked sarcastically. "Jeff's just dropping Gretchen off. Now *there's* the woman you oughta be worrying about."

She turned away, bestowing her brother with a glare. "Why is it," she demanded, "that men shit their pants at the idea of a woman in a battle—but have no trouble at all sending Mata Hari into the lion's den?"

Mike laughed. "Mata Hari? Get real! Gretchen's not going to be batting her eyes at any diplomats and generals."

His sister's gaze was unwinking. "No. That'd be safe, compared to what you want her to do."

Mike looked away. To his relief, Gayle came to his rescue. "Give your poor brother a break, Rita," she said, chuckling. "He backed us up, didn't he, push come to shove?"

His sister's reply was inaudible. But Mike wouldn't have heard it, anyway. He had caught sight of Gretchen, still kissing her new husband as she stood alongside Jeff's motorcycle. He almost laughed again, seeing the shocked expressions on the faces of the German burghers and their women alongside the road. *In public! Outrageous!*

"You ain't seen nothing yet," he whispered. "Notable men and women of Germany—*heeere's* Gretchen!"

Chapter 38

Reluctantly, Jeff let her go. "Be careful," he whispered, giving Gretchen's waist another quick hug.

"Me?" she demanded, frowning half-jocularly. "You are ze one goink in battle. Not me!"

Jeff was not mollified. "Still—"

Gretchen grabbed the back of his head and drew his face to hers. A quick, firm kiss followed. Then she stepped back, patting him on a plump cheek. "Go, husband. Come back to me. Safe."

Jeff sighed. When she wanted, his wife had a will of iron. He knew full well that this was one of those times. He still didn't understand why Gretchen had been so quick—so eager—to accept Mike and Melissa's proposal. But he hadn't questioned her at the time, and he wasn't about to do it now.

So he satisfied himself with a quick glance at her bodice and vest. The garments had been designed slightly oversize. Between that, and Gretchen's impressive bust, the 9mm automatic resting in the shoulder holster was quite unnoticeable.

His wife laughed. "Not to stare at *mein* tits!" she exclaimed, shaking her head and wagging a finger. "Vat *skandal*!" Then, very softly: "Do not vorry, husband. *Go*."

A moment later, Jeff was roaring off. He made it a point to do a wheelie as he passed a small group of young men standing by the road. The local toughs, by their look.

They were suitably impressed—not so much by the acrobatics of the machine as the ferocious scowl on the face of the very large man who rode it. That, and the odd but deadly looking weapon slung over his shoulder. Jeff would have been quite shocked—and utterly pleased—had he known the impression he made on those bravos.

They saw nothing of a shy young man in his leather-jacketed form. Just a killer. The fact that he wore spectacles made him seem all the more dangerous. *The better to see his victims, no doubt.*

One of the young toughs was not as intimidated as the others. After the motorcycle's roar faded, he cast an eye on the woman standing by the road staring after it.

"Good-looking," he mused. "Very."

"Forget it, Max," hissed one of his friends.

Max leered. "Why, Josef? Who knows? Her man might be dead before the day is over."

Max's friends gathered around, crowding him close. "I said forget it," repeated Josef, punching Max in the shoulder. The gesture was not playful in the least. "He might not, either. And even if he is, what of the others?"

Max let it go. The woman had disappeared into the crowd, by now. And he didn't like the way in which Josef was gripping his dirk. "Just joking," he mumbled. But he made himself a silent promise to pursue the matter. Alone.

An hour later, their bikes perched atop a small ridge, Jeff and Larry Wild spotted the oncoming mercenaries through their binoculars.

Well—Jeff did. Larry was too busy admiring the scenery. "God, this is a pretty place," he murmured admiringly. He pulled the binoculars away from his eyes for a moment, to get a panoramic view of the Saale valley. The Saale was a small river, originating in the hills of the Thuringen Forest. In its northward course, flowing down the valley to which it had given its name, the river passed through Jena on its way. The valley was flanked by red sandstone and chalk hills, half-covered with grapevines. This was wine country, and it was as pretty as such areas usually are.

"Forget the *vino*," muttered Jeff. "Trouble's coming."

Startled, Larry's eyes followed the direction of his friend's binoculars. Even without the aid of his own, Larry could now see the cloud of dust.

"How many?" he asked.

Still holding the binoculars pressed to his eyes, Jeff shrugged. "Hard to say. That's not an army, so much as it is a mob. If there's any marching order at all, I can't tell what it is."

By now, Larry had his own binoculars back in place. "Not too many cavalry," he commented. "Mike'll glad to hear that."

"I don't think there's any *cavalry* at all," snorted Jeff. "Just maybe two dozen guys who managed to steal horses and ain't real good at riding them yet. Call themselves 'officers,' I bet. The Scots'll go through 'em like a chainsaw."

After a few more seconds of observation, Larry chuckled. "I do believe you're right, buddy of mine. I do believe you're right."

Jeff lowered the glasses and reached for his radio. A moment later he was giving Frank Jackson directions to the ridge. He and Larry had already determined that it was the best position from which to command this portion of the valley. It was the only high ground in the area and, what was even better, the road into Jena passed by at the foot of the ridge. They were hoping that the veteran Frank would agree with them, with all the tender pride of youthful war-gamers putting abstract skills to concrete practice.

Frank did. Heaped them with praise, in fact, insofar as Frank's terse remarks could be called "heaping." But Frank Jackson was one of those people who ladled with a teaspoon, and Jeff and Larry were more than satisfied.

The next few minutes were taken up with preparing the American positions. Mike kept the APC and Mackay's cavalry out of sight, hidden beyond a curve in the road. They would be used to pursue and capture the defeated enemy. He stationed Heinrich and the German contingents across the road itself. They would form the barrier to the oncoming mercenaries.

The new German recruits constituted about half of Mike's infantry force. They were still organized into their own units, under newly elected officers. Heinrich was in overall command.

Mike had intended to integrate the army immediately, rather than keeping the Germans in separate contingents. But experience had taught him that the process was going to be protracted. The problem was not "social," and involved no prejudice. The American and German soldiers were getting along quite nicely, as it happened— especially after a notable barroom brawl in which several American and German soldiers marched into the Club 250 and taught the resident rednecks who was who and what was what. Dan Frost and his deputies had tossed the lot of them into the town's jury-rigged jail thereafter, but the event had crystallized the army's growing sentiment of comradeship.

No, the problem was purely military, and purely simple.

Germans couldn't *shoot.*

Blast away, yes. Stand their ground like lions, yes.

Aim? Hit a target? Not a chance.

Squeeze the trigger? You must be joking! An arquebus has no "trigger." Just a heavy hand-lever closed with a jerk—*after* shutting your eyes to protect them from powder burns.

Heinrich and his men were veterans, and their habits were deeply ingrained. With the exception of a handful of the youngsters, none of the Germans had been able to adjust to modern rifles. The attempt to train them had simply produced frustration on all sides.

In the end, Mike had taken the practical course. "Screw it," he told Frank. "Just arm them with shotguns loaded with lead slugs. We'll use them for close action."

The Germans had been ecstatic. They took to shotguns like bears to honey. The shotguns were more accurate than arquebuses, even after the chokes were sawn off to produce cylinder bores which would handle solid slugs. But the Germans didn't give a damn about accuracy, anyway. They had survived as long as they had because each and every one of them was a devotee of the First Principle of Smooth-bore Battle:

Rate of fire. That was Moses and the prophets, as far as the German soldiers were concerned. *Rate of fire.* Victory in battle went to the men who stood their ground and blasted away the most. Simple as that.

The American invention of bayonets was icing on the cake. None of them, any longer—arquebusier or pikeman—had to worry about the reliability of the other. All were now both in one.

Pump-action shotguns, fitted with bayonets—those, if nothing else, sealed the allegiance of Heinrich and his men to the new order. Their love for the marvelous devices was so great that it even reconciled them to the grotesque eccentricities of the Americans. Such as—

The German soldiers were careful not to ogle Gayle as she and two of the other women passed down the lines handing out extra ammunition pouches. Nor did they seem to pay any attention to Rita—unseemly attention, at any rate—when she took up her position as the unit's radio operator. Heinrich and his men, for all their crudities, had long ago learned the First Principle of Mercenary Armies: *Don't piss off the toughest guys around.* Which exalted status the Americans still had, in general—and one American in particular.

Rita's brother, of course, was their commander. But what was more important—much more—was that her husband stood in their own ranks. In the center, in the front line—as befitted a man who had gained the absolute confidence of his new comrades. And a man whom *none* of them—not the biggest and toughest veteran—would even think of challenging. Easy-going, he was—true, true. Not a friendlier man in the company!

Good thing, too. Seeing as how he was as big as a walrus and could bench-press a horse. So, at least, thought the man's German comrades. When the man himself had explained to them that he wasn't *quite* up to the standards of "professional football," he single-handedly killed—quite inadvertently—any chance that football would become a popular sport in the new society. In this new universe, it would be Tom Simpson, not Abner Doubleday, who caused the astounding popularity of baseball. A reasonable sport, baseball, playable by reasonable-sized men.

But Tom Simpson now had other accomplishments to his credit. One, in particular: it had been he, in truth—far more than the shotguns—who truly welded the German soldiers into the American army.

Tom Simpson, in the first months after the Ring of Fire, had been something of a lost sheep. His allegiance to Mike's course of action had completed his estrangement from his own parents. Yet, there had seemed no real place for him among Mike's crowd.

Not that Mike didn't make many offers. But Tom, stubbornly, turned them down. He had had enough nepotism and favoritism to last a lifetime. For a while, Tom thought of dabbling in business. But, in truth, he knew he had none of his father's executive skills. Nor, perhaps because of his rich birth, did he have the hardscrabble instincts of a true entrepreneur—which were an absolute necessity in the raw and booming commercial world springing up in southern Thuringia.

He had volunteered for the army, of course, as soon as Mike put out the call. But, there too, he had found no ready place. For all his size and incredible muscle, Tom was a rich kid from the city. Among his country-boy fellow soldiers, he quickly become famous as the worst marksman anyone had ever seen. The jests were never made in a nasty spirit—Tom was a popular figure—but they stung nonetheless.

Finally, more out of desperation than anything else, he volunteered to join the new contingents of German troops being formed. And there, as much to his surprise as anyone's, he found the home he was looking for.

Tom, it developed, had a knack for learning foreign languages; in the field, at least, if not in a classroom. What was more important— much more—was that he discovered he had the right temperament for the work. He liked the German soldiers, and they liked him. He was easy-going, unflappable, friendly—and fearless.

True, that fearlessness had yet to be tested in a gun battle. But there was not a man in Heinrich's contingent who doubted the outcome. Fear, they knew, came from the mind, not the bullet or the pike. In the way such men have, many had tried to intimidate Tom in the first weeks.

Size be damned! Size isn't everything. Toughness is a thing of the *mind.* So, in the first few weeks after Tom joined their ranks, Heinrich's toughest veterans tested his alpha-male mettle.

Heh.

Tom never had to raise a hand. He was accustomed to the ferocious intimidation on the football fields of the nation's top universities. In the *line*. And he had been very good at it. His body wasn't *quite* up to the standards of professional football, but his mind certainly would have been.

By the time the battle of Jena began, the thing was settled. Tough Tom—*gut Thomas!*—stood in the front line, in the center, where he belonged. His comrades took strength and courage, seeing his huge form standing there.

Because *that* was what won battles, in the end. Not firepower and fancy marksmanship. Strength and courage.

So, needless to say, no one ogled his wife. But once the other women were gone, scampering up the ridge, some gave vent to their true sentiments.

"The Americans are *crazy*," grumbled Ferdinand, one of Heinrich's lieutenants. "You watch—those silly bitches'll start screaming as soon as the first gun goes off."

Glumly, Ferdinand stared up the slope. The bulk of the American soldiers, he knew, were positioned just over the crest of the ridge. "Then those soft-headed American men will drop their own guns and spend all their time trying to calm the women down."

He shifted his gaze, now staring up the road. Perhaps half a mile away, Ferdinand could spot the first enemy horsemen coming into sight. "You watch," he concluded sourly, "we'll wind up doing all the fighting." He stroked the sleek shotgun in his hands, finding solace in that wondrous rate of fire.

Heinrich, examining the same horsemen, sucked his teeth. "Maybe," he grunted. He lowered the binoculars and looked up the ridge. He spotted Frank almost at once. Two women—girls, in truth—were standing next to him. One of those girls, Heinrich knew, was Frank's own niece. He and Frank had become very friendly, over the past few months, and Heinrich knew full well that Frank shared his own reservations. On the other hand . . .

"I admit the damn girl can shoot," Frank had told him once. Grudgingly, true. But given Frank's definition of "shooting," Heinrich understood just how much praise was contained in that sullen admission.

He looked away. "Maybe," he repeated. A slight smile came to his face. "Then again—maybe not."

At that very moment, as it happens, Jeff and Larry were heaping their own praise onto Mike and Frank. And there was nothing grudging or sullen about it. The two young men had just realized what Mike intended, by positioning most of his American troops on the reverse slope of the ridge, just below the crest. They would be invisible to the enemy there, until he summoned them forth.

"Man, that's slick, Mike!" exclaimed Larry.

Mike jerked a thumb at Frank. "Tell him, not me. He's the pro— I'm just following his advice."

The adulation was transferred to Jackson. "Just like Wellington at Salamanca," intoned Jeff.

"And Le Haye Sainte," agreed Larry sagely.

Frank scowled. "Common fucking sense, is what it is. I learned this trick from a sergeant in Nam. I think he learned it from the NVA. So who the hell is Wellington?"

Jeff and Larry goggled at him for a moment. Then, in a small voice, Jeff said: "He's the guy they named your favorite boots after."

Now, Frank was impressed. "Oh," he said. "*Him*. Good man! Whoever he was."

And, at that very moment, Gretchen struck the first blow against a different enemy. A much less concrete foe, in her case—and a much harder one to vanquish.

"All right," said Mathilde, one of the women in the shack. Her voice was hesitant, uncertain. She glanced quickly at the four other women huddled on pallets against the walls. Two of them were Mathilde's sisters; the other two, cousins. Both her cousins and one of her sisters were nursing babies.

Mathilde's own fears and doubts were mirrored in their faces.

"I do not ask you to take great risks," Gretchen said immediately. "Nothing you are too scared to do. But I think you will find everything much easier by tomorrow. After the battle is won, Jena's high and mighty notables will not be so quick to accuse anyone of witchcraft."

The women in the shack stared at her. They were still frightened, Gretchen saw. They had been frightened and nervous since the moment Gretchen approach Mathilde and one of her cousins. The two young women had been part of the crowd watching the American army march past. Gretchen had singled them out within a minute of Jeff's flamboyant departure. She had been guided less by instinct than by her own hard experience. She knew how to recognize desperate women—and, what was more important, women who still retained their backbones.

Frightened, yes; nervous, yes. But Gretchen knew her choice had been well-aimed. The women had still listened, as she spoke, with neither protest nor any attempt to drive her out of their miserable dwelling in Jena's worst slum.

Mathilde and her extended family were part of the great mass of poor women whom the war had driven into dire straits. All of them were refugees from the Palatinate, who had found a sanctuary in Jena. The adult men in the family were all dead or gone, except for Mathilde's crippled uncle. He was sleeping quietly in the next-door shack.

Mathilde and the prettiest of her cousins supported the family by prostitution. Jena was a good town for the trade, what with its large population of young male students, most of whom were from Germany's nobility and prosperous burgher class. But if Jena was a sanctuary, it was a precarious one. Women of their kind were only tolerated so long as they kept their place. For almost a century, since the witch-hunting craze began, it was wretched creatures such as they who were the first to be accused of witchcraft. The accusation was almost impossible to disprove, even if the area's notables were willing to listen to protestations of innocence—which, more often than not, they weren't in the least.

"Trust me," Gretchen stated. "After today, the notables will be much less full of themselves."

"You are so sure?" asked one of the cousins. Her voice, for all the meekness of its tone, held a trace of hope.

Gretchen gave no answer beyond a level gaze. But that was enough. For all their fears, the women in the shack were quite dazzled by her. They could tell she was one of their own kind. Yet the woman seemed so—so—

Sure. Confident. Poised.

Powerful. They had never seen a woman like that. Not once. Not from their own class . . .

"All right," said Mathilde again. This time, the words were spoken firmly. "We will do as you say, Gretchen. We will start here, with us. There are some others we can talk to, also." Mathilde glanced at her sisters and cousins. "Hannelore, I think. And Maria."

One of her sisters nodded. Mathilde's cousin Inga, the other prostitute, smiled. As if a dam had burst, she began to speak quickly and eagerly:

"And the students will be easy. There are at least three I can think of at once! Joachim, Fritz and Kurt—especially Joachim. He's very nice, and always wants to talk to me afterward. He thinks a lot about politics, I know that, even if I can't follow half of what he says. I wish he wasn't so short of money all the time so he could come more often."

Mathilde laughed, a bit coarsely. "He comes often enough, girl! What kind of idiot whore lets her customer owe her money?"

Inga flushed. "I like him," she replied stubbornly. "So what if he can't always pay at the time? He never cheats me. He always gives me what he owes whenever his parents send him money."

Mathilde didn't press it. She rather liked Joachim herself, actually. But mention of his name brought up another concern.

"For the students it will be easy, this—what did you call it?"

"Committees of Correspondence," said Gretchen.

"Yes. For them, easy. But for us? Inga is the only one who can even sign her name."

Gretchen scanned the women in the room. "You are all illiterate?" Five nods came in reply.

Gretchen sat up straight. Since she had the only chair in the shack, she practically towered over the others. The height, and her own size and posture, made her seem like a hearth goddess.

"Then that is the first thing we will change." Her eyes fell on the youngest woman in the shack. A girl, really. Her name was Gertrude, and she was Mathilde's youngest sister. She had just turned fifteen, and already showed signs of becoming as attractive as Mathilde. Under normal circumstances, she would become a prostitute before she saw another birthday.

But circumstances had changed. The family had been adopted by a hearth goddess, and she made her first decree.

"Gertrude will accompany me back to Grantville. We will put her to school."

There was no protest. The first Committee of Correspondence was still fearful, still uncertain, still groping for clarity and understanding. But their timid fingertips could feel the first touch of hope. And, besides, women of their class did not argue with a goddess. Not even a goddess who spoke in their own tongue. *Especially* not such a goddess.

Mathilde cleared her throat.

"You will speak to the students, then, after we—" She fumbled at the unfamiliar terms: "*organize a meeting?*"

Gretchen smiled. "Me? Nonsense! Well, not alone, at least." She snorted. "Stupid boys. They'll think of nothing but what I look like naked."

Soft laughter filled the shack. Gretchen's smile returned, wider than ever—and more than a little wintry. "No, no. I will come. But I will bring my husband with me. Better that way. He's an intellectual himself, which I most certainly am not. The students will understand him better."

Inga's eyes were very wide. "I saw him, when you came into town. Oh!" She snickered. "They'll be so *scared* of him, too."

Gretchen's heart warmed, for a moment. She would be sure to mention that comment to Jeff. He would be pleased, very. She liked pleasing her husband, even if the whole matter was male foolishness. But she let none of that show. Her eyes were cold and grim. "Yes, they will. *Sehr gut!*"

Chapter 39

Mike knelt down next to Julie Sims. Frank's niece was sitting cross-legged next to a small tree at the crest of the ridge, just a few yards from its highest point. Mike didn't recognize the tree. Some kind of elm, he thought. The leaves had not yet been touched by autumn color.

Julie's rifle was propped against her shoulder, the butt nestled against her inner calf. The rifle was a Remington Model 700, firing .308 rounds, with an ART-2 scope. The gun was a larger caliber than was used in biathlon competition in the modern era, but it was the rifle Julie preferred for hunting. Her father had bought it for her three years earlier.

Next to her was Karen Tyler, the girl who would serve as her observer. Karen was raised up on her knees. A pair of binoculars were slung around her neck, but at the moment she was studying the oncoming mercenaries through an M49 spotting scope. The expensive optical piece had been Frank Jackson's contribution to Julie's fledgling biathlon ambitions, along with her skis. For all Frank's crabbing, Mike knew, he adored his niece as much as any of his own sons.

"You're sure about this?" asked Mike. He spoke very softly, so only Julie could hear.

Julie's lips twitched, but her eyes never left the landscape below the ridge. "What? Are you going to lecture me too?"

Solemnly, Mike shook his head. "Look at me, Julie." For all the softness of his tone, the words were full of command. Julie turned to face him. As always, Mike was struck by her classically "all-American country girl" features. Peaches-and-cream complexion, light brown hair, blue eyes, open face, snub nose. No one except a man in love with her would ever call Julie Sims "beautiful." Just—good-looking.

Mike nodded at Karen, now exchanging the scope for the binoculars—just as James Nichols had trained her. Use the binoculars for scanning the area, the scope for pinpointing target locations. He could see the little notebook by her knee in which Karen had scrawled key target areas and wind direction. The target area page was full. There were only two words on the opposite page: *no wind*.

"This isn't target shooting, Julie. Or deer hunting. This is sniper work. In the past few weeks, James trained you the way he was trained when he was in the Marines, after he volunteered for sniper school."

Julie said nothing. Her face was expressionless. "Did you ever wonder why he never finished the training?" he asked gently.

Nothing. Mike sighed. "He told me—and I'm willing to bet he told you, too. He thought being a tough guy and a good shot would be enough. It isn't. They make sure you understand that. And you can drop out any time you want, without prejudice."

Nothing.

"When he did finally understand it, he dropped out. He just didn't have the temperament. And I know I wouldn't, either. One shot, one kill—and you're killing men, not animals. Men with faces you can see."

Finally, an expression came to her young, almost angelic face. But Mike couldn't quite interpret it. Sarcasm? No, it was more like whimsy; or maybe, wry amusement.

"Did Uncle Frank ever tell you the story," she asked, "about the first time I went deer hunting? How I cried like a baby after I shot my first buck?"

Mike nodded. Julie's expression grew very wry.

"You know why? The deer was so pretty. And it had never done me any harm." Julie cocked her head toward her observer, a girl no older than she. Another recent high-school graduate. Slender, where Julie was not, but otherwise—peas from a pod.

"Hey, Karen! Those guys look pretty to you?"

Karen shifted her gum into a corner of her mouth. "Nope. Ugly bastards. Mean looking, too. Look more like wild dogs than cute little deer."

Julie bared her teeth. The smile was far more savage than anything belonging on the face of an eighteen-year-old, male or female. "That's what I thought. Hey, Karen! Watcha think they'll do—to you and me, I mean—if they get their hands on us?"

Karen was back to chewing her gum. Her words came out in a semi-mumble. "Don't want to think about it, girl. But I'll tell you one thing. Won't be trying to sweet-talk us into the backseat of a car. Not likely."

The smile left Julie's face; but, if anything, the sense of whimsy was even stronger in her eyes. She gave Mike a level gaze.

"That's the whole problem with allowing men into combat," she said solemnly. "You guys are just too emotional about the whole thing."

Mike chuckled. "All right, Julie—enough! Just checking."

"S'okay, Mike. I like you, too. But I'll be fine. Just give me the word, and I'll start dropping the bastards."

Mike shook his head slightly. The gesture was more rueful than anything else. He rose to his feet. "How far are they now, Karen? I make it six hundred yards."

" 'Bout right," came the reply. "A little less, those first horsemen. The crossroad is right around five hundred fifty yards, and they're almost there."

"You two got your locations fixed?" Both girls nodded. "Okay, then. I want to wait a bit. Don't want to scare them off before the Scots can circle. I want that army captured, not running off to attack some other town."

Mike turned his head, looking for Mackay. Mackay was standing next to Frank Jackson some fifteen yards off. Mike had asked the Scottish commander to stay with him as an adviser. Mackay had agreed readily enough. Much more readily than Mike had expected, in fact. At the time, Mike had ascribed that willingness to nothing more than Mackay's confidence in Lennox. But now, seeing the Scotsman staring at Julie, he realized that Mackay had an interest of his own.

Mike managed not to smile. He had noticed the way in which Mackay, in times past, had tried not to ogle Julie in her cheerleader costume. The Scotsman had been quite discreet about it, in fact, despite the bare legs and Julie's exuberant athleticism. Mike found it amusing that Mackay was doing a much poorer job of maintaining his gentlemanly couth, seeing Julie now in her baggy hunting outfit. The Scotsman seemed utterly fascinated by the girl.

Mike cleared his throat. "Uh, Alex?"

Startled, Mackay jerked his gaze away from Julie. "Aye?"

Mike pointed toward the still-distant mob of mercenaries. "How close do they need to be? For Lennox to be able to surround them before they can make their escape?"

Mackay, for all his own youth, was a seasoned cavalry officer. He took no more than a few seconds to gauge the problem. "Four hundred yards," came the confident answer. "Once all of them have passed the crossroad. That'll do nicely."

Mike turned back to Karen and Julie. Karen nodded. Julie ignored him. She was giving Mackay an odd look. Then, quickly, looked away and hefted her rifle. There might have been a slight flush on her cheeks. Maybe.

Mike strolled back to the top of the ridge, where Frank and Mackay were standing. Frank was studying the mercenaries on the level ground below through his own set of binoculars. When Mike came up alongside the Scotsman, he said casually, as if commenting on the weather: "She's got a boyfriend, you know."

Mackay's flush was not slight in the least.

Mike did smile, now. "Frank doesn't think much of him, though."

Jackson never took the binoculars away from his eyes. "Worthless snot, you ask me. Thinks 'cause he was the captain of a high-school football team that he's some kind of bigshot for life. Probably wind up flipping hamburgers for the next thirty years."

He lowered the eyepieces. His face was quite expressionless. "Rather see her get hooked up with a more substantial sort of man, myself. Even if he ain't as pretty as a homecoming king."

Silence. Mackay's eyes were riveted on the mercenaries, as if he had never seen enemy soldiers before. His lips were pressed tightly shut.

Frank glanced at him. "Your teeth bothering you? Why don't you pay a visit to the town's dentist? It'll hurt, mind you—he's pretty well out of anesthetic. But I'm sure he could fix them up."

Mackay's flush deepened. Mike knew that the Scotsman's teeth made him nervous in the presence of American women. For this day and age, Alex's teeth weren't in bad shape. But by American standards, they were something of an eyesore.

Mackay's preoccupation caused him to lapse into the dialect of his youth. " 've thought on it," he muttered. "I'll no mind t'pain."

The last statement was flat, firm. Mike didn't doubt him for an instant. Men of Mackay's time had standards of pain acceptance that veered just as widely from those of Americans as their dental condition. "Anesthetic," to a man like Mackay, meant half a bottle of wine—and glad to get it.

Behind his lips, Mike could see Mackay's tongue running over his teeth. " 'Tis no the pain. S'the expense. I dinna ken if I can afford it."

Frank made a faint snorting sound. More of a sniff, perhaps. "Hell, don't worry about that, Alex. Your credit'll be good with him."

"Credit?" Mackay's eyes widened. "*Credit?* I don't even know t'man!"

"I do," stated Frank. "He's my brother-in-law. Henry G. Sims, DDS." Jackson nodded toward the sniper. "Julie's father, as it happens. And he don't think any better of little old Chip-shit than I do. As it happens."

The binoculars went back up to his eyes. "So go see him, why don't you?"

"Good idea," concurred Mike. He gave Mackay a friendly slap on the shoulder. "Good idea."

As Gretchen was about to leave the shack, a young boy came rushing in. She recognized him—one of Mathilde's two younger brothers.

"Max Jungers is outside!" hissed the boy. He leaned over, his face anxious and intense. Gretchen saw the difficulty with which he was controlling his impulse to point.

Her eyes flitted to Mathilde. Mathilde's own face was tight with apprehension.

"Shit! I thought he'd decided to leave us alone."

"Who is Max Jungers?" asked Gretchen.

The words came out in a quiet, tumbling rush, from all of the women at once. When they were done, Gretchen nodded. Local tough. Hooligan. Thief. Cutpurse. Would-be pimp.

"The usual," she muttered. "He has bothered you?"

The women nodded. Mathilde's little brother was staring at her with open eyes. "I think—" he squeaked. Then, clearing his throat: "I think he's not here for that." The boy hesitated, as if abashed. "I think—"

Gretchen chuckled. The sound was as humorless as a razor blade. "Me?"

The boy nodded. The gesture was quick, frightened.

Gretchen rose from her chair. "Well, then. I should go speak to him. Since he came all this way to see me."

Three seconds later, she was striding out of the shack. The women watched her go, gaping. There they squatted, for a moment, before the reality registered. Like a little mob, they rushed to the door and stared out.

Max Jungers, sure enough. He had apparently been lurking at the corner. Now, seeing Gretchen coming down the narrow street, he smiled and ambled toward her across the cobblestones. His hand was resting loosely on the hilt of a dirk scabbarded to his waist.

"Shit!" exclaimed Mathilde again. "There's going to be trouble!"

Her cousin Inga nodded sadly. "It's too bad. I liked Gretchen."

Mathilde stared at her. "Are you mad? Don't you understand *yet*?"

"Four hundred yards!" snapped Karen. Before the last word was spoken, Julie's Remington erupted. Less than a second later, the most flamboyantly caparisoned mercenary "leader" was hammered out of his saddle. Julie was using her match ammunition. The 173-grain boat-tail round punched right through the front of his cuirass and took a goodly piece of his heart with it through the backplate.

Julie was not particularly tall for an American girl—five and a half feet—but she weighed a hundred and forty pounds. The shapeliness of her somewhat stocky figure was due entirely to muscle. She absorbed the recoil with no difficulty at all. A quick, practiced, easy motion jacked another round into the chamber.

"Target area six!" snapped Karen. "Three hundred fifty yards! Hat— green feather!"

Julie was standing, to give herself maximum ease of movement. At that range, she was not worried about accuracy. It took her not more than three seconds to bring the next target into her scope.

Crack! The head beneath a green-feathered hat spilled blood and brains. The horseman slumped sidewise out of the saddle.

"Fuck," grunted Julie. "*Missed!*"

Mackay's eyes were like saucers. Mike was amused—and half-appalled. "She was aiming for what James calls the 'sniper's triangle'— both eyes down to the breastbone," he explained. "That shot was a little high."

Karen: "Area three! Three hundred fifty again! Big old floppy hat!"

Crack! A cavalryman was driven out of his saddle onto the rump of his horse. A red stain appeared on his cloth coat, just above the belt buckle. Behind him, a much larger pool of blood spilled down his mount's tail.

"*Shit!*" screeched Julie. She jacked another round into the chamber. The gesture was angry, frustrated. Her uncle hurried toward her. In the distance, Mike could see the cavalryman clutching his stomach. His legs flopped uselessly, trying to hold him onto the horse. Mike realized his spine was severed. A second later, he was toppling off the horse. He hit the ground like a sack.

"Five ring at six o'clock," said Mike softly. "She's off a little." He glanced at Mackay. The Scotsman had transferred the wide-eyed stare to Julie.

Frank was at her side now. Karen started to call out another target, but Frank waved her down. With one hand on Julie's shoulder, Frank was speaking urgently into his niece's ear.

Mike could just hear the words. "Take it easy, baby. Just buck fever, that's all it is. The bastards are going down. You aren't wide, just off your elevation. Easy to fix. Just take a breath—relax—that's it."

Julie took a deep breath and began easing it out. Another. She flashed her uncle a quick, thankful smile. Frank smiled back for an instant, before frowning ferociously.

"And don't let me hear you using that kind of language again, young lady!" He started wagging his finger.

"You?" demanded Julie. "Foul-mouth Frank himself? Ha!"

Cheerily, now—smiling—Julie looked to Karen.

"Call 'em out!"

Karen was right on the job. "Area one! Four hundred yards! The fatso!"

Crack! A heavyset officer lost the proverbial pound of flesh—right from the heart itself. The shot was perfect.

And so were the rest. *Crack! Crack!* Down, down.

Frank reloaded for her while Julie rested her shoulder. She was back to work in seconds.

Crack! Crack! Crack! Crack!

"Aye, an' she's t'true Queen o' Hearts," whispered Mackay.

When Gretchen was fifteen feet away from Jungers, she stopped. So did he, leering cheerfully. He took his hand from the dirk and planted his arms akimbo.

"Well now, girl—it seems to me—"

"Did you see my husband?" interrupted Gretchen.

Jungers broke off. For an instant, his face was still. Then, just as quickly, the leer was back. More of a sneer, really.

"The big fat one? Not worried about him."

"No reason to be," agreed Gretchen. She nodded, then smiled. The smile was very thin. Like a razor.

"He would have tried to reason with you. That's why I love him so." Gretchen reached into her bodice and removed the 9mm. The motion was easy and relaxed. So was the way she levered the slide. So was the way she slipped into a firing crouch, and brought the pistol up in a two-handed grip. She had spent hours and hours on the firing range, over the past few weeks, being trained by Dan Frost.

Jungers' eyes widened. But he never thought to reach for his dirk. He didn't recognize the pistol for what it was, until the first shot was fired. But that shot blew out his cerebellum along with his teeth, so the thought was fleeting.

Gretchen stepped up four paces, aimed at the body lying on the street, and fired again. That round went into the heart. There was no need for it, but Dan had trained her to go for the body mass shot. "No headshots unless they're wearing armor," he had insisted, over and again. Gretchen was feeling a little guilty. She just hadn't been able to resist wiping that leer away.

The mercenaries were truly a mob by now, milling aimlessly. Their pikes bristled in all directions, like a porcupine. Dozens of arquebuses were fired at random, blasting at nearby shrubbery.

"I'll be damned," hissed Mike. "They don't even realize what's killing them."

"*At this range?*" choked Mackay. "They've not a thought in the world!" The young commander gave his head a sharp shake. He was finally able to tear his eyes away from Julie and look down the slope behind him. Far below, Lennox's upturned face was staring back, waiting for the command.

Alex whipped off his hat and waved it. Lennox spurred his horse into motion, bellowing his own commands. Within thirty seconds, the Scots cavalry was pounding around the eastern end of the little ridge, aiming to encircle the left flank of the mercenaries by using the crossroad.

In those thirty seconds, Julie extracted three additional hearts. Then there was a pause. The mercenaries had finally realized that only cavalrymen—officers—were being targeted. Every man on a horse who was still alive had clambered off. Most of the men wearing fancy headgear had removed it like so many snakes.

Mike heard Karen muttering. "Have to just pick 'em at random now. Okay. Area three! Any—"

"Hold up!" shouted Mike. "Hold up, Julie! That's enough!"

He raised his binoculars. The mercenaries and their camp followers were crowded into a rough, packed circle. Julie's long-range massacre had confused them utterly. They had assumed themselves to be under attack from nearby skirmishers, and had taken position to charge in any direction once the enemy was spotted. By the time they saw the Scots cavalry pouring out from behind the ridge, it was too late to even think of fleeing. Most of them were on foot, and the cavalrymen didn't dare get back on their horses.

Mike turned. Gayle was right there, handing him the CB. "Okay," he ordered into the radio. "APC move up. Remember, guys—I want a surrender, not a slaughter. So start with the loudspeakers."

Below, the APC's engine roared into life. Hearing the sound behind them, Heinrich and his men immediately cleared a path down the middle of the road. Seconds later, the APC went charging through the gap. The German at the loudspeaker microphone was already bellowing out the terms of surrender.

"You are surrounded. Lay down your weapons. Quarter will be given to all unarmed men. Your women and your possessions will not be touched. Lay down your weapons. New terms of enlistment will be offered. Pay—good pay—food and shelter. Only to unarmed men. Lay down your weapons. Quarter will be given—"

On and on, over and over. By the time the APC reached the mercenaries—still hundreds of yards from the ridge—many of them were beginning to lay down their pikes and firearms. To the north, the Scots had finished the encirclement and were beginning to trot forward. Hurriedly, all the mercenaries began to disarm.

"A combination of the old and the new," mused Mike. Changing sides was common practice in this day and age, for surrendered soldiers. Even if APCs and rifles which could slay unerringly across a fourth of a mile were almost like magic. "Old and the new."

He turned to Mackay, but saw that the Scotsman's mind was elsewhere.

"God in His Heaven," whispered Alex. "I've been in—what?—call it six battles. Never killed that many men. Not in all my days put together."

Mike followed his eyes. Julie was leaning against the tree. So was her rifle. She was staring at the enemy, her arms crossed over her chest. Her face was blank as a sheet. Frank put his hand on her shoulder and gave it a little squeeze. That gesture brought Julie's own hand up, covering her uncle's. Other than that—

Nothing.

"Can you handle this, young man?" asked Mike softly.

Mackay never looked away. His tongue, again, swept teeth under tight lips. "Where does this dentist do his work?" he asked.

"I'll take you there myself." Mike smiled. "As it happens, I don't think any better of her boyfriend than Frank or Henry."

"There will be trouble," muttered Mathilde. She was now standing alongside Gretchen, not ten feet from Jungers' body. Mathilde plucked at Gretchen's sleeve. "Come. He was nothing but garbage. If we are not here when the Watch arrives, they will not question anything. Just another street killing."

Gretchen swiveled her head. Her eyes widened slightly. "Oh, but I want them to," was her reply. And she refused to budge thereafter, for all of Mathilde's pleas.

"And maybe not," concluded Heinrich. He grinned at Ferdinand. "So what do you say now, wise man? Ever been in such an easy fight in your life?"

Heinrich spread his arms and looked down, inspecting his body. "Look! Not even a speck of dust. Much less blood and guts."

Ferdinand glared at him. But not for more than a moment or two. Then he raised his head and gazed at the girl standing by the small tree atop the ridge. He heaved a deep sigh.

"Ah . . . ! I still say—*ah!*"

He rubbed his side. Even beneath the heavy cloth, Ferdinand could feel the ridged scar tissue. A pike had done for that, years ago, somewhere in Bohemia.

Suddenly, he snatched the helmet off his head and raised it high. "*Joo-li!*" he cried. "*Let's hear it for Joo-li!*"

The cheer was echoed instantly by all the men in the German contingent. Almost two hundred helmets were raised high—a good number of them atop bayonets.

"JOO-LI! JOO-LI! JOO-LI!"

The watchmen who formed Jena's constabulary trailed after Gretchen like minnows after a shark. The Chief of the Watch scurried at her side, trying to match her striding steps. His hands fluttered with protest.

"There must be an investigation!" he exclaimed. "An investigation!"

"*Absolutely!*" boomed Gretchen. "My husband will insist!" She smiled down at the short, portly Chief. "You remember him, perhaps? The large man on the motorcycle? With the shotgun?"

The Chief of the Watch *had* seen him, in fact. And he could guess—not that he wanted to—as to the meaning of the strange terms "motorcycle" and "shotgun."

"A very short investigation," he muttered. "Only a formality."

"I think not!" boomed Gretchen. "My husband will insist otherwise!"

Again, she smiled. "And I, of course, must obey his every wish."

Finally, Julie's face gained an expression. She blushed with embarrassment, hearing the cheers coming from below in thick German accents. Then, blushed deeper still. The American soldiers now climbing up the ridge were cheering themselves. *Julie! Julie!*

Frank managed to sigh and grin at the same time. "So, niece of mine. How does it feel—being cheered yourself, for once, instead of leading them?"

"Feels great," came the immediate response. Julie was now grinning herself. Then, catching sight of one of the faces coming up the slope, the grin faded.

"Oh, *damn*," she grumbled. "I was afraid of that. Chip's sulking again."

Frank looked away. "He's good at that. I've noticed."

Julie cast a suspicious glance at him. "Are you criticizing my boyfriend, Uncle Frank?"

"Me? God forbid. Nothing else, I've got too much sense to tell a young lady what kind of man she oughta latch onto."

The suspicion was replaced by a mischievous little gleam. "God forbid, my ass!" Then, Julie sighed. "Oh, hell. I'm beginning to think— I don't know. Maybe Chip's a little—I don't know. Too young for me. Too immature. What do *you* think, Uncle Frank?"

"Not for me to say," was the reply. "Not for me to say."

"God forbid," agreed Julie. "God forbid."

When Gretchen's husband arrived back at Jena, leading the triumphant American army on his motorcycle along with his friends, he did *not* demand a full investigation into the circumstances regarding the death of one Max Jungers at the hands of his wife.

Not at all. He more or less demanded, instead, that a fair piece of Jena be turned into rubble. Offered to do it himself, in fact, insofar

as the very frightened Chief of the Watch could interpret his snarling phrases. And his friends, apparently, were offering to help.

So, when they arrived, did the Americans riding in the awesome
APC. So did the Americans marching alongside the thousands of
captured prisoners and their camp followers.

So did the Scots cavalry—with the sole quibble that *all* of Jena
would look better, loose stone piled on charred beam.

The Chief of the Watch—all of the town's notables, in fact, who
had gathered hastily by now—had no difficulty at all understanding the Scotsmen. The Scots accent was heavy, but their command
of German was excellent. And whatever slight misunderstanding there
might have been was promptly cleared up by the German contingent
in the American army, who added their own cheerful recommenda-
tions. Most of which involved the sort of gruesome details which only
hardened mercenaries can send tripping so lightly off the tongue.

Fortunately—*danke Gott!*—the American commander was a less
irascible sort of man. Slightly.

"Bad," muttered Mike angrily. "Very bad!" He glared at the cluster of frightened notables. "One of our women *molested*—after not
more than *a few hours* in this town? Just visiting old friends and
distant relatives?"

He snarled. *"Very bad!"* Then, visibly restraining his fury: "But—
No doubt the town itself was not responsible."

Heinrich interpreted. A small sea of nodding heads greeted that
last sentence. Mike responded through clenched teeth.

First, to Heinrich: "Interpret precisely!"

Then, to the notables: "This scoundrel. Jungers, his name? He has
friends? Accomplices?"

Eagerly, the notables offered up the sacrificial lambs. Names were
named. Faces described. A particularly disreputable tavern
mentioned—specified—described in detail—its location precisely
depicted—offers of help to find the way—

The APC rumbled down narrow streets, followed by perhaps a
hundred American soldiers. The large and well-armed husband stayed
behind, surrounded by several hundred equally fierce-looking friends
and comrades. Fortunately, he seemed preoccupied with comforting
his timid, trembling, terribly upset wife. So, at least, the notables
interpreted the beautiful young woman's shaking shoulders and
heaving chest. The husband's broad smile, of course, was nothing
more than a man trying to settle his wife's nerves.

By the time the APC reached its destination, the tavern had long
since emptied. Not even the owner of the ramshackle stone building had stayed behind.

Wise choice. The Americans—in and out of the APC—put on a

splendid display of firepower. The large crowd of Jena's citizens who watched were most impressed. And even more pleased. The tavern's reputation was well deserved.

So, the incredibly rapid rifle fire which shattered all the windows and pockmarked the soft stone walls was cheered exuberantly. The Claymore mine mounted on the APC's front armor which blew the heavy wooden door into splinters was greeted with gasping applause. And the pièce de résistance—the grenades lobbed into the interior which turned a tavern into so much wood-and-glass wreckage—produced squeals of glee and even, here and there, some dancing in the streets.

When it was all over, everyone's good mood had returned. The notables as much as the Americans. It was not surprising, therefore, that the town's high and mighty were quick to accept Mike's new offer.

Perhaps—in addition to trade and commerce—

Perhaps—and the value of exchanging knowledge and pooling printing facilities—

—and, of course, now that he thought about it, perhaps a closer joining of forces to protect everyone against the ravages of the coming winter—

—it occurred to the American leader—

—perhaps—

—that Jena could use a bit of help, patrolling the streets and keeping the ruffian element under control.

Wunderbar!

As they left town, one of Jena's now-fawning notables made so bold as to ask Mike a question. Heinrich interpreted again.

Mike looked up at the banner flying from the APC. It was a modification of the U.S. flag. The same thirteen red-and-white stripes. But the blue field in the corner contained only a single star. A small one, for the space, nestled in the upper left.

"We call ourselves the United States," he explained.

The notable conferred with Heinrich, making sure that he hadn't misunderstood the plural. Again, he asked a question.

"Oh, there's just one state. At the moment." Mike pointed to the single star. "That's Grantville, and the surrounding area."

He beamed down at the notable. "We expect to add others. I think Badenburg and its countryside will be joining us soon. Certainly hope so!" Again, he pointed to the flag.

"Then there will be *two* stars."

Again, the beaming smile. "You grasp the logic?"

And there he left the notable. Staring at the flag, as it passed slowly out of sight.

Chapter 40

When they got back to Grantville, the town was in an uproar. So was Badenburg and the entire surrounding area.

A huge army had just passed through, the day before. Gustav Adolf's Swedes, moving like the wind.

"He went right through Thuringia," Rebecca explained to Mike and Alex. She had been waiting for them outside the high school, where the emergency committee was about to go into session. "He captured Erfurt on October 2, without a fight. That city belongs to the elector of Mainz, you know."

"Not any longer, it doesn't sound like," mused Mike. He frowned worriedly. "That bothers me, being caught by surprise like that. A lot. I screwed up. We had most of the army out of town. If—"

Mackay interrupted. "And what else were you going to do, Michael? The mercenaries attacking Jena had to be dealt with. That was a given."

The Scotsman shook his head firmly. "This is what war is like, man. You think you can predict everything? Cover all the possible dangers? Ha! You'll be doing well if you're right half the time."

Alex stared to the south. His own face showed none of Mike's fretting and self-condemnation. Rather the opposite, in fact. "The king must have caught everyone by surprise," he said admiringly. "Not the custom, to maneuver that quickly. Especially after a great victory. Most armies would have spent months resting on their laurels."

Mike was still frowning. Mackay studied him for a moment, before adding softly: "You must be willing to face something squarely, Michael Stearns."

Mike's eyes came to him. Mackay continued. "You simply don't have enough men, Mike. And that will not change. Not soon enough, at least. You can certainly defeat a force much greater than yours, in any battle for which you are prepared. But—"

His hand swept in an arc. The broad gesture indicated not simply the hills in the immediate vicinity, but the entire region. Rolling, hilly, heavily wooded Thuringia. "You can not guard against everything. Especially an opponent which can move quickly. I have said this to you before, but I will repeat it. Do not think for a moment that these slow and clumsy tercios are all you will ever face. Or that all of your enemies will line up so neatly for your rifles. I wouldn't. The Finns wouldn't. The Croats wouldn't."

Mike sighed. "I know, Alex." He took a deep, slow breath. "There's too much of a tendency, for us, to think we can handle everything with our modern weapons. Or new ones we could design, if we devoted enough resources to it. But you're right. That road leads to folly."

He smiled whimsically. "Probably wouldn't work anyway. Be a good idea for us to keep Little Big Horn in mind. Not to mention Vietnam. Hardware will only get you so far."

Mackay's face was blank. The names meant nothing to him. But Rebecca nodded. She had been devouring books on American history for months.

The whimsy faded from Mike's face, along with the smile. His expression became almost bleak. "And even if it did succeed—"

"That would be even worse," stated Rebecca, completing the thought.

"Yes," said Mike firmly. "Win the battles and lose the war. This world does *not* need another set of conquistadores. I want to bring America into it—*my* America—not some English-speaking version of Prussia."

Mackay's face registered confusion. "Prussia? The Prussians aren't—"

Mike chuckled. "Not today, Alex, no. Sorriest Germans around, this day and age. But just stick around for a couple of hundred years." The bleakness in his face deepened. "If we don't succeed—you'll see all of Germany under a boot heel, soon enough."

"And worse," whispered Rebecca. Her father had never been able to finish Morris Roth's book on the Holocaust. She had.

Mike shook his head, as a horse shakes off flies. "Over my dead body," he muttered. "What we need is a *political* solution."

He gave Mackay a shrewd glance. "You'll be reporting to Gustav Adolf soon, I imagine."

The Scots officer nodded. "Yes. Not sure when, though. There's no point in galloping all over the countryside until the king sets up quarters somewhere. But soon, yes."

"Put in a good word for us, Alex, if you would. I'd just as soon not get the Swedes on our backs."

Mackay smiled. "I shall," he replied firmly. "The best word possible." Beneath his lips, his tongue ran over his teeth. "Got no choice," he chuckled. "You've got the only dentist I know of."

Ed Piazza emerged from the door. "The meeting's about to start," he announced.

Mackay turned away. Although he often attended those meetings, he would not on this occasion. The Americans, he knew, were coming to a turning point. Like any family, they needed a moment of privacy.

"Good luck," he said.

"What was that about?" asked Rebecca, as she and Mike walked down the corridor to the committee's conference room. "Is Alex having some problems with his teeth?"

She grimaced. Rebecca's own teeth had been in splendid condition, by the standards of the day. But she had still spent a few hours in that torture chamber. Luckily, she had moved on the matter very quickly—before the anesthetic was entirely gone.

"Poor man," she sympathized.

Mike laughed. "Poor man, my ass! There's nothing at all wrong with his *teeth*, Becky, other than cosmetics. It's his heart that's the problem."

Startled, she glanced up at him. Mike was grinning very broadly. "Oh, yes. The Scotsman is a smitten man. I know." He reached his arm around her waist and drew her close. "I recognize the symptoms."

It didn't take Rebecca more than two seconds to understand. She tucked her own arm around Mike's waist, and matched his grin. "Poor man," she concurred. "Mind you, I am a bit surprised. I thought he would be scared off. Once he saw past those magnificent knees."

Mike shook his head. "Not Alex. A very *substantial* fellow, he is."

"Do you think—?"

"Who knows? Her uncle thinks well of him. And even her father, it seems. But God forbid the girl should listen to the voice of wisdom and maturity."

Rebecca snorted. "What woman in her right mind would listen to *such*?" She smiled slyly. "This requires feminine sagacity."

They were at the door, and relinquished the embrace. Rebecca paused before entering. "I will speak to the lady," she announced.

Mike eyed her skeptically. "And say what? Your own words of wisdom?"

"Absurd," she replied. Idly, her fingers stroked her hair. "I said nothing of 'wisdom.' Only *sagacity*."

She swept through the door. Over her shoulder: "You would not understand, Michael. You do not read enough poetry."

"Not *any*," grumbled her fiancé. Thereby, quite unknowingly, proving her point.

Once he entered the room, Mike pulled up a chair and sat down at the conference table. Glancing around, he saw that the entire committee was already gathered except Frank Jackson.

"Frank will be along later," he explained. "Along with Gretchen Higgins. They're seeing to the new prisoners." He turned back to Rebecca, who had taken her usual seat next to Melissa. "I'd like to start the meeting with a report on the Swedish movements."

Rebecca clasped her hands on the table, as she always did when giving a report. Then:

"Gustav Adolf left a garrison in Erfurt—after stripping the town clean of all its hard currency—and marched straight south. He passed through Arnstadt on the seventh. Yesterday. He did not stop, however. According to reports from some of the hunters, he was driving his army very hard. By now they must be south of the Thuringenwald."

Rebecca's face was creased with worry. "The Swedes have stripped the entire central province of the bulk of its stored food. They paid for it, mind you. There was no looting." She laughed harshly. "Except for the archbishop's gold in Erfurt, of course, which is what they used to buy their provisions."

Willie Ray Hudson snorted. "Great! So everybody in central Thuringia's got a pocket full of money and no food. Except us, and Badenburg. We were apparently too far east for the Swedish quartermasters to reach in the time available."

"And winter's a-coming," muttered Nat Davis.

Mike held up his hand. "Later for that. I want to get filled in on the political situation first. Who did Gustav leave in charge of Thuringia?"

"Well, most of it officially belongs to the Saxe-Weimar brothers," said Rebecca. "But Bernard, according to reports, is staying with the Swedish army." Again, that harsh laugh. "It seems he has developed a bit of a military reputation and finds that profession more interesting than taking care of the people he supposedly rules."

"What a surprise," sneered Underwood. "Goddam noblemen!"

Mike grinned at him. "Hey, Quentin—it's okay by me. The fewer noblemen hanging around here the better, as far as I'm concerned."

Rebecca cleared her throat. "Wilhelm, on the other hand—he is the oldest—stayed behind. He has set up his headquarters in Weimar. But the word is that he will not be staying long. He is supposed to recruit eleven thousand men. Field Marshall Banér is to raise an equivalent number in Erfurt. Added to the forces Banér already has, the Swedes think that should be enough to go after Pappenheim while the king himself continues south after Tilly. Pappenheim is apparently running an independent operation now."

Mike did not press Rebecca for an explanation as to the sources of her information. He didn't need to. Her father and uncle were both experienced spies, and by now they had created a network throughout central Germany. The network was broader than that, actually. Working through the Jews scattered all over Europe, the two brothers had informants penetrating large parts of the entire Holy Roman Empire.

He tapped his fingers on the table. "It sounds as if Wilhelm will be leaving soon also."

Rebecca nodded. Mike's finger tapping turned into a decisive little rap. "So. The long and the short of it is this."

His eyes slowly scanned the room, while he held up his fingers one at a time.

"*One*. The war has now moved south of Thuringia, over to the other side of the Thuringenwald. *Two*. Official 'order' has been restored in Thuringia—and is about to be removed again. *Three*. Most noblemen in the area—the ones active in political life, anyway—are either gone or going. The Catholic ones will have fled and the Protestants are seeking fame and glory with the Swedes. *Four*. The economic situation in the province is going to be desperate in a few weeks. *Five*. On the other hand, the area is flush with hard currency."

He turned to Rebecca. "That about sums it up, I think." Again, she nodded.

Now, Mike slapped the table top with his palm. The hard, cracking sound matched his voice.

"Wonderful! Couldn't have asked for anything better!"

Everyone was staring at him. Mike laughed gaily. "And will you look at you?" he demanded. "Problems, problems—that's all you see."

He clenched his fist and held it half-raised. "Now's the time," he stated firmly. "While the cat's away, the mice will play. The war's come and gone until next spring, at the earliest. Probably next summer. The only thing that's going to matter between now and then—six to eight months—is who can keep this province's people alive. Alive—and *by God* well!"

Quentin Underwood was the first to see Mike's point. That was not surprising. As often as he and Underwood clashed in the committee meetings, Mike had found that his former mine manager usually had a better grasp of economic realities than anyone. Moreover, unlike most of the Americans, Quentin's hardheadedness did not lead him to flights of fancy concerning American military supremacy. As a young man serving aboard an aircraft carrier in the South China Sea, he had gotten a good lesson in the limits of hardware. The technological disparity between the aircraft which flew off that carrier and the men they bombed in the forests below had not been substantially different from that between Grantville's Americans and seventeenth-century Germans. Once before, in another universe, Quentin Underwood had seen machinery defeated by men. He intended to be on the other side of that equation, in this new world.

"You're right!" he exclaimed excitedly. "And the timing couldn't be better, from our point of view. We're *set.*"

Underwood began counting on his own fingers. "First, we're out of the woods on the power plant. The coal's been coming in for the last week."

Bill Porter nodded. "Enough of it for the time being, anyway. Once that steam locomotive gets finished, we'll be flush. We should be free and clear until next summer, when critical parts might start going. And by then the new power plant should be ready to go on line."

Underwood continued. "Second, we've got more food coming in than we'll need ourselves." He chuckled dryly. "It's kind of amazing how many little farms there were tucked away all through these hills and woods. Every one of which is now eager to sell their produce, since we've brought some security and stability back into southeast Thuringia."

Willie Ray snorted. "What's so surprising about that? Think farmers are stupid?"

Quentin ignored the quip. "Three, the machine shops are roaring full blast. Three shifts, round the clock—seven days a week."

Nat David grinned. "Had to start hiring lots of German help. Take me awhile, training them to be modern machinists. But I'm only hiring men with metal-working experience and there's a lot of them in this area. Biggest problem I've got is a shortage of metal."

Ed Piazza picked up the thread. "Not much longer, Nat. Uriel Abrabanel just told me there's at least four suppliers ready and willing to start shipping in raw material—as soon as we can come up with the hard currency." He laughed dryly. "Credit's not real big in Germany, this time of the millennium."

"We'll fix that," growled Underwood. He glanced at Mike questioningly.

Mike smiled and turned a lazy eye on Rebecca. She straightened a little in her chair and said softly:

"To sum up, the economic situation looks very promising. With electrical power guaranteed and the town's production facilities in full operation, our only problem is the shortage of hard currency and the primitive state of banking and credit in Europe at this time. As to that—"

She sat up very straight. "My family has been discussing the matter—my very *extended* family—and has come to a decision. My uncle Uriel will stay in Badenburg, since he is well situated there. But several of my relatives will be arriving here soon, including three of my distant cousins. Their names are Samuel, Moses and Francisco. Samuel's father is a prominent banker in Italy. Moses' father is a financial adviser to Emperor Ferdinand in Vienna. And Francisco's grandfather is Don Joseph Nasi, who was formerly—"

Mike laughed. "The Ottoman Empire's effective foreign minister! And the nephew of Doña Gracia Mendes, who transferred her business—Europe's largest banking and gem-trade concern—from Portugal to Turkey after the expulsion of the marranos. Did quite well, I understand."

Everyone except Rebecca was goggling at Mike. He shrugged. "I listen to my National Security Adviser, folks. That's why I spend so much time with her."

Rebecca clasped her hands demurely. "He is a good student, too." She smiled. "Very attentive."

A little chuckle went up. Rebecca's smile became wintry. "When the Spanish expelled the Jews, most of them went to Istanbul. The Ottomans welcomed them, you see, especially since many of the Jews who came were experts in science and technology. Gun manufacturing, among other things. Sultan Bayazid is reported to have said: 'You call Ferdinand a wise king, he who impoverishes his country and enriches our own?' "

"There's a lesson here," murmured Piazza.

Rebecca turned her eyes toward him. "There is, you understand, a condition."

Piazza snorted. "I should hope so! Citizenship, rights, liberties, the works."

"*More*," said Rebecca firmly. "We Jews must be allowed to break out of the economic ghetto in which Europe has forced us. Money-lenders can get rich, but they live on the sufferance of princes."

"Not a problem," growled Underwood. "Matter of fact, if any of your relatives has got some capital to put up—for which they'll get stock and a working partnership if they want it, me and Ollie Reardon and Greg Ferrara have been thinking about—"

Bill Porter looked alarmed. "Quentin, we need the coal—"

"Relax!" snapped Underwood. "I wouldn't be doing much of it myself. I've got relatives too, you know. My son-in-law's—"

Ferrara chimed in. "I wouldn't be doing much either, except giving some technical advice. But we really *do* need to start building a chemical plant. Sulfuric acid is about as basic for modern industry as steel"—for a moment, his face looked aggrieved—"even though most people don't realize it, and—"

Mike rapped the table with his knuckles, in first-class schoolmaster form. Melissa grinned. "Later!" he said. "Enough!"

The hubbub settled. "Christ, let you eager beavers get started on all your pet business schemes and we'll never get anywhere!" His smile took the sting out of the words. In truth, Mike favored most of those schemes. But he was also a firm believer in the old saw: *First things first.*

"The *first* thing—in fact, the *key* thing," he said forcefully, "is to resolve the political issue. I think it's time to call the constitutional convention—and then have another election. This 'temporary emergency committee' has gone as far as it can."

Silence fell on the room. Nat Davis puffed out his cheeks. "Are we ready for that?" he asked uncertainly. "I haven't really given it much thought, to be honest."

Melissa snorted. But the sarcastic remark about to issue from her lips was cut short by James Nichols.

"We're ready, Nat." James glanced at Melissa, Ed and Willie Ray. "Actually, the subcommittee finished drafting our proposal last week. Everything got put on hold because of the crisis in Jena. But—yeah, we're ready."

Hudson nodded. Piazza reached into his briefcase and began hauling out stapled sheets of paper. He gave Mike a questioning glance.

"Pass 'em around, Ed. It's time."

The ruckus started long before anyone got through the material. Mike was not surprised—talk about mixed blessings!—to see that Underwood led the charge.

"I don't like this crap!" snapped Quentin. "Not one damned bit! Why'd you waste your time on this silly shit about at-large elections? Why the hell aren't we—"

As always, Melissa charged into the fray as eagerly as Underwood, and just as bluntly. "Screw you, too! At-large elections are way better than geographic representation—in the lower house, at least."

Mike intervened before the usual Melissa–Quentin fracas could reach thermonuclear proportions. "Cut it out! *Both* of you!"

Sullen silence fell over the two disputants. Mike suppressed a sigh. Each in their own way, Quentin and Melissa were invaluable, but there were times . . .

He decided to start with Melissa, since even though he basically agreed with her it would help to keep the issue focused. Concrete, not abstract.

"Whether or not at-large as opposed to residential representation is better or worse in the general scheme of things is neither here nor there. This isn't a constitution for thirteen colonies scattered across half a continent. It's a constitution for one geographically small colony, about as concentrated and packed with people as Holland. Or Calcutta. And we're not in the same situation as the Founding Fathers were in 1789. We're still back in 1776. *Our* revolution's just starting."

So much for generalities. Now he shifted his attention to the real problem, which was Underwood. "Quentin, you're letting sentiment get in the way of practicality. I had pretty much the same reaction, when I first heard about this idea. But the more I thought about it, the better it sounded. We're in a completely fluid situation here. People move constantly from one place to the next. You know that as well as I do. How can you register somebody to vote in a refugee center? When—hopefully—they'll be living somewhere else in a few weeks. The big advantage to at-large elections—"

No good. Nat Davis and Greg Ferrara were barging in now, hollering on the side of what Mike called "sentiment." Mike's attempt to remain Washingtonian lasted about three minutes. Thereafter he was bellowing with the rest of them.

All except Rebecca, of course. She adopted what might be called a Shakespearean stance. Or Oxfordian. Such, at least, seemed the best interpretation of her occasional muttered remarks:

Tomorrow and tomorrow and tomorrow . . . last syllable of recorded time . . . sound and fury, signifying nothing . . .

"Are you all finished?" she demanded, perhaps half an hour later. The surliness in her tone—which, from Rebecca, was unheard of—brought everyone up short.

"Children!" she snapped. "Squabbling over your toys!"

She glared around the room. "What *difference* does it make? You have your Bill of Rights—no quarrel there. You have your citizenship requirements—no quarrel there either. You have your elections and all the other trappings of democracy—any arguments over *that* petty matter?"

Silence. "So what is it then?" In a little singsong: "'I think we should register people at-large. I think we should register them by residence.'" She took a deep breath. Then:

"*Who gives a shit?*"

Dead silence. Rebecca *never* used that kind of—

"Ha! As I said—*children.*"

At that moment, the door opened and Frank Jackson entered the room. Behind him came Gretchen.

Rebecca pointed dramatically at the new arrivals.

"Ask them!" she commanded. "Go ahead!"

After the issue was explained, Frank spoke first. "Don't much care," he said, shrugging. "Six of one, half dozen of the other. So I figure since Mike'll be running the show—he's got my vote anyway—let him have what he wants."

Gretchen was terser still. "Vat he says," she stated, pointing at Frank.

Gretchen and Frank's remarks, combined with Rebecca's profanity, had produced a sharp break in the room's tension. The members of the committee stared at each other, for a moment. Then, collectively, they heaved a sigh and relaxed.

Mike cleared his throat. "Look, I'm not trying to make pronouncements about abstract political principles. I'm just trying to give us a political system that does the best job for our current needs. We can always hold another constitutional convention later, when circumstances change. Remember what I said. We're at the equivalent of 1776, not 1789. The Constitution which our old United States adopted came out of years of experience and discussion. *After* the revolution, not at the start of it. So let's give ourselves the same breathing room. For now, I want to keep our eyes focused on the struggle ahead of us. *Today. Right now.*"

Mike nodded toward Gretchen. At Frank's quiet insistence, the young German woman had taken a seat at the table. "The reason I asked Gretchen to sit in—which I plan on making a permanent thing, by the way—is because later on in the meeting I want you all to hear her report. As far as I'm concerned, the work that Gretchen's started is going to be a lot more important, in the long run, than any victories we win on a battlefield. Or whether we register people to vote at-large or by residence."

He almost laughed, seeing the simultaneous looks of discomfort which came over the faces of Melissa and Quentin. Each in their different ways, both people were a bit aghast at the way Mike and Rebecca were shaping Melissa's original proposal. Melissa was upset because practice was proving to be a lot *messier* than theory. And, she already understood, was going to be a lot bloodier. Her semi-romantic idealism about the "underground" was now in the firm grip of a woman who had no romanticism about it at all. Just a determination to *win*, driven by an iron will.

Quentin, of course, had never been fond of the theory in the first place. He found himself in the peculiar position of helping to lead a revolution—a task for which, temperamentally, he had no sympathy at all. By nature and habit, Quentin Underwood was a man of the establishment.

Mike turned his eyes upon him. Quentin and Melissa formed the poles of the committee. Both of them were often unhappy with the way Mike drove things forward. But Melissa's support, at least for the moment, was a given. If nothing else, she had no alternative. Quentin, on the other hand—

Underwood heaved a sigh. "Oh, hell. All right, Mike. I'll go along with at-large elections, much as it rubs me the wrong way."

The victory was only half won. Mike gave Underwood his own sharp eye. "Not good enough, Quentin. Not good enough by half. 'Going along' is one thing. Standing up and being counted is another. We've already decided to call for new elections for delegates to a constitutional convention, since that voice-vote 'election' a few days after the Ring of Fire was too casual and too far back. You're bound to be elected one of those delegates, Quentin. But how are you going to *run*?" Mike pointed to the proposed constitution in front of him. "Based on *that* platform? Or someone else's?"

He didn't bother to specify the "someone else." There was no need.

Underwood returned Mike's stare with his own. Everyone else in the room found themselves holding their breath. They had reached a decisive moment, they suddenly realized, without anyone other than Mike—and maybe Rebecca—seeing it coming. For months, the group of people in that room had worked together as a team. But—

In the universe they had left behind, Quentin Underwood—capable, narrow-minded, intelligent, stubborn, energetic, hard-driving manager that he was—would have been a natural ally of John Simpson. *Establishment. Tory through and through.* Would he break ranks now?

"Cut it out, Mike," growled Underwood. "Do I look like an idiot? If Simpson was running this show, we'd have been dead by now."

Suddenly, he grinned. That cheerful expression was not seen often on Quentin's face.

"So. You thought up a name yet?"

Mike's face was blank. Quentin's grin widened. "For our political party, dope. Gotta have one, if you want to be president of a revolution-in-progress. None of that above-the-fray Washington business for *you*, young man!"

Blank.

"What a genius," chuckled Underwood. "Leave it to a UMWA *mi-li-tant*." The chuckle grew into a soft laugh. "This calls for managerial skills. I think we oughta call ourselves the Fourth of July Party."

"Fourth of July *Movement*," came Melissa's immediate riposte.

And that, of course, startled another wrangle. But Rebecca wasn't reduced to quoting verses. The argument was sharp, short—and ended in an overwhelming victory. Everything else against Melissa.

Fourth of July Party it was. The announcement was made the following morning, along with the declaration that the constitutional convention was to go into session.

❖   ❖   ❖

Simpson protested immediately, even though he had been calling for the convention for weeks. "To bridle the Stearns military dictatorship," as he had often put it.

No matter. The iron heel of democracy was on Grantville's neck. The victim of that tyranny reacted as could be expected.

Politicking! Whoopee!

Chapter 41

"Americans ae a daft breed," stated Lennox. Firmly, he drained his mug; and, just as firmly, set it down on the table. "No daft enough, howe'er, t'keep brewin' they sorry excuse f'r beer. So I will make allowances."

The man sitting across from him at the large table, Moses Abrabanel, ignored the remarks. He was gazing about the main room of the recently opened and jampacked Thuringen Gardens. He seemed in a bit of a daze. So did the man sitting next to him, his distant cousin Samuel. For all their relative youth—both men were still short of thirty—they were experienced negotiators and men of affairs, accustomed to navigating the corridors of power in Vienna and Italy. At the moment, however, they seemed like country rubes.

Smiling, Lennox glanced to his left. Balthazar returned the smile with one of his own. Clearly enough, the two "old America hands" were enjoying the discomfiture of the newcomers. Moses and Samuel had arrived only a few days earlier, and were still in a state of semishock.

Some of that was caused by their own folk. The small number of Jews who had settled in Grantville over the past months had acclimatized with a vengeance. To a degree, that was expected. The Jews were all Sephardim who, unlike the Ashkenazim of eastern Europe, had a long tradition of cosmopolitanism. The saw "When in Rome . . ." might have been invented by them.

Still—

It was hard to know what startled Samuel and Moses the most. Perhaps the open manner in which Grantville's practicing Jews were overseeing the construction of their new synagogue. The temple was being built in the rehabilitated shell of an abandoned building right in the middle of town. Perhaps. But—

The night before, Michael Stearns had spent hours in Balthazar's living room, engaged in a frank and freewheeling discussion with the two Abrabanel representatives as well as Balthazar himself. This, of course, was as it should be. But Rebecca had spent the hours with them—and participated just as fully as anyone else.

So much was bad enough. *Then!* When the discussion was finally ended, Rebecca's father retired for the night—with his two young male relatives firmly in tow. Rebecca, on the other hand, had remained behind.

Unchaperoned? Shocking! Her father permits this? And a gentile! Shocking!

Remembering the expressions on his relatives' faces, Balthazar hastily drained his own mug—more to quench his outright laughter than his thirst. Moses and Samuel would have been considerably more shocked, he knew, if they had wandered into the living room a few minutes later. They would have found Rebecca planted in Michael's lap, engaging in a *most* unseemly form of American behavior. For all his own cosmopolitanism, Balthazar himself had been shocked, the first time he accidentally stumbled across his daughter engaged in that particular practice. He had not intervened, although he did speak to Rebecca the next day. But she had defended herself vigorously and, under the circumstances, Balthazar had let the matter pass. He allowed that the American term for it had a certain rough charm. "Necking," they called it.

But most of Moses and Samuel's discomfiture was caused by the Americans themselves.

First and foremost, of course, was the manner of American female dress. Much of which was prominently displayed at this very moment in the Thuringen Gardens.

Samuel was trying not to ogle a young woman standing at the bar nearby. The woman was exchanging words with Rebecca, a discussion which seemed to amuse both of them. Given the shapeliness of her figure, brazenly displayed in tight-fitting blouse and pants, the task was clearly straining the young man's will.

Lennox came to the rescue, in a manner of speaking. "Nae that one, laddie," he said, shaking his head in solemn reproof.

Flushing, Samuel looked away. "She is married? Engaged?"

"Nayther, at t'moment." There was an interruption, as one of the barmaids arrived and plunked a pitcher of beer on the table. "On the house," she said in thickly accented English. "Compliments of the campaign." Then she was off, plowing through the mob. The woman was stout and well past her youth. Like most of the barmaids at the Thuringen Gardens, she had been hired for her tenacity and determination as well as her experience. She was a former tavern-keeper herself, accustomed to maneuvering through rowdy throngs—and glad to do it again, now that she was earning more money than she'd ever dreamed of.

"At t'moment," repeated Lennox. He gave the young woman in question a brief inspection. "Th'lass 'as risen soom in status lately, as it 'appens, an' her former young man took it puirly. So 'e was unceremoniously given t'boot."

He saw Rebecca give the woman a little nudge with her elbow, after glancing at the door. Smiling thinly, Lennox turned away and refilled all the mugs. "Bu' I daresay there'll be another along soon." His eye caught motion, heading toward him. "An' speak o' t'devil."

Mackay pulled up a chair next to Samuel and dropped into it. He seemed exhausted.

"Beer?" asked Lennox, pushing a mug toward him.

"*Yes.*" The word was almost hissed. "Please!" Alex was having a bit of difficulty talking. His mouth seemed stiff. But not so stiff that he wasn't able to drain the mug at one quaff. Wordlessly, he extended it for a refill. Lennox obliged, and the refill went the way of its mate.

Mackay lowered the mug. A slight shudder rippled his shoulders. "There's a man who'll never lack for work," he commented grimly. "Worse comes to worst, the Inquisition would treasure his talents."

Lennox grunted. "Bad again, eh?" Mackay shrugged. Lennox shook his head. "Madness, what men will put theyselves through. D'ye think 'tis worth it, lad?"

"Do find another chair, would you?" murmured Balthazar to Samuel. "I think the young lady is coming for a visit."

Lennox turned his head. Sure enough. Julie Sims was bouncing over with her inimitable stride. He was amused to spot Rebecca moving away through the crowd. Like a snake in the grass, having made her strike. *Treacherous Eve!*

"Hi, Alex!" Julie called out. Samuel hastily arose and offered her his chair. Smiling, she accepted, while Samuel went in search of another.

The smile, transferred to Mackay, became very wide. "Daddy tells me you've been coming to see him," she said, without preamble. "So lemme have a look."

After a moment's hesitation, Mackay open his mouth. Slightly. Julie shook her head firmly. "Come on, Alex. Show me."

Wider. The head shaking continued. Wider. Continued. Alex sighed. Gaped.

Julie half rose and inspected his teeth from close range. Nothing casual about that examination, either, as you might expect from a dentist's daughter.

She sat back down. "Looking good," she announced. The smile thinned, and the amusement in her eyes was replaced by something very warm. "That must hurt an awful lot," she said softly. The statement was not one of commiseration, however. It was more in the way of an assessment. The look which accompanied the words seemed to belong to someone much older than eighteen.

"It's crowded in here," she announced abruptly. "Would you like to take a walk?"

"Yes," replied Alex. "I would."

After they were gone, Moses said tentatively: "She seems a bit on the bold side."

Lennox snorted. "She's got more counselors an' advisers th'n fuckin' Emperor Ferd'nand hisself. No tha' she needs 'em." He cocked an eye at Moses; there seemed to be a twinkle there. "Ye'd be bold too, lad, if ye c'ld drop a man at four hundred paces wit' ae single shot." He sipped on his beer contemplatively. "Which, as it 'appens, I saw 'er do not so long ago. 'Bout a doozen times."

And there, of course, was another source of amazement. Neither Moses nor Samuel was personally familiar with firearms. Few Jews were, in that day and age. By law, most realms which tolerated Jews also forbade them the practice of carrying arms. But they were quite familiar with gun-handling *men*. Moses and Samuel had each been chosen for this mission because of their experience with mercenary armies, as well as their command of English. It had not taken them more than a few days, after arriving in Grantville, to drastically revise the far-flung Abrabanel family's initial estimation of American military capability.

Revised—*up*. Way up. Moses and Samuel soon realized that the striking power of the Americans, dependent as it was on their dazzling motor vehicles, was somewhat limited in range. But anywhere within reach of the rapidly expanding network of roads surrounding Grantville, they had little doubt that the Americans could shatter any but Europe's largest armies.

True, thought Samuel and Moses, the Americans remained vulnerable to cavalry raids. Neither the imperial Croats nor the king of Sweden's Finns would collide head-on with American firepower. But raids are not conquest. Should the Abrabanel family make the decision to—here, another peculiar American term, *invest*—in Grantville, their fortune would be secure enough.

"Deadly faeries," murmured Lennox. He started to add something, but was interrupted by a shout coming from the platform at the other end of the huge room. The platform was designed for musicians, but today it had been taken over by the political campaign which was hosting the festivities.

The Fourth of July Party was about to start its first rally. Mike Stearns was climbing onto the platform and advancing toward the microphone.

And that, of course, was the principal source of the newly arrived cousins' amazement. Again, Lennox and Balthazar exchanged the knowing glance. Old America hands.

Lennox refilled all the mugs. "Brace yeselves, lads. Ye've never seen ae folk so enchanted wit' speeches."

He settled back in his chair. "Ae daft breed."

Chapter 42

Mike started his speech by going straight to the point.

"There's only one issue in this campaign. Forget all the blather about at-large election. And why is Simpson so worked up about what he calls the 'principle' of residential election, anyway? Back in the old days, what with his globe-trotting and his villa in Spain and his penthouse in London, I'm sure he never cast anything *except* absentee ballots."

The large crowd in the Gardens laughed. Mike waved his hand, as if brushing aside an insect.

"But that's all a red herring. The only thing Simpson *really* cares about is the same thing I care about—the franchise." Again, he made that brushing motion with his hand. "Oh, sure, there's other stuff. Lots of it. Our refugee policy, our economic policy, our foreign policy— you name it, and Simpson and I are on opposite ends. But all that's for later. *This* election is for delegates to the constitutional convention. The convention won't be deciding matters of policy. It will settle something far more important, which is simple. *Who decides in the first place?* Whatever policy is implemented, by whatever person or party—who gets to decide which person or party holds office? That's the franchise, and the franchise is ultimate power. And *that's* the issue. The only issue."

Mike turned from the microphone and glanced at Rebecca, standing toward one side of the stage. She came forward, holding two documents in her hand, and passed them to Mike.

The first document which Mike held up was a few pages, stapled together.

"This is *our* proposed constitution." He nodded toward a group sitting at a nearby table. "Ed, Melissa, James and Willie Ray drew it up, and the emergency committee as a whole approved it."

A call went up from one of the tables in the back. "Underwood, too?"

Mike nodded. "Yes. Quentin's running for delegate based on this proposal."

A little murmur went up from the crowd. More than a little, actually. The news of Underwood's allegiance was significant, and everyone knew it. In times past, as manager of the largest working mine in the area, Quentin had been the proverbial "big man in town." The biggest, in truth. Unlike many of the town's businessmen, Underwood was not an independent proprietor. But his actual power and influence had been far greater. No locally owned small business in Grantville had had anything like the payroll of the mine, nor the purchasing power of its manager.

Some of the UMWA members in the tavern were not exactly thrilled by the news. They were more accustomed to seeing Underwood on the other side of a picket line. But none of them were stupid, and all of them were accustomed to thinking in tactical terms. *First things first. Better the manager—home-grown boy, comes down to it— than that stinking out-of-town miserable CEO son of a—*

Harry Lefferts summed it up: "Bet Simpson's dick turned into a pickle when he heard *that*."

His packed table erupted in laughter. "That leaves him all the little old ladies and the used car dealers." More laughter. "Oh, yeah—I forgot. I hear the temperance people are backing him one hundred percent, too." Uproarious laughter now. The town's alcohol consumption, never low, had reached epic proportions with the massive influx of German refugees. "Temperance," for seventeenth-century Germans, meant no beer with breakfast.

On the stage, Mike was continuing. He held up the other document Rebecca had given him. It constituted a very thick bundle.

"And these are the amendments demanded by Simpson and his crowd." His expression exuded sarcasm. "If you can use the word 'amendments' to refer to something four times longer than what they're supposedly amending. Their delegates are running on this proposal—because it *is* a different constitution altogether. You want to know what it is? Really? It's a Jim Crow constitution, that's what."

He began thumbing through the sheets and reading portions of the amendments. "'Absolute command of English, ascertained by duly appointed election boards . . . includes satisfactory literacy, ascertained by the same boards.'" Mike scanned down; chuckled. "This one's my favorite: 'aspirants for voting rights must demonstrate a sound knowledge of American history, to the satisfaction—'"

He dropped the sheets onto the floor, as if they were unclean. "I'm sure *I* couldn't pass those tests—not given by the kind of 'boards'

Simpson has in mind. Jim Crow boards, that's all they'd be." He grinned. "I imagine they'd even flunk Rebecca."

"Yeah?" demanded Lefferts in a booming voice. The young miner rose—well, staggered—to his feet. "Put Simpson on Becky's talk show then! Let's all watch her clean his fucking smartass clock!"

The tavern erupted with laughter and applause. For weeks, Rebecca's thrice-weekly roundtable discussion had been the most popular of all the TV shows. Hands down.

"She offered!" came a woman's voice. The crowd craned their necks. At a table near the side, Janice Ambler stood up. "She offered—*eight times,*" repeated the TV station's manager. "Simpson turned her down."

On the side of the stage, Rebecca was hanging her head in embarrassment. Then, hearing the loud cheer which went up in the tavern—and continued, and continued—she force herself to raise it. She was learning, slowly, not to assume an automatic pose of modesty when her prodigious intellect was publicly praised. But she was still unaccustomed to such praise, after all these months. So she was unable to control the flush in her cheeks. Fortunately, with her dark complexion, the involuntarily reaction went largely unnoticed.

Lennox spotted it, of course, as did Rebecca's relatives. Her father sipped his beer complacently. Lennox grunted. "Did I mention they was daft? Praisin' female brains in pooblic!" He guzzled his own beer. " 'T'will all end badly—mark my words."

Mike was giving a peroration now, but Lennox's words drove over it at his own table. "Ye can ignore t'is portion o' t'speech, lads. 'Tis a lot o' silly business 'boot t'grand tradition o' West Virginians an' how they seceded from a sorry lot o' aristocratic secessionists when t'slave-owning bastids attempted to undermine t'will o' America's 'onest an' stalwart yeomanry—"

His summary made no more sense to the Jewish diplomats at the table than what they could grasp of Mike's own speech. But if they missed the specifics of the thing, they did not fail to grasp the essence of it.

"The man is *serious* about this," muttered Moses. His eyes roamed the huge room, scanning the crowd packed everywhere. For all their easy intermingling, Moses could easily distinguish the Americans from the Germans, and both from the Scots. Others were unknown to him. A small party of men at one table, acting very ill at ease, he found impossible to place.

"Mennonites," whispered Balthazar. "A few hundred of them arrived just two weeks ago. The Americans gave them a grant of unused land in the foothills. Those are their elders."

"Deadly serious," stated Lennox. He wiped beer from his lips. The gesture carried an unmistakable aura of satisfaction. "T'man's daft, lads, but make no mistake 'boot one t'ing. He is a faery, right an' true."

"Will he win this contest?" asked Samuel.

Lennox gave him a cold gaze. "Didna ye hear me? A *faery*, I said."

At the same moment, if in a different way, Underwood and Henry Dreeson had come to the same conclusion.

Leaving the Chamber of Commerce meeting, Underwood remarked: "That went better than I'd expected."

Dreeson smiled. "Not me, Quentin."

The former-and-still mine manager eyed him skeptically. "I know that bunch, Henry. They're about as conservative as dinosaurs. Hell, they even make me look like a wild-eyed radical."

The town's mayor shook his head. "That's not fair, Quentin. Dinosaurs are extinct, and that's one thing those boys don't intend to be."

They came out onto the street, and took a moment to button up their jackets. November had come in chillier than they were accustomed to.

Dreeson looked up and down the street. "Look at it, Quentin. Notice anything different?"

"Sure! The street's packed with people. Business is booming." Underwood glanced up at the row of old, multistory brick buildings lining both sides of Grantville's small downtown "main drag."

"I can remember when half of those buildings were vacant," he mused. But the statement was accompanied by a scowl. "Still—the place is a lot rowdier, too. Dan and his deputies are really earning their keep now. He told me the other day he's starting to feel like Wyatt Earp or Bat Masterson, trying to keep a Wild West boom town under control."

But Dreeson's eyes were elsewhere. He was watching a small mob of children romping through the street. With only an occasional bus coming through, Grantville's streets had become pedestrian avenues.

"I was thinking about the kids," he said softly. "It broke my heart, Quentin. All those years, in this town I was born in, grew up in, and love so much. Plan to die in. Seeing so many of the young people leave, like they do—did—all over Appalachia."

The elderly mayor drew in a deep breath. The cold autumn air seemed to invigorate him. "Damn and blast Simpson and all his Cassandra screeching." Dreeson nodded back toward the building they had just emerged from. "Sure, they're nervous. Nervous as hell. But they'll back us up. Business is booming, even if it is crude. And the kids are back. In droves."

❈   ❈   ❈

Two other people, walking down a different street, were also finding the chill air invigorating. Or, perhaps, it was simply their own company.

"It won't be easy, Alex," said Julie. She stopped at a corner and turned to him. Her hands were tucked into the pockets of the jacket she had put on as they left the tavern. Julie's expression was severe, in the excessive manner of a girl trying to be a mature woman. "I don't need another twitchy boyfriend."

The Scotsman's freckled face was twisted by a wry smile. "I trust you'll allow me the occasional lapse?"

Taking Julie's chuckle for an affirmative, the smile became much less wry. "I'm not a boy, Julie, despite my looks. I've seen more ruin and destruction in my life than I care to think about. I think it gives a man—me, at least—a certain perspective."

The smile vanished, replaced by his own excessively severe expression. "For my part, you must understand that I am sworn to the service of the king of Sweden. No matter what you may have heard about mercenaries, I take that oath seriously. So—"

Julie took her right hand out of the pocket and placed fingertips on his lips. " 'Nough. I understand. You don't need a fretting female. You'll be gone a lot, and may never come back."

He took her hand in his own and kissed the fingertips. Then, taking them gently away: "Not willingly. But mine is a risky profession. No way around that."

They set off again, now walking hand in hand. Julie's steps, as always, had a certain bounce to them. More than usual, perhaps.

"You'll allow me the occasional lapse?" she asked.

Her first lapse came less than two minutes later.

"*Tomorrow?*" she exclaimed.

Mackay shook his head. The expression combined regret, apology—and stubbornness.

"I must, Julie. I was in Jena when the king passed through Thuringia, so I was unable to report. I can delay no longer. Gustav Adolf has established a temporary headquarters in Würzburg. But I don't know how long he'll be there. He's moving very fast, while the imperialists are still off balance. So I must be off—"

"Tomorrow!" she wailed.

If the horde of children who burst around the corner and swarmed past them some time later thought there was anything odd about two people embracing in public, they gave no sign of it.

Probably not. They saw a lot of that, these days.

Chapter 43

November was a whirlwind.

The first storm of winter, when it hit, seemed but a minor distraction. No one in Grantville or the surrounding area was worried about surviving the winter. Not any longer. Even with the influx of new prisoners-turned-immigrants from the battle at Jena, there was more than enough food and shelter.

"Shelter," of course, was often crude. The area surrounding the power plant had become a small town in its own right. The power plant's steam provided a ready source of heat, which was piped through a crazy quilt of hastily erected log cabins so closely packed together that they constituted a seventeenth-century version of a housing project. But, for all its primitive nature, the housing would keep people alive during the winter. And the crowded conditions provided another incentive—not that Germans of the time needed one—to quickly seek work which could provide the wherewithal to move into better quarters.

The problem, actually, was more a shortage of good housing than the wages to pay for it. Grantville had become a classic boom town. The coal mine was running full blast by now, using hordes of pick-and-shovel miners in place of the absent modern equipment. So were all the established industries, especially the machine shops. Even the school's technical training center had become a production facility—and the students, most of whom were now German youngsters, learned their trades all the quicker for it.

New businesses and industries were springing up like mushrooms. Most of them were of a traditional nature. Construction, of course, occupied pride of place. But the Thuringen Gardens soon had competitors, and lots of them, even if it was still the largest tavern in town.

Food, in the end, turned out to be much less of a problem than Mike and his people had feared. In addition to the grain stocked up during the fall, two new sources of provender had turned up.

The first was trade. In the mysterious way that these things happen, coursing through the consciousness of a nation's masses far below the notice of its political and military overlords, word had spread throughout Germany. There was a place . . .

A market for food, textiles, metal, minerals. Almost anything, it seemed. Paid for with hard currency—gold and silver—if you so desired. Or, if you were smarter, with wondrous new products. Fine metalwork; strange, silky garments; most of all, ingenious toys and dolls and devices made of some substance called "plastic." Luxury goods! Grantville's pharmacies and knicknack stores, oddly enough, proved to be the town's biggest trade asset. In weeks, they unloaded half-useless toys and gadgets which had cluttered the shelves for months.

Some of the German traders—the smartest ones—moved their base of operations to Grantville. And found, soon enough, that investing in manufacture was even more profitable than trade. The way was led by Georg Kleinschmidt, the merchant who brought in the first shipment of nails and spikes. Seeing the massive amount of wood construction going up, he cheerfully abandoned trade and sank his new small fortune into building a nail factory. His partner was Keith Trumble, an American car dealer. The American, realizing that his former business was a lost cause, provided his offices and small showroom as the facilities. While his fellow car dealers moaned and groaned, and flocked—small flock—to Simpson's campaign rallies, Trumble greeted the new reality with good cheer. Making nails was harder work, true; and dirtier. But at least he didn't have to tell lies anymore, or dicker with his customers. There was a line at the door every morning.

The other source of food brought pure joy to West Virginians. Fall was deer hunting season. But in seventeenth-century Thuringia—

A *license?* What is that?

Limits? None. Except, of course, that it is strictly forbidden to hunt on land owned by the aristocracy, which comprises most of the forests and all—

Fuck the aristocracy. They don't like it, let 'em try to arrest us.

The game in the Thuringenwald was plentiful. And the deer were quite unaccustomed to rifles which could hit a target at several hundred yards.

Julie Sims alone brought in enough venison to feed hundreds. But that feat—in her eyes, at least—was eclipsed by her new boyfriend's. The day after Alex returned from Würzburg, Julie took him hunting.

She carried her beloved Remington .308, but Alex satisfied himself with a double-barreled shotgun loaded with slugs.

Julie scoffed at his choice of weapons. But Mackay was not fazed. He had no chance of equaling her marksmanship, anyway. And, truth to tell, he was not concerned with deer. Mackay, unlike Julie, was familiar with the forests of his time. He brought the shotgun along in case—

When the boar charged out of a thicket, Julie stood her ground. But she fumbled, trying to bring the long-range rifle to bear. No matter. Mackay dropped it at five yards—*bang bang*—cool as could be. Julie didn't stop talking about it for weeks.

Her bragging precipitated the first duel in Grantville's modern history. Her former boyfriend, Chip, still sulking and nursing his romantic wounds—well, injured pride; he had the amorous instincts of a bullfrog—took umbrage.

Fueled by too much beer on one particular evening, Chip saw fit to challenge Mackay on the floor of the Thuringen Gardens. The Scotsman, a gentleman even if he was not legitimately born, naturally accepted. He probably would have done so even if he hadn't consumed more than his share of the Gardens' excellent home brew.

The confusion began immediately. Chip, a football player raised on a twentieth-century American diet, was much larger than the little Scotsman. So, boldly, he advanced and felled Mackay with a fist.

Not even bothering to inquire as to the challenged party's choice of weapons!

Mackay, outraged by the American's uncivilized conduct, immediately made his choice of weapons. He sprang up from the floor (a punch in the face?—to a man who has faced a *dentist?*), drew his saber and began chasing Chip through the premises.

Progress was slow, both for pursuer and pursued. Chip, needless to say, scampered through the crowd as if he were scrambling for the goal line. Which took a lot of scrambling, since the crowd grew rapidly as word spread into the streets. *Fight! Fight!*

Mackay, fortunately, did not use his saber to clear a path. Still polite, for all his inebriation and murderous purpose, he asked the avid onlookers to step aside. Finally—this took perhaps two minutes—he cornered Chip in the area of the Gardens given over to the pool tables.

Chip, of course, was now armed. He took a mighty swing at Mackay with a pool cue. Alas, he quickly discovered that a pool cue is a truly pitiful weapon to use against an experienced cavalryman—even on foot—armed with a saber. The pool cue was transformed into toothpicks in a matter of seconds.

The end seemed near.

Fortunately, one of Dan Frost's deputies intervened. *Unfortunately*, the deputy was Fred Jordan who, it transpired, had imbibed perhaps too much of his Scottish friends' attitudes (along with German beer, inasmuch as he had been off duty). So he took it upon himself to rule Mackay's choice of weapons legal and legitimate and ordered the duel to continue—with the proviso, of course, that Chip be provided with a saber.

More confusion emerged. Chip did not possess a saber. A dozen Scots cavalrymen immediately offered the use of their own. Confusion was now rampant, propelled by Chip's cries of outrage and indignation. The bold young man, it developed, also lacked the knowledge of a saber's use.

Mackay—ever the gentleman—immediately switched his choice to pistols. Adding insult to injury, he offered to match his wheel lock against any modern sidearm of Chip's selection. At any range the American chose.

By now, sobriety was beginning to arrive. By now, Alex was in a cold fury. By now, Chip was *not*. Young Chip, belatedly, was realizing that the braggadocio of a former high-school football team captain was no match for the serious intent of a professional soldier.

Wheel lock against a modern pistol? At any range? Given those two men, the outcome was a foregone conclusion.

"He's trying to kill me!" wailed Chip.

Unkind words were muttered in response, here and there in the huge crowd which was now packing the Gardens. Many of them— again, insult piled onto injury—by the Americans in the crowd. *Good riddance* was a particular favorite. So were: *Pride goeth before a fall* and *Look before you leap*.

By the time Dan Frost arrived, the betting was running in favor of the Scotsman. But Dan put a stop to the whole thing immediately. City ordinances, he explained, expressly forbade dueling.

Mackay, ever the law-abiding man, immediately proposed transferring the locale of the duel to the woods, beyond the city limits. The odds began running heavily in his favor.

But Mike arrived then, and made a general ruling. No dueling, period. Anywhere in American territory.

"As you say, my lord," was Mackay's response. Bowing stiffly, he stalked off, never casting a glance at his erstwhile opponent.

The opponent, for his part, spent the next several days in an attempt to extract honor (if not glory) from his own part in the affair. To no avail. Not even his closest friends on the former football team sided with him.

"Cut the bullshit," said Kenny Washaw, the high school's former tight end. "And grow up, while you're at it. Or you'll wind up flipping hamburgers the rest of your life."

"What there is of it," added the former left tackle. Steve Early, that was. Unkindly: "Which won't be much, you keep picking fights with guys who carry sabers and spend hours in a dentist's chair without anesthetic. I don't care how little they are."

Simpson, of course, tried to make an issue out of the "duel." *Another example of the lawlessness brought on by the Stearns regime!*

But it fell flat. No one had actually gotten hurt, after all, saving Mackay's black eye. And, once again, Simpson misjudged his audience. Hill people have their own sense of justice—humorous, but grim for all that—which runs heavily toward bragging about the shrimp in the family tree who showed the local bully who was who and what was what.

Then, the memory of that little fracas was swept aside by the arrival of the Abrabanel representative from exotic and far-off Istanbul. Half the town turned out to greet him. Well, the American residents.

Some of them, of course, were there in an official capacity. But most of the crowd was, for the moment, utterly uninterested in general matters of high finance and foreign policy. One question—and one question only—was uppermost in their minds.

Grantville's supermarkets had run out of coffee weeks ago. To the shock and horror of its American residents, it was discovered that in that day and age coffee was almost unknown. Could only be obtained, in fact, from one source.

Turkey.

So, a somewhat bewildered Don Francisco Nasi found that his first item of business, upon his arrival, was negotiating the establishment of a coffee trade.

But he was not that bewildered. Francisco was younger than either of the other representatives of the Abrabanel family who had recently arrived. He had just turned twenty-six. Yet it soon became clear that he possessed in full measure the talents of his grandfather and the illustrious matriarch, Doña Gracia Mendes, who had created the fortune of their branch of the Abrabanels.

In the week following his arrival, in the course of almost nonstop negotiations with Mike and the committee, Francisco led the Abrabanel representatives with a firm hand. Perhaps because of his upbringing in Moslem Turkey, Francisco was much less taken aback than either Moses or Samuel at the undoubtedly outlandish character of the Americans and their new society.

"Who cares?" he demanded. The slim and handsome young man scanned the faces of the other Jews gathered in the Roths' living room. The Roths themselves were absent. Politely, they had felt it best to let the Abrabanels discuss family matters in private.

Francisco gazed at Rebecca, for a moment. There was, perhaps, a faint shadow in his eyes. Even in far off Istanbul, they had heard of the beauty and intelligence of Dr. Balthazar's daughter. Francisco had been enjoined by his family to seek a bride also, in this journey.

But, if there was a shadow, it was gone quickly enough. Francisco was a seasoned diplomat—a budding statesman, in truth, for all his tender years—not a lovesick shepherd. He had never found it difficult to look truth in the face. And the cold-blooded Machiavellian in him saw the other side of the matter. The Americans would soon be bound by ties of blood, as well as trade and statecraft. Francisco *believed* in ties of blood, as much as he believed in the sunrise. They had kept his family going for centuries.

"Face reality," he commanded. "Where else, since the Almoravid dynasty ruled Sepharad, have we had such an offer?" He reached for his cup, and sipped the precious coffee he had brought with him.

Then: "Nowhere. Not the Ottomans, even. We have done well in the empire, of course. Very well. But we still exist only on the sultan's sufferance." He snapped his fingers. "A new sultan—"

He left the words unspoken. There was no need. "There is a time for boldness, too," he stated. "This is such a time."

He turned to Moses, who had proven to be the most hesitant of the representatives. That was not surprising, of course. *His* branch of the family lived in the heart of the Habsburg beast.

"You may stay in the shadows," Francisco stated. "The Americans are not seeking material goods from the Catholic domains anyway. Just a loan—which you can easily supply in secret."

"They insist on absurdly low interest," grumbled Moses.

Rebecca began to speak, but her father stilled her with a quick hand on her arm and a cautioning glance. *Let Francisco handle it. Your interests are compromised.*

Francisco finished his coffee, and shrugged. "So? Take advantage of their offer, then. *Invest.* I intend to do so myself. We have been moneylenders long enough."

Moses and Samuel exchanged a hesitant glance. "It is—not customary," complained Samuel.

"No, it isn't," replied Francisco. Harshly: "What is *customary* is for Jews to lend money to princes, or serve the Christian aristocracy as their rent collectors. Then, when the princes are done with their wars—or the peasants rise up in rebellion—it is the Jews who burn."

He placed the cup down so forcefully that it almost broke the saucer.

"Enough, I say! I have the full backing of Turkey's Abrabanels." He was polite enough not to add: *who are the largest and richest branch of the family.* "Whatever your decision, I have made ours. We will take all necessary precautions, of course. No reason to publicly tweak the noses of the Christian rulers. But we *will* provide the Americans with the support they ask. Hard currency, loans, trade, investment."

Francisco paused, and made his own final decision. "*More.* We will begin to immigrate here. I will stay myself."

That announcement froze everyone. Francisco was the rising star in the Abrabanel firmament. Guaranteed, if he stayed in Istanbul, a life of power and luxury and splendor.

Perhaps he read their minds. He smiled. "Until the next sultan . . ."

The smile vanished, replaced by a look so stern it seemed quite out of place on his young face. His eyes moved back to Rebecca.

"There is a condition," he stated stiffly.

Rebecca inhaled so sharply it was almost a hiss. She knew full well Francisco's other purpose in coming to Thuringia. It would have taken no genius to deduce it, even if her father had not been notified in advance.

She found herself struggling fiercely to keep anger out of her own stiff face. She was almost shocked, then, to realize how much she had internalized the American way of looking at things. *If this man thinks he can demand—*

Francisco, as if realizing her thoughts, shook his head. "When is your marriage to Michael Stearns to take place?" he asked.

The question caught Rebecca off guard. "I—we—" she fumbled. Then, quietly: "We have not set a date."

"*Set it, then,*" commanded Francisco. "That is my condition."

Rebecca stared at him. For one of the few times in her life, she was quite at a loss for words.

Francisco's stern expression softened. "Please, Rebecca. Do it now. For all of us." He spread his hands, as if to explain the obvious. "I believe in ties of blood."

Moses and Samuel, true to their cautious instincts and training, made no final pronouncements that night. But it was obvious to all that Francisco had settled the matter.

The meeting broke up soon thereafter. Rebecca had to leave. Her roundtable discussion show was on the air again that night. Francisco walked her to the door, and offered to accompany her to the school.

Rebecca hesitated. She had no desire—none at all—to offend Francisco. Or to bruise his sentiments further. So, for a moment, she fumbled with the explanation that Michael always walked her—

Again, Francisco was a mind reader. "He seems a magnificent man," he said gently. "We Turkish Sephardim, you know, are quite accustomed to marrying outside the faith."

Rebecca's smile lost its shy hesitance. "Thank you, Francisco. For whatever it may be worth, had the circumstances been otherwise, I would have been quite happy to become your wife. I think you are quite magnificent yourself."

He nodded, with all the aplomb of a courtier raised in the formalities of the Ottoman court. "I thank you for that, Rebecca Abrabanel."

Rebecca cast hesitation aside. "But I have a cousin in Amsterdam. She is very pretty—very intelligent, too—her name is—"

Francisco held up his hand. "Please! Allow me a day or two to wallow in my heartbreak." A chuckle took all the sting out of the words. Then a thoughtful expression came to his face.

"Besides," he mused, "it would be best to leave that aside, for the moment. I am here now, to stay. Perhaps I should give some thought to following your own example. Ties of blood."

Hesitation—to the winds!

"Even better!" exclaimed Rebecca. "There is a young schoolteacher— Gina Mastroianni—very good family, as Americans count such things—a good friend of mine, she has become—she is even prettier than my cousin—smarter, too, in all honesty—and—"

Francisco was laughing aloud, now. "Be off!" he commanded. "Later!"

Obediently, Rebecca skipped down the steps. But, by the time she reached the bottom, a new enthusiasm had come. She turned around.

"Be sure to watch the show tonight, Francisco! There will be a great opportunity to invest! Watch!"

"How does she get away with it?" grumbled Piazza. As usual, he was attending the roundtable discussion as part of the live audience in the recording studio.

Sitting next to him, Mike grinned. "What's the matter?" he whispered. "Think the TV executives we left behind—not to mention the sponsors—would have choked on this show? Not suitable for a popular audience?"

Piazza grunted sarcastically. He started to reply, but fell silent. The show was starting.

"Welcome to tonight's roundtable discussion," began Rebecca. She was practically bouncing in her chair from enthusiasm. "Tonight's show, I think, will be grand!"

She introduced the participants with a quick pointing finger. "Most of you, of course, already know Greg Ferrara from his many appearances on the show. Next to him is Ollie Reardon, the owner of one of Grantville's machine shops. And next to him is Jerry Trainer. Jerry is Quentin Underwood's son-in-law and was studying for a degree in chemical engineering before the Ring of Fire—ah—*interrupted* his education."

A little laugh went up from the audience. "But he finished enough, I'm quite sure!" said Rebecca firmly. She broke off for a moment, translating the introductions into German. When she resumed in English, her enthusiasm seemed to rise.

"Tonight we're going to discuss their proposal for building a chemical factory, and they will explain the importance of it for our future." Bouncing like a puppy, now: "Especially sulfuric acid! Isn't that grand?"

"How does she get away with it?" demanded Piazza. "The worst of it is—don't take this bet!—she'll keep the whole damned audience."

And, indeed, she did. The German audience, anyway. Some of the Americans turned away from their TV sets. But not one German.

A half hour into the show, watching Greg Ferrara at his blackboard explaining the critical importance of sulfuric acid to practically all industrial chemical processes, a German farmer turned his head to the man sitting next to him in the Thuringen Gardens. His neighbor at the table, a German coal miner, had his eyes glued to one of the elevated TV sets scattered throughout the huge tavern.

"Sounds dangerous," commented the farmer.

The miner snorted. "More dangerous than a coal mine? And with the wages they're talking about?" He emptied the pitcher into his mug and looked around for a barmaid. "Besides—"

He spotted the woman he was looking for. "Gesine—*bitte!*" He waved the empty pitcher. "*Und* a telephone!"

A minute or so later, Gesine appeared with a fresh pitcher and a cordless telephone. The coal miner accepted the second as easily as the first. He was an "old America hand" himself, now. Telephones were easy.

When the call-in section of the show started, the coal miner was the first one to be sent through. In the studio, Rebecca listened carefully to the man's question, carried over the loudspeakers. Since most of the question had been asked in German, she translated.

"He wants to know if you'll be offering employees the option to purchase stock."

"Oh, sure," came Ollie Reardon's immediate response. "Got to do that, these days, or you can't hire anybody." The machine-shop owner spotted Mike in the audience and grinned. "And we're not even going to try to stop the UMWA from organizing the place. Don't need any extra wars."

The audience laughed.

"And she's getting away with it again," muttered Piazza. But he was laughing himself.

Later that night, Mike wasn't amused in the least.

"You don't have to let anyone tell you what to do, Rebecca," he growled. Sitting on the armchair across from her, he began to clench his fists. "Especially not about *this*."

On the couch, Rebecca shook her head. "I am not concerned about that, Michael. Only about you. How do you feel—*yourself*?"

He looked away. For a moment, his eyes roamed the interior of the living room of his family's house. After the show, they had come here—at Rebecca's request—rather than the Roths' house. Mike's mother, sister and brother-in-law had already gone to bed. So had the German family which occupied what had once been Mike's bedroom. Not needing the space, Mike had set himself up in the small room which had once served his mother for her sewing.

He brought his eyes back to her. "It was your desire to wait, sweetheart. You wanted time."

"*Yourself*," she commanded.

The half-clenched fists opened. "Oh, hell," he whispered. "I wouldn't have waited a day."

She smiled. "Good. It is settled, then. We will get married as soon as possible." Half-eagerly; half-timidly: "Tomorrow?"

He was still frowning. Rebecca made a little fluttering motion with her hand. "Enough time!" She almost giggled. "Even for me!" Then, seriously: "And Francisco is right, Michael. I also have a responsibility to my family. They will be risking much. I know it is hard, sometimes, for you to understand this. But we have survived, in part, because we can also be cold-blooded when necessary."

The term "cold-blooded" went very poorly with the warmth—the heat—in her voice. "Tomorrow," she whispered.

Mike heaved a deep breath, almost clenching his fists again. He did press them very firmly into the armrests.

"No," he said forcefully. "Not until after the election. The convention is about to take its final vote, and we're going to win—*hands down*. I'll call for immediate elections. Give it—say, a month for campaigning. No, six weeks would be better. Then we can get married."

"Why?" Rebecca demanded. She slid forward to the edge of the couch, her whole posture pleading. "*Why so long?*"

Mike's expression, for all the love so obvious in it, was set like stone.

"Because, sweetheart, I will see you—*finally*—elected to office in your own name. Before you take mine."

Rebecca groped for the logic. When she found it, she burst into tears.

Mike rose and came to the couch, enfolding her in his arms. "Not so long," he whispered. "Six weeks. Maybe two months."

But Rebecca was already wiping away the tears. She turned her face into his neck and pressed open lips against him. "I love you," she whispered. "And we will *not* wait two months. Not for everything."

She rose and extended her hand to him.

"I have never seen your bedroom. Show me."

Chapter 44

Everywhere, the whirlwind.

A new nation would be born that winter. Three days later, the convention would ratify the new constitution—without amendments—by a seventy-eight percent majority. Mike would announce new elections with the same blow of the gavel with which he closed the convention. The election "season" would last through December, but it was more in the nature of a triumphal parade than a contest. With the franchise now extended to most of Grantville's German residents, the outcome was a foregone conclusion. After the way in which he had conducted his campaign against the constitution, Simpson had alienated every German in the area except the pure halfwits. Now, he even lost a large number of his American supporters. Sensing the tide, they bowed to the inevitable.

Mike's decision to allow weeks for the campaign proved to be a wise one. The conclusion was foregone, true—and had been from the first day. But Mike knew the difference between "winning" an election campaign and forging a political structure. The weeks of constant campaigning allowed him and his supporters time and opportunity to sink real roots in the new nation's budding growth.

The process proved complicated and contradictory, as these things do in the real world. The Fourth of July Party was really more of a coalition than a political party. Over the weeks, the different underlying factions had time to sort themselves out. Which, from Mike's point of view, was all to the good. "Unity" is a splendid word, but not when it comes at the price of clarity. That there would be political factions in the new United States, just as there had been in the one left behind in another universe, was as certain as the sunrise. Better to have them out in the open, where the public could gauge their programs, than hidden away in murky shadows.

His own position was somewhat peculiar, and more than a bit awkward. Mike now commanded a personal allegiance—*especially* from the "new" Americans—which would have allowed him, had he so chosen, to force through anything he wanted. Whatever else they disagreed on, Melissa Mailey and Quentin Underwood—the publicly recognized leaders of the Fourth of July Party's respective "left" and "right" factions—were both heard, on more than one occasion, to grumble about "Bonapartism." But not even Melissa or Quentin used the term seriously. No one who knew Mike Stearns was really worried about "a whiff of grapeshot." So, much like George Washington before him, Mike tried as far as possible to stay out of the immediate factional fray. And he accepted compromises, as a prospective president, that his younger persona would have sneered at.

At one point in the campaign, that brought him in serious collision with his own power base. The UMWA, now as always, formed the heart of Mike's support. Early in the campaign, the union voted overwhelmingly to demand that a law be passed requiring the unionization of all businesses employing more than ten workers—of which there were now quite a few, and obviously more to come.

Mike was initially inclined to agree, but Rebecca convinced him otherwise. "Most of our citizens are now Germans," she argued. "They do not understand what you mean by a 'trade union.' They think of it as a *guild*. And a guild is a very different thing altogether. It is very oppressive."

She was right, and Mike quickly saw the logic. He had noticed himself—and been uneasy about it—that the UMWA's support was coming entirely from the older, established German craftsmen. The young men—not to mention the young women—were implacably hostile to the proposal.

He tried to explain it to the UMWA at a local meeting. "Guys, our new people think of this idea as a way of imposing master-craftsman rule over the apprentices. That's why we've had so few young people knocking on our door. They want out. They're not looking at the thing from our perspective, they're—"

No use. Frank supported him. So, to his surprise, did Harry Lefferts and most of the younger miners. But it should not have surprised him. Unlike the middle-aged miners who formed the majority of the UMWA, Harry and the other young miners had made a lot of friends among young German workers and understood their viewpoint. But the local union was adamant, and Mike's public refusal to support their proposal produced a considerable strain in relations.

The strain lasted for months, until events proved Mike was right.

Soon enough, the arrogance of some of the new "captains of industry" triggered off a rapid change in attitude among young Germans. Once again, the UMWA was back in full swing, organizing new shops like mad—and this time, with Mike's full support. Which, of course brought him into a clash with Underwood and *his* faction.

So be it. Such is the whirlwind which brings new societies onto the historical stage. Forging a nation does not happen in a test tube. It happens in the real world, sweeping real people into the political arena for the first time, bringing with them all the accumulated baggage of centuries. Turbulent, chaotic, confused—*messy.*

So be it. Mike was not dismayed. Not in the least. A basket full of puppies is messy too. Which is simply nature's way of saying: *Alive and well.*

Even the new political structure was messy. Half-formed, half-shaped, a thing of big paws and big ears and precious little in the way of real flesh.

The new constitution allowed for an upper and lower house—the Senate, and the House of Representatives. Like the original Senate, the upper house gave representation to states as such, regardless of comparative population. The only difference was that each state got one senator instead of two. But the "upper house" was more fiction than fact. The "United States" still contained only one state—Grantville.

So there was only one Senate seat open in this election, although, of course, everyone was hoping for a future expansion. If nothing else, it seemed almost certain that Badenburg would soon be adding another star to the flag. And the students in Jena—with the tacit support of the town's poor quarters—were already demonstrating in the streets. The students were even chanting the name of their future Senator: Jeff Higgins. The fact that Jeff did not technically reside in Jena, for all the frequency of his and Gretchen's visits, did not concern them in the least.

Nor did it need to. The convention had decided that apportioning seats by residence, in an area as geographically small but densely populated as Grantville and southern Thuringia, would be absurd—at least for the moment. So all elections, for all seats, were held "at large."

Mike came in with eighty-seven percent of the votes for president. Except for Rebecca, every single member of the emergency committee was elected to the House by a similar landslide. To her astonishment—and chagrin—Melissa got as many votes as anyone.

"So much for my standing as a rebel," she was heard to mutter. But she consoled herself with the thought that Quentin had gotten—

by half a percentage point—a higher margin than she. So she was *still* the underdog, in a manner of speaking.

And Rebecca? Her contest was a moot point. Simpson and his followers didn't even try to run against her. She was elected unanimously, as the sole Senator of the United States.

But that night in his bedroom, weeks earlier, Mike had been swept up in a very different whirlwind. From the months of ever-growing physical intimacy, he and Rebecca had become quite familiar with each other's bodies. So there was little in the way of surprise or discovery, beyond the act of intercourse itself. Which, even for the virgin Rebecca, no longer held much mystery—and no fear at all. But their first night in bed was still a whirlwind.

Or just the wind itself. Beginning with a tornado, perhaps, but settling, as the hours passed, into something as steady and unvarying as the trade winds.

As dawn crept through the curtains in his window, Mike reflected that his grandfather had been right after all.

"Anticipation," he murmured. "God, that was *great.*" He pressed Rebecca's nude form against him, reveling in the sensation.

"Hmm?" she murmured drowsily. Neither of them had gotten any sleep. Her eyes half-closed, Rebecca kissed him. Reveling herself, not so much in the sensation as the knowledge that it would be hers for a lifetime. "What did you say?"

"Anticipation," repeated Mike happily.

Rebecca's eyes opened all the way. "What nonsense!" she exclaimed. "You did not *anticipate* anything at all."

She rose on her elbow, grinning down at him. "It was so amusing, watching you rummaging through your dresser with such frantic abandon."

Mike's answering grin was embarrassed. "Well . . ." Justify, justify: "I wasn't expecting—you didn't give me any warning—I thought I might have some old ones lying around—"

"Oh, marvelous!" she laughed, slapping his chest playfully. "I have seen those things! They look grotesque enough even when they are new!"

Sheepishly, Mike shrugged. "I was just trying to protect you—"

She silenced him with a very passionate kiss. They weren't that tired. One thing quickly led to another.

"It does not matter, anyway," she whispered later. "Even if—" Happy chuckle. "In two months, nothing would show. And even if it did, I am sure I would not be the first bride in Grantville waddling down the aisle in a loosened wedding gown."

She laughed, very happily. "Hillbillies! You have no *respect.*"

Part Five

And what shoulder, and what art,
Could twist the sinews of thy heart?

Chapter 45

Striding out of the Schloss, the enormous palace of the Archbishop-Electors of Mainz which he had appropriated for his own use during these past winter months, Gustav II Adolf caught sight of the Rhine. The flow of the river—clear, clean, simple, straightforward—brought a certain relief to his spirit.

He stopped abruptly, to admire the sight. Behind him, his little escort of advisers stumbled to a halt. Fortunately for them, none of the advisers actually collided with the king. There would have been no royal repercussions, of course. Gustav was not that kind of monarch. But as enormous as he was—and the king had gained considerable weight during the months of physical idleness and diplomatic feasting—it would have been somewhat like running into an ox. Startled king; bruised adviser, sitting on his ass. Contemplating the futility of trying to move the king of Sweden when he chose otherwise.

"No, Axel," said Gustav firmly. He did not take his eyes off the Rhine. "Let Wilhelm and Bernard Saxe-Weimar rant and rave all they want. I am not sending an expedition to Thuringia."

"Wilhelm is not 'ranting and raving,'" demurred Oxenstierna. "He is simply expressing concern over the situation in his duchy. You can hardly blame him."

Gustav scowled. "I don't care how polite he's being—which his brother certainly isn't! The answer is still *no*."

The king rubbed his hands briskly. There was no snow on the ground, but it was still only mid-March. The temperature was chilly. "I've gotten soft and tender," grumbled Gustav. "All this easy living in the south!"

Just as briskly, he turned and faced his advisers. They were all Swedish, except for Sir James Spens.

To Axel: "No, no, no. In this, the dukes of Saxe-Weimar are proving to be as petty as any German noblemen. In their absence—*protracted* absence, let me remind you—the people of their principality have seen fit to organize themselves to survive the winter and the depredations of the war." Half-angrily: "What were they supposed to do, Axel? Starve quietly, lest the tranquility of the dukes be disturbed?"

Oxenstierna sighed. His long-standing, half-amicable quarrel with the king of Sweden on the subject of aristocracy had intensified over the past year. And the chancellor of Sweden was losing the argument. For a moment, trying not to grit his teeth in frustration, Axel silently cursed his German counterparts. *With friends like these, who needs enemies?* In truth, the chancellor did not really disagree with his monarch on the specifics of the matter. Axel wouldn't wish the German nobility on a pack of dogs, except as provender. Still—

"Gustav," he said firmly, "the issue is not petty. And it can't be shrugged off as another instance of aristocratic fatuity. For all intents and purposes, power in southern Thuringia—every single report agrees on *this*, whatever else they are in dispute over—has been seized by a republic." His lips tightened. "They even chose the Dutch United Provinces as the model for their own name. The 'United States,' if you please!"

The king began to speak, but Axel held up his hand. The gesture was not peremptory—there were limits, even with Gustav II Adolf—but firm for all that. The monarch acceded politely to the wishes of his chancellor, and held his own tongue for the moment.

"The issue is a general one," continued Oxenstierna. He snapped his fingers. "I care *that* for southern Thuringia. But what if the example spreads? Or simply starts to panic the surrounding principalities? We have enough problems with nervous German allies as it is. Let the Protestant princes start fretting over revolution, and the yoke of the Habsburg empire will start seeming more like a shelter than a burden."

Standing a few feet away, Torstensson snorted. "As if the Saxons or the Prussians needed an excuse to be treacherous!"

Oxenstierna cast the artillery general a quick glare, but Torstensson stood his ground. More—he pushed back. The young general snapped his own fingers. "And I care *that* for the tender pride of the German aristocracy. Any one of those noblemen"—he glared himself—"and I do not except the Saxe-Weimars or Hesse-Cassel—will abandon us quickly enough, given the opportunity."

A small murmur of protest began to arise from the other generals. "That's not fair, Lennart," said Banér. It seemed a day for scowling. A fair example now adorned the face of the field marshal. "Bernard is an arrogant ass, sure enough. But Wilhelm is another story."

The king intervened, before the dispute could get out of hand. Let the personal character of Bernard of Saxe-Weimar assume center stage, and hot tempers would invariably result. For all the undoubted military ability which the young duke had demonstrated over the past year, the Swedish generals found him insufferable as often as not. *Arrogant ass* was the mildest of the epithets which Gustav had heard his officers use.

"All of that is also beside the point," stated the king. To Banér: "Johann, I share your personal estimate of Wilhelm. I think quite highly of the man, as it happens." Gustav gave Axel a quick, half-humorous glance. "Wilhelm is the one exception to my general condemnation of the German breed. If I didn't know better, I'd swear he was a Swedish nobleman."

A little laugh went up. With the exception of the Scotsman, all of the men standing in that little group near the Rhine were members of the Swedish aristocracy—and proud of it.

It was also, apparently, a day for finger snapping. Now the king added his own thick-fingered version. "*That* for this whole argument." He glanced again at Oxenstierna—and this time, with no humor at all. "I *do* care about Thuringia, Axel. For two reasons."

Solidly, stolidly: "First, because I am a Christian before I am anything else. My title, my lineage, my trappings—all these came from the hand of God, and no other. I have not forgotten, even if other monarchs have, that the Lord gave us that power for a purpose. Let others ignore their duty, I shall not. If a king or a prince or a baron cannot see to the needs of his folk, then he is not fit to rule. It is as simple as that. God's punishment on such men is evident in all the pages of history. Where are the Roman emperors *now*?"

The foregoing words, pious and heartfelt, had been spoken with neither heat nor pride. The next words, Gustav II Adolf spoke fully erect, his pale blue eyes alive with his own lineage. In that moment, peering at his subordinates down a majestic and powerful nose, the immense man was every inch the king.

"Secondly, because I am *Vasa.*" The name of Sweden's ruling dynasty rolled across the flagstones of the terrace. For an instant, it almost seemed as if the Rhine rippled in response.

"Vasa!" he repeated. The name was both a reminder and a challenge. A reminder to himself, a challenge to—

Gustav stared at his underlings. The gaze was not a glare. Not quite—there was too much iciness in the thing. A glacier does not glare; it simply *is*.

"Do not forget," he said softly.

Under that gaze, his subordinates did not flinch. But they did seem to shrink a little. The Vasas had established their rule over Sweden by many methods. Among those, of course, had been political and military skill. But there had also been—proven time and again—their instant readiness to break the aristocracy to their will.

Gustav Adolf had been named after his grandfather, the great Gustav Vasa who founded the dynasty and created the modern nation called Sweden. His grandfather's contempt for nobility was a matter of historical record—as was the result of that contempt. The Swedish aristocracy had been broken, bridled, disciplined. Accepted back into royal favor only after they demonstrated their willingness to work alongside the new dispensation. In Gustav Vasa's realm, the four estates had all been listened to—the peasants and the citizens of the towns as much as the nobility and the clergy. If anything, Gustav Vasa had favored the rising middle class—and been rewarded, in return, by a state treasury flush with silver, a powerful fleet and army, and Europe's finest, if not largest, munitions industry.

Vasa. Upon his accession to the throne at the technically illegal age of seventeen—made possible by a special dispensation of the *riksdag*, the Swedish parliament, engineered by Oxenstierna—Gustav II Adolf had agreed to a compromise whereby some of the privileges of the aristocracy were restored. And he had kept his promises. Unlike his grandfather, who favored commoners, Gustav II Adolf generally appointed only noblemen to high office. Yet, beneath the surface, the reality remained the same. The power of the dynasty rested on Sweden's people, not its aristocracy—and the latter knew it as well as the former.

Vasa . . .

"It is settled," stated the king. "Thuringia will be left in peace, to manage its own affairs. If Wilhelm and—ha!—Bernard can make an accommodation, excellent. But it is their business, not ours. I will *not* send a single soldier to enforce the will of Saxe-Weimar on the province."

"We already have soldiers on the scene," pointed out Torstensson mildly.

Gustav cocked his eye. "Mackay?" He shrugged. "A few hundred cavalrymen."

Spens began to speak. The king shot him a quick glance, and the Scottish general closed his mouth.

The king's eye moved on to Oxenstierna. Having made his point, Gustav would now sweeten the thing. "I will speak to Wilhelm personally, Axel," he said. "I will give him my assurances that, regardless of what happens in Thuringia, the family of Saxe-Weimar will not be abandoned by me." He chuckled harshly. "Who knows? Wilhelm, unlike his younger brother, is sagacious enough to realize that being the duke of a petty principality is not, all things said and done, the highest goal to which a man might aspire in this new world."

He clapped his hands, announcing a change in subject. The clap turned into another brisk rubbing of the palms. To ward off the cold, of course. But the motion also conveyed a great deal of satisfaction. So does a craftsman gesture, contemplating a new masterwork.

"And now, gentlemen—Tilly! The latest report indicates that the old man is stirring again. He's left Nördlingen and is moving against Horn at Bamberg. Wallenstein, meanwhile, is also back in business."

Torstensson laughed. "Big business! Has ever a mercenary general in history gotten such a contract? Who is emperor and who is lackey now, I wonder?"

His laugh was echoed by the other generals. News had recently arrived of Wallenstein's terms for accepting Emperor Ferdinand's plea for help. After Breitenfeld, the Habsburgs had been desperate, and Wallenstein had driven a devil's bargain. The Bohemian general had the emperor's formal agreement that he was in exclusive command of all military power in imperial lands. Wallenstein had also been granted civil power over all imperial territory in the possession of Ferdinand's enemies—including the right to confiscate lands and do with them as he wished. That meant booty on a gigantic scale, for all his officers. Mercenaries and adventurers could become landed noblemen overnight, in the event of victory—and why not? Hadn't Wallenstein himself set the example, in the early years of the war?

Gustav continued. "All accounts have Wallenstein assembling a huge new army. You can imagine what wolves are gathering around his banner!"

General Tott grunted. "They'll make Tilly's men look like gentle lambs."

The king nodded. "When that army moves, they will ravage everything in their path. But they will not move for weeks yet. I propose to deal with Tilly first."

He began issuing orders, facing each man in turn.

"Axel. I want you to return to Alsatia. We've got enough of a force there to keep the Spanish Habsburgs from getting ambitious. And take Bernard with you." He chuckled, seeing Oxenstierna's grimace of distaste. "Please! He *is* a very capable military commander, after all. And I'd much rather have him there than stirring up trouble about his precious Thuringia."

"Which he hasn't even bothered to visit in years," muttered Torstensson.

As if his low voice were a cue, the king turned to Torstensson next. "Lennart, you'll be staying with me in this campaign. Tilly will be using the tributaries to block my advance up the Main. I expect we'll see a lot of gun work, to clear the fords."

The young artillery general frowned. "My guns are getting pretty badly worn, Your Majesty." Scowling: "The ordnance facilities in these blessed Rhenish archbishoprics are a joke."

Spens cleared his throat. The king seemed to ignore the sound, except that his next words came in a bit of a rush. "Don't worry about that. I think I've found a new supplier. I expect to have new guns arriving within a month or two. The ones you have should last that long."

Torstensson nodded. The king turned to General Tott next.

"Return to the Weser. Keep an eye on Pappenheim. Our Saxon allies will help you readily enough with that." Another nod. Then, Banér:

"And you, Johann, I want back on the Elbe. That'll keep our Prussian friends half-honest, if nothing else. But I also need you there in case the Poles get ambitious or Wallenstein decides to move directly on Saxony."

The immediate measures taken, the king went back to rubbing his hands. "That's it, then." To Spens: "Stay behind a moment, would you, James?"

The signal was clear enough. Within seconds, the Swedish officers had all left, hurrying to set their new orders into motion.

Gustav examined Sir James Spens silently. The Scotsman occupied a peculiar position in the king's forces. He was, simultaneously, the Swedish ambassador to England as well as the English ambassador to Sweden—*and* one of Gustav's top military commanders in the bargain. The multiplicity of functions indicated the king's high regard for the man, but of those functions it was Spens' military position which was paramount. In truth, there was not much in the way of diplomatic exchange between Sweden and England. The island, for all its official Protestantism, had maintained an aloof and standoffish attitude toward the war raging on the Continent.

When all was said and done, Sir James Spens was Gustav Adolf's man. Like most of the Scotsmen who figured so prominently in the Swedish service, Spens' allegiance was highly personal. Unlike the Swedish officers, Spens had no ties of family or class to dilute his loyalty to the Swedish crown. For that reason, Gustav often used him in matters which were of a delicate political nature.

"I am concerned about the continuing allegations of witchcraft," stated Gustav forcefully. He waved his hand. "Yes, yes, James, I realize that the reports come from tainted sources. For the most part. But I am still concerned. There are so *many* reports."

Sir James shrugged. "What would you, Highness? Do you expect Catholic mercenaries thrashed by a handful of Scots and their

American allies to praise the military prowess of their opponents? Witchcraft is the easiest thing in the world to shout from the rooftops. And the hardest to disprove."

Gustav stroked his massive nose, thinking. "I'm well aware of that, James. Nevertheless, the thing is odd."

The Scottish general chuckled. "Odd? Say better—*fantastic*. A colony of Englishmen from a future America find themselves planted in the middle of Thuringia? It's a thing of fable! The tales of Rabelais and Sir Thomas More come to life."

Still stroking his nose, Gustav muttered: "You believe Mackay still, then?"

Spens nodded firmly. "Absolutely. I've known him since he was a lad of five. I took him into my service more from my own high opinion than from the fact his father is an old friend."

He studied the king intently for a moment. Then: "You were there when he gave his report at Würzburg, Your Majesty. Not three months ago. Did he strike you as a liar—or a witling?"

"Neither," came the instant reply. "'A most promising young officer,' I called him last year. Axel was quite sarcastic about it, given my unfamiliarity with the young man. But that was my impression then, and certainly nothing since has predisposed me otherwise."

He sighed heavily. "But I am concerned, James. I have more than enough problems as it is. Treating with mysterious colonists from the future—a fable, as you say!—is a bit much to add to the brew." His voice trailed off into an inaudible mutter.

The Scotsman said nothing. From long experience in Gustav's service, he knew the king was talking to himself now. Gustav II Adolf was no more immune to hesitation and uncertainty than any man. He was simply much better at dealing with it than anyone Spens had ever met.

As always, the process was brief. Within a minute, the king had stopped stroking his nose and was standing erect.

"So be it. God's will, clear enough. Is Satan so powerful he could transplant a colony from the future? I think not!" He went back to rubbing his hands. "Besides, one cannot fixate on the problems. There is also the opportunity."

Spens took the moment to fortify the king's resolve. "*Corpus Evangelicorum,*" he murmured.

Gustav smiled faintly. "You are the only man I know besides myself, James, who manages to say that phrase without lifted eyebrows."

Spens returned the smile with a grin. "And why not? I think a north European Protestant confederation under the leadership of Sweden would be a splendid solution to the war. And much else. Sweden gets its long-sought Baltic supremacy, the Holy Roman Empire gets its peace, and the north Germans—finally—get a chance to build a real nation instead of a princes' playground."

The king cocked a quizzical eye. "You do not share the general presumption that the result would be a Swedish tyranny?"

"What nonsense! Forgive me for saying so, Your Majesty, but there is simply no way in the Lord's green earth that a million and a half Swedes could maintain a genuine tyranny over ten times that many Germans. Not for long, in any event."

He shook his head. "I've lived in Sweden. You're a practical lot, comes to it. I imagine a Swedish-led north European confederation would soon enough resemble Sweden itself. Which is the best-run kingdom in the world, in my humble opinion."

"Mine also!" exclaimed Gustav cheerily. "And not such a humble opinion, either."

He clapped Spens on the shoulder. "Good enough, James. We'll stay the course. Who knows? Thuringia may well be destined to play a role in all this. But send another courier to Mackay immediately. You heard Lennart. We're going to need those new guns more quickly than I'd thought. It'll be interesting to see if Mackay's boasts about the manufacturing talents of his new friends are justified."

Spens nodded. The king continued. "Also make sure to pass along my congratulations to him. The Dutch money is rolling through very nicely. Yet another reason to leave Thuringia in peace, eh?"

"Is it not?" agreed Spens lightly. He cleared his throat. "If I may be so bold, Your Majesty, I think a promotion is in order as well as congratulations. Mackay now has a full thousand cavalrymen under his command, wearing your colors."

"So many?" Gustav shook his head with bemusement. "Well, then— of course. Colonel Mackay, from this moment forth! Nothing less!"

He and Spens shared a small laugh. As they began walking away from the palace, the king added: "And also tell him to escort the new guns to me as soon as possible. In person. I want to talk to him." Gustav hesitated, then shook his head firmly—almost vehemently. "No! I want more." He reached out with his hands, as if groping in the dark. "I want something more tangible than simply a personal report. I want—"

Grope, grope.

"An American?"

"The very thing!" exclaimed the king. "I want to *see* one of these fabled folk!"

Chapter 46

Ollie Reardon, the owner of the machine shop, wasn't sure if he was amused or aggravated. Both, he decided.

"Why is he wasting time cutting the outside of the barrel?" demanded Mackay. The Scots officer was practically dancing with impatience. "We don't have time for cosmetic adornment!"

Studying the work being done at the lathe, Ollie pursed his lips. The lathe operator, Jack Little, had been a machinist for longer than Alexander Mackay had been alive.

Guess which one of them knows what they're doing? But for all the irritation in the thought, Ollie decided to explain. Politely.

He pointed to the large casting. The butt end of the future cannon was held in the lathe's jaws; the front, already center-drilled, was held steady by a live center projecting from the tailstock. The two trunnions were rotating so rapidly they formed nothing more than a blur. Soft bronze could be machined at a much higher RPM than steel. Jack was making a very shallow cut a few inches long near the end of the barrel—a skin cut, as it was called.

"There's nothing cosmetic at all about what he's doing. He needs a machined surface for the steady rest. Unless the end of the barrel is held steady, it'd take forever to drill out the internal diameter. Just holding the casting at one end, the chatter would be ferocious."

Mackay frowned. "What's a steady rest?"

Ollie suppressed a sigh. He pointed to a fixture sitting in a rack at the end of the lathe's ways. The fixture, which could be swung apart on a hinge, formed an open circle some ten inches in diameter. Three adjustable columns ending in ball bearings projected into the center at 120-degree intervals. Two of them would cradle the piece from below; the third, from directly above.

"That is," he growled. "You set it on the ways, clamp it down, and then bring the bearings to ride on the machined surface which Jack's cutting right now. Steadies the piece and holds it true for the next operation, which, on these three-pounder barrels, is drilling out the bore." The precisionist soul of a machinist surfaced. Frowning: "We really *ought* to be reaming it, for the finish cut—we'll use a boring bar for the six-pounders—but those cast iron cannonballs are so sloppy and uneven there's no point. We'd be trying to make a silk purse out of a sow's ear."

Mackay flushed. "I see." With obvious embarrassment, he tugged at his short beard. "I see," he repeated.

Next to him, Julie grinned. "Any more questions, big shot?" She turned to Ollie and shrugged. "You got to make allowances. He's still trying to adjust to his magnificent new status."

The grin widened. "*Colonel* Mackay, no less. And he only just turned twenty-three!"

"Stop it, girl," grumbled Alex. "I was only—"

Ollie clapped him on the shoulder. "Congratulations on your promotion, by the way. I'm sorry I wasn't able to make it to the celebration at the Gardens yesterday, but—"

A little salt in the wounds, here. "I was here till midnight, making sure we were set up to run the new castings. No time for *me* to be carousing all night."

Mackay's embarrassment deepened. He *had* caroused all night. His grumpy attitude this morning was the direct result.

"Sorry," he muttered. Then, rallying what was left of his dignity: "Well, since everything is obviously under control, I think I'll be on my way."

Ollie let no sign of his relief show. In truth, he liked the Scotsman, and was willing to forgive the man being an occasional fuss-budget. Besides, Ollie understood as well as Mackay what was riding on this first shipment of new guns to the king of Sweden. So, politely—even affably—he escorted the Scotsman and his girlfriend to the door.

Memory of something he'd heard this morning suddenly surfaced. "Oh! And congratulations on your engagement, also."

Julie beamed happily and showed off the new ring on her finger. "Nice, isn't it? Alex found it in Eisenach, when he was there last week."

Mention of Eisenach caused Ollie to raise an eyebrow. He hesitated, wondering if he should ask—

"There's no big secret about it, Ollie," said Mackay. "Eisenach's almost certain to come in. They're just dancing around for a bit, waiting to see what Gotha decides." The Scotsman snorted. "And *they're* dancing around waiting on Erfurt, and Erfurt is dancing on Weimar. But it should be all over soon enough."

"That'd give us—what? Six stars on the flag, instead of two?"

Julie butted in before Alex could speak. "Eight, I bet! Word is that Mike and Becky's trip to Saalfeld and Suhl was a big success too!"

Ollie started. "I didn't know they were back. Saalfeld, huh? That'd give us a boost on the chemical side, what with the mines in the area. And—"

Mackay, his voice filled with satisfaction, completed the thought: "And that would almost certainly bring in Gera. The United States would have all of Thuringia's major towns, then. In the south of the province, anyway. Every last one."

But Ollie's mind was already elsewhere. "I'm thinking about Suhl. That town would give us control of the entire Thuringenwald. And what's probably more important is that it would stabilize our ordnance industry. A hundred years ago, you know, Suhl was the biggest armament center in Germany. Still has a lot of capacity left." He pointed over his shoulder with a thumb. "We got those castings from Suhl, as it happens. Be nice to see them part of the family."

Less than a year ago, the Scots nobleman Alexander Mackay would have been astonished to see a manufacturer and a former schoolgirl discussing matters of foreign policy. Today, he didn't even take notice of it. On that happy note, Alex and Julie left the machine shop and entered the street.

Immediately, another discussion on foreign policy erupted. Mackay launched a preemptive strike before Julie could raise the subject anew.

"You are *not* going—and that's final."

"Ha! We'll see about that! *You* don't get to make *that* decision— *Colonel, sir!*"

The two lovers glared at each other as they worked their way down the street. Their progress was slow, partly because they were immersed in the argument, but mostly because the street was very crowded. By April of 1632, Grantville's population density bore a closer resemblance to Calcutta than the small town in West Virginia it had once been.

The preemptive strike having failed, Mackay launched his next salvo.

"Impossible," he stated. "Your father would insist on a chaperone. For that matter, *I'd* insist on a chaperone. And there's—"

He stumbled for a moment, trying to force words through Julie's ensuing sarcastic remarks about his drastic change in attitude on the subject of chaperones—which he *certainly* hadn't been concerned about the night before; quite the contrary! Hadn't it been *he* who found that deserted—

Rally, Scotsman! "—no other woman be going," he concluded.

Julie looked smug. Mackay felt the pit opening beneath him.

"I don't like it," growled Mike. "Not one bit."

Rebecca said nothing. She simply sat there on the couch, relaxed, hands clasped in her lap, and returned her husband's scowl with a patient smile. Three months of marriage had brought a deeper intimacy into their relationship. Intimacy—and a much better knowledge of each other's habits and foibles.

So, where the fiancée would have argued, the wife simply let the husband argue with himself.

It wasn't much of an argument. The advantages to her proposal were blindingly obvious.

"I don't like it," he repeated. "You're pregnant and it's wartime. God knows what you'd run into."

Blithely, Rebecca ignored the issue of her pregnancy, other than running her hands down her waist to show that it was still as slim as ever. But the rest seemed to call for a response.

"Michael, all reports agree that Tilly has fallen back on the Danube. The Lower Palatinate and Franconia are firmly in Swedish hands, as is most of Würtemburg. We would encounter nothing on our way to Gustav Adolf's camp except for a few bands of stragglers and deserters. None of whom, as you well know, pose any threat to the expedition. Not with Mackay's cavalry *and* Tom's dragoons as an escort."

Silence. Rebecca decided to add a sweetener. "And since your sister *insists* on accompanying Tom," she added, smiling, "I would be chaperoned. So you would not even have to worry about my fidelity."

For all his fretting, Mike couldn't stifle a laugh. "What a relief! Boy, will *that* help me sleep easy at night."

The humor broke the tension. "All right," he sighed. "I agree it's the best response. I'd like to go myself, of course, but—"

Rebecca was already shaking her head. "That *is* impossible. I know you do not like to hear this, Michael, but the fact remains that your personal authority is key to our negotiations with the other cities in Thuringia. We *must* weld them into the new nation quickly, before the war takes another turn. For the worse, quite possibly. You have stressed that necessity over and again. In this day and age, diplomacy is a thing between specific persons, not abstract political entities. Without you—*here*—none of the cities will be confident in any negotiations."

Mike's fears made a last feeble sally. "The same could be said if I'm not there to meet—"

Again, Rebecca was shaking her head before he finished the

thought. "We are not *negotiating* with the king of Sweden, Michael. We are simply making an appearance." She smiled. "I suspect Gustav Adolf simply wants to make sure we are real, and not figments of a deranged Scotsman's imagination."

Mike smiled. "Or he simply wants to make sure we are not witches." His eyes, examining his wife, were full of love—and, truth be told, immense satisfaction. "Witches," in seventeenth-century Europe, were not something out of a Walt Disney movie. They were not beautiful stepmothers. They were hideous crones. Which Rebecca was most certainly not!

Accurately reading the look in her husband's eyes, Rebecca decided the moment was right to bring up another matter. "In that respect, I think we should add another person to our party. Ed Piazza will bring assurances of middle-aged male sagacity and stability. Tom Simpson, of course—especially accompanied by his pretty young American wife—will bring the appearance—the *reality*, I should say—of martial strength and vigor." Modestly: "I will do what I may." Then, raising her eyes to the ceiling as if a thought had just come to her: "But I think—something more—"

Mike grinned. "Cut it out, you schemer."

Rebecca lowered her eyes and studied her husband. Michael often insisted that she was smarter than he was. Rebecca thought he was wrong. Quite wrong. True, there was no comparison between their respective intellects, measured in what might be called "book learning." But Rebecca had not been reared in the poisonous doctrine of "IQ tests." She measured intelligence by the concrete standards of her own time—in that respect, at least, she had not acclimatized to American notions. A man's mind could not be separated from the man himself.

"I love you so much," she whispered. Then, ruefully running fingers through her thick black hair, she confessed her sins.

"Mackay'll shit a brick," predicted Mike. He scratched his jaw. "But—you're right. If there's any person in the world who could convince Gustav Adolf that we're not witches, it'd be a high-school cheerleader. Especially *that* one."

The happy thought was replaced by another. "As long as he doesn't see her shoot. And how are we going to keep her from bringing that damned rifle along?"

The doting husband scowled at the brilliant wife. "So, genius. Any bright ideas on that score?"

Silence.

"Ha!"

Chapter 47

The king was convinced of one thing within five minutes. Try as hard as he might—and he did, for he was a conscientious man as well as a pious one—Gustav II Adolf simply could not imagine the girl named Julie Sims as a witch.

"Impossible," he muttered under his breath. His eyes moved away from Julie and settled on the other two women sitting at the table. Even in the light thrown out by oil lamps and candles, their features were quite visible. The abandoned farmhouse had been set up as a temporary headquarters, and the modest interior was very well lit. Gustav normally satisfied himself with nothing more than was needed to read and write dispatches—and perhaps his beloved Grotius and Xenophon, if there was time. But when he heard that the American delegation had arrived at his camp, he had hurriedly requisitioned as much lighting as was available.

He wanted to *see* these people.

After his eyes left Julie, he squinted at the slender blond woman sitting next to her. The leader's sister, they said. But he did not spend much time on that examination. Cut from the same cloth as the youngest, obviously. Also pretty, also—*not a witch*.

His eyes lingered for a moment on her husband, standing next to her. The man was not sitting for the simple reason that none of the rickety chairs in the farmhouse could be trusted to support his incredible bulk.

Precious little of it fat, either, came the thought. For one of the few times in his life, Gustav had met a man who was obviously bigger and stronger than himself. He was finding the experience a bit disconcerting. Also a bit comical. The king's reaction to the man named Thomas Simpson, once he recognized it, almost made him laugh.

Much as he imagined a male seal might react, encountering a male walrus for the first time.

He suppressed the thought firmly. They were not beasts, this was not rutting season—and the man, in any event, was being a model of decorum. His eyes moved to the other man sitting at the table. The other *American*, that is. Alexander Mackay was also sitting at the table, as was a man named Heinrich. But those two were familiar to Gustav. Mackay in person, Heinrich by type.

It did not take the king more than a few seconds to assess the American. His name was Ed Piazza, and he was a type of man quite familiar to Gustav also. High-placed adviser, counselor, factotum. Cut from the same cloth as Axel, Gustav imagined—whatever the difference in origin.

Finally, his eyes came to rest on the central figure in the American delegation. And that she *was* the central figure, the king did not doubt for a moment. Gustav II Adolf was as experienced a diplomat and politician as he was a general. At the invitation of his father, Charles IX, he had sat in meetings of state since the age of eleven. He had long ago learned to read the subtle signs which indicated power and preeminence.

He was fascinated by her. Part of his interest, of course, was due to the woman's sheer beauty. But only a small part. Gustav was by no means immune to such things. His illegitimate son, product of a passion for a Dutch lady during his rambunctious youth, was serving as an officer in this very camp. But—certainly by the royal standards of his day—Gustav II Adolf was not given to lechery.

Partly, his fascination was due to the fact that the woman was obviously a Jewess. Gustav was familiar with Jews, to a degree, though they were rare in Sweden. But his interest was not so much in her faith as in her position. A Jewish adviser, yes—though court Jews of that sort were invariably male. But a Jewish co-ruler?

Now, *that* was interesting! Mackay had explained this to him, once, in a letter. But Gustav's mind had not really encompassed the reality until this moment. *Freedom of religion . . .*

"I am skeptical," he pronounced. "I am opposed to the Inquisition and all its works, mind. Nor have I placed any burdens on Catholics in areas I have conquered—beyond squeezing the coffers of the bishops. Or Jews, for that matter. But I do not believe a realm can remain stable without an established Church."

The woman named Rebecca Stearns replied. "Experiment with it then, Your Majesty. Use us as your laboratory. We will accept any religious minorities you find troublesome."

Seeing the surprise in the king's face, Rebecca smiled. "The American approach is the opposite, Your Majesty. We believe stability is found in fluid motion. Which lasts longer—the mountains or the sea?"

He stared at her. Abruptly: "You consider yourself an American? You were not born there, I am quite certain. England or Holland, judging from the accent."

Rebecca nodded. They had been speaking in German, since the king's spoken English was poor. "Both," she replied. "I was born in London but spent much of my girlhood in Amsterdam."

She gestured at her companions. "I only encountered this folk a year ago, when they—when my husband—rescued my father and me, yes. I consider myself an American now."

"Ah."

A smile came to her lips. "In most things, at least. Not all." The smile widened. "But, then, that is true of most Americans—the majority of whom are now people who were born and raised in this time and place."

"Ah." Mackay had told him this, also. And—again—the king had not quite believed. But now, seeing the ease of a Sephardic woman in her new identity, Gustav realized that his Scots officer had spoken the simple truth.

Can it be done? he wondered. He mused, for a moment, on the woman's earlier words. *Which lasts longer—the mountains or the sea?*

Gustav was a man of Scandinavia. He knew the answer.

Now, his eyes went to Mackay himself. The Scots officer had taken a chair next to the open-faced, pretty girl named Julie Sims. The king did not miss the subtle proprietary hints in the postures of both young people, and found himself smiling broadly.

"And you also, I see, Alexander."

There was perhaps a slight flush in the Scotsman's freckled face, but the officer's eyes remained steady.

"I am sworn to your service, Gustav II Adolf of Sweden." The words were spoken in a clipped, almost hostile manner. No, not hostile—simply challenging. The king understood the concept of honor which lay beneath. Quite well. Perfectly, in fact.

He raised a hand in a gesture which was not so much placatory as reassuring. "I am pleased to hear it, Alexander. Not that I doubted, mind you." He ran the hand over his short-cropped blond hair. "But, over time, loyalties can change. All I ask, if you find that happening, is that you give me your resignation. Until then, I ask no questions."

Mackay nodded stiffly.

The next few minutes were taken up by a discussion of the Ring of Fire. Gustav had already gotten a description of it from Mackay—in more than one letter—but he wanted to question the Americans themselves. So, with Rebecca acting as his interpreter, he asked many questions. And he listened very carefully to the responses.

The questions were firm, the responses were not—and it was *that*, more than anything else, which finally convinced the king. Within a very short time, Gustav was certain that the Americans, for all their mechanical wizardry, were as mystified by their situation as anyone else.

He was immensely relieved. All his deepest fears vanished. And began to be replaced with the first calculations for the future.

No witchcraft. Mackay was right. As for the rest—

Gustav swiveled in his chair and glanced at the two men standing toward the rear of the farmhouse. They had remained there at his request. Gustav had wanted to make a private assessment of the Americans, before pursuing anything else. But the matter had taken much less time than he expected, and he was satisfied that he could press onward. What he had thought would be a mystery, had proven otherwise. Or, rather, had proven to be the familiar mystery of divine providence.

With a little wave of the hand, he summoned the two men forward. *As for the rest—*

Who are we to question God's will? And who else could create such a Ring of Fire?

Which was quite as it should be. Gustav felt a rush of warmth for the Americans sitting across the table from him. They too—even this most outlandish folk he had ever heard of—were God's creatures, after all. Able to marvel at His handiwork, but not to understand it.

"As it should be . . ." he murmured.

The two men arrived at the table. "Sit," he commanded. With a pointing finger, he introduced them. "Wilhelm of Saxe-Weimar, the eldest duke. And Lennart Torstensson, my artillery commander."

Torstensson was obviously on the verge of bursting into speech, but Gustav restrained him with a sharp glance. *First things first.*

"You have created a difficult situation for me in Thuringia," the king said abruptly, speaking to the Americans. "Wilhelm here is one of my few reliable German allies, and you seem to have expropriated his duchy out from under him. This is—very awkward."

The Jewess cast a quick glance at Saxe-Weimar. Then, squaring her shoulders, she began to speak. But Wilhelm interrupted her before she was able to utter more than a few words.

"Please! I do not wish to add to the king of Sweden's problems." Wilhelm gestured with his head toward the door of the farmhouse. "Tilly's army is encamped less than two miles away, on the opposite bank of the Lech. The king intends to force the crossing tomorrow. This is not the time for political wrangling among his allies."

The last sentence produced a sudden stillness. *Silence.* Then, within seconds, it brought a pronounced easing of tensions at the table. The duke of Saxe-Weimar had now stated openly what had heretofore not been addressed. The fact that no one—not the king, not the Americans—had challenged the statement proved its truth. The new American regime was now accepted—in word as well as in deed— as an ally of Gustav Adolf. The nature of that alliance, of course, had yet to be determined.

Wilhelm continued. "May I suggest that we therefore leave aside, for the time being, any discussion of the future status of the province." He squared his own slender shoulders and looked directly at Rebecca. "I ask two things only. The first—"

He stumbled to a halt. For an instant, his features seemed to twist slightly. Chagrin? No—shame.

"I have been told that there was no starvation in the province, during the past winter. This is true?"

After Rebecca translated, the middle-aged American male cleared his throat. He began to speak, in halting German. The Jewess aided him past the rough spots. "No one has starved. Actually—by our best estimate, which is admittedly very crude—we think the population of southern Thuringia has quadrupled. Since we arrived a year ago."

The statement was met by blank, wide-eyed stares from Wilhelm and the two Swedes at the table. *Quadrupled? In central Germany? During* this *war?*

Hastily, almost apologetically, Piazza added: "Not natural increase, of course! Well, some. But there were so many refugees from elsewhere."

Wilhelm's shoulders slumped. He wiped his lowered face. "Thank God," he whispered. "That much is not on my soul, at least."

He raised his head. "That is my first request, then. Please do your best to continue providing that shelter and comfort. As for the second—"

He managed a smile. A thin smile, true, but a genuine one nonetheless. "I would appreciate it if you would do nothing—take no public stance—which forces me to make public defense of my rights. As the king says, that would be—awkward."

The Americans exchanged glances. It was obvious to Gustav that they were groping for a response. And equally obvious—this took not more than five seconds—to whom they turned for leadership. Soon enough, they were all staring at Rebecca, waiting for her to speak.

Gustav found a certain satisfaction in seeing, once again, that his keen political eye had not failed him. But he found a much greater satisfaction—a reassurance, in truth—in the fact that it was a person in their delegation who was *not* born an American to whom they turned. Mechanical wizards, yes. Wizards, no.

Rebecca spoke softly. "I cannot say anything specific, Duke. Not here, and not now. I do not have the authority. But this much I can say: the legal documents which guide the United States—we call them the Constitution and the Bill of Rights—are not . . ." She hesitated; then: "Let me put it this way. They are concerned with the positive, not the negative. They *establish* rights and responsibilities, rather than take them away. If you see what I mean."

Simultaneously, Wilhelm and Gustav smiled.

"How diplomatic," murmured the king happily. "Such a nice turn of phrase."

He cocked his head at Saxe-Weimar. "Wilhelm?"

The duke made a little gesture with his hand, wriggling fingers, to accompany the wry twist of his lips. The combination was subtly comical. "As you say, Your Majesty. A nice turn of phrase, indeed. I imagine we can spend quite a bit of time parsing that phrase."

He glanced at the door. "More than long enough, I should think, to see Tilly and Wallenstein done for." He brought his eyes back to Rebecca. "Afterward . . ."

"Is *afterward*," said the king firmly. "Good enough!"

He turned now to Torstensson. "All right, Lennart," he growled. "Spit it out."

Lennart was speaking before the king even finished. Unlike Gustav, he was fluent in English.

"How did you manage it?" he demanded. "Those bores are perfectly identical!" Scowling: "It's impossible! Absurd, even—I don't have cannonballs to match that precision."

Piazza smiled and leaned over. Rummaging in a bag at his feet, he brought out some sort of peculiar instrument.

"Ollie thought you might ask." He extended the instrument to Torstensson. The thing, for all the evident precision of its manufacture, vaguely resembled a sort of clamp. Hesitantly, the artillery general took it in his hand.

"It's called a micrometer," said Rebecca. Quickly, drawing on her own briefing from Ollie, she explained the basic workings of the gadget. "Precision screw—each turn of the barrel records precisely one-fortieth of an inch—point-oh-two-five inches, as machinists prefer to say—each little mark—see here? how it matches against this other?—measures exactly one-thousandth of an inch—"

"One *thousandth*?" choked Torstensson. He rotated the barrel back and forth, staring at the matching lines. "How can you make something this precise?"

"We can't," replied Rebecca. "Not easily, at least—although our experts think we could, over time, make something equivalent."

Now it was her turn to grope for words. "To do so would require machines which we do not have. And machines to make those machines—which we also do not have. The Ring of Fire brought only what was available in the town of Grantville. Sooner or later, many of our machines and instruments will wear out. They cannot be replaced, not directly. The computers, for instance, presuppose an entire electronics industry—"

She broke off, realizing that she was using meaningless terms, and went directly to the point. "We call it *gearing down*." She pointed to the micrometer in Torstenson's hands. "With that—which will last a very long time, if it is not abused—we can make simple cannons which are far more precise and accurate than guns made anywhere else. And there are other items we can make."

Tom Simpson interrupted. His German, though not up to Rebecca's fluent standards, was much better than Piazza's. "Rifled muskets, for instance, using Minié balls. Possibly some simple breechloaders." He chuckled. "There's quite a wrangle going on, among the gun buffs. Some want a Ferguson, some a—"

He broke off, seeing the renewed looks of incomprehension. Those terms, also, were meaningless. "Never mind," he said. "The gist of it is this. We can't recreate the world we left behind. But we *can* make things which are far in advance of anything here and now."

Smoothly, Rebecca took over. "That's part of it, Your Majesty." Half-apologetically: "Not to speak ill of your own munitions industry in Sweden, of course, but we can provide you with a much closer supply of good ordnance. Better ordnance, in all truth."

All traces of apology vanished. *"And money."*

Those words—truly magic!—brought dead silence to the room. Money was the essential blood of warfare, far more than pikes, horses, guns and powder—or even soldiers. For the Swedes, especially, the perennial shortage of cash was their biggest handicap.

"How?" demanded the king. He cocked his head skeptically. "I assume you are not offering a direct subsidy?"

Rebecca laughed softly. "Please, Your Majesty! Do I look like Richelieu?"

"Not in the least," muttered Torstensson. The young artillery officer was having a harder time than his monarch keeping his attention focused on Rebecca's mind.

Rebecca ignored the admiring remark. She pressed on: "A subsidy, no. But we can serve you in two other ways. First, southern Thuringia is rapidly becoming an economic center for Germany. Very rapidly, given the chaos in most of the Holy Roman Empire. Construction, manufacturing, commerce—all these are growing by leaps and bounds. The end result, among other things, is that we can provide your army with most of the supplies you need—"

"Food, too?" asked Torstensson. "And what about horses and oxen?" The professional soldier's mind had come back in focus.

Rebecca nodded. "Both. I might mention that American seed and livestock is better than the German, and they have begun a careful breeding program to preserve the strains. And we can offer you much better prices than you could get anywhere else—especially for the ordnance."

She gestured at the micrometer, still in Torstenson's hand. "Our metal-working methods are not simply more precise, they are also much faster and more efficient than anything you could find anywhere else in Europe. Or anywhere in the world, for that matter."

She hesitated for an instant, thinking. Then: "Gunpowder itself, for the moment, we cannot supply directly. Nor textiles, in any quantity. But because of the stability we have brought to the area"—she gave a quick, half-stubborn/half-apologetic glance at Wilhelm—"merchants and traders are pouring in. We cannot supply gunpowder or textiles, but we can definitely serve as a conduit for them. And, again, at a better price than you would find elsewhere."

Gustav rubbed his nose. "What you are proposing, in essence, is that Thuringia—your part of it, at least—can become my supply center and depot. Sweden's arsenal in central Germany."

"Yes," stated Rebecca firmly. The king gave her a shrewd look. She shrugged. "We understand that this will probably bring the wrath of the Habsburgs down on our heads."

Tom Simpson chuckled. "They'll be in for a surprise, if they try to hammer *us* under."

Mackay frowned. "It's not that simple, Tom. A cavalry raid can do a lot of destruction, even if it does no more than pass through the area. And it's a lot harder to stop."

The huge American got a mulish look on his face. Mackay tightened his jaws a bit. "Listen to me, Tom! If I were your opponent, I assure you I would be a lot harder to counter than one of Tilly's clumsy tercios."

Rebecca interrupted the developing quarrel with a sharp gesture. Gustav, watching, was impressed at the instant obedience the gesture produced. There was more to the woman's authority, he realized, than simply the fact she was the wife of the American commandant. Much more, he judged.

The king spoke again. "You mentioned a second form of financial assistance."

Rebecca's head swiveled back to him. For a moment, she stared with dark eyes. Gustav realized that the woman was judging *him* now.

When she spoke, her words were clipped, abrupt. "Are you familiar with the Abrabanel family?"

Gustav nodded. "Quite familiar. My assistant, Sir James Spens, has had any number of dealings with them in the past."

"Sir James?" exclaimed Rebecca. "I know him! Not well, myself. But my father thinks quite highly of him."

Gustav's eyes widened. "Your father?" Belatedly, he realized that he had not inquired as to the woman's *maiden* name.

"Abrabanel. My father is Balthazar Abrabanel."

The king laughed and clapped his thick hands. "Well—no wonder you're such a marvel! Balthazar for a father, and Uriel for an uncle." He grinned at her. "What was it like, being raised in such an atmosphere of cunning and intrigue?"

She grinned back. "Very nice, actually, Your Majesty. You know my father and uncle?"

Gustav shook his head. "Not personally. Only by reputation." He eyed her with renewed respect—and understanding.

"Am I to understand that the *entire* Abrabanel family has decided to throw its lot in with the Americans?"

Rebecca nodded. "Even the Turks. *Especially* the Turks, actually. Don Francisco Nasi has been residing in Grantville—our capital—for a number of weeks now. He has announced he plans to stay permanently."

Again, silence filled the farmhouse, while that news was absorbed. The Europeans in the room—Swede, German and Scot alike—understood the implications immediately. They were not peasants, for all that they might share some of the general prejudice against Jews. Those men, especially the king, were familiar enough with banking to know what Abrabanel allegiance to the United States provided. Put bluntly, the finest financial network in the world.

"Loans," mused Gustav. His gaze sharpened. "Interest?"

Rebecca's response came with a smile so broad it was almost a grin. "Five percent, annual interest. For a war loan. Four percent for anything else."

The king almost choked. "*Five percent?*" His pale blue eyes were practically bulging. "*Annually?*"

Rebecca shrugged. "The Americans—" She broke off; then, with a little laugh: "*We* Americans, I should say, have convinced the Abrabanels that a large and steady business is preferable to the occasional windfall." She repeated, very firmly: "Five percent. For you, that is. For Gustav II Adolf. Others will find the rate higher."

She looked away, brushing her thick hair with light fingers. Demurely: "Quite a bit higher, I imagine."

Suddenly, the king was roaring with laughter. "Five percent!" he halloooed, rising, almost lunging, to his feet; shaking his great fist at the heavens.

"*That* for Richelieu!"

Gustav lowered his fist. His own grin was matched by Torstensson's and Mackay's. Even Wilhelm, he saw, was smiling widely. The king of Sweden took a moment to admire the man's spirit as well as his brains. For all intents and purposes, the duke of Saxe-Weimar had just heard a death sentence passed on his hereditary claim to Thuringia—and he was quite intelligent enough to realize it. Once let a Thuringian republic establish its financial and commercial dominance, and the province's nobility would be lucky if they managed to maintain as much power as the Dutch. Even the mighty Spanish Habsburgs had broken on that rock, for well-nigh a century. Yet the man was spirited enough not to quail at the prospect.

And why should he? Wilhelm of Saxe-Weimar was also sworn to the service of the king of Sweden. A monarch who was not known to be miserly toward his trusted subordinates—and a monarch whose prospects had just received a mighty boost.

Gustav swiveled his head toward Torstensson, as if to bring the artillery commander under a gun himself.

"*Corpus Evangelicorum*," the king stated boldly. "What say you now, skeptic Lennart?"

Chapter 48

Rebecca and Ed Piazza remained in the farmhouse the next day, while Gustav Adolf prepared to move against Tilly. They would spend the entire day, and the next, working with the king's quartermasters to organize the new Swedish logistical base.

The rest of the delegation went with the Swedish army. Tom and Rita and Heinrich, who had spent the previous weeks working with the machine shops to get the cannons ready, went with Torstensson. Insofar as the new United States had anything resembling an "artillery officer corps," those three were it. Mike and Frank had urged them to take whatever opportunity they might find to get acquainted with the artillery practices of the current day—the best of which, by universal acknowledgment, was embodied in Torstensson's Swedes.

"The key is the hostlers as much as the artillerymen," Torstensson informed them, as they watched the Swedish guns being brought into position. "My horses and wagons are owned by the artillery stable."

The information meant nothing to Tom and Julie, but Heinrich started. Unlike the two Americans, he was quite familiar with the practices of the day. "You mean—?" He pointed to the hostlers guiding the horses forward and unhitching the cannons.

Torstensson nodded. "Army men. Mine—all of them, to a man." His lip curled in a magnificent sneer. "Not a single one of them is a misbegotten wretched coin-counting—" The rest trailed off into muttered obscenities.

Heinrich chuckled. He turned to Tom and Julie and explained.

"Every other army I know uses civilian contractors to handle the horses and wagons in the artillery train."

Tom's eyes widened. "That's crazy!" he grunted.

As always in the field, whenever possible, Tom spoke in German.

Torstensson, hearing the words, grinned. But his humor vanished at once, seeing the American guns being brought up to the earthworks. A moment later, he was bellowing new orders, seeing to it that the new cannons were properly placed. Right in the center of the line, under his watchful eye.

Torstensson intended to test those guns today. He had had his men selecting cannonballs since daybreak. He wanted to take advantage of those perfect bores by using the best cannonballs in his arsenal, the ones which were the roundest and made the best fit.

"Half again the range, I'll wager," he said softly, staring at the enemy entrenchments across the river.

Gustav Adolf was studying the same entrenchments, from a position further up the river. Trying to, at least. His myopia made the exercise a bit pointless.

His bodyguard, Anders Jönsson, was standing to his right. One of Anders' unofficial jobs was to serve as his king's eyes. He leaned over and whispered: "Tilly's got all his men in those woods beyond the marsh, just as you expected. I can't see a one by the riverbank itself."

Gustav nodded. The gesture was more one of frustration than agreement, however. He wished he could see for *himself.*

He heard a feminine sound. The American girl—Julie Sims—was clearing her throat.

"Uh, sir—uh, I mean, Your Majesty—uh—"

He turned and peered down at her. She and Mackay were standing to his left. The girl herself was right at his elbow.

"Yes?"

Again, she cleared her throat. Then, in halting German: "Why don't you wear spectacles, sir? I mean, Your Majesty?"

Anders hissed. A few feet behind, the Scottish bodyguards stiffened. *There was going to be a royal explosion!*

For an instant, the king felt his hot vanity surging to the fore. But there was something about the innocent, open, pretty face which disarmed the fury. Gustav restrained himself.

"Impossible!" he barked. "I tried, once. The spectacles flew off my nose at the first clash of the sabers."

Julie tried to speak again. But she had apparently reached the limit of her German. She whispered hurriedly to her fiancé. His face a bit pale—like all of Gustav's soldiers, Mackay was well aware of the king's sensitivity on this subject—the Scotsman translated.

"She says that she didn't mean normal spectacles, Your Majesty. She was referring to the kind of sports spectacles that—" Here, Mackay stumbled himself. *How to explain a basketball game?*

He managed, more or less, and in the process described to the king of Sweden the special goggle-style spectacles which young American athletes wore.

Gustav's eyes widened. "Impossible!" he repeated. "Absurd!"

His temper was rising, now. He glared at the impudent girl. The glare transferred itself to the peculiar firearm in her hands—then, to the telescope mounted upon it. Despite his irritation, the king recognized the superb craftsmanship embodied in both the firearm and the optical piece.

The girl seemed quite properly abashed by now. Perhaps in an attempt to mollify the royal outrage, she held up the weapon. "Would you like to look?" she asked.

Scowling, Gustav took the weapon and held it up for inspection. Despite the peculiarities of the thing, its use was clear enough. A moment later, he had the butt nestled against his shoulder and was peering through the telescope.

His annoyance vanished at once. "Marvelous!" he exclaimed. The clarity of the image was far better than anything he had ever seen through a telescope. He spent perhaps a minute, gaily swinging the rifle back and forth, before settling to serious business.

The next few minutes were devoted to a careful inspection of his opponent's position. The Swedish and the Bavarian armies were located on opposite banks of the Lech, just south of the small river's confluence with the Danube. Here, the river passed through a low, marshy plain, flanked by higher land on either side. Tilly had marshaled his forces in the elevated woods beyond the marsh. Clearly enough, the old Catholic general was confident that the boggy terrain on the river banks would impede any Swedish advance badly enough to prevent a crossing. His flanks were well anchored by fortifications, and he had his own batteries drawn up in the center. It was, to all appearances, a well-nigh impregnable position.

But—

The king smiled grimly, as he studied a particular stretch of the river through the telescope. Directly opposite the high ground where Torstensson was positioning his seventy-two guns, the Lech made a wide loop. The river's meandering course had left a spit of land projecting toward the Swedes on the opposite bank. If a strong force could be moved across the water, onto that spit, under the cover of the Swedish guns, the king would have his bridgehead.

The king lowered the rifle. "Just as the Finns reported," he murmured to Anders with satisfaction. He turned to Julie and handed back the weapon.

"Splendid telescope," he said. "Though I found that peculiar flaw a bit distracting."

Mackay translated. Julie frowned—insult her scope!—and demanded an explanation. Mackay translated. The king explained: *Those two black lines meeting right in the center of the eyepiece.* Mackay translated. Julie—royal temper be damned—growled her response. Mackay translated.

The king erupted anew. "Nonsense!" he bellowed. Waving a great hand angrily: "That's five hundred yards!"

Imperiously, he pointed to Mackay and spoke to Julie. "Give this braggart that gun!" To Mackay: "Now—sir. Make good your boast!"

Mackay swallowed. Then, explained. The king's eyes bulged. *Her?*

Mackay nodded. The stare was transferred to—to—this—*this impudent female!*

Julie had had enough. She hefted the rifle. "Tell that fathead to pick his target," she snarled.

Mackay translated, more or less. He did not include the term "fathead." Gustav II Adolf glared at the enemy across the river, selecting his target. He couldn't see well enough, alas, so the king was forced to rely on Jönsson.

"There's a very fine-looking officer near that one grove, Your Majesty. Dramatic fellow, judging from his posture."

Mackay began to translate, but Julie's German was good enough to understand the gist. The rifle was into her shoulder, her eye at the scope.

The king, watching, began to hiss. For all his indignation, Gustav was far too experienced a soldier not to recognize the casual expertise with which the girl—

Crack! The flat, unfamiliar sound startled the king. His head swiveled to Anders. The bodyguard's face seemed a bit pale.

"Well?" demanded Gustav.

"Dead on, Your Majesty. Right through the heart, I think. Hard to tell, at that distance. But he's down for good, that's certain."

"Nonsense! Luck! Another!"

Anders called out another target. A few seconds went by. *Crack.*

"Another!"

Crack.

"Another!"

Crack.

"Ano—" Gustav fell silent. The silence lasted for well over a minute. At the end, he heaved a sigh. Then, suddenly, he broke into a smile.

"Ah, Mackay—" The Scotsman, face very pale, stared at his sovereign. The king, for his part, was staring at Julie. Still smiling.

Julie was *not* smiling. She was glaring at Gustav with grotesque disregard for all proper etiquette in the presence of royalty.

"I believe I have offended your fiancée," he said. "Under the circumstances, it might be best if you explained to her the provisions of the dueling code. Can't challenge a ruling monarch. Simply isn't done. Besides—"

He chuckled. "Explain to her that as the challenged party I would have the choice of weapons. Sabers, for a certainty!"

When Mackay translated, Julie's ill humor evaporated instantly. For a moment, she and the king of Sweden exchanged grins. Watching, Anders thought of a chipmunk and a bear beaming in mutual approval.

But he kept the thought to himself. He even managed not to smile at his king's next muttered words.

"Witchcraft—nonsense! What woman needs to be a witch, when she can shoot like *that*?"

A moment later, Torstensson's guns began to fire, and his amusement vanished. Anders knew the king's plan for the coming battle. No one had asked his opinion, of course—he was merely a bodyguard—but the veteran had a firm one nonetheless.

Gustav II Adolf proposed to force a river in the face of a powerful fortified enemy, in defiance of all established military wisdom of the day.

Madman!

"Too high!" bellowed Torstensson. "Still too high, damn you!"

The gunners at the American cannons swore angrily. Again, they fumbled at the—*cursed newfangled!*—things which the Americans called elevating screws. They were accustomed to adjusting the tangent elevation by simply levering up the breech and inserting quoins. Admittedly, the new system was quicker, and certainly much easier. Probably more accurate, too. But the gunners did not have the hang of it yet, and they kept overshooting. Some of that inaccuracy, of course, was due to the simple fact that the American guns, with their tight-fitting balls in perfect bores, had a greater range than they were accustomed to. As was the custom of the day, "aiming" was simply a matter of gauging the distance and the angle of the barrel.

Tom turned to Heinrich and whispered, "Remember, when we get back, to talk to Ollie about setting up some kind of sights and elevation lines."

Heinrich nodded. He did not need an explanation of the terms. The German mercenary—*former* mercenary; like Tom, he now held the rank of captain in the regular U.S. army—had spent much of the past winter in the machine shop. He had become quite familiar, even comfortable, with American notions of precision and accuracy.

Finally, the gunners got it right. The next salvo of cannonballs hammered straight into the earthworks sheltering Tilly's batteries.

Those earthworks had already taken a beating from the traditional guns. Now, with the flat and powerful trajectories of the new cannonballs adding their own force to the bombardment, the enemy fortifications were beginning to come apart.

"Take a while, still, to smash them up," stated Torstensson. He smiled grimly. "But they won't be doing any shooting themselves, that's for sure."

He turned, cupped his hands around his mouth, and shouted to the orderly waiting on the slope above. An instant later, the man was spurring his horse toward the king's position upstream.

Torstensson went back to overseeing his guns. "Up to the Finns, now," he said. Cheerfully: "But those sullen savages won't be able to whine about their covering fire. Not today!"

He bestowed a look of approval on Tom and Heinrich. "Splendid pieces!" His eyes then moved to the very attractive American woman standing at their side. A similar thought crossed his mind, but he left it unspoken. Lennart Torstensson had already come to the same conclusion as Tom Simpson's own mates. Not a good idea, irritating a man who could probably *lift* one of those marvelous cannons.

An idle question came. He leaned over and murmured to Tom: "I'm curious. What would be your weapon of choice? In a duel, I mean."

The very attractive woman's husband replied instantly.

"Ten-pound sledgehammers."

Not a good idea.

"Now, now!" bellowed the king. On the marshy ground below, Swedish engineers led hundreds of soldiers in a rush to the river bank. The "rush," needless to say, was a slow and sodden kind of thing. The terrain was bad enough, even if the soldiers hadn't been hauling a multitude of freshly cut logs.

Despite the marshy ground, the engineers were soon throwing a crude bridge across the water. The work was not suicidal, due to the heavy covering fire of Torstensson's guns, but it was still dangerous. Within five minutes, several of the engineers had been wounded or killed. Gustav scowled unhappily. Tilly's men were simply sticking their arquebuses over the ramparts and firing blindly. But an occasional round, he supposed, was bound to find a target.

The king heard the American girl whisper something to Mackay. The Scotsman passed the remark along.

"Your Majesty, Julie says that most of the damage is being done by some skirmishers in the woods."

Gustav squinted at the line of trees. The term "sniper" was

unknown in that day, but all armies had contingents of lightly armored skirmishers using hunting pieces. Those weapons, since they were not part of the line and were not concerned with rate of fire, were rifled. Their accuracy was still not great, but it was not laughable either.

"She is certain?"

Mackay nodded. Then, after a moment's hesitation, he added: "She is also offering to—ah, the expression she favors is 'take them out.'"

The king smiled thinly. "You are afraid I will be offended by such an offer? My royal dignity insulted?"

Mackay pursed his lips. The king's smile widened.

Then, disappeared entirely—replaced by a ferocious scowl. "Well, I am—and it is!" He shook himself like very large dog. Still scowling: "But not half as much as seeing my engineers struck down."

The scowl faded. With royal dignity, Gustav turned to Julie and gave her a small bow. "If you would, Miss Sims. I would be much obliged."

Julie stooped, dug into the backpack she had brought with her, and hauled out the spotting scope and the binoculars. A moment later, Mackay was festooned with the optical equipment.

"Call 'em out, Alex," Julie commanded. She brought the rifle up.

As he watched the ensuing slaughter, the king of Sweden was not sure which disturbed him the most. Seeing the casual ease with which a young American girl from the future struck down men at a third of a mile—or the casual ease with which her Scots fiancé of the time assisted her in the task. The first introduced a very bizarre and rather frightening new world. The latter opened the entire book.

Crack!

"Left fifty paces! By the tree! Red feathered hat!"

Crack!

Like steel pages turning.

As evening fell, the Finns surged onto the nearly completed bridge. There were three hundred of them, volunteering in eager anticipation of the ten rix dollars promised as bonus. Each man carried a bundle of damp straw which, set alight, soon covered the end of the bridge and the opposite riverbank with thick smoke. Under that concealment, the work of finishing the bridge was done and the Finns charged onto the opposite bank. Hastily, they began erecting new earthworks, turning the spit of land into a fortress.

Tilly ordered his guns to begin a desperate attempt to destroy the new bastion. Desperate, because after hours under Torstensson's counterbattery fire, there was not much left of the Catholic artillery.

"Damn those Swedish guns!" he roared. "They're even worse than they were at Breitenfeld!"

Through the night, under cover of darkness, smoke and Torstensson's batteries, the king led his army across the bridge onto the spit.

From there, through the course of the day—April 16—the Swedes used their numbers to establish a solid position along the entire bank. Gustav Adolf had successfully forced the river. There remained only two choices for Tilly: retreat, again—or launch a final assault.

He chose the latter, and led it himself. Late in the afternoon, atop his white charger, Tilly thundered down the slope. Thousands of cavalrymen and infantry came in his wake.

The struggle which followed, for all its brevity, was no mean affair. Gustav led his own cavalry in a coun07charge and the Swedish infantry, at many points along the line, clashed head-on with their Bavarian counterparts. Had the battle been restricted to those forces, Tilly might still have won.

But, it wasn't. Throughout, from their position on the opposite bank, Torstensson's guns kept up their deadly fire. Now exposed on open ground, Tilly's men were being butchered.

"Damn those Swedish guns!" snarled Tilly again. And so, too, came a bitter self-reproach: *I should have listened to Wallenstein.*

It was the old general's last thought. One of Torstensson's cannonballs shattered his thigh. His valiant charger staggered under the blow but kept its feet. Slowly, unconscious from shock, Tilly toppled from the saddle. In the years to come, men who saw would say it was like watching a tree fall. A great, gnarled oak, finally come to the end.

As Tilly's men carried him to the rear, Aldringer took command. But Aldringer fell within minutes, wounded in the head. By now, the imperial forces had suffered four thousand casualties, and the men lost heart. Night was falling, and they took advantage of the darkness to retreat back into their fortified camp near the Danube. The next day, under the command of the elector himself, Tilly's army retreated to Ingolstadt. Maximillian of Bavaria had had enough of Gustav II Adolf.

"Let Wallenstein try to handle him," he snarled. "Let bastard Bohemian deal with bastard Swede!"

When Gustav heard the news of Tilly, he sent his own body-surgeon into the enemy camp. "Do what you can for the old man," he commanded.

"Won't be much," grumbled the surgeon. "Not from the description of the wound." But he obeyed.

Torstensson was not entirely pleased. "Let the butcher of Magdeburg bleed to death," he growled. The savage expressions on the faces of the other Swedish officers surrounding Gustav made clear their agreement.

The king said simply: "Last of a line. A great line, for all its sins." Then, as if struck by a thought, he turned to the young girl standing a few feet away.

"And what do you think?" he demanded. The girl responded with a shy smile.

"I think you're a nice man," came her reply.

Gustav II Adolf was quite taken aback. "Nice man," he muttered, as he walked away. He shook his head. "Nice man. What kind of thing is that to say—*to a king?*"

Tilly died two weeks later.

The last of a line was gone, and another line was stepping forward to challenge the King of Sweden.

Wallenstein, now. Wallenstein and his wolves.

Part Six

When the stars threw down their spears,
And water'd heaven with their tears

Chapter 49

Cardinal Richelieu set the letter down on the bench in his garden. For several minutes, sitting next to it, he stared down at the detested thing.

Since he had been appointed head of the Royal Council on August 13, 1624, the cardinal had pursued a consistent policy in foreign affairs. Officially, of course, he had expressed his full support for the Counter-Reformation and the assault on Protestantism. Such was necessary, if nothing else, to retain the allegiance of the Catholic fanatics led by the Capucin Father Joseph and those organized in the secret society called the Company of the Holy Sacrament. But, underlying that pious surface, was Richelieu's true aim: *strengthen France.* And that meant, first and foremost, humble the Habsburgs— especially the Spanish branch of the family, who ruled the greatest military power in Europe.

All in ruins . . .

Without lifting his head, he asked the man standing nearby: "It is true, Etienne?"

Etienne Servien nodded. He was one of the cardinal's *intendants,* the special agents who maintained Richelieu's iron rule over France. Officially, the intendants were nothing but minor functionaries, appointed directly by the crown. In reality, they were the cardinal's private army of enforcers, spies, dictators by proxy. Servien had just returned from a protracted mission. First, to Vienna; then to Brussels; and along the way—

"Yes it is," he said. "I spent a week in Thuringia myself, Cardinal. Most of it in Grantville. It's all true."

"Witchcraft?"

Servien shrugged. "My opinion? No. Not, at least, in minor things.

I spoke to many of the German residents, and none of them believed the American arts were more than those of superb mechanics. Several of the ones I spoke to have begun learning those arts themselves, in fact. As to the thing in large? Who knows? They call it the Ring of Fire, but no one seems to understand what it was. Divine intervention is the accepted explanation."

The cardinal's eyes moved to a bed of flowers. Beautiful things. For a moment, he pondered the Lord's handiwork.

But not for long. Richelieu believed in few things, beyond France and its glory. Establishing French supremacy was his lifelong ambition, and his beliefs were yoked to that purpose. Absolute monarchy, of course, was necessary to that end; as was religious conformity. Beyond that—

The Lord's handiwork is what I say it is.

"Witchcraft," he stated. "Sorcery, pure and simple. Satan's hand clutches Thuringia today."

Servien bowed. "As you say, Cardinal."

Richelieu patted the letter with his fingertips. He was tempted to crumple the thing in his fist, but the cardinal was not a man to ignore reality. No matter how detestable.

"Very well," he said. He rose to his feet, adjusting the great robes of office. "We will accede to the Spanish request."

Demand, he thought sourly.

"Take the silver to Bernard of Saxe-Weimar, Etienne. Make sure he understands the conditions of his new service."

Servien's face twisted into a grimace. "He's a hothead, Cardinal. Unruly."

Richelieu waved his hand impatiently. "We can deal with Saxe-Weimar's undisciplined nature on a later occasion. For now, I simply need him to move his forces aside so that the Spanish troops have a clear line of march on Thuringia. He can manage that easily enough, even with Oxenstierna in the vicinity. There is so much chaos in Germany today that Bernard can justify his movements a hundred different ways."

The cardinal began pacing slowly through his garden. Servien walked by his side.

"There will still be no way to keep the tercios hidden," remarked the intendant. "Not marching all the way from the Spanish Netherlands."

Richelieu shrugged. "That hardly matters. From the reports, I suspect the Spanish will be defeated in any event. Probably all the better, if their approach is foreseen. It will distract attention from the real blow."

Servien's eyes widened. "Wallenstein has agreed?"

"Yes. I received his letter three days ago. He expects to be locked with the Swedes very soon now. Probably at Nürnberg. A siege will last for months. More than enough time to use his Croats for this purpose."

The grimace returned to the intendant's face. "Cardinal, I've seen those works. The thing they call a 'power plant,' in particular, is built like a castle. There's no way a cavalry force will be able to reduce them. Not significantly—not in a raid, for sure."

Richelieu smiled faintly. "I am not concerned with that." Shaking his head: "You worry too much about the mechanics of war. A paltry business, that. *Money*, Etienne—that's the key. I could tolerate the king of Sweden, armed with his fancy new weapons. I could even tolerate a rich new republic—a little republic—in central Germany. We've managed to live with the Dutch, after all. Given time, given that they remain small, I expect we'll consume them soon enough."

He walked on a few paces before continuing. "What I *cannot* tolerate is Swedish power dominating central Europe, standing on financial bedrock. A poor Sweden will never be dangerous. Obnoxious, yes; dangerous, no. A *rich* Sweden—rich from its new connection with this bizarre United States—is a different matter altogether. Better a powerful Habsburg dynasty than *that*. Whatever else, the Habsburgs can always be counted on for disunity."

He stopped abruptly, and scowled at an inoffensive rose bush. "I cannot touch the Abrabanels in Turkey. Not even—as you know—in Vienna."

Servien nodded. That had been part of his recent mission. To convince Ferdinand II to dispense with his court Jews, and execute the Abrabanels in particular. But in that purpose, the intendant had failed.

There had been no condemnation of Servien in the cardinal's words, however. Richelieu had not expected a Habsburg emperor to destroy his court Jews in the middle of a war—certainly not at the urgings of his French enemy.

The cardinal continued: "I may be able to have the Italian branch eliminated. Hard to say, especially dealing with Venetians. But they are the least important, in any event. The key is destroying them in Thuringia."

The intendant began to speak again—another demurral, judging from his expression—but the cardinal waved him silent. "Yes, yes— I know the Croats won't be able to kill all of them. Not in the time they'll have. It doesn't matter. They will savage the place so thoroughly that whatever Abrabanels survive will soon enough take their business elsewhere." His thin lips grew thinner: "*Jews*, you understand."

Servien nodded. "Half the greedy Germans will pack up also. Half, at the least." His own lips grew thin: "Merchants. Manufacturers. Rats in a granary set on fire."

"Yes." Richelieu leaned over and sniffed the roses. "Exactly."

"That still leaves us a mess with the Spaniards," muttered Servien. "We'll have let them into Germany."

"Please, Etienne!" The Cardinal continued his sniffing. "Give me a moment to enjoy God's handiwork, before you spoil the rest of my day."

Several weeks later, in his fortified camp outside Nürnberg, Wallenstein *did* crumple a letter.

"*Idiot,*" he hissed. He tossed the message into the fire. The roaring flames in that great fireplace—as ever, Wallenstein had appropriated the largest mansion in the area—consumed the paper in an instant.

The imperial army's top commanders were standing as far away from the fireplace as possible, while staying within speaking range of Wallenstein. In the heat of a July evening, they found the flames oppressive. Absurd, even. But Wallenstein always insisted on a fire, no matter the time of year.

"Idiot!" repeated Wallenstein. He clasped his hands behind his back and stared at his officers. His next words were spoken in savage, singsong mimicry: "'Kill all the Jews in the town.'"

Piccolomini barked a laugh. "Ha! Easy to say—for a cardinal! What does that shithead think we're dealing with? Unarmed civilians in the Inquisitor's chambers?"

Next to him, General Sparre sneered. "And how in God's name are the Croats supposed to find them?" he demanded. "Especially in that grotesque place! Read the street signs? The ignorant bastards are illiterate."

"Wouldn't matter even if they weren't," muttered General Gallas. He lifted his heavy shoulders. The gesture was not so much a shrug as a twitching off of insects. "Does Richelieu seriously think you can order Croat cavalry to kill *selectively*?" He snorted. "They might spare the dogs. Probably not. Jews *are* dogs, after all—ask any Croat."

The salon echoed with coarse laughter. The huge portraits on the walls, mediocre for all their size and splendiferous frames, stared down with disapproval. The disapproval was odd, perhaps. The obscure line of petty barons who had—involuntarily—given up their ancestral mansion for Wallenstein, had been noted for little beyond coarseness. But such men, when they pose for a provincial artist's work, almost invariably frown. An attempt at grandeur, perhaps; or simply holding in their bladder.

Wallenstein strode over to the table at the center of the salon. The table was quite out of place in the room's furniture. It was a great, heavy kitchen table, wrestled into the salon by soldiers on the day Wallenstein took possession of the mansion. The chairs and couches which had already been there were fragile and fancy things, imported from Vienna. They were even more fragile now, but no longer very fancy—not after Wallenstein's officers had spent the past days inflicting spurs and spilled wine upon them.

The table, on the other hand, was more than sturdy enough to support cavalry boots and flagons, as well as the huge map which covered most of its surface.

When he reached the table, Wallenstein spread his hands and leaned over the map. His officers gathered around him. After a minute or so, Wallenstein stretched out a long, bony finger and pointed to a spot.

"There? A demonstration."

That would be Piccolomini's task. The Italian general leaned over and studied the area indicated.

"If it's just to be a demonstration, yes. Anything more—"

Wallenstein shook his head. "Please. I am not a cardinal, who thinks war can simply be counted in coins. He may choose to shrug off the accounts, but I do not. Every army which has gone straight at the Americans has been broken like a rotten twig. And those accounts come from Tilly's veterans, not a pack of stinking monks and priests." He resumed his study of the map. "I do not expect you to actually take Suhl. This is just a feint, to draw off some of their forces."

The generals around the table relaxed. Not the least of the reasons Wallenstein had become the greatest military figure in the Holy Roman Empire was that he commanded the allegiance of his own men. If for no other reason, because he did not ask mercenaries to attempt the impossible. All of those officers had personally heard the reports. Impenetrable steel vehicles, without even horses to be slain; a preposterous rate of fire; rifles which could kill unerringly across a third of a mile; even some kind of gun which could pour out bullets like a rainspout.

"Simply a demonstration," Wallenstein repeated. He gave Piccolomini a sharp glance. "A genuine demonstration, you understand? They'll get suspicious if there's no contact at all. There must be a reasonable number of casualties."

Piccolomini shrugged. "I can spare a few hundred. I'll use those Swabian fucks. They've been nothing but a pain in the ass since they got here, anyway. Do them good to be bled."

Wallenstein nodded. Keeping his right forefinger on Suhl, his left forefinger moved across the map to the west, coming to rest on the spot marked "Eisenach."

"The Spaniards should manage to take Eisenach. If they fail, they can retreat into the Wartburg."

General Gallas sniffed. "I still can't believe the Americans haven't stationed a garrison in the place. Old as it is, the Wartburg's still the strongest castle in Thuringia. Idiots."

Wallenstein shook his head. "I do not share your attitude, I'm afraid. If the United States is not stationing a garrison there—so obvious!—there must be a reason for it. And I think it would be foolish to assume the reason is simple incompetence."

"Short of troops, probably," mused Piccolomini. "Every spy we've sent into the area reports that they maintain only a small permanent army." He sniffed himself, now. "Merchants and bankers—and, God help us, *manufacturers*. That's what they are, nothing more. I don't care how fancy their weapons are, they don't *think* like soldiers."

Wallenstein rose to his full height. He was a tall man, very thin. Now at the age of forty-eight, his dark hair had receded to form a widow's peak. A long and prominent nose was offset by high cheekbones and, beneath a slender mustachio and above a goatee, a mouth whose lower lip was so thick and out-jutting that it suggested Habsburg bastardy. It was a forbidding face, cold and unexpressive. The face, combined with the stature, gave Wallenstein more than a passing resemblance to the popular image of Mephistopheles.

"I don't think like a soldier either," he said. His dark eyes scanned the officers around him. Coldly: "That's why you work for me, not I for you."

The officers did not bridle at that cutting remark. Partly, because it was the simple truth. Mostly, because bridling at Wallenstein was dangerous. The Bohemian general—military contractor was a better term—would tolerate discussion, argument, even quarrel. He gave short shrift to officers who couldn't learn to accept his authority. And when it came to "short shrift"—there, too, Wallenstein did not think like a soldier. The man had the soul of an assassin, not a duelist.

"It doesn't matter," he stated forcefully. "Whatever the reason—whether it's incompetence, lack of men, or, as I suspect, because the Americans know something we don't—it'll be the Spaniards who make the discovery. Not us."

His officers nodded in unison. The collective gesture exuded all the satisfaction of mercenaries who expect to collect their pay while others do the dying.

Wallenstein leaned back over the table. Again, his two forefingers spread wide. "The Spaniards, in force, at Eisenach. Piccolomini, you here—in a solid demonstration at Suhl. That should be enough to draw aside all significant opposition. Then—"

He removed his finger and slashed up the map with the edge of his right hand. "The Croats—right through the heart of the forest. The hunters we hired assure me there is a good trail, passing through uninhabited terrain. The Croats should get within striking distance before they're even spotted. Nothing to oppose them but the town's constabulary."

He leaned over the table and reached for a smaller map. Grasping it between thumb and fingers, he drew the map to cover the larger one.

"Here," he said, pointing. He cocked his head at Gallas, under whom the Croat light cavalry served. "Make sure the Croats understand. The main blow is to fall *here*."

Gallas studied the place indicated on the map. It was a very good, very detailed map of the town—small city, now—called Grantville. Dozens of spy reports had gone into its making, over the past few weeks.

Gallas' face was creased with a slight frown. "Not the town itself?"

Wallenstein shook his head. "No. Oh, certainly—make sure a sizeable force of cavalry ravages the town, as best they can." He chuckled harshly. "If they can butcher a few Jews, so much the better. But the main blow must come *here*."

He leaned back and, once again, stood erect. "Cardinal Richelieu can prate about money and bankers and Jewish financial wizards all he wants. *That* place is the heart of the United States. I have studied all the reports and come to that conclusion. That is where this new serpent lairs, and that is where it hatches its offspring."

Again, he stooped; and, again, pointed with a devil's finger.

"*There. Raze it to the ground. Kill everyone. Even the dogs, if they find any.*"

His own laugh, when it came, was as coarse as that of any of his officers. "Who knows? Might be a Jew in disguise."

Chapter 50

"I don't like this," growled Gustav Adolf softly. He gave the letter in his hand a little flick of the fingers. "Not in the least."

He raised his eyes and peered at Torstensson. "Lennart, can you think of any good reason Bernard would be engaging in such maneuvers? That far to the south?"

The young artillery general started to make some sarcastic remark—*wanted to admire his reflection in Lake Geneva*—but restrained himself. He could sense that the king was genuinely concerned. He nodded toward the letter in Gustav's hand.

"Axel has no suggestions?"

Gustav shook his head. "No. But he's worried, I can tell."

Standing on the walls of the redoubt which the Swedes had built where the river Rednitz entered Nürnberg, Torstensson turned and stared to the northwest. The king copied the movement. Both men were groping in their minds, trying to visualize the terrain in the Rhineland. *What could Bernard of Saxe-Weimar be thinking?* There was no logical reason for him to have moved his troops as far south as Cologne.

Their eyes passed over, but ignored, the huge complex of fortifications which surrounded the city. Most of those fortifications were crude earthworks, and most of them were new. Like the redoubt itself, they had been erected hastily over the past month.

As soon as he entered the city on July 3, Gustav had used the labor of Nürnberg's inhabitants to build those fieldworks. The citizens had not complained—not in the least. Nürnberg had allied itself to the king of Sweden, and they were well-nigh ecstatic to see him make good on his promise: *Nürnberg will not be another Magdeburg.*

Gustav Adolf had arrived not a moment too soon. The huge army which Wallenstein had assembled in Bohemia was marching on the city. Sixty thousand strong, that army was—the largest force ever put into the field in the course of the long and brutal war. Tilly's Bavarian troops, now under the direct command of the Elector Maximillian, were marching to join him—perhaps another twenty thousand men. And Pappenheim, whose Black Cuirassiers had spent the spring and early summer in Westphalia, was reported to be coming as well. Pappenheim's route was unclear, but the Swedes assumed he would take advantage of Gustav's withdrawal to Nürnberg to march through Franconia. If so, Nürnberg was threatened from three sides: Wallenstein from the northeast, Maximillian from the south, Pappenheim from the west. An army of one hundred thousand men was about to threaten Nürnberg with the fate suffered by Magdeburg.

While the inhabitants of the city frantically erected their fortifications, under the direction of the Swedish engineer Hans Olaf, Gustav had led his army back into the field. For days, the Swedes had maneuvered against the oncoming enemy forces, slowing their advance and buying time for Nürnberg. But on July 10, at Neumarkt, the Bavarian and imperial armies had finally merged.

Although he was outnumbered four to one, Gustav had continued to challenge Wallenstein to meet him in the open field. Wallenstein had declined. The Bohemian military contractor preferred the surer, if slower, methods of siege warfare. Steadily, surely, inexorably, his enormous army had moved into positions threatening the city. But, by then, the feverish program of fortifications had erected a new wall around Nürnberg, replacing the inner walls of the city. Gustav's line of defense, hastily erected but well designed, was too large for even Wallenstein to surround.

So, the Bohemian had been forced to "besiege" Nürnberg by erecting what amounted to a "counter-city." Through the rest of July, Wallenstein's men had been set to work erecting a gigantic armed camp a few miles to the southwest of the city. Using the Bibert River as a central water supply, Wallenstein had erected fieldworks with a circumference of a dozen miles. The strong point in those fieldworks, directly facing the Swedes, was a wooded hill on the north. That hill was called the Burgstall. It rose some two hundred and fifty feet above the Rednitz river, flowing past its eastern slope. In effect, the Rednitz served as a moat, and the wooded hill was capped by an ancient ruined castle named the Alte Veste. Wallenstein had turned the Alte Veste and the entire Burgstall into a fortress. Palisades and ditches sprouted like mushrooms on the hill, with clear lines of fire for the heavy guns positioned on its slopes.

Then—nothing. Time after time, Gustav had sallied from Nürnberg, challenging Wallenstein to open battle. Wallenstein declined. "There has been enough fighting," he told his generals. "I will show them another method."

Cold-blooded like no man of his time, Wallenstein's method was simple. Hunger and disease, soon enough, would strike both armies. Men would die in the thousands, and then the tens of thousands— and he had a lot more men than the king of Sweden.

"Treason," whispered Gustav. "It can only be treason."

Torstensson frowned. He detested the younger duke of Saxe-Weimar, true. But—*treason*?

"I can't—" The young general hesitated. "I'm afraid I can't see the logic of that, Your Majesty." He pointed to the west. "It's true that Bernard's left the door open for the Spaniards, if they choose to come through. But even if that's his purpose, what's the point? The Lower Palatinate is still blocked. For a Spanish army to threaten us, they'd have to—" He stumbled to a halt, his eyes widening.

The king nodded. "March through Thuringia," he concluded grimly. "Which, of course, would be an incredibly roundabout way of threatening Nürnberg. But what if they have no intention of coming this far? What if, Lennart, their purpose is not to march *through* Thuringia, but simply to attack it?"

Torstensson's head swiveled. He was staring north, now, instead of west. "Maybe," he mused. "That, at least, would make Bernard's maneuvers sensible—assuming he is committing treason." Torstensson squinted. "But, even so—what's the point?"

The artillery general's shoulders twitched. The gesture was more an expression of exasperation than a shrug. "I have never seen the Americans in action. But judging from every report we've gotten— and I've heard Mackay myself—they can shatter any army which comes at them directly. Especially those hide-bound Spanish tercios."

The king snorted. "Yes. But ask yourself this, Lennart—*has anyone told the Spaniards?*"

Now, Torstensson's eyes were very wide. Like all of Sweden's top commanders, Torstensson was privy to the complex and tortuous diplomatic maneuvers which his king had been forced to engage in over the past two years.

"Richelieu," he murmured.

Gustav nodded. "That would be the conduit, sure enough. Richelieu has the money, and the patronage, to offer Bernard an exceptional price for turning his coat. Alsace, probably, to replace his precious Thuringia. Or Lorraine. A word to the Spanish—who have been chafing to get into Germany for years, on any pretext—and there we have it. An open road for a Spanish army from the Low Countries to strike at Thuringia."

"But Richelieu's been trying to keep the Spanish *out* of Germany since he took office," protested Torstenson. The protest was feeble, however. The quick-witted artillery general was already working through the logic. He began stroking his beard, thinking aloud: "Hostility to Spain has been the keystone of his foreign policy, true enough. But now that your position in central Europe has become so strong, he may be thinking of a counterweight."

"Precisely. And ask yourself—*why* has my position grown so strong?" Gustav made a little dismissive gesture with his hand. "Not my army. Richelieu is a money man, not a soldier. To him, bullion rules the world."

Torstensson's beard stroking grew vigorous. "Yes. *Yes.* Thuringia's the key to that, too. As long as the Americans hold it firmly, we have a secure logistics base and a reliable source of cash. It's made us completely independent of any foreign pursemasters." His lips pursed. "Well—it *will*, I should say. Take a few months before everything settles in. But Richelieu is a man to think ahead, if ever one lived."

He dropped his hand from the beard and turned to face his king squarely. "But I still don't see what Richelieu hopes to accomplish. Unless he simply wants to see a Spanish army battered and bleeding."

Gustav grinned humorlessly. "He certainly wouldn't lose any sleep over *that*." The king shrugged. "I don't understand the logic myself, Lennart. But I can smell it. Something's up."

He paused for a few seconds. Then, slowly, a wicked smile began spreading across his face. His blue eyes seemed to dance and sparkle.

"The very thing!" he exclaimed. He planted his hands on his hips and, grinning now, said to Torstensson: "I believe we should send a small expedition to Thuringia to investigate. And I know just the man to lead it!"

Torstensson frowned. "Who? One of the Scottish colonels? Or perhaps—" The meaning of that wicked gleam in his king's eye finally registered. Torstensson's own eyes almost bulged. "*Not—*"

"The very man!" cried the king gaily. "Captain Gars!" He clapped his hands. "He'll be ecstatic at the prospect, too—I can assure you of that. Captain Gars is every bit as sick of this miserable siege as I am. And there's plenty of time for him to go and come back before anything happens."

The king turned his head and glared at the distant Burgstall. "You know as well as I do, Lennart, that Wallenstein has no intention of offering me battle. That spider intends to just sit there—for months, if need be—while everyone dies around him. He counts men like a spendthrift counts coin."

Again, he clapped his hands. "Yes! Plenty of time for Captain Gars to carry out the task. More than enough."

Torstensson was scowling ferociously, now. "Your Majesty," he protested, "you haven't used Captain Gars for anything of that nature in years!"

The king matched the scowl with one of his own, even more ferocious. "What?" he demanded. "Are you saying you have no confidence in the man?"

Torstensson started. "Well—no. Of course not!"

The king's gaiety returned. "Done, then!" He gave Torstensson's shoulder a hearty pat. "Done! Captain Gars it is."

The decision made, Gustav moved at once. He turned to his bodyguard, Anders Jönsson. "You heard?"

Stolidly, Jönsson nodded. The king continued: "Get Captain Gars a cavalry detachment, Anders. A good one. The captain is partial to the *Västgöta*, as you know. And make sure he has plenty of Finns and some Lapps."

Gustav grinned cheerfully. "And I do believe I'll assign you to the captain as well, Anders." He waved a thick hand in the direction of Nürnberg. "There obviously won't be any danger to *me*, in the midst of these great fortifications. Will there?"

Stolidly, Jönsson shook his head.

"Excellent," said the king. He began walking away briskly, heading for the stairs leading down from the redoubt. Almost bouncing with enthusiasm, it seemed. Over his shoulder: "Captain Gars will be so delighted!"

When he was gone, Jönsson and Torstenson stared at each other.

"Captain Gars," muttered Jönsson. "Wonderful."

Torstensson's expression was a mix of concern and amusement. "Do take care of him, Anders, will you?"

The response was stolid, stolid. "That madman? *Impossible*."

Chapter 51

"What the hell are they *doing*, Heinrich?" demanded Tom Simpson. The big American captain was peering over the top of the parapet which had been erected across the road leading into Suhl from the south. The hastily built field fortifications were positioned at the northern edge of a large meadow. The meadow was about two hundred yards long and slightly less than that in width. A small stream ran through the center of it, bisecting the road.

His commanding officer shrugged. A pair of binoculars was slung around Heinrich's neck, but he was not using them. The oncoming mercenary soldiers were already entering the meadow, and in plain view.

Tom raised his own binoculars and scanned the meadow. After a few seconds, he lifted the eyepieces and began slowly studying the woods which covered the hills beyond.

"I don't like it," he muttered.

Next to him, Heinrich smiled. If he had any professional criticism of his inexperienced junior officer, it was that Tom *insisted* on finding complexity where, more often than not, there was none. "Too much football," he murmured.

Tom lowered the binoculars and peered at him suspiciously. "What is that supposed to mean?"

Heinrich's sly smile widened. "What it means, my friend, is that you keep thinking you are on a playing field. Facing enemies who are working out of a fancy play book."

Except for the English phrases "playing field" and "play book," Heinrich had spoken the last two sentences in German. The language made the English sports terms particularly incongruous—which was exactly what Heinrich had intended.

Tom snorted. "And what do you know about play books? Every time I've tried to explain football, you either fall asleep or order another beer."

Like Heinrich, Tom now also spoke in German. His command of the language had improved faster than that of any adult American in Grantville. It could not be said that Tom was fluent yet—not quite—but he was already able to participate in any conversation.

"That's because it's too intricate," retorted Heinrich. His hands zigzagged back and forth. "This one goes that way, that one goes this way"—his forefinger made a little twirling motion—"the other one runs around in circles to confuse the opponent—ha! It's a wonder you didn't all collapse from dizziness."

Tom grinned. "Not *my* problem. I didn't go anywhere except straight ahead—right into the guy in front of me."

"Excellent!" cried Heinrich. He slapped Tom on the shoulder with his left hand while he pointed at the meadow with his right. "Then you shouldn't have any difficulty with *this*. They come straight at us—good soldiers!—and we knock them flat. What is to understand?"

Tom's grin faded, replaced by a scowl. "Dammit, Heinrich, it doesn't make sense! They have got to know by now—"

Heinrich cut him off. "No, they don't! Tom, listen to me. You have no experience with these mercenary armies. Those men"—he jerked his head toward the meadow—"have probably had no contact with Tilly's. And if they did, they would have ignored anything a *stupid Bavarian* had to say."

He could tell that Tom was not convinced. Heinrich chuckled. Pointing now with his chin, he indicated the woods beyond the meadow. "What? You think there are cavalrymen hidden in the wood? Bringing their clever maneuver to fruition. Waiting to pounce when the time is right?"

Tom hesitated. Heinrich smiled. "Double reverse? Is that what you call it?"

"All right," the American grumbled. "Maybe you're right." He lifted his head over the parapet again. Softly: "We'll know soon enough. They're starting to cross the stream."

Lazily, Heinrich raised his own head and studied the enemy. "Swabians, I think. Sorry ignorant bastards."

Tom's lips twitched. "*All* of them?"

"Every Swabian ever born," came the firm reply. Then Heinrich's own lips moved. Twitched, perhaps. "I'm from the Upper Palatinate, you know."

"As if you haven't told me enough times. Funny thing, though."

Tom's heavy brows lowered. "I was talking to a Westphalian just the other day, and *he* swears that everybody from the Palatinate—Upper or Lower, the way he tells it—is a natural born—"

"Westphalians!" sniffed Heinrich. "You can't believe a word those people say. They're all goat-fuckers, for a start. Bastards, too, every one of them."

Tom started to make some quip in response, but never spoke the words. For all the relaxed casualness in Heinrich's stance and demeanor, Tom understood the sudden squinting of his eyes. During their badinage, the German veteran had never taken his gaze off the enemy. Tom envied him that relaxed poise. Personally, he felt as tight as a drum.

"Seventy yards," Heinrich murmured. "Good." He raised the whistle hanging around his neck. But before blowing into it, he gave Tom a sly smile.

"How do you say it? Oh, yes—*play ball.*"

The whistle blew. An instant later, three hundred U.S. soldiers rose from behind the parapet and began pumping lead slugs into the Swabians.

Five minutes later, the gunfire ceased. Heinrich swiveled his head. The sly smile was back.

"How do you say it? Oh, yes—*blowout*, I believe."

Tom made no reply. He appreciated the humor, but couldn't really share it. Unlike Heinrich, Tom Simpson was not a veteran of a dozen battlefields. He kept his eyes firmly focused on the enemy soldiers stumbling in retreat, so that he wouldn't find himself staring at the corpses mounded in an innocent meadow. Or a pleasant stream, suddenly running red.

"Why'd they do it?" he whispered. Again, his eyes ranged the woods beyond. "Shoulda had cavalry. Tried a flanking attack or something."

The reply was a given. "Swabians. What do you expect?"

As it happened, there *were* horsemen in those woods. But they were not Wallenstein's cavalry. They were Lapps, in service to the king of Sweden. Gustav Adolf believed, quite firmly, that Lapps were the best scouts in Europe.

He was quite possibly right.

The Finn who was in command of the Lapp scouting party reined his horse around. "Interesting," he said. "Come. Captain Gars will want to know."

Captain Gars raised himself off the saddle, standing in the stirrups. His head was cocked, listening for the sound of gunfire coming from the north. But there was none. The gunfire he had heard earlier that day had not lasted for more than a few minutes.

"How many?" he asked gruffly.

The Finnish scout waved his hand back and forth. "The Swabians, maybe two thousand. The other side?" He shrugged. "A few hundred, no more. Hard to say, exactly. They fight like skirmishers."

The last sentence, almost barked in his rural-accented Finnish, was full of approval. The scout, like most Finns and all Lapps, thought the "civilized" method of warfare—blast away, standing straight up, practically eyeball to eyeball—was one of the surest signs that civilization was not all it was cracked up to be.

He finished with a grin: "Smart people, these Americans. Whoever they are."

Captain Gars grunted. "It's all over, then?"

The Finn snorted. "It was a bloodbath. If the Swabians weren't so stupid they'd have run away after a minute."

"No chance they can take Suhl?" The scout's only response was a magnificent sneer.

Captain Gars nodded. "Not our concern, then. But this other—"

He twisted his enormous body in the saddle and looked toward the small group of Lapp scouts sitting on their horses a few feet away.

"Two thousand, you say?" As with the Finn himself, the captain spoke in Finnish. Few Lapps knew any other language beyond their own.

The head Lapp scout grimaced. "We guess, Captain. They follow narrow trail. Way ground chewed, must be two thousand. More. Maybe."

"And you're sure they're Croats?"

Again, the Lapp grimaced. "Guess. But who else? Good horsemen."

Captain Gars peered into the distance, looking slightly east of north. The Thuringenwald was a dense forest in that direction. Largely uninhabited, by the Lapps' accounts. The kind of terrain that good light cavalry can move through unobserved, as long as they carry enough provisions. The Lapps had spotted the trail less than two miles ahead. If their assessment was accurate—and Captain Gars thought Lapps were the best trackers in Europe—a large body of cavalry had broken away from the army marching on Suhl, moving into the forest east of the road.

Croats were good light cavalry. The best in the imperial army. Captain Gars decided that the Lapp was probably correct. Who else would it be?

The captain was not familiar with this particular area of the Thuringenwald. But, even given the roughness of the terrain, he estimated that a cavalry force of that size could pass over the crest of the low mountains within two days. Certainly not more than three. In straight-line distance, the heart of southeast Thuringia was not more than forty miles away.

Or Saalfeld, possibly, if the Croats angled further to the east. But the captain did not think Saalfeld was their target. Saalfeld could be approached far more easily from the opposite direction, following the Saale river. With the king of Sweden's army concentrated in Nürnberg, there was nothing impeding Wallenstein from sending an army directly against Saalfeld.

There was only one logical reason for a large cavalry force to be taking this route.

"They're planning a surprise attack on Grantville," he stated. "A major cavalry raid. Not to conquer, but simply to destroy."

Sitting on his horse next to the captain, Anders Jönsson heaved a sigh. He had already come to the same conclusion. And, what was worse, already knew for a certainty what Captain Gars would decide to do.

"We'll follow them." The words seemed carved in granite.

Anders appealed to reason. "Two thousand, the Lapp says. We've only four hundred."

"We'll follow them," repeated the captain. He glared at Jönsson. "Surely you don't intend to argue with me?"

Anders made no reply. *Surely, he didn't.*

Captain Gars spurred his horse forward. "And move quickly! The enemy is already half a day's march ahead of us."

Chapter 52

Mike decided to take out the field guns first. His confidence as a military commander had grown enough that he didn't wait to check with Frank. The Spaniards, in the manner of the day, were moving the artillery into position ahead of the infantry. Smoothbore cannons firing round shot needed a flat trajectory to be effective in a field battle. There was no way to do that with a mass of infantry standing in front of them. Mike understood the logic, but he still found the idea vaguely absurd.

"Talk about being exposed," he muttered. He lowered the binoculars.

"Orders, chief?" asked his radio operator.

Mike grinned. "I'm never going to get used to that expression coming from *you*, Gayle." He extended his hand and took the radio.

"*Harry, this is Mike. Move out the APCs. Take Route 4 and then turn south onto Route 26. The Spanish are positioning the field guns east of the road. You can cut right between the artillery and the infantry.*"

Harry Lefferts' voice crackled out of the radio. "*What about the cavalry?*"

"*We'll worry about them later. Frank can hold his ground easily enough, even if he doesn't use the M-60. We've got a chance to nail the artillery right now.*"

Lefferts' response, like the entire exchange, was sadly lacking in military protocol.

"*Gotcha. Will do, chief.*"

In the distance, coming from the grove northwest of that stretch of Eisenach's walls, Mike could hear the sound of the APC engines firing up.

His grin came back. "And I'll *sure* as hell never get used to it coming from Harry."

Gayle matched the grin. "Why not? Ain't you just the proper budding little Na-po-lee-own?"

"Give me a break," snorted Mike. "The day I become a military genius is the day hell freezes over." He handed the radio back to Gayle. "Call Frank and tell him about the change in plans. I want to go talk to Alex."

Gayle nodded. Mike turned away from the redoubt's wall and hurried toward the stairs leading to the compound below. By the time he reached the level ground where the cavalry was waiting, taking the wide stone steps two at a time, Mackay and Lennox were trotting forward to meet him.

After Mike explained the new situation, Alex grimaced. Lennox scowled. Mike found it hard not to laugh. The Scotsmens' expression combined varying amounts of amusement and exasperation.

On the part of Lennox, mostly exasperation. "Soft-hearted Americans," he grumbled. "Ye'd do better—"

"Enough," commanded Mackay. "*General* Stearns is in command."

Lennox subsided, but it was plain enough that he was not a happy man. Mike decided to explain.

"I realize we'd have a better chance of smashing the whole army if I waited. But our first responsibility is to ensure the safety of Eisenach. Without those guns, the Spaniards don't have a chance in hell of breaching the walls."

Lennox refrained from making the obvious rejoinder. *They don't have a chance in hell anyway.* Alex tugged at his beard. "I assume, then, that you'll be wanting us to chivvy the bastards after the APCs rip up the guns?"

Mike nodded. Alex's beard tugging grew vigorous. "And are you still determined . . . ?"

"Yes," came Mike's firm reply. "Drive 'em toward the Wartburg, Alex. And don't expose your men more than you need to. I want to keep our casualties as low as possible."

It was plain enough from his expression that the young Scottish officer was not happy with Mike's plan. But he refrained from argument. Alexander Mackay most definitely did *not* think Mike Stearns was a "military genius," but he also believed firmly in the principle of command.

A moment later, Mackay and Lennox were starting to issue orders to the cavalry. Within seconds, the marshaling area was a beehive of activity. The packed earth was rapidly chewed up still further by a multitude of stamping hooves.

The Eisenach militiamen staffing the gates were the only foot soldiers in the area. But they were able to start working the gate mechanisms from within the protection of the stone gatehouse. Mike was out in the open. He scampered back toward the stairs and started climbing them—again, two steps at a time. Being on foot in an area where a thousand horsemen were moving their chargers into position was not anywhere he wanted to be. *Squash. Oops. Sorry 'bout that.*

Once he was back at the redoubt wall, Gayle offered him the radio again. He cocked an eye. "Problems?"

"No," replied Gayle. "Except Frank told me to tell you that you're a soft-hearted wimp."

Mike smiled. He brought the binoculars back up to his eyes. "Yeah, I know," he murmured. "It's a dirty job, but somebody's got to do it."

As he studied the Spanish tercios beyond the walls of Eisenach, Mike's smile faded. There were six tercios in that army—approximately twelve thousand men, he estimated—along with two thousand cuirassiers positioned on either flank. It was not a huge army, by the standards of the day, but it was sizeable. Big enough to have turned the farmland across which they marched into barren devastation. Mike could see the burning farmhouses in their wake. Fortunately, the inhabitants had long since taken refuge within Eisenach's walls. But the destruction was still savage enough.

The Spanish infantry was 500 yards away. The Spanish commander had brought his infantry to a halt just short of the road, while he moved his artillery into position across it. Clearly enough, he intended to begin his attack on Eisenach with a cannonade.

That road ran north to south, just west of the city. It was now officially designated as U.S. Route 26. Route 4, the road along which Harry was now leading the ten APCs, intersected Route 26 about two miles to the north. The Americans, following their own traditions, had insisted on giving a proper nomenclature to all the roads in the new United States—which now included all of southern Thuringia from Eisenach to Gera. The native Germans thought the custom was bizarre, but they went along without complaint. Compared to everything else about the Americans, numbering roads was small potatoes. And the Germans had noticed that roads which were given "official status" were invariably widened and properly graded. Graveled, too, more often than not. So the farmers were happy enough with the change. Easier on their carts and draft animals.

"Soft-hearted," mused Mike, speaking to himself. "No, Frank, not really. It's just that I know the cost of being anything else."

He lowered the binoculars and turned his head to the northeast. Not more than three seconds later, he saw the first of Harry's APCs thunder from behind the low hill which had hidden their approach.

"God, I'm sick of this," he muttered.

Gayle misunderstand his frown. "Something wrong with the APCs?"

"No, Gayle," Mike replied softly. "Nothing at all. Harry'll rip right through 'em." He glanced at her. "*That's* what I'm worried about."

It was Gayle's turn to frown. Clearly enough, she didn't understand.

And that's what I'm worried about the most, thought Mike. He brought the binoculars back to his eyes, focusing on Harry's blitzkrieg attack. *Give it a few years. Cortez and Pizarro, coming up. Hidalgos true and pure.*

"*Fire!*" shrieked Lefferts, riding in the armored cab of the lead APC. His words, carried over the CBs to all the APCs coming behind, produced an instant eruption. On both sides of the armored coal trucks, the rifles poking through the slits began firing. Most of those weapons were bolt-action or lever-action, but a goodly number were semiautomatics. The rate of fire which they produced fell far short of automatic weapons, but it still came as an incredible shock to the Spanish soldiers gawking at the APCs.

The U.S. soldiers on the right side of the trucks, facing the Spanish infantry, were simply trying to fire as many rounds as rapidly as possible. Aiming was a moot point. The front ranks of the tercios were less than thirty yards from the road. At that range, firing into a mass of tightly packed men, almost every round hit a target.

The soldiers on the left side of the trucks, facing the field guns, did take the time to aim. They needed to kill the gunners and the rammers, who were individual targets rather than a mass. But since the range was just as short—shorter, in the case of the bigger guns—aiming was not difficult.

The voice of the radio operator in the rearmost APC came over the CB in Harry's vehicle. "We're into the zone!" she cried.

Harry immediately issued new orders. "*Stop the column!*"

The drivers of the ten APCs braked to a halt. All of the vehicles were now "in the zone"—positioned right in the middle of the Spanish army, with clear lines of fire on both sides. The APCs were facing south on Route 26. The Spanish infantry was now separated from the artillery by the armored coal trucks. Now that the vehicles were no longer moving, the rifle fire intensified and became more accurate.

The result was a one-sided slaughter. Several of the tercios managed to get off coordinated arquebus volleys, but the gesture was futile. Even at point-blank range, the thick steel of the APCs was impervious to slow-moving round shot. The Spaniards might as well have been throwing pebbles.

The tires were somewhat more vulnerable, but not much. Few of the Spanish bullets hit the tires, anyway, and those only did so by accident. The Spaniards had no experience with American vehicles at all—most of the soldiers were still gawking with confusion—and never thought to shoot for the tires. Even the few bullets which did strike the tires caused no real damage. Coal truck tires were not, to put it mildly, fragile and delicate; and, again, the slow-moving round shot of seventeenth-century firearms was poorly equipped to rupture them.

There was one American fatality. By sheer bad luck, a bullet came through one of the firing slits and hit the man positioned there. He died instantly, his head shattered by the .80-caliber round.

The damage wreaked by the U.S. soldiers, on the other hand, was horrendous. Within a minute, those artillerymen who had not been shot down were sprinting away from the guns, seeking nothing more than refuge in the distant woods. Seconds later, the soldiers on that side of the trucks stopped firing. There were simply no more targets available.

On the other side of the APCs, the firing continued. By their nature, tercios were so tightly packed that it was impossible for men in the front ranks to simply run away. The soldiers standing behind them formed an impassable barrier. Moreover, these were *Spanish* pikemen and arquebusiers. Spanish infantry were universally acknowledged as the best in Europe. Even by the standards of the time, those men were ferociously courageous. *Stand your ground and take it* was as ingrained in them as their native tongue.

Three of the tercios even managed to launch pike charges. Stumbling over corpses, the Spaniards leveled their fifteen-foot spears and lunged onto the road.

The charges had no chance of destroying the APCs, of course. That would have required grenades, which the Spanish soldiers did not carry. But the pikemen might still have disabled the vehicles as effective military instruments, by the crude but simple expedient of sticking pikes into the firing slits and forcing the U.S. riflemen to retreat against the opposite walls.

But they never got that far. As soon as the first ranks of the tercios stepped onto the road, the Claymore mines positioned along the sides of the APCs erupted. A hail of cannister and shrapnel literally wiped them off the road. In an instant, hundreds of men were dead and dying.

That stunning blow was too much, even for Spanish soldiers. The men who survived stumbled back. By now, the pikemen and arquebusiers behind them had begun to retreat, leaving space for the front ranks to follow. Within two minutes, chased along by continuous rifle fire, the entire Spanish infantry was in headlong retreat.

When Mackay's cavalry sallied from Eisenach, the retreat became a rout. The Spanish cuirassiers, as brave as the foot soldiers, launched

a countercharge. But the effort was futile. As soon as the Spanish
cavalry emerged in clear view, Frank ordered his infantrymen to open
fire. Those U.S. soldiers were stationed in rifle pits and behind palisades a hundred yards in front of Eisenach's walls. They were firing
at exposed horsemen from a range of two hundred yards. Before the
lead elements of the Spanish cavalry could reach Mackay's oncoming charge, they had already been bled badly.

Mackay hit them like a hammer. Although Mackay's forces were
still technically part of the Swedish army, they were for all practical
purposes the U.S. cavalry—and had been equipped accordingly. Most
of his horsemen—the big majority of whom were now Germans, not
Scots—had been equipped with an American revolver or automatic
pistol. Matched against the wheel locks and sabers of the Spanish
cavalry, the outcome was a foregone conclusion. The Spanish cuirassiers were shattered within less than three minutes. The survivors
raced away, stunned by the firepower they had encountered.

Mackay could have given pursuit, which would have produced yet
more carnage. But he held back his forces. He had his doubts about
Mike's battle plan, but he was too well trained to break discipline.

Fifteen minutes after the APCs opened fire, the Battle of Eisenach
was over. The broken Spanish tercios and their cavalry escorts were
retreating in complete disorder. While Mackay and his men chivvied
them toward the distant Wartburg, the U.S. soldiers in the APCs
dismounted and took possession of the Spanish field guns. Before
another fifteen minutes had passed, the gates of Eisenach were wide
open and hundreds of conscripted farmers were starting to hitch up
the captured cannons and haul them into the city.

The Spanish commander, meanwhile, had managed to bring a
semblance of discipline back to his army. It did not take him long
to reach the obvious conclusion. They had been half-destroyed in a
field battle. It was time to seek shelter within fortifications.

Where?

Where else? The ancient castle called the Wartburg was in plain
view, perched atop a hill to the south. The Spaniards had already taken
possession of it, in fact. On the march in toward Eisenach, cavalry
units had investigated the castle and found it deserted. The Spanish commander had been dumbfounded at the news. Were these
Americans utterly insane, not to garrison the strongest fortress in the
region? But he was more than happy to take advantage of his enemy's
stupidity.

Through his binoculars, Mike studied the retreat of the Spanish
army until he was satisfied that they were definitely making for the
Wartburg. By the time he finally lowered the eyepieces, Greg Ferrara

and the leaders of his special artillery unit were gathered around him on the redoubt.

"We're a go?" asked Ferrara.

Mike nodded. "They should be forted up by nightfall. We'll start the special effects at midnight. Come dawn, we'll start lobbing the bombs."

That announcement produced instant frowns on the three young faces peering at him. Larry Wild, Jimmy Andersen and Eddie Cantrell, plain to see, were not pleased.

Hell hath no fury like a wargamer scorned.

"No," Mike said. "I am *not* starting the bombardment until daybreak."

"We should take advantage of darkness," complained Jimmy. "Create more confusion."

Mike forced down his scowl. But he couldn't restrain the sigh. *Is there anything in the world as bloodthirsty as a kid?*

"That's exactly what I'm trying to *avoid*, Jimmy," he said forcefully. He pointed to the retreating Spanish army with the hand still holding the binoculars. "Those men may just be so many toy soldiers to you, but they're not to me. They're *people*, dammit!"

The three youngsters flinched from the genuine anger in Mike's voice. Mike drove home his point. "It's going to be bad enough as it is. At the very least, I want to make sure that men trying to surrender can do it. Not get destroyed simply because they couldn't find their way out of a castle in pitch darkness. Do you understand?"

There was no response, beyond sulkiness. Chagrin, mixed with frustration.

"Get going, boys," commanded Ferrara. The three youngsters scampered off the redoubt with great eagerness.

Mike muttered something. Ferrara cocked at eye at him. "What did you say?"

Mike shook his head. "Never mind."

Ferrara left, then. Mike stared at the Wartburg. The grim castle seemed to return his gaze with its own baleful glare.

"Hidalgos true and pure," he muttered again. "There has *got* to be a better way."

Chapter 53

"Are you *sure?*" squeaked Julie. "I mean, like—*positive?*" Her next words came in a rush. "I thought I just had a flu or something. It's been going around, you know. Bad one. Sick to my stomach, that's all. I woulda gone to Eisenach except Alex insisted I see you and Mike backed him up. Wouldn't let me go." She glared at the doctor, as if to say: *This is all your fault!*

James Nichols managed to keep a completely straight face. It was not easy. The face of the young woman perched on the chair in the examining room was a study in contradictions. Anxiety, chagrin, apprehensiveness—all of these warred with outrage and indignation.

"Those things are supposed to *work*," she snarled.

James opened his mouth. Julie drove right over him. "They are!"

Again he tried to speak. Julie drove right over him.

"Alex is going to *kill* me," she moaned. "I promised him we had nothing to worry about!" She pressed her hand over her mouth. Mumbled: "What am I gonna do?"

James thought he could get a word in edgewise, now. "Julie, you're supposed to use a diaphragm with contraceptive—"

"The stores ran out!" she protested. Imperious demand: "What was I supposed to do?"

Abstain, came the whimsical thought. But James squelched it. The likelihood of someone as vigorous as Julie Sims abstaining from sex with her fiancé ranked somewhere below the proverbial snowball in hell. And James was hardly in a position to criticize. Leaving aside his own reprobate youth, his relationship with Melissa was neither platonic nor blessed by the sanctity of matrimony.

On the other hand, he thought wryly, Melissa was fifty-seven years old. For them, contraception was a moot point.

"Oh, Jesus, he's gonna *kill* me," Julie whimpered anew. Now she pressed both hands over her mouth. Gargling sounds emerged.

James managed a paternal frown. "Why?" *Hrmph, hmrph.* "I should think Alex is the one to be worrying. Your father—not to mention Frank!—aren't exactly going to be—"

Julie gargled protest through her hands.

"I didn't quite catch that."

She took the hands off her lips and opened them wide, cupping them around her mouth as if to impart a secret.

"It was my idea," she hissed. Seeing the expression on the doctor's face, Julie laughed. The sound was perhaps a tad hysterical. Well, semihysterical.

"You think it was *Alex*? Ha! That proper fellow? Oh, God!" The laughter swelled. Yes, definitely semihysterical. "It took me *weeks* to wear him down!"

For a moment, her eyes grew dreamy. "He's such a sweet guy," she whispered. "It was a nice change, not having to fend off the sweaty mitts."

Julie slumped in her chair. "He's gonna kill me." The words carried all the gloomy surety of a Cassandra.

James cleared his throat. "You do have a couple of options. The first is an abortion." Hastily: "I don't do abortions myself, but Doctor Adams can handle that. So can Doctor Abrabanel, for that matter. At your stage of pregnancy, it's not a difficult procedure."

Julie gave him a sharp glance. "If it's so easy, why can't you do it?" Then, seeing the stiff look on his face, she giggled. "Don't tell me!" Giggle, giggle. "Boy, I bet that was a donnybrook. When you told Melissa, I mean."

James shrugged. "Wasn't a donnybrook at all. She has her principles, I got mine." His own eyes got a bit dreamy. "We get along pretty well, all things considered."

Abruptly, Julie shook her head. "Abortion's out anyway. I don't approve of it myself. So what's the other option?"

"It's obvious, isn't it? Get married."

Julie was back to wailing. "He's gonna *kill* me!" Her hands went back over her mouth. Gargle, gargle.

James scratched his head. "I don't get it. The way I heard it, he's been *trying* to get you to set a date."

Again, the hands popped open. "He has!" she hissed. The hands closed. Gargle.

"So what's the problem?"

Julie took a deep breath, sucking the air through her fingers. Then, slowly, eased it out. She removed the hands, dropped them into her lap, slumped her shoulders, and heaved a sigh worthy of Cassandra. Unheeded, again.

"You don't get it. It's the principle of the thing. By the time—" Her eyes narrowed, as she did some quick calculations. "By the time we got married—couldn't be sooner than next month, at the earliest—maybe not till September 'cause he's gotta go right away to see the king of Sweden as soon as he and Mike get done whipping those Spanish clowns—"

Calculate, calculate. James was struggling to keep a straight face again. He wasn't sure which amused him more—Julie's insouciant assumption that the Spaniards would be trounced, or her blithe reference to her fiancé's familiarity with royalty.

"Yeah," she concluded. "That's what I thought. We couldn't get married until sometime in September." She puffed out her cheeks and cupped her hands a foot away from her belly, in a parody of a pregnant woman.

"For Christ's sake, Julie! You can't possibly be serious. That early in the second trimester? Nothing would show at all."

"It would six months later!" she snapped. "Big time!"

James shrugged. "By then you'd be married. So who cares? Wouldn't be the first time—"

"That's the whole point!" Wailing: "You *know* how sensitive Alex is on account of he's illegitimate! You know! He's told me once, he's told me a thousand times: 'No child of mine will ever be bastard born.'" Even in her despair, she managed quite a good rendition of Mackay's Scottish accent.

Julie's logic had completely eluded James, by now. "I don't get it," he muttered. "If you're married when the child is born, then he—or she—isn't—"

"It's the *principle* of the thing!" she wailed. "Don't you understand? And nobody can get hung up on principles like a damn Scottish Calvinist!"

She was no longer even slumped in her chair. Just puddled in it, like a quivering blob of anxiety.

"He's gonna kill me," she squeaked. "I'm *dead*."

James' struggle for dignity collapsed, finally. He just couldn't resist. "Make sure you tell him at five hundred yards, then."

Julie's ensuing words were not uttered in a squeak. Rather the opposite. James consoled himself with the thought that he had, as was a doctor's duty, elevated his patient's spirits. In a manner of speaking.

Shortly thereafter, he ushered Rebecca into the same examination room.

"Julie seems out of sorts," she commented. "Is something wrong?"

James' lips twitched. "Nothing serious." He helped her into the chair.

"Oof!" said Rebecca. She gave the doctor a quick smile. "Thank you. I feel so awkward."

She gazed down at her belly. "Philosophically, I do not approve of this," she pronounced. "It seems such a foolish way to go about the matter. By the time a woman can get accustomed to her condition, it is gone." Her dark eyes grew very warm. "Soon."

James nodded. "Six to eight weeks. Can't be sure with a first pregnancy."

Rebecca lifted her head, smiling. "We did not waste any time, did we, Michael and I?" She broke off, laughing softly. "It will be such a scandal! The baby will be born barely seven months after we were married."

The thought did not seem to disturb her. Not in the least. James grinned.

"There seems to be a lot of that going around, these days."

It didn't take Rebecca more than two seconds to make the connection. In a movement which bore an uncanny similarity to Julie's, she clapped her hands over her mouth.

She laughed softly. Gargled.

"Poor Alex!" she mumbled through her fingers. She took the fingers away and cupped her hands around her mouth. "Julie will *kill* him," she hissed.

James threw up his hands. "Women! I can't follow your logic at all!"

He stalked over to his own chair and sat down in it heavily, then glared at Rebecca. "Explain *your* reasoning, if you would."

Rebecca dropped her hands into her lap. Her brow furrowed.

"Is it not obvious? Julie will be convinced that Alex will be furious with her because I am quite certain—I know none of the details, mind you, but I *do* know Julie—that she convinced him pregnancy was not to be feared."

Rebecca ran fingers through her hair, thinking. "Yes, that would certainly be the way it would have happened. Alex is too much the gentleman to have urged the thing upon her. She would have been the seductress, not the seduced one. *Then—*"

Thinking, thinking. "Of course, it is obvious. She will now tell Alex, convinced that he will lose his temper. You know how Julie is! By the time she tells him, she will have worked herself into a fury because she will be convinced that Alex will be furious with her. Like a firearm, primed and loaded. Alex, of course, will say something wrong. Under the circumstances, that is a certainty, since anything he says will be wrong as far as Julie is concerned. *Then—*"

She beamed. "The logic is impeccable. Julie will kill him. Hopefully, of course, she will only slay him with words. Since, I trust, she will not have given him the news at five hundred paces."

Seeing the expression on the doctor's face, Rebecca frowned. "Is something wrong, James?"

Nichols shook his head. "Nope. I'm just glad you're on our side." He snapped his fingers. "*That* for Richelieu!"

Gretchen leaned over the bed and kissed Jeff on the forehead. She could feel the fever through her lips, but was not concerned. Not any longer.

Jeff's eyes opened. Smiling, Gretchen sat on the bed and bent her head down. Her lips began to part.

Jeff twitched his head aside. "Don't!" he protested. "You might catch—"

"Nothing," she whispered. She took his face in strong hands and turned it back to her own. The kiss which followed was gentle. But it was also lingering, and not platonic in the least.

"Nothing," she whispered. "Nothing but a fever. I just returned from seeing Dr. Nichols. He assured me that you have none of the symptoms of the plague."

"Even so—" Jeff tried to push her away. He was too weak to succeed in that task. His wife did not push easily. "The flu is bad enough, Gretchen! You don't have my resistance to it!"

She rose slowly and shrugged. Gretchen understood the medical logic behind her husband's words. Dr. Nichols had explained to her at considerable length. People of her time did not have a built-up resistance to strains of disease carried by those born in the future.

She began to disrobe. Gretchen understood the logic, but she did not agree with it. She had her own way of reasoning, which was more tough-minded. *Much* more.

"Best I develop it, then," she murmured. Now nude, she slid under the sheets and pressed herself against her husband. Her movements were gentle, not passionate. But they were no more platonic than her earlier kiss. Since Jeff had contracted influenza, two days earlier, she had been forced to sleep with the children. Her husband had insisted. Now, she practically wallowed in the sensation of his body against hers.

Feebly, Jeff tried to protest again. Gretchen put her hand over his mouth. "Be quiet," she whispered. "I will contract this disease sooner or later, anyway. So why not get on with it?"

Jeff sighed and closed his eyes. His fears for his wife were warring with desire for her nearness. Desire won. He enfolded her in his arms and drew her closer still.

"Oh, yes," Gretchen murmured a few minutes later. "There's something else. Dr. Nichols tells me I am definitely pregnant."

Jeff's eyes popped open.

"What, husband? You are worrying again? It happens, you know." She snuggled closer. "I will be fine, and the baby also. And look at it this way—at least there will be no scandal. *Our* baby will not be born at a questionable time."

She chuckled. "Unlike some others, I suspect."

Captain Gars drove his men well beyond sundown. Only when the last glimmer of dusk faded, and the forest was black with the night, did he relent.

"Make camp," he growled, climbing down from his horse. His movements were stiff and heavy. The past two days had been brutal, as hard as the captain had kept up the pursuit. And if his men thought the notion of four hundred cavalrymen pursuing two thousand was bizarre, they kept their thoughts to themselves. Captain Gars was not one to listen to reason.

"No fires," he commanded. "Not following Croats. Eat the food cold."

None of his soldiers complained. Captain Gars was not one to listen to complaints, either. And besides, he was sharing the same cold food and sleeping on the same naked ground.

When the men were settled down, Anders Jönsson approached him. The captain was sitting on his bedroll, staring at nothing.

"And tomorrow, Captain? What then?"

Captain Gars lifted his head. "Tomorrow we will rise before sunup. There is no time to lose. The Croats will reach Grantville by mid-morning at the latest."

He paused, thinking. "I am certain, now, of their plan. Everything makes sense. The Spaniards that Saxe-Weimar let through, the seemingly pointless attack on Suhl. Diversions to draw off the American army. The Croats are the thing. They will strike a town filled with women and children. Their purpose is pure slaughter and destruction."

Jönsson frowned. "To what end?"

The captain shrugged. "Ask someone else. That is the way men like Wallenstein and Richelieu think. I am skeptical of such reasoning, myself." He smiled faintly. "But then—what do you expect? I am a madman. It is well known."

Chapter 54

The witching hour started at midnight. From loudspeakers positioned at five places surrounding the Wartburg, music suddenly blared forth. A wooded hill in seventeenth-century Thuringia was blessed with the popular tastes of a much later era.

Harry Lefferts' tastes, anyway. Somehow—Mike never was clear on the exact chain of command involved—Harry had gotten himself appointed DJ for the occasion.

He began, naturally, with the Rolling Stones' "Sympathy for the Devil," then, followed with "Satisfaction" and "Street Fighting Man."

So far, so good. The arguments started thereafter. To the disgust of the teenage American soldiers in the army, Harry, despite his own relative youth, turned out to be a Classic Rock enthusiast. He followed the Stones' openers with various selections from Creedence Clearwater Revival and the Doors.

Then—

"I can't believe this antique shit," hissed Larry Wild. The young "artillery specialist" was making the final adjustments to one of the catapults, working in the light thrown out by an electric hang lamp. Greg Ferrara was directing the work. The crew which would actually fire the contraption was standing nearby, next to the portable generator.

Larry's voice was bitter, aggrieved—betrayed. *"Bob Dylan?"*

The strains of "Positively Fourth Street" finally ended. Larry heaved a thankful sigh, as did Eddie Cantrell. But the third member of the "special artillery unit" did not share their relief.

"It's gonna get worse," predicted Jimmy Andersen gloomily.

Sure enough. Southwest Thuringia, at that very moment, was rocked with—

Larry and Eddie shrieked in unison. *"Elvis Presley? You gotta be kidding!"*

Alas, Harry turned out to be a devotee of the King, so the torment of the special artillery unit was protracted. By the time the first catapult was assembled and ready, they were trembling with outrage.

Then, torment became torture. Over the loudspeakers, Harry announced he was taking requests. Instantly—despite all of Greg Ferrara's squawks about military discipline—the trio scurried through the woods, bound and determined to bring reason and sanity back into the world.

Not a chance. By the time they reached Harry's impromptu "music HQ," the small clearing was thronged with soldiers eagerly calling out their requests. The noncommissioned ranks of the U.S. army were still primarily composed of middle-aged UMWA members, and Harry cheerfully bowed to their veteran wisdom.

Larry and Eddie groaned. Jimmy staggered and reeled.

Reba McEntire?!

Desperately, as "The Heart Is a Lonely Hunter" echoed across war-ravaged central Europe and added to that poor land's agony, Larry and his friends tried to rally support among the soldiers who now formed the bulk of the U.S. military.

No use. Many of those soldiers, of course, were youngsters like themselves. But, by August of 1632, the ranks of the U.S. army were primarily filled with Germans, who, as it developed—especially the younger ones—had become something in the way of country-western fans. They liked Reba McEntire just fine, thank you.

Ferrara finally managed to drive his underlings back to work. Feverishly—anything to keep their minds off the pain—they worked their way around the hill, readying the other two catapults. But then, done with that immediate task, the youngsters could bear it no longer. Despite all of Ferrara's protests about the "chain of command," they marched in a body to the army's central HQ, determined to bring their complaints to the very top.

And, again, met the stone wall of officialdom.

"Sorry, guys," said Mike. "Can't help you." He glanced at his watch, turning his wrist to bring the dial into the light thrown by the gas lantern hanging at the entrance to the field tent. "Yeah, what I thought. It's two o'clock in the morning. The preliminaries are over. Time for the main program."

He grinned down at the three aggrieved youngsters. "All that other stuff," he waved, "was just the warm-up. Now we'll get to the *real* psychological warfare."

They stared up him, uncomprehending. Mike's grin widened.

"Becky put it together," he explained.

At that moment, the sounds of a very different music erupted over the hillside. The three boys standing in front of him flinched.

"Jesus," whined Jimmy. "What is *that?*"

A few feet away, Frank Jackson laughed. "And you thought your stuff was 'out there'!" Frank shook his head. "Forget it, boys. Becky's about ten times smarter than you, and she's got all those centuries to pick from."

He cocked his head, listening. "Horrible stuff, ain't it?"

Mike pursed his lips. "It's pretty good, actually. If you listen to it in the right frame of mind."

Frank chuckled. "That's just the accommodating husband speaking, Mike. Like me pretending *nuoc mam* don't taste like rotten fish."

Jackson twitched his head. "I hope there ain't much of *this* selection. Gross violation of the rules of war, what it is."

Mike smiled. "Just a few minutes. Even Becky'll admit that a little of Berg's *Wozzeck* goes a long way."

To the Spanish soldiers in the Wartburg, the eerie cacophony of *Wozzeck* seemed to last a very long time. The soldiers crammed into the castle were filled with anxiety. For two hours, now, they had been subjected to that incredible aural bombardment. For the soldiers standing on the ramparts, it had been even worse. The blinding glare of the spotlights which Ferrara and his teenage "tech warriors" had jury-rigged, sweeping endlessly back and forth across the castle, added visual assault as well.

As always with Spanish armies, the troops were accompanied by officials of the Holy Office of the Inquisition. Ten priests, now standing on the ramparts alongside the soldiers, hissed their fury.

Fury—and fear. The Spanish branch of the Inquisition, which answered only to the crown of Spain, was an order of magnitude more vicious and unrestrained than the Papal Inquisition. But they were by no means mindless thugs. The Spanish Inquisition had developed secret police techniques to a level of sophistication which would not be surpassed until the Tsarist *Okhrana* of the late nineteenth century. By the standards of the seventeenth century, they were considered the unrivaled practitioners of what a later age would call "psychological warfare."

They had just met their master. Their mistress, rather. It was a pity, perhaps, that they did not understand the historical irony involved. A young woman from the cursed race which the Inquisition had hounded for two centuries was about to pay them back in full measure. Her own intelligence, coupled to the entire musical tradition of a later Western world, would complete the task which rock and roll and country-western had begun.

The selection from *Wozzeck* ended. As the next piece began blaring in the night, the Inquisitors heaved a small sigh of relief. At least this music—whatever it was—had some logic.

Their relief lasted not more than a minute. There is a logic to Mussorgsky's *Night on Bald Mountain*, true enough. But it was not a logic which appealed to them. Neither did the grinding, ominous strains of the same composer's "Bydlo" from *Pictures at an Exhibition*.

Rebecca built from there. Grieg's short, sharp, thunderous "In the Hall of the Mountain King" came next. As the popularity of that portion of *Peer Gynt* grew, over the years after its composition, Grieg himself had come to detest the thing. "The worst kind of Norwegian bombast," he once called it. But on that night, the savage Nordic triumphalism of the piece served Rebecca's purpose well enough.

Tremble, lords of the dungeon! Trolls and Vikings are at your door!

A Russian variation on the theme followed. The heroic choral strains of "Arise, ye Russian People" from Prokofiev's *Alexander Nevsky* filled the air, succeeded immediately by the driving fury of "The Battle on the Ice." On the ramparts of the castle above, the Spanish variation of the Teutonic Knights suffered, in their minds, the same disaster which had befallen the butchers of Pskov centuries earlier on the real ice of Lake Chud.

The Inquisitors tried to dispel their own growing terror by driving their soldiers into action. Shrieking and bellowing, they forced shivering Spanish arquebusiers to the ramparts. Dragging them by the neck, in some cases, ordering them to fire at the Satanic music and spotlights.

Given the inaccuracy of arquebuses, the command was foolish enough. Given the accuracy of the weapons in the hands of the devils in the darkness, it was sheer folly.

"Take them out!" commanded Mike. He studied the ramparts through the binoculars. The spotlights were now focused on the priests and soldiers lined along the battlements, illuminating them clearly. "Aim for the inquisitors!"

Alexander Nevsky ended, immediately replaced by the conclusion of Prokofiev's Piano Concerto no. 3. The wild exuberance of the music from the third movement served as a backdrop for the rambunctious enthusiasm of the U.S. snipers. Julie Sims was not among their number, true. But if Julie was the best sharpshooter in the U.S. army, there were many other very fine ones. Within two minutes, all of the Spanish soldiers had retreated from the battlements. They left behind twenty of their own dead—and seven inquisitors.

"A daft breed," grumbled Lennox. He and Mackay had tried to seek shelter from the auditory storm in the HQ tent. To no great avail, as loudly as Harry was playing the music. "A guid thing I slept earlier. Get nae sleep now."

Alex shrugged. " 'Tis better than rap music."

Lennox snorted. "Anyt'in' is better'n *tha'* crap!"

Another piece blared over the loudspeakers. Lennox flinched.

Mike, seeing the motion out of the corner of his eye, turned his head and grinned.

"That's from something called *The Rite of Spring*," he explained. "Becky's real fond of it."

"Glad she's no my wife," muttered Lennox under his breath. "Even if t'lass does look like Cleopatra."

Mackay smiled. He stepped forward, coming alongside Mike at the tent's entrance.

"I'm curious," he said. "Rebecca's been with you lunatics for not much more than a year." Alex gestured into the darkness with his chin. "So how has she managed to learn so much of your music?"

Mike shrugged. "Beats me. Her father helped, of course. Balthazar's gotten to be a fanatic about classical music. Says he's sick to death of stupid lutes." He hesitated, torn between pride and a desire not to seem like a doting husband. But, since he was both proud of his wife—fiercely proud—*and* a doting husband, the struggle was brief.

"I don't know, Alex. How she managed that, along with all her reading, and everything else? I just don't know." His chest swelled. "The only thing I know for sure is that Becky's the smartest person I've ever met. Or ever will, I imagine."

Mackay nodded. "True enough. Still—"

He froze. "What is *that*?"

Mike listened, for a moment, to the sound of Leontyne Price's powerful soprano. Then, laughed. "Don't you like it? It's called the 'Liebestod.' By a guy named Wagner."

Alex pursed his lips. "Incredible voice, I grant you." He grimaced. "But it sounds as if the poor woman is dying."

"She is." Mike turned his head, staring at the battlements above. Gaily: "And she takes her sweet time about it, let me tell you."

And so it went, through the night. The program which Rebecca had prepared followed the "Liebestod" with a whole dose of Wagner. She detested the composer, as it happened—as much for the histrionics of his music as for his personal vileness and anti-Semitism. But she thought the music suited the occasion. So, striking their ears like lead mallets, the Spanish soldiers forted up in a German castle were assaulted by the ultimate in Teutonic bombast. "The Ride of the Valkyries" came next, followed by all of the orchestral grandiosities from the *Der Ring des Nibelungen*: "Entry of the Gods Into Valhalla,"

"Wotan's Farewell," "Siegfried's Funeral March" and—last but not least—the "Immolation of the Gods."

When it was over, Frank Jackson sighed with relief. "Good thing they lost World War II," he growled. "Can you imagine having to listen to that shit forever?"

Mike snorted. "You think *that* was bad?" He glanced at the eastern horizon. The first hint of dawn was appearing in the sky. "Try listening to *Parsifal,* some time."

He raised the binoculars and studied the battlements. They were still shrouded in darkness, except where the spotlights flashed across the walls. There was not a soldier in sight.

"Becky made me do it, once. All five hours of the damned thing."

Jackson frowned. "Why? I thought you told me she hated Wagner."

"She does. She just wanted to prove her point."

A new, very different strain of music came over the loudspeakers. Mike glanced at his watch. "Perfect timing," he said softly. "What the French call the 'pièce de résistance.'"

Frank cocked his ear. "What is it?"

"According to Becky, this piece of music captures the heart of war like nothing else ever composed." Mike stepped out of the tent and strode into the clearing beyond. Seeing Ferrara standing nearby, he signaled with his hand. The former science teacher nodded and turned to his youthful subordinates. Partners in crime, rather.

"Time to start the fireworks, boys." Grinning, Larry, Eddie and Jimmy scampered off, each headed for one of the catapults—and the rocket stands which stood near them.

Mike returned, walking slowly and pausing at every step. He was listening to the music. By the time he got back to the tent, Frank's face seemed strained.

As well it might be. Shostakovich's Symphony no. 8 was well underway now, blasting the horror of a war-ravaged Russia of the future across the war-ravaged land of today's Germany. Stalin had wanted a triumphalist piece, to celebrate the growing tide of Soviet victory over the Nazis. But Shostakovich, though a Soviet patriot himself, had given the dictator something quite different—the greatest symphony of the twentieth century. And if the piece as a whole transcended the year 1943, the third movement did not. It was a pure, unalloyed, cold-eyed *shriek.* Terror and agony and heartbreak, captured in music.

The first rockets sailed from their launching pads and began exploding over the ramparts. The explosive charges in the warheads were not designed for destruction so much as for show. Instead of splattering the castle with shrapnel, they shrouded the Wartburg with sparkling dazzle. A glaring, flaming accompaniment to the Symphony no. 8—a visual promise, added to a musical one. *This is what awaits you, soldiers of Spain.*

Dawn arrived, and the third movement screamed into silence. The last rockets flared in the sky.

Silence. Stillness, at last. Mike waited, studying his watch. He and Rebecca had decided on five minutes of peace. A "tension-builder," she had called it.

When the five minutes were up, Mike gave the order and the catapults began to fire. An ancient design, coupled to modern materials, hurled cannisters onto the battlements of the Wartburg.

These first missiles, though they contained a small explosive charge, were still part of the psychological campaign. They burst over the castle and showered leaflets onto the thousands of soldiers huddled inside the walls. The leaflets were written in Spanish and German, calling on the soldiers to surrender and promising good treatment to those who did.

Over the loudspeakers, Spanish-speaking soldiers in the U.S. army called out the same terms of surrender. *Food. Water. Good treatment. No atrocities. Recruitment—at good pay—for those who choose to join the army of the United States.*

When the catapult barrage ended, the voices calling over the loud-speaker were replaced by more music. Rebecca had selected these pieces also; choosing, this time, for a different purpose. The Span-iards had been given one alternative. Now, the other.

The tranquil strains of "Morning Mood" from Grieg's *Peer Gynt* filled the dawn. To Mike, and Frank, and Mackay and Lennox, and all the U.S. soldiers surrounding the castle, the music came like a balm. They could well imagine its effect on the Spaniards.

"Morning Mood" faded away. In its place came music even more serene, spreading with the daylight. Like peace and hope, after the night.

Frank seemed transfixed. Gently, seeing his friend's face, Mike said: "Becky thinks this is the most beautiful piece of music ever written. Though she admits it's a matter of taste."

"She's got good taste," whispered Frank. "Makes me think of a bird, soaring through the sky."

Mike nodded. *The Lark Ascending*, by Ralph Vaughan Williams, had been inspired by the composer's own beloved English countryside. But it filled the air over central Germany as if it belonged there.

"As it does," said Mike softly. "As it does. Here—and everywhere."

He turned his head, looking to the east. There, somewhere under the rising sun less than a hundred miles away, his wife would be in their kitchen. Rebecca was an early riser. Mike knew that she would have already prepared breakfast for her beloved father, even though she was moving more slowly these days due to her pregnancy. The German family which had once lived in Mike's house had found new lodgings, and Balthazar had moved in with them. He and Mike's invalid mother got along well, and Balthazar wanted to spend the rest of his days watching his grandchild grow up.

"Here—and everywhere," Mike repeated. His voice was very soft, and very loving.

The Lark Ascending faded away. Frank cleared his throat. The sound was regretful. More like a sigh than anything else.

"They won't surrender," he said. "Not yet."

Mike shook his head abruptly, banishing thoughts of love and tranquility.

"No, they won't," he said harshly. He turned to face the castle. "But I don't think it'll take much. Just a touch of the fire."

As it happens, Mike had misjudged. Rebecca had risen much earlier than usual, that day. Melissa had asked her to come to the school early that morning, to discuss something before classes started.

So, at the very moment when Mike ordered the catapults to start firing again, Rebecca was walking along Route 250. She had just left the outskirts of the town and was enjoying the solitude and the tranquility of early morning.

Others were *not* enjoying the morning.

When Jeff awoke, he discovered that his fever had broken. But he still felt lousy. His whole body ached.

Gretchen came into the bedroom, carrying a bowl of porridge. She was already dressed, wearing, as always, her beloved blue jeans and sneakers.

"Eat," she commanded, driving down her husband's protest. "You will need your strength today." She smiled. "You'll have to fend for yourself until evening. I promised Dan Frost I'd help teach his new batch of recruits."

Gretchen's smile twisted, became slightly derisive. "German girls! Still don't really believe a woman can use a gun."

Jeff had wondered why Gretchen was wearing her bodice and vest. She usually preferred a simple blouse, especially in warm weather. He eyed the heavy garments, looking for the pistol. He couldn't spot it. Gretchen's pregnancy was still not showing in her belly. But Jeff thought it was definitely showing itself in her already impressive bust.

It was a happy thought. Gaily, Gretchen slapped his head. "And stop staring at my tits! What a scandal!"

❖   ❖   ❖

Four hundred West Gothlanders, Finns and Lapps were also not happy that morning. Captain Gars had roused his little army long before daybreak, and driven them ever since. The pace he was setting, on horseback through an unknown forest, varied between recklessness and downright insanity.

But they uttered no protest. There would have been no point. Captain Gars was not one to listen to the voice of caution, and he had a will of iron.

A madman. It was well known.

The car pulled up alongside Rebecca. James leaned out of the window. "Want a ride?"

Smiling, Rebecca turned. "Good morning, James. Melissa." When she spotted Julie Sims, sitting in the back seat, her smiled widened. Not too much, she hoped. "Julie." Rebecca shook her head. "No, thank you. I am enjoying the walk."

James nodded. He had expected the answer. As one of the town's two doctors who could drive a car, James was exempt from the ban on private motor vehicle operation. He always drove Melissa to school and would spend the morning there attending to the medical needs of the students. Often enough, he had passed Rebecca walking alongside the road, offered a ride, and had the offer declined. Rebecca liked to walk.

"See you later, then."

As the car pulled away and disappeared around a bend in the road, Rebecca's smile became a wide grin. Now that Julie could no longer see her, she made no attempt to hide her amusement.

Poor girl! So frantic, when there is so little need.

Julie, she knew, would have spent the night at Melissa's house. In her anxiety over her unexpected pregnancy, Julie would have gone to Melissa for advice and comfort, talking so late into the night that Melissa would have invited her to sleep over.

Melissa and James' house, now. The doctor had moved in with her months ago. The prim and proper schoolteacher was making no attempt any longer to disguise their relationship. And if that indiscretion scandalized the town's more prudish residents—not to mention the bigots—it had the opposite effect on others. Over the months, Melissa Mailey's status among her students and former students—especially the girls—had undergone a sea change. She had become something of a surrogate mother. Or, perhaps, a beloved aunt. Relaxed, confident, serene—*approachable*, in a way the schoolmarm had never been. Her house had become a haven and a refuge for such.

Rebecca resumed her morning promenade, still smiling. James had grumbled to her, once, that he sometimes felt he was living in a boarding home for wayward girls. But Rebecca had not missed the warmth and affection under the gruffness. Julie, she knew, was a particular favorite of his. Last night was not the first time she had slept on the couch in their living room.

Rebecca made her slow way along the side of the road, full of good cheer. Even her waddle pleased her. She would be glad enough, of course, to resume her former svelte figure when the time came. But for all things there is a season. She was looking forward to being a mother.

She breathed in the clean air. A line from one of her father's favorite plays came to her. It fit her mood to perfection. So much so that she shouted it gaily to the hills around her:

"*O brave new world, that hath such people in it!*"

After he finished his breakfast, Jeff rose from the bed. He was feeling a bit energetic himself. He was sick of being sick, and wanted to *do* something. Anything.

Staring out of the trailer's kitchen window, his eyes fell on the dirt bike parked outside. Grew thoughtful.

The decision came within seconds. He wasn't foolish enough to try riding in rough terrain, as poorly as he still felt. But a little spin would do him some good. He scurried about and got dressed for the occasion, not forgetting the leather jacket.

By the time he went out the door, he had already decided on his destination. The school was only two miles away, a quick and easy run on the best road in the world. Jeff thought it would be nice to drop in on Ms. Mailey. Just to say hello, before he came back to his cursed sickbed. Why not? Dr. Nichols had told Gretchen that he wouldn't be infectious anymore.

He had already straddled the bike when he remembered something. For a moment, scowling, he almost decided to leave it behind. Rules and discipline be damned!

Habit dies hard. The bike was now, officially, the property of the U.S. army. Jeff was a soldier in that army, even if he was usually on detached duty working with Gretchen and her less-than-official underground. But he was still required to carry a firearm when using a military vehicle.

Better safe than sorry. Some busybody might spot him. Jeff hurried back into the trailer, got the shotgun, and stuck it into the bike's saddle-holster. An instant later he was roaring off, enjoying the breeze.

On the steep slope above Route 250, hidden in the trees, four Croat horsemen stared at the road below. They were the advance scouts for the oncoming imperial cavalry, send ahead to study the approaches.

There had been a half dozen of them, in the beginning. But now that the town's layout and the school had been examined, two had already returned to report. The others had been about to follow. But then, spotting movement on the road, they had moved forward to investigate.

One of the horsemen took his eyes off the woman and scanned the road. "She's alone," he murmured.

One of his companions nodded. The gesture was quick, eager. "A Jew bitch too, by the look of her." His hand fondled the hilt of his saber. "Two for one," he chuckled savagely. "We can spill her big belly after we're done."

Chapter 55

"Light 'em up!" commanded Ferrara. His words were carried over the radio to all three catapults. Almost simultaneously, three cannisters were flung into the air. Propelled by the relatively gentle motion of the catapults—gentle, at least, compared to a cannon—the cannisters soared through the sky in a looping trajectory. The catapults had been specifically designed for this purpose. The fragile cannisters could not withstand the shock of gunpowder—and nobody wanted to be in the vicinity when their contents were spilled.

The missiles cleared the walls of the castle with no difficulty. The timed fuses went off just before the cannisters landed. Each cannister contained five gallons of napalm. Hellfire erupted across the fortifications and the thousands of soldiers huddled within.

Greek fire was back—with a vengeance.

"Fire at will!" shouted Ferrara. The next round of napalm was lobbed a bit more raggedly. The three different crews had practiced with the devices, but there was a slight difference in their proficiency. Again, hellfire spread across the battlements of the castle. By now, the upper fortifications were a raging inferno.

A man appeared on the walls, burning like a torch. It was impossible to tell, from the distance, whether he committed suicide or simply stumbled to his death from sheer agony.

Watching, Mike winced. He could already hear the swelling shrieks of the Spanish soldiers burning to death inside the castle.

"That is some nasty shit," muttered Frank. "Been so long I'd half forgotten."

A new voice came over the radio, instantly recognizable. Hilda was the only German woman who had so far enlisted in the U.S. army and made it past Frank's screening. Since her English was good, if heavily accented, she had been assigned to serve as a radio operator.

"The main gate is opening! Main gate is opening!"

Mike raised his binoculars. Sure enough, he could see the heavy gate starting to swing aside. A moment later, waving pikes and arquebuses, a mob of Spanish soldiers surged through.

That gate was the only entrance to the castle from which large bodies of men could issue quickly. For that reason, Frank had positioned the M-60 to cover it. The men manning the machine gun didn't wait for orders. There was no need. Frank's instructions had been crystal clear: *If they come out armed, kill 'em.*

The M-60 stutter-stutter-stuttered. The packed mob of soldiers were cut down as if by a scythe. Stutter-stutter, stutter-stutter. Stutter-stutter-stutter.

Mike lowered the binoculars and looked away. In less than a minute, the M-60 had left a small hill of bodies. The gate was almost blocked by the corpses. The Spaniards who survived had stumbled back into the castle.

He watched another cannister of napalm explode over the battlements. The entire castle now resembled a bonfire. The resemblance was an illusion, more than a reality. The Wartburg was stone, not wood, and the lower levels of the castle would still be untouched by the flames.

An illusion—so far. Even stone castles will burn, if given enough of a start. Not the walls themselves, of course. But all castles are full of flammable substances. Wooden beams, furniture, tapestries, textiles—with enough napalm, the interior of the castle would be a firestorm within an hour. Nothing at all would survive. Over ten thousand men, thinking they had found a haven, had discovered instead a hideous deathtrap.

Mike opened his mouth, about to issue the command to cease fire. Then, seeing Frank's cold eyes on him, he fell silent.

No choice. The Spanish army trapped in the Wartburg still outnumbered the U.S. forces by a large margin. Until they surrendered— marched out, unarmed—Mike could not afford to ease up the pressure. So, tightening his jaws, he said nothing.

Burn and burn and burn. The first men started popping out of the castle; stumbling through a multitude of exits, even scrambling down the walls. Most of them were unarmed. The few who still carried weapons dropped them quickly enough, when they heard the voices shouting at them in Spanish. They had no thought but survival—anything to escape the holocaust which the Wartburg had become.

Now, dozens of unarmed Spaniards started pouring out of the main gate, pushing aside the mound of corpses by sheer weight of numbers. Then hundreds.

"It's done," said Frank. Mike nodded and gestured at Ferrara. A moment later, Ferrara passed along the order. The catapults stopped firing.

Mike stared at the burning castle. There was no way to stop the conflagration now. By the next day, the Wartburg would be a gutted ruin.

He tried to find humor somewhere. Whimsy, at least. "You know," he mused, "that's probably a historical monument, in the world we came from. Makes you feel a little guilty, doesn't it?"

"Not me," snorted Frank. "A castle is a castle is a castle. Just a robbers' den, far as I'm concerned. Thieves braggin' about their thievin' great-grandfathers. Good riddance to the whole lot."

Mike didn't know whether to laugh or sigh. In the end, he laughed.

"What can I say? You're right."

When Rebecca saw the horsemen charging out of the trees, her jaw dropped. Sharp terror held her frozen. Part of her mind was paralyzed, but the rest had no difficulty understanding what was about to happen. The grinning savages racing their horses down the slope were not even bothering to unsheathe their sabers. They would keep her alive, for a while.

Rebecca Abrabanel, the Sephardic maiden of a year ago, would have still been standing in the road, petrified with terror, when the Croats took her down. The Becky Stearns of the present, heavy with child, was rummaging in her large handbag within seconds, whispering thanks to her hillbilly husband.

Mike had insisted that she learn to use a gun. Obediently, Rebecca had tried. Tried, and failed. Failed, at least, insofar as accuracy was concerned. Whatever her other qualities, even her husband had finally agreed that she couldn't hit the broad side of a barn.

So be it. There are guns for barns, too. Harry Lefferts had been delighted to provide her with one. "A gift for a pretty lady," he called it, with Appalachian gallantry.

When the first Croat was ten yards away, Rebecca hauled the sawed-off shotgun out of the handbag. At five yards, she cut loose with the first barrel.

Five yards, with a sawed-off twelve gauge loaded with buckshot.

She missed. Completely. Didn't even scratch him.

The *horse*, on the other hand, was killed instantly. The pellets ripped the beast's throat wide open. Its legs buckled, spilling the rider.

An animal as big as a horse, moving at that speed, has too much momentum to be stopped by any handheld firearm. Squawling with anger and fear, Rebecca managed to dodge the horse. But her now-ungainly figure could not avoid the rider. He plummeted into her shoulder, knocking her to the pavement.

The impact dazed her, but she managed to hold onto the shotgun. Lying half-sprawled on the road, she shook her head. Her long black hair spilled loose and free. For a moment, her only thought was a sharp fear for her unborn child.

That fear was driven out by another. She felt a hand seize her hair. An instant later, with a vicious jerk, she was hauled to her feet.

Off her feet. The Croat was a powerful man, and filled with rage. He didn't quite understand what had happened to his comrade, but he had no doubt who was responsible. He started hauling Rebecca onto the saddle.

"Fucking Jew-bitch!" he shrieked.

Rebecca didn't understand his language. She didn't need to. She still had the shotgun.

The Croat's fury fled, then. Replaced, not by fear but simple astonishment. He stared at the hard object pressed into his groin. He had time to recognize it as a firearm of some kind, before Rebecca pulled the trigger and blew his testicles off. Along with his penis, his lower intestinal tract, his bladder, and a portion of his spine.

Her hair released, Rebecca collapsed back onto the pavement. She landed on her posterior. Again, the impact dazed her a bit—and then, flattened by the leg of her victim's skittering horse, she was momentarily stunned. Her eyes were still open, and she could see. But her mind could not process the data.

She saw that the horseman on the other side was blinded, his face splattered with blood and flesh. The Croat was clawing at his face, trying to clean away the gore. Out of action, for the moment.

The first horseman, the one whose mount she had killed, was just starting to move, groaning. Also out of action, for the moment.

The other Croat, the last of the four, was not. He was preoccupied, true, bringing his startled horse under control. But the mount was a warhorse, accustomed to the sound and flash of battle. The Croat reined him in. Then, snarling at Rebecca, drew a wheel-lock pistol from its saddle holster. He was not thinking of rape, any longer. He was just going to kill the Jew-bitch.

Rebecca still had the shotgun in her hand, but both barrels had been fired. She twisted on her hip, desperately searching the pavement. There were more shells in her handbag. When she spotted it, lying by the side of the road, she was flooded with despair.

Too far. She could hear the clatter of the Croat's horse, as he guided it toward her. He was about to shoot. Despair was washed aside by simple sadness. *I so enjoyed my life.*

Her mind grew dull, now that there was no hope. The adrenaline was wearing off, and she had taken a brutal hammering. She was simply waiting, like a stunned ox, for the sound of the final gunshot. She was so dazed that she never noticed the much louder sound that was filling the road.

The Croat did, however. He was no longer even thinking about Rebecca. He was just staring at the bizarre vehicle racing toward him.

Fury unleashed. *Chooser of the slain.*

Now, it was a savage horseman's turn to be frozen in place. It was not the mount itself which produced that terror, but the man atop it. The Croat had never encountered spectacles on a killer. *The better to see you with.*

When Jeff heard the first gunshot, he was simply puzzled. Puzzled, and a bit outraged. That had been a shotgun. Twelve gauge, by the sound of it.

What idiot's firing a shotgun by the side of the road? he wondered. *The school buses will be coming through any minute!*

The second shot went off just as he was rounding the bend, and everything became clear at once. He didn't recognize the woman lying on the road, nor did he recognize the horsemen. Not Scots, for sure, but who they were he did not know.

Nor did it matter. The uncertain boy he had once been, not so very long ago, had done well enough on his first battlefield. That boy was gone, long gone. Replaced by a man who was no longer a stranger to violence. And, perhaps more important, was married to a woman whose soul was tempered steel. Not married for long, true. But more than long enough for Gretchen to have rubbed off. Mercy be damned.

He raced down the final stretch. He saw one horseman firing his wheel lock at him. Jeff had no idea where the bullet went.

At the last second, he almost laid the bike down bringing it to a skidding stop. The horses, terrified by the strange noise and sight, whinnied and skittered. The two men still mounted were completely preoccupied with staying in the saddle.

Almost leisurely, Jeff dismounted and drew the shotgun. The magazine was full, loaded with slugs. He glanced at the woman, and recognized her immediately. He held out his hand, palm down, and made a little patting motion.

"Stay down, Becky!"

The man on the ground was rising to his feet. Jeff decided to take him out first. He pumped a round into the chamber and brought the shotgun to his shoulder in one easy motion.

Clickety—boom! The Croat was back on the pavement, dead before he landed.

The two men still on horseback had brought their mounts under control. The one who had fired at him earlier was drawing a new wheel lock. The other already had one in his hand.

Jeff grinned, as savagely as might Harry Lefferts. "It's called rate of fire, motherfuckers!"

Clickety—boom! Clickety—boom!

Two bodies landed on the asphalt with sodden thumps. The horses raced off. Jeff glanced at Rebecca to make sure she was unhurt. She smiled feebly, then lowered her head. He decided she would keep, until he made sure of the enemy.

He strode toward the men lying on the highway. One of them was clearly dead. The slug had blown his chest apart. The other—

Jeff wasn't quite sure. Mercy be damned. *Clickety—boom!*

He turned away and hurried toward Rebecca. By the time he reached her, she was starting to rise. Then, she collapsed back to her knees.

Now deeply concerned, Jeff tilted her face up. Rebecca's dark eyes seemed very wide. Dazed looking. He thought she was in shock. She was mumbling something, but he couldn't make out the words.

Jeff hesitated, unsure what to do. She needed medical attention, clearly enough. The closest place for it was the school, not half a mile away. And Dr. Nichols would already be there. He and Melissa always showed up early in the morning. But how was he to get Rebecca there? She was obviously in no condition to walk.

For a moment, longingly, Jeff looked at his bike. Then shook his head. In Rebecca's dazed state, that would be sheer folly. She'd fall off, sure as shooting.

Again, she mumbled something. This time, he understood the words.

"Stop the buses," she was saying. "Stop the buses."

Jeff's uncertainty vanished. Of course! The school buses would be passing through any minute. They'd be jampacked, of course, as many kids as there were in town nowadays. But room could certainly be made.

He half-helped, half-hauled Rebecca to the side of the road. She was shaking her head, still mumbling: "Stop the buses, stop the buses." Then, after covering her with his jacket—you were supposed to do that with people in shock, he knew—Jeff hesitated again. What else should he do, besides wait for the buses?

His eyes fell on the bodies littering the road. "The kids don't need to see *that*," he muttered. Quickly, he went over to his bike and rolled it to the side. Then, he hauled the bodies off the pavement and rolled them down the far slope toward the creek. Not completely out of sight, but as close as he could manage in the time available.

As he was finishing with the last corpse, he heard the sound of the first bus approaching. He scrambled up the bank and lunged into the road, waving his arms. His efforts were wasted, however. The bus was already coming to a stop. The driver had spotted Rebecca on the side of the road.

Hurriedly, Jeff lifted her up and half-carried her to the bus. The driver had opened the door and was calling at the children to move back, make room. As Jeff heaved Rebecca onto the step leading into the bus, she held out a hand and tried—feebly—to block him. "No, no," she mumbled. *"Stop the buses."*

Jeff shook his head. The gesture combined worry with amusement. "Boy, are you out of it! I *did* stop the bus, Rebecca. I'm putting you on right now."

Still, she tried to block him. But Jeff was having none of it. "She needs to see a doctor—*now!*" He carried her into the bus by main force and set her on a seat made vacant by the driver.

"Get her to Doc Nichols right away," Jeff ordered, ignoring the driver's babbled questions. "I'll explain later."

He hopped out of the bus, turned, and waved his arm vigorously. *Move, goddamit!*

The driver obeyed. The door closed with a hiss and the bus rumbled into motion. Jeff hurried over to his bike. By the time he started it up, a line of buses was coming down the road from town. He preceded them into the school's parking lot as if he were leading a parade.

As hundreds of schoolchildren started pouring off the buses, Jeff plunged through the entrance. Half running, he made his way through the corridors. He was at the clinic less than a minute after parking his bike.

Rebecca was already there, perched on an examination table, with Nichols in front of her. Jeff's leather jacket was draped over a nearby chair. As he started pulling it back on, Jeff heard someone behind him. He glanced back and saw that Ed Piazza and Len Trout were coming through the door, their faces full of concern. Trout had replaced Piazza as the school's principal months ago, given Ed's general responsibilities. But, at his insistence, Piazza had kept using his old office.

The driver, Jeff realized, must have spotted the bodies. Not to mention the blood and gore all over the highway. He would have charged right into the principal's office and told them.

But, for the moment, Jeff's concern was all for Rebecca. He turned back. To his surprise, he saw that she was staring at him. He was even more surprised to see that the dazed look was gone. Instead, her eyes were filling with tears.

"Oh, Jeff," she said softly, "why did you not *stop the buses*?"

His face must have shown his confusion. Rebecca shook her head sadly. "I wanted to send them all back to town, where they would be safe."

Jeff's jaw started to sag. Rebecca wiped the tears away with a trembling hand. Then, straightened her shoulders.

"Never mind," she said firmly. Her eyes were now dark with purpose. Not dazed in the least. "What is past is past."

Startled by the iron in her voice, Nichols stood erect. Rebecca glanced at him, then Piazza, then Trout.

Her eyes came back to Jeff. For a moment, they softened. "Thank you for saving my life, Jeffrey Higgins. Now, we must see to the lives of the children."

"Oh, Jesus," whispered Jeff.

Rebecca nodded. "Yes. They will be coming soon."

Captain Gars took his eyes off the trail for a moment, glancing at the sky. It was a very brief glance. Driving a horse down such a trail required concentration.

"Now," he growled. "They'll be starting the attack now." He cocked his head, shouting at the men following.

"Faster!"

Chapter 56

As she watched Julie's energetic rearranging of the chairs in her classroom, Melissa Mailey found herself laughing.

Julie's head popped up. "What's so funny?" she demanded. Then, seeing the way Melissa was looking at her: "You're laughing at me!"

Melissa brought fingers to her lips and forced silence upon herself. "Am not," she mumbled.

"Are too!"

As she studied the aggrieved expression on Julie's face, Melissa tried to think of a way to explain. A way that would make sense to an eighteen-year-old who was only a few months removed from being a schoolgirl. It was difficult. Melissa wasn't sure that anyone under the age of fifty could understand it. But she decided to try.

"I just thought it was funny, seeing the eager way you were helping me. When I remembered how hard it was to get you—*any* of you—to do the same thing when you were still in school."

To Melissa's surprise, Julie understood at once. The young woman's face broke into a smile. "Oh. That's not so hard to figure out. Back then you were Miz Mailey. Today you're—" The smile became very shy. "Now you're *Melissa*."

Melissa Mailey tried to fight down a sudden surge of maternal warmth. Tried and failed. Her eyes started to tear. In what seemed an instant, Julie was across the room and hugging her.

"I like you so much better this way," Julie whispered.

Melissa returned the hug with one of her own. "So do I," she said softly. "So do I, Julie."

For a few seconds, Melissa treasured the embrace. She had no children of her own, and never would. But, since James Nichols had come into her life, she had found herself changing in ways she would never have imagined. Her view of the world was still the same, at bottom, but it was so much less—*brittle*. After half a lifetime living among West Virginians, Melissa Mailey had finally adopted them for her own.

Melissa stroked Julie's hair. "Don't worry about Alex," she murmured. "I keep telling you—"

She broke off. Tensed. The sound of babbling voices—frightened voices—was coming from the corridor outside the classroom.

Julie heard also. She straightened and turned her head. "What's going on?"

James Nichols surged into the room. He gave Melissa a quick smile, but his eyes were focused on Julie.

"Can you handle a .30-06 semiautomatic?" he demanded. "We've got two of them, but they're the only rifles in the whole damned school."

Melissa gasped. So did Julie. Melissa's gasp came from shock. Julie's, from sheer outrage.

"Is that a *joke*? I can shoot anything!"

James Nichols was, by nature, a smiling man. It was one of the reasons Melissa loved him. But she had never seen such an incredible grin on his face. "Those poor bastards," he laughed. "Did they ever pick the wrong day to piss off pregnant women!"

The steel pillars holding up the weather awning in front of the school's main entrance were not really load-bearing structures. The bus knocked them aside like so many sticks. By the time Jeff slammed on the brakes and brought the bus to a halt, the awning had collapsed onto the bus' roof.

Jeff didn't bother removing the keys from the ignition. Even if they got into the bus, the Croats wouldn't know how to drive it. He hopped out and took a quick look at his handiwork. It didn't take him more than a few seconds to decide that the main entrance was almost completely blocked off.

Good enough. They'll pay hell, trying to charge through a school bus.

The bus gave a little lurch. The driver of the next bus wasn't taking any chances on leaving gaps. He had deliberately bumped his bus into the rear of the one Jeff had positioned in front of the door.

A moment later, the same bump was repeated. Repeated again. The drivers of the third and fourth buses were doing the same. Then the fifth driver, and the sixth.

But Jeff didn't wait to see the results. He plunged through the big doors of the entrance and raced toward the principal's office. Rebecca had set up her HQ there, despite the relatively cramped space, in order to take advantage of the communication facilities in the school's administration center.

When he charged into the office, Rebecca was talking on the telephone.

"One moment, Dan," she said calmly. Rebecca raised her head, eyes questioning.

"We're set!" said Jeff.

Rebecca nodded and resumed her conversation. "We have now blocked off the entire front of the school with a line of buses. We shall be doing the same with the rear entrances. The students and faculty in the technical center are moving equipment to block the entrance to their building. That will leave only the glassed-in walkway between the school itself and the technical center as an easy access route. We have no way of blocking that, but we will try to improvise obstructions on the inside."

She fell silent, listening to something the police chief was saying. Then: "No. We are evacuating the auditorium completely. We will collect as many students as possible in the classrooms on the second floor. But there is not enough space for all of them, so we will put the older students in the gymnasium."

Again, she fell silent for a few seconds. Then: "Not much, Dan. Two rifles. Eleven pistols and revolvers in the personal possession of teachers. And Jeff has his shotgun and—"

She gave him a questioning glance. Quickly, Jeff flashed his fingers. "He says he has fourteen rounds left."

She paused, listening to something Dan was saying. Jeff could hear Dan's loud voice coming over the telephone, ringing in her ear. *Grarr! Grarr! Grarr!*

Rebecca shrugged. "Yes, I know. It is a pitiful arsenal. A stupid oversight on our part. In the future, we shall certainly do otherwise. But we have nothing else at the moment, except"—her lips quirked—"a plentiful assortment of kitchen utensils and baseball bats."

Suddenly, Jeff saw Rebecca stiffen. "No! Dan—you cannot! They will certainly be attacking the town also. Until we know where the attack is concentrated, it would be pure folly for you to bring an expedition here. These are *Croats*, Dan. The best light cavalry in the imperial army. They will not line up for you neatly like a tercio. If they see you coming, they will set an ambush. They will swarm any caravan of vehicles on the open road. And you do not have any APCS. They are all with the army in Eisenach. Wheel-lock pistols are quite capable of butchering people trapped in an automobile. And if you emerge, you will be sabered and lanced. As long as we are behind walls—here as well as in town—we have a chance."

Grarrgrarrgrarr.

"Dan, that is stupid! *Think.* What good is a rescue attempt that never arrives? You will all die for nothing. What you must do is smash the Croats attacking the town *first.* Then you can send a rescue expedition."

Grarrgrarrgrarr.

Rebecca's lips tightened. "Dan—listen to me! They are coming— *now.* Get off the telephone—*now.* See to the town! We will hold them off here as long as possible. Do not make any attempt to rescue us until you have defeated the Croats in the town!"

With a motion as decisive as her voice, she placed the telephone back on its cradle. Immediately, she turned to Jeff.

"The most dangerous place will be the gymnasium. We will not be able to keep the Croats out of the ground floor of the building for very long. The buses will slow them down, and make a mass charge impossible, but—"

Jeff nodded. "They'll smash in the windows to the cafeteria, first thing. There's enough space between the buses and the wall to move single file. Once they're in the cafeteria, all bets are off."

He glanced at the large vestibule beyond the administration office. The door to the cafeteria led directly into it. From there, the enemy would be able to reach the gymnasium as well as the administration center itself. To reach the classrooms on the second floor, they would have to use the stairwells. Jeff could hear the clattering sound of desks and cabinets being moved into place, blocking those access routes. The obstructions could be removed, but there were enough sidearms—and the two rifles in the hands of James and Julie—to make that a bloody business for cavalrymen trying to force their way up a flight of stairs.

But there was no way to block the gymnasium, beyond locking the heavy doors. The doors and locks were solidly built, true. Impossible to break through simply with shoulders or boots. But the Croats would smash them in soon enough. There were simply too many ways they could improvise a battering ram.

Jeff grimaced ruefully. He had provided them with battering rams himself, he realized, by knocking down the pillars supporting the weather awning. He drove the thought aside. *The fog of war,* Clausewitz called it. The friction of a battlefield, where actions produced unintended consequences.

"Will do," he announced firmly. He hefted the shotgun. "This is the best weapon for that area, once they break in."

He gave Rebecca a stern look. "You're going upstairs. *Now.*"

She nodded. "Yes. I had thought to remain here, where we have communications—"

"No way, Rebecca! Once they break through, this office is a death trap!"

Ed and Len Trout charged in. Both of them were holding pistols. "They're coming!" shouted Piazza. "From the north, over the ridge. One of the kids just spotted them."

"Hundreds of 'em," growled Trout. "Over a thousand, probably."

Ed marched forward and took Rebecca by the arm. "Let's *go*. You're going upstairs, young lady—this second!"

Unresisting, Rebecca allowed herself to be led away. Her eyes remained on Jeff. Soft, dark, gleaming with sorrow and apology. She had condemned him to death, and knew it.

He gave her a cheerful grin. Made the attempt, anyway.

"Relax, Becky! It'll be okay." He propped the butt of the shotgun on his hip and tried to assume his best Clint Eastwood spaghetti Western imitation. The good, the bad and the ugly—all rolled into one. With spectacles.

Rebecca's eyes teared. "Hidalgo, true and pure," she blessed him.

Once they left the office, Piazza gently handed Rebecca over to Trout.

"Get her upstairs, Len. I'll stay with Jeff and the kids in the gymnasium."

"*No.*"

Ed was startled. He stared up at the tall, balding figure of the school's former vice-principal. Trout was glaring down at him.

"I'm the principal of this school now, Ed, not you." He jerked his head toward the stairs. "Upstairs. Becky and the teachers will need you up there."

Jeff was emerging from the office. Trout started walking toward him. Over his shoulder, repeated in words of iron: "*Upstairs, Mr. Piazza.*"

Ed stared at him, his mouth half open. Rebecca placed her hands on his shoulders, turned him, and started moving him toward the stairs.

"Come along, Edward." She managed a little smile. "We are in a school, you know. We dare not disobey the principal."

Piazza's mouth was still open when Jeff and Len Trout entered the gymnasium. A moment later, hearing the heavy locks sliding into place, he closed his lips. "Jesus Christ," he whispered. "I've known Len Trout for twenty years."

The sentence was like an epitaph.

"We'll give the bastards another Matewan," Dan snarled. "With cherries on top."

He pointed to the bridge over Buffalo Creek. The bridge was now blocked off by one of the school buses which served the town as its public transportation. "Get the recruits over there, Gretchen. You stay with them, you hear? As long as you're there, they won't lose heart."

Gretchen nodded and started bellowing orders. A few seconds later, her 9mm gripped in her hand, she was leading the young Germans who were being trained as new police officers onto the bridge. There were eighteen of them, four of whom were female. All of them were armed with shotguns and revolvers and, like Dan and Gretchen, were wearing bullet-proof vests.

The bridge and the three-way intersection next to it was the center of Grantville. The intersection formed something in the way of a small plaza. The buildings on all sides were two and three stories tall. People were still pouring into those buildings from all the houses and trailers on the north side. Many of the men and some of the women were carrying rifles and other firearms.

Fortunately, Rebecca's warning had come in time to evacuate the part of town directly in the path of the oncoming Croats. It had also enabled the police force to organize the citizens into an impromptu militia. True, most of the able-bodied men and women were with the army in Eisenach or Suhl, but there were still plenty of people who could use a gun—especially firing from within buildings. Rebecca's plan still grated Dan Frost's soul, but he had bowed to the logic of it.

The police chief turned to Fred Jordan, one of his deputies. Before he even asked, Fred was answering. "They're all in place, Dan." Jordan swept his outstretched hand in a half-circle, indicating the buildings lining the intersection. "Got deputies in every one. They'll organize the other people with guns. Biggest problem we're having is keeping the hotheads from charging right off to the school."

Dan nodded. He studied the intersection for a few seconds. "Good enough. All we need is something to draw their attention and suck 'em into the ambush."

He was already marching toward the intersection before he finished speaking. For a moment, Fred was rooted in place. Then, realizing what the chief intended, he started hurrying after him.

Hearing his steps, Dan turned around. "Get out of here, Fred," he said quietly. "Take position in one of the buildings. We don't need two people for this."

Fred started to squawk a protest, but Dan waved him down impatiently. "Do as I tell you, dammit!" His face twisted into a wry grin. "As long as this town seems bound and determined to make me Wyatt Earp, I may as well do it up right."

Lowering the radio, Mike's face was ashen. "Oh, Christ. We've been *suckered.*"

Frank Jackson, Harry Lefferts and Alex Mackay were gathered around him. Frank turned his head and glared at the Spanish prisoners being herded into a makeshift "prison camp." The camp was nothing more than a large stretch of farmland below the Wartburg's hill. The prisoners were held in place not by fences but by the crude expedient of guns pointing directly at them. Even the guns did not surround them completely. The area to the west of the prisoners was bare and open. But the three catapults were standing by, ready to lob hellfire into their midst in case of any trouble.

"All this?" Frank demanded. His voice was choked. "They sent an entire fucking *army*—just to get a clear shot at Grantville?"

Mike sighed. "Yes, Frank. That's exactly what they did. That—and the army that marched on Suhl. Just diversions, that's all."

Silently, Mike cursed himself for an incompetent fool. He glanced at Mackay. "It's not as if you didn't try to warn me," he muttered.

The Scottish colonel shook his head. "You are missing the point, Mike. The problem is not that you made a mistake." He pointed to the Spaniards. "That *is* an army. Had you not come here to meet them, they would have been no diversion at all. They would have sacked Eisenach and poured into Thuringia. And if Heinrich and Tom hadn't done the same in the south, Suhl would now be burning."

Half-angrily: "So what else could you do?"

Mike said nothing. Again, Mackay shook his head. "You must face a reality. You are simply too *small*, Mike. Half of Europe—no, two-thirds of it!—is now arrayed against you."

He jerked his head toward the prisoners. "The Spanish army is perhaps the most powerful in the world. On land, at least. If they ever get over their obsession with reconquering Holland, God help the rest of Europe." Pointing to the southeast. "And now Wallenstein has amassed that huge army outside Nürnberg. A hundred thousand men, he must have by now—a force equal to the population of Thuringia."

He shrugged. "And if you defeat all of them, then what? Can you march into Spain and Austria and crush the Habsburgs in their lair? And what about Richelieu, and the power of France? They are also now your enemies, clearly enough."

He waited. Mike was silent. Mackay moved his stare to Frank and Harry. They, too, said nothing.

"If you do not destroy the Habsburg dynasty—*and* the French, *and* the Papacy and the Poles and the Russians, for that matter—they will remain an ever-present threat. And you have no way of doing that. Before too long, the ammunition for the M-60 will be gone. Within a year, even with your capacity for reloading, you will run out of ammunition for your modern rifles. Long before the Habsburgs will run out of money and soldiers. Then what? How long can you hold

Europe at bay, even with *your* technology? The powers arrayed against you can *gear up* while you gear down—and they are immeasurably larger than you are."

Silence.

Mike heaved a sigh. "Yeah, Alex, I know. I've been thinking about it a lot, lately." He managed a rueful smile. "It's about all I think about, in fact."

"Well, think about it later," snapped Frank. "We've got today to deal with. What do you want to do?"

Frank's question broke through Mike's paralysis. He stared at the Spanish prisoners for a few seconds. Then:

"Let 'em go. All of them except the officers and the priests. We can keep those locked up in Eisenach for a few weeks. March the rest of them straight west for maybe ten miles and then send them on their way. Tell them we'll kill any who turn back."

Jackson started to protest but Mike waved him silent. "We haven't got time to mess around with them, Frank!"

Alex was nodding his agreement. "I can leave you Lennox and a few hundred cavalrymen to ride flank. The rest of my men and myself will start back to Grantville." He left unspoken the obvious: *Not that cavalry can get back in time to do any good.*

Mackay's support crystallized Mike's determination. "Right. Frank, you and the infantrymen stay here, until you're sure the Spaniards are gone for good. Harry, gather up the APCs and cram as many men into them as possible. We're heading back right now."

He glanced at his watch. "Even on that road, the APCs can make it back in three or four hours. So let's go!"

He left unspoken the obvious: *Not that three or four hours will be in time either.*

Chapter 57

Most of Grantville's residential areas were south of Buffalo Creek. The Croats had begun their approach to the town on that same side of the creek. But their commanders, wanting to maintain surprise, had crossed the creek miles downstream and circled to the north. There, in the uninhabited hills between the town, the school and the power plant, the imperial cavalry had been able to move unseen.

Almost unseen. They did encounter a small crew of tree trimmers, engaged in clearing foliage away from the power lines. Croat light cavalry were superb woodsmen, so the tree trimmers were caught by surprise. The three men in the crew were butchered within seconds. The cavalrymen were prepared to linger over the woman, but an officer arrived and demanded dispatch. For all their well-deserved savage reputation, the Croats were not undisciplined freebooters. They made only token protest before decapitating her.

Once they reached the northern outskirts of Grantville, the commanders of the cavalry detachment sent against the town—about a third of the entire force—ordered the charge. Whooping their war cries, seven hundred Croats began pouring through the small streets, lancing and sabering—

Three dogs, a cat, and Mrs. Flannery. As pigheaded and irascible as she had been throughout her eighty-one years of life, the widow had refused to evacuate. The Croats found her standing in her yard, shrieking the same imprecations at them which she had visited on her neighbors for decades. The cavalryman who cut her down even hesitated for five seconds, he was so bemused by the sight.

For a few minutes, the Croats' attack was delayed as the cavalrymen smashed into the deserted houses, looking for victims. *Kill everyone*, they had been told. *Especially Jews.*

The qualifier, as Wallenstein's officers had foretold, was pointless. The Croats had only the vaguest notion of how to distinguish Jews from gentiles, and they were not, in any event, a soldiery given to making fine distinctions. As far as they were concerned, the operative phrase was: *Kill everyone.*

But there was no one to kill.

"Empty—again!" barked the officer, as he led his men out of yet another house. His commanding officer was waiting on the street outside, perched on his horse. While the officer made a hurried report, his men amused themselves with vandalism. But even the vandalism was petty—smashed windows and sabered furniture—since the cavalrymen were under orders not to linger.

The commander's snarl was ferocious. "They've been warned." He pointed to the center of town, whose taller buildings were clearly visible not more than two hundred yards away. "But they can't have gotten far. Gather the troops!"

It was the work of another few minutes to round up the soldiers from their futile house-wrecking. By the time the Croats reassembled, several of the homes were starting to burn. But even the arson was petty. The cavalrymen had been expecting a lightning strike aimed at massacre. They had brought little in the way of incendiary supplies and were not given enough time to set proper fires.

"Charge!" the commander bellowed. The order was relayed to the separate detachments gathered in the streets. Seven hundred Croats pounded toward Grantville's center, shrieking with murderous fury.

The fifteen hundred Croats surrounding the school were also shrieking, but theirs was a frustrated fury. Coming down onto the school from the ridge to the north, they had found no easy access into the buildings. Nor had they expected any. Their scouts had already reported that the school's vulnerability was on the south side.

Then, after circling, the Croats discovered the buses blocking off the entrances. For a moment, they milled around in confusion, hundreds of horses stamping their hooves on unfamiliar pavement. Within a minute, the large parking lot south of the school was covered with soldiers, staring at the bizarre yellow contraptions barring their way.

The officers gathered in a knot around the general commanding the entire expedition. Angrily, the general was stroking his mustachioes, examining the unexpected barricade.

"There must be a gap!" he snarled. "Between those—those *things*—and the building. Dismount and—"

❧   ❧   ❧

James waited until the officers had gathered. He and Julie were positioned at the open window of a classroom on the second floor, facing to the south.

"I'll take the guy in the middle," he said, sighting down the barrel of the .30-06. "You take—"

Julie started firing. *Crackcrackcrackcrack.* By the time James took out the general—a perfect shot, right in the middle of the sniper's triangle—four of his officers were already dead.

Julie ejected the magazine and slapped in another. *Crackcrack.* Two more. *Crack.* Another.

The sole surviving officer spurred his horse into motion. It did him no good at all. Julie tracked him for not more than a second.

Crack.

"Jesus Christ," whispered James. He turned his head and stared at the girl next to him.

She responded with a glare. As she started reloading her rifle, she chanted in a little singsong: "'Can you handle a .30-06 semiautomatic, Ju-lie?'"

Nichols grinned. He extended his own rifle to her. "Tell you what, Julie. Why don't you do the shooting and let me reload for you?"

"Good idea," she growled.

Captain Gars heard the first shots just before he reached the road. A wide road, it was, paved with some peculiar substance. Perfectly flat. The finest road he had ever seen in his life.

He turned his head to the northwest, listening. Anders Jönsson drew his horse alongside.

"Not far," stated Anders. Captain Gars nodded. He reached down and seized the hilt of his saber in a huge hand. Anders sighed. The captain, obviously enough, had no intention whatsoever of using his wheel-lock pistols. Saber, as always.

The rest of the Swedish cavalry was pouring onto the road. Captain Gars drew his saber and lifted it high. *"Gott mit uns!"* he bellowed, and spurred his horse into a gallop.

Within less than a minute, four hundred West Gothlanders, Finns and Lapps were thundering down what had once been—and was still named—U.S. Route 250. Heading west, following a madman.

"Gott mit uns!"

"Haakaa päälle!"

The Croats hit Grantville's downtown like a log hits a saw.

As soon as his horse debouched onto the main street, the commander spotted the figure of a lone man in the plaza to the east. The man was standing still, facing them. One hand was holding an object—a weapon, perhaps—while the other was planted on his hip. He seemed to be wearing some sort of uniform, with an odd-looking breastplate, and his hat had a certain "official" air about it.

The open target was irresistible, after the frustration of the past quarter of an hour. The commander drew his wheel lock and waved it forward. "Attack!"

As he led the charge, some part of the commander's mind noted that the entrances to the buildings had all been blocked off by various means. The sight filled him with good cheer. Blocked doors meant that people were hiding inside. Like chickens in a coop, waiting for slaughter.

Dan hefted the pistol in his hand, watching the oncoming cavalrymen. For a moment, he was tempted to draw the weapon in his holster and shoot two-handed. The notion appealed to his sense of history. Sid Hatfield, by all accounts, had fought so at Matewan. A weapon in each hand, as he gunned down the company goons from the Baldwin-Felts detective agency.

Firmly, he suppressed the notion. True, family legend claimed that Sid Hatfield, the sheriff who led the coal miners in their shoot-out with the company goons at Matewan, had been a distant relative. But Dan was skeptical of the tale. Practically everyone he knew claimed to be related to the Hatfield clan, the West Virginia half of the famous Hatfield–McCoy feud.

Still, Dan was tempted. Whether or not Sid Hatfield was a blood relative, he was most certainly an ancestral spirit. Company goons or Croats, his town was under attack.

But that was in the old days, when police officers were not really professionals. So Dan resisted the amateurish whimsy, and brought up the .40-caliber automatic in a proper two-handed grip. The first line of horsemen was forty yards away.

The first wheel locks were discharged at him. Dan ignored the shots. As inaccurate as the weapons were, especially on a galloping horse, he would only be hit by blind chance.

As he started squeezing the trigger, Dan forced another thought out of his mind. That was a much more difficult struggle. Dan disapproved strongly of cruelty to animals, and he was especially fond of horses. Still—

Professional.

He emptied the twelve-round clip, methodically mowing down the horses in the front of the charge. Most of his shots struck the cavalry mounts in the chest or throat, killing several of them outright. Even those horses that were only wounded stumbled and fell, spilling themselves and their riders. Then other horses, uninjured by bullets, began stumbling over the corpses. Within half a minute, the charge had piled up like water hitting a dam.

Long before those thirty seconds expired, however, the street had become a charnel house. As soon as Dan's first shot went off, the deputies and armed citizens in the upstairs windows began firing their weapons. The range was point-blank, and the street below was packed with horsemen. Due to their excitement and fear, many of the citizens—and not a few of the deputies—missed practically every shot they fired. It hardly mattered. It was almost impossible for a bullet not to hit something.

Screaming rage and terror, the Croats tried to return fire with their wheel locks. But the contest was hopelessly one-sided. Not only were the wheel locks inaccurate, but the men firing them were mounted on pitching horses. Any shot which struck home did so by pure luck. The residents of Grantville perched in the upper stories of the downtown buildings suffered only eight casualties. None were fatal, and only two of them were actual bullet wounds. The rest were cuts caused by shattering glass and splintered stone. And one freak concussion: when a heavily framed velvet portrait of Elvis, shot loose from the wall, landed on the head of a woman huddled below.

Dan had planned to retreat, as soon as he fired off his first pistol. But now, seeing that the charge had been stymied, he stood his ground. Carefully, almost gently, he laid the empty automatic on the street next to his feet. Then he drew the pistol from his holster and started shooting again.

One of the officers who had been in the forefront was just now rising to his feet, shaking his head. The man was still dazed from his spill. He stumbled, and fell to his knees. His head came up, staring at the uniformed man who had so shockingly—*one man!*—shattered the charge.

Dan would have passed him up, if the man had managed to lose his hat. But Croats treasured their headgear—none more so than officers—and the hat was firmly attached by a drawstring. It was a very fancy, elaborate hat, replete with feathers. A commander's kind of hat. Even the bullet which came in between his eyes and blew out the back of his head didn't dislodge the thing.

Again, methodically, with a proper two-handed grip, Dan began killing the dismounted cavalrymen who had been in the first rank. He had intended to save a few rounds to cover his retreat. But by the time he came to the last few rounds, he saw that retreat would be unnecessary. Downtown Grantville, like a giant-scale Matewan, had become a death trap for arrogant outsiders. Already, he could see the Croats beginning their retreat.

Rout, rather. There was no discipline or order in the mob of horsemen galloping off to the east. Just five hundred panicked cavalrymen, leaving two hundred dead and wounded behind, driving down a road which led to no destination they knew. Just—*away.*

Dan heard the engine of the bus blocking the bridge start up. He spun around.

"Goddamit, Gretchen—*wait for me!*"

Gretchen had positioned all the German police recruits in the bus, ready at the windows to cover Dan's retreat if necessary. Then, seeing the way the battle was going, she ordered the driver to start the bus.

The driver was an elderly man, confused and frightened by the situation. Seeing that he was useless, Gretchen seized him by the scruff of the neck and manhandled him out of the bus. Then, scanning the large crowd which had gathered south of the bridge, she bellowed: "I need someone who can drive this thing!" She repeated the words in German.

"*I can! I can!*"

Gretchen recognized the voice even before her little brother forced his way through the mob. Hans was grinning from ear to ear. "I can drive anything!" he called out proudly, racing toward her.

Gretchen hesitated. Her brother loved to drive and was very good at it—measured, at least, in his ability to get from one place to another in a minimum amount of time. But he had an extremely nonchalant attitude toward what the American driving instructors called "defensive driving." His operating motto behind the wheel was: *You can't live forever, anyway, so why not get where you're going?*

Her hesitation was brief. Time was of the essence, and she could think of no one who would get the bus to the school quicker. "All right," she growled. "But be careful." Even to her, the words sounded absurd.

Hans clambered aboard and flung himself eagerly into the driver's seat. "Where to?" he demanded, starting the engine.

Scowling, Gretchen studied the main intersection. The plan which Dan had developed, to pursue the fleeing Croats directly, was obviously impractical. The street was so littered with the bodies of horses and men that it would take a quarter of an hour—at least—to clear a pathway. Already, she could see that the buses which Dan had held waiting a few blocks away were arriving on the scene, ready to load the deputies and other armed men in the buildings. But until the obstacles were removed, her bus was the only one which could go into immediate action.

She was about to order Hans to follow the road just south of Buffalo Creek, running parallel to the street down which the Croats were retreating, when she spotted Dan racing toward them. The police chief was supposed to ride one of the other buses, but he had obviously reached the same conclusion as Gretchen.

For a moment, so great was her furious determination to punish the invaders and protect the school, Gretchen almost left him behind. But she managed to restrain herself. Dan Frost was the best pistol shot in town, for one thing. And she'd *never* hear the end of it.

"Wait a moment," she said. In the few seconds it took Dan to reach the bus, Gretchen hurriedly explained her new battle plan to Hans and the recruits.

As soon as Dan came aboard, Hans closed the door and sent the bus lurching ahead. Dan grabbed the upright post by the door to keep from falling.

When he saw Hans at the wheel, the police chief hissed, *"Oh, shit."*

"He can drive anything," stated Gretchen firmly.

The bus careened around the corner. Frantically, Gretchen grabbed the overhead rail. "Anything," she repeated. Not as firmly.

Hans took the next turn like a charging cavalryman. The rear right wheels of the bus hammered over the curb, half-spilling the recruits out of their hastily taken seats.

"Oh, shit," repeated the police chief. He was now holding onto the upright with both hands. His knuckles were white.

On the next turn—*whang!*—Hans massacred a stop sign. "Anything," prayed Gretchen. *"Gott mit uns."*

Chapter 58

Harry Lefferts was so distracted by the news coming over the radio that he almost lost control of the vehicle. The road down which the column of APCs was racing, Harry's in the lead, was very far from a modern highway. The coal truck's front tires hit a huge pothole and Harry hastily fought the sudden skid.

Mike held his breath but didn't say anything. Once he was sure that Harry had the vehicle back under control, he leaned forward and returned the radio to its bracket.

"So the town's okay," he sighed, with some relief, but not much. And that little relief vanished almost instantly. In truth, Mike had not been too concerned about the town. Between Dan and his police force, and the fact that the town's residents were heavily armed, he had expected the enemy to be driven off readily enough. Grantville had become a seventeenth-century German version of a Wild West boom town. The Croats had simply discovered what the Dalton gang or any number of old American outlaws could have told them: *"Treeing" a town is a lot easier said than done.*

Harry echoed his worried thoughts. "What do you think about the school?"

Mike rubbed his face. "I don't really *want* to think about it. They don't have many weapons. And even if they've blocked off the entrances like we were told, that still won't hold off the Croats for more than a few minutes."

Silence followed. Halfway between Eisenach and Grantville, a column of APCS drove to the east. All the men and women in those vehicles—crammed with every soldier who could possibly be fit inside—were silent. There was nothing to say. The fate of their children was out of their hands.

     ❧   ❧   ❧

The horde of Croats milling around on the parking lot south of the school was bellowing like a herd of enraged bulls. Enraged—and terrified. Many of them were already dismounting, and the rest were frantically trying to force their horses away from that hideous window.

For a time, they had tried to return fire. But it was hopeless. Twice they had managed, by sheer weight of hastily "aimed" pistol volleys, to drive the terror away. But destruction returned, almost at once. Four rounds to a magazine, fired as rapidly as James could reload. And while the school only had two rifles, there had been plenty of ammunition.

Crackcrackcrackcrack. Crackcrackcrackcrack. Like Death, wielding his unstoppable scythe, reaping men with each sweep like so many fistfuls of grain.

A few of the Croats, by now, understood that the murder was being rained upon them by a demon. A monster taking the form of a girl. A pretty one, too, to make the horror worse. But not many. Those Croats who were foolish enough to spend time studying the window usually died within seconds.

As he kept reloading and swapping the rifles, James Nichols was almost in awe. Abstractly, he could understand what he was seeing. The girl had trained for the biathlon, after all. The emphasis in that sport was on short-range shooting, not long-distance. And there was an absolute premium on firing quickly and moving to the next target. But the doctor still knew that he was in the presence of something truly special.

Julie Sims' face held no expression at all, beyond concentration. None. She was completely in the zone. A pure killing machine. At that short range, even shooting rifles she had not sighted in, she never missed. Not once.

To James Nichols, watching, it was almost like a religious experience. An angel had materialized, and declared every man within a hundred yards to be hers by God's will.

The scythe swept again. *Crackcrackcrackcrack.* The angel of death reaped and reaped.

Coming out of a side road, the bus careened onto U.S. Route 250 just behind the last fleeing Croats. They were approaching the eastern outskirts of the town. The school was two miles away.

Dan had already used a shotgun butt to smash out the front window on the opposite side from the driver. "Step on it!" he commanded. Then winced.

"*Hallooooo!*" shrieked Hans, shoving the gas pedal to the floor. The bus surged ahead, rapidly gaining on the Croats.

"God help us," muttered the police chief. He braced himself in the stairwell of the bus and brought up the shotgun. Behind him, Gretchen stood ready with another. Behind her, perched in their seats, all the German police recruits had their own shotguns ready.

Seconds later, the bus came within range and Dan fired. Another angel of death began sweeping its scythe.

Hans was forced to slow the bus while he steered around—and over, often enough—the bodies littering the highway. But he was able to speed up again soon. The panicked Croats had now left the highway and were desperately trying to escape the terrifying machine behind them.

Those who fell off to the north side of the road made their way to safety. The area there was wide enough to allow them to escape. But those who drove their horses off the south embankment found themselves in a death trap.

Buffalo Creek paralleled Route 250 not more than thirty yards away. As soon as he saw the road was clear of corpses, Hans stepped on the gas again. Within a minute, the bus was pulling alongside the mob of imperial cavalrymen pounding along the bank of the creek, looking for a ford.

By then, Dan and Gretchen had a recruit positioned in every window on the right side of the bus. At Dan's command, the recruits started blasting away with their shotguns. The Croats were driving their horses much too fast—along treacherous ground—to even think of returning fire with their wheel locks. And there was nowhere to escape.

Hans slowed down again. The bus rolled up the road at thirty miles per hour, while the recruits poured slugs and buckshot into the Croats stumbling their horses down the creek bed. The result reminded Dan of a photograph he had once seen; old, sepia images of buffalo herds slaughtered by hunters firing from a train.

Now desperate, the imperial cavalrymen drove their horses into the creek and tried to force their way across to the wooded hills on the opposite bank. But there was no ford here. True, since the Ring of Fire the water level had dropped considerably, but Buffalo Creek was still more in the way of a small river than a stream. A number of Croats drowned in the attempt, as did an even larger number of their horses.

Dan let them go. It was plain enough that these enemies had been whipped senseless. They had no thought at all beyond making their escape. He was much more concerned for the school, still a mile away.

"Step on it!" he commanded.

Hans did; Dan went back to muttering prayers.

A large number of Croats had finally pushed their way into the narrow space between the buses and the front wall of the building. They were packed like sardines, but at least here they were safe from that incredible rifle in the upper window.

It was the work of but seconds to smash in all the windows of the cafeteria with pistols and sabers. A moment later, the Croats surged into the school building.

Captain Gars led the charge up the slope toward the school, Anders Jönsson by his side. He could see hundreds of Croat cavalrymen milling around in apparent confusion.

"Not too late," he grunted. He grinned at Anders. "Good, no?"

Then, waving his saber: "Forward! Forward!"

Behind him thundered the battle cries:

"*Gott mit uns! Haakaa päälle!*"

Some of the imperial cavalrymen wasted time searching the kitchen. But most of them poured out of the cafeteria into the vestibule. From there, led by subofficers, they began fanning out.

Some of them charged down the corridor leading to the technical center. But they immediately encountered an obstruction. Other Croats, by now, had smashed their way into the glassed-in walkway between the school proper and the tech center. Within seconds, they were trying to force the door into the center itself.

Trying, and failing. The door had been blocked by the simple expedient of backing a fork lift against it. Outside, the imperial cavalrymen slammed their shoulders into the door with futile fury.

The cry went up: "Find a battering ram!"

Other Croats charged up the stairwells leading to the classrooms on the upper floor. They could hear the shrieks and screams of frightened children coming from above, and knew that their target was finally within reach.

But at the top, they encountered barricades and men armed with pistols and revolvers. Flurries of gunfire erupted—sharp crack versus the boom of wheel lock.

One of the schoolteachers was shot in the arm. Ed Piazza, firing over the barricade with his pistol, was also struck down. A heavy wheel-lock bullet punched between two filing cabinets and ricocheted into his chest, shattering his ribs and penetrating a lung.

Instantly, Melissa was kneeling at his side, desperately trying to staunch the flow of blood. To her relief, Sharon Nichols pushed her way forward carrying a first-aid kit. Between the two of them, they fought to save Ed's life while yet another schoolteacher took up the pistol and entered the bloody fray at the top of the stairs.

The battle was brief. The gunfights, again, were entirely uneven. The Croats coming up the stairwell were in the open, completely unprotected, and the disparity in rate of fire was impossible to overcome. Wheel-lock pistols took even longer to reload than arquebuses, whereas the schoolteachers were wielding automatic pistols and revolvers.

Soon enough, the Croats retreated to the vestibule, where they vented their frustration wherever possible. A dozen Croats charged into the library and began smashing the furniture, the computers, and spilling the books. Others visited the same wreckage on the administration center. Still others, in the vestibule itself, went at the huge display case lining the west wall. Smashing glass instead of skulls, spilling athletic trophies instead of blood, and carving photographs instead of faces.

Other imperial cavalrymen, meanwhile, had been slamming shoulders and boots into the wide doors on the northeast side of the vestibule which led into the gymnasium. They could see through the cracks of the doors, and knew that their prey awaited them beyond. But the doors were too solid to push through.

Again, the cry went up: "Find a battering ram!"

Julie spotted the motion of the oncoming new cavalry at the same time as she heard them shouting. Something about those battle cries seemed familiar to her—quite unlike the screeching of the Croats.

But her mind was entirely on her shooting. She had a fresh magazine in the rifle. Julie brought the iron sights to bear on the huge man leading the charge, and started to squeeze the trigger.

Stopped. There was something—

She lifted her head and peered. Julie's eyesight, as might be expected in a sharpshooter, was phenomenal—considerably better than 20/20.

"Jesus Christ," she whispered. "I don't fucking believe it."

The corner of her eye caught motion. A band of Croats—perhaps ten in all—had also spotted the new threat and were charging to meet it.

Julie swung the rifle. *Crackcrackcrackcrack.*

"Switch!" she squealed. James had the other .30-06 in her hands within seconds. The angel of death went back to the field, reaping with a fresh scythe.

Desperately, Anders tried to drive his horse ahead of Captain Gars, in order to shield him from the oncoming Croats.

No use. The captain always rode the finest horses in Europe.
The madman! cursed Jönsson.

Captain Gars raised his saber, ready to strike. *"Gott mit uns!"*

The first rank of charging Croats was suddenly hammered aside,
falling from their saddles like so many dolls. Neither the captain
nor Jönsson understood what had happened. They had heard a
sound, like a great tearing of cloth, but did not recognize it as rifle
fire.

No matter. Other Croats were upon them. Captain Gars matched
saber against saber in his usual style. Sheer strength and fury smashed
aside his opponent's weapon and then, in the backstroke, took the
imperial cavalryman's arm off at the shoulder. The arm fell one way,
the Croat was flung off the saddle to the other. He would bleed to
death soon enough, never recovering from the shock.

Anders, as always, began with his wheel locks. Four of them he
possessed; one in each hand, two in their saddle-holsters. He used
them all in the first few seconds, desperately trying to protect Captain Gars from the Croats encircling him.

The wheel locks now fired, Anders dropped them and took up his
saber. There was no time, in this furious cavalry melee, to reload and
crank the firing mechanism on the clumsy weapons.

Captain Gars struck down another Croat, then another. His powerful blows fell like the strikes of an ax. But he was almost surrounded
now.

The great tearing sound ripped through the sky again. And, again,
Croats were smashed off their saddles. Anders could see the blood
erupting from their chests, and suddenly understood that they had
been shot in the back.

From above, somewhere. His eyes ranged up, and immediately
spotted the window. The window, and the figure standing in it.

Anders, unlike the captain, had good eyesight. When he understood what he was seeing, he lapsed into blasphemy.

"Jesus Christ," he whispered. "I don't fucking believe it."

Next to him, in the sudden pause in the action, Captain Gars
grinned savagely. His eyes swept the scene, taking in what he could.
Which was not much, given his myopia.

"It goes good, eh?" he demanded.

A broad smile spread across the face of Anders Jönsson. *"Very*
good, Captain Gars. I believe an angel is watching over us."

Upstairs, Julie squealed again. *"Switch!"*

In the years to come, the Västgöta would speak with awe of Captain
Gars' final charge against the Croats. Like a Titan, he was, smashing

aside the savages like so many toys. The Finns, more superstitious, would claim that his saber had become a magic sword—striking down enemies long before they were within range.

The Lapps kept their opinion to themselves. They were only nominally Christians, and had found that it was unwise in the presence of devout Lutherans to speak too freely of their tribal spirits. One of which, quite obviously, had ridden the captain's shoulders that bloody day.

Only Anders Jönsson and the captain himself understood the truth. Anders, because he had seen the angel for himself; the pious captain, because he recognized her handiwork.

"Gott mit uns!" he bellowed again, resuming the charge. And, indeed, God went before him. Slaying every Croat who stood in the captain's way, as if a mighty hand shielded him from harm.

The vestibule was so jammed with cavalrymen that it took a full minute to haul the awning support into position. Then, shrieking curses and commands, another full minute to clear a space for the impromptu battering ram.

Finally, the ram went to work. *Boom. Boom.* The doors began splintering.

When the bus was a hundred yards from the driveway leading up to the school, Croat cavalry began pouring down the slope.

Away from the school. As if they were panicked.

Dan leaned forward. "What the hell—?"

An instant later, he was shouting new orders. Gretchen saw to it they were carried out. Police recruits were again perched in the windows, their shotguns and revolvers in hand. Screaming with unprofessional rage, they began their new slaughter.

When they reached the driveway, Hans almost overturned the bus making the turn. But he never lost his good cheer. "Hallooooo!" he shrieked, driving the bus straight through the horde of imperial cavalry pouring away from the school. He crushed several Croats under the wheels and almost overturned the bus again, driving over the corpse of a horse. But the recruits were back at the windows in seconds, blasting away on both sides, wreaking havoc and carnage. Gretchen, in a fury, slammed open the rear window and started firing her automatic at the Croats fleeing toward Route 250 and Buffalo Creek. She only missed twice.

Once he reached the parking lot on top of the slope, Hans slammed on the brakes. Dumbfounded, he stared at the scene.

Equally dumbfounded, Dan stared with him. The entire area in front of the school was a cavalry battle. Bands of Croats were engaged in a desperate struggle with bands of other soldiers. Saber against saber; wheel lock against wheel lock.

The police chief had no idea who the other soldiers were. But he didn't care. He could recognize an ally when he saw one—and his allies were winning.

"Shoot the Croats!" he roared.

As if his voice were a signal, all of the Croats still on horseback in front of school suddenly broke. As it happened, they still outnumbered their Swedish and Finnish opponents—by a considerable margin—but it mattered not at all. Captain Gars' hammer blow from the rear, coming on top of their own frustration, had broken their spirit. Within a minute, leaving hundreds of dead and wounded behind, the imperial cavalry was in full rout. Many more men died or were crippled, spilling from horses driven too recklessly down the slope.

They were sped on their way by gunfire from the bus, but not for long. With Dan leading from the front, and Gretchen driving from the rear, the police recruits stumbled out of the bus and began racing for the school entrance. It was obvious enough, just from the sounds of shouting, that there were still enemies within.

Captain Gars and Anders, with dismounted Västgöta and Finns following, moved down the narrow space between the line of buses and the side of the school. There were still dozens of Croats in the cafeteria, but none of them were looking at the broken windows. They were all piled against the door to the vestibule, eagerly awaiting their chance to join the charge into the gymnasium. From the splintering sounds accompanying the booming battering ram, the slaughter was finally about to begin.

Inside the gymnasium, Jeff stood alone in the middle of the floor. He hefted the shotgun in his hands, staring at the big double doors. The doors were starting to splinter, and he didn't think the lock was going to last more than a few seconds.

Len Trout was still finishing the task of shepherding the students onto the upper rows of the tiers of benches. Only one set of benches had been lowered: the one against the north wall of the gym, farthest from the doors. The principal had crammed as many students as possible onto the top rows. A line of the oldest boys was standing guard on the lower benches, armed with nothing better than baseball bats.

"All we can do," muttered Trout. He turned and strode to the center of the gym, taking position next to Jeff. He levered the slide on the automatic and checked quickly to make sure the safety was off.

"All we can do," he repeated.

Jeff said nothing. He couldn't think of anything to say that wouldn't sound melodramatic and corny. So he decided to spend these last moments of his life simply thinking about his wife, and hoping that their unborn child would enjoy the world as much as he had.

The lock on the door gave way and the doors slammed open. Murder poured into the room, shrieking death and destruction.

"*Gott mit uns!*"

Captain Gars' battle cry signaled the attack. With the captain and Anders leading the way, the Västgöta and Finns surged through the windows into the cafeteria.

The Croats still in the cafeteria were caught completely by surprise. By the time they spun around, Captain Gars was upon them, like a grizzly bear savaging his prey, with another roaring at his side. Between them, the captain and Anders cleared a path to the door. The Croats who fell away from that berserk saber charge were swarmed under by the captain's soldiers.

"*Gott mit uns! Haakaa päälle!*"

"That's it, Julie," said Nichols, handing her the rifle. "You've got a fresh magazine. The rest of the ammunition is gone."

Julie leaned the empty .30-06 against the wall, seized the other, and charged for the door. By the time she got to the corridor, she was already shrieking her own battle cry.

"Make way! Make way! *Goddamittohell—clear a path!*"

In her frenzied drive through the mob of students and teachers in the corridor, Julie did not actually use the gun butt to hammer herself a path—though the claim would be made afterward, by students knocked down by her charge. But the truth was quite otherwise. A hundred-and-forty-pound cheerleader was simply doing an excellent imitation of a fullback twice her size.

James followed. For all his concern—he knew the damned girl was heading back into action—he couldn't restrain a smile. Then, as he neared the end of the corridor where Julie was frantically clambering over the barricade at the stairwell, he caught sight of Melissa's pale face and the smile vanished.

She saw him at the same time. "Oh Jesus, James—*hurry*. Ed's been shot!"

"Get those fucking buses out of the way!" bellowed Dan Frost. When he saw Hans squirrel into the lead bus through a broken window, he cursed under his breath. That bus was the one which Jeff had planted directly in front of the school's main entrance.

"Not *that* one, Hans! It's blocked by the others."

He started toward the bus, pointing with his finger to the ones further down the line. "You gotta move those others first before you can—"

Hans had his own ideas about how to move a bus. His theory leaned very heavily on kinetic energy, and gave short shrift—*no* shrift, actually—to repair costs. Half a minute and much wreckage later, the bus pulled away. The entrance to the school was open.

Croats began pouring out, desperate to escape the furious charge of the Swedes coming through the cafeteria. But by the time they emerged, Dan and Gretchen had already formed the police recruits into a new line, standing to one side, shotguns reloaded and ready, leaving an apparent path to freedom and safety.

It was a firing squad, for all practical purposes. Of the hundred or so imperial cavalrymen who managed to get out of the school building before the Swedes and Finns cut them down, less than half ever made it out of the parking lot.

When the firing ceased, Dan and Gretchen led the police recruits into the school. Tried to, at least. But there was no way to force themselves past the men who now filled the vestibule. Captain Gars' Västgöta, those were, still following the madman.

Coming down the stairs, Julie met four Croats coming up. The Croats were not even looking at her. They were coming up the stairs backward, frantically trying to fend off twice their number of Finns.

The scythe swung—*crackcrackcrackcrack*—and her way was clear. The Finns at the bottom of the stairs, gaping, simply moved aside. There was something inexorable about the way the young woman came down the stairs, trampling over the bodies she had put there. Christianity was more than nominal, among Finns, but they still retained memories of their pagan traditions.

No man in his right mind will stand in the way of Loviatar, Goddess of Hurt, Maiden of Pain.

Jeff blew the front rank of Croats into bloody shreds. *Rate of fire.* At that range—less than fifteen yards—the heavy shotgun slugs punched through the light armor of the imperial cavalrymen as if it were tissue paper.

Frantically, he started reloading the shotgun. Len Trout stepped in front of him and leveled the automatic. Again, the Croats charging into the gymnasium encountered that incredible rate of fire.

But Len was no marksman. For all his courage, he was not an experienced gun handler. Half his shots missed.

Five Croats went down, true, even if three of them were only wounded. But there were still more than enough to drive through the hail of pistol bullets. Less than a second after he fired the last shot in the magazine, the first saber cut Len Trout down. A head wound, bloody but not fatal. But the next saber slash almost removed his head entirely, hacking halfway through his neck.

Trout's killer died himself, then. He and all the men at his side. Jeff's shotgun was reloaded and back in furious action. Rate of fire. *Clickety-boom*, over and again, coming so fast it sounded like thunder.

And now the shotgun was empty, and it was over. Jeff still had a full magazine's worth of ammunition left in his pockets, but he would never have the time to reload before the Croat sabers arrived.

The first Croat charged up, saber held high. Jeff went to meet him. The Croat had time to be amazed at how quickly the big man in front of him moved, before the butt of the shotgun shattered his jaw.

A saber cut into Jeff's right shoulder, knocking him to the floor of the gym. Instantly, his entire arm and side were soaked with blood. The muscle was cut through to the bone. Only the tough leather jacket had kept that sword stroke from amputating his arm entirely.

Half-dazed by the shock, Jeff stared up at the man who had slashed him down. Snarling, the Croat raised the saber again.

Then, to Jeff's amazement, the Croat's head exploded. Cut in half, rather, by a saber which descended like the hammer of an ancient war god. The Croat was driven to his knees. A twist of the powerful wrist holding the saber broke the blade lose from the skull and cast the victim aside.

Jeff found himself staring at a huge man, grinning down at him. Immense, he was. Tall, broad, heavy as an ox. His pale blue eyes, peering down over a powerful nose, were gleaming like glacier ice.

Captain Gars led the charge into the gymnasium, still roaring his battle cry. Anders was at his side, roaring the same. Not half a step behind came dozens of the Västgöta and Finns. Walls which had once rung to the sound of cheerleaders' slogans now shook with the fury of the Northmen.

Gott mit uns!

The captain himself cut down the Croat who had been about to kill the young American on the floor. Then, standing over him like a protective idol, he bellowed commands to his soldiers. It was the work of less than fifteen seconds to drive the rest of the Croats to the rear wall of the gymnasium.

Led by Anders, the Västgöta flooded the area in front of the tiered seats, protecting the students. At the captain's command, his Finns moved forward against the enemy.

At the end, the surviving imperial cavalrymen—perhaps twenty in all—tried to surrender. They received the traditional Finnish terms. *Haakaa päälle!*

Julie and Gretchen reached the broken doors of the gymnasium at exactly the same time. Dan Frost was a few steps behind.

As soon as she saw Jeff, Gretchen raced to his side. By now, several of the students trained in first aid were clustered about him, removing his jacket and staunching the wound. Gretchen forced her way through, knelt, and cradled his head in her lap. Weeping as she had not wept in years.

"S'okay," her husband mumbled. He even managed a wan smile. "S'okay, sweetheart—honest. Nothing but a little flesh wound." Then his eyes rolled up and he fainted.

Julie stood in the doorway, staring at Captain Gars. Her eyes seemed as wide as saucers.

The captain was also having a wound tended to. Nothing major, to all outward appearance. But at Jönsson's insistence, the captain had removed his buff coat and blouse. His upper body was bare and exposed. Very pale-skinned he was, with a carpet of blond hair on his chest. Thick muscle bulged under layers of fat.

"You see?" he grumbled. The captain pressed the heavy flesh aside, exposing the cut along his ribs. The gash was shallow, and perhaps three inches long. Plainly enough, it would soon be nothing but a minor blemish on a torso which was already heavily scarred. Captain Gars seemed utterly oblivious to the blood soaking his hip.

"It's nothing," he insisted. Anders sighed with exasperation and handed him a scarf. The captain pressed the cloth against the wound.

Motion caught his eye. Captain Gars turned his head and squinted at the person coming toward him. When the figure finally came into focus, he grinned.

Julie covered the last few steps in a rush. A moment later, equally oblivious to the blood, she was hugging the huge body of the captain fiercely. Much like a chipmunk might embrace a bear.

The captain seemed startled, at first. Then his fierce warrior's face softened. After a few seconds, he was returning the embrace. A bit gingerly, at first. Afraid, perhaps, that he might crush the girl in his arms. But then, as he felt the muscle beneath his hands and remembered the sheer force of her spirit, the embrace grew warm and tight.

"Iss all right," he murmured, in his thick and awkward English. "I not bad hurt."

Julie's head popped up from his chest. Craning her neck, she glared at the captain.

"You could have gotten killed!" she squealed. "What are you—
crazy?"

"Yes," stated Anders gloomily. "The captain is a madman. It is well
known."

When Rebecca came into the gymnasium a minute later, Julie was
still hugging the captain. *And* still chastising him for his reckless folly;
loudly, and in no uncertain terms. Captain Gars himself didn't seem
to know how to handle the situation. Apparently he was a man
unaccustomed to being scolded. But Anders Jönsson and all the
Västgöta were grinning from ear to ear.

Finally! Someone to call the madman to his senses!

Rebecca burst into soft laughter. Dan Frost, standing next to her,
was frowning with puzzlement.

"I don't get it," he hissed. "Does Julie know that guy from somewhere? They say his name's Captain Gars."

Rebecca choked off the laughter. "Oh, yes. They've met before."

She stared at the immense man in the center of the room. Her own
eyes softened.

"What a lunatic," she murmured. "He has not done this in many
years. Not since he was a young man, according to the history books."
Again, she laughed.

Dan was scowling fiercely. "I still don't—"

"Captain Gars," said Rebecca. "To the best of my knowledge, he
is the only king in history who ever actually did it outside of fable.
Travel in disguise, I mean, assuming the pose of a simple soldier. The
books claim that he scouted half of western Europe in that fashion."

The police chief's eyes widened. His jaw sagged.

"Oh, yes," chuckled Rebecca. "Captain Gars. Gustavus Adolphus Rex
Sueciae."

Part Seven

Tiger! Tiger! burning bright
In the forests of the night,
What immortal hand or eye,
Dare frame thy fearful symmetry?

Chapter 59

By the time they reached Grantville, Mike had reached his conclusion. He didn't much care for it, in many ways. But he knew it was—by far—the best alternative.

If nothing else, listening to Harry Lefferts' monologue during the drive from Eisenach had convinced him. Once they got word over the radio that the imperialist raid had been driven off, with light casualties, everyone in the relief column had been able to relax. Cheerfully, enthusiastically—even gaily—Harry had spent the last two hours explaining all the many ways in which the United States could be made safe from any future invasion or attack.

Barbed wire. Land mines. Fortresses along every approach bristling with Gatling guns—*we can make 'em, Mike, I'm telling you!*—and napalm catapults. *Greg says we can make phosphorus bombs too—way better'n napalm!* A much bigger army—*universal draft, goddamit!*—and a massive expansion of the military college which they had already decided to launch. Oh, and lots more. Observation balloons, and powered hang gliders for recon. *Even poison gas, maybe.*

Outside of the poison gas, Mike had no particular problem with any of Harry's specific ideas. But, taken as a whole, he understood the inexorable logic involved.

Festung Amerika! Fortress America, and everything that went with it.

When the relief column reached the center of Grantville, driving slowly through the cheering crowd, Harry stopped the APC. He turned to Mike, smiling broadly.

"So, chief—whaddaya think?"

Mike did not return the smile. "What I think, Harry, is that your proposal is just Simpson all over again. Only bigger."

Harry's smile vanished, replaced by a look of bewildered outrage. The young coal miner *detested* Simpson!

Mike couldn't help but chuckle. At that instant, Harry reminded him of a small boy, accused of liking *girls*.

"Think it through, Harry." Mike listened to the roar of the crowd, for a moment. Even through the steel plate armor, the sound penetrated easily. There was nothing about that sound that Mike disliked, in and of itself. It was just the roar of a triumphant nation, saluting its soldiers. Nothing to fear—as long as it ended soon enough.

But if it went on, and on, and on . . .

Festung Amerika. But there was not enough room for America in a fortress. Certainly not one as small as Thuringia. Not Mike's vision of America, at least. Soon enough, Fortress America would need to expand. The militarist logic would inevitably guide that expansion. *Living space*, to be seized from its neighbors. Everything else would follow, like a glacier moving to the sea. *Drang nach Osten. Amerika über alles!*

It was obvious that Harry still didn't understand. Mike began to sigh with exasperation, but forced himself to control his impatience. Like a schoolteacher, explaining things again. And again. And again— as long as it took.

That image brought a smile to his face. *Yes!*

He bestowed the smile on Harry. "Didn't you wonder? Why Wallenstein sent most of his Croats against the school—instead of the town?"

Harry frowned. "I dunno. He's a murderous bastard, from what everybody says."

Mike shook his head. "No. I've been reading about him, in the history books. He wasn't—isn't, I should say—a sadist, Harry. Not at all. He doesn't eat babies for breakfast. He's just utterly cold-blooded and, without a doubt, the smartest man on the other side. Smarter than Richelieu, even."

Someone started pounding on the door of the APC. Demanding that the soldiers emerge, so that the crowd could greet them properly.

Nothing to fear. As long as it ended soon enough.

Mike started unlocking the door. "Think about it, Harry. Think long and hard. The reason Wallenstein wanted to destroy the school more than anything else is because he understands us better, I think, than we often understand ourselves. He knows what's *really* dangerous."

Now unlocked, the door was swung open from the outside. A sea of cheering faces appeared, and the sound of applause became almost deafening.

Before he climbed out of the APC, Mike gave Harry a glance. The young miner still didn't understand. But, apparently, Harry didn't much care. Whether he understood or not, Harry Lefferts *did* know who he had confidence in.

"So, chief," he shouted. "You got another plan?"

Mike grinned. "I think I do, as a matter of fact." He turned and started climbing out of the truck. Before his feet touched the ground, a multitude of hands had picked him up and were carrying him around the intersection in gleeful triumph.

Mike returned the applause with waving hands and a big grin. *A man could get to enjoy this*, he thought. *Like a snake, digesting its prey.*

He turned his head and stared to the east. The school was in that direction, not far away. He was burning with impatience to get there. To see his wife, of course. He knew that Rebecca was unharmed— she herself had been the one to make the last radio call—but he still wanted to hold her, and hold her, and hold her.

Beyond that—

I've got to talk to a captain. And hope—and pray—that he's every bit the madman that everyone says.

Chapter 60

"You are insane," growled Gustav Adolf. He waved his heavy hand in a circle. "Your mind is as jumbled as this room."

The library was still a scene of semiwreckage. The students had not finished rearranging the books when Mike had arrived at the school and immediately insisted on a private meeting with "Captain Gars." There were now only three people in the room: Mike, Gustav and Rebecca. All of them were seated on armchairs arranged in a half circle.

The king glared at the tall man sitting across from him. Blue eyes locked against blue eyes. "A *madman*!"

Mike's German was more than good enough to understand. He didn't wait for Rebecca's translation before matching the royal glare with one of his own.

"Am I?" Snorting, almost sneering: "Or is the true madman a Swedish king who thinks he can establish a *Corpus Evangelicorum* in central Europe? A *Protestant* confederation—when most of his Protestant allies are unwilling and his own conquered territory consists mainly of Catholics?"

After Rebecca translated, Mike stretched out his hand and swept it south by west. The fact that his finger was actually pointing at bookcases in a library did not prevent the monarch from understanding the gesture.

"What do you propose to do with Franconia?" he demanded. "Or the 'Priests' Alley'?"

The king was silent. Mike pressed on. "Or with the Palatinate—*both* the Upper and the Lower? Or with Swabia and Württemburg?"

Gustav's heavy jaws tightened. "There *must* be an established church."

Again, Mike didn't need to wait for the translation. He shrugged his shoulders. "For a *Corpus Evangelicorum*, well and good. As long as it's restricted to Lutheran north Germany. Pomerania and Mecklenburg you control directly. Brandenburg–Prussia and Saxony are *technically* your allies. If you can convince them to join, Lutheranism is not an issue."

Mike waited for Rebecca to translate. The king glowered at the use of the word "technically," but issued no verbal protest. What was there to say?

Mike continued. "But how do you propose to establish Lutheranism as the official church of *central* Germany? Most of which, except for Hesse-Kassel and Thuringia, is Catholic."

The king was now glaring fiercely. Mike matched the glare. "And *we* control Thuringia. And *we* will not accept an established church. The separation of church and state is one of our fundamental principles!"

Glare.

Glare.

Rebecca managed not to laugh. Just barely. Melissa had once explained to her the "modern" notion of the so-called *alpha male*. At the time, Rebecca had found the logic of the argument highly suspect. But now, watching her husband and the king of Sweden, she admitted that the concept had a certain validity. Other than the fact that they were matching wills over power rather than females, the two men in the library reminded her of nothing so much as a pair of bull walruses during mating season.

She decided to intervene with the voice of feminine reason. Rebecca wasn't quite certain where Michael was going with his argument—they had barely had time to exchange an embrace and a few words before he insisted on this private meeting with "Captain Gars"—but she thought she could guess. Many times—many times—Michael had spoken to her of his greatest fear. That the new United States he was trying to forge would become another of Europe's tyrants instead of a school for humanity's future.

"Perhaps—" She cleared her throat. "Perhaps a compromise might be possible."

Two pairs of glaring blue eyes were now transferred to the female in the room. Rebecca managed to bear up under the burden. Quite easily.

"Yes, I think so." To the king, in quick, velvety German: "You must remember, Your Majesty, that my husband is accustomed to the clarity and simplicity of his traditional political arrangements." To Michael, in quick, hissing English: "Get off your high horse!"

Neither man quite understood what she had said to the other. They were suspicious, but . . .

Rebecca struck while the iron was confused.

"Yes, a compromise! In those principalities of the future realm—let us, for the moment, simply call it the *Confederation of Europe*—which are *directly* ruled by the Vasa dynasty *as such*, Lutheranism will of course be the established religion. But in those principalities—"

Mike and Gustav both erupted. Mike with a loud snort, the king with words.

"Nonsense!" bellowed the king. "The principle of monarchy cannot be compromised! Intolerable!"

Rebecca glided through his outrage unscathed. "Well—of course not. But, Your Majesty, remember that the principle of monarchy resides in your personage as Gustav II Adolf Vasa, King of Sweden. *Not*—"

She slid in the knife: "—in your persona as *Captain Gars*."

The king's jaws snapped shut. Michael goggled at her.

"Captain *General* Gars, I should say," Rebecca continued. "The title will naturally be hereditary, running through the Vasa line of Sweden. But since the captain general, as such, is not a king . . ."

She let the words, and the implication behind them, trail off into silence. Michael, unaccustomed to the arcane logic of feudalism, was confused. But the king, after a moment, began to smile. The blue glare in his eyes faded, replaced by thoughtfulness. He *did* understand the logic.

"Hm," he mused. "Interesting. As a purely military figure, the captain general would have no personal prestige bound up with any particular church. A monarch derives his authority from the hand of God, and must naturally support God's lawful church. But a captain general *could*—speaking abstractly, for the moment—leave strictly religious matters to the parsons." A bit sourly: "And priests, of course."

Mike had been able to follow the German exchange well enough. "*And* the rabbis," he insisted.

Gustav cast him another glare, but it was brief. He waved a thick hand. "Yes, yes—surely. Once the principle is established, the rest follows."

Rebecca twisted the blade. "And I *do* think it is time—long overdue, in fact—for Captain Gars to receive a promotion."

Gustav burst into laughter. "Scheming woman!" For a moment, he stared at her admiringly. His eyes drifted down to her swollen midsection. "If the child is a girl," he chuckled, "I assume you plan to name her Circe."

Rebecca laughed. After a moment, so did Michael.

The king began stroking his big nose. "Hm. Hm." The stroking stopped. The glare returned.

"But what about this other nonsense!" he snapped. "This preposterous idea that only the *lower* house—the estate of the commons, if you will!—has exclusive control over taxation and the state treasury?" His voice rose to a bellow: *"Absurd! Utterly unreasonable!"*

Michael snapped back: "Bad enough I'm willing to give you a stinking House of Lords, just to keep your lousy noble allies! You want the worthless parasites to decide how much they get *taxed*, too?" His own bellow was as impressive as the king's: *"Not a chance! Power must remain in the lower House! Let the damned nobility be satisfied with their frills!"*

Bellow.

Bellow.

The king of Sweden roared like a lion, defending the divine right of kings and the principle of aristocratic precedence. The president of the United States snarled like a tiger, insisting on the primacy of the popular will. *Royalty must rule, not simply reign!* was matched with *Millions for defense, not one cent for tribute!*

It went on for quite some time. On and on. Several hours, in fact.

Now and again, Rebecca's voice slid through the verbal maelstrom, like a blade between ribs. The roars and bellows would fade, replaced by *hms* and *wellIgottathinkaboutthats*, until they resumed their former fury. But, always, the ground would shift a bit.

Outside the library, the vestibule quickly became packed with the other members of the U.S. government. Within an hour, every elected official living in Grantville had arrived at the school. The crowd became so large that it was necessary for most of them to gather in the cafeteria. At periodic intervals, Representatives eavesdropping on the raging quarrel in the library would give hurried reports.

At first, Melissa and her supporters gathered around one table, while Quentin and his faction collected at another. But eventually, as if by unspoken agreement, the two of them met privately in the vestibule.

"I'm worried, Quentin," admitted Melissa. "I think I understand what Mike's trying to do. If the United States is part of some great Confederation of Europe, we'll have breathing room. It'd buy us time to grow and—" She groped for words. "And teach. Instead of turning us into a garrison state."

Quentin nodded. "Yeah. And if I'm following the latest twist and turn in the debate, Mike just got half of Franconia added along with the rest of Thuringia. I think he's shooting for all of it, too." For a moment, his eyes grew a bit dreamy. "Be one hell of an expansion in the market, that's for sure. Every business in the U.S. will start growing by leaps and bounds. The railroads alone—" He broke off, scratching his chin worriedly. "Still—"

"Still—" echoed Melissa. She sighed heavily. "But it sounds like he's trading political principles for military security and economic expansion."

She sighed again. "Well, that's not fair. He hasn't budged an inch on the Bill of Rights. Mike wouldn't. Not on that. But I'm worried he'll give so much else away in return that—"

Quentin snorted. *"Mike?"* He laughed drily. "Melissa, I used to negotiate contract provisions with that pigheaded SOB. Not to mention about a million grievances."

The mine manager scowled. "I'm not worried about *that*. Mike negotiates like a pit bull. He'll give you your leg back, sure—*after* he's swallowed the meat. It's just—" He heaved his own heavy sigh. "Oh, hell. It's just that I'm a conservative, and I *don't* approve of radical changes. And what Mike's proposing—" He threw up his hands. "I mean—*Jesus!* I don't care what you call it—a friggin' *king*?"

For a moment—a rare moment—he and Melissa shared a common outrage and a common opinion. Then, simultaneously, they burst into laughter.

"Well," chuckled Melissa. "Look at it this way, Quentin. If you and I can manage—*somehow*—to get along, then maybe those two can do the same." She peered through the glass doors of the library. Gustav and Mike were now on their feet, standing nose to nose, roaring and raging and gesticulating wildly.

"Testosterone!" sneered Melissa. Her eyes fell on Rebecca. "Thank God for feminine reason."

Quentin snorted. He began to make some sarcastic remark. Then, as his own eyes fell on Rebecca, the remark went unsaid. The snort became a chuckle. "Believe it or not, I agree with you." Glowering: "Just this once."

It was done. The initial round, at least.

Gustav Adolf was now sprawled on his chair, relaxed and at ease. "Axel will be furious with me," he said, smiling ruefully. "He will accuse me of being a half-witted peasant, swindled by a Gypsy."

Mike glanced at the doors of the library. Every inch of the glass seemed to be filled with faces.

"I'll probably catch hell myself," he admitted. "They'll be calling me the new Benedict Arnold. Selling out my country to a foreign crown."

His eyes came back to meet those of the king. They did not seem noticeably chagrined, either of them.

"Don't care!" snapped Mike. "If I have to, I'll call for new elections and run against all of them." Half-savagely: "And I'll *win,* too!"

The king grunted. The sound was full of satisfaction. "Spoken like a Vasa!"

The future hereditary Captain General of the United States matched stares with his future President. There was a richness to that silent exchange. Acceptance of future quarrel—bitter quarrel, often enough. Recognition of mutual necessity. Understanding that the road would be full of pitfalls and controversy. Respect—even admiration. And, underlying everything, a shared desire to end a continent's torment and shape a better world out of its ruins.

"Thank you for saving our children, Captain Gars," said Mike softly.

The king nodded heavily. His eyes seemed to twinkle. He turned to Rebecca. "Your husband is such a scoundrel, you know. He thinks I don't understand his scheme. He thinks I will *continue* to safeguard his offspring, simply by giving them a world large enough for them to grow. Grow straight and strong, as big as giants."

Rebecca smiled, but said nothing. The king chuckled. "And you as well!" He clapped his hand to his forehead in a histrionic gesture. "The poor Vasas of the future! They will toil away, sweat pouring off their brows, shielding this monster growing in their midst."

Rebecca smiled, said nothing. The king grimaced like a thespian. "Oxenstierna will denounce me for a fool! He will accuse me of attaching a parasite to the body of Sweden and its Confederation. *Corpus Evangelicorum,* feeding the worm within! I'll never hear the end of it!"

Rebecca smiled, said nothing. The king returned her smile with one of his own. And, this time, there was nothing histrionic in the expression at all. It was a gentle smile; calm, and confident.

"So be it," pronounced Gustav II Adolf. "An unborn child is also a parasite, if a man wishes to see things in that manner. But I do not."

He planted huge hands on his knees and rose slowly to his feet. Now standing erect, the king of Sweden seemed to fill a library for schoolchildren like a giant in his own right. And, like a giant, he roared his simple challenge—to himself as much as to his world.

"Vasa! Always Vasa!"

Chapter 61

Alex Mackay and his cavalrymen arrived in Grantville the next day. Immediately, upon learning that his beloved fiancée—crazy girl!— had been involved in the thick of the fight at the school, Alex went in search of her. Desperate to assure himself that she was truly unharmed.

But his betrothed was hiding from him. "He's gonna *kill* me when he finds out I'm pregnant," she moaned. "I'm *dead.*"

"Leave the matter to me," intoned her new protector. "No harm will befall you."

Nor did it. When Alex finally found Julie, hiding behind the huge form in the library, the king of Sweden set him straight.

"Won't tolerate such behavior on the part of one of my officers," gruffed Gustav, in blithe disregard of his own not-entirely-reputable history. "Bastardy is a shame before God!"

As it happens, Alex was not angry with Julie at all. He was quite delighted at the news, in fact. But he had no time to reassure his betrothed. The king marched him directly to the parson and oversaw the rest of the preparations himself. Karen Reading was quite overwhelmed by his presence. Overwhelmed—and ecstatic. Her bridal shop had just gotten a *royal* boost.

They were married the following day. The king himself stood in the groom's party. For all the impromptu nature of the event, most of the town showed up for the wedding. Julie and Alex were quite popular, which accounted for some of the crowd. But most of them came to get a glimpse of Gustav Adolf. Or *Captain General Gars*, to use what would soon become his correct title whenever the king of Sweden visited the United States in an official capacity. Word of the negotiations was spreading rapidly, and everyone wanted to make their own assessment of this mysterious new figure in their political pantheon.

On balance, they were quite impressed. The more so when it was announced that the Captain General had given his finest horse as a gift to the groom, and an actual *title* to the bride. Julie Mackay, nee Sims, former cheerleader, sharpshooter in the U.S. army, was now also the baroness of a small domain somewhere on the edge of Lappland in northern Sweden.

The king also promised her a pair of skis. "You will need them," he assured her, "if you ever plan to visit the place. The hunting is excellent, incidentally. But I do not propose to provide you with a new rifle. Anyone else, but not you. Your rifle is already the best in the world."

A week later, Axel Oxenstierna arrived in Grantville. Just as Gustav II Adolf had foreseen, his chancellor was apoplectic when he heard the king's new political plans. Axel ranted and raged, desperately trying to convince his monarch that a Confederation of Europe with a *republic* planted at its center—*don't think I'm fooled by this Captain General rigmarole! and you gave them Franconia also?*—would assuredly be the death knell—*sooner or later!*—for the aristocracy of Europe.

But the king refused to budge. After two days, he took Oxenstierna to visit a place in Thuringia. A place called Buchenwald.

"In another universe, Axel, this will be a place of slaughter." Gustav's heavy jaws clenched. "And by no means the worst!" He pointed to the east. "The real killing will take place in Poland and Russia. At places called Auschwitz and Sobibor and Treblinka."

He glared at his chancellor. "In *that* universe, my new president's grandfather will be forced to fight his way into this place, that a handful might survive. And do you know why?"

Now, the king pointed to the northeast. "Because in *that* universe, chancellor of Sweden, I will die. Less than three months from now, at a battlefield called Lützen." His lips quirked. "Leading a perhaps reckless cavalry charge."

The brief moment of humor vanished. Gustav took a deep breath, resting his hands on the pommel of the saddle. His eyes scanned the entire landscape; unfocused, as if he were looking in his mind's eye at all of Europe. "My death will end any chance of rescuing Germany from the clutches of the princes. You will try, Axel—strive well, and mightily—to salvage what you can. But it will not be enough. Germany will be doomed to the centuries which came after, and the world will be doomed to *that* Germany."

He sat erect in the saddle. "Not now! No longer! Not in *this* universe!"

His next words ended any further argument. "I understand God's will, Oxenstierna. It was for this purpose, in His mercy, that He created the Ring of Fire. This, and no other. Only a blind man, or an impious one, could fail to understand that *now*. So I will hear no further words on this subject. Do you understand, chancellor of Sweden? I am *Vasa!*"

Axel bent his head. Accepting, if not the wisdom of his king, the will of that king's soul.

Accepting the will, of course, did not mean accepting all the fine points. So, in the weeks which followed, Axel Oxenstierna—Sweden's canniest diplomat—immersed himself in the final negotiations. And, by the end, found himself in much better spirits. True, he disapproved in principle of the entire scheme. But Oxenstierna was a practical man, also. And he had discovered, in the political shrewdness of such men as Ed Piazza—now recovering from his injuries—and Francisco Nasi and the Abrabanel brothers, as well as Michael Stearns and *especially* his wife, a new asset for the cause of his king.

So, although he remained dubious of the final outcome, Oxenstierna could still console himself with a certainty.

Tremble, lords of Germany. A new breed has come into the world.

A month after her wedding, Julie would use the best rifle in the world. As the armored column of the United States smashed its way through the imperial fortifications which Wallenstein had erected on the Burgstall, Julie took out Wallenstein himself.

The king of Sweden did not approve, of course. By the semifeudal military protocol of his day, deliberately targeting an enemy commander was considered low and foul. But the Captain General was already beginning to accept some of the attitudes of his U.S. soldiery. To whom it seemed far more sensible—not to mention *moral*—to shoot the commander of a vicious army like you would a rabid dog.

So, the Captain General made no protest while Julie and her spotter went to work.

"It's a good one thousand yards, girl," muttered Karen. "This Wallenstein character sure as hell don't believe in leading from the front."

Karen could make out the figure easily enough through the spotting scope, standing on the battlements of the Alte Veste.

"Are you sure it's him?" asked Julie.

"Yep. There's a portrait in one of the books in the school library. I musta studied it for an hour, memorizing his ugly face. That's him, all right."

Reassured, Julie studied the enemy commander through her scope. He *was* an ugly bastard. Reminded her of a cartoon version of the Devil. "Wind?" she asked.

"Hard to tell," muttered Karen. "Nothing here, but on top of that hill?" She shrugged. "Start by figuring no wind. I'll try to spot where the first bullet hits."

Silence followed, while Julie gauged the elevation. The shot was at the outermost limit of the rifle's range. It would require her utmost skill and concentration. She blocked everything out of her mind— the sound of the APCs smashing through the lower fortifications, the fiery flares of napalm clearing the side trenches—everything except the devil in the distance.

As always, squeezing the trigger, her shot came as a bit of a surprise.

"Four feet off!" cried Karen. "Nine o'clock! That's wind! Elevation's dead on!"

Julie had seen it herself. One of the officers standing to Wallenstein's right had been struck down by a bullet in the chest. Wallenstein himself, his mouth open, was staring at the man's body.

Julie adjusted for the wind. Wallenstein's head came back around, staring directly at her. His mouth was still open.

The sniper's triangle. *You're dead, motherfucker.*

The only thing that saved Wallenstein's life was the extreme range. The shot was perfect. But, traveling that distance, the bullet slowed enough to go transonic. It began to tumble, and missed by inches. Wallenstein's jaw was shattered, instead of his throat.

The imperial general's head spun, spraying teeth and blood on his subordinates. He staggered into General Gallas' arms.

"Damn," growled Julie. She jacked another round into the chamber. Fired again.

That shot splintered Wallenstein's shoulder. Gurgling with pain and fear, Wallenstein tried to shout orders to Gallas: *Put me down, you idiot!* But he could not get the words through his mangled mouth, and Gallas was too confused to understand what was happening. Wallenstein's frantic attempt to force Gallas to the ground brought the general's own head into the path of the next bullet. Now finally in the safety below the battlements, Wallenstein stared at the pieces of Gallas' brains scattered over the stones.

Good riddance was his last thought, before pain and shock dragged him into unconsciousness.

A thousand yards away, sighing regretfully, Julie lowered her head and muttered a few curses. The Captain General knelt by her side and consoled her with a heavy hand on the shoulder. Due to the sports spectacles which Julie had presented him as her own gift, Gustav's eyesight was good enough to have followed the action.

"No matter," he said. "He will not be there to rally his men. All that matters."

The Captain General raised his head and studied the battle. The U.S. armored column had now broken through the outer fortifications on the lower slope of the Burgstall. The M-60 in the lead APC was shattering the counterattack coming down from the Alte Veste. Thousands of Swedish cuirassiers and Finnish light cavalry were pouring into the breach. For a mile on either side of the armored thrust, Swedish pikemen and arquebusiers were launching a massive charge. The Captain General smiled, seeing the U.S. infantrymen at the fore of that charge. Even from the distance, he could hear their incredible rate of fire.

"No matter," he repeated. "Wallenstein's army will break—and very soon. We are on the verge of an even greater victory than Breitenfeld. Trust me, girl. I am experienced in these things."

Julie raised her head and glared at him. "And I suppose you're going to lead another idiot cavalry charge?"

Gustav II Adolf, King of Sweden and the Baltic Territories, newly crowned Emperor of the Confederated Principalities of Europe, and Captain General of the United States, shook his head.

"Please! Do I look like a madman?"

When Mike returned from the Alte Veste that evening, the Captain General ordered him to return home. He would brook no argument.

"I command the armies of the United States in the field!" he roared, driving over Mike's protest. "That was the agreement!"

He settled down, a bit. "Besides," he gruffed, "there is no further need for you here. The battle is won—decisively. And you have a situation at home. We just got word over the radio."

Mike's face paled. The Captain General chuckled. "Relax, man! It happens. A bit early, in this case, but that is not so unusual in a first—" The rest of the words went unheard. Mike was already racing out of the command tent, looking for his vehicle and official driver.

Hans got him back to Grantville in record time, even on those roads. The pickup, of course, needed extensive body work afterward. But they were still late. The baby had been born many hours earlier.

"Relax, fer Chrissake," said James, as he trotted alongside Mike down the corridor of the town's new hospital, trying to keep up with the frantic new father. It was a long corridor. The hospital had only been completed two months earlier, and its builders had planned for the future. Halfway down, Mike almost trampled Jeff as he emerged from one of the wards, his arm in a sling. Gretchen, coming right behind her husband, called out a greeting. But Mike only responded with a vague wave of the hand.

"She's fine," the doctor insisted. "No complications at all. So's the baby."

James gave up. "It's a girl, by the way!" he shouted after Mike's retreating back.

"Isn't she beautiful?" whispered Rebecca, cradling the sleeping baby in her arms. "Kathleen," she murmured.

That was the name they had agreed on, if the child was a girl. But Mike had been thinking about it during the endless drive back from Nürnberg with ferocious concentration, trying to keep his mind on future hope rather than today's fear.

"No," he said, shaking his head. Startled, Rebecca looked at him.

Mike smiled. "We can call our next girl Kathleen. But this one—" Gently, he stroked the tiny head. "This one I'd like to name after a promise kept. So let's call her Sepharad."

Rebecca's eyes filmed with moisture. "Oh, Michael," she whispered. "I think that would be wonderful."

She reached up her free hand and drew Mike's head down. But halfway through the kiss she started laughing.

"What's so funny?" he demanded.

"Sepharad!" she exclaimed. "It's such a splendid name. But you know they'll be calling her Sephie before she's two months old."

Laughing, laughing. "Hillbillies! You have no *respect*."

Author's Afterword

The town of Grantville and the characters who populate it are purely fictitious. But Grantville, along with the nearby consolidated high school, is inspired by the real town of Mannington, West Virginia, and its surroundings.

Many years ago, I lived in northern West Virginia (Morgantown, to be precise), and I revisited the area in preparation for this novel. I'd like to thank the many people there who provided me with their help. I'd especially like to single out Paul Donato and Dave James for the hours they gave me, both at the time of my visit and in many phone calls later.

Paul is the principal of North Marion High School, which is the model for the high school which figures so prominently in *1632*. He took the time, on a day when the school was closed due to a winter storm, to give me an extended tour of the high school and its facilities. Although I did not hesitate to make whatever changes were needed to fit the plot, the high school in the novel is true in essence to the one which really exists—down to the television station and the decor of the cafeteria. And yes, North Marion High *did* win the West Virginia AAA state football championships in 1980, 1981 and 1997—along with a number of other athletic and academic awards. The great trophy case which the imperial cavalrymen shatter in frustration toward the end of the book really exists, and it is just as large and impressive as depicted.

In a day when public high schools never seem to get any notice or attention until something goes wrong, let me take the time here to remind everyone that the vast majority of America's high schools are alive and well. As a boy, I attended a consolidated rural high school—Sierra Joint Union, near Tollhouse, California—and it was much of a piece with North Marion in West Virginia. Public schools, and high schools in particular, remain the principal forges of America's youth. Let others whine about their shortcomings and faults, I will not. You can have your damned playing fields of Eton, and all the other varieties of that exclusionary "vision." I'll stick with the democratic and plebeian methods which built the American republic, thank you.

Dave James is the chief of Mannington's small police force, and he was very helpful to me in preparing the material for the novel. Beyond the specifics he provided me concerning the police department, he was also a fount of information concerning the town and its environs.

In addition, I'd like to thank Herb Thompson, the manager of the power plant near Grant Town, for his explanation of the workings of a modern power plant. Also: Billy Burke, the WV State Executive Director for the USDA's Farm Service Agency; David Adams and Amy Harris, respectively the manager and a pharmacist at one of Mannington's largest drug stores; and Mike Workman, a former coal miner and currently a professor at West Virginia University.

It's a bit awkward for a writer to thank his publisher, without seeming like a sycophant. But simple honesty requires to me to thank Jim Baen. Jim gave close editorial attention to this novel from beginning to end, and his many suggestions and criticisms helped to improve it immensely. In particular, I owe him a debt of gratitude for restraining me when my emotions ran a tad too high. The historical villains of this story were every bit as vile as I depict them, and I sometimes found it difficult not to give them their just desserts in gory detail—down to a splendid scene involving a guillotine. But *1632* is a sunny book, when all is said and done, and Jim helped me to remember that.

Beyond that, the mentioning of specific names becomes difficult. There are just too many of them. But I need to thank, in general, all the many people who participate in Baen Books' very active chat room (www.baen.com/bar/ — "Hang Out at Baen's Bar") and who responded to my request for input. And, in particular, I want to thank Pam ("Pogo") Poggiani for reading the manuscript and helping me ferret out the factual or historical errors which are such a potential menace to writers of alternate history. Any errors which may remain are entirely my responsibility. There are at least a dozen which are gone, thanks to Pam's eagle eye.

Leaving aside possible errors on my part—which I strove mightily to avoid—the historical setting of this novel is accurate. The town of Badenburg is my invention, as are all the German characters, such as Gretchen Richter, whose social class puts them beyond the reach of history's notice. The rest of the places mentioned are real, as are all of the major historical figures such as Gustavus Adolphus and his generals, Axel Oxenstierna, Tilly and Wallenstein and *their* generals, John George of Saxony, Cardinal Richelieu and Emperor Ferdinand II. The Scottish officer Alexander Mackay is fictitious, but the prominent role of Scotsmen in Gustav Adolf's army was very much as I depict it. Likewise, while Rebecca and Balthazar and all the other specific members of the Abrabanel family who figure in the novel are my creations, the Abrabanel family itself is not. The Abrabanels were, indeed, one of the great families of the dispersed Sephardic Jews of Spain and Portugal.

More generally, the American characters who populate *1632* are all figments of my imagination. But I like to believe they are a faithful portrait of the American people. Part of the reason I chose to write this novel is because I am more than a little sick and tired of two characteristics of most modern fiction, including science fiction.

The first is that the common folk who built this country and keep it running—blue-collar workers, schoolteachers, farmers, and the like—hardly ever appear. If they figure at all, it is usually as spear carriers—or, more often than not, as a bastion of ignorance and bigotry. That is especially true of people from such rural areas as West Virginia. Hicks and hillbillies: a general, undifferentiated mass of darkness.

The second is the pervasive cynicism which seems to be the accepted "sophisticated" wisdom of so many of today's writers. (Not all, thankfully.) I will have no truck with it. Of all philosophies, cynicism is the most shallow and puerile. People may choose to believe that no young man like Jeff Higgins would ever make the decision concerning Gretchen which is portrayed in the novel. Yet that episode, like many in the book, was inspired by real life. A young American infantryman, who encountered a prostitute caring for her family during the Italian campaign in World War II, made exactly the same decision—and, like Jeff, made it within hours. Do not ask me his name, or where he came from, because I do not remember. I ran across the story in a history book which I read as a teenager. The specifics I forgot long ago, but I never forgot the incident. He may have been a boy from West Virginia or Kansas—but he could just have easily have come from the mean streets of New York. If there is one human characteristic which truly recognizes neither border, breed nor birth, it is the courage to face life squarely.

As for the coal miners who are central to the story, people may think the portrait unrealistic. That is their problem, not mine. I never had the honor of being a member of the United Mine Workers of America. But in my days as a trade-union activist, I had many occasions to work with the UMWA and its members. I know the union and its traditions, and those traditions are alive and well. That is as true of the Navajo miners in the southwest and the strip miners in Wyoming as it is of the Appalachian core of the union. I began this book by dedicating it to my mother, who comes from that Appalachian stock. Let me end by rededicating it to UMWA Local 1972 of Sheridan, Wyoming, especially to Dan Roberts and Ernie Roybal; and to Maurice Moorleghen, who came up from District 12 in southern Illinois to lend a hand.

Eric Flint
East Chicago, Indiana
August 1999